Wonderful

S.C. STEPHENS

Wonderful
By S.C. STEPHENS

WONDERFUL

S.C. STEPHENS

Copyright © 2023 by S.C. Stephens

Cover design © Hang Le (byhangle.com)

Editing by Madison Seidler Editing Services (madisonseidler.com)

Formatting by HMG Formatting (hmgformatting@gmail.com)

First Edition: 2023

Library of Congress Cataloging-in-Publication Data

Wonderful – 1st edition

ISBN: 979-8-8548-3721-7

BOOKS BY S.C. STEPHENS

THOUGHTLESS SERIES

Thoughtless

Effortless (Book 2)

Reckless (Book 3)

Thoughtful (Thoughtless alternate POV)

Painful (Effortless alternate POV)

Wonderful (Reckless alternate POV)

Untamed (Book 4)

RUSH SERIES

Furious Rush

Dangerous Rush (Book 2)

Undeniable Rush (Book 3)

CONVERSION SERIES

Conversion

Bloodlines (Book 2)

'Til Death (Book 3)

The Next Generation (Book 4)

The Beast Within (Book 5)

Family is Forever (Book 6)

STANDALONE BOOKS

Collision Course

It's All Relative

Under the Northern Lights

Something Like Perfect

For my very patient readers.
Thank you for keeping these characters in your hearts for so long!
I hope you enjoy the final part of Kellan's story.

Chapter 1

MY WIFE, MY LIFE

Kiera Allen married me last night. A part of me still couldn't believe it, and as my mind slowly shifted from slumber to awareness, I began to wonder if the last twenty-four hours had just been a really long, elaborate dream. Not that my dreams were usually that pleasant. I had a lot of emotional baggage, and my subconscious loved to unpack it while I was sleeping. But yesterday...if that was just a dream, then it was the best one I'd ever had.

Not only had Kiera agreed to be my wife, fittingly in the place where I'd first laid eyes on her, but I'd also met with my...father. Gavin Carter. It was still strange to link the word "father" to him. I'd avoided any sort of personal attachment for so long, resisted meeting or even talking to him for so long...and now...now we had plans for breakfast. It was all so surreal, almost more so than Kiera marrying me. Or my band getting a record deal and recording an album. That was still a work in progress. In fact, I was only here in Seattle for Kiera's graduation, and I had to be back in Los Angeles to continue recording on Monday. God... maybe the entire last six months were just a dream.

Cracking open my eyes, I looked around the room. Generic art, cream-colored walls, a large TV on the dresser directly across from the bed...this wasn't my bedroom. This was a hotel room.

The hotel room Kiera and I had booked for our wedding night. A smile crept over my face as I accepted the fact that I hadn't dreamt my marriage. My smile grew as I felt Kiera's warm, naked body beside mine on the bed. Definitely not a dream. *Fuck. She really married me.*

I inhaled a slow, deep breath, letting the contentment I felt inside me touch every cell of my body. This was what I'd always wanted—someone I loved who loved me back, wholly and completely...the girl of my dreams wrapped in my arms. I could die happy right here, right now. But I genuinely hoped that didn't happen. I wanted more of this. So much more. Eternity wouldn't be long enough.

Turning toward Kiera, I reached over and placed my hand on her leg. Closing my eyes, I savored the feel of her as I ran my fingers up her smooth skin. She stirred under my touch, slowly returning to the real world, leaving her dream life behind. I kind of hoped she'd dreamt about us, about all the things we'd done last night, about all the things we could do from here on out. I was reluctant to leave her again, but I was also excited because I knew it was only a temporary separation. Kiera was going to join me in L.A., and then she was going to go on tour with me. We wouldn't have to go through another long, painful division. I really couldn't wait to start our new life together.

Kiera stretched out her body, then placed her hand over mine. I cinched her fingers tight, holding her to me. My lips pressed against her shoulder, and she wriggled her back against my chest, trying to get even closer. Since we were about as tangled as two people could get, we really couldn't get much closer. Well, I supposed there was *one* way we could be closer...

Kiera pulled on our joined hands, lifting them to her lips and placing a soft kiss upon my wedding ring. A soft laugh of contentment escaped me. Maybe she'd also thought last night was a dream. A perfect, amazing dream.

I ran my lips up her neck, feeling a surge of energy rush through me as I did. When I got to her ear, I whispered,

"Mornin', Mrs. Kyle." Just saying her new name made my heart start to beat faster. *Mrs. Kiera Kyle...my wife.*

Kiera rolled in my arms, twisting to face me. My chest squeezed in a weird yet wonderful way as her features came into view: the flawless, creamy skin, the faint rosy blush highlighting her cheeks, the ever-shifting hazel eyes that were damn near glowing with adoration, the alluring curve of her lips, drawing me in, promising me comfort, seduction...hope. She was beautiful. No, she was *breathtaking*. Everything I could have asked for in a woman. But her face wasn't why I loved her. Kiera saw me, understood me, accepted me. She wanted me to grow and wanted to be there for me as I did, through the good times and the bad. She loved me for *me*, the person behind the face, behind the body, behind the job. She loved the core of who I was, flaws and all, scars and all, and that meant everything to me. *She* meant everything to me. There was nothing I wouldn't do for this woman.

"Good morning, Mr. Kyle," she demurely said. Then she giggled. It was adorable. "I can't believe we just did that, Kellan."

I knew exactly what she was referring to, but I couldn't let her say something like that and *not* tease her. "What? Have mind-blowing sex? That really shouldn't surprise you. Every time with you is incredible." Incomparable, life-changing, soul-altering...I could go on and on.

She bit her lip in response to my comment, her cheeks only marginally growing pinker. "I wasn't talking about that." Her other hand lifted, and her finger traced my jaw. "I meant getting married."

I know. I feel the same way. Sitting up on my elbow, I looked down at her in awe. Then my gaze shifted to the band of silver around my finger, and the awe I felt grew a hundredfold. "'Til death do us part," I told her. And not a day sooner.

Kiera's finger on my jaw ran down my neck, then down my chest. My muscles involuntarily clenched as her touch sent a sparking current through me. Her eyes began to burn as she studied me, as she felt me. "My parents won't accept you as my husband until you walk me down the aisle, you know."

Knowing she was right, that most people wouldn't consider us truly married until we had a ceremony and a signed piece of paper, made me laugh in a lighthearted, carefree kind of way. It seemed such an inconsequential detail in my mind—Kiera was already my wife, 100 percent—but I also understood the need to make it legally binding. And I wasn't opposed to making things official, I'd just been too impatient to be her husband to wait for the formality.

I shifted our bodies, moving on top of her, and Kiera lightly ran her fingers down my back. The soft caress reminded me of not-so-soft touches, of wild, near-frenzied passion, of releasing so much pent-up desire that it had almost unhinged me. I shuddered at the memory, my body instantly hardening.

"And I will," I told her. I kissed her neck, then her collarbone. "I will give them the ceremony they want..." My lips slowly drifted to the top of her breast. "I'll give you the wedding of your dreams, Kiera." I locked my lips around her nipple, swirling my tongue over the sensitive skin. Her breaths grew ragged, and her fingers shifted to weave through my hair. God, I loved that.

Releasing her, I looked up. Her eyes locked on mine; the heat in them made me ache. Smiling, I kissed between her breasts, then started my way down her stomach. I felt her abs clench, felt her fingers tighten in my hair, felt her breath stop for a moment. She wanted me to keep going, wanted me to taste her, and fuck, I wanted that too.

Loving how much I turned her on—how much she turned *me* on—I gave her a knowing, satisfied smile. *You're putty in my hands right now, and I love it because every day I'm putty in yours.* "I'll give you everything, Kiera, but until I can do it properly..." I playfully licked the rim of her belly button, then ran my tongue down her lower abs. She squirmed beneath me, letting out a groan that made my body pulse, then she pushed my head down. Clearly, I wasn't getting where she wanted me to be quickly enough. Her eagerness made a soft laugh escape me. Avoiding what she wanted, I kissed down her inner thigh instead as I finished my sentence, "...we may as well enjoy the perks." I stopped denying her then and shifted my mouth over so I could give us what we both wanted.

An erotic, needy noise filled the air as I tasted her desire for me. Her hips rocked beneath me, and her hands clutched at anything on me they could touch. Her moans turned into vague words, and the passion coming from her nearly undid me. I wanted to stop so I could drive into her. I wanted to keep going so I could drive her over the edge. A throaty groan escaped me as I debated what to do, then Kiera's hand found one of mine, and we clenched each other's fingers tight. Kiera's breath picked up in a pattern I recognized, and I instantly knew exactly what I wanted. It was what I always wanted—to please her.

Seconds later, Kiera's hand in mine squeezed tighter while her other one tangled in my hair, holding me to her. My body throbbed as I heard her release, felt it...tasted it. It damn near made me delirious. As she came down, I rose up, placing fevered kisses upon her skin as I worked my way back up her stomach.

Her breaths evened while mine grew erratic. I needed her so badly. Her fingers dislodged from mine, and she placed her hand on my cheek, holding my gaze. My eyes locked with hers. I wasn't sure what she saw in my expression, but she bit her lip as she studied me. Then her other hand was on my hip, pulling, encouraging. I leaned down to kiss her while simultaneously pressing inside her. I had to break away from her mouth as the pleasure overwhelmed me, and I dropped my head to the crook of her neck with a deep groan. Then we were moving together, and it was...ecstasy.

I lost myself to her—to the softness of her skin, the warmth of her body, the silkiness of her hair, the enticing sounds escaping her lips. I let her take everything from me, every part of who I was, because I knew I was safe with her. Sheltered. Protected. Loved. I opened my heart as far as it would go, lowered all my walls so I could fully experience this with her. Our breaths were in sync, our bodies were in sync, our hearts, our minds, everything.

Right as I felt the buildup becoming uncontainable, I found her hand again and clenched it tight. Her nails dug into my shoulder as her body stiffened beneath me. She held her breath for a second, then made an erotic sound that shoved me right over the brink. Our laced fingers tightened together as the euphoria burst through me, and I was gasping and groaning—undone and so very, very happy. *Every morning should start like this.*

Kiera wrapped her arms around me, holding me tight against her body while we recovered. My heart was racing, my breath fast in her ear. Smiling, I kissed her neck. "Can we do that every morning?" I asked, echoing my thoughts.

She laughed, her hand lazily threading through my hair. "Probably not."

"Well, that's a damn shame," I told her, nestling into her body.

She laughed again, then turned to kiss my cheek, and I sighed, utterly, completely, profoundly content.

We dozed a little after that, then woke up and made love again, then finally accepted the fact that our wedding night/morning was over, and we really needed to get back to the real world. With sloth-like speed, we got up and got dressed. Kiera seemed reluctant to leave, though, as she stared at the messy covers of our mammoth bed; it looked like a tornado had ripped through our room, and that made me smile. A lot.

Wrapping my arms around Kiera's waist, I kissed her ear and said, "We should go. I told Gavin I would have breakfast with him today, and we're already really late...It's more like brunch now."

Kiera looked over her shoulder at me, a prideful smile on her face. I knew she was thrilled that I was letting Gavin in, giving him a chance. I wouldn't be giving him anything without her interference. I owed her a lot for pushing through my stubbornness, forcing me to face him. Assuming things with him went well, of course. A part of me still expected the ground to fall out from under me when it came to him. It was a little terrifying to feel that way. Okay, a lot terrifying. But I was trying to be hopeful.

Kiera twisted her body and wrapped her arms around my neck. Her eyes were adoring as she ran her fingers through the back of my hair. Giving me a soft kiss, she said, "I'm sure he'll understand that your wedding night ran a little long."

With a satisfied sigh, I clutched her tight to me. *Wedding night.* It was still so surreal. Kissing her head, I told her as much. "I still can't believe you're my wife."

Kiera nuzzled into my chest, and I felt my heart expanding in a way I didn't even know was possible. Then she suddenly stiffened and pulled away from me. "You're right, we should go," she said, her words rushed.

There was an adorable pout on her lips, like she didn't really want to go anywhere, and heat was burning in her eyes. She wanted more of me. I loved how insatiable she could be sometimes. It was clear she was trying to hide it, though. Because of our responsibilities? Or was she embarrassed that she still wanted me. She shouldn't be. If she wanted me every ten minutes, I'd love to hear about it. God knows I wanted her every ten minutes.

The conflicted look on her face made a crooked smile grace my lips. "You want to have sex again, don't you?"

Pink tinted her cheeks, and she pushed me away from her. "I think we broke enough records last night...and this morning." She looked away. Definitely embarrassed. And she had no reason to be.

Squatting, I gently grabbed her chin and forced her to look at me. "Do you want to have sex with me?"

Her eyes flicked back and forth, and I knew she wanted to look away again, wanted to hide. But surprising me, she focused her gaze on my face and said, "Yes."

Her admission made me grin. Good. She should be able to talk about this stuff with me. Openly, freely, whenever and wherever she wanted to talk about it. We were partners. In this, in everything. "Was that so hard to admit?" I asked her, genuinely curious.

Kiera's eyes almost closed, but she willfully kept them open. "Actually, yeah, that was a little mortifying."

Mortifying? It shouldn't be mortifying for her to talk to me. I wanted her to be able to discuss anything with me, especially when it came to sex. But I also understood discomfort; I'd felt it a few times myself. And I knew the one thing that had helped me get through it was exposure. The more times she talked to me about things she didn't want to talk about, the easier it would get for her. And there was no time like the present to get started.

Pulling away from her, I said, "I want you to ask me to have sex with you...right now."

Her jaw dropped. "Kellan..." Then she tried to hide her body like she was naked or something. She wasn't. She was wearing the short, tight dress her sister, Anna, had lent her for her graduation, a dress I was very reluctant to return. "I've asked you for sex before...Why are you purposely embarrassing me?"

I'm not. That's not my goal right now. With a sigh, I locked eyes with her. "You've asked me in the heat of the moment when we were heading in that direction anyway. I want you to feel comfortable enough to ask me anytime, anywhere."

She raised an eyebrow at that. "Anywhere?"

I gave her a playful grin. "*Any*where."

A flash of annoyance crossed her face as she exhaled in a grunt. It was quickly replaced by reluctance, then acceptance. Hands stiff at her sides, she inhaled a deep breath, held it, then let it go. Lifting her chin, she nervously said, "Kellan, will you have sex with me?"

I was so proud of her that I was almost bursting at the seams. I contained the smile, though, and let her words seep through me instead. They ignited me instantly, and I let myself imagine saying yes, imagine pulling that dress off her, imagine pushing her back onto that messy bed...

But no, we really did need to get going. All I could do for her now was tease her a little.

Slowly sliding my eyes down her body, I lingered on all the places I wanted to explore before finally returning to her face. I stepped forward, my hips pressing into hers. Leaning down, I said in her ear, "That is the hottest thing I've ever heard you say."

Her eyes slid closed, and her breath stuttered. Seeing her reaction made it really difficult not to cave into her request; my body was already on board with that idea, blood surging in all the right places. I sucked her earlobe into my mouth, and she moaned. That almost sealed the deal for me, but fuck, we really did need to leave. Fortifying myself, I whispered, "But we have to go." Then I grabbed her hand and yanked her forward, breaking the spell. For both of us. Otherwise, we might not ever leave this room.

She frowned as I pulled her toward the door. So cute. A light laugh escaped me as I told her, "I'm sorry, Kiera, but you'll just have to be unsatisfied for a while." Tilting my head, I grinned. "That's sort of...karma...for all the times you've left me aroused and alone."

"You're mean," she murmured, looking genuinely disappointed. The fact that she looked that way made me surprisingly happy; it took some of the sting out of my all-too-true statement. I removed the rest by quickly kissing her cheek.

"Hmmm, maybe I am," I said. Wanting my next words to sink in, I grabbed her ass and pulled her into me, closing all the distance between us. She made an insanely erotic noise as we came together. Running my nose along her jaw, I mentally reminded myself that I was saying no right now. It was exceedingly difficult to remember that. "Because I'm really looking forward to teasing you all day," I breathed into her skin.

Her body shuddered in response, but she pushed me away, annoyed. "You suck."

Loving the effect I had on her, I laughed as I opened the door.

Kiera grabbed her purse, then looked back at the bed again. With a frown, she said, "Wait, Kellan. Should we make the bed before we go?"

Confusion swept over me as I pondered her question. Why would we make the bed in a hotel room? But then I understood. It was painfully obvious that a good time had occurred in those twisted sheets, and she wanted to hide that fact. I couldn't help but smile at her. "You're so adorable," I said. My grin turned devilish as I looked over at the bed again. "No, we're leaving the room like it is. I want the world to know what happened here... on the night we consummated our marriage." My eyes returned to hers, and she let out a soft, happy sigh. Because I couldn't help myself, I added, "Besides...it's hot."

She rolled her eyes in the most fantastic way, but she left the bed exactly as it was and followed me out of the hotel room.

I was absurdly buoyant as we drove home...to *our* home. I literally couldn't think of another moment in my life when I'd felt this content, this fulfilled, this completely, blissfully at peace. I felt like I could take on anything, do anything, become anything. I felt like nothing could possibly touch my good mood. I was high on life, and I never wanted to come down.

Turning onto my street, I carefully navigated the narrow, car-lined road to my house. When I got there, I saw a bright red Jetta parked in my driveway. *Odd.* A frown curved my lips as I pulled up next to it. I mentally flipped through all the people I knew and what they typically drove, but the vehicle wasn't registering with me. Apprehension pricked my stomach as I shut off the Chevelle.

"Hmmm," I said, cracking open my door. This could be nothing, a random friend who'd decided to drop by, or this could be bad. And by the crass bumper sticker on the car, I was leaning toward bad. Damn it. Why today?

Kiera looked a little forlorn as she got out of my car and walked with me to the front door; she must have also surmised that this would be bad. I wasn't entirely sure what was going to happen, but I already felt like apologizing. Containing a sigh, I tried the front door and found it unlocked. I pushed it open, stepped inside, then held out my hand for Kiera as she followed me, subtly letting her know that whatever this was, I loved her and only her. My history wanting to see me for some reason didn't change that fact. Kiera clasped my fingers a little firmer than she usually did, and I gave her a tight, apologetic smile.

As Kiera stepped to my side in the entryway, closing the front door behind her, I scanned the living room. The first thing I noticed was the expression on the faces of Kiera's parents. They were still in town, visiting for Kiera's graduation, and they did not look happy as they sat on the couch; Caroline looked uncomfortable, Martin looked pissed. Of course, he almost always looked that way around me. I wasn't his favorite person. I didn't think it was me making him look that way right now, though, because the next thing I noticed was a pair of long, feminine legs dangling over the side of Kiera's favorite chair. Crap.

The person sitting there heard the door and tilted their dark head back to look at us. A very familiar face greeted me, and my stomach dropped. Oh fuck. Joey. My slightly unhinged, melodramatic ex-roommate/ex-lover who'd run off in a huff after she'd caught me in bed with another woman. Great. What was she doing here? Goddamn it. Of all the people to randomly show up at my house while Kiera's parents were here—while *Kiera* was here—Joey was the absolute worst one. She was not a good person, and she did *not* like me.

"Shit," I muttered, nervously glancing at Kiera. Would she understand if I asked her to go upstairs? Would she do it without questioning me? Probably not. And if she questioned me, Joey would have a field day with her. Fuck. *How do I get through this without it blowing up in my face?*

Deciding I'd rather have Kiera beside me, I squeezed her hand and led her into the living room. *Might as well get it over with.* Joey's deep brown eyes narrowed as I stepped in front of her. I really wasn't sure why she despised me so much. Because I'd slept with someone else? So did she. We were never together, we were never a thing, we'd just fooled around on occasion. And that was all it had ever been between us—mindless, emotionless, just-for-fun screwing. It made absolutely no sense to me that Joey was so bent out of shape about it when she didn't give two shits about me. I was a toy to her, one she hadn't wanted to share. Apparently. I wish I'd known that before I slept with her.

Joey's bright red lips pursed in disdain as she stared at me. "Well, fuck me, Kellan Kyle." She smirked, then added, "Oh, wait, you already did."

My stomach clenched as she crassly announced our relationship to the room. Damn it. This was not a good way to start my marriage...and it definitely wasn't going to help me win over Kiera's dad. Ignoring Joey's comment, I shifted my attention to my new in-laws. "Martin, Caroline," I warmly said. Then my eyes reluctantly swung back down to the girl I wished would leave. "Joey."

Kiera stiffened beside me, and I knew she'd placed the name. A flash of guilt went through me, but I tried to ignore it. I hadn't even known Kiera when I'd gotten together with Joey, and I'd been...desperate at the time. Sad but true. Already hating this, I asked Joey, "What are you doing here?"

She leapt to her feet. Her long black hair flowed around her shoulders as she crossed her arms over her chest and lifted her chin in self-righteous indignation. "Where the hell is all my stuff, Kellan?"

That was why she was here? To collect all the crap she'd abandoned years ago? Seriously? My momentary disbelief shifted to wariness. All her stuff was gone because Kiera had gotten rid of it. She'd removed the furniture to refresh the space, cleanse it of its demons, so to speak. And I loved the fact that she'd done that for us, for me, since she'd turned the room into a sort of writing den, a place where I could work. It was sweet, thoughtful, and there was no way in hell I was going to let Joey know any of that. And why the hell would she expect me to still have her shit anyway? That was so long ago.

Annoyed, I told her, "You've been gone for two years. I tossed it."

Her near-black eyes grew fiery, and she shoved my shoulder hard enough to jerk my torso. "You what? That wasn't yours to get rid of, asshole!"

Heat surged through my veins as I took a step forward. "You ran out. It's not my problem if you left everything behind! My house isn't your personal storage unit."

Joey gave me a dismissive wave, like she didn't give a rat's ass what I thought. "Whatever, Kellan. I don't need your temperamental crap. If you don't have my stuff, then you can just pay me for it." She gave me a wry smile. "Fifteen hundred should cover everything."

I didn't know what was funnier—*her* calling *me* temperamental or her thinking her beat-up furniture was worth fifteen hundred dollars. Before I could respond to her absurd demand, Kiera made a grunting noise of disbelief, capturing Joey's attention.

Glaring at Kiera, Joey snidely asked, "Who the hell are you? Kellan's flavor of the hour?"

My blood instantly boiled. I saw Martin rise to his feet, heard him say something about not talking to his daughter that way, but I was too pissed to truly listen to him. Dropping Kiera's hand, I stepped right into Joey's personal space. "Be very careful, Josephine. That's my wife you're talking to."

Joey's eyes widened as she backed up a step. But then the wary look shifted into one of disbelief, then amusement. She started laughing. "Oh my God, are you serious? You, the biggest manwhore I know, actually got married? What a joke."

Folding my arms over my chest, I quickly counted to ten, calming myself down before I did or said something stupid. Joey needed to leave. Now. And if agreeing to her price got her out of my house, then it was well worth the cost. Jerking my thumb at the door, I told her, "Fine. I'll get you fifteen hundred for the furniture. Now get the hell out."

Joey had a defiant smirk on her face and an odd gleam in her eye; seeing it made me nervous. She shook her head at me. "Oh, I don't think so...not anymore, Kellan."

I wasn't sure what she meant by that, but I was sure I wasn't going to like it. While I tried to understand Joey's endgame, Kiera lost her temper. She walked right up to Joey, hands clenched into fists like she wanted to slug her. "You heard him! You'll get your money. Now go back to whatever hole you crawled out of."

I cringed as Joey glared at Kiera. Joey was not the type of person to let a remark like that slide. My body tensed in preparation; if Joey made one move toward Kiera, that would be it...I'd forcibly remove her from my home.

Still stabbing Kiera with her eyes, Joey said to me, "I have something of yours that I'm returning." Her gaze shifted back to my face. "Since I have no use for it." Confusion swept over me; I had no idea what she was talking about. Had she stolen something of mine? If she had, I hadn't missed it. Seeing my befuddled expression made Joey smile. "And if you want it back...sweetheart...then you'll double my price."

Kiera yelled at Joey, calling her nuts, but icy dread was running up my spine. Joey knew something...something I couldn't remember. She was pretty positive she had leverage over me, and if she felt that way, then she probably did. Fuck. What was I missing? What did she have?

Eyes glued on me, Joey leaned over and grabbed her bag off the chair. Curiosity kept me silent as I watched her open the bag, reach in, and pull out something...small. Joey held it between her thumb and finger, smiling at me, as what it was—and what was on it—instantly flooded my brain. Oh...fuck. She was holding an SD card from her camera, the camera we'd used to make a sex tape what felt like a million years ago. Shit. I'd completely forgotten all about that fucking tape. Jesus Christ...if Kiera found out what that was...

"Fine, I'll give you three thousand," I quickly told her. *Just don't tell the room what that is.*

Joey smiled at me like she'd heard my internal plea, but thankfully, she handed me the SD card without comment. Wrapping my fingers around it, hiding it, I pointed at the door. "I'll get it to you tomorrow."

Joey patted my cheek in a condescending way. "You better... 'cause I will make your life a living hell if you don't." Then she gave Kiera a look that made my blood freeze solid. Fuck, she really could live up to that threat. If Kiera ever saw this, if she ever knew...but...damn it. While making a sex tape wasn't something I particularly wanted Kiera to know about, I couldn't keep it from her. And besides, there was no way she wouldn't ask about the card after this. I had to tell her, and I *really* wasn't looking forward to that conversation.

I closed my eyes in defeat. "Get the hell out of my house, Joey." *You've done quite enough.* I opened my eyes so I could drive this last part home. "And don't ever come back here."

She ignored the heat in my glare and twisted to wiggle her fingers at Kiera's parents. Joey already knew she'd won. She'd screwed me, and that in and of itself was satisfying to her; the money was just a bonus. Everyone was quiet as she left the house. The silence was full of tension...and questions.

I heard Joey's car pulling away, and I forced myself to relax. Wishing we'd never come home, I shoved the card into my pocket and slapped on a smile. "I'm sorry about that," I said to Martin and Caroline. "I hope she didn't give you too much trouble while we were gone."

Martin still looked upset as he stiffly sat on the couch. "I'm more concerned about what the two of you were doing last night than your tawdry friend." He looked between Kiera and me. "What's this about you running off and getting married? Have you lost your mind, Kiera?"

Martin patted Caroline's hand. Caroline looked like she was about to cry, her jade eyes glistening, but oddly, having them upset over our marriage was kind of a relief; anything to stop them from asking me about the thing currently burning a hole in my pocket. Somehow, I knew I wouldn't get so lucky with Kiera. I tossed her a nervous, worried look, praying she wouldn't bring it up right now. Or ever. I'd be happy with that too. *Let's talk about the wedding*. Hell, I'd rather talk about our wedding *night* at this point.

I gestured toward the couch, hoping Kiera would sit down and get absorbed in a conversation with her parents, one that would make her forget all about the thing I was hiding. Wanting out of the room—and needing to reassure myself that Joey was truly gone and that she hadn't fucked with my car before leaving —I pointed at the door and told Kiera, "I'll be right back. I want to go check on my car, make sure Joey didn't mess with it." God, if she touched the Chevelle…Just thinking about it caused me physical pain. Both meaning it and wanting to lighten the mood in the room, I added, "If she keyed my baby, you may need to restrain me, 'cause I might kill her." I laughed as I made my escape, even though this wasn't funny.

Kiera didn't let me get two steps before she asked the one thing I'd hoped she wouldn't. "What's on the SD card?"

My forced smile left me. *Not now. Please.* "It's nothing. Don't worry about it, Kiera."

That didn't appease her. Stepping closer, she reached for my pocket like she was going to pull out the card and pop it into something so she could watch it. That *could not* happen. I backed away from her, and Kiera's face tightened in anger. She really didn't like it when I hid things from her, but I couldn't talk about this now, here. Not with her parents listening. They'd definitely never like me if they knew what I'd just purchased from my ex.

Kiera repeated her question, hell-bent on an answer. "What's on the card?"

It was almost like the idea of another secret between us had made her completely forget that her parents were here. Hoping to remind her, without actually reminding her, I leaned in and said,

"Can we talk about this later...in private?" *It won't be another secret, I promise.*

I saw conflict in her eyes. And pain. Like she couldn't stop herself, the dreaded question escaped her lips again. "What's on the card?"

There was an edge to her voice that was crawling under my skin. She was never going to let this go. She was going to poke and prod until I told her, so I might as well fucking tell her. The words erupted from me without a second thought. "What do you think it is, Kiera? We filmed ourselves screwing!" Fuck. Goddamn it...I hadn't meant to say that.

Kiera's mouth dropped open, and her face paled. I really wanted to take the words back, but I couldn't. They were out there, inflicting pain and revulsion on everyone who'd heard them. Me and my big fucking mouth.

Kiera's eyes watered in a way that tore at me. I hadn't wanted to say it like that. I'd wanted to be gentle about it, ease her into the conversation with a couple hundred apologies first. Not vomit the cold truth all over her. "You made a sex tape with her?" she whispered, her voice full of hurt.

Before I could answer, Caroline cleared her throat. Kiera's eyes widened, and I knew she'd suddenly remembered our guests. I reached out for her, wanting to fix this in some way. "Kiera, I can explain." I wasn't sure what there was to explain—a sex tape was pretty self-explanatory—but I didn't know what else to say.

It didn't matter, though, because Kiera didn't want to hear it. She held up her hands, warning me to keep my distance. Tears dropped onto her cheeks, killing me. *I'm so sorry.* Before I could say it, Kiera turned from me and ran toward the stairs. I begged her to wait, but she didn't. She ran into our room, and I heard our door slam shut.

Married one day and already doors were being slammed shut again. Not a promising start.

Chapter 2

FAMILY

I wasn't sure what I should do. I knew I needed to go talk to Kiera, but I felt like I should give her some time to calm down. Plus...I wasn't sure what to say. Except *I'm sorry,* and that didn't feel like enough. Kiera already had to tolerate my past constantly rearing its ugly head and biting her on the ass. This—a visual, graphic reminder of who I used to be—felt like too much. Was this what finally drove her away from me? I hated not knowing, I hated her being upset and alone, and I really hated feeling her parents' eyes on me. I might or might not have just lost Kiera, but I was fairly certain I'd just lost them. Goddamn it.

Inhaling a deep breath, I pulled my gaze from the stairs and slowly twisted toward the couch. Caroline's eyes were wide as she stared at me; she occasionally flicked glances at my pocket, and I had an undeniable urge to hide my sin from her. Shifting my hips slightly, so the SD card was as far from her as I could get it, I looked over at Martin. His light brown eyes were narrowed in anger as he studied me, and I knew he was furious with me for hurting Kiera. I was too. For once, we agreed on something.

I held up my hands in a placating position. "That wasn't supposed to happen. I didn't mean to tell her like that..." I felt stupid just saying it. Was there a *good* way to tell your wife you had a sex tape with another woman in your pocket? No...there really wasn't.

Martin crossed his arms over his chest. "What on Earth were you thinking, Kellan? How could you have been so reckless. Filming something like that...you had to have known it would get out one day, that it would hurt people you care about." I opened my mouth, but he continued before I could respond. "It was irresponsible of you and disrespectful to your future...bride." He frowned on the word "bride," and I had a feeling he was just as upset by that as he was by the tape.

I paused for a moment, debating how best to explain myself, then I simply gave him a small nod in surrender. I really didn't have a good argument anyway. *It sounded like a good idea at the time* wouldn't win him over. Sighing, I shook my head. "I should go talk to her. Explain..." *Somehow.*

Martin gave me a stiff nod. Caroline smiled encouragingly. I started walking toward the stairs, then stopped and headed into the kitchen. I wanted this damn thing out of my pocket before I did anything else. Opening a junk drawer by the stove, I found a lighter shoved in the back. Flicking it on, I carefully burned the edge of the SD card before tossing it in the trash. That should make it unreadable, right?

When I was upstairs, I lightly tapped on the bedroom door, then cracked it open. I paused before entering; I probably shouldn't assume I was welcome. "Kiera...can I come in?"

I heard movement, then a soft, "Yeah."

Hesitating, I tried to determine her level of unhappiness, but that one word wasn't giving me a lot to go on. "You're not gonna...throw anything at me, are you?"

She laughed. Taking that as a good sign, I pushed open the door and stepped inside. Small smile on her face, Kiera shook her head at me. "No, it's safe."

Closing the door behind me, I made my way over to the bed. That was when I noticed what Kiera was doing. I stopped moving as I stared at her, ice flooding my veins. She'd taken off her wedding ring, and she was holding it in her fingers like she was debating what to do with it. The world started closing in on me as the thought of her giving it back to me crashed around my brain. *Did I finally lose her? No...I can't handle that.*

Both wanting and not wanting to know where her head was at, I quietly asked, "Are you leaving me?" *Fuck. Please say no.*

My gaze was glued to the ring in her hand while my heart pounded in my chest and my eyes burned with tears waiting for permission to fall. Kiera immediately slid the ring back on her finger, breaking its hold on me, and I slowly lifted my eyes to her face. There was sympathy in her expression, but I wasn't sure what that meant. Soft smile on her face, she held her arms open in invitation. "No, of course I'm not leaving you."

I wanted to believe that, wanted to believe this hadn't changed us and we were still having the beautiful, peaceful day we'd woken up to, but how could she not think differently of me? She had to be hurt, had to be upset, had to be...reconsidering. Seeing my confusion, my hesitation, Kiera sat up on her knees and grabbed my T-shirt. She pulled me into her, lacing her arms around my neck. Her tenderness relaxed me, and I melted into her embrace, wrapping my arms around her tight. In my ear she told me, "I was remembering all of the reasons why I love you so much. I was appreciating everything you do, and everything you are. I was falling in love with you, all over again."

Her words were everything I wanted to hear, but I was still shocked at hearing them. I drew back so I could look at her. "You find out, the day after we get married, that I have a sex tape with another girl...and *that* makes you fall in love with me again?" Because I still couldn't quite believe it, I felt her forehead. She had to be ill, it was the only logical explanation.

Kiera laughed and pulled me onto the bed until I was lying beside her. "Well, no, the tape doesn't thrill me, but..." she paused to rest her head on my shoulder, "there is so much about you that does, and I won't let this one thing ruin it...ruin us."

Relief and understanding hit me hard. She was letting it go, she was willing to work it out with me, she was staying with me. Thank God. Smiling, I kissed her forehead. "Have I told you today how much I love you?"

She cuddled into my side, tossing a leg over mine and resting her head on my chest. Heaven. "Probably, but I'll never get tired of hearing you say it," she said.

We were quiet for a moment, enjoying each other's comfort, and then I broke the silence and apologized. "I'm really sorry, Kiera. I never meant for you to find out about that."

She shifted to look at me, concern on her face. "I don't want you to hide things just because you think the truth will make me unhappy. We've gotten into trouble too many times that way already."

That was certainly true. I nodded. "You're right. And I think I would have told you eventually...although definitely not the morning after our wedding night." That was a conversation that absolutely could have waited...until our tenth anniversary. Maybe our twenty-fifth. Of course, I would have had to remember the tape with Joey to tell her about it. Mentally kicking myself, I confessed my cluelessness. "But to be honest, I kind of forgot about the tape with Joey."

"How do you forget making a sex tape with your roommate? I would have thought something like that stood out," she asked, studying my jawline.

Right...I supposed it *would* have stood out if it had been my one and only time doing something like that. But it wasn't. Great. Kiera wasn't going to like this. Seeing the suspicion in her eyes when she looked up at me, I sighed and shook my head. "I really am sorry, Kiera. She asked...I didn't care. I didn't really say no to a whole lot back then and she—" Closing my mouth, I forcefully stopped myself from going into unnecessary detail with her. *Keep it brief, keep it simple, keep it apologetic.* "I wasn't thinking about the future, about what I was leaving behind...and I'm sorry." *So very sorry.*

She sat up. Eyes slightly narrowed, she said, "That's not the only tape you made, is it?"

I instinctively cringed, and I could see the weariness in her eyes as I nonverbally answered her question. "I'm so sorry, Kiera."

Disbelief was all over her face as she crossed her arms and shook her head. "Oh my God...I married Ron Jeremy."

I tried not to laugh, I really did, but I couldn't help it. Her comparing me to a porn star was just too funny. Kiera lightly smacked my shoulder when the laugh escaped me. The disgruntled look on her face was adorable, but I knew the feeling behind it was genuine; she wasn't happy about this. Honestly, I wasn't either, but there wasn't anything I could do about it now. I couldn't recall every person I'd made a tape with, and some I'd never gotten their names, so there was no way for me to even begin collecting those tapes. It was what it was. All I could do now was comfort Kiera and hope this didn't bite me in the ass later.

Sitting up, I grabbed Kiera's hands and wrapped her arms around my waist. Holding her to me, I rubbed my palms up and down her back in a soothing pattern. It worked, and I felt her relax against me. She was quiet a moment, then she said, "They'll never all stay hidden, Kellan. Not once your band hits the airwaves. Not once your name is well known. Once people know they can make money off of you...those tapes will be everywhere."

I wanted to assure her that wouldn't happen...but I couldn't bring myself to give her false hope. She was probably right. If the D-Bags ever became something more than what we were now, the past I'd shared with a handful of girls would become a path to pseudo-fame and potential wealth. And sadly, I didn't know the girls well enough to know if they'd turn that down. God, I was an idiot. I kind of wanted to go back in time and slap myself. Or punch myself. In the junk.

I gave Kiera a remorseful smile. "I know...and I can't apologize enough."

Kiera's expression was one of sympathy, and I was a little surprised to see it. I thought she'd be angry or disappointed, but she just seemed...sad. "It's not *my* body being peddled, Kellan. You don't need to apologize for something you did years ago. I just...I feel bad that your intimate life is going to be so...public."

Her worrying about *me* in all of this was heartwarming, but my body being exposed like that wasn't what I was worried about. "I don't care about that." I cupped her cheek. "I just don't want it to hurt you."

She leaned into my hand and let out a long, steady breath. "Well, at least I'll be prepared for it." She smirked, and I loved seeing the humor behind the expression. "And it's not like I'm *ever* going to watch them."

I had to laugh at that. No...she definitely shouldn't ever watch them. Roles reversed, I couldn't watch her and keep my sanity intact, so I had to believe it would be the same for Kiera. Well, at least I could protect her from that. But still...if tapes started coming out, if people started talking about them...would she feel differently about us being together? Could she really handle this? Handle me? God, I hoped so.

Like she could see that my mind was still spinning, Kiera gave me a warm smile and playfully said, "You're such a whore."

Amusement and relief flickered through me as I shook my head at her. If we could joke about it, then we were okay. Not wanting to worry about it anymore, I pulled her back down to the bed so we could cuddle a little longer. She melded into my body, more on top of me than beside me, and I smiled as I rubbed her back. Making all of those sex tapes...those moments didn't even come close to the thrill of just *holding* Kiera. From the very beginning, being near her had unraveled me.

I could have lain in bed with her all day, reveling in her comfort, but we did have things we needed to do today, people we were supposed to be visiting with. A fact I was reminded of when our door was knocked on, and I heard Caroline's concerned voice. "Kiera, honey, is everything okay?"

Removing myself from underneath Kiera, I stood up. Kiera looked a little disappointed, but she sat up and told her mom, "Yeah, come on in."

My stomach tightened with unease when Caroline walked into the room. Up until this point, she'd seemingly liked me; I wasn't sure if she still did. She gave me a smile, but there was uncertainty in her green eyes. She didn't trust me, that was obvious. And understandable, I supposed.

Kiera beamed at her mom like nothing in the world was wrong, but I could tell Caroline wanted to have a serious conversation with her. Knowing that would go smoother if I wasn't present, I leaned over and kissed Kiera's cheek in goodbye. "I'm going to go call Gavin...and check on my car. I'll see you in a minute."

Kiera nodded at me and kissed my fingers. I left the room with a strange feeling in my stomach. A part of me wanted to know what Caroline was going to say about me...the rest of me didn't. I was pretty sure it wasn't going to be flattering. Hopefully, I had a lifetime to make it up to Caroline, to prove to her and Martin that they were wrong about me. Kiera was safe in my hands. I would never do anything to hurt her. Well, anything from here on out. My past occasionally socking her in the gut was an entirely different story.

Martin was glaring at me when I stepped off the stairs. Still angry then. I knew I should talk to him, or more accurately, listen as he vented his frustrations on me, but I really did want to check on my car, and I needed to call Gavin. I gave him a "just a minute" finger, then headed outside before he could object. I exhaled a deep breath once I was out of the house, glad for the momentary reprieve from his judging eyes, then I headed over to the Chevelle.

I was on edge as I walked around my car, inspecting her. If Joey so much as chipped the paint so help me God...Thankfully, my baby looked the same as when I'd parked her. Guess Joey didn't have a death wish after all. Although she was seriously pushing it. I was *not* looking forward to meeting up with her tomorrow. Fuck.

Feeling slightly better, I pulled out my cell phone as I headed back to the house. Calling Gavin made me nervous for an entirely different reason, and I had a really hard time hitting the connect button. I'd never called him before. Never texted him either. Not talking to him was still far more natural than talking to him, and I had to clear my throat about a dozen times as the phone rang. *Relax...it's fine, you're fine.*

Right. Totally fine.

I almost hung up, but just as I moved the phone, I heard the line pick up, heard Gavin's voice in my ear. "Kellan...hello, I'm glad to hear from you."

My heart thudded in my chest as I paused on my doorstep, hand on the doorknob. I swallowed again so I could speak. "Um...yeah...hey." Rolling my eyes at myself, I took a step back and tried to sound more like a fully functional human being. "I was just wondering...would you want to come over to my place for breakfast? Kiera's parents are in town visiting, and I'd love for everyone to meet."

"I would love that," he answered, and I could hear the smile in his voice.

"Okay, uh, good. Sorry, I would have called sooner, but Kiera and I...well, we got married last night. We've been...celebrating." I had to smile after saying that to him; Kiera would kill me if she could hear me.

Gavin softly laughed. "Well, congratulations. I'm sorry we missed the ceremony."

A trickle of guilt hit me, then I felt surprised for feeling guilty. Cringing, I told him, "We didn't have an actual ceremony. We just...exchanged rings at Pete's. But that's enough for me. She's my wife."

He laughed again. "And in the end, that's all that really matters. But...if you ever do decide to make it official...I would love to be there. We all would."

My throat damn near closed up on me, and I had to swallow again to relieve the pressure. "Yeah, of course. Kiera wants that, so...yeah, I'll let you know when."

"Thank you, Kellan," he warmly told me.

My eyes started burning, and I shook my head in annoyance. Why was talking to him yanking me from one emotion to another? I went my entire life not talking to him, and I'd been fine. Well, mostly fine. What had changed?

I'd finally let him in...that was what had changed. And it fucking terrified me.

Not wanting to dwell on that, I gave him directions to my house. He told me he'd be there in about thirty minutes and after our goodbyes, I disconnected the call. Letting out a burst of cleansing air, I opened my front door and was immediately met with Martin's cool voice. "Kellan, I'd like to have a word with you, please."

Containing a sigh, I nodded at Martin, then shut my front door and solemnly walked back into the living room. When I was in front of him, I quietly said, "I'm sorry about Joey. I didn't know she'd—"

Martin cut me off. "That's not what I want to talk to you about." He lifted his eyebrows. "You married my daughter without telling us? Without inviting us? Without...asking my permission?"

My lips twitched with that last one, but I wisely didn't comment on it. Instead, I told him, "We didn't intentionally exclude you. It was kind of a...spur-of-the-moment thing. We were at the bar, I asked her to marry me right then and there. We exchanged rings...and now she's my wife."

His brows bunched in confusion, and he started to open his mouth. Knowing exactly what he was going to say, I shook my head and objected to his unspoken argument. "No, I married her. I consider what we did binding. She's my wife in all the ways that matter, and that's a commitment I take very seriously." Maybe not in the past, when it had applied to others, but when it applied to me, when it was *Kiera*...absolutely.

I held eyes with Martin, wanting him to understand me, wanting him to believe me. His lips pursed as he thought. "So... you married my daughter—*in a bar*—with no officiant, no license, and no family present? That's not nearly good enough for my daughter. You know that, right?"

I gave him a polite nod. I was very aware that wasn't enough. "We're going to have a ceremony, going to make it official. I just... I couldn't wait another day to marry your daughter."

He sighed, then slowly shook his head; his hair seemed to be getting grayer by the second. "If you *are* going to be her... husband...then you will show her more respect than you did that young woman in your house earlier. What you two do in private...will *remain* private. Do you understand me?"

My eyes widened at that, but I gave him a nod. Of course I wasn't going to make a sex tape with Kiera. I would never risk her being exposed like that. Ever. But after what he'd just witnessed, I couldn't really blame him for being wary.

Martin went on for a few more minutes, explaining everything he expected from me as a husband. He never once said anything I even remotely objected to, so I just gave him thoughtful nods and let him say his piece uninterrupted. Whatever got him to accept this, accept *me*.

Kiera and her mom came back downstairs when Martin was finishing up. The look on Kiera's face stole my breath. I wasn't sure what she was thinking about, but whatever it was...she was practically glowing as she walked over to me. She was so beautiful, so wonderful, so...mine.

Stepping to my side, she wrapped her arms around my waist. Grateful she wasn't upset, I folded my arms around her and took a moment to drink her in—the dark, wavy hair resting over her shoulders, the warmth in her hazel eyes, more brown than green today, the way her lips were curved in a loving, secretive smile, the way her thumbs stroked my sides as she held me—everything about her captivated me. I could have stared at her all day, but Martin, maybe uncomfortable watching our affection, cleared his throat.

Kiera blinked, like she'd been in a daze too. When she looked over at her dad, he asked, "Everything...okay?"

Kiera nodded, a bright smile on her face. Martin sighed, either confused by her shifting moods...or disappointed by her choice of spouse. I was betting on the latter.

Maybe seeing that her dad needed some reassurance, Kiera let go of me and hugged him. Martin made a sullen comment about our wedding at the bar, then he frowned at me and quietly said, "Are you sure about this, Kiera?" I could only assume that by *this* he meant *me*, and I had to admit, that stung a little.

Beaming, Kiera told him, "Absolutely, Dad." It thrilled me to hear her say that, but it made Martin frown in an almost petulant way. Yeah, definitely disappointed by her choice of spouse. It was going to be a long, uphill battle to make him like me. Good thing I was persistent.

The conversation switched to Gavin after that, and I relayed my information to Kiera: Gavin would be here soon...and my car was completely fine. Thank fucking God.

Kiera and I killed time waiting for my family to arrive by listening to Caroline plan our "official" ceremony. She seemed to have some strong opinions on what Kiera should do, like she'd been thinking about this for a while. It made me wonder if she'd started planning Kiera's wedding when Kiera had started dating Denny. Maybe. Or maybe she'd been dreaming of this since the day Kiera was born. I liked that thought better. A lot better.

The more Caroline talked about colors and dress designs, the more I could picture it...and the image of Kiera in a sparkling white wedding dress, walking down a flower-petal-strewn aisle to me...well, damn. That was a sight I couldn't wait to see.

The visual was so intoxicating that the sound of my doorbell chiming took a second to register with me. When it did, adrenaline instantly flooded my veins. Fuck. Gavin was here. Even though I'd seen him less than twenty-four hours ago, I was suddenly, exceedingly nervous. I wanted this to go well, wanted my relationship with him to go well. I just...*wanted*. And wanting things was dangerous territory for me.

My heart was racing in my chest. Wanting to calm it down, and myself, I let out a long, steadying breath as I stood up. My hands were clammy, a fact that really annoyed me. Nerves weren't something I had a lot of experience with, so I wasn't the best at dealing with them. I didn't want this to be a big deal, but my body disagreed; my stomach was practically doing somersaults.

Irritated with myself, I wiped my palms on my jeans before making my way to the door. I had to wipe my hands two more times and roll my shoulders to ease the escalating tension inside me. Clenching and unclenching my fists, I exhaled a short, forceful breath as I prepared to open the door. *I can do this. No problem.* Slapping on a breezy smile—like my insides weren't twisting me in knots—I quickly pulled open the heavy wood before I could overthink it and completely freeze up.

Gavin's deep blue eyes were the first thing I saw—eyes that were eerily similar to mine—and my entire body tensed. *Shit, maybe I can't do this.* Throwing my heart out there for him to step on felt too...perilous. But then Gavin gave me a warm smile, and just like that, my nerves melted, and my stomach settled. Peace flowed into me. And happiness, so much happiness. *Yes. Yes, I can do this.*

"Good morning, Kellan," he said, holding out his hand for me.

Grinning, I clasped it. "Mornin', Gavin." Releasing his palm, I gestured inside. "I'm glad you're here. Come on in."

Gavin nodded and stepped inside. His head turned this way and that as he scanned my home, and I was struck with the strangest feeling of surrealness as I watched him. My biological father was inside my house because I'd *invited* him here; I'd never anticipated this day happening. Ever.

Shaking away the bizarreness of my life, I turned to greet my half-siblings: Hailey and Riley. My sister was giggling as she waved at Kiera. Hailey was the first family member I'd met, back in December when she'd introduced herself at a concert. That first meeting hadn't exactly been an easy one for me but being friends with her now was effortless. Hailey was a genuinely good person, and funny, smart. The two of us talked a lot, and I had to say, as far as siblings went, I'd gotten pretty lucky with her. When Hailey saw she had my attention, she tossed her arms around me in a fierce hug. With a laugh, I squeezed her tight, then released her so she could walk further into the house.

Riley was right behind her, staring up at me with wide eyes. Like Gavin, my little brother was a new relationship for me; we'd only finally met yesterday, although I'd occasionally relayed messages to him through Hailey. The expression on Riley's young face, the way his sky-blue eyes were absorbing me, it was even more bizarre than my father being here. I wasn't sure why, but the kid seemed to idolize me. Amused, I rumpled his messy hair, then shut my front door.

Stepping around my new family, I indicated the living room. "Please, have a seat."

Kiera and her parents stood from the couch when we approached, and I took a moment to introduce everybody. Martin gave Gavin a firm, appraising handshake. Caroline giggled when it was her turn, then tried to hide it by clearing her throat. That made Kiera smirk, and Martin instantly switched positions with Caroline so he would be the one sitting next to Gavin on the couch instead of her. Interesting. I was pretty sure Caroline found me attractive, and Gavin...well, he was basically an older version of me—same height, same lean build, same dark blue eyes, same strong jawline, same thick hair...although his was much shorter, and as my barber would say, far more "respectable" than my shaggy mess. I had to wonder if Caroline finding Gavin attractive too would make it even more difficult for Martin to bond with me. I hoped not. There wasn't much I could do about the way Gavin and I looked.

Riley plopped himself onto the floor while Hailey squeezed Kiera in a hug. Gavin was having a quiet conversation with Martin and Caroline, and I loved seeing it—loved seeing *all* of it. Smacking my hands together, I told the room, "Well, I'll get started on brunch since it's getting close to lunch time." With a laugh, I again apologized to Gavin for missing breakfast. "I'm sorry I was so late in calling you."

Gavin looked at me, then his gaze swung over to Kiera, and he smiled. Kiera's cheeks grew rosy as Gavin nodded at her. "Yes, I hear you got married last night. Congratulations."

I could tell Kiera was embarrassed. Her cheeks grew even redder as Hailey squealed in excitement. "You're part of the family now, Kiera! Like it or not!"

Since Hailey clearly wasn't upset about missing our wedding —something she'd asked to be invited to—I had to assume Gavin had explained our informal ring-swap at the bar and told her we'd be having an official ceremony later. What Hailey had just said, though...warmed me.

Walking up to Kiera, I removed her from Hailey's arms and gave her a soft kiss. I took a moment to just look at her, appreciate her, then I repeated my sister's sentiment. "Like it or not."

I pressed my lips against hers again, and when I pulled away Kiera dazedly murmured, "Like."

Good. Because I absolutely *loved* it.

Chapter 3

MARRY ME?

Kiera and I fumbled our way through making breakfast. Or at least we tried to muddle our way through it; Hailey ended up taking over for us. Then she chided me on being so nervous she could smell it. I wasn't nervous, per se, just...anxious. I wanted things to be *just right*.

And they were.

Hanging out with my family and Kiera's—it was one of the best afternoons that I'd ever had. One of the top five moments in my life, excluding all my moments with Kiera, of course. I helped Riley play a song on my guitar, won and lost a handful of board games, learned about even more family members I had back east, and even had a sort of heart-to-heart talk with Gavin about Joey basically blackmailing me. That last one was a little embarrassing —not really something I'd wanted my father to know about— but almost everyone else in the house knew about it, so...yeah.

All in all, it was a perfect day. Even with Joey disrupting it, even with snapping at Kiera, and even with my bandmate, Griffin, barging into my house that night like he owned the fucking place, it was perfect.

Saying goodbye to Gavin at the end of it was surprisingly difficult. A weird, sad-happy feeling filled me as I watched him say goodbye to Kiera and her parents. He approached me last, and my gaze lowered to the floor as my thoughts spun. Finally, I looked up and said, "I'm really glad you came all the way over here just to...see me. Thank you for that. It means more than you know." There was a horrid ball of awkward tension in my chest after saying it, but it was the truth. Not many people would have traveled thousands of miles just to spend a day with me, and up until him, no one I was related to would have done that. It meant a lot to me that I was worth his time.

Gavin bunched his brows as he stared at me, his midnight eyes deepening with concern, like he understood just how little I'd been cared for over the years. Then he tossed his arms around me, and this time, I returned the gesture. "Of course, son," he said, patting my back. "There's nothing I wouldn't do for you, Kellan. Nothing."

That made my throat cinch tight, and I had to swallow about five times in a row. Gavin released me, then smiled as he stepped back. "Call me whenever you need to, okay?"

I nodded at him, then smirked. "I'm sure we'll speak frequently," I said, referencing his relentless calling and texting.

Gavin chuckled as he reached for the doorknob. I stopped him with a hand on his arm. When he looked back at me, I grimaced. "I just wanted to say...I'm sorry...about your wife. Hailey told me a while ago; I just didn't feel comfortable enough to mention it." My eyes drifted over to Kiera, standing a few feet away, saying goodbye to Hailey and Riley. God, if I lost Kiera like that... "I can't imagine anything worse than what you went through," I said, returning my focus to him.

Gavin looked back at Kiera for a second. Soft smile on his face, he shook his head at me. "Yes, you *can* imagine worse, Kellan. You lived it," he whispered. "And I'm so sorry."

A brief flicker of pain tightened my chest, but it wasn't nearly as bad as when we'd talked about this at the bar. I gave him a brief nod, and he placed his hand on my shoulder. "Thank you, though," he said. "It's been hard...without her. But...I haven't been alone." A warm smile lightened his face as Riley and Hailey stepped over to us.

Hailey looked between us with a curious expression, but she didn't ask what we'd been talking about. Riley stepped right up to me and tossed his arms around my waist. His level of comfort at showing affection made me laugh, and I gave him a quick one-armed hug. He was grinning when he pulled away. "Hey, next time you're in my state, do you think you could come do a concert at my school?"

"Ry," Hailey said with a frown. "Don't ask him to do that."

A chuckle escaped me as Riley frowned at her. "It's just a question, Hail." He looked back at me, and his cheeks faintly reddened. "There's this girl in my class...and I think she'd think it was pretty awesome if I got a rock star to play in our gym."

Gavin sighed at his son while I laughed a little harder. Leaning down, I said, "She might already think you're pretty awesome. Maybe you should just ask her out and see? You could show her that song I taught you. Girls dig guys who can play guitar." I flicked a quick glance at Kiera, just in time to see her bite her lip and look away. Yep. The guitar had a seductive power all on its own.

Gavin instantly put a hand on Riley's shoulder. "When you're older, Riley," he said, frowning at me. "He's only ten, Kellan. He doesn't need a girlfriend yet."

Riley's gaze snapped to Gavin's face. "Whoa, Dad. No one mentioned the g-word. I just...I think she's pretty." The grin after he said that made me laugh again. And made Gavin sigh again.

Leaning past Riley, I quietly said to Gavin, "If you haven't covered it already, you may not want to wait too much longer on the birds and the bees speech."

Gavin gave me a wry smile. "Yeah, I'm realizing that." Opening the door, Gavin shepherded Riley through it. As they left, I heard Riley say, "Birds and the bees speech? Does he mean that gross sex stuff that the older kids talk about? 'Cause I'm not doing that. Ever."

I snorted a laugh as I shook my head. *Never say never, Riley.* Hailey was laughing as she approached me; behind her, Kiera was laughing too. "I think you just aged Dad by about ten years," Hailey said, wiping tears from her deep blue eyes.

I shrugged, then held my arms open. Hailey gave me a hug, then pulled back and patted my chest. "I'm glad you stopped being stubborn," she said with a smirk.

Pursing my lips, I looked over at Kiera. "I wouldn't say it was me."

Kiera shrugged as she approached us. Ducking under my arm, she shook her head. "I only did what you secretly wanted me to do." She grinned at me while I frowned at her. No, she did exactly what I *didn't* want her to do...but in the end, it was the right call.

Smirking, I kissed her head. "Yes, dear," I murmured.

Hailey nodded her approval, then she pointed a stern finger at me. "I'm not missing the wedding, got it? I fully expect an invite."

Grinning, I made an X over my heart. "I promise, you'll get one."

She made a small squeal of excitement, then darted out the door after her father and brother. Kiera looked up at me after she left. "I like her."

I laughed as I closed the door. "Yeah...I do too."

It was really late, so we headed upstairs to go to bed. Martin and Caroline followed us up. Caroline disappeared into the guest room, to fall asleep on Kiera's old, uncomfortable futon. Martin stood in the doorway a moment, staring at Kiera and me in our doorway. Kiera gave him a bright smile and a wave, but I could tell from the look on his face that he really wanted to order Kiera to sleep in a different room than me. He couldn't, though...this was my house, and I was sleeping with my wife tonight.

He sighed when I gave him a small wave, then I disappeared into the room with Kiera. Shutting the door behind us, I slowly shook my head at my overprotective father-in-law. At least he had

Kiera's best interest at heart. I couldn't fault him for wanting to shield her from harm; I wanted that too.

Grinning, Kiera grabbed my T-shirt and pulled me toward the bed. "Did you have a good day?" she asked.

"I had the *best* day," I told her.

Kiera's legs hit the edge of the bed and she shifted to crawl on top of it, my shirt still clenched in her fingers. A light laugh escaped me as I followed her onto the mattress. "Good," she said once we were lying down. She nestled into my shoulder, her hands darting under my shirt to stroke my skin, her legs tangling with mine. Closing my eyes, I pulled her close, rubbing her back and running the tips of my fingers up and down her thigh. *Every day should end this way.*

But it couldn't. I was leaving tomorrow, and Kiera would be staying here for a time. And I was going to miss her, so fucking much.

I didn't want to waste a single second of our precious time together sleeping, and Kiera didn't seem to want that either. We talked instead. About her family, about my family, about what the future could hold for us. There was so much possibility now, and feeling that way made me so...buoyant. I'd never expected this from life, *any* of this, and I was just so incredibly grateful for it. I never—not for a single minute—wanted to take any of it for granted. Take *her* for granted. Which brought to mind something that I did sort of feel bad about.

In my nervousness about asking Kiera to be my wife, and in my impatience to skip over everything and just be married already, I was pretty sure I'd forgotten to actually ask her if she wanted to marry me. I ran through last night in my mind, trying to remember if I'd ever officially "popped the question," but I hadn't. I'd taken the roundabout, passive-aggressive, sneaky way to ask her without really asking her, and that didn't sit right with me. She should have it all, every single sappy moment.

Smiling, I kissed her hair. "Kiera?" She peeked up at me, and I immediately asked her the question I should have asked her at the bar. "Will you marry me?"

An adorable expression of confusion marked her features as she sat up on her elbows. "What?"

I grinned. "Will you marry me?"

Her gaze drifted to our fingers, to our rings. "Didn't we already get married?"

Her acknowledging what we'd done as legitimate made me so happy, and I laughed as I told her, "Yes, but I just realized that I never actually proposed to you." Studying her face, I tucked a strand of hair behind her ears before stroking her cheek. "And you deserve a proper proposal."

More proper than just casually asking her while lying in bed together. She needed a moment—*the* moment. The hearts and flowers, story to tell your friends, a memory to look back on for all time moment. And I hadn't given her that yet. But I still could.

Mind made up, I gently pushed her away so I could stand. She seemed confused, and she tried to pull me back, but there was something I needed to do first. I walked around to the other side of the bed, closer to where she was lying. I couldn't take my eyes off her, and oddly, knowing what I was about to do, watching her watch me so intently...it made nervous energy slam right into me. Logically, I knew I shouldn't be nervous, I knew what her answer was going to be, but yeah...my heart was pounding.

I let out a calm, steadying breath, then I slowly sank to one knee. The confusion on Kiera's face instantly disappeared once she realized what I was doing. Her eyes grew heavy with tears as she stared at me. She quickly swiped them away, but seeing the emotion made it difficult for me to speak. I could feel the moisture building in my own eyes as I willed my throat to relax. "Kiera Michelle Allen, will you do me the absolute honor of being my wife? Will you marry me?"

Even though she was already nodding, my heart wouldn't

stop racing. Kiera reached down and grabbed my face, kissing me. "Yes, of course, yes," she said, kissing me over and over.

A weird swell of relief hit me as I let her pull me back onto the bed, back into her arms. We both laughed, we both cried, and I marveled at this beautiful creature who'd just agreed to be mine for the rest of her life. Goddamn. I was so fucking lucky.

We kissed for a while, until the room brightened with daylight, and I heard the door to the guest bedroom open. When we heard Martin's heavy steps in the hallway, Kiera and I simultaneously pulled away from each other and looked at our closed door. I could sense him out there, trying to see through the door, trying to watch me...trying to be Kiera's chaperone through the wood. It gave me the weirdest feeling, like I was doing something really scandalous, even though I was in *my* bed with *my* wife.

Martin finally shuffled off, his steps retreating downstairs. The fact that I'd kind of won that round and he hadn't busted in here and removed me from Kiera made me a little giddy. I was grinning when I looked back at her. "Why do I feel like I should be hiding in the closet?" I asked.

Kiera smiled at my comment, slightly tilting her chin up, making her neck an irresistible draw. My hips pressed against hers as my lips found her skin. Desire flickered to life throughout my body, and I instantly wanted to do a lot more than just kiss her. Kiera shifted her head, giving me better access, and I slowly worked my way down her neck. Her legs wrapped around mine, holding me tight. She squeezed the hand that was holding one of mine while her other one threaded through my hair. I was just about to push up her shirt when she murmured, "Mmm... because you're a villainous boy who is only using me to satisfy his baser instincts."

That stopped me cold. Well, damn. Pulling back, I asked her, "Is that really what your dad thinks of me?" *Still*?

I knew he'd thought that way back in December, but I felt like we'd...kind of bonded since then. Maybe. A little. Hopefully. Had the tape with Joey done more damage than I'd realized? He knew that was years ago...I wasn't that guy anymore; didn't he see that?

Kiera seemed a little thrown by my sudden mood shift. "Uh, I don't...no...I don't think so."

She was saying no, but I could hear the truth in her words. It was a yes, a big, fat yes. I shifted to her side, and she twisted to face me. "Yeah, he does. He thinks all I want from you is sex, and that I have a different version of you in every city that I visit." *He thinks I'm a whore. He thinks I'm cheating on you. And I really haven't done much to convince him otherwise.*

Kiera frowned at me, but I could tell she was analyzing what I'd said, and she was looking for something that wasn't true in my statement. And she wasn't finding anything. Finally, she said, "I'm sure he doesn't think it's *every* city."

Right. *I'm only a whore in* almost *every city.* Great.

With a frown, I hopped out of bed. Kiera let out an annoyed grunt as she sat up. "Now what are you doing?"

Instead of answering her, I walked over to the dresser and started taking off clothes. Kiera blatantly stared as I stripped. *Blatantly.* Her eyes were wider than normal, and her mouth was popped open, like even after all this time, seeing my bare body took her breath away. It was flattering...and extremely amusing.

I shook my head at her when I was finished. "You do know that if I stared at you the way you stare at me, I would get yelled at."

Leaning down, I gave her a soft kiss. "I would never yell," she said, "but yes, I know." I smirked at her as I straightened, and she giggled as she told me, "Life is full of unfairness." She paused to frown. "Like you leaving me right now. Where are you going?"

Smiling, I attempted to fix my messy, bed-head hair. Or make it messier. Whatever. "I'm going to go show your dad that there is more to me than he thinks. My *only* interest isn't sleeping with his daughter." I gave her a playful wink, then made my way to the door. Hand on the knob, I turned back to her lying on my bed like a freaking goddess. "Although that really is what I would like to be doing right now." My eyes scanned her body, head to foot, and she rubbed her legs together like I was killing her just by doing that. Damn. I sighed as I willed my body not to react to her eagerness. Lifting my eyes back to hers, I said, "See the sacrifices I make for you?"

I crooked a grin at her, then quickly left the room before I changed my mind and let myself be the villainous boy her dad thought I was.

When I got downstairs, I met up with Martin in the kitchen. He looked me over as I stepped into the room. "You're up early," he said.

I gave him a warm smile. "This is actually kind of late for me. I'm an early riser."

He lifted his eyebrows at hearing that, clearly surprised. He shouldn't be; I'd woken up at nearly the same time as him during my visit over the holidays. "Well, that's good. As my grandfather used to say, a surefire key to success is to get a jump on the day."

Biting back a smile, I nodded. My father would have certainly agreed with that. Not that I was going to mention John Kyle to Martin; I'd rather not talk about him if I could help it. Martin pointed at the coffee that had just finished brewing. "I found where everything was...hope you don't mind."

I shook my head. "Not at all. My home is your home."

He gave me a teeny-tiny smile as I grabbed us some mugs from the cupboard. I poured some coffee for him, then some for myself; Martin left his black, same as me. He walked into the living room, so I followed him. Martin sat on the couch while I took the comfortable chair.

He took a small sip of his coffee, his eyes speculative. "So... this band thing. Do you really think you can make a living off of it?"

I forced myself not to smile, but I kind of failed and the corner of my lips curled up in amusement. "I think we'll make out okay." With a three-record deal, we shouldn't starve or anything. Hopefully.

Martin frowned at my answer. "Well...don't feel like you're stuck in that career path. There are a lot of other things you could do. Have you ever considered college?"

"Uh...well...no, not really. I mean, I sat in on one of Kiera's classes once, and that was fun, but going to college, being a student...I just don't see much point in it for me." I shrugged. "*Music* is my path. It's the only thing I've ever really wanted to do."

His frown deepened as he took another sip of his coffee. "Kellan, son, sometimes life doesn't work out the way we want it to. Sometimes you have to do things you don't want to do just to get by, to survive."

Staring into my coffee, I nodded. "I know. I'm not delusional about this. If it doesn't amount to anything, if it's not enough to give Kiera the life she deserves..." My voice trailed off as I looked up at him. "I'll do whatever I have to do to take care of her. I promise."

Martin's eyes were glued on mine for long, silent seconds. Then, finally, he smiled. "That's good to hear," he said.

I felt like dancing, 'cause damn, he smiled at me...and for a positive reason. I was fully taking that as a win.

We talked about less serious stuff after that, and I smiled to myself as I heard the shower turn on upstairs. Caroline had joined us in the living room, so I knew it was Kiera in the bathroom. I tried really hard not to picture her naked while I visited with her parents. I did *not* succeed.

Thankfully, the phone ringing in the kitchen disrupted my steamy thoughts. "Excuse me," I said, standing. I felt like humming as I walked into the kitchen, and my spirits were high when I brightly answered the phone. "Heeeeello."

"You're chipper," a disgruntled feminine voice answered. "I almost forgot how much you love mornings. That should have been my first clue that there was something seriously wrong with you."

I let out a long sigh, my mood fizzling with the exhale. "Joey...what do you want?"

"My money. You're paying me today, remember?"

Right. "Yeah...give me twenty minutes, and I'll meet you somewhere."

"I'll be at your house in ten," she coldly stated.

"No," I instantly snapped. I didn't need a repeat of yesterday's awkwardness. "Don't come here. I'll meet you up the street, at the corner."

She made a scoffing sound. "Seriously? We're gonna do this like we're making a drug deal?"

"If that's the way you want to look at it, sure, but I've got family visiting—I don't want you swinging by the house again."

"Oh..." she cooed, her voice mocking. "Did I make your *wife* mad? Did she refuse to fuck you last night?"

Tension instantly flooded my body, and my fingers clenched the phone so hard that I thought I might break it. "Joey..."

She continued like I hadn't just growled her name in warning. "You poor thing...it's probably been quite a while since you've had to get yourself off. You could have called me, Kellan. I would have helped you scratch that itch."

I'm sure you would have. My jaw tightened as my teeth ground together. "The corner. Ten minutes." Then I hung up the phone before she could respond.

"Fuck," I murmured. I did *not* trust that Joey wouldn't show up here anyway, just so she could stir shit up. I needed to get out of here—remove myself, remove the temptation. But how to leave...alone. I knew Kiera would want to come with me, and I really didn't want that. She shouldn't have to hear about Joey and me, any more than she already had, and I was positive Joey would say something...awful.

Dashing upstairs, I heard that Kiera was still in the bathroom. Maybe if I was quick, I could race out of here without her even knowing I'd left. But she'd worry if I took off without saying anything. Stewing on that, I grabbed what cash I had in my rainy-day fund—it wasn't nearly enough, so I grabbed my checkbook too. I looked around my room as I contemplated what to do about Kiera, and then I spotted an old pair of sneakers peeking out from under the bed. Maybe I could tell her I was going for a run. And actually...that sounded like a great idea. I had a feeling I'd need the release after talking to Joey. Mind made up, I quickly changed clothes.

I was just tying my shoes when Kiera stepped into the room. I did a double take when I saw her. She was wrapped in a tiny, barely-there towel, and I swear, it was the same towel from that very first meeting in the hallway. The memory of that moment seared me as I stared at the alluring hipbone peeking its way through the crack in the fabric. Jesus. Now I really didn't want to leave.

I went back to tying my shoes, but my mind was still in the past, to the look in her eyes when she'd scanned my body, to the feeling in my chest when I'd scanned hers. It felt like a lifetime ago now, and at the same time, it felt like only yesterday. I really wanted to move aside that damn towel and kiss her hip. To begin with.

Kiera caught my amusement. "What?" she asked, closing our door.

My thoughts were getting pretty provocative, so I shook my head. "Nothing," I said. *Nothing we have time for.* Standing, I told her part of my plans, "I'm going to go for a quick run."

"All right." Her brows furrowed in concern. "Everything okay?"

My thoughts were still deeply in the gutter, and I couldn't stop myself from visually caressing her body. When my eyes returned to hers, I knew Kiera could see the desire in them; I could certainly see the interest in hers. *Damn Joey. Damn company.* Why couldn't we be alone right now?

Closing the door on my pleasant ideas, I told her, "Everything's fine. Just need to do a little maintenance." Smiling, I reached up my shirt and patted my abs for emphasis; Kiera's eyes tracked the movement, and I could have sworn she looked...jealous. Walking over to her, I pinched her ass. "Wouldn't want to get all flabby now that I'm married," I murmured.

My fingers started slinking under her towel; guess I hadn't completely closed that door after all. Kiera giggled as she batted my hand away. Lacing her arms around my neck, her eyes filled with love as she gazed at me. "I'd rather have you flabby than gone," she said.

I let myself fall into the warmth of her kaleidoscopic eyes as I pulled her close. Mesmerized, I heard myself say, "I just need..." Realizing I was about to tell her the complete truth, I let that trail off unfinished. Fuck. I should just tell her exactly what I was doing. It wasn't like it was a surprise. She knew I was meeting Joey today. But she would want to come, and I did *not* want her to be there. Feeling like shit, I quickly told her, "I need a little fresh air."

I gave her a kiss on the cheek, and she nodded as she removed her arms from around me, letting me go. The guilt tore at me, and every step I took toward the door was more difficult than the last. I put my hand on the doorknob and turned it, but I couldn't make myself open the door. I couldn't leave with this half-truth between us. Resting my head against the hard wood, I muttered, "Damn it, I can't do this."

I heard Kiera say my name, and I inhaled a deep, cleansing breath as I turned to face her. She was not going to like what I'd done, or what I was about to do. I stared at her for long seconds, wondering if I was doing the right thing by saying something. If she wouldn't let me go on my own, this might lead to a fight. Maybe absolute honesty wasn't the best policy. But fuck...for us, with our fucked-up skeletons tossed about the yard for each of us to see...it was the *only* policy. We wouldn't work any other way. I knew that, I really did, I just...didn't want to deal with the consequences of the truth right now.

Kiera looked scared, and I hated the fact that I was freaking her out by not saying anything. Her mind was probably making this worse than it really was. But even still, I had to make sure 100 percent truth was what she wanted. I took a step toward her. "You said complete and total honesty, right?"

She nodded, and I looked away as I debated how to tell her what I'd just done without her getting pissed, or without her turning this into an argument about coming with me. I didn't have time for an argument. Maybe I should tell her later, after I got back. But Kiera was tired of waiting, and she wanted an answer. "What is it?" she asked, her voice quiet.

Accepting the approaching fight, I looked back at her and confessed. "I'm sorry. I purposely misled you right now. I'm not leaving the house because I want to exercise, or because I want air. I need to do something...and I need to do it alone." There. If I simply didn't elaborate, then I wasn't lying, and she couldn't argue to come with me. It was underhanded, sure...but effective.

Kiera was still upset, though, and her eyes instantly turned fiery. "You...lied to me? About what? What exactly do you need to do alone?"

Damn. I should have known vagueness wouldn't work. She'd simply argue about wanting to know what we were fighting about. I held up my hands like that would somehow hold back her anger. "See, I wanted to avoid this reaction, that's why I lied. But we're trying to do the honesty thing, so I changed my mind and decided to tell you the truth. So don't get mad."

She instantly zipped past mad to flat-out pissed. "But you haven't told me the truth. You haven't told me anything. You're being vague and mysterious...and I don't like that."

True. But still...I didn't have time for this. I closed my eyes as weariness settled over me. "It would have been easier to just keep walking." I knew I shouldn't have said it the instant I did. Wondering if she was epically angry now, I was slow to reopen my eyes. Fury blazed in hers as she tapped her foot, waiting for an answer. So much for being vague. "Joey called while you were in the shower. I'm going to go meet with her, and I want you to stay here with your parents."

She looked stunned by my proclamation. "No! I don't want you to meet her without me. I'm coming with you!"

Yep. I knew it. I knew she'd want to come with me. But that *wasn't* happening. I shook my head, hoping she'd listen to me for once. "I don't want you anywhere near her. I want you to stay here."

By her face, you'd think I'd just ordered her to obey my every whim without question. "You're not the boss of me. If I want to go—"

Her words sparked something dark in me, and with a soft sigh, I turned to leave without letting her finish. That ticked her off even more, and she grabbed my elbow, jerking me back around. "Hey, I wasn't done talking to you."

The darkness inside me shifted into anger, and I said something rash as heat simmered in my stomach. "I know I'm not the boss of you, Kiera. I got that loud and clear when Denny walked back into your life, and you didn't say a word to me. But you're not the boss of me either, and if I want to do this on my own, then I will." My anger flared with each word, and when I was finished spouting cold truths, I stormed from the room.

And instantly regretted it.

Chapter 4

SAYING GOODBYE

The second I was downstairs, I wanted to turn around and go apologize to Kiera. I shouldn't have said that to her. True or not, it was a dick move to use the past against her like that. I needed to leave, though. If I waited too long, Joey would come *here*, and that was the last thing I wanted; I'd rather have Kiera mad at me for a little while than have Joey in my house again.

After telling Kiera's parents that I'd be back in a bit, I headed outside. I jogged up the street to the corner, but I didn't see Joey. *Good. I beat her here.* I kicked at a pebble on the sidewalk as I waited for her, wondering just how pissed Kiera was right now. I had some serious groveling in my future.

A few minutes later, Joey's Jetta pulled up to the curb. Joey stepped out of the car, and her gaze scanned the street before settling on me. She looked disappointed that I was alone, and I was instantly grateful Kiera hadn't come with me.

She strutted over to me with a smirk on her face. "Got my money?" she asked, flipping her ebony hair over her shoulder. Her eyes drifted down my body, lingering on my crotch.

I turned my hips slightly, and she peeked up at me, her dark eyes sparkling in amusement. Frowning, I reached into my pocket and pulled out the cash I'd brought. Knowing it wasn't nearly enough, I told her, "This is all I had on me. I'll write you a check for the rest."

Her lips pursed as she took the money and quickly counted it out. "Are you fucking serious? This is only five hundred bucks. I don't want a twenty-five-hundred-dollar check from you. It'll probably bounce."

I gave her a dry expression. "It won't."

She lifted an eyebrow. "Like I'm gonna take your word for it." She got a devilish look in her eye that I knew really well. Shoving the cash into her pocket, she stepped closer to me and put a hand on my chest. "You know, there are other ways you could pay me..."

She lifted her other hand, aiming for my junk. I quickly stepped back before she could reach me. "Don't," I brusquely said.

Pursing her lips, she crossed her arms over her chest. "Why not? You used to love it when I touched you like that. Remember?"

My eyes narrowed. "That was a long time ago. Things are different now."

"Right," she said with a scoff. "You're *married*. What the hell is so special about that girl anyway? 'Cause I didn't see anything overly remarkable about her. Really, Kellan, you could do *so* much better."

She was crawling right under my skin...and I knew that was exactly what she wanted. Inhaling a deep breath, I attempted to calm down. "I didn't come here to discuss my wife. I came here to pay you, that's it." Before she could say another word, I pulled out my checkbook and started writing her a check. The sooner we got this over with, the better.

"What the fuck do you think you're doing?" she snapped, her hands dropping to her sides. "I said I didn't want your worthless check."

I glanced up at her. "This is the only way I'm going to pay you, take it or leave it." Finished with the check, I handed it to her.

"This isn't what I want," she bit out, not taking it.

My face hardened, along with my voice. "Well, I don't have any more cash, and I'm not going to fuck you, so this is all I've got."

She let out a mocking laugh. "Like I actually *wanted* to have sex with you. I was joking." She tilted her head to the side. "Or maybe I was curious to see if you'd do it. You *are* incapable of being with just one person after all."

My anger flared. "You don't know anything about me, Joey." Not really. She'd barely scratched the surface of who I was.

She smirked at my statement, then rolled her eyes. "I know enough. And one day, that wife of yours will know too. And what a sad day that will be for her." A sadistic smile crossed her lips, and I had to resist the urge to wipe it off her face.

Fuming, I held the paper out to her again. "Just take the check. If you don't trust that there's enough money in the account, then I'll drive to the fucking bank with you, but I swear to God I'm not trying to screw you over." *I just want you out of my goddamn life.*

Heat flared in her eyes as she snatched the check out of my fingers. Done with this conversation, I was just about to turn and leave when she suddenly reached out and smacked my face. No, not smacked. The bitch curled her fingers and scratched me with her long, pointy nails. "You already screwed me over," she snarled.

I could feel the radiating burn of the fresh cut, could feel the wetness on my cheek. I was stunned stupid for a second, and then the fury hit me, and I could barely stop myself from slapping her back. *Fucking psychotic bitch.*

I almost wanted to get into it with her. Ask her how I'd possibly "screwed her over" when we were never together in the first place. I mean, fuck, she'd been dragging a guy into her bedroom on the night she'd "caught" me with another woman. It wasn't like I could cheat on her when she was on a fucking date. But from the gleam in Joey's eye, I could tell that was exactly what she wanted me to do. She wanted me to go after her. She wanted me to fight with her. She wanted this to escalate so she could revel in the chaos. Too bad I had better things to do.

"Fuck off, Joey," I seethed, my hands clenching into fists. I twisted to leave, then paused and looked back at her. Her dark eyes narrowed as she watched me. "Don't *ever* talk to me again. Me or my wife."

I wasn't ready to go home yet, so I took off down the street in an easy jog that quickly turned into a hard run. My face burned, the pain intensifying as sweat rolled down my cheek. It pissed me off, and I pushed myself even more, trying to melt away the anger with fatigue. By the time I was utterly exhausted, my mood had evened. I headed home, hoping Kiera wasn't still mad at me; I really didn't have it in me for another fight.

My cheek was throbbing when I opened my front door. I knew I couldn't hide the injury from Kiera forever, but I really wanted to look at it before she saw it. Maybe it wasn't as bad as I feared. Maybe if I took a shower and cleaned the blood off, it would barely be noticeable. I doubted that, but I held onto the hope as I stepped into the entryway.

Everyone was staring at me, and I made sure to hide my cheek; I really didn't want Kiera's parents seeing it. Inhaling a deep breath, I closed the front door. Kiera was going to flip out when she saw the scratch, especially if she saw it right now, all raw and bloody. I really wasn't sure how she was feeling at the moment—this could make things worse between us. Her face looked apologetic, though, as she set down her notebook and stood up. Still, I didn't want her to see it yet.

As she started approaching me, I told her, "I need a shower before I head out to the airport." That didn't stop her from walking my way. Turning from her, I quickly sprinted up the stairs. She said my name, confusion in her voice, and I tossed out, "I'll be right back...just need to clean up."

I felt like a chickenshit coward, but it was a necessary distraction to get a moment alone before seeing her. And technically, I hadn't lied about anything I'd just said. I'd told the truth about needing to rinse off, so at least there was that. Right.

Flicking on the bathroom light, I turned my head to get a look at the damage. Fuck. *Joey got me good*. There was a swollen, bloody red line from the top of my cheek down to my jaw. I was a little surprised there was only one line...although looking closer, I could see two faint parallel red lines that hadn't quite gone deep enough to draw blood. I supposed I should consider myself lucky.

"Kellan?"

Hearing Kiera's voice in the hallway, I instinctively turned to look at her. Her eyes instantly widened, her jaw dropping. "She hit you?"

Glancing back at the mirror, I too-late realized that she could see the cut in the reflection. I sighed. Damn it. I should have closed the door. I'd wanted to clean it before she saw it, lessen the severity, but I supposed it didn't matter; a cut was a cut. "I'm fine, Kiera."

She gingerly grabbed my face, turning me to get a better look. "She drew blood. That bitch drew blood!"

"It's fine." Because I didn't want her to be too upset, I smirked and added, "It's not the first time a woman has cut me." She didn't find my reference to our hot little moment in an espresso stand amusing. Her eyes started watering. My small smile faltered as I stared at the compassion on her face. "Things...didn't go very well. Maybe you should have tagged along after all."

Although I wasn't sure if her presence would have changed anything. It probably would have made things worse. Kiera seemed to agree. She gave me a hard look as she tenderly cupped my unharmed cheek. "Maybe it's better that I didn't. I probably would have gotten arrested for assault."

A portion of my smile returned at the image of Kiera going off on Joey. I'd never allow it to happen, but still, the visual was appealing. "I'm sorry I was sort of an ass to you. I just didn't want you involved in her ugliness."

Her eyes scanned my face as she stroked my cheek with her thumb. "I'm not involved with her, I'm involved with you, and I wanted to be there to support you."

Her words got to me, and my gaze dropped to the floor; I'd never had anyone offer that kind of support before. Not really. The guys had backed me up on occasion, and I knew they'd go to blows for me, but this was different somehow. Deeper. It meant a lot to me, and I felt kind of bad for denying her that opportunity. And yet, I still didn't want her anywhere near Joey. "I know," I told her. "I just...I know her, and I knew how she'd be." I lifted my eyes to her face. "Especially now that she knows what you mean to me. I wanted to protect you."

A loving smile on her face, she kissed my chin. "I'm not weak. I can handle it."

Considering everything about my past that she'd already handled, I had to admit that was true. Giving her a warm smile, I sat on the bathroom counter. "I know you're not weak. I think I'm the weak one. I needed to know you were safe, protected. I didn't want you to have to hear..." Not wanting to remind her about all the things Joey could tell her, I let that thought die. "This was all about me, Kiera...and I'm sorry."

Her lips curling into a half-smile, she wrapped her arms around my neck. "You can stop apologizing, you know. I forgave you a while ago."

That surprised me. And delighted me. "Yeah?" I said, enclosing her in my arms.

She shrugged as she moved closer to me. "Of course. You and I aren't always going to agree; we're not always going to get along." She shifted her hands to my cheeks, careful of my cut.

"And...I am so proud of you for telling me the truth when you really wanted to lie. That means more to me than...well, that means everything."

Emotion laced her voice, and I understood why. We had done so much damage to each other by not being honest. I never wanted to go back to that gut-wrenching time when so many lies and secrets had been between us. I was so grateful that I'd told her the truth; the tiny spat was well worth it. I nodded in her hands, agreeing with her on every level.

Kiera asked what happened, and I told her the basics of the story. When I was finished, I rolled my eyes. "She's a touch crazy. I don't know how I ever lived with her." Kiera gave me a questioning look that clearly said, *How could you have slept with her?* Thankfully, she didn't ask that...because I really didn't have a good answer for her, and she wasn't entirely wrong. I should have hooked her up with Griffin instead. He kind of deserved her brand of crazy.

Knowing I needed to get my butt in gear, I kissed Kiera's head. "I just want to shower now, get ready to go."

There was a sad look on her face as she moved away from the counter so I could hop off of it. I understood that too; I didn't want to go. But I had to. I turned on the shower, and Kiera shut the bathroom door. I smiled to myself, happy that she was staying. Kiera hopped on the counter while I fiddled with the water. When it was ready, I started undressing. Kiera stared at me the entire time, and when my shirt was free, her eyes locked on my tattoo and a warm smile touched her lips. She loved my tattoo. *I* loved my tattoo. It was something private and special between us, one of many private and special things we had between us.

I paused with my hands on my track pants as I thought over our life before I'd left on Justin's tour—before everything had changed. My world had been so small back then, and there had been countless hours for Kiera and me. Mornings together, driving her to and from school, afternoons spent together doing nothing and loving it, lounging around at Pete's while she worked, our cherished, lazy days off together...the simplicity of it all tightened my chest with fear and anxiety. If I did this—made an album and released it to the masses—if that somehow worked and the band got noticed, if the band got big...would I be setting a match to that simple life, never to return to it again? I almost couldn't bear that thought.

Kiera's eyes met mine, her brows furrowed as she watched me. "Am I making a mistake?" I asked her. Seeing her confusion increase, I expanded my question. "Making an album, going on tour...am I making a mistake?"

Kiera jumped off the counter and approached me. I took her hand, lacing our fingers together. "All I want is a quiet life with you," I told her. "What I just signed up for...isn't exactly a quiet life." And what happened today only emphasized that fact. If fame found me, I'd hear from Joey again. I'd probably hear from *all* of them. But if I let this go...

But letting it go filled me with a different sort of anxiety. An anxiety laced with sadness. As much as I told myself I didn't want this life, I deeply *did* want it.

Kiera's face was a picture of sympathy, and I knew she understood the division inside me; she probably had similar thoughts. Reaching up, she almost imperceptibly stroked my cut. "Kellan, your life will never be quiet, no matter what you do."

A laugh escaped me. I supposed she was right. Joey attacking me had nothing to do with my upcoming fame. As far as I knew, she wasn't even aware of the success our band had found on the road. Fingers crossed she somehow never found out. Fat chance of that. If she was back in town, someone would tell her. The minute she stepped inside Pete's, she'd know.

Kiera placed her hand on my chest, holding my gaze. "You belong on a stage. It's what you were born to do." As I absorbed that statement, Kiera gave me a soft kiss. "We will just have to find moments of quiet in the chaos, and we're pretty good at that."

"Yeah...we are," I said, returning her kiss.

Speaking of moments of quiet in the chaos...

Pulling back, I tilted my head toward the shower, inviting her in with me. She pursed her lips like she was debating it, but then she shook her head and gave me a goodbye kiss. I frowned at her answer, even though I understood.

Kiera smirked at me as she gathered my dirty clothes. I quickly removed the rest of what I was wearing and gave it to her. "Thank you for the pep talk," I said, kissing her cheek.

She had a hard time keeping her eyes on my face. So cute. "You're welcome," she told me, faintly blushing.

I was smiling as I stepped into the shower. Until the water hit my face, then I was swearing. Kiera jumped on the opportunity to tease me about my pain tolerance. I rolled my eyes as she left the room, but then I grinned and shook my head. Served me right, I supposed. Lord knows I relentlessly teased her.

Kiera was visiting with her mom when I was done showering; I could hear them discussing flower arrangements in our guest room. Kiera wasn't a fan of being the center of attention, so I had to believe she was *not* looking forward to an official wedding ceremony. I was positive she would go through with it, though. For her mom. For me. I loved that.

My phone chimed with a message just as I was finishing getting dressed. Grabbing it, I saw the message was from Gavin. I opened it without hesitation...and then marveled over the fact that I could do that now. It was kind of a long message, and I was still reading it as I headed across the hall to the spare bedroom. Every line I read tugged at something inside me, filling me with a warmth I hadn't even known was possible to feel. It struck me, all the way down to the core of who I was, to that lonely, forgotten child who'd just wanted someone to say they cared. And the last thing he said...

"What is it?"

I looked up to see Kiera watching me with curious eyes. My smile felt enormous to me as I tucked my phone into my pocket. A part of me wanted to respond to the message...but I literally didn't know what to say. "That was Gavin. His plane is just about ready to take off. He wanted to thank me for meeting with him... finally...and let me know that I could visit him anytime I wanted." As I thought of his last words, a weird feeling surged through me. Letting out a small laugh, I dropped my gaze to the floor. "He said he...he loves me."

I peeked up at Kiera as the strange feeling grew even stronger. I wasn't sure how Gavin could possibly love me—he barely even knew me—but hearing him say that, hearing...*my father*...say that, it patched something inside me. How long had I wished for a parent to say those words to me? My entire fucking life. That was how long.

Still, the oddity of it was hard to wrap my mind around.

Maybe seeing my confusion, my uncertainty, Kiera stood up and walked over to me. Wrapping her arms around my waist, she said, "Of course he loves you. You're his son."

Words escaped me before I even realized I was saying them. "That doesn't mean anything." And wasn't that the fucking truth.

Kiera's eyes glistened, the green in them a deep jade, and I could practically feel the empathy radiating from her. Brushing a strand of hair off my forehead, she leaned up and told me, "I will always love you, Kellan. Your heart is safe with me."

I greatly appreciated the fact that she didn't try to argue my statement. She knew as well as I did that there was no arguing with it. I also appreciated her words—more than she would ever know. A hopeful yet painful ache ripped through me as I pulled her into a tight hug. "Promise?" I whispered.

She squeezed harder, like she really would never let me go. "I promise." She pulled back to rest her forehead against mine. "Not loving you isn't possible. Trust me, I tried."

I had to smirk at that. So very, very true.

Kiera and I were softly kissing when someone behind me loudly cleared their throat. We both twisted to see Martin staring at us from the doorway. "Something going on?" he asked, a forced measure of pleasantness in his voice.

Not wanting to lose any ground I'd made with him this weekend—if I'd made any at all—I let go of Kiera and shook my head. "Everything's fine...just getting ready to leave."

You would have thought I'd just told Martin I was throwing him a party by his reaction. Clapping me on the back, he brightly said, "Well then, anything I can help you with?"

His eagerness to get rid of me made me laugh. "No, I'm good, thank you," I told him, after kissing Kiera's head. Stepping away from her, I clapped Martin on the shoulder, then headed back to the bedroom to get my stuff.

Not too much later, I was pulling the Chevelle into the parking lot at Pete's so everyone could say goodbye to the band before we headed back to Los Angeles. I was a little melancholy as I handed Kiera the car keys, and I made a small misstep by mentioning to Kiera that we should have the Chevelle garaged when she left Seattle and joined me in California. By the look on both Kiera's face and Martin's face, it was obvious she hadn't told him about that yet. Oops.

Martin tried to talk to Kiera about it, but my bandmates started showing up and the conversation was lost. Matt and Griffin arrived first with Rachel and Anna in tow; Evan and Jenny arrived a moment later. A warmth filled me when everyone was together again. We didn't get to hang out as a complete group nearly often enough. I was really going to miss this when we hit the road, miss everyone we were leaving behind. But I'd see them all again. Of that, I was certain.

Kiera flashed her wedding ring at her best friend, Jenny, and the perky blonde instantly squealed and hugged her. I had to laugh at their excitement, especially when they started jumping up and down like they'd just won the lottery. All the guys glanced at me with confused expressions on their faces. I shrugged at them, 'cause I didn't get it either.

Rachel and Anna joined the mix, and then all the girls were

admiring Kiera's ring. I shook my head as I watched them; it was literally the same ring Kiera had been wearing since Christmas. Why it was so fascinating now was a bit of a mystery to me. And that thought instantly made me want to get Kiera a new ring. Her band was beautiful, sure, and perfect for what I'd originally purchased it for, but Kiera deserved a diamond. A breathtaking, spectacular diamond. Yes. This was happening.

Smirk on my face, I looked over at Evan, my drummer and closest friend. *You don't know it yet, but you're gonna help me go ring shopping.* Evan was smiling at Kiera, but he must have felt my stare because his dark eyes shifted to look at me. My grin grew, and his brows furrowed in confusion. Laughing, I looked away. He was gonna kill me when I told him what we were doing. I couldn't wait.

My gaze settled on my guitarist. Matt's pale blue eyes were wide as he watched the girls, and all the blood drained from his face when he heard his girlfriend let out a dreamy sigh and say, "You're engaged." Rachel seemed enraptured by the idea, but clearly, the thought of following in my footsteps freaked the fuck out of Matt. I barely contained a snicker as I looked back at my wife.

Shaking her head, Kiera told Rachel, "No...we're married."

Jaws dropped everywhere, and all the guys zeroed in on me again. I grinned at them, shrugging again. Evan and Matt shrugged back—Griffin rolled his eyes—and that was about it. The girls reacted a lot differently. Jenny's face shifted into a mixture of anger and betrayal. "What? You got married? Without me?"

Anna let out an amused snort. "Relax. They exchanged rings at the bar. They're not really married."

That made me frown. It was real to me. Real to Kiera too. And she immediately told her sister so. "We're married in our hearts, where it matters. The legal stuff will come later."

Griffin tossed a disgruntled look at me, then decided to join the conversation. Making the same sound Anna had, he said,

"Please, you guys aren't married." He crossed his arms over his chest and stared me down. "No bachelor party, no marriage. That's the law."

I rolled my eyes at my bassist, and he scowled at me. I instantly smiled. He was doing more to win me points with Martin than anything else I'd done this weekend. *Keep talking, Griffin. Please.*

Kiera wasn't as amused as me, though. Crossing her arms, she told him, "That is *not* a law, Griffin."

He looked over at her, annoyance clear on his face. "Well, it should be. No T and A, no ball and chain." He gave Kiera a creepy smirk, and I almost wanted to shake his hand. *Thank you, Griffin. I think you just completely erased the whole Joey incident.*

Kiera looked like she wanted to slug him. She didn't, but Anna did. Well, she smacked the back of his head. Griffin frowned at her, irritated. "What? It's a fair sacrifice. If you've got to be with one chick for the rest of your life, then you should at least get to go out with a bang. Or two. Or three."

Evan and Matt both rolled their eyes at the same time, and for the first time ever, Rachel looked pissed; there was a flush to her bronze skin, and her almond eyes were narrowed in anger. Her expression matched Kiera's. And Martin's. Jenny shook her head at Griffin while Caroline just...gaped. I fought back a smile. Fucking Griffin...but damn, he made me look so good.

Anna was the only one, besides me, who didn't react negatively to what he'd said. Amusement on her face, she lifted a dark eyebrow at him. "Really? Would you want some jackass to do that with our daughter?" Her hand drifted to her stomach, and Griffin's eyes followed.

He spoke so quickly that I knew the words were coming out without a conscious thought. "Fuck no. I'll chop the little bastard's balls off if he tries that kind of shit on my girl."

Surprise made me blink. Damn. Never thought I'd hear him admit something like that. He lived and breathed casual sex and often encouraged everyone else to as well. But apparently, not when it came to his kid. Maybe there was hope for him yet.

Anna smiled like she'd known all along what was hiding deep inside him. "Hmmm," she said, then she kissed his cheek while he stood there, dumbfounded and contemplative.

I grinned as I watched Griffin's wheels turning. Or trying to turn. Griffin wasn't all that great with self-reflection. Still, it was obvious Anna had given him something to think about. She really was perfect for him. Hopefully, he realized that before he completely fucked things up with her.

We had a little time before our ride to the airport was due to arrive, so we headed into the bar to have one last drink at Pete's. Well, one last drink for now. I fully intended on returning to this bar. It was just as much a home to me as my actual home. More so.

I waved at the day crew as I stepped inside the large rectangular building. Troy let out a wistful sigh when he saw me, and I bit back a smile. It didn't matter if I came here in the morning or at night, either way the bartender had the hots for me. At least Troy was a hell of a lot more respectful than Rita.

All of us started heading to the band's unofficial table near the stage. Kiera froze up on me as we walked, coming to a complete stop. I glanced down to see her staring at something, and my gaze shifted to look. Then my jaw dropped. Denny—the friend I'd stabbed in the back by having an affair with his girl-friend—was here, waiting at the table. Waiting...for *me*?

He stood when he saw he had our attention. A small smile was on his face, and I was struck by how different he seemed. His dark hair was a little longer than he used to keep it and was styled back from his face in a more professional kind of cut. His clothes were nicer, better kept. His facial hair was thicker, not nearly a beard, but more than just stubble. He stood taller, prouder, and there was an undeniable well of wisdom in his deep brown eyes that made you want to hear what he had to say. He just seemed more confident now, more self-assured, like he had everything in his life figured out. Denny was only a couple of years older than me, but at the moment, he seemed more like ten.

I scoffed at the fact that he was here, waiting for me, and he smiled wider as I approached him. When I was close enough, I pulled him in for a one-armed hug. "You came to see me off?" I asked, still stunned that he'd do that. Sure, we'd made up recently, but honestly...there was nothing in this world that could truly make up for what I'd done to him. Words weren't enough, actions weren't enough. He should slug me every time he saw me, and it never ceased to amaze me that he didn't.

Denny shrugged as he stepped back. "You guys are about to hit it big. This might be the last chance I get to see you."

I had to look away. Even now, he still believed in me. God, I was such a dick for ever hurting him. "I don't know about that." I paused to look back at him. "But I'm glad you're here."

Kiera gave him a brief, friendly hug after that, and surprisingly, the embrace didn't bother me. That part of their relationship was over. Long over. Denny greeted the rest of the guys, then we all crowded around the table. I couldn't help but notice Caroline glancing between Denny, Kiera, and me with a confused expression on her face. I had to wonder if she knew everything that had happened between us, and if she did, if she was just as mystified as I was that we were all...civil. *Yeah, I know, join the club.*

Emily was working our section today, and she brought the table the round of shots I'd ordered—plus apple juice for Anna. Once everyone had their drinks, Matt lifted his glass to make a toast, and everyone followed suit. He opened his mouth to say something, but of course, his cousin verbally ran right over him. "To fame, fortune, and scores of loose women!" Griffin stated, glee on his face.

Since none of us were about to toast to that list of asshole items, no one, except Griffin, moved their raised drink. While Griffin downed his alcohol, I glanced at Martin; he looked so pissed. I loved it. It kind of made me wish Griffin was by my side every time Martin was around. But that would require Griffin to be around me even more than he already was. So...no.

After Griffin smacked his empty glass on the table, Matt continued like nothing had just happened. "To good friends and good music. May we always have both."

Now that, I could drink to.

Chapter 5

CELEBRATING

Eventually the guys and I had to say goodbye to all the people we were leaving behind and make our way to the airport. I felt a strange mixture of joyfulness and sadness as I watched Seattle disappearing from view. That had been...the best weekend of my life. Even with Joey showing up. Even with the scratch she'd left me that was still burning my face. Best weekend, hands down. I couldn't stop smiling, and I couldn't stop missing Kiera. Already.

Evan was sitting on the far side of the cab from me, by the other window. He leaned over Matt in the middle seat and poked my shoulder. When I turned to look at him, he said, "I guess congratulations are in order. You got..." His brows furrowed. "Married?"

I laughed at the odd look on his face, then nodded. "Yes, I did. Thanks."

Matt turned to look at me too. "Yeah, congratulations, Kell." He looked a lot calmer about the whole thing now that Rachel wasn't around.

Griffin was sitting in the front seat by the driver. Twisting around, he tucked his dirty-blond hair behind his ears and made a disgruntled noise. "Married...whatever."

I narrowed my eyes at him but let it go. Evan shook his head at Griffin, then looked back at me. "We'll go out when we get back to L.A. Celebrate."

"Sounds good," I said, nodding at him.

Griffin's face suddenly shifted into one of true excitement; his light blue eyes were practically glowing with eagerness. "Dude, yeah, that's a great idea. Strip club here we come!"

"Now you're happy for me?" I asked, lifting an eyebrow.

He nodded. "If it means boobs, then yeah, I'm thrilled for you."

Rolling my eyes at him, I looked back at Evan. I simply stared at him for a moment, my expression neutral. Evan grinned at me. "I know," he said. "You want to go to a bar."

Griffin groaned while I grinned. "Damn it, Evan. Does it matter what he wants? What about *us*?"

Evan indicated me with his hands, the flame tattoos on his forearms twisting with the movement. "Well, it is for *him*, so I feel like, yeah, it does matter what he wants."

Griffin shot us both a blank look, then focused his attention on Matt. "What about you, cuz? You want boobs, or do you want beer that we can get any-fucking-where?"

Matt glanced at me, smiled, then looked back at Griffin. "Beer," he stated.

Griffin flipped him off. "All of you suck."

We all started laughing, and Griffin flipped us off with both hands. As the laughter died down, Griffin said, "Hey, Kell, what happened to your face?"

I frowned as I remembered. Fucking Joey. I opened my mouth to tell him...something...but before I could, he got his own idea about what happened. "Did Kiera do it? She get a little...carried away?" He wriggled his eyebrows just in case I wasn't sure what he meant. I was about to tell him no, but he again beat me to the punch. "Shouldn't the claw marks be on your back, though...unless..." His eyes lit up in a way that was mildly disturbing. "Duuuude...nice."

He held out his fist for me to bump. I ignored it. And him. And his questions.

Shaking my head, I looked out the window. Were we there yet? I sensed eyes on me, and when I looked back, Evan was staring at me, scratching his super-short dark brown hair while he bit his lip. He clearly wasn't going to ask, but I could tell he was really curious. Rolling my eyes, I told him, "Joey paid me a visit. She was upset about...her furniture being gone." It was slightly a lie, but it was also the truth, if you boiled the truth down to its basic facts. It was all I wanted to say about it, though. I'd rather not tell him that I made a sex tape with her...especially with Griffin listening. He'd probably jump out of the cab and track her down so he could watch the damn thing. Because fuck...there were probably more copies out there. I highly doubted Joey had given me the *only* one, and that meant I'd paid her for no reason. Goddamn it.

While I mentally kicked myself, Griffin latched on to my comment, confirming my instinct not to say anything in front of him. "Joey...damn...I miss that girl. Or I miss that girl's ass." High in the air, so we could all see, he mimed grabbing Joey's ass. I stopped looking at him when he started repeatedly jerking the imaginary ass toward his hips. I couldn't block out the moaning, though.

As Matt leaned forward to try to stop Griffin's disturbing display before he got us kicked out of the cab, I quietly murmured, "God, I can't believe he's going to be a dad."

Evan heard me. He nodded and let out a long sigh. "We should have sterilized him years ago."

A laugh escaped me, and I subtly held up my fist for Evan behind Matt's back. Evan laughed as he bumped it. The two of us were quiet for a moment as Matt and Griffin started talking about family stuff. Apparently, Griffin's parents wanted him to visit while he was down in L.A., but he hadn't yet. When Griffin started complaining that his parents' place didn't have a pool, Evan leaned toward me.

"Hey," he said, his voice low. "I don't usually put much stock in anything Jackass says..." He jerked his thumb at Griffin. "But he mentioned something about you having two dads now? Do you know what the hell he's talking about?"

I laughed as I glanced up at Griffin. "Yeah...actually, I do." Returning my eyes to Evan, I told him the whole sordid story about Gavin, then I told him about everything I'd been going through the last six months. Telling him was easier than I ever thought it would be, and I didn't know if that was because it was Evan, and he already knew the darkest parts of my past, or if it was because I'd finally accepted Gavin as family. Maybe a combination of both.

Evan looked stunned when I was finished. "Damn, man. I don't know if *I'm sorry* is the right thing to say, or if *I'm happy for you* is better. I'm sorry you had to go through that. But I'm happy it worked out for you." His brows furrowed. "And I'm a little annoyed that you didn't tell me while it was happening. Or before it happened. Or after it happened. Or *ever*."

I cringed at the look on his face. "I'm telling you now?"

His dark eyes narrowed. "Uh-huh. Because Griffin spilled the beans."

True. I let out a long sigh. "I'm sorry. I just...I didn't know how to deal with it, so I...didn't deal with it," I said with a shrug.

Evan's expression leveled, and he nodded. Smiling, I said, "Thank you, though. That means a lot."

He nodded again, then raised his pierced eyebrow. "Any other family issues you're not dealing with that I should know about?"

Since he did in fact know everything, I laughed and shook my head. "No...that's it, I promise."

He eyed me for a second, then nodded. "Okay. If that changes, let me know."

I smiled, then nodded. "Deal."

. . .

The flight to L.A. was uneventful, and before I knew it, we were back in the recording studio, continuing to work on the album. Recording an album was an interesting yet tedious process. It was like the world's most fastidious rehearsal session. Starting, stopping, recording, rerecording; it was enough to test anyone's patience, but it was especially hard on Griffin. Every second he was getting more and more annoyed, and I could tell he was practicing an insane amount of self-control. It was pretty huge of him not to make a scene, and it almost made me want to take him to a strip club as a thank you. Almost.

When we were done with our session, everyone looked exhausted. I thought sleep might trump our hastily made celebration plans, but when we were back at the label's house, lounging in our semi-private living room, Evan looked at me and asked, "So where should we go?"

Griffin instantly raised his hand. Ignoring him—and his obvious answer—I shrugged. "I don't know. Suggestions?" I said, only looking at Evan and Matt.

Griffin jumped off the couch and waved his hand high in the air as he bounced on his toes; the grin on his face was enormous. Also ignoring him, Evan smiled at me and said, "I think it's only fitting to go back to where this all started." He indicated the four of us with a swirl of his finger.

Matt flicked a glance at Griffin. He was holding his elbow now, supporting his wildly-waving raised hand, and making whimpering noises. I was honestly shocked he hadn't spoken yet; *that* was how badly he wanted us to call on him. I knew we should probably throw him a bone since he'd been on his best behavior today *but*...messing with him was too much fun. Matt seemed to agree with me. Ignoring Griffin's display, he turned to Evan and said, "Good idea, what did you have in mind? The place where we did our first show?"

Griffin started waving both of his hands now. Evan smiled at Matt. Shaking his head, he said, "No...I was thinking of a place that was important to us before that."

Matt rubbed his jaw, murmuring, "Hmmm," while I bit my lip to stop from laughing at Griffin. He was getting pissed; his cheeks were turning red. And now he was jumping.

Still ignoring him, Matt snapped his fingers. "Oh, what about that one place—"

Griffin finally lost the battle with his patience. Dropping his hands to his sides, he let out a loud, annoyed exhale, cutting off Matt's idea. "Jesus Christ!" he sputtered. All of us instantly started laughing. Eyes narrowed, Griffin pointed at each of us in turn. "I've said it before, and I'm sure I'll say it again—all of you fucking suck!" We kept right on laughing while he kept right on glowering. Then his expression shifted into a devilish grin. "Where we *should* go is back to that strip club where we all met. That was the true start of this band...so it's only right and natural that we return there." He nodded his head, a solemn look on his face, like we'd only be doing our civic duty to head over there. Like it would be a sacrifice or something.

After blankly watching him for a second, Evan returned his eyes to me. "I was thinking we should go to The Rusted Pipe."

I instantly grinned, loving the idea. "Oh yeah, that sounds perfect." The Rusted Pipe was basically our version of Pete's down here, although it wasn't nearly as nice as Pete's. It was a hole-in-the-wall, falling apart, dive bar, but at the time, it had been all we'd been able to afford. We'd spent *a lot* of time there.

Griffin groaned at our choice as he collapsed onto the couch, but Matt and Evan were smiling just as brightly as I was. We'd made a lot of good memories in that bar, much like we had at Pete's. It wasn't home like Pete's was, but it was damn close. I had to wonder if we'd still know anyone there; it had been ages...

Thirty minutes later, we were pulling into the parking lot. We'd borrowed one of the label's sedans to get there, and Griffin was oohing and aahing over the plushness of the car. All it did for me was make me miss the Chevelle. And Kiera. The two were intrinsically linked now.

From the outside, The Rusted Pipe looked even worse for

wear than before with faded paint, gouges in the exterior walls, and half-lit neon bar signs. It almost looked like it should be condemned, but lights were on inside and music was pumping out into the street, so the place was clearly still open for business. The four of us eyed each other with trepidation as we approached the door—this could possibly be a bad idea—then we shrugged off the feeling and stepped inside.

We instantly had to step aside as a beer bottle thrown against the wall next to us shattered into a million pieces. Someone yelled at someone to *take it outside*, and Evan looked over at me with furrowed brows. "Maybe we should go somewhere else."

Griffin was instantly in our faces. "You know where we could—"

A loud voice booming over the noise of the bar cut off Griffin's repeated attempt to get us to go to a strip club. "Holy fucking shit, Kellan Kyle, back at The Pipe. Never thought I'd see that."

We all twisted to look at the owner of the voice, and when I saw who it was, I instantly grinned and felt like staying. "Damn... Cody, you're still here?"

Cody smiled at me from behind the bar. He was a huge guy, all muscle and attitude, with a shaved head and eyes so dark they were almost solid black. I really wasn't all that surprised to see him; he'd been a fixture here before us, and I had a feeling he'd be here long after everyone else. He confirmed that when he said, "Shit, I'll be here until the day I die. You know that." He patted the bar in front of him. "Come on up, have a seat."

I looked back at the guys, but they all seemed more comfortable now that we'd spotted a familiar face. Well, all except for Griffin. He was still moping. Not seeing any real objections, I headed up to the open stools at the bar. The inside of The Pipe was mostly how I remembered it. A handful of grungy, rickety tables, most of them full of guys who were either ancient or way too young to be here, and a few eager-looking women, all of them staring at me now. There was an old-school dart board in the corner, a clunky jukebox with a decent assortment of classic rock, a dusty pinball machine that rarely ever worked, and the cheapest beer in town.

"Same as usual?" Cody asked when we sat down.

I laughed that he remembered our order, although that also wasn't very surprising. We tended to drink the same thing, and like I said, we came here *a lot*. "Yeah, thanks."

He raised a dark eyebrow at me. "Are you finally old enough to drink here?"

My smile was light and breezy. "I was always old enough to drink here." Not true, but Cody knew that. He'd always known that, and he'd never once cared.

Cody smirked. "Right." He set our beers down in front of us. "So what brings you back to this dump?"

"Feeling nostalgic, I guess," I said with a shrug.

Evan grinned and bumped my shoulder. "Kell's getting married, we're celebrating." I looked over at him with a frown on my face, and he instantly amended his statement. "Er, I mean he *got* married...so we're celebrating." I smiled at him, and he shook his head, amused.

Cody's jaw dropped. "Wow. I did *not* expect that. I remember when you were here all the time...you left with a different girl every single night. And I mean *every* single night. I don't think I ever saw you leave alone. Ever. It was impressive, truly."

The guys were all sniggering at this point while I pursed my lips at Cody. *Thanks for basically calling me a slut.* "Yeah, well... things change."

Cody grinned, then poured shots of whiskey for us. He handed one to each of us, then poured one for himself. "Well, congratulations, Kellan. If you're happy with just one girl, then I'm happy for you."

I clinked his glass, then we all downed our shots. It was bottom-shelf whiskey, and it tasted like it. But the thought was nice. After his drink was gone, Cody smirked and said, "I'll never, ever join you on that path, and I think you're crazy for giving up what you had, but...I'm happy for you anyway. Someone's got to bite the bullet, as long as it's *not* me."

Griffin raised his empty glass. "A-fucking-men," he said, motioning for Cody to pour another shot.

I rolled my eyes at them, then smiled, thinking of Kiera. Despite what they thought, I wasn't giving up anything by being with just one girl. Quite the opposite. I was gaining *everything*. My grin grew as I wondered what Kiera was doing right now. Probably entertaining her parents. Or maybe sleeping. Maybe thinking of me. I hoped so.

Griffin suddenly smacked my shoulder. "Knock it off. We're drinking, not whatever the hell that sappy look on your face was all about."

Frowning at him, I reached over and grabbed his newly filled shot glass. I downed it while he gaped at me, then I let out an exaggerated, "Ahhhh."

Griffin narrowed his eyes, murmuring, "Asshole." Then he turned to Cody and ordered another one.

While Cody poured it, laughing to himself, I jerked my thumb at Griffin. "If you think my life is shocking...dipshit here is about to be a dad."

Griffin frowned at my word choice. Cody almost dropped the bottle of whiskey. "Damn. I feel like I should say sorry." He looked over at Evan and Matt. "This is a sorry moment, right?"

We were nodding, but Griffin looked offended. "Fuck you guys. This is awesome. I'm gonna be the best dad there is. And my baby mama is smokin' hot, so my kid is gonna rule the world. Enjoy your freedom now, boys, while you've still got it."

I glanced at the guys, but just like me, they seemed confused as to how attractiveness equaled rulership. We all knew it wasn't a conversation worth starting, though, so none of us asked Griffin to explain.

Cody seemed truly stunned by what he'd said. Pointing at Griffin, he looked over at us. "*He* was with a hot girl? Really?"

Griffin instantly protested. "Hey, fucker. I'm with hot girls all the goddamn time. Hot girls *love* me."

Cody ignored him, still looking at us. I shrugged. "Yeah...he's right on this one. Anna is...incredibly hot." I shrugged again. "None of us are sure how it happened...but it did."

Griffin turned his protest toward me. "Dude, what the fuck? You owe me a drink for that, asshole."

I laughed at the look on his face, then motioned at Cody. "You should probably just leave the bottle."

Cody unscrewed the cap and set it down in front of me. Griffin instantly grabbed it and took a swig, his eyes locked on me in challenge. I just laughed again.

The night sped by, probably because when we twisted around in our seats to face the room, we kept spotting people we knew; they trickled into the bar on an almost hourly basis, and every single one of them remembered us and were shocked to see us. They all wanted to buy us a drink, and that made me think we probably should have taken a cab. Thankfully, Matt switched to water so he could drive our drunk asses home.

Being back at our old stomping grounds was fun, but in a weird way, it made me miss home even more. If I could somehow make Pete's magically appear in Los Angeles, I would. In a heart-beat. Evan echoed my thoughts as we were stumbling up the walkway to the label's house. "That was fun, but I'm glad that's not where we hang out anymore." Grinning, he shook his head. "The Pipe doesn't hold a candle to Pete's."

Matt smirked as he watched us trip over nothing. "Yeah, Pete's is the best," he said. His grin grew. "Home of the D-Bags." He shook his head like he still couldn't believe Pete was going to do that for us. It blew my mind too. I just couldn't articulate that at the moment.

Griffin grunted. He opened his mouth to say something, then frowned and sat down. On a berm. "Fuck walking. I'm sleeping here," he slurred.

He immediately lay down on the bark, plopping his head on

his arm. Matt sighed while Evan and I just stood there, staring at Griffin. 'Cause damn, that didn't sound like an unreasonable plan. It sounded way better than walking up a bunch of stairs.

Evan must have seen the decision in my eyes, because when Matt leaned down to pick up Griffin, he put his shoulder under my arm; it was only then that I realized I'd been starting to sit. "Nuh-uh," he said. "You're not sleeping outside, man. Kiera would kill me. Then Jenny would kill me."

I grinned as I looked over at him. "Kiera...I love her so much..."

He let out a laugh as he helped me plod to the door. "I know. I figured as much when you married her."

I started laughing, which made him laugh. The two of us were in hysterics by the time we got to the stairs. It got especially bad when we gave up on trying to walk up them and dropped to our hands and knees so we could crawl instead. From behind us, I heard Matt mutter, "Jesus..." as he helped Griffin up the stairs. It just made me laugh even more.

When I got to the top step of our floor, I flopped onto my stomach, since sleeping right there sounded fabulous. I couldn't even remember the last time I slept. It wasn't last night. And real-izing that made me feel like I'd been hit by a brick wall, a brick wall of exhaustion.

Matt kicked my shoes, jostling me. "No," he said. "Go to your room."

Turning onto my back, I looked up at him. There were three blond heads above me, all with Matt's signature short, spikey cut. "Why?" I murmured, my eyes closing.

He kicked my shoes again, forcing my eyes open. "'Cause you can't sleep there." With a sigh, he shook his head. "God, I hate being the only sober one." I laughed, making the three Matts frown. Adjusting how he was holding Griffin, Matt said, "Come on, Kell. I gotta get him into a bed. I need you to do this on your own." He pointed somewhere ahead of me. "Like Evan. *He* managed to make it to a bed. I think." He frowned again.

"Okay," I said, holding up my thumb. Then I closed my eyes and got comfortable.

"Goddamn it," I heard Matt grumble. Everything was quiet a moment, then I heard him say, "Stay right there, Griffin." Then I felt Matt reaching into my front pocket and pulling out...something.

"What are you doing?" I mumbled.

"Motivating you," he answered. I forced my eyes open to see Matt standing over me, calling someone...on *my* phone. Griffin was leaning against the wall behind him; he looked asleep. And that sounded amazing. As my eyes slipped closed again, I heard Matt say, "Hey, Kiera. No, it's Matt." I reopened my eyes and frowned at him. Why was Matt talking to my wife?

Matt smiled at me as he talked to Kiera. "Everything's fine, I just need your help getting Kellan into his bed." Kiera must have said something because Matt started laughing. "We took him to a bar to celebrate your marriage. He, uh, got a little carried away, and now he's got it in his head that he's gonna spend the night on the stairs."

I reached out my hand for the phone. Matt stepped away. Walking back to Griffin, he kept talking to Kiera. "Well, I figure he'll want to talk to you more than he wants to sleep on the floor. That's my hope anyway." Matt laughed again as he put his shoulder under Griffin's. "I know," he said, walking away from me...with my wife still on the line. *What the hell?*

Grunting, I made myself get up and follow him. I shuffled behind him a few paces as he made his way to the bedrooms. He kept looking back at me while he talked to Kiera. "Yeah, he *is* following me. This works like a charm." When he got to my bedroom door, he paused to open it, then said to Kiera, "Okay, we're here. I'm gonna go, he'll be on in a sec. Thanks, Kiera." Then he tossed the phone into my room.

"Night, Kell," he said, grinning at me, then all three of him finished helping Griffin to his room.

Frowning, I trudged into my room to find my phone. It was

on my bed. Perfect. I flopped onto the mattress, then brought the phone to my ear. I could hear Kiera laughing, and my lips instantly flipped into a smile. "Hey, beautiful...I'm sorry if he woke you."

"It's fine," she giggled. "I couldn't sleep anyway. I miss you," she said with a sigh.

"I miss you too," I murmured. "Want me to sing to you?"

"No," she said. "I want you to go to sleep."

"Okay," I muttered, shutting my eyes. "See you in my dreams..."

"Always," she said, a smile in her voice. "I love you, Kellan."

I mumbled something that was supposed to be, "I love you too," but I had no idea if that was what I actually said.

My head was pounding the next day. A fact that delighted Matt. I'd never seen him quite so chipper as he cranked up the music in the living room, grinning ear to ear as he watched Evan, Griffin, and me wince. We managed to get through that day's recording session, but just barely; everyone was pissy, even Matt at that point, and I made a mental note not to go out drinking again until the album was done. And Kiera was with me. I'd much rather follow her to my bedroom than Matt.

Over the next several days, I grew more and more impatient for Kiera to join me. But unfortunately, she had a few responsibilities that she had to take care of before she could.

First, her parents were in town for a few more days, so she was still playing host at our house...and slowly being driven insane by her overprotective father and wedding-obsessed mother. She was as ready for them to leave as I was for her to join me.

Second, she wanted to give Pete a full two-weeks' notice before she left the bar...unlike the last time, when we'd broken up and she'd bailed on him without warning. Pete had never held a grudge against Kiera for that, but I knew she carried around a lot of guilt for it. I did too, to be honest, because it was as much my fault as hers.

The last thing Kiera needed to take care of was for Anna. She had an important doctor's appointment coming up, and Kiera didn't want to miss it; knowing how hard all of this was for Anna, I thought Kiera's support at the appointment was probably a good idea.

So yeah, Kiera had several good reasons for not joining me right away—important things that she really couldn't miss. I just had to continue being patient. At least there were a few things to help me pass the time.

"Hey...Evan." Evan looked my way with raised brows, and I smiled once I had his attention. "There's something I need help with."

He instantly frowned. "No."

That made me frown. "What do you mean no? You don't even know what I need help with."

He got this knowing look on his face, like he could see right through me, and he wasn't amused. "You've got that gleam in your eye. Whenever you get that look, it means *one* thing."

I fought back a smile as I tried to look innocent. "What are you talking about?"

He sighed, then rolled his eyes. "You want to go shopping, and you want me to come with you because you think it's hilarious to make me do something I hate."

A snicker escaped me. "I wouldn't say I *make* you. So...come with me?"

He crossed his arms over his chest. "No. You'll be fine on your own."

I tilted my head. "I could get mugged on my own."

He raised a dark eyebrow at me. "You'll be fine. But if you're really worried about it, then take Griffin with you."

My frown returned. "Griffin? That's who you want guarding me? You've seen him practicing kung fu downstairs, right? When he tried kicking the couch and fell over?"

Evan laughed. "Dumbass," he muttered, shaking his head.

Sitting on the edge of the couch cushion next to him, I pressed my palms together in a prayer position. "Please?"

He sighed. "Why do you want me to come with you?"

I smiled. "Because I like hanging out with you."

"And...?" he said, waiting.

I bit my lip so hard that I almost drew blood. "That's it, no other reason."

Evan eyed me for a minute, then stood up. "You're such a liar, but fine...whatever." I stood up with a grin while he sighed dramatically. "And where exactly are we going?"

"Jewelry store," I said with a laugh, twisting on my heel as I headed for the stairs.

Evan groaned, but he followed me.

After grabbing one of the label's loaner cars, we made our way into town. By the fourth jewelry store, I could tell Evan was done with our little excursion. "Sorry, man," I said with a laugh. "I really didn't think it would be this hard to find the right ring."

He rolled his eyes at me, let out a long, annoyed sigh, then switched it to a tired laugh. "It's fine. And I should probably start looking for a ring too."

That got my attention. "Are you finally gonna pop the question?"

He shrugged. "I don't know. Maybe. Someday. When the moment's right. But I should probably be ready for whenever that might be." He laughed. "You know, like how you used to always have a couple of condoms on you, just in case."

The saleswoman's eyes widened as she stared at us, then back down at the case. I frowned at Evan comparing an engagement ring to a condom, then laughed at what was actually a pretty good comparison. "Yeah...you should always be prepared for the moment, whatever that moment might be." Words to live by.

The saleswoman's cheeks flushed with color, and she very subtly excused herself. Her reaction reminded me of Kiera, and a soft chuckle escaped me. I looked over at Evan; he had his lips pressed together, and his cheeks were a little red too. "Oops," he said. "Guess I've been hanging out with Griffin too much lately."

Laughing a little harder, I nodded at the case. "See anything Jenny would like?"

With a sigh, he rubbed his buzz-cut head. "I don't know. They all look the same to me. What do you think?"

I looked over the case again, thinking of Jenny and her tastes. And that was when I saw it...the perfect ring for Jenny...that just so happened to be sitting next to the perfect ring for Kiera. The one I wanted for Kiera had a large, round diamond in the center that was surrounded by a ring of smaller diamonds; it was a little extravagant, but elegant too, and absolutely stunning, just like Kiera. The one for Jenny was a bit more artistic, with the band curving down to a sharp point, like a widow's peak, and a modest, pear-shaped diamond tucked in the V. "There. Those two."

Evan's eyes widened. "She doesn't need *two*."

I smirked at the panic in his expression, then explained. "The one on the right is for Kiera, the one on the left is for Jenny."

Evan bent over to look closer. He peeked up at me, and the smile on his face was enormous. "Yeah...those two. They're perfect."

Slapping him on the back, I looked around for the embarrassed saleswoman. She had a couple of sales to ring up. Now I really couldn't wait for Kiera to get here.

Chapter 6

FINALLY

Time trudged by. *Trudged*. It never ceased to amaze me how cruel time was. Racing by when you wanted it to slow down, trickling along when you wanted it to move faster. I swear it was the universe's cosmic way of giving everyone the middle finger. *Yeah. Hilarious, Universe.*

But finally, after eons of waiting, the day I'd been anticipating for weeks was here—Kiera was on her way to Los Angeles. I just needed to go pick her up from the airport, and then I'd be with her again, for an indefinite amount of time. Finally.

I scanned my bedroom one more time before I left, triple-checking to make sure everything was perfect. It was. The empty dresser drawers were waiting for Kiera's things, the clumps of candles were giving the place a romantic feel, and the enormous bed was, for once, perfectly made. The bed was actually the most important part. Not because it was a bed and I couldn't wait to use it with Kiera, although that was certainly true, but because of what was *on* the bed. I'd scattered a bunch of red rose petals on the covers, tossed some extra ones on the floor. Then over the petals on the bed, as skillfully as I could, I'd made a heart out of white petals, and in the center of the heart was the engagement ring I'd purchased for Kiera. It was an impossible-to-miss presentation, and I couldn't wait for Kiera to see it. Then I couldn't wait to mess up the bed. All those flower petals stuck to our naked, slightly sweaty bodies was a really appealing image.

A voice in the doorway distracted me from my pleasant thoughts. "Hey, time to go get Kiera?"

I turned my head to see Evan walking into the room. As he studied my romantic display, I nodded. "Yeah, just about."

Stepping to my side, he looked at me with an expression on his face that was half amusement, half sympathy. "Is she feeling better? Jenny told me about her last night at Pete's. Sounds like she tied one on pretty good."

I gave him a tight smile. *Yes, she did.* And I hadn't been there, and even though it was hypocritical for me to be upset about that, since I'd been drunk several times without her, I was. A little. But discovering *who* had been with her that night was almost worse than me not being there for her. I'd called her that evening, and Denny had answered her phone. *Denny.* He had helped her home. He had stayed the night with her. He had been there for her. And yet, nothing had happened. Kiera had openly confessed to me that Denny had been taking care of her, told me it meant nothing, and I'd spent the entire night singing to her. Even though she'd been completely plastered at the time, she'd been good, he'd been good, and the more I thought about it, the better I felt. Friendship truly was the only thing between them now, and I was glad Denny had watched over her. I was glad she hadn't been alone.

My smile widened. "Yeah, the headache finally wore off, I think." I paused to frown. "Of course, now that she has to live with Griffin, it will probably come back. Stronger than ever."

Evan laughed. "Yeah, that's a pain we all have to endure. She'll get used to it." Pausing, he clapped my shoulder. "This is nice, Kell," he said, indicating the bed. "I think she'll like it."

He was softly smiling at the display I'd laid out on the bed, but as I watched, his expression changed. Now he seemed...

annoyed. Frown on his face, he looked over at me but didn't say anything. "What?" I asked, confused.

He motioned at the bed again. "You make every single one of us look bad. You know that, right?"

I grinned at him. "Are you failing in the romance department? I could give you some pointers if you want? Help you keep the spark alive?"

Rolling his eyes, he started leaving the room. "My spark is just fine," he tossed over his shoulder.

I unintentionally sniggered, and without looking back at me, Evan extended his hand behind him, middle finger raised. I laughed a little harder as I shook my head. "Just offering," I told him.

I took one last look at the prepared room, then grabbed my welcome sign for Kiera and headed out. Carefully closing my bedroom door, I turned to see Matt talking to Evan by the couch. I looked around the living room, but I didn't see Griffin anywhere. Damn it. I really didn't feel like wrangling him, and Anna was coming down with Kiera. I had to imagine she would expect Griffin to be there. Maybe. It was really hard to tell with those two.

Stepping up to Matt, I asked, "Where's Griffin? We need to go."

Matt frowned as he turned to me. "He said he was going down to the pool."

I gave him a blank stare. "Did you remind him we had to go to the airport? That Anna was on her way?"

He nodded. "Yep, I did." By the way he pressed his lips together, I could tell he was annoyed at his cousin.

"Do I want to know what he said?" I asked.

Matt smirked. "He said Anna could take a cab. He said that made more sense, and he didn't see the point in picking her up."

"*And?*" I said. I knew there had to be more to it than laziness.

Matt rolled his eyes. "And there's supposed to be a wet T-shirt contest happening later." He gave me a tight grin. "He doesn't want to risk missing it."

He doesn't want to pick up the woman who is having his child because he doesn't want to miss seeing the outline of some random girl's breasts? I didn't bother saying it out loud because I knew Matt was thinking it too. Matt and I just stared at each other for a second, then I said, "Do you think she'll dump him before or after the baby?"

Matt grinned. "My money's on before. There's just no way she stays with him the whole time."

Evan turned his head to Matt. "I'll take that bet. A hundred bucks says it will be after the baby."

Matt raised a pale eyebrow at him. "Really? You think she'll hold out that long?"

Evan grinned like he knew something. "You're forgetting that the jackass is about to go on tour with us. He won't be around to piss her off. They'll stay together simply because she'll forget what he's like."

Matt rubbed his chin. "Damn. You make a good point." He thought about it a moment, then shook his head. "I stick by my original assessment, though. He'll annoy her over the phone. It's a done deal."

Evan laughed, then stuck out his hand. "All right, it's a bet."

Before Matt grabbed his hand, accepting the bet, he looked over at me. "You want in on this?"

I gave them both a small smile. "Sure...but I bet they stay together. I think they'll make it." A bold declaration since they weren't really together anyway...but I was feeling hopeful today.

They both gave me wry, disbelieving looks, then Evan said to Matt, "He's just feeling all sappy 'cause he's giving Kiera her ring today. You should see his room...it's like a Hallmark movie threw up in there."

I raised an eyebrow at Evan's description of my display. "I really will help you if you want me to."

Evan narrowed his eyes, then laughed. Matt laughed too, then clasped Evan's hand, and then mine. "All right, game on," he said. After a pause, he gave me a sad smile. "But...for the sake of my future relative...I really hope you win, Kellan."

A sigh escaped me. "Yeah...I hope so too."

After saying goodbye to Matt and Evan, I headed to where the loaner car keys were being stored downstairs. There was only one set of keys left on the rack, and it was for a shiny convertible thing that was a bit on the small side. Not ideal for picking up people from the airport. Hopefully, the girls hadn't brought much luggage with them. I was fairly certain Kiera had packed modestly, but Anna...who knows.

It was mid-morning on a Friday, but the label's house was already swarming with people. Some I sort of knew, some were still complete strangers. And that was pretty typical for this place. It was like a bar that never closed. I waved at a couple of guys that I knew as I hopped into the car, then I was off to get my girl.

I couldn't stop smiling as I drove to the airport. Even when I got stuck in traffic, I had a grin on my face. There was this almost electric feeling of hope and eagerness inside me, like everything was going to be great from here on out. Like I would never have a bad day again. I knew that wasn't true—I would probably have multiple horrible days in my future—but knowing that didn't alter the fact that I felt...impervious.

Grabbing my sign after I parked, I made my way into the bustling airport with a jaunty spring in my step. A quick glance at the *Arrivals* sign told me Kiera's plane had just landed. Perfect. I made my way to a spot where I was sure she would see me, then when travelers started filtering into the room, I thrust my sign high into the air like I was at a concert, and I wanted the band to see me. It was an over-the-top display, but with Kiera's tendency to be overly nervous about everything, I thought she'd appreciate not having to look too hard to find me. And when she appeared a second later and spotted me instantly, she genuinely seemed to appreciate it.

Her beautiful face melted into an expression of joy and relief, and moisture was clear in her hazel eyes, even with the distance between us. She flew to me, then jumped into my arms so quickly that I had to drop the poster board to catch her. Her arms and legs wrapped around me, squeezing me tight, and I closed my eyes as I drank her in—the softness of her curves pressing against me, her tender lips touching my neck, the floral notes of her shampoo...I paused the world and took a long moment to just savor it. Savor her. *My wife.*

A light laugh escaped me when it became clear that Kiera had no intention of ever letting go of me. And I was perfectly fine with that. She pulled back to look at me, and I was mesmerized by the warmth in her eyes. "Miss me?" I asked, tilting my head up to kiss her.

She smiled brightly in answer, then her lips lowered to mine. Our mouths moved together, and I was instantly flooded with memories of her, flooded with emotions for her. Love surged through my veins like it was a living thing, tingling my skin, doubling my heartbeat, warming my entire body. I could have stayed this way forever, locked around each other, our lips tenderly pressing and retreating, our fingers softly exploring...

It was only when Kiera started wriggling away from me that I realized my hand had drifted down to her ass. Not something she approved of in such a public space. Oops. I frowned at her anyway once her feet touched the floor. "Hey, I was enjoying that."

She smirked at me. "Yeah, I know."

Her hand came up to rest on my stomach, and my frown evaporated as I grabbed it and laced our fingers together. With a soft laugh, I bent down to pick up my discarded sign. Kiera pointed at it when I straightened. "I like your sign."

"I thought you might," I said with a smile. I'd made the sign look like the ones professional drivers used to pick up their clients—just Kiera's full name in large black letters. I figured she'd get a kick out of me pretending to be her servant. Although it really wasn't pretending for me. Anything she wanted, I would try to make it happen for her. All she had to do was ask.

She smiled tenderly at me for a moment, then her eyes drifted back to the sign, and she pursed her lips. "But just so you know, I'm not going by Mrs. *Kellan* Kyle. It's too old-fashioned."

I forced myself *not* to smile as I looked down at the sign in my fingers. I'd written it that way to intentionally tease her a little. And because...it still blew my mind that she'd married me, and I wanted the whole world to know *exactly* who she'd chosen to spend the rest of her life with. Old-fashioned, sure, but meaningful...to me.

Looking up at her, I said, "What? It's endearing to take your husband's full name, isn't it?" My thumb was stroking her wedding ring, and I just couldn't stop smiling at her.

The look on her face matched how I felt, but she subtly shook her head. "It's sexist, Kellan. I have my own name. I don't need to assume yours." Her other hand reached up to my chest, and her fingers traced the tattoo of her name. It made a shiver go through me, and I wished we were somewhere private so I could take off my shirt and let her do that against my bare skin. "Just your last name," she whispered.

I couldn't get my mind off of bare skin now. Her body sprawled atop my mattress, my fingers feeling every curve, my lips tasting every delicious inch of her. Desire and loneliness were hitting me hard as I stared at her mouth. It had only been a couple of weeks, and we'd definitely gone a lot longer, but I suddenly needed her more than anything. We'd made love over the phone just a few days ago, an erotic night where she'd shocked the hell out of me by asking for photo-evidence of how hard I was for her, and a night where I'd shocked the hell out of myself by figuring out how to send her that picture without hanging up on her, but it wasn't the same. Nothing was the same as actually being with her, holding her in my arms, feeling her body move underneath mine.

I really shouldn't be thinking about that right now, but the look on Kiera's face wasn't helping anything. Her eyes burned as she watched me drag my teeth over my bottom lip, and she seemed like she was ready and willing to risk getting arrested for indecent exposure. Damn.

An irritated shout nearby broke our heated contact. Thankfully. "Thanks, Kiera! I nearly gave birth trying to get my carry-on down!"

Kiera and I looked over to see Anna storming our way. She looked pissed. Her green eyes were fiery as she puffed at a dark lock of hair that was getting in her way. Weird. I'd completely forgotten she was on the plane too. And apparently, Kiera had as well. We did that sometimes, forgot all about the world around us. I wasn't sure if that was a good thing or not.

Dropping Kiera's hand, I stepped forward. "I guess I should help."

Kiera's voice stopped me. "Is Griffin here?"

I looked back at her, unsure what to say. *He didn't want to risk missing a wet T-shirt contest* seemed like a bad idea. Kiera already hated Griffin, no need to add fuel to *that* fire. I didn't want to lie, but I also didn't want to upset her with unnecessary details about my bandmate. This total honesty thing was tricky.

But ultimately, this was Griffin's drama, not mine, and I really didn't want to get into his issues right now. "He...decided to wait at the house," I said with a shrug.

Kiera frowned in annoyance, then she rolled her eyes and let it go. Griffin being inconsiderate was nothing new to her.

When we finally arrived at the label's house, Kiera eyed the impressive spread with awe on her face. Then her gaze fell on some of the people loitering around outside, and she frowned at me. I had to believe that reaction was because of what the people were wearing. Or *not* wearing. Most of the people were in bathing suits, barely-there bathing suits. Like the woman strolling past the front of the car with tiny scraps of clothing covering the essentials, and that was about it. The outfit didn't leave much to the imagination, or anything really. Right. In all the times Kiera and I had talked, I'd forgotten to mention the party-like atmosphere at the house. Honestly, it kept slipping my mind. While the scantily clad women were a constant distraction for Griffin, they didn't even register with me. And they definitely weren't on my mind when Kiera's sultry voice was in my ear.

Knowing I should have mentioned it already, I turned to Kiera and answered the question that had to be rolling around her brain, because she had to be wondering who the hell these people were. "It's the record label's house. Any artist on their label is welcome to come here, and some of them invite guests. Actually, almost all of them invite guests...at all hours of the day and night." I had to roll my eyes at that. I didn't mind a good party, but I was ready for this one to end. Thankfully, the chaos usually didn't drift upstairs to our floor. I'd probably go insane if it did.

Kiera's frown deepened after my explanation, and I gave her an *I know and I'm sorry* shrug. It was what it was.

Returning my borrowed sunglasses to the car's visor clip, I hopped out of the vehicle and started grabbing luggage. As I did, a couple I'd met once or twice walked by the car. The guy raised his chin at me while his girlfriend looked me over with a seductive gleam in her eye. "Hey, Kellan," she said, her voice low and provocative—a clear invitation. Her boyfriend either didn't notice or didn't care. Probably didn't care since his eyes were locked on Anna's chest.

I nodded a greeting at the woman whose name completely escaped me, then glanced over at Kiera, hoping that interaction hadn't upset her. Kiera was used to girls coming on to me, but they were usually wearing a lot more clothes when they did. The blonde's bikini was even smaller than the previous girl's bikini, and that was saying something.

Kiera gave me an impassive look, then she minutely shook her head, and I could see her subtly relaxing, like she was making herself let it go. I was grateful for her acceptance since there was literally *nothing* I could do about the people walking around here.

Even nearly naked, they had just as much right to be here as me. And Kiera. She was part of the craziness now too.

Kiera and Anna both looked awestruck when we walked inside the house. I understood the feeling. This place screamed money. But it did it in a way that was...discomforting. Cold, clinical, museum-like. The style reminded me of my parents' place, my childhood home. Everything inside that house had a sterile, don't-touch-me feel to it, and even when I'd been small, I'd instinctively avoided touching almost everything. It had made me feel like a visitor in my own home, although that might have been because of how my parents treated me, to be honest. Either way, that distaste for staged elegance had stuck with me, and every piece of art on the walls here, every overpriced rug on the floors, and every uncomfortable piece of furniture, filled me with an odd sense of revulsion; I'd love to replace the couch downstairs with my lumpy, tattered sofa. Put some life into this place.

Thankfully, the second floor had a homier feel to it. And it was quieter. It was almost a home within a home, one filled with D-Bags. Or two of them, at least. Just moments after the three of us walked in, Evan and Matt stepped into the living room from the second-floor deck. Matt was bouncing a water balloon between his hands, smiling as he told Evan, "Nice toss." I instantly cringed as I glanced at the balloon, and I silently prayed that Matt didn't drop it or accidentally pop it. Because it wasn't filled with water.

A few days ago, Griffin had pissed off Matt while they'd been fighting about...something. I wasn't even sure what they'd been bickering about. Evan had helped Matt come up with a very childish form of retribution: milk stink bombs. They'd filled a bunch of water balloons with milk, vinegar, and I'd heard something about eggs, then they'd left them on the deck to rot in the sun. I could only imagine how godawful they smelled now. In fact, I was pretty sure I could faintly smell the one in Matt's hand. He better not fucking drop it. The living room would never smell the same.

Matt and Evan noticed the girls and immediately moved in for hugs. After Anna hugged them, she glanced around with an expectant look in her eye, then she turned to Matt. "Where's Griffin?" she asked, frowning as she rubbed her stomach.

Matt looked at Evan, then me. I could see the question in his pale eyes, the indecision about what he should or shouldn't say to Griffin's somewhat significant other. We might have jokingly placed a bet on their odds, but none of us wanted to see Anna and Griffin break up, and the truth might make that happen. But it wasn't our job to safeguard Griffin, and Anna was going to find out sooner or later. I gave Matt a miniscule nod, and he turned to Anna. Jerking his thumb behind him, he said, "He's by the pool."

Evan grinned. "Look for the annoyed one with sour milk dripping down his face."

Matt let out a snort as he lifted his palm to Evan. "Damn fine shot, man." I shook my head as they high-fived, then I looked over at Kiera. Her face was scrunched in disgust as she eyed the balloon in Matt's hand. *Yes, I know. It's gross. I hope you realized what you were signing up for.*

Anna seemed pissed for a second, then she got a devilish look in her eye. Smooth smile on her face, she held out her hand to Matt. "Would you mind if I borrowed that?" she asked, her voice deceptively sweet.

Matt laughed as he handed it to her. "Be my guest."

Charming smile on her face, Anna walked out to the deck. Matt and Evan waited a few seconds, then followed her with glee on their faces. I shook my head again, then looked down at Kiera. "Want to see our room, or watch Griffin be assaulted?"

Kiera bit her lip, halfway hiding an adorable smirk. "Wow, that's actually a really hard choice."

I laughed as I grabbed her hand. Then I led her toward our new bedroom. "Well, I've had enough of Griffin lately and not nearly enough of you." *And I have something to show you.*

Opening the door for her, I let her walk past me into the room. Her eyes briefly scanned the space before snapping to the bed and staying there. A smile crept onto my lips when I heard her make a soft sound of surprise. I stepped up behind her after closing the door. "Do you like it?" I whispered in her ear.

As she silently nodded, I shifted my gaze to the brilliant red petals scattered over the floor, over the bed. The contrasting white petals were shockingly bright against the black comforter, and it made the ring box in the center of it stick out all the more.

I pulled her forward, toward the box. She paused for just a moment so she could remove her sandals and feel the flower petals on her bare feet; I loved that. I led her to the edge of the bed, then reached over and grabbed the ring box from the center of the rose petal heart. Kiera tracked me the entire time. Her eyes were glossy, and she was stone silent, at a loss for words; I loved that too.

Soft smile on my face, I sank to one knee in front of her. Maybe it was because I'd done this so many times now, but I wasn't nervous. At all. I only felt complete and total bliss as I calmly said, "Kiera Michelle Allen, will you be my wife?"

As I opened the box for her, the tears in her eyes fell onto her cheeks. She was nodding at my question, but her focus was glued on the ring. Her eyes opened fractionally wider as she stared at it, and her mouth popped open like she was well and truly stunned. I could tell she liked it, but she was still processing the fact that I'd purchased it. This was *not* something she would ever ask for, not for herself, not in a million years. If she was going to object to any part of this, it would be the ring's cost, which was a substantial chunk of change. Even *I* would admit that. But I didn't have any qualms about this. None. And it was important to me. I wanted the physical representation of our relationship to be breathtaking because...*she* was breathtaking. The very least my parents' money could do was buy something beautiful for the woman who meant *everything* to me.

Carefully pulling the sparkling ring out of its box, I grabbed her trembling left hand and slipped it over her ring finger. It seemed like the new ring had been intentionally designed to go with her promise ring, and it thrilled me to see how well they complemented each other. This was meant to be.

Kiera was still just staring at the ring, a dazed expression on her face. I lightly laughed as I stood up. I'd hoped to surprise her, but I was pretty sure I'd absolutely floored her. When she finally wrapped her mind around what had happened, she looked up at me and said, "You didn't need to do that. My old ring was fine." She cringed right after she said it, like she hadn't meant *that* to be the first thing she said.

The embarrassment on her face made me smile. "Yes, I did," I told her, wrapping my arms around her waist.

She shook her head. "Don't get me wrong, this is...unbelievable...but I was content with the old band. You didn't have to do this."

Her refusal to let me lavish her was sweet, adorable even. It just made me love her even more. But still, I *needed* to do this for her. "Yes, I did," I repeated.

"Kellan—"

I cut off her objection with my lips on hers. "Yes, I did, Kiera," I murmured against her mouth. She deserved more than the simple ring I'd given her. She deserved this moment—the extravagance, the romance, the once-in-a-lifetime feeling. I couldn't deny her this any more than I could deny being in love with her. And I'd never been very good at that.

Kiera finally stopped objecting as our mouths moved together. I squeezed her tighter, pulling her into me, and her fingers drifted up, wrapping themselves around the longer strands of my hair. It was such a familiar feeling; one I'd been missing for far too long. *I can't believe she's finally here. For good.*

I deepened the kiss as the ache of loneliness swelled inside me. Kiera made the softest, most erotic noise as my tongue brushed against hers, and my body instantly responded, blood surging to all the right places. Kiera's fingers left my hair, and I felt them tugging at my shirt. Knowing what she wanted, I paused to pull the fabric off me. Her fingers were instantly on my bare skin, tracing the lines between the various muscles, electrifying me. Then she leaned forward and placed a kiss on the tattoo over my heart. Something about the gesture filled me with peace, warmth...belonging. Like she was claiming me, or more accurately, approving the claim I'd pronounced when I'd etched her name into my skin. She was accepting my declaration, giving herself to me. And that was all I'd ever wanted.

Tenderly cradling her head, I held her to my chest, closed my eyes, and just...cherished her.

And that was when I felt her tongue drawing a circle around my nipple. Then she closed her mouth over it, lightly dragging her teeth across it, sending a bolt of lightning straight to my cock. *Well, damn.* My eyes snapped open. Kiera was biting her lip, looking up at me with a playful but heated expression on her face. Her eyes were greener in the bright sunlight streaming into the room, and they practically smoldered as she watched me. A grin curled my lips as I began slowly, teasingly removing her shirt. But after I pulled it off, I was the one being smacked in the face with seduction.

The bra she was wearing was one I hadn't seen before; it wasn't even a *style* I'd seen on her before. It was lacy and sexy and it pushed her breasts together in such an appealing way that I couldn't stop staring. Leering. That was what I was doing. Because damn...it was hot. My body was throbbing.

I knew she wasn't wearing this for herself; she was wearing it for me, to give me something special. It wasn't necessary—I didn't need *any* help getting turned on around her—but it was sweet, thoughtful. Still, I couldn't stop myself from teasing her. When I finally pulled my gaze from the enticing view she'd just given me, I met her eye. There was amusement on her face, and right behind it, desire. I absorbed how gorgeous she was for a second, then I shook my head and playfully told her, "You didn't have to do that. I liked the old one just fine."

Kiera laughed at me using her point against her, then she

tugged on the waistband of my shorts, pulling me closer. "Yes, I did," she murmured, kissing me.

A soft laugh escaped me at hearing her use my words against *me*, but then she was deftly unbuttoning my shorts and slipping her hand inside to feel me, and all I could do was groan as her fingers curled around me. *God, yes.*

Wanting so much more, I gently pushed Kiera back onto the bed. She sat on the scattered petals, almost directly over the heart, and my body pulsed with need as I stared at the erotic image in front of me. An incomplete image: she should be sprawled on top of the petals in her underwear. *That* was something I needed to see. Grabbing the bottom of her stretchy shorts, I yanked them off her. My entire body froze when I saw her underwear, and I let out a low groan. Holy. Fucking. Shit. The underwear was new too, and again, not at all her style—tiny, with thin, hardly-there straps across her hips, and fucking see-through. *See. Through.*

I was not prepared for this today. My body reacted to the visual so strongly that I had to mentally order myself to calm down, or else this was going to be extremely disappointing for her. She had to do this to me *now*? When I was already suffering from weeks of being without her? Jesus Christ. I swear she gave my willpower too much credit sometimes. Irritation touched my lips as I peeked up at her. "Are you trying to make this last about five seconds?" She let out an adorably innocent giggle, and I grinned, both loving and hating the imagery in front of me right now. "You're killing me, Kiera." I paused to kiss her stomach. "You're actually killing me."

My lips traveled down her stomach, toward that wonderous underwear, and Kiera's breath noticeably quickened. She shifted on the bed, scooting up so she could lie down, then she reached out a hand for me, asking me to join her. Be with her. Warmth swelled in my chest as I took in her invitation, the love in her eyes, the petals sticking to her skin, and that damn overly provocative underwear. "You're so beautiful...do you know that?"

A flush swept across her cheeks, and she looked away from

me. No. She didn't know that. Or she didn't believe it. How could she not believe it, after all this time? Removing my shoes and shorts, I crawled onto the bed with her. Lying beside her, I tenderly touched her chin and made her look at me. "Do you know that?" I asked again.

As I expected, she shook her head. A sigh escaped me as I ran my fingers through her hair. If only she could see what I saw. "Well, I do," I whispered. *Every day I see your beauty, and every day you blow me away.*

I brought my lips to hers, wanting to show her how I felt, wanting her to feel what she did to me. Rolling on top of her, I pressed my hips into hers. A sensual noise left Kiera's lips, igniting me. Our kiss grew heated as my hardness pressed against her softness. I wasn't sure how much of this I could take, but I also never wanted it to end. My heart was already racing, my breath fast as sensation overloaded me. Leaning down to her ear, I told her, "I love you." She quietly whimpered with lustful hunger, her fingers clawing into my skin.

Unhooking her bra, I quickly removed it so I could see the breasts that had been haunting my dreams. I ran my tongue over her nipple, curling my lips over the peak. Kiera's erotic exhale was loud, stimulating. It made me ache so much that I wasn't sure I could keep teasing her. She squirmed beneath me, her breath fast and needy, then she subtly pushed my head down. *Fuck, yes.* I could hold out for this. Wanting what she wanted, I wrapped my fingers around the ridiculously tiny straps of her underwear, then pulled them off her. I teased her, tasted her, brought her right to the edge, and then I couldn't take any more.

Ripping off my boxers, I moved over the top of her. I was sliding inside her before my mouth even made it to hers. *Heaven...absolute heaven.* Kiera groaned as I pressed in deep. "Oh God...I've missed you," she said, her voice wavering with emotion.

I had to pause as the connection overwhelmed me. Head resting at the base of her neck, I told her, "You never have to miss me again." The truth of those words filled me with lightness. *Never again*.

I pulled back, then pressed forward again, slowly, deliberately. Every movement was like liquid, electric fire surging through me, pleasure and an aching pain woven together so tightly that it was impossible to separate them. My body begged to go faster, to satisfy the wanton need building inside me, but I didn't. I kept it slow, torturous, prolonging the glorious agony. The restraint was making me shake, but it was also driving Kiera crazy, and I could tell she was close. If I could just hold out, I could give her a couple of releases, double her pleasure. I wanted that, wanted it more than I wanted my own satisfaction, so I kept up the steady rhythm despite how badly my body was protesting. *Just keep going...don't think about coming, just don't think about it*.

But then Kiera's body stiffened under me, and she let out a long cascade of irresistible moans, and I felt her body tightening around me in a delicious way that I just...couldn't...resist. I lost the fragile hold on my willpower, and the euphoria hit me hard and fast; all I could do was groan and swear and melt into Kiera's body as I gave into it.

I lay against her afterward, both blissfully happy and slightly disappointed. At myself, of course. Kiera rubbed my back as she made a soft, purring sound of contentment. Smiling, I decided to confess my failure to her. "Sorry, I was going to try to give you a twofer, but I couldn't hold out." Lifting my head, I pointedly raised an eyebrow. "I blame it entirely on the underwear." Seriously. How could she do that to me? *I'm not Superman, Kiera*.

She laughed at my comment, then gave me a sweet kiss. "If the first one is done right, I don't need two," she said.

That made me grin, laugh, and feel absurdly happy. Shifting to her side, I pulled her close and spent a few glorious moments just kissing her. Pulling back, I noticed the stray petals covering both of us. They were just as alluring as I'd thought they'd be. Plucking a few off her breast, I told her, "Give me a minute, and I can probably change your mind about that." I was pretty sure I could hold out now. I was definitely willing to try, at any rate.

But unfortunately, I didn't get the chance to try anything, because right at that moment, our bedroom door slammed open. What the actual fuck?

Chapter 7

A MEETING

Kiera screamed and looked for something to hide herself with. Unfortunately, we were on top of the covers, so the only thing around to truly shield her with was me. Shifting over, so I was on top of her, I did my best to hide all her important bits. Then I glared at the person interrupting our moment. *Someone better be dying, or the house better be on fire.* Those were the only two scenarios I'd accept.

But when I saw it was Griffin rushing up to the bed, I knew neither of those two things had happened; the glee on his face when he locked eyes with me made it especially obvious. *That's it...I'm going to kill him.* "What the fuck, Griffin?" I snapped.

Looking like he was standing in my living room and not my bedroom, he bounced on his toes, eagerness all over his face...a face dripping with sour milk so pungent that it was already making me nauseated. "Kellan, you're not gonna believe who's here!" he said, his expression joyful, but oblivious.

You're right. I can't believe that you're *here.* Chucking a purple pillow at him, I snarled, "I don't care! Get the fuck out!" I could practically feel Kiera willing herself to be invisible beneath me. Her embarrassment was almost a physical thing in the room, tightening around my chest and filling me with rage. But aside from yelling at Griffin to go away, there was nothing I could do for her. Standing up and pummeling my bassist was *not* an option at the moment.

The pillow struck Griffin in the face, but he looked more confused than anything else, like he really didn't understand what he was interrupting. Fucking moron. Brows bunched, he told me, "Dude, you're gonna care when you see her. Get the fuck out of bed, lazy-ass!" For some reason, saying that opened his eyes to the fact that I wasn't alone. His gaze shifted from my face to take in Kiera beneath me. He grinned in a way that was about to shorten his lifespan. "Hey, Kiera...it's good to see you."

Un. Fucking. Believable. I almost hopped up to punch him in the face, but all that would do was give him a better view of Kiera. Hating my options, and hating that Kiera was going to suffer because of my options, I called for help. "Matt! Get your cousin out of my fucking bedroom before I toss him off the fucking balcony!"

It took longer than I liked for Matt and Evan to stride into the room. They both looked mortified to be in my bedroom when they *knew* what was going on, and they both respectfully didn't look at the bed. And that right there was why both of them would never have anything to fear from me. Griffin might not live to see tomorrow.

I heard Kiera groan in embarrassment, ratcheting my anger even higher. And then Anna appeared in the doorway, grinning and giggling as she blatantly stared at us. Goddamn it.

Matt and Evan had to physically drag Griffin from the room, and he fought them the entire way. "Dude, they can bone later! He needs to see who's here!" Looking back at me, he grinned as he added, "She's asking for you, dude. You!"

I had no clue who he was talking about, and I really didn't care. It could be the fucking Queen of England, and I wouldn't fucking care.

Matt smacked the back of Griffin's head. "Remember what we said about giving Kellan some space when Kiera got here...

because of that *thing* he was going to give her?" From the blank look on Griffin's face, it was clear he did *not* remember that conversation. Matt hit him again, murmuring something about Griffin being a moron, then he tossed out a, "Sorry, Kell!" and mercifully closed the door.

The boiling anger in my stomach started quieting to a simmer with Griffin's absence. Kiera's fingers dug into my skin as her wide eyes sought mine. "Oh my God! That did *not* just happen, did it?"

God...if only that had been a dream. I rubbed her back with a sigh. "Unfortunately...it did." I gave her an apologetic cringe. "Sorry, I forgot to lock the door." A laugh escaped me, even though none of that was funny; I was just grateful it was over. "I was a little preoccupied," I told her.

Kiera glared at me a little, presumably for the laugh. Then she looked confused. "Do you know what he was talking about? Who's here to see you?"

Clueless, I shook my head. "No idea." I turned to look at the door where I could hear Matt reprimanding Griffin on the other side. Good, he deserved a Matt Lecture. "I suppose I should go see, though."

Putting our clothes back on took a while with all the flower petals stuck to our bodies. I would have loved to take the time to playfully peel each one off Kiera's skin, tenderly replacing it with my lips, but apparently, there was somewhere I needed to be. And some*one* I needed to deal with.

Once I was ready to go, I inhaled a deep breath, praying for patience and restraint, then I gave Kiera a kiss on the forehead and told her, "Stay here. I'm gonna go kill Griffin."

By the beaming grin she gave me, I knew she had no intention of missing out on me going off on Griffin. I honestly wasn't sure what I was going to say to him. Because I honestly wasn't sure what I could possibly say that would actually alter his future behavior. And him walking in on us like that was something that I needed to *never* happen again.

There was only one thing I could think of that might get through to him. Kiera might not like it. The guys might not like it either. But I needed Griffin to *listen*. I was done fucking around.

Griffin had his shirt off when we got into the living room. He was scrubbing milk out of his chin-length hair with it while Matt and Evan snipped at him; I couldn't hear what they were saying, but they both looked mad. Anna did too as she tapped her foot while she waited to talk to Griffin. Jackass was pissing off everybody today, and there was still a whole lot of today left.

Griffin looked up when he sensed me coming. He smiled like he was thrilled to see me. "Dude—"

Wanting him to understand that I was pissed, I cut him off by putting my hands on his chest and shoving him back, hard. Not expecting me to get physical, I caught him completely off guard, and he crashed right to the floor. His smile instantly evaporated. "What the fuck, Kell?"

In the space of one heartbeat, the room flooded with tension as everyone waited to see what I would do. Matt and Evan's eyes on me were especially penetrating; I could practically feel them digging into my skin, begging me not to take this too far. As I stared at Griffin on the floor, I did my best to rein in my anger. This wasn't about picking a fight with him. This was a message, one I wanted him to take seriously.

Griffin rolled his eyes as I stared at him. Not a good start. "Relax," he said. "Besides your ass, I didn't see anything."

I didn't care about my ass, and what he did or didn't see wasn't the point. Slowly and deliberately, I pointed at the hallway that led to the stairs. "Grab your shit and get out."

I could feel the weight of my words shocking the entire room, and that was why I'd said it—to shock him into listening. But it didn't work. Griffin looked more amused than anything; he snorted as he jauntily got back on his feet, and my hands unintentionally clenched as I watched him. "Oh, come on, Kell." He pointed over to my bedroom. "It's not like I knew she was here."

Moron. He knew Anna was coming in today. Did it really never occur to him that Kiera would be on the same flight? Anna muttered words that echoed my thoughts. Griffin ignored her, crossing his arms over his chest in a gesture of defiance. "Besides, you can't kick me out of the band, dude."

Like hell I couldn't. The real question was *should I*? And he really wasn't helping me answer that question. Even more annoyed now, since he wasn't taking me seriously, I stepped closer to him until we were toe to toe. "Why the hell would I keep you?" I growled, almost meaning it.

Griffin had the balls to smirk at me. He sank his weight onto his hip, looking completely relaxed. "Because I'm the shit, and you know it." Then he gave me a smile that reminded me of a little kid. "And we're best friends," he said with a shrug.

Those words, combined with the look on his face, made it really fucking hard to stay mad at him. Closing my eyes in defeat, I took a step back. Some of my anger might have fizzled, but I still needed him to hear me. Breathing deep, I opened my eyes and tried to give him a hard look. "If I am anywhere with my wife —*anywhere*—you knock and wait for permission to enter. Can your tiny fucking brain comprehend that?"

He shrugged like it was no big deal. "Fine, whatever, dude."

Irritated at his casual response, but glad he'd agreed, I turned around and grabbed Kiera's hand; her cheeks were still bright red. That didn't help my mood. Neither did Griffin's carefree reaction of coming up to me and slinging an arm around my shoulder, like we really were the best friends he'd claimed we were. And yeah, in a way, I supposed we were. Maybe we weren't *best* friends, but we were definitely family, and that bond was just as deep. Honestly, it wasn't the gesture that was annoying me, it was more the fact that he smelled like a fucking cesspool.

"So, can I show you who's here now?" There was giddiness in his voice again.

Needing away from his stench, I shoved him off me. He frowned at me like he was offended. "Hey, come on, I'm sorry for barging in on you, okay? I just got excited." He bounced on his toes, eager again, and I instantly wondered who in the world could have gotten him so riled up. His next words partially explained it. "I mean, how often do you get to meet a porn star!"

A porn star? Why would a porn star want to meet *me*? I was about to ask him, but then I saw Matt roll his eyes. "She's not a porn star, Griff. Stop calling her that."

Griffin glared at his cousin. "Tomato, tom*a*to, dude. She had sex on tape. I got off on it. Boom—porn star."

Those words made Kiera close her eyes and pinch her nose like she had a headache. Understandable. I wasn't enjoying the visual either. Matt rolled his eyes again while Griffin turned back to me. "And she's asking to see you...by name! Can you believe that shit?"

Done with this weird, uninformative conversation, I stopped walking and addressed the entire room. "Who the hell is he talking about? Who's here?"

Evan scratched his head, looking a little unsure and a little blown away. "Uh, Sienna Sexton."

My mouth fell open as I absorbed that. Sienna Sexton was a pop culture icon, a name everyone knew. Her songs were all over the radio, and yeah, her sex tape was all over the Internet, or so I'd been told. I hadn't watched it because Matt was right; she wasn't a porn star, and that tape wasn't supposed to be public. Her dickhead ex had leaked it without her permission, and that just made it feel...wrong to me. Her story was sort of a cautionary tale about trust. And considering the fact that I'd just been essentially blackmailed about the same thing, I really wished I'd paid more attention to it.

She was a huge star. Why the hell was she asking for me?

I looked between Evan and Matt, trying to figure it out. "Are you serious? Sienna Sexton? *The* Sienna Sexton? Why does she want to see me? How does she even know who I am?"

They both looked just as clueless as I felt. Matt shook his head. "Don't know, man. She just came in with her entourage a few minutes ago and asked to see you." He pointed above us. "They're waiting upstairs for you. Which we were going to tell you about when you were done…giving Kiera…you know." His cheeks flooded with color as he sheepishly looked over at my wife. "I like the ring. It's really beautiful on you, Kiera."

I could practically feel Kiera dying at my side as she murmured, "Thank you."

Anna came over to examine Kiera's ring and gush over meeting a pop star. I was still just standing there, floored. How in the world had I gotten the attention of Sienna Sexton? It didn't seem possible. I was a nobody. Was someone messing with me?

Griffin looked thrilled that I was finally interested. He slung his arm over my shoulders again, bringing his odor right beside my nose again. "So can we go now?" he asked.

The closer he got to me, the more I felt like I was going to heave. "You smell awful. Could you shower first?"

Griffin tossed Matt a dirty, accusatory look, then said, "Yeah, just give me two secs."

He jogged to his room, leaving the door open in his haste. I waited until I could hear the water running, then I told Matt and Evan, "Let's go." I couldn't keep the satisfied smile off my face. While threatening to kick Griffin out of the band had fallen flat, I was pretty sure being denied the chance to meet a "porn star" would make an impression on him. Served him right. And besides, I had a feeling this meeting would be a whole lot more professional if Griffin wasn't there. We'd fill him in later. When he was cleaner. And calmer. And started respecting people's privacy.

As I walked beside Kiera, I noticed one last petal buried in her hair. Seeing it made me deliriously happy. I almost wanted to leave it, but I knew Kiera wouldn't want to meet a pop star like that. I handed it to her after plucking it from her long locks. She gave me the sweetest smile, then asked if I was serious about kicking Griffin out of the band. *No. Not really. Maybe.* I asked her if she wanted me to, and while she seemed to genuinely contemplate that, she ended up shaking her head no. I understood the feeling. Griffin might drive everyone crazy from time to time, but he still belonged. He was a D-Bag through and through.

When we got upstairs, there were two burly guys in suits blocking the hallway. From the earpieces, steely expressions, and rigid stances, they were clearly security. Weird. I'd never met anyone who needed security like *this*. It drove home the fact that the person in the next room was a big deal. And it again made me wonder why she wanted to see *me*.

Not sure what I was supposed to say to get by them, but knowing they wouldn't let me squeeze between them, I said, "I'm Kellan Kyle, this is my band. Ms. Sexton asked to see us."

The guard spoke to someone through a microphone in his sleeve, then stepped aside so we could pass. Lana approached us in the hallway. I instantly felt more at ease seeing her here. Lana had been the one to "discover us" on Justin's tour, and the guys and I had spent a lot of time with her while we'd been finalizing which songs should go on the album. Over the last several weeks, I'd really come to trust her judgement, and her opinion, since she knew a hell of a lot more about this business than I did. Even though she worked for the label, I felt like she was on our side.

Dressed impeccably as always, her dark hair swept up in a loose bun, Lana gave me a warm smile as she drew closer. "Kellan, boys."

"Lana," I said in acknowledgment.

Lana swished her hand behind her, to the living area on this floor. "Miss Sexton would like to speak with you, Kellan, if you're free?" A mischievous look gleamed in Lana's deep brown eyes as she glanced over at Kiera. From the small smile on her face, I knew Lana was aware of why I'd been preoccupied. She must have been the one who'd told the guys that Sienna was here, asking for us, for me. *I wonder if she heard us in the bedroom.* Huh. Oh well. Worth it.

My lips started to curl into a smile, amused that Lana would even subtly allude to what we'd been doing, but I stopped myself before a full grin grew. It was time to be professional. "Of course."

Lana led us into the living room where a couple of people were making drinks and a guy in a nice suit was sitting on the couch. I focused on him since he was the one who seemed out of place here. Sienna's manager maybe?

I felt Kiera squeeze my hand as she looked around the room for Sienna; she wasn't in here, but she had to be nearby. Kiera had been a nervous wreck when she'd met Justin for the first time, so I had to imagine she was freaking out right now. I squeezed her hand back, letting her know I was here, and this was nothing for her to worry about. Underneath it all, Sienna was a human being, just like us.

Lana led us right to the couch, to Sienna's manager. Weird. Guess we had to go through him first. The blond, blue-eyed, sharply dressed man stood and extended his hand to me. "Kellan, nice to meet you. I'm Nick Wallace, VP of Vivasec Records."

Oh shit. Not Sienna's manager. Why was the vice president of the label here? Meeting me? Was this normal? I felt like it wasn't, and that made a weird, cautious feeling crawl up my spine. Maintaining my professionalism, I held onto my questions as I released Kiera's hand so I could shake Nick's. "Nice to meet you."

Before any other words could be spoken, three people entered the room from a set of doors that led outside. Two of them I'd never seen before. The third one was Sienna. I'd never seen her in person, obviously, but she was one of those celebrities that seemed to be everywhere, so she was instantly recognizable to me. Long, black hair, creamy olive-tan skin, high cheekbones, large, dark eyes, full pouty lips—she was exotically beautiful; no one on Earth could deny that.

I was so struck by the oddness of being in the same room with her that it took me a minute to realize she was in a bikini. Sure, she had a cover-up on over it, but it was see-through and did nothing to hide the fact that most of her body was on display.

Tight, trim, curvy—it was exactly the type of body you'd expect from a celebrity. Yeah, it was definitely a good thing I'd left Griffin behind.

Sienna's eyes instantly locked on me, and she raised both hands as she made a beeline for where I was standing. When she spoke, a British accent flavored her words. "Kellan, I am so excited to meet you. I'm a huge fan." She grabbed my hands with both of hers, then leaned up and kissed one cheek and then the other. It was weird. I'd never had someone greet me that way. Her words were even stranger, though. *Huge fan?* How had she even heard me?

She pulled back to look at me, and the expression of eagerness and interest on her face was so startlingly familiar that it threw me. *She's looking at me like my fans do.* But she was the biggest pop star on the planet, so that made no sense to me. I shouldn't even be on her radar, but apparently, I was.

It was all just so...bizarre.

I didn't know what to say to her. I usually just smiled at my fans and told them thank you, but that didn't seem like quite enough in this instance. We were peers, in a way, so I should reciprocate, right? "Uh, thank you. I'm a...huge fan too." Fuck. Was that polite and professional, or did I sound like a suck-up tool? But it wasn't exactly a lie. I mean, maybe *huge* fan was a stretch, her style wasn't exactly my preferred style, but I certainly respected all she'd accomplished. I was a fan of her work ethic. And her talent. Her voice was undeniably spectacular.

Sienna seemed to take my words exactly as spoken. She stepped back with a giggle. "Ah, love, aren't you a sweet one."

While Sienna's friends turned on a TV, I introduced Matt and Evan. They both looked wide-eyed and starstruck as Sienna shook their hands. Interestingly enough, she didn't kiss their cheeks in greeting like she had mine. That concerned me a little. What exactly was Sienna hoping to get from me? Because if it was more than just this meeting...she was going to be disappointed.

I was about to introduce Kiera when Anna stepped forward.

Grabbing Sienna's hand, she gushed, "Anna Allen, mega fan. You're practically my idol."

That made me grin. Yeah, I could totally see Anna worshipping her. Sienna gave her a polite smile, then patted her protruding stomach. "You due soon, love?"

Anna frowned like she was offended. "No, November..."

Sienna cocked a questioning eyebrow at me. "Yours?" she asked, clearly meaning the baby.

I flicked a quick glance at Anna's stomach, then shook my head. Slinging an arm over Kiera's shoulders, I drew her into my side. "Mine," I stated.

Kiera smirked at me for my possessive answer, then surprised me by calmly extending her hand to Sienna. Although her fingers were trembling a little. "Kiera...hi."

Sienna's smile minutely dropped as she examined Kiera and me as a couple, and I had the weirdest sensation that even though she'd asked about Anna's baby, she'd really been hoping I was single and available. *Sorry, I most definitely am not.* Sienna's momentary disappointment vanished as she shook Kiera's hand. "Nice to meet you."

While I was happy Sienna was being courteous to my wife, I was ready to know what was going on. "You...wanted to see me?" I asked.

She clasped her hands together, her eyes sparkling with excitement. "Yes! I have a proposition for you. One I think would be in your best interest. Yours and mine." She grinned and pointed at me with her laced fingers. "I want you," she stated.

While her words sounded somewhat suggestive, I was pretty sure this wasn't about sex. She wouldn't make *that* kind of proposition in front of the VP of the label. Right? I really hoped not. Turning her down with an audience like this would be... awkward. For everyone.

Nick spoke while I was still trying to figure out what she *really* meant. "As you know, Sienna is the label's largest star." Sienna winked at that, and Nick smiled before continuing. "She's been listening to your finished tracks, and she's impressed, to say the least."

Well, I supposed that explained how she knew who I was, but what were they getting at? Before I could ask, Nick gestured at Sienna with both hands, like she was a game show prize. "We've been looking for a way to rejuvenate Sienna's sound, add some kick to it."

Sienna nodded, smiling brightly at me. "Something new...fresh."

Nick tilted his head as he continued. "We've been looking for a collaboration that would blend well with her unique style." He swung his hands to me. "And that's where you come in."

I blinked in surprise. Sienna collaborating with an artist certainly made sense for her career, but was she really asking to team up with *me*? I had to be misunderstanding them. "Me?" I asked.

Nick clapped my shoulder like we were buds. "Yes. Your sound is exactly what Sienna's been looking for. And we have the perfect song for you—'Regretfully.' Sienna's already recorded her half of it. We just need you," he finished with a shrug.

Damn. So they *were* asking to team up. But something about the look on Nick's face, and honestly, the look on Sienna's face, wasn't sitting right with me, and every cell in my body flared with caution. They kept singling me out—asking for *me* by name, saying they wanted to work with *me*, but the band wasn't just *me*, and I wasn't interested in a solo project. If that was what was on the table here, then my answer was an easy one: no.

Making sure I was understanding them properly, I indicated Matt and Evan. "You mean all of us, right?"

Sienna's smile was pure innocence. "Of course."

Right. Maybe I was being paranoid, but I didn't entirely believe her.

I could feel Matt and Evan's eager energy beside me. They knew what this could mean for our band. I did too, but I couldn't shake the feeling that there was more going on here, something I wasn't understanding. And I also knew that this could be too much, too fast. Sienna was a huge star; being tied to her right off the bat would throw us headfirst into public awareness. We'd have no chance to warm up to fame, to get used to being in the spotlight on a global scale. It would just be right there in our faces, blinding us. Maybe. I supposed if the song sucked, things for us wouldn't change too much. I really wasn't sure. All I knew was this felt...important. And I wasn't sure what to do.

Feeling pressure being placed squarely on *my* shoulders, I looked over at Kiera. She had the same shocked, almost overwhelmed expression on her face. She knew what this might mean for us too. I chewed on my lip as uncertainty filled me. I'd been hoping for a slow build, a chance for the guys and me to grow into this life. Would saying yes destroy that? Would saying no be stupid?

Matt and Evan were being quiet, waiting for me to say something. I still wasn't sure what to say, and I needed time to think. "Our styles are very different. Can I hear the song first, make sure it's a good match...for us?"

Nick's face instantly changed, hardened. He clearly didn't like me having an opinion about this, and that filled me with a dark kind of dread. He was the VP of the company...if I said no to this, could he kill our deal? He gave me a tight, obviously annoyed smile. "Absolutely."

"Come," Sienna said. "I'll play it for you." Then she grabbed my hand and pulled me toward a piano in the corner of the room. I wanted to disengage from her, but that cautious feeling was still pricking me, and it suddenly felt really important not to offend her.

Sienna sat on the piano bench and began playing. Evan and Matt joined me beside the piano, listening intently. The melody was interesting, not quite a ballad, not quite a fast song, but in that tricky in between area. Sienna's voice filled the room, and I really paid attention to the lyrics. I had to admit, they were good;

it was something I could see myself singing. The song was about a relationship ending—badly. It was something I could relate to, something I could draw from internally. That wasn't truly necessary when performing, but it definitely helped.

As the song continued, Evan started drumming a beat with his fingers, and I could tell Matt was spinning something in his head. I tried to hear what they were hearing, tried to hear our sound meshing with what Sienna was playing...and I could. And it was good. If we did this, it could be a *really* good song, a massive hit. Which brought me right back to the beginning of my worries. *Should* we do this?

Sienna finished the song, looking at me with expectant eyes. Matt and Evan were looking at me in the same way; by their smiles, I could tell they were sold. They didn't seem to be at all concerned with what instant success might do to us. Of course, the downside might not have crossed their minds yet.

As I grappled with uncertainty, I felt a hand on my back. I twisted around to see Lana standing there, a friendly smile on her face. I minutely relaxed, seeing someone who could give me some real advice. Like she could see my doubt, Lana raised an eyebrow and said, "This is one of those once-in-a-lifetime moments that we talked about, Kellan. I would say yes if I were you."

I gave her a smile and a nod in thank you, and I felt a small piece of the weight being lifted from me. A part of me knew she was right. Career-wise, this was a no-brainer. But the band was my family, *Kiera* was my family, and I didn't want to do anything that might jeopardize their health and safety, their security and happiness. The "career" wasn't worth it if they suffered...if Kiera and I suffered. Because honestly, that was my truest, deepest fear. That somehow this decision would damage what Kiera and I had, and that scared the living fuck out of me.

Kiera looped her arm around my waist. Grateful for her presence, I returned the gesture. "What do you think?" she asked.

Knowing everyone was intently watching me, I told her the straight-up truth. "I don't know. What do you think?"

She hesitated for a moment like she was debating what to tell me. Then she shrugged. "I think it's incredible. I think it would be a waste of your talent to say no."

I was a little surprised to hear her say that because I could see the trace amount of fear in her eyes. She was worried about what this could mean for us too, but it wasn't going to change her answer, wasn't going to change her truth. And I knew she was right. We couldn't run from an opportunity like this. *I* couldn't run from an opportunity like this. I owed the guys too much for that.

Kiera was being brave right now. I needed to be brave too. I gave her an appreciative smile, then looked back at Nick. "I guess we'll get to work on it first thing."

Chapter 8
MY HAPPY PLACE

My mind was spinning when we got back to the second floor, trying to process everything that had just happened, trying to imagine what our future might look like now. I had no idea. Things had been vague and cloudy ever since we'd left on that tour with Justin, and my old life was feeling further and further away. As I sat on the couch with Kiera, I kept thinking about Pete's. About playing at the bar, hanging out with my friends, flirting incessantly with Kiera. I'd given it up before I'd been *ready* to give it up, and all of this...it really made me miss it.

But I knew I couldn't stay in the past forever. Time relentlessly moved forward, and I had to move forward with it. At least Kiera was by my side now. She would be my constant, my compass, my true north. Whatever happened with the band, whatever Sienna's fame might mean for us, that fact wouldn't change for me. Kiera was my home, my happy place, my quiet in the chaos. This *wouldn't* change us. I wouldn't let it.

Griffin was pissed at me for not waiting for him, and he spent the next hour sulking in the corner. I was positive I would hear all about how much I sucked later, when he got past the ignoring me phase. But thankfully, that wouldn't be tonight because Anna was in a...frisky mood after meeting her idol, and the pair disappeared into Griffin's bedroom.

After they left, my mind started wandering again, worrying. The displeasure on Nick's face when I'd asked to hear the song was stuck in my head, and I couldn't help but wonder what he would have done if I'd said no.

"Can you believe it, Kell? Sienna Sexton wants to do a song with us. *Us!*"

I roused myself from my thoughts to look over at Matt. He and Evan were both grinning at me with mile-wide smiles. Kiera looked up from her writing notebook to give me a soft smile of encouragement. She hadn't asked about my introspective mood, just quietly supported me while I'd processed. I appreciated that. The silence was soothing.

My lips twisted into a lopsided grin. "I hate to burst your bubble, Matt, but I'm pretty sure we're all having some weird, shared dream and none of that actually happened."

Matt snorted at me, then frowned when we all heard the telltale sound of Anna and Griffin reuniting. "If that's true, then this dream is about to turn into one of my nightmares." He paused to let out a weary sigh. "I do *not* want to listen to those two go at it again. Let's get out of here. Go celebrate."

I glanced down at Kiera, to ask if she wanted to leave, but she was already nodding, eager to get away from the loud lovebirds. Looking back up at Matt, I nodded. "Sounds good."

As we all stood from the couch, Matt smiled at Kiera and said to me, "We should take Kiera to The Rusted Pipe. Show her where we used to hang out."

I frowned as I considered that. The Rusted Pipe wasn't the greatest bar, and it *definitely* wasn't in the greatest neighborhood. "I don't know. The Pipe is kind of...sketchy." If only we could take Sam with us too. *Nobody* would mess with us if that tank was nearby. And thinking that made me miss Pete's. Again.

Kiera smiled like Matt had just suggested Disneyland. "I

don't care if it's sketchy. I want to see where young you used to hang out."

I smirked at her enthusiasm. "Young, *broke* me...just keep that in mind."

She laughed a little, then bit her lip. It made me want to suck on it. Her gaze drifted to my mouth. "No judgement, I promise. But I want to see it." She lightly patted my stomach. "And I'm not worried, you'll keep me safe."

The way she was looking at me stopped my breath for a second. There was so much adoration in her eyes, like I walked on water or something. It mystified me...blew me away. And I knew she was right—I would fight until my very last breath to keep her safe. "All right, fine," I told her, a humoring tone in my voice.

Kiera grabbed her purse, then we all headed for the stairs. Just in time too because Anna and Griffin were *really* getting into it now. As we speed-walked down the stairs, Matt tossed over his shoulder, "We're taking a cab this time. I'm not gonna be the only sober one again. You guys suck when you're drunk."

Evan laughed while I made an affronted noise. Kiera smirked at me, rolling her eyes. Then she said, "At least with me here, getting him into bed won't be such a challenge." She instantly realized how provocative her statement sounded, and her cheeks went beet red.

Matt's eyes widened, but he faced front and didn't say anything. Evan chuckled, shaking his head, while I tried my best not to burst out laughing. I was *not* successful. I had to stop on the last stair and hold onto the railing as a fit of giggles grabbed hold of me.

Kiera's eyes drilled into me as she fisted her hands, ramming them into her hips. "It's not *that* funny," she murmured.

Trying to calm myself, I inhaled a deep breath and slowly shook my head. "It's not that it's *funny*. It's that you're so fucking cute, I just can't stand it." She didn't look amused. Reaching out, I grabbed her waist and pulled her into me. "Oh, God...I'm so glad you're here." I nuzzled into her neck, and she finally relaxed, melting into my arms. I kissed her neck, my lips tenderly tracing the curve up to her ear. Kiera let out a soft moan, igniting me. I was just wondering if we should turn around and go back upstairs, when I heard someone loudly clear their throat.

I looked up to see Evan standing there, an amused look on his face. "We still leaving?" he asked.

Kiera's cheeks flushed again, and she spun in my arms. "Yes. Yep. We're going. Let's go."

She stalked away from me, and I smiled as I stared at her backside. Yes. I was *extremely* glad she was here. Evan laughed at the look on my face, then playfully socked me in the shoulder. "Come on, let's go drink."

Lana was still here when we walked into the downstairs living area. When we told her what we were doing, she mentioned that the label had drivers available upon request. Good to know. She arranged one for us, and then we were on our way.

When we got to The Rusted Pipe, Kiera's eyes widened as she looked over the exterior. If she thought that was bad...

Smiling, I laced my fingers with hers and led her inside. An odd look was on her face when she glanced around the dimly lit interior of the bar; it was an expression of both fondness and mild alarm, like she was picturing a younger version of me in every corner of the room, but she was also keeping an eye on the exit, just in case she had to run for her life. So cute.

I nudged her shoulder, and she looked over at me with a smile. "You weren't lying about this place," she said, stepping closer to me so that her entire side pressed into mine.

Grinning, I lifted my eyebrows. "Are you judging now?"

She laughed as she peered up at me. "No. Just wondering if you'll have to come into the bathroom with me to hold the door closed."

My grin grew downright devilish, and she poked me in the ribs as she giggled. Matt and Evan were already heading for the bar, so Kiera and I followed. Cody was working again, and he shook his head when he saw us. "You guys are gonna be regulars again, aren't you?"

I shrugged as I pulled out a stool for Kiera. "Maybe. For a little while."

Cody's dark eyes were trained on Kiera as she sat down. His gaze locked on to her wedding ring when she put her hands on the bar. "You must be Mrs. Kyle," he said. "Nice to meet you. I'm Cody." His eyes focused on her face for a moment, then slid down her body.

Kiera flushed a little, uncomfortable with Cody's scrutiny. So was I. Cody better lift his gaze before I lifted it for him. "Nice to meet you too," Kiera said.

Cody's eyes finally swung back to me as I sat down. "Damn, Kellan. Now I kind of get it. Not saying I want that life...but I get it."

I smirked at him, then frowned when I saw him wink at Kiera. Seriously? "Thanks, man. Now stop flirting with my wife."

His expression was instantly horrified...in a totally fake way. "I would never..." He grinned, then fucking winked at her again. If he did it a third time, he was going to lose the ability to ever do it again.

Like he knew he was testing my patience, his demeanor changed into a more professional one, and he addressed all four of us. "Your regulars? Or is it another special occasion?"

Matt was practically bouncing on his seat; he was so giddy. "Dude, you are *not* gonna believe what happened to us today." Matt filled Cody in on our odd, dreamlike day, and by the end of his story, Cody was floored.

"Holy shit," he murmured. "You guys are actually gonna make it. All the way make it. Fuck...that's crazy." He instantly reached into his pocket and grabbed his phone. "Crowd together. I need a picture of you guys for the wall. You're gonna make us famous."

I had to frown at that, but I did what he asked and leaned into Evan's side so that the three of us were in the frame; Kiera leaned in the opposite direction, so she wasn't in the photo at all. Not too surprising. She avoided the spotlight even more than Matt did. When Cody was finished with his picture, he frowned and looked behind us. "Where's Griffin?" he asked, like he just now noticed we were short a D-Bag.

Matt grimaced. "He's...busy."

Kiera peeked around me to look at Matt. "Should we have waited for him and Anna? I mean...it's his moment too. I feel kind of bad now."

I rubbed her back while she frowned, and I couldn't help but be genuinely impressed by the fact that she actually did seem to feel bad. About *Griffin*.

Matt snorted, and I looked over at him. "No," he said. "Those two aren't going to be done for a long, long time." His pale eyes shifted to me; there was a mischievous glint in them. "Griffin got some..." His voice trailed off as his gaze slid back to Kiera. Closing his mouth, he shook his head. "Never mind," he murmured, looking embarrassed.

I could practically feel the curiosity oozing out of Kiera. Curiosity mixed with trepidation. "He got what?" she asked, then she cringed like she hadn't meant to ask him, but that damn impulsive mouth of hers won again.

If Matt didn't want to say it, then I was pretty sure Kiera wouldn't want to know it...but damn if I wasn't curious too. I lifted my eyebrow at Matt, giving him a slight nod when he gave me a questioning look. Matt's cheeks reddened a little, but he grinned. He spoke to all of us, but his gaze stayed fixed on Evan and me. "He finally visited his parents last week, and while he was there, he swiped some of his dad's Viagra." He started laughing. "He wants to see if he can get a four-hour erection."

Kiera bit her lip as Cody, Evan, and I cracked up. Then she started laughing too. Shaking my head, I said to Matt, "But isn't that a bad thing? Does he know that?"

Matt laughed so hard that his eyes watered. "Yeah, but he doesn't see how that can possibly be a bad thing."

Evan was dying now. Matt patted his shoulder. Once he pulled himself together, Evan looked over at me with a sigh. "God...is it wrong that I'm kind of curious to see how that goes?" He started laughing again, then looked past me to Kiera. "Sorry, Kiera," he murmured.

She shook her head as she laughed with him. "It's fine." All of a sudden, the humor left her face, and she locked gazes with me. "You don't think he would take more than one, do you?"

That made Matt and Evan lose it again, but Kiera looked genuinely concerned. "I should call Anna...see if he's okay." She looked a little nauseated by the idea.

I put a hand on her arm to stop her from reaching for her phone. "Anna wouldn't let him injure himself," I said with a laugh. "I'm sure he's fine. *Just fine*," I added with a raised eyebrow.

The nauseated look on her face sharpened, then she sighed. "God...I can't believe *that's* my nephew's father..."

Kiera's statement got Matt's attention. "Nephew? He's having a boy?" His face slackened as his eyes widened. "Jesus... there's going to be two of them."

That revelation killed the humor real quick. Shaking his head, Cody set a bottle of whiskey in front of us. "I'll just leave this here," he said.

When we were pretty deep into the bottle, I suddenly remembered my vow not to drink to excess until the album was finished, but of course, at that point, I didn't really care. The four of us spent the rest of the evening celebrating. We drank, we ate, we laughed, we tried really hard not to hit people while playing darts, and we occasionally sent a prayer out into the universe for the health, safety, and sanity of Griffin's unborn child.

We decided to head home a little before the bar closed for the night. Matt called our driver while I wrapped Kiera in my arms, holding her close, where I preferred her to be. She kept her arms tucked into her chest, letting me surround her, absorb her. I smiled as I kissed her head.

"It's not as bad as you made it sound," she murmured, looking up at me.

I tilted my head as I examined her. Her eyes were a little unfocused, her smile loose and easy. "Is that because you're drunk?" I asked.

She laughed, then shook her head. "No. It's because the bathroom closed and locked properly. And it was surprisingly clean," she added with a grin.

A soft laugh escaped me as I leaned down to kiss her. "Who knew all it took was a clean bathroom to impress you."

"That and the locks," she said against my lips.

I paused to laugh again. "Right." Pulling back, I let out a dramatic sigh. "Man, I could have saved myself so much time if I'd only known that earlier."

She pursed her lips at me in an adorable expression of *That was inappropriate and not true, but I adore you, so I'm going to let it go.* It just made me laugh harder.

Our car arrived, and Kiera and I climbed into the backseat. Kiera giggled as she partially sat on my lap. She twisted around to face me, slipping her arms around my neck. Definitely tipsy. Evan sat in the backseat with us. He eyed how Kiera was sitting and then frowned at me. He raised an eyebrow, and I knew what he was saying without him even opening his mouth. *Am I going to have to watch you two make out the entire trip back?*

I smiled at him in answer. *No, you absolutely don't have to watch. You've got a window right there.*

Evan rolled his eyes and looked out the window like he'd heard me suggest it. I could see him smiling in the reflection, though. And then Kiera's lips were on mine, and I really didn't care if he was smiling or not. I tried to keep our kisses soft and sweet, tried to keep my hands in only appropriate places, but I'd been drinking a lot too, and willpower was *not* my strongest asset.

Before I knew it, we were getting far too friendly for where we were. She was fully on my lap now, grinding against me and letting out soft moans that were quickly unraveling me. My body surged with need, the lust breaking apart my buzz and scattering my thoughts. I knew Kiera wouldn't want such a public memory when she sobered up, I knew my bandmates wouldn't want this memory *right now*, so I forced myself to push her shoulders back. She stared down at me with parted lips and heat in her eyes, and I had to remind myself that I was doing the right thing. Leaning up, I said in her ear, "We're almost home. I'll satisfy you there, I promise."

Her eyes got wider as my words pierced her desire. She tossed a quick glance at Evan beside us and Matt in the front seat. Both of them were staring fixedly out the side windows, and the music in the car was much louder than it had been a moment ago. Color filled Kiera's cheeks as she sank her head to my shoulder. "Damn it," she mumbled in my ear.

The seldom heard swear made me laugh. As I rubbed her back, I willed my body to calm down. For now. "Don't worry about it," I told her. "They understand. If their girls were here, they'd be all over them too."

Kiera pulled back to look at me. She got more comfortable in my lap but didn't move to leave it. "I wish they could be. I wish everyone could be together."

I smiled at her thoughtfulness as I glanced at my bandmates. Matt looked back at us, tentatively at first, then more deliberately when he saw that we were finished with the foreplay. Evan looked over at us too. He smirked at me, shook his head a little, then looked back out the window.

Turning back to Kiera, I smiled and told her, "Someday, we will be." Then I coaxed her over to her seat and helped her buckle up. Safety first and all that. Once she was secured, I grabbed her hand and moved over to speak in her ear since the music was still cranked up. "You know, I think I robbed you."

Her brows bunched together as she tried to understand what I meant. "Robbed me? Robbed me of what?"

I grinned at her bemused expression. "A honeymoon. We got

married, then went our separate ways, and now we're here...we didn't get to take one. I feel like I robbed you."

She smirked at that, then smiled. "At least we had a wedding night."

Flashes of that evening flitted through my brain—warm skin, soft sighs, fast breaths, indescribable bliss; I had to shift how I was sitting as the memory consumed me. "One night wasn't enough. I want a full week of wedding nights." Or two. Or a month. Or a year. Or ten.

Kiera ducked her head as she giggled at my suggestive remark. Then she sighed. "I know you're busy, and I know what you're doing is important. I don't need a honeymoon, Kellan."

Nuzzling into her neck, I kissed her skin before telling her, "It's not about what you need. It's about what you deserve. And you deserve a honeymoon." I lifted my head to look at her, tucking a dark strand of hair behind her ear. "*We* deserve a honeymoon. We deserve some time that's just ours, no one else's. Right?"

She smiled as she gazed at me, then she slowly nodded. "Yeah, you're right."

I kissed her nose, then gave her a lopsided smile. "I know."

She playfully smacked my shoulder, then leaned her head against it. Heaven.

As I'd predicted, Griffin was fine after his pharmaceutical adventure, and he was all too happy to share his insights on the experience with me. I was all too happy to listen because if he was talking about his junk, then he wasn't bitching at me for leaving him behind for the meeting. In fact, he seemed to have forgotten all about the Sienna incident. Probably because she spent the next several days at the house, and Griffin had numerous opportunities to talk to her. Or more accurately, to hit on her.

When Griffin wasn't trying to pick up the celebrity, he was

getting berated by Anna. Not for flirting with Sienna. Oh no, Anna didn't care about that. No, she was pissed at Griffin for giving her a boy. It would seem Anna was just as concerned about the prospect of two Griffins as we were. She was just a lot more vocal about it.

"No, it's not a good thing. I wanted a girl!"

Opening my eyes, I lifted my head to see a bikini-clad Anna storming over to a nearby patio table, Griffin just a couple of steps behind her. Kiera and I had been enjoying some quiet time by the pool, sunbathing, but quiet didn't last long around here. Especially with those two in the house. I mindlessly twisted Kiera's wedding ring in a circle around her finger while I watched Anna and Griffin repeat an argument that I'd heard at least six times already.

Griffin was frowning at Anna, annoyed at her lack of excitement about the sex of their baby. "Well, I'm cool with a boy. I think it's awesome. Instead of Myrtle, we can call him Myrt or Mort...Mortimus." Anna grimaced while I smirked. Mortimus. God, the guys and I were going to have to name this baby, I just knew it. But then Griffin got struck with an idea and tossed out, "Maximus!"

Maximus? Well, it was definitely a step up from Mortimus. I felt Kiera's eyes on me and glanced over at her. She looked delicious in her solid black tankini. All the areas it covered had my mind spinning, my imagination percolating. I just wanted to roll it up her stomach and kiss every inch of her. Kiera smiled at me and shrugged, amused but accepting Griffin's name choice. I smiled back at her, mimicking her gesture of *Yeah, okay, whatever*.

Anna snorted at Griffin. "Maximus...like the gladiator?"

Griffin gave her a suggestive smile. "Well, he will be a slayer." Then he acted out the "slaying." That led to Anna laughing and grabbing Griffin's shorts, pulling his body into hers. Then the foreplay started: kissing, groping, what little clothes they were wearing being tugged on.

Kiera stopped watching, turning her eyes back to me, while I studied them a little longer to see if they were going to stop, or if we should leave. When Anna pulled Griffin's hand out of the back of her bikini, I felt like it was okay to stay. Closing my eyes, I relaxed into my lounge chair.

The moment after I'd finally tuned out the sound of Anna and Griffin making out, a voice on the other side of me said, "Are those two really a couple? He's hit on me about a dozen times."

Recognizing Sienna's accented voice, I opened my eyes and looked up to see her frowning at Anna and Griffin. I could understand the confusion on her face because she wasn't exaggerating. Griffin hit on her every chance he got. "That depends on your definition of 'couple.'" I shifted to look at them. Griffin was still palming Anna's body, kissing her wherever he could, but he kept flicking glances Sienna's way too, like he wasn't sure if he should try again with Sienna or keep working on his sure thing. Jackass. "We're all still trying to figure them out."

"They're not as exclusive as the two of you then?" Sienna said.

"No, definitely not," I answered, kissing Kiera's wedding ring. Kiera wasn't just my "sure thing." She was my forever, and that was infinitely better.

Sienna sat on the chair beside me, flipping onto her stomach as she lay down. I noticed her bodyguards standing a few feet away, actively scanning the yard. I also noticed how closely they watched Griffin. That almost made me smile. *Wise choice, boys.*

Kiera fidgeted in her lounger, adjusting the bottom of her swimsuit. When I looked over at her, she was blatantly staring at Sienna, a slight frown on her lips. I had to believe she was comparing herself, or convincing herself that she didn't measure up, or something equally foolish. I kept my eyes trained on Kiera as I stroked her ring finger, reminding her that she had nothing to worry about when it came to Sienna. Or anyone. I was hers, and I loved her exactly the way she was.

When I was just about to tug on Kiera's hand to get her to look at me and not Sienna, Sienna spoke again. "I'll be heading back to London in the morning. Would the two of you like to have dinner with me tonight?"

I glanced back at Sienna and instantly returned my eyes to Kiera. Sienna had unhooked her top, and with her head resting on her arms, a lot of her body was exposed; I didn't want to strengthen Kiera's insecurity by looking too long.

I was a little surprised by Sienna's offer, but she'd been nice and astoundingly down-to-earth the few times we'd spoken, and we were working together now, so maybe the invitation wasn't all that odd. I honestly had no problem hanging out with her—she was just a person after all, same as anyone—but I had no desire to make Kiera uncomfortable. This might be more than she could handle, so it was up to her if we said yes or not. And truly, as long as Kiera was by my side, either answer was fine by me.

Kiera surprised me by saying, "Yeah, sure...sounds great."

Sienna let out a chipper sounding, "Fabulous," and Kiera's lips pursed a little, like she was second-guessing her answer. She also wouldn't stop staring at Sienna. Honestly, she was leering more than Griffin. Okay, not true. Now that Sienna was almost naked, Griffin's attention was laser-focused on her. I was pretty sure the only thing stopping him from coming over was Anna holding his hand as she sat in a chair beside him. Of course, Anna was watching Sienna too.

Rolling my eyes, I tugged on Kiera's hand. Her gaze finally shifted to my face, and her cheeks colored a little. I smiled at her embarrassed reaction, then tilted my head toward the pool. "Swim with me?" I asked.

Her eyes drifted down my body, and the flush to her cheeks brightened. *Ah, yes, she has a thing for me wet.* Well, that was something I definitely wanted to encourage. Dropping her hand for a second, I stood up, then extended my palm to her. She grinned as she took it, and I pulled her to her feet. She laughed a little as she steadied herself, her hand drifting to my bare chest.

I kissed her sun-warmed head, then turned around and started leading her to the other end of the pool, the deep end. I felt eyes on me the entire way. One set I knew was Sienna's. Another set was Anna's. I met Anna's gaze. She swept her eyes over me, wriggled her eyebrows, and mouthed, *Hot*. Laughing, I shook my head at her.

Once Kiera and I were at the deep end, I turned to face her, wrapping my arms around her. A soft smile lifted her lips as she laced her arms around my neck. I leaned down to kiss her, then shifted my mouth to her ear. "Hold your breath," I murmured.

She instantly said, "No," and attempted to push me away, but it was too late. I already had a tight grip on her, and we were already falling into the pool. She screamed as we descended.

Since she hadn't been ready for it, I let her go the instant we broke through the water. She came up immediately, sputtering and slapping the surface, looking for me. I swam away from her, just my eyes above the waterline as I watched her. After tipping her head up, slicking back her hair, Kiera straightened and gave me *I'm going to kill you* eyes. I grinned as I popped my head all the way up. I had a thing for her wet too, and she looked...incredible right now.

"Don't be mad," I said, a playful smile on my face.

She gave me a lopsided grin. "I'm not mad. Come closer."

I pursed my lips at that, but I ventured closer...because how could I resist her asking me to be near her? She just gave me a sweet smile as she treaded water, waiting for me. But then, the second I was close enough, she swept her arm out, sending a small tidal wave of water into my face. Game on.

Hours later, the playful cavorting in the pool shifted into playful cavorting in our bedroom. I was just thinking we should skip dinner altogether and stay in bed all night when Kiera slipped away from me and disappeared into the bathroom to take a shower. I couldn't stop smiling as I listened to the water running. Things might be changing, but right at this moment, everything was perfect.

When Kiera came back into the room, I was still just lying in bed, smiling at nothing. She giggled when she saw that I hadn't moved. "Are you going to get ready to go?"

I pulled back the sheet, inviting her into bed with me. "I am ready to go," I told her, my smile suggestive.

Her eyes swept over me before quickly darting away. "I'm pretty sure you'll need to be wearing more than that, Kellan."

Standing, I came up behind her and wrapped my arms around her towel-covered waist. "Not for what I had in mind," I whispered in her ear.

A shudder went through her body, but she quickly snapped out of it. "You should get ready...and I need to figure out what I'm going to wear." She suddenly looked forlorn.

I snuck my hand under the towel, placing it on her bare stomach. "I know what you can wear."

The forlorn look disappeared as she twisted around and frowned at me. Mission accomplished. "Go," she said, pointing a stubborn finger toward the bathroom.

"Yes, ma'am," I grinned.

By the time I'd showered, dressed, and scuffed up and styled my hair, Kiera was still debating what to wear. Looking more than a little unhappy with her options, she finally settled on a long, flowy dress that I quite liked; it just...fit her right. With the loose waves she'd put in her hair, and the minimal makeup that emphasized everything I loved about her, she looked amazing. I told her as much, and for once, she didn't argue with me. Just smiled and said, "Thank you." I was glad she let me compliment her. She was beautiful, and she should know she was beautiful. All the way to her core.

We walked out into the living area when we were ready to go. Griffin was annoyed that he couldn't come, so he ignored us. Evan wrapped an arm around Kiera and told her she was a doll. That seemed to remind Kiera about something, and she scampered back to the bedroom. While she was gone, I spotted something that reminded *me* of something. There was a vase of pink roses resting on a small table by the slider. There were fresh flowers all over this house, and they were usually roses. Seeing them always brought to mind the display I'd made when I'd given Kiera her ring.

Walking over to the vase, I plucked one of the petals. I knew Kiera was nervous about tonight, even though she was trying to act like she was fine. Rubbing the silky petal, I wondered if seeing this would make her think of our romantic moment, make her momentarily forget her nerves. Or it might remind her about Griffin walking in on us, and that wasn't necessarily a bad thing. Nothing in the world could possibly be as embarrassing as that moment for her. In comparison, everything else was a piece of cake. So maybe Griffin had done us a favor after all. Not that I was going to thank him for it.

Chuckling to myself, I walked over to Matt. "Hey...you have a Sharpie in your room?"

Matt's brows bunched as he looked up at me, then he reached into his pocket and handed me one. I smirked as I took it. "You just walk around with a Sharpie in your pocket?"

He shrugged. "What? It's my favorite pen. Or marker. Whatever. They're handy. I want it back," he finished, pointing at me.

Shaking my head at him, I glanced up to see Kiera walking over to Evan with something in her hand. She gave him whatever she was holding, and they started talking. Since she was distracted, I returned my attention to the petal in my fingers. I was going to write *I love you* on it, but then decided on something cute instead. Working quickly but carefully, I drew an eye, a heart, and an animal that I hoped she realized was a female sheep. It wasn't the best drawing, but the two of us were pretty good at Pictionary, so I had high hopes that she'd get it.

Stuffing the petal into my pocket, I handed Matt his precious Sharpie right as Kiera approached us. Not wanting her to think too much about that exchange, I grabbed her hand and began pulling her away. She gave Matt an *I miss you* message from Rachel before leaving with me, and I saw a light flick on in his eyes as he nodded and waved goodbye. From the secretive smile on his face, I had a pretty good idea where Matt's night was heading. That was all but confirmed when I saw him stand up and pull his phone out of his pocket. Ah, my protégé. I was so proud of him.

Kiera's nerves spiked in the car on the way to the restaurant; I could tell by the way she was ceaselessly bouncing her feet. I handed her the petal in my pocket, and she instantly relaxed when she looked at it. She peered up at me with eyes that radiated love, and my heart squeezed as I wrapped an arm around her, drawing her into my side. That look was all I needed. Today, tomorrow, or sixty years from now, that look would always be it for me. She would always be it for me.

Chapter 9
DINNER / DESSERT

When we got to the restaurant, Sienna's bodyguard let us out of the vehicle. His fierce eyes scanned the crowd hovering nearby, watching for any sign of danger. It was weird to be around that kind of intensity outside of a bar. It made me miss Sam again. *I should call Pete's, have Jenny buy him a shot for me.* I could easily picture the half amused, half annoyed look that would be on his face if Jenny gave him whiskey from me.

Smiling at the thought, I held Kiera's hand as we followed Sienna toward the restaurant. There was a man in a suit by the door, holding it open as he greeted her. Sienna thanked him, but she paused a ways from the door and waited for Kiera and me to join her. I gently stroked Kiera's thumb with mine as I smiled at her. She looked a little nervous as her eyes darted from the fancy restaurant to Sienna's body-revealing outfit to the crowd of looky-loos watching us enter the building. I had to admit, that last one was a little strange to me, especially when I noticed that a lot of the people in the crowd had cameras out and were taking pictures of Sienna standing tall and proud as she waited for us.

Seeing that level of fame was strange, and I couldn't help but wonder if that kind of attention would happen to Kiera and me one day, if random people would be taking *our* picture everywhere we went. It was a mildly disturbing thought. Sure, I was used to a small amount of fame and recognition, but nothing on Sienna's scale. I had to wonder how Kiera would feel about it if it happened to us. She wasn't big on being in the spotlight, so being ambushed by cameras all the time would be absolute hell for her. Maybe I could shield her from it...somehow. But then again...the odds of us being *that* interesting to people were really, really low. Even after doing a song with Sienna, we'd most likely still be a relatively unknown group of guys, easily dismissed and overlooked. And I was fine with that.

When we reached Sienna, she looped her arm around my elbow, attaching herself to my side. The photographers snapping pictures of her went crazy, shouting her name and asking her to turn their way. She ignored them. Smiling up at me, she said, "Ready? I'm starving." I gave her a polite smile as I debated how to get her to release me. Pulling away or asking her to take a step back seemed really rude. Before I could think of anything, Sienna leaned around me, and said to Kiera, "You're going to love this place. The food is to die for."

I looked over at Kiera. She was smiling softly at Sienna, and she didn't seem overly upset that the superstar was glued to my side. Annoyed, sure, but it was a resigned sort of annoyed, like she also understood that I couldn't just shake her off. Figuring politeness was the best way to get through this, I let Sienna hold my elbow as we continued to the doors. Kiera glanced behind us and frowned as she spotted the photographers still snapping pictures. Her cheeks flushed with color, and I knew she wasn't enjoying the aftereffect of being in Sienna's spotlight. Not wanting her to worry about it, I squeezed her hand in two tight pulses. Her uncertain eyes flashed up to mine, and I gave her a crooked grin and a quick wink. Even more color flooded her cheeks, and she bit her lip and lightly shook her head, a soft laugh escaping her. I grinned at her response and pulled her into my side.

Sienna disengaged herself from my elbow to step through the door, patting the doorman's shoulder in the process. Releasing

Kiera's hand, I rested my palm on the small of her back as we followed. The inside of the place was just as nice as I'd expected it to be: prim, proper, plush, and a bit pretentious. It made me feel like I was interrupting something just by being here. This really wasn't my scene. It wasn't Kiera's either by the look on her face. I had a feeling, if I asked her if she wanted to go to The Rusted Pipe instead, she'd leap at the chance to leave. Sienna was certainly comfortable, though, a breezy expression on her face as she elegantly sat down at a linen-covered table.

Having dinner with Sienna was surprisingly effortless, and even Kiera seemed at ease around her after a while. Sienna was a good conversationalist and shockingly open and down-to-earth. She talked about the annoyance of maintaining a lean, fit image for the public, something that maybe wasn't required of her, but was definitely encouraged by all those photographers following her around. She talked about the pressure her parents had placed on her growing up in the business and how it had felt to be a constant disappointment to them. That was something I could relate to since everything I'd ever done had let my parents down in one way or another. Sienna even talked about her leaked sex tape, about how it had felt to have her ex betray her like that. She told me that this business required a thick skin, and I didn't doubt it. Then she told me, "No regrets. It's the only way you'll survive in this town."

There was something about the way she said it that made that strange sense of caution resurface. This was a woman who would fight tooth and nail to keep what she had—no matter who got in the way. That kind of ambition was both admirable...and terrifying. I only gave her a warm smile in response, though, because I had no intention of getting in her way. And really, once she left tomorrow, we'd probably never see her again.

Even still, by the time we got back to the house, Sienna felt more like a colleague than an unapproachable celebrity, and I could see us all hanging out again sometime. Maybe.

Sienna walked up the stairs with us, her bodyguard trailing a few steps behind. "Goodnight, loves," she said at our floor. She smiled at both of us for a moment, then she leaned up and lightly kissed my cheek.

I had no idea if that was a custom thing or a flirting thing. I also had no idea if saying something to her was rude or not. I tried to school my features, but I could feel myself fighting a frown. Kiera's hands on my arm tightened a little as she said, "Have a good flight tomorrow, Sienna."

Sienna tossed an untroubled grin Kiera's way. "Thank you. It was lovely to meet both of you." Her eyes shifted to me, and there was a glint in them that was both familiar and completely foreign, like she was hitting on me yet being completely professional at the exact same time. Not being able to completely decipher her intentions was a little disorienting, to be honest. I didn't like it.

Sienna continued upstairs, and Kiera let out a sigh as she pulled me toward our living room here at the house. "Did you have fun?" I asked her, a bit of trepidation in my voice.

Kiera heard the uncertainty and looked up at me with a small frown on her face. She glanced back at where Sienna had left us, then she sighed again and forced a smile to her face. "Yes...that place was a little ridiculous, but yes, I had a good time."

I laughed at her assessment of the restaurant, relieved that she wasn't too upset over the cheek kiss. "I agree. I mean, don't get me wrong, the food was good and all, but it was a little stuffy for me. And damn if I'm not still hungry." I could have eaten about three more plates of what they'd served us...but not at their prices.

Kiera giggled, her hand going to her stomach. "Me too." She stopped walking and turned to face me. "I'll go make us some sandwiches. Back in a minute." She softly pressed her lips to mine in a brief kiss. Pulling back a little, she studied my face, then she returned her mouth to me and kissed me with a vengeance. She even grabbed my neck and held me to her—like I wanted to be anywhere else but attached to her. Her tongue brushed mine and a groan escaped me. I suddenly wasn't hungry...for food.

When she finally pulled away from me, we were both

breathing heavier, and my hands were on her waist, my fingers digging into the fabric of her dress as I restrained myself from ripping it off her. Or ripping it to shreds. Kiera's eyes were glazed as she looked me over, and I had to fight the desire to grab *her* neck this time and pull her back to me. "Be right back," she whispered. Then she bit her lip and minutely moved toward me before turning on her heel and dashing away.

Well, damn.

My body was surging with white-hot, desperate energy as I watched her leave. Then someone in the room cleared their throat. Shaking the desire off my face, urging my body to calm down, I looked over to the couch where Matt, Evan, Anna, and Griffin were sitting, watching a movie. Or at least, they *had* been watching a movie—now they were all watching me.

Evan smirked at me. "Good dinner?" he said.

I grinned at him in answer. "Apparently." I pointed at the TV. "You guys might want to turn that up."

Anna, Matt, and Evan chuckled at that. Griffin shot up off the couch and started walking toward me. I instantly headed for my bedroom, but he caught up to me. Slinging an arm over my shoulders, he secretively glanced back at the couch; only Anna was still watching. "Sooooo," he said, drawing out the word for a couple of seconds.

"So what?" I asked, shrugging off his arm.

He glanced at the couch again, then lowered his voice. "Did you see her boobs?"

I narrowed my eyes at him. He meant Sienna, right? Either way, why the hell would he ask me that? "We went out to dinner," I stated, confusion and sarcasm in my voice.

Griffin's brows bunched like he didn't understand my tone. Or my answer. "Yeah, I know. So did you see her boobs or not?"

Tilting my head, I studied his face. Seriously? What kind of dinner did he think we went to? Because I couldn't think of any other way to answer, I again stated the obvious. "We went out to dinner."

He let out an annoyed huff as he tucked his hair behind his ears. "I know that. So did you?"

I debated leaving him standing there, looking at me with confusion on his face, like *I* was the idiot, but I was too floored by his question to let it go. "We. Went. To. Dinner."

His light blue eyes narrowed in annoyance. "Why do you keep answering the same way? It's a yes or no question, dude."

I tossed up my hands. "No."

Griffin crossed his arms over his chest, eyeing me from head to foot. Then he rolled his eyes. "You *so* did. God, I hate you." He immediately gave me a devilish grin. "I want details later."

With that, he turned around and walked back to the couch. I could only gape at him, mystified by the murkiness of his mind. Anna was laughing when I glanced her way, like she knew what he'd asked me. I shook my head at her, then pointed at him and made a circle motion by my ear. *He's crazy.* She snorted at me, nodding as she placed a hand on her stomach. I smiled at her reaction. At least Griffin amused her.

After taking off my shoes and socks, I climbed onto the bed and relaxed against the headboard, waiting for Kiera to rejoin me. I hummed to myself while I rested, swishing my feet back and forth and idly spinning the wedding ring on my finger. Just when I was about to go downstairs and see what was taking her so long, Kiera toed the door open and stepped inside; a bright smile was on her face as she held a tray practically overflowing with food.

"You really were still hungry," I laughed.

Closing the door with her heel, she shrugged. "Everything looked good."

Kiera walked over to me, paused to slip off her shoes, then set the monstrous tray on the bed. She instantly got a thoughtful look on her face and darted back over to the door, locking it. Apparently, she wanted privacy tonight, and she didn't trust that Griffin had learned his lesson. Smart. Her bold move would have made me laugh, but I was too distracted by the spread she'd assembled. As she returned to me, I stared in disbelief at the numerous little sandwiches nestled between clusters of grapes, strawberries, crackers, cheeses, and some sort of creamy dip. At the back of the tray was a bottle of wine and two empty glasses. Staring at the display made me wish we'd stayed in and done this all night. I couldn't stop the image of licking that dip off her skin...running a strawberry between her breasts. My body hardened as I indulged in the fantasy.

Head still lowered, I peered up at her. "I don't think I'm hungry anymore."

Kiera softly exhaled as she took in my provocative expression. She chewed on her bottom lip as she scanned every inch of me. I could almost feel where she was looking, like her gaze was a physical caress against my skin; it made me ache. Leaning forward, I grabbed her hand and yanked her toward me. She laughed as her body collided with mine. Sitting up, I twisted my body and pulled her onto the bed. Her laughter increased as I leaned over her, circling my fingers around her wrists, pinning her under me.

She looked over at the forgotten tray beside us. "Kellan...the food."

I kissed her neck, reveling in the heat of her skin. "What food?" I playfully asked.

She made a soft, erotic sound as my lips worked down her neck. "That food..." She pointed a trapped finger at the tray, but her tone told me she really didn't care about the food anymore.

Smiling, I shifted one of my legs between hers. She sucked in a breath as my thigh pressed against her. "I don't think it's going anywhere," I whispered, working my way across her collarbone.

"I had no idea snacks were such a turn on for you," she murmured, her voice sounding light, airy...distracted.

A laugh escaped me, and I paused in kissing the hollow of her throat to look at her. Kiera's cheeks flushed a beautiful shade of peach when our eyes met. She gave me a small, embarrassed smile, and shaking my head, I kissed her nose. "It's not the snacks that turn me on, it's the beautiful woman who brought them to me."

Kiera sighed and lifted her head to kiss me. I indulged her in a long, luxurious melding of our mouths and bodies. I released her wrists, and her hands instantly smoothed up my arms and into my hair. My fingers ran down her side, over the ridges of her ribs, down to the curve of her hip. Our breath picked up as I pulled her leg over mine, and somewhere in the back of my mind, I registered that the movie in the living room was blaringly loud now. Perfect.

My hand slipped under Kiera's billowy dress, and my palm slowly slid up her thigh. Kiera hurriedly unfastened my dress shirt, ripping it open when she got to the last button. Then she started exploring my torso, outlining every muscle with the tips of her fingers. Mine tightened around her underwear as I watched her face. There was so much heat in the emerald of her eyes that it made me feel like I'd been dunked in fire. Euphoric, heavenly, lustful fire.

She tugged on my shirt, pulling it off my shoulders. I felt frantic and needy as I helped her remove it, like I was going to lose it if I didn't have her soon. The fact that I could still feel that way with her was gloriously intoxicating. Kiera pushed against my shoulder, urging me onto my back, away from the forgotten food. I let her adjust me where she wanted me, scooting back so that I was still sideways on the bed but more in the middle of the mattress. Kiera's lips traveled down my chest, and my eyes fluttered closed as I absorbed the sensation of her soft mouth on my skin. Kiera moved down farther, and I clenched my abs so I could feel her tongue flick between the grooves of the muscles. A pulsing ache crashed through me with every touch, and I honestly didn't know how much more I could take.

Kiera's fingers shifted to my jeans. Once she unbuttoned them, I helped her slide them off me. Then my underwear. Then her dress, her underwear. Once we were both bare, I decided to fulfill my earlier fantasy. Seemed like a wasted opportunity if I didn't. Reaching over, I stuck my finger in the dip. Kiera watched me with confused but lascivious eyes. When I dropped my finger to her chest, drawing a straight line right over her breast, she closed her eyes and let out a groan of understanding and anticipation. I followed the path of the dip with my tongue, luxuriating on her nipple for far longer than necessary. I couldn't decide what tasted better—her skin or the strawberry flavored dip. Both. Definitely both. The blended flavor was now my new favorite.

My body throbbed with need, every pulse telling me to stop it and drive into her already, but Kiera's reaction was too exquisite for me to stop now. She let out loud, breathy exhales as she squirmed beneath me. One of her hands ran down my back, her nails slightly digging into my skin. Her other hand ran up my neck to my hair, her fingers threading through the strands before aggressively fisting them. Practicing as much restraint as humanly possible, I continued drawing patterns on her, then slowly licking them off. Kiera murmured my name and begged me to take her. That was almost my undoing...but I hadn't even gotten to the fruit yet. I was just about to move on to the berries when she suddenly pushed against me, forcing me onto my back again. Breath fast, eyes wild, she straddled me, then instantly pushed herself onto me, sinking me inside her...taking me. *God, yes.*

A groan escaped me as we connected, and my hands drifted to her hips, holding her to me, pulling her closer, deeper. Kiera let out a breathy moan, and as we started moving together, all coherent thought left me. All that existed was the feel of her soft skin, the sound of her fast breath, her sensual noises, and the incessant, building pressure that I both wanted to maintain and wanted to relieve. The world fell away as we held each other, moved against each other, absorbed each other. The need for more pushed us harder, faster, then Kiera grabbed my hand, squeezing tight as she let out a noise that pushed me right over the edge. I clenched my fingers laced in hers, feeling her wedding ring dig into my skin as everything in my body tightened. We rode out the ecstasy together, holding on to the connection for as long as we could, until finally Kiera's body went limp against mine, spent and satiated.

I put a hand on her low back, stroking the ridge there as I

worked on breathing normally again. Kiera kissed my neck, then let out a girlish giggle. Sliding off me, she rolled toward the food. I looked over at her with a raised eyebrow as she nonchalantly started making a tiny sandwich out of cheese and crackers. "Done with me, so she eats." She glanced back at me with a smirk on her face. "No snuggles?" I asked, crooked smile on my face.

Kiera grinned and rolled her eyes. Then she pressed her back against my side, snuggling into me while simultaneously eating her cracker-wich. I laughed as I slung my arm around her body, pulling her into me. "I'll take it," I murmured. "Beats snuggling with Griffin any day."

Kiera laughed, then straightened and twisted to look at me. "Wait. When—and *why*—were you snuggling with Griffin?"

Chuckling, I kissed her shoulder. "It's best not to ask." She pursed her lips at me, and I laughed again. "Don't worry...we were wearing clothes."

Kiera shook her head at me, then shivered. It was a little chilly now that there wasn't any friction keeping us warm. Looking around, I spotted a throw blanket that was slowly sliding off the bed. I grabbed it before it could escape and draped it over our bare bodies. Once we were warm, I pointed at the tray of food. "Pass me a sandwich?"

Kiera gave me an adorable, teasing grin. "Done with me, so he eats."

I instantly shook my head. "Nope. I am in no way done with you. Screw food, let's do that again." My lips immediately attached to her neck, but she pushed me away, laughing. She handed me a sandwich with an amused look of defeat on her face. *Don't bluff with sex, Kiera. I will* always *call you on that.*

We made it through damn near half the food on the tray, and most of the bottle of wine, and fell asleep exactly where we were, lying on top of the covers, sideways on the mattress, wrapped in each other's arms. It was the perfect end to an odd but amazing long weekend.

. . .

The next day, Anna went back to Seattle, Sienna went back to London, and the guys and I went back to work. We still had to finish recording the songs for our album, but we started working on Sienna's song too. The melody was already written, so it didn't take us long to learn it. Although both Matt and Evan had several little changes that they wanted to make so that it sounded more like one of ours. Thankfully, the label approved everything they wanted to tweak. I couldn't imagine Matt and Evan performing a song they didn't like. I knew they would do it, since they were professionals, but I also knew they'd be miserable doing it, and it might come across that way to people listening. Griffin I wasn't too worried about; he still moped about not being lead guitar. Sometimes there just wasn't a good way to satisfy him.

When I wasn't working on the album with the guys, I showed Kiera some of the places in Los Angeles that were important to the formation of the band. Not Griffin's beloved strip club, of course, but other interesting locales: where we did our first show, where I'd purchased the Chevelle, where Evan and I had lived...and the coffee shop where I used to work. I was sure she'd get a kick out of that last one.

Kiera looked surprised and amused when I stopped us in front of the shop and showcased the door for her. "And this is Buzzed, where I used to work." It was a small, locally owned coffeehouse with a handful of locations around the city. It was one of those trendy places that only the locals knew about, making it relatively tourist-free. That was a very important fact to some of the customers, but honestly, it didn't matter in the slightest to me. I just liked the name.

A smirk was on Kiera's lips as she peered through the windows. "I just can't get over the fact that you used to work in a coffee shop."

I frowned as I looked down at her. "What? I love coffee."

Kiera laughed as she turned to face me. "Yeah, I know," she said, her gaze adoring as her cheeks slightly flushed. Biting her lip, she shook her head. "Maybe it's just the idea of you having a regular job that's hard to picture." Her brows bunched as she tried to visualize me behind a counter, pouring drinks...the nonalcoholic kind.

I chuckled at the look on her face. "Well, I did have to eat, and until the band started taking off, the only other thing I could have done for money would have gotten me arrested, so regular job it was."

She instantly pursed her lips and the adoration in her eyes shifted into annoyance. "Really?" Her voice was thick with irritation and disbelief that I'd gone there. I knew I shouldn't have, but the opening she'd left me was too large to resist. As was that sarcastic, rhetorical question.

"Yes," I answered her with a bright grin. "You'll be happy to know I never once charged for my services. I was very philanthropic with my time." I ended with a playful wink. *Please don't smack me for saying that. I'm just kidding. Sort of.*

Thankfully, Kiera just stared at me for a second, then she slowly shook her head. "Sometimes you're so sweet. Other times you're so...Griffin."

"Ouch," I said, laughing. She had a point, though, as much as I hated to admit it. "Well, while I will *always* be a giver, the only person I want to give anything to now, is you." I gave her a soft smile, then leaned in and said, "That makes me a step up from Griffin, right?"

She tilted her head as she thought about it, and I frowned. Was it seriously something she had to consider? Kiera laughed as she studied the annoyance on my face. "Yes...ninety-nine percent of the time, you are much better than Griffin."

I smiled. Then frowned. "Wait...one percent of the time he's better than me? When? Name *one* time."

She laughed so hard that she couldn't answer me. Rolling my eyes, I opened the door. One percent of the time, my ass.

Kiera was still laughing as we stepped inside the coffee shop. I frowned at her, and she poked me in the ribs until I smiled.

Shaking my head, I wrapped an arm around her waist, pulling her into my side.

"Well, there's a face I will never forget...Kellan Kyle. It's been an age and a half."

I looked up at the counter to see the owner of the store, and my old boss, Stella. She was just as I remembered her—long, silver hair pulled into a loose bun, a warm but teasing smile, and a mischievous twinkle to her brown eyes, like she was in on everybody's inside jokes. "Hey, Stella. It *has* been a long time. How have you been?"

Smiling wider, she finished wiping off her hands on a rag, then set it down on the counter. "Good, can't complain. You?" Leaning in, she asked, "You finally take up modeling, like I said? You know you have the face for it."

Kiera looked like she was agreeing with Stella's assessment as she scanned me up and down. Rolling my eyes, I shook my head at Stella. "No. Standing there making weird faces at a camera sounds about as appealing as sitting at a desk all day."

Stella laughed at my argument. "But what about the other models, Kellan? I figured that part of it would be right up your alley."

Kiera's smile instantly shifted to pursed lips and bunched eyebrows. Clearing my throat, I indicated her to Stella. "Not anymore. Stella, meet my wife, Kiera. Kiera, my old boss, Stella."

Stella's eyes widened as she extended a hand to Kiera. "Wife? Someone got him to settle down? Well done, my dear, you've accomplished something I thought was truly impossible."

Kiera bit her lip as she flicked a glance up at me; her face was an odd mixture of joy and discomfort, but she politely took Stella's hand. While they briefly shook, I frowned at Stella. Maybe bringing Kiera to all the places I use to frequent when I was...a lot freer with myself...wasn't the best idea. "Thanks, Stella. Way to make me look good in front of my wife."

She laughed, then swished a hand at me. "You know I'm joking. Sort of." She pointed a finger at me while raising an eyebrow at Kiera. "This one was such a hopeless flirt when he worked here. He'd bat an eye at one of the girls and get them to make all his drinks for him."

Kiera laughed, looking over at me like she could easily picture me doing that. "Did he now?" she murmured.

Crossing my arms, I narrowed my eyes at my old boss. "No, that's not true. I did my fair share."

Stella grinned at me. "Of flirting? Yes, yes you did." While I pursed my lips at her, she turned back to Kiera. "His tips were ridiculous, though, which is why none of the girls complained too much about making his drinks for him."

My mouth dropped open as disbelief washed through me. "I did my fair share," I repeated.

Stella raised a pointed eyebrow at me. "You sat on the counter and played your guitar."

True. I had spent a lot of time here doing just that. Grinning, I lifted a shoulder in a shrug. "People like ambiance. I was setting the mood." And no one had ever complained about it, not even my coworkers. That was probably because I got even more tips when I was playing, and I shared them with everyone. Maybe I'd been an unrepentant flirt, but I was also a generous flirt. That had to count for something.

Kiera laughed as she wrapped her hands around my elbow. While I smiled down at my wife, Stella let out an exaggerated sigh. "I honestly don't know why I hired you." I looked back at her with an arched eyebrow, and she smirked as her eyes skimmed over my face. "Damn it...yes, I do. I don't suppose you need your old job back?" she asked, her expression hopeful.

I laughed at the eagerness on her face. "No...my other one is going pretty well."

Kiera bounced on her toes. Pride on her face, she told Stella, "He's making an album. He just recorded a song with Sienna Sexton."

"Sienna Sexton? Seriously?" Stella asked, pride on her face too.

I shrugged, feeling a little uncomfortable with the silent praise in their expressions. "Yeah..."

Stella's eyes misted, making me even more uncomfortable. "Well, that is...really impressive, Kellan. Congratulations."

My gaze drifted to the floor. "Thank you," I said, peeking up at her. After a long moment of both Stella and Kiera studying me with admiration on their faces, I pursed my lips and said to Stella, "Can we be done talking about me now, and maybe get some of your should-be-world-famous coffee?"

Stella laughed, then nodded. "Of course." She lifted a gray eyebrow at me. "Would you like to make them?"

Grinning at her, I shook my head. "No."

She laughed again. "Can't say I'm surprised by that."

When our coffees were ready, Kiera and I sat down at a quiet booth to drink them. Stella joined us for a bit, eager to tell stories about me. Kiera was on the edge of her seat, listening to tales of a younger me, even the tales of a flirtatious younger me, although she frowned at me a lot during those stories. Playful frowns, but still.

As we were leaving, Kiera looped her arm through mine. She looked up at me with an amused smile. "I can't believe you charmed your coworkers into making your drinks for you. You *are* a hopeless flirt."

I frowned at how Stella had portrayed me. "She's exaggerating...I did my fair share. Ask Evan. He used to come in all the time. We'd work on our songs between customers."

Kiera cocked an eyebrow at me in a look that spoke volumes. I chewed on my lip as I considered the fact that maybe I *had* taken advantage of the situation. A little bit. "Okay...maybe I took a *few* liberties. But I was much more helpful than she made me sound." I smiled as I stared straight ahead. "You know me, I always aim to please."

Kiera sighed, then laughed and squeezed me tighter. "Yes, I am well aware of that, Mr. Kyle."

Grinning down at her, I kissed her head. "Good...Mrs. Kyle."

Then I unlinked our arms so I could wrap mine around her waist and squeeze her tight. *Mrs. Kyle*. I didn't think I'd ever get used to the thrill it gave me to call her that. Hopefully, I'd get to call her that for the rest of my life.

When we got back to the house, Kiera had a giddy smile on her face as she darted upstairs to grab her new laptop so she could write for a little bit. Jenny had told me once that writing was what Kiera was meant to do, and I believed her. I hadn't read anything of hers yet, but the look on her face when she was writing, the content sigh she let out when she was done...it was the way I felt after a good show. Or even a bad one. It was a calling being fulfilled, and that was a beautiful thing to see.

I moved toward the stairs to join Kiera, but a voice calling my name stopped me. When I turned, I expected to see one of the various houseguests, but it was Lana coming my way. I smiled at her as she stepped up to me.

"Good, I didn't miss you," she said, a friendly glow of warmth brightening her expression.

"Are you leaving?" I asked.

She nodded. "I'm heading out to check on a couple of bands that are making a buzz. I doubt I'll find another *you* so soon, but I'm always hopeful." Her smile grew. "Making dreams come true is the best part of my job." Her expression softened as she paused. "Telling hopeful artists no is the worst part."

I nodded in understanding. I had to imagine that would be difficult. Unless the artist in question was an a-hole like Paul. Then it would be cathartic. "Well, good luck. And thank you again for everything."

She gave me a warm smile. "It was an honor to be the one to find you." Cocking a dark eyebrow at me, she said, "Before I go, Sienna asked me to give you her number, just in case the two of you ever need to talk about your collaboration."

Surprise washed through me. "Oh, um...sure." Since I didn't feel like programming the phone, a feat I'd reluctantly mastered on the bus, I handed my cell to Lana. "Here. Go ahead and put it in."

She smirked at me, then messed around on the phone for about two seconds before handing it back. "Good luck on the album, Kellan. I know it's going to be amazing." She patted my arm in friendship, then made to step around me. Stopping, she looked up at me. There was reluctance on her face, and it worried me to see it. "I probably shouldn't say this, but you should be careful of..." She let that thought trail off, then shook her head and said, "Just be careful. This business can be tough on beginners. Success is all some people care about, and they'll do anything to get it. *Anything*. Just keep your eyes open, okay?"

There was sympathy and concern in the depths of her brown eyes as she studied me; she looked like she wanted to say more, and she also looked like she'd said too much. I had no idea how to respond, no clue what to feel except...worried. I nodded at her while I tried to decipher what she was really saying. I wanted to ask her to explain what she meant, wanted to know if she had something—or *someone*—specific in mind, but from the antsy look on her face, I had a feeling she wouldn't, *couldn't,* clarify.

She patted my arm again, then continued on her way, and as I watched her leave, I had the weirdest feeling that I'd just lost my only ally here.

Chapter 10

APPEARANCES

By the end of July, the guys and I were finished with our part of the album, including the song with Sienna. There was just one more thing we had to do...and I wasn't all that thrilled about it. The label wanted the four of us to be on the album cover, and we had a professional photoshoot lined up for later today. Looked like I was making weird faces for a camera after all. Stella would be thrilled to know that.

Hailey laughed into the phone as she listened to me complaining about it yet again. When I was done, I could practically see her shaking her head at me. "You're being ridiculous, Kellan. The band should absolutely be on the cover."

"You're just saying that because you want to use it to get your friends all riled up," I said with a smile.

Hailey let out a soft giggle, confirming my suspicions. "Well, that *is* one of the perks of being related to you. You should hear some of the things they say about you." She paused a moment, then quickly added, "On second thought, no, no you shouldn't."

"I can only imagine," I laughed.

Hailey shared my mirth for a moment, then sighed. "I can't believe you're not even on the radio yet, but you've already recorded a duet with one of the biggest pop stars in the industry. I'm so proud of you, Kellan."

That now-familiar sensation of happiness and discomfort washed through me at hearing her praise. Shaking my head in disbelief, I rested my elbows on the balcony railing that over-looked the pool. "Thanks...sometimes I can hardly believe it myself. It might not amount to anything, but it *is* a good oppor-tunity for the band." Lana's vague warning flashed through my brain, and I frowned as I murmured, "The guys are excited."

Hailey must have heard the trepidation in my voice. "Are you?" she asked. "This could turn you into a massive star practi-cally overnight. Are you okay with that? Is Kiera?"

Straightening, I looked back through the slider. I could see Kiera sitting on the couch, typing on her laptop. Happy, content, and completely out of the spotlight, where she wanted to be. Would she be okay if this song stripped away her anonymity? Forever? I didn't want that for her, but if it was inevitable, I hoped she'd be able to handle it. I hoped she'd still be happy.

"We're...prepared, I guess." Twisting back around, I shook my head. "But honestly, that probably won't happen. The song could flop, or it might do well for Sienna, but our name won't stick, and people will just associate the song with her. A lot of different things could happen. This isn't a guarantee for us."

"Oh, Kellan," Hailey said, her voice warm and amused.

"What? You know I'm right," I stated. "That's not the way the world works."

I could hear her smile when she spoke again. "Maybe for us mere mortals it doesn't work that way, but trust me on this one... you're going to stand out just as much as she does. Maybe more. People will notice. Everyone will notice."

Even though she couldn't see me, I smirked into the phone. "Everyone? I seriously doubt that."

"I know you do. Which is why it's going to be so much fun to tell you *I told you so*. You have no idea how excited I am." She barely finished saying it before she started laughing.

"Are all sisters brats? Or am I just blessed?"

"Blessed, for sure." She was still giggling.

"All right" I told her, feigned annoyance in my voice. "Well, it was good talking to you, but I've got to go stare at a camera lens now."

"Good luck. Love you."

"Love you too." The words were out of me before I even registered saying them, before I'd even fully registered Hailey's words to me. I was shocked at how easily they'd slipped from my tongue, and even more shocked that I didn't regret saying them. I *did* love Hailey. A deep, brotherly love that had slid into place almost instantly. It scared me a little to feel that way, but I did my best to push the fear down as far as I could. I didn't want my insecurities to get in the way of our relationship. And the reason I had the strength to do that was because of the warm, wonderful woman in the next room, typing out her bestseller.

Smiling at that thought, I tucked my phone into my pocket and left the balcony to go join her. Kiera glanced up as I closed the balcony door behind me. "How's Hailey?" she asked.

"She's good. Ridiculous, but good."

Her brows bunched as she tried to puzzle out why I'd said that. Chuckling, I pointed at her computer. "How's the writing going?"

The smile on her face turned enormous. "Good. Great. I don't know...I like it." She laughed and shrugged at the same time, and I smiled at her joy.

Sitting on the couch beside her, I thought over the words she was writing, the story she was putting down. *Our* story. The heartbreak, the pain...the love. I was eager to read it but really nervous too. And I already knew there were a lot of sections I wouldn't be able to read. Basically, everything between her and Denny. I just didn't think I could do it. Not all of it, at least. But...there were also things about *me* I wasn't sure I wanted to read. And there were things about me that I hadn't considered her writing about before...personal things. Things I wasn't ready to share with the world. I had no idea what she was including about me and what she was glossing over. And I also wasn't sure if I had a right to bring it up with her. It was her work, her art, asking her to change it seemed wrong. She had certainly never asked me not to write songs about her, and not all my songs about her were nice. But this was different. This wasn't about our history *together;* it was about my history...alone.

Kiera had gone back to her typing as I'd quietly watched her. I glanced around the room, but we were alone. Griffin and Matt were down by the pool, and I was pretty sure Evan was in his room. "Kiera," I started, my voice hesitant.

Not pausing from her typing, she brightly said, "Yeah?"

Struggling with confliction, I didn't say anything else. Kiera noticed the odd silence and stopped writing to look at me. Her brows furrowed as she studied my expression. "Are you okay?" she asked.

Still unsure if I had a right to say what I wanted to say, I cringed and pointed at her computer. "I was just...the story you're writing...there are a lot of things..." I sighed, feeling more frustrated with every word leaving my mouth. *Do I ask, or do I leave it?*

Kiera closed her laptop and twisted to face me. "What?" She chewed on her lip, looking nervous. "Did you change your mind about the book? Does it bother you?"

I shook my head as I looked her over. "No...not that you're writing it, no." She bunched her brows, confused, and I sighed. "It's just...there are things about me...that I don't talk about. That people...don't know." A knot formed in my throat, and I had to pause to swallow. "Things I don't *want* people to know..."

Her eyes widened as she understood what I was saying. "I know that, Kellan. I would never write about your secrets. I left all of that out. *All of it,*" she repeated, stressing the words.

A relieved sigh left me. She wasn't writing about the abuse. She wasn't writing about the lie my parents told the world, the truth they shoved down my throat. She wasn't writing about *that* part of my misery. Thank God. "Okay, thank you. I feel bad saying anything. I just...it's so..."

Her hand came up to cup my cheek. "I know. I still think you should talk about it with someone, but I would *never* force you to talk about it...in this way."

I nodded, feeling heaviness settle around me. I really wasn't sure if talking about it was something I'd ever be able to do, but it meant a lot to me that she wasn't including that in my "character's" backstory. True, she'd changed our names to protect us, but a lot of our friends already knew the book was based on real events—they knew it was about Denny, Kiera, and me. And I wasn't ready for them to see *all* of me yet.

Needing the tension in the air to change, I smirked at her. "Does this make my character boring now? Readers might want you with the Denny character."

She smirked right back at me. "Trust me, your character is anything but boring. And they will still love you...just as much as I do."

A small smile was stuck on my face as I shifted my gaze to the floor. It was a weird thought, that people might like me because of what she was writing. Maybe fame would find me through *her*...and then she'd only have herself to blame. Shaking my head in amusement, I peeked up at her. "We should probably get ready for that...*thing*." And saying that instantly made me frown. Stupid photoshoot.

Kiera laughed at my expression, then slid the laptop off her legs. "It's going to be fine, rock star. I promise."

My frown deepened as her amusement grew. "You don't know that," I told her.

Standing, she extended her hand to me. "True. But that's what you're always telling me, isn't it? And your advice is usually good, so I think you should take it."

With a smirk, I grabbed her hand and pushed myself up, then I yanked her into my body and wrapped my arms around her.

"*Now* you start listening to me," I said, dropping my lips to the curve of her neck.

She shuddered under my touch, her breath coming out in a rush. Smiling, I dragged my lips up her neck, occasionally flicking her skin with my tongue. "We should go, Kellan. We can't be late..."

"It will be fine. I promise," I murmured in her ear, echoing her words. I nibbled on her earlobe, and she let out the most fantastic moan. Then she pushed me away.

She gave me a disapproving look, and I gave her the most innocent smile I possessed; she rolled her eyes at seeing it. "Still think I give good advice?" I asked her, cocking an eyebrow.

Smirking, she shook her head. "I guess it depends on the situation."

I still wasn't excited about the photoshoot, and as we made our way to the studio in one of the label's convertibles, I tried my best to convince Kiera that having the band on the cover was completely unnecessary. Some of my favorite covers didn't include the band members. In fact, most of them didn't. Kiera, like Hailey, disagreed with me. Or maybe it was my choice of a replacement subject that she disagreed with.

"A duck? Really?" she asked, tucking a misbehaving strand of hair behind her ear.

The look on her face made me want to laugh. I supposed a duck was an odd choice, but it was the first thing that had popped into my head...and now I kind of loved it. "What? Ducks are sexy...right?" I gave her a mischievous grin. She rolled her eyes, and I finally laughed. "They've got those long, flat bills, plump bellies, wide, webbed feet. What could be hotter than that?"

I could feel her eyes on me as she analyzed my ridiculousness, then she let out a loud laugh. "Um, just about anything."

Turning my attention from the road, I smirked at her. "We'll just have to agree to disagree on this one."

There was an awaiting argument in her expression, but her phone rang before she could vocalize it. Digging it out of her purse, she glanced at the screen, then answered it. "Hey, Denny. How are you?"

She played with her necklace while I turned down the radio so she could hear him better. Then she said, "I'm great. Why do you sound weird?"

I flashed Kiera a concerned glance as I took a right turn. Had something happened? I tried to remember the last time I'd talked to Denny. We'd texted a few times, but our last in-depth conversation had been a while ago. Kiera shrugged at my unasked question, then furrowed her brows. "Of course," she told him. "Why? Did something happen? Is Anna okay? Is the baby?"

That immediately got my attention, and I felt my heart surge with dread. Kiera's face quickly shifted into relief, though, and she shook her head at me. I relaxed as I realized Anna and the baby were fine. Kiera expressed her relief to Denny, then asked him something about tabloids and gossip sites. Following just her side of the conversation wasn't very illuminating, but it seemed like Denny was concerned about Sienna, someone's boyfriend, and a...picture? Whatever it was, it was affecting Kiera—her jaw dropped, her cheeks paled, and she looked a little nauseated.

Then she told Denny, "It's not what it looks like. I was there, you just can't see me."

Now I was even more confused. Clearly, this had something to do with Kiera too. I just couldn't figure out how the pieces fit together.

Kiera looked a little stunned as she told Denny goodbye. We'd arrived at the studio while she'd been talking, and as I shut off the car, she stared at her phone with her mouth popped open in surprise. Her reaction made my stomach tingle with nerves. What the hell was going on?

"Kiera, are you okay?" I asked her, worry working its way up my throat.

She looked over at me, still seemingly dazed. "I'm fine," she quietly said.

I frowned at her stock answer; I'd used that one a lot myself, and more often than not, it meant, *No, I'm not fine, but I don't want to talk about it.* Unfortunately for Kiera, I wasn't going to let her dodge so easily. "Honestly, you're fine?"

My question snapped her out of her startled state, and she minutely pursed her lips in annoyance. I had a feeling she wanted me to take her at her word and drop this, but she couldn't; my question had effectively cornered her into telling me the truth. We had an honesty deal in place, and I was asking her to honor it. Finally, she told me, "I don't know what I am."

I nodded in understanding. "Okay, can you tell me what that was about? Maybe we can figure out what you feel together."

As I returned my sunglasses to the clip on the visor, Kiera bit her lip and held up a finger, asking for a minute. I held her hand and tried to wait as patiently as I could for her to be ready to tell me. Every second was a little more torturous, so I distracted myself by playing with her wedding ring.

Finally, Kiera twisted in her seat to face me. She studied my eyes, and there was a trace amount of sadness in her expression. "Talk to me," I whispered, feeling that familiar worry nibbling away at my stomach.

She shook her head like she was annoyed at herself, then gave me a reassuring smile. "Denny was just concerned about me because there's a photo of you and Sienna running rampant on the Internet. Everyone on the planet thinks you're her new 'unknown' boyfriend. Apparently, the photo is convincing. Denny didn't directly say so, but I think he thought you were stepping out on me." She started to laugh, but the sound quickly morphed into pain, and she swallowed numerous times, like her throat had closed up.

Seeing her distress tore at me, but the situation she'd just mapped out was so confusing it threw me; I had no idea what she was talking about, what people were gossiping about. "Photo?" Kiera's forlorn expression suddenly registered with me, and I was hit with a ball of anxiety. Shit. Did she believe the rumor? "You know I'm not, right? I'm not interested in her...at all. You know that, don't you?"

She nodded, and her hand reached up to cup my cheek. I saw love and reassurance in her eyes...but I also saw fear. "I know." Inhaling a deep breath, like she was cleansing her thoughts, she indicated the studio with a tilt of her head. "Should we go get this photoshoot over with?" A very forced smile graced her lips. "Maybe you can request a duck for the background?"

I knew she was pretending to be fine, knew this was bothering her more than she wanted to admit. I hated that it was. Sienna meant nothing to me. Kiera was my world—always had been, always would be. "Kiera," I started, as she got out of the car.

She cut me off with a raised hand. "I'm fine. Honestly. Can we just...not talk about this anymore? It doesn't matter anyway. It's not true."

I was glad to hear her say that, to hear her acknowledge that the rumor was complete crap, but her reaction still worried me. I nodded, granting her the time she needed to process this, but the conversation wasn't over. And what the fuck was this photo everyone was obsessing over anyway? I couldn't recall ever posing for pictures with Sienna. And that was when I remembered it. I hadn't posed for a picture with her, but there had been photographers outside the restaurant when the three of us had gone out to eat. But I was holding Kiera's hand at the time... wouldn't it be painfully obvious that I wasn't with Sienna when I was holding another girl's hand? Unless, of course, they'd cropped Kiera out. And obviously, that was exactly what had happened. Great.

I debated what to do about the photo as we walked into the building. Leaving it as rumor and innuendo seemed wrong to me, but I didn't know how to fix it. Make a statement? But who would I make a statement to? Plus, I didn't see how talking about it publicly would help anything—nobody knew who I was, and if memory served me right, all the photographers had of me was a vague profile shot. No, a denial would need to come from Sienna to have the most impact. Good thing Lana had given me her number.

Kiera and I met up with the rest of the guys once we were inside. Matt looked uncomfortable as he took in the large, white backdrop, the assortment of people adjusting lights and equipment, and the various makeup stations awaiting, well, us. Evan looked curious but unfazed as he glanced around the room. Griffin looked downright giddy; he was giving cocky little chin nods to every girl he made eye contact with, like he was positive every single one of them wanted him. I saw more than a few roll their eyes at the gesture.

As we all just stood there, wondering what we were supposed to do, a small man, holding a camera, pointed at us and said, "Ah, the talent arrives." There was a condescending tone to his voice that I didn't care for. The distaste doubled when he snapped his fingers at a woman standing a few feet away. The blonde was instantly at his side, not looking at all displeased by the way he'd summoned her, like she was used to it. Dick.

Wiggling his fingers at us, he told her, "Fix them."

Fix them? God, I hated this already.

The woman looked over at her team of assistants, and they all started heading our way. Dread filled me as they approached. I tried to convince them that we didn't need to be "fixed," that we looked fine as we were, but my objections were ignored, and before I knew it, I was wearing someone else's clothes, my hair was ridiculously over-styled, and my makeup artist, Bridgette, was dabbing some sort of creamy shit on me. I felt like a tool.

While Bridgette worked on my face, the photographer came over to inspect her progress. He seemed pleased with what he saw until his gaze dropped to my hands. "No, that needs to be removed," he said, pointing to my wedding ring.

"Excuse me?" I asked, raising my eyebrows. What the fuck did he care if I was wearing a wedding ring?

The photographer pursed his lips at me, clearly not happy that I was questioning an order. "The label doesn't want any of you to appear to be...taken. Sales drop twenty percent or more if the artist is married and unavailable, especially when that artist is the lead singer, so ring off." He made a go-ahead motion with his hand, his face showing impatience.

I opened my mouth to object, but he sighed in annoyance and cut me off before I even began. "It's not up for debate. It's what the label wants, so it's what the label is going to get." When I didn't move right away, he sighed again. "The sooner you remove it, the sooner we can both continue on with our day. You're wasting everyone's time, but even worse than that, you're wasting *my* time."

He stood there, staring at me, clearly not going anywhere until I did what he said. Feeling annoyed but stuck, I reluctantly pulled the ring off my finger. He pursed his lips, then pointed at my pocket and made another go-on motion with his hand. A slice of anger shot up my spine as I shoved the ring into my jeans. I held up my empty hands, showing him that I was being compliant. He gave me a tight, unamused smile. "Great. Now we're getting somewhere."

He looked up at Bridgette, dramatically rolled his eyes, then continued on to the other guys. My hands clenched into fists as I watched him leave. Asshole. Once he was gone, Bridgette leaned forward and said, "Don't take it personally. Frank's like that with everyone. Little Man Syndrome we call it." Standing straight, she gave me a conspiratorial wink.

Feeling my hands relax, I laughed at her assessment of him. Cocking my eyebrow, I asked, "Does this little bonding moment here mean we can skip the makeup, and I can go?"

She stared at me for a moment, then she started laughing. "Oh God, you're cute. Now relax your face." I sighed as she returned the sponge to my skin, then tried to do what she asked. The sooner this was over with, the better.

After what felt like a lifetime, Bridgette was finally done with me, and I was allowed to leave her station. But not before she gave me firm orders not to touch my hair or my face, because God forbid, I mess up my makeup. Feeling ridiculous, I walked over to Kiera. Her eyes widened as she took me in, and I felt my mood lightening. Her gaze started on my hair, then drifted over my body, taking in the borrowed frayed jeans, the studded belt, and the tight leather jacket, before returning to my hair. She nibbled on her lip as she studied me, and I could tell she was enjoying what she was seeing. It made me want to grin at her, but I was too annoyed by the amount of crap on my face. I really wanted to go to the bathroom and wash it off, but I had a feeling Bridgette would kill me if I did. Then she'd make me endure that whole process again.

Kiera frowned when I stepped in front of her. "You look great. What's wrong?" she asked.

"I'm wearing makeup. I feel like an idiot."

Leaning forward, Kiera studied my face like it held the answers to a test she was preparing for—or like I was a dessert she wanted to dive into. Her voice a little breathy, she told me, "I can't even tell. You're fine."

I brought my hand up to run it through my hair, then remembered Bridgette's warning and stopped. "I'm wearing eyeliner…and I'm pretty sure she put lipstick on me." Not to mention whatever the hell she'd wiped all over me.

Kiera grinned, and while there was a hefty dose of humor in her expression, there was desire there too. "You look incredible… darn near delectable."

The look on her face was turning me on, and that wasn't necessarily a good thing, considering how tight my pants were. Still, if she wanted me, I was hers. Wrapping my arms around her, I playfully said, "Yeah? Would you like a bite?" I flashed a glance around the room to see if anyone was paying attention. When I saw that nobody was looking our way, I leaned down to Kiera's ear. "We could disappear for a few minutes."

Kiera pushed me back, but from the simmering heat in her eyes, I could tell what she really wanted to do was grab my jacket and pull me closer. Showing a lot of restraint, she told me, "I think Bridgette would have my head if I messed up her handiwork."

Very, very true. But a small price to pay to be with her. I gave Kiera a suggestive onceover as I sucked on my lip. Ignoring the fact that I could taste whatever the hell product Bridgette had brushed on me, I told Kiera, "Yeah, but just think about it...every time you see the album cover, you'll know, without a doubt, that *you* put that smile on my face." And now I really wanted this to happen.

My hands slid over her ass, and I couldn't resist giving her a gentle squeeze. Kiera's eyes fluttered closed, and she made a soft noise that generally led to all sorts of good things, but the moment was ruined by Frank snapping his fingers and shouting, "Let's do this, people!"

Kiera's eyes immediately snapped open, and she looked a little startled, like she'd forgotten where we were for a moment. Chuckling at her expression, I released her. Kiera quickly recovered, and grabbing my hand, she kissed my cheek. Her eyes drifted to my naked finger. "Where is your ring?" she asked.

Annoyance ran up my spine as I remembered that conversation. Patting my front pocket, I told her, "Label doesn't want us to advertise that we're not single. Apparently, sales drop twenty percent if we're off the market. Or so Frank says." I pointed him out, so she would know I was talking about the photographer.

Kiera frowned, her expression matching my mood; irritation was buzzing through my veins. I supposed I could understand the label wanting the best start for us, but I didn't see how their statistic could possibly be true. Fans would buy the album for the music. Who we were—and if we were single or not—was completely irrelevant. I was happily married, and I wasn't embarrassed about that fact. Hiding it made it seem like Kiera was my dirty little secret or something. And she wasn't. Not anymore, not ever again. Frank could kiss my ass.

Mind made up, I cast a secretive glance around the room. Making sure Frank and Bridgette weren't watching, I slipped the ring back on my finger, where it belonged. "What the fuck do I care what people think, right?" The playful grin slipped off my face as I recalled the rumor that was already circulating. While I didn't care if people knew I was married, I did care if they thought I was dating someone I wasn't. "I do care about that photo with Sienna, though. I'll take care of it, Kiera."

She started to say something, but someone yanked my arm and hauled me away before she could. I was wrangled into position in front of the backdrop where the guys were already waiting. Evan laughed when he noticed my peeved expression. I flipped him off, and he laughed even harder. Matt and Griffin were sniggering too. Assholes.

Frank started shouting directions at all of us: stand here, stand there, head down, head up. I suppressed a sigh with each one and did what he asked as soon as he asked it. I figured if I was perfectly compliant, he might not notice my wedding ring. And it seemed to work. I expected him to yell at me to take it off with every shot, but he never did, and by the middle of the shoot, my amused smirk was genuine.

My mood improved even more once we were done. After Frank thanked us all for our cooperation, highly implying that we should leave now, I drifted over to Kiera, the guys trailing after me. Kissing her cheek, I told her, "I'm gonna go change and wash this shit off my face."

While she laughed at my sullen remark, Griffin stepped to my side. "Hey, you think they'll let us keep these clothes?" He gave Kiera a smug smile. "I am *so* getting laid tonight."

I wasn't too surprised by his comment, but Kiera was instantly livid; I could practically feel the anger radiating from her. She wanted a *happily ever after* for Anna, especially now that she was pregnant, but Griffin was not and never would be Prince Charming. The cold truth was...I was probably going to lose that bet with Matt and Evan. And Kiera was probably always going to hate Griffin.

Just as I thought that, Kiera spat out, "You make me sick!"

I braced myself to intervene if Griffin took that the wrong way, but he seemed more confused than anything. "What's your problem?"

Kiera's hands curled into fists, and I instantly worried that I might have to restrain *her*. Or maybe I'd just let her hit him. "You're about to have a baby with my sister, and you're still putting your...Hulk...into anything that lies still long enough. It's disgusting!"

Griffin stepped past me to stand in front of Kiera. My hands instantly moved to restrain him, but his hands were on his hips, his posture annoyed but non-threatening, so I held back. "I'm a rock star," he said. "I'll fuck anything I want to fuck. It's what we do."

Venom in her eyes, Kiera shook her head and looked between Matt, Evan, and me. My body tensed as I waited for this to either explode or dissipate. But it was clear Kiera wanted to speak her mind, so I stayed silent and let her. Eyes returning to Griffin, she said, "No, it's not."

Griffin looked over at me and rolled his eyes in that conde-scending way I was oh-so-familiar with. "Oh, please. Just because you pussy-whipped him doesn't mean you can pussy-whip me." I narrowed my eyes at him, and he smirked at me before shifting back to Kiera. "Besides, it's not like Anna isn't out banging every guy that she wants to. And do you see me getting all bent out of shape about it?"

He was right, and Kiera knew it; her expression fell a little, the anger in her eyes cooling, morphing into something that almost resembled sadness. "She's not like that anymore. She hasn't been with anyone but you since she got pregnant. You're the only man she talks about now."

Griffin looked floored by that news; I was too, to be honest. It was pretty obvious by Griffin's face that he and Anna didn't discuss their relationship status. Ever. He looked like he'd honestly never even considered that Anna was committed to him. I couldn't tell how he felt about it, though, other than surprised. "Really?" he asked, disbelief still etched on his face.

He glanced around at all of us watching him, and he suddenly looked...ashamed. That was almost as shocking to me as Anna's fidelity. Griffin didn't do shame. Or regret. Or reflection. But as he studied us, he seemed to be doing all of that, and he was hating it. Tossing his hands in the air, he looked back at Kiera. "It's just fucking. What's the big deal?"

Sadness on her face again, Kiera shook her head. "You're both going to be parents, Griffin. That's a life-changing event, one that Anna is scared to death about. And here you are, living it up, still banging babes left and right. Do you even care about what she's going through? You enjoy having sex with Anna, but do you care about my sister at all?"

Griffin just stared at Kiera, but his face was completely blank —blank in a way I wasn't used to seeing. He was genuinely absorbing her words, I could tell, and he also wasn't happy about what it was doing to him. If I had to guess, I'd say he was finally experiencing guilt.

After a long, silent moment, he scoffed and told her, "I was just joking. Relax the fuck up, Kiera." Then he stomped off.

Once he was gone, Matt turned to Kiera, a look of surprise and pride on his face. "I can't be sure, but I think you just gave him food for thought." Grinning, he extended his hand to Kiera. "Nicely played, Mrs. Kyle." They briefly shook hands, then Matt clapped Evan's back and they trailed off after Griffin, lightly laughing.

Wrapping my arm around Kiera, I pulled her close. "It's adorable that you still try."

She smirked at me, then her gaze drifted to my chest. "Griffin did ask a good question. Think they'll let you keep the clothes?"

Her gaze drifted even lower, and I grinned as I leaned down to her ear. "I don't need to keep them...they're just in the way."

I left her with that image in her head, and she was clearly indulging in it; her breath was coming faster, and her eyes were closed. When she reopened them and looked at me, there was so much heat in her expression that I wondered if I should pull her into the changing room with me. Damn. Now I really wanted out of these clothes. Smiling to myself, I hurried after the guys.

The instant I rejoined them, Griffin rounded on me. "What is up with your girlfriend?" he snapped.

"Wife," I automatically corrected.

He flipped me off with a derisive smirk on his face. "Whatever she is, why the hell is she raggin' on me? Tell her to back the fuck off."

I let out a long sigh. "She's just worried about her sister, Griffin."

He dismissively waved his hand. "Anna is fine; there's nothing to worry about there."

Matt raised an eyebrow. "You don't think Anna might expect more from you now? Since, you know, you're about to be parents?"

Griffin narrowed his icy eyes at his cousin. "Wouldn't she ask if she wanted more? She hasn't asked, ergo, she doesn't care."

Matt grinned. "Ergo? Did you get a word-of-the-day calendar?"

Griffin smirked. "Dad did. I stole that too."

While Matt laughed, I tilted my head at Griffin. "Why don't *you* ask Anna?" I said, refocusing the conversation.

Griffin looked at me like I'd just suggested he pour fire ants all over himself. "Dude, if she doesn't care if we're exclusive, why would I bring it up? She's letting me be free, man. That's a win-win...win-win-win."

Matt and Evan shared a look as they tried to puzzle out what that meant. I clapped Griffin on the shoulder. "But it also means that she's free to keep looking around too. What if she meets someone else? What if they fall in love? What if that guy marries her? What if that guy ends up raising your kid?"

Griffin's jaw dropped. "Fuck. That."

I shrugged at him, and he shook his head, looking disgusted

by the very plausible scenario I'd just mapped out for him. He walked away looking sickened and frustrated...and worried.

Once he was across the room, Matt stepped up to my side. "I almost want to call you out on interfering with our bet, but since I want you to win, I'll let it slide." I smiled at him, and he smiled back, then we bumped fists and watched as Griffin silently stewed.

Chapter 11

DO YOUR JOB

The first thing I did after leaving the photoshoot was call Sienna so I could talk to her about saying something publicly about that photo of us. When she picked up, I thought I'd have to explain who I was, but Sienna instantly knew it was me. Surreal, but I supposed it wasn't all that surprising. If Sienna had wanted Lana to give me her number, then it made sense that she had asked Lana for mine as well. And being as important to the label as she was, Lana probably hadn't felt like she could refuse her. Not for a nobody like me, anyway.

Our conversation was polite and civil, and by the end of it, Sienna agreed to say something. Kiera didn't look convinced when I relayed the news to her. She seemed to think Sienna wanted me in a more-than-professional way. I didn't think so, but I couldn't for-sure tell when it came to her. It was entirely possible that Sienna might be interested in me. Didn't matter, though. I was *not* interested in her.

I tried to put it out of my mind after that, but it kept popping up, and even though Sienna did release a statement saying that the guy in the photo was "just a friend," everyone was still talking about it for some reason. And speculating on our relationship. And coming to the wrong conclusion. Even my friends fell victim to the hype. Or one of them did, at any rate.

"I hate you. I hate you so much; there aren't enough words to express how much I hate you. *That's* how much I hate you."

Pulling a beer out of the fridge, I looked over at Griffin standing beside me, scowl on his face, arms crossed over his chest. I stared at him a moment, then pointed at the open fridge. "Want a beer?"

He narrowed his pale eyes at me. "Don't you want to know *why* I hate you?"

Closing the fridge, I shrugged. "Not really. You say you hate me about three times a week, so I'm kind of used to it." Grabbing a bottle opener on the counter, I popped off the cap to my beer. Griffin watched me with heat in his eyes as I tipped back the refreshing beverage.

"Sienna," he said. "I've seen the picture, heard what people are saying. You're *screwing* her? Seriously?" The look he gave me was one of complete disbelief. "You knew I wanted her first, and you broke your damn monogamy rule just to piss me off. That's why I hate you." He slowly shook his head, disgust on his face.

I swallowed another mouthful of beer as annoyance shot up my spine. Lowering the bottle, I told him, "I didn't break *anything*, Griffin. The photo was taken when we all went out to dinner—Sienna, me, and *Kiera*. She was there, but they cropped her out. The rumors aren't true. Nothing has or ever will happen between Sienna and me. I love my wife."

Griffin studied me intently, looking for any sign that I was lying. "Really? Nothing happened? 'Cause you can tell me...I'll get over it. It's not the first time I've had your seconds." He gave me a quick onceover before glancing down at himself, frown on his face. "It's annoying as fuck, but whatever. I'm not going to *not* sleep with her because of that. I just like to know beforehand. Also...what kink is she into? Got any tips for me?"

My eyes narrowed as I stared at him. "Nothing. Happened."

He pursed his lips at me. "I don't know if I believe that.

Because I know for a fact you saw her boobs that night. You still owe me details, by the way."

I slammed my beer on the counter so hard that some of it came out of the top. "Oh my fucking God, Griffin. All we did was go out to dinner. *Dinner*. That's it."

Griffin held up his hands. "Okay, fine, I got it. You didn't fuck her, and you didn't see her naked. Damn, calm down, Pollyanna." He eyed me for a second as I wiped off the counter with a nearby towel. "So you really don't want to have sex with her? Like...ever?"

Striving for patience, I let out a long sigh. "No, I don't. I love my wife, and I don't want anyone else. I'm completely faithful to Kiera, and I always will be."

He gave me a puzzled expression. "That's still so weird, man. You're a rock star, and you look like..." Pausing, he indicated my face with his hand. "You could probably have anybody. Or every-body." He smirked. "All at the same time. Why would you give that up?"

I smiled at the confusion on his face. "Because I found some-thing better." His expression turned oddly thoughtful. Seeing an opportunity, I said, "You could try it and see for yourself. You might like it."

His lips shifted into a sly grin. "Sex with Sienna? Yeah, I'm working on it."

I gave him a flat look. "No. Monogamy. With Anna."

He made an affronted noise. "Dude, get off it." Kiera walked into the kitchen then, and Griffin instantly pointed at her. "And you get off it too." Then he turned around and left the room, shaking his head and mumbling to himself.

Kiera frowned as she met eyes with me. "Do I even want to know what that was about?"

I smirked at her. "Monogamy."

She tilted her head at me, confused, and I let out a light laugh. "He came in here all pissed, thinking I slept with Sienna." I lifted an eyebrow at her as she wrapped her arms around my waist. "Apparently, he wanted her first, and he was annoyed at me for jumping the line." Anger flooded Kiera's face as she glared back at where he'd disappeared. Oops. Probably shouldn't have mentioned that to her. She hated him enough as it was. Bringing my finger to her chin, I refocused her attention on me. "But I convinced him I didn't sleep with Sienna and won't ever sleep with Sienna. Because I love you."

She smiled warmly at me for a moment, then frowned. "I'm not all that surprised that he believed it at first. It took some explaining with some of the girls too...and Denny." Sudden worry marked her features. "Do Matt and Evan think you—"

"No," I interrupted. "They know I would never..." A heavy sigh escaped me. "I'm so sorry, Kiera. I know this is awkward."

She chewed on her lip for a moment, then smiled. "It's not true, so it doesn't matter, right?"

"Yeah, I guess." Irritation pricked me at using such an indecisive word. "Yes," I said more firmly. "It doesn't matter at all."

But a couple of weeks after that, I learned that Kiera and I were wrong. It did matter. To some people, it mattered a lot.

We were about to leave on a promotional tour for the album. The itinerary for it was so jam-packed that it had Matt freaking out on an almost daily basis. "They can't be serious about this, right?" he said, showing it to me for the hundredth time. "This is insane. If one tiny thing goes wrong..." His voice trailed off as his eyes drifted to Griffin sitting on the couch, playing a videogame.

I clapped Matt on the shoulder. "It'll be fine." Leaning in, I quietly added, "We'll have help with him."

He gave me a small smile, but it quickly fell off his face. "We should talk to someone about this."

Griffin let out a loud groan as he set down his controller. "Dude, stop bitching about it. Your stress is more stressful than the schedule. Relax, okay? Or I'll be forced to relax you." He grinned like he was daring Matt to test him.

Matt sighed, but he put the schedule away.

Griffin smirked and patted the couch cushion beside him.

"Come on, come blow some shit up with me. It'll take your mind off it."

Matt stared at him a moment, then nodded and walked over to grab another controller. As he sat down, Griffin cocked his head at me. "You want in on this, Kell?"

I shook my head. "No, Kiera and I are going down to the pool." Just as I finished saying it, Kiera emerged from the bedroom dressed in a swimsuit and a pair of shorts. I grinned as she walked my way. "Hey, beautiful."

She gave me a demure smile as her eyes drifted to the T-shirt and board shorts I was wearing. "Hey, yourself. Ready?"

As I nodded, Griffin partly turned his head toward the bedrooms and yelled, "Evan! Stop whacking it and come play videogames with us!"

Kiera instantly grimaced at Griffin, and I instantly wished we'd left five minutes ago. I heard an annoyed sigh from Evan's room, then he appeared in the open doorway. His deep brown eyes locked on mine, and his expression was so unamused that I had to laugh. Evan cracked a smile, then rolled his eyes. Walking into the living room, he muttered, "Grow up, Griffin." Griff snickered in response.

Evan gave Kiera an apologetic smile, then studied the game Matt and Griffin were playing. "The object is to kill Griffin, right?" he asked Matt.

Matt smiled, his eyes glued on the screen. "Isn't it always?"

As Evan grabbed a controller, Griffin made a sound of confident disbelief. "Please. You can't kill a god, remember?" Then he scowled as his character on the screen abruptly fell face first to the ground, dead. "Goddamn it, Matt."

Matt snorted. "Me one, god zero." He shifted to look at Griffin. "You're right, I do feel better."

Kiera laughed, then grabbed my hand and started pulling me downstairs, where we could be alone. Hopefully.

It was hot outside, so Kiera and I wasted no time getting into the water. We swam for a while, played for a while, then cuddled for a while. We were holding each other in the shallow end when Griffin came out of the house and interrupted our quiet time. He looked puzzled as he approached the stairs leading into the pool. He wasn't wearing swim clothes, so I was pretty sure he wasn't here to join us. Unless he planned on going commando, and if that was the case, then he could have the entire pool to himself. But all he did was stop at the edge of the stairs and scratch his head like he was confused. I had no fucking clue what he was doing until he shrugged and tapped his knuckles on the railing dividing the steps. Oh my God...he actually remembered my warning about knocking. And even more shocking—he was doing it.

It took a lot of willpower, but I managed to stop myself from laughing. "Yes?" I said, like we were in a room, not a pool.

"That dude from the record is here. Wants to talk to you."

That got my attention, and the humor fell right off me. Setting Kiera beside me, I stood up. "Which dude?"

Griffin's eyes immediately locked on Kiera's chest, and his lips lifted into a slight smile. Shrugging, he said, "I don't know. The uppity one in a suit."

Annoyed that he was openly ogling my wife, I stepped in front of her to block his view. Hopefully, that would help him focus, because this sounded important. "Nick? The vice president of the label?"

Now that he couldn't see Kiera, Griffin raised his eyes to mine. "I don't know. Sure."

Irritation shot up my spine that he didn't know for sure, but it was quickly replaced by dread. "The uppity one in a suit" had to be Nick, and I wasn't entirely sure why I felt uneasy about that. After all, the last time I'd spoken with him, it had led to a great opportunity for the band. If he wanted to talk to me again, it was probably about another great opportunity. I shouldn't be worried. And yet...

Kiera and I quickly dried off and put our cover-up clothes back on. I briefly considered going back to our room to shower and change but keeping Nick waiting probably wasn't a good idea. Griffin led us upstairs to the room where we'd met Nick and Sienna last time. Nick was on the couch, just like before. Matt and Evan were sitting on a couch across from him, looking both nervous and excited. Nick stood as I approached him. Noticing that Kiera wasn't beside me anymore, I glanced back to see her just outside the room, talking to Griffin. Or listening to Griffin talk to her. She had an annoyed look on her face. I wanted to go save her from him, but Nick was greeting me. I had to stay.

"Kellan," he said, extending a palm. "It's good to see you again."

"Likewise," I replied, shaking his hand. Like Griffin had said, Nick was in a full suit, complete with a bright red tie. I wasn't an expert on suits, but it shouted money to me. In fact, everything about him felt like a statement. Not a single strand of blond hair was out of place, not one scuffmark marred his shiny shoes, and there wasn't a speck of dirt under his neatly trimmed nails. I instantly felt a little unkempt beside him, which was probably exactly how he wanted me to feel.

He indicated an open space on the couch beside Evan. "Please, have a seat." With a nod, I sat down, leaving a space for Kiera. Nick smiled as he returned to his spot on his couch. "I was just telling your bandmates how great the finished album is," he said. "Truly spectacular. If success was based on talent alone, it would definitely be a hit."

"But it's not," I said, both as a statement and a question.

Nick frowned. "No, it's not."

He opened his mouth to say more but paused when Kiera and Griffin entered the room. Nick smiled as they sat down, a forced, impatient smile. His eyes drifted over Kiera as she nestled into my side. "Making good use of the home's amenities, I see," he said, taking in her swimsuit top and wet hair. His eyes shifted to me. "That's good. You'll need your rest now to get you through the launch."

I glanced at Kiera. She had an uneasy, uncomfortable expression on her face. It matched the uncertainty churning in my stomach. I gave Nick a brief nod, acknowledging his comment, then waited for him to explain what we were all doing here.

Nick's expression brightened once he had our attention. "I have good news. Great news." He paused as he leaned forward, letting the air fill with expectation. "Diedrick Kraus just agreed to shoot the video for 'Regretfully.'"

I secreted a look at Matt. The name wasn't ringing a bell for me, but it might for him; he followed the industry a lot more than I did. Matt's brows were furrowed, though. Clearly, he was clueless.

Nick spoke in the silence. "You have no idea who that is, do you?"

Speaking for the group, I told him, "Sorry, no."

Nick dismissed my apology with a wave. "Diedrick Kraus is the genius behind some of the greatest music videos of our time. He's exclusive. Hard to come by. We gave him a sample of your song, and he wants to direct it. No, he fucking insisted on it." He pointed at me. "Diedrick's got a couple of days available at the end of the month, Sienna's got a tiny break in her schedule, and we'll squeeze it in for you during the promotional tour." Smile on his face, he lifted his hands. "I swear the stars aligned for this."

Surprise washed through me as I glanced at the guys. "We're making a music video? Do people even still watch those?"

I thought I heard one of the guys let out a soft snort. I supposed it was kind of a dumb question, but I was barely ever online, so I never saw anything. Matt sometimes showed me videos, but he always showed me concert footage. He said a band's true talent was only evident when they played live, so why watch anything else. *I guess.* All I knew was that filming a music video sounded like doing a really long, obnoxious photoshoot, so already I wasn't too excited about this.

Nick frowned at me. "Yes, they do." He suddenly grinned in an overly animated way that was kind of creepy. "And we've got an opportunity here to stir the hornet's nest."

171

The hair rose on the back of my neck as wariness coursed through me. "I have no idea what that means."

Nick gave me a look like he thought I was slow. "It means we're going to cause some serious buzz with this video. Ever since the public caught wind of you and Sienna in that photograph, there has been a firestorm of interest. Everyone is curious about Sienna's new man."

"I'm not her man," I immediately stated.

Nick kept going like I hadn't even opened my mouth. "We're going to fuel the flames of Kellan and Sienna madness and ride the hype to the top of the charts."

His words, mixed with the excitement on his face, filled me with dread. I didn't like the sound of this. At all. Lana's vague warning suddenly flashed through my mind, and my stomach felt like someone was clenching it tight. There were a lot of different ways to interpret his statement, though. I needed clarification. "What do you mean?"

Nick spread his fingers, his pale eyes glowing with avaricious delight. "We're going to play up the romantic portion of the song, make the video seriously hot. Naked bodies, deep kisses, moaning and groaning, whatever we can get away with. Anyone who watches it will immediately need to take a very cold shower. The buzz around you and Sienna is going to skyrocket."

What. The. Hell? The direction he wanted to go with the video made absolutely no sense to me. He wasn't serious, was he? *I can't do any of that.* "The song is about a breakup," I spat out, hoping I'd somehow misunderstood him.

Nick nodded, a sly smile spreading over his face as he steepled his fingers under his chin. "Yes, and what great breakup didn't start off with a fiery romance?"

Shit. He was serious. He wanted me to basically get it on with Sienna. My heart pounded in my chest as I studied him, my stomach churned. There was no way I could film something like that. How could he even suggest it without asking my opinion first? Because he didn't give a shit about my opinion, that much was obvious. Well, fuck. *How the hell do I get out of this?* If I flat-out refused to do it, what would that mean for our future? I supposed it didn't really matter, because there was no way on Earth I could say yes. I couldn't do that to Kiera. Fuck. I couldn't even look at her yet. I was too scared of what I might see on her face. She was rigid beside me, like she'd been frozen solid. I didn't even want to imagine what she was thinking right now, what she was feeling. She had to be sick to her stomach, just like me.

Hoping Nick would understand, I began the process of bursting his bubble. "I'm married. I can't do that."

Griffin instantly volunteered. "I can!"

Yes, please, let Griffin do it. But Nick clearly wasn't interested in Griffin as his leading man. His eyes hardened as he glared at me, and the expression on his face had me instinctively tensing, preparing for a fight. "I'm not asking you to have an affair with the woman. That part is entirely up to you." He smirked as he threw a glance Kiera's way, and a burst of rage flashed through my body. Fucking asshole. I opened my mouth to tell him exactly what I thought of his entire proposal, but he continued speaking before I could. "I'm merely asking you to film a *fictional* video with her to a song that you've already recorded, a song that we own, by the way." The heat running through my veins suddenly shifted to ice. By his tone, it was clear that he meant he owned me just as much as he owned the song. And fuck...maybe he did.

As I swallowed a sudden knot in my throat, Nick pushed back on his thighs, preparing to stand. "Entertaining the masses is part of your job description, and sometimes that includes acting. If we'd known you were...unwilling...to do that, we wouldn't have signed you." He stood up and took a step toward me, so he was towering over me. "All I'm asking for here is for you to suck it up and do your fucking job. And in case you couldn't tell...I'm not really asking."

He left immediately after that, but the menace in his words lingered. And the meaning: *Do this or you're done.* Jesus. This was it. The one moment that our entire career hinged on, and for some reason, the moment was entirely dependent on me—on what I would or wouldn't do to my wife. It wasn't right. My personal life and my career should be separate. He had *no* right to force me to do this. None.

The air was chokingly thick with tension as I sat and stewed. I could feel my friends' discomfort, Kiera's concern. I still couldn't look at her. *What the fuck do I do?*

Griffin, oblivious to the mood in the room, suddenly said, "Dude! You get to film-fuck Sienna Sexton! High five!"

He had the audacity to hold up his hand to me, like I would actually high five him for that. All the anger in my stomach shot out my eyes to drill into him, but he didn't even notice my mood. He was too excited about the whole thing...so excited he wasn't even jealous. Yet. I was sure that would come later. If I did this. Fuck. *I can't do this.*

I can't. I can't. I can't.

No...I won't.

Decision made, I stood up. Staring at the doorway where Nick had gone made the heat in my chest swell into fiery rage. "This is bullshit." *And I'm not doing it. Fuck it. Fuck it all.*

In my haste to get out of the room, I roughly brushed past the others sitting on the couch. Evan said my name, concern clear in his voice, but I ignored him. He wasn't going to like my decision, none of them were, but they weren't the ones being asked to cross a line. And there was no way in hell I was going to willingly cross that line. Kiera would never forgive me. *I* would never forgive me.

I fled to my bedroom and immediately grabbed my bag and Kiera's. After setting them on the bed, I began ripping open dresser drawers and grabbing shit. Kiera and the guys walked into the room as I was shoving shirts into my bag.

"What are you doing?" Kiera's voice was soft, cautious, and careful, like she thought I might bolt any moment. Or snap. I was buzzing with so much adrenaline that I felt like I could do both.

Trying to keep calm, I met eyes with her. "Pack your stuff. We're going home. I'm done."

Griffin was instantly pissed. "What the fuck, Kellan?"

Before I could respond to Griffin, Evan put his hand on my shoulder. A warning and an attempt to soothe me. I wasn't in the mood for either. As I brushed him off, Matt softly said, "We signed a contract, Kellan. We can't just walk away."

My fury instantly shifted to him. "Then they can fucking sue us! I'm not whoring myself out for them. I'm going back to Pete's. Are you guys coming with me or not?"

Matt flinched at my words, at the look on my face and the heat in my voice. Evan looked torn. So did Kiera. Griffin just looked shocked. And mad. "You are the biggest fucking pussy—"

Before he even finished his insult, I was striding his way, my arm pulled back to shove the rest of those words right down his fucking throat. Evan blocked my way, his hands on both of my shoulders now, firmly pressing me back. I didn't want to see the look in Evan's eyes, the sympathy, worry, or even disappointment, so I kept my gaze on Griffin. Matt had a hand on his chest, keeping him away from me. Griffin's eyes were narrowed in anger, but I was the one about to come unglued. *Fuck. You.*

Kiera's voice broke the tense stillness in the air. "Could you give me a moment with my husband, please?"

Rage still pounding through me, I whipped my head around to glare in her direction. Because that didn't sound like she was on my side. And out of all of them, I thought she would be the one who understood, who *agreed*. What the fuck did she want to talk about?

Evan released me, and I heard someone dragging Griffin out of the room. Before he left, he yelled, "You talk some fucking sense into him, Kiera! *This* is bullshit!" My eyes narrowed at hearing that, but I couldn't stop staring at Kiera. Did she agree with Griffin? Seriously? *What the actual fuck, Kiera?*

The door closed, and she took a step toward me. There was a level of calmness in her hazel eyes that lit a fire in my stomach.

Why was she so relaxed about this? And what the fuck did she think we needed to talk about? There was no discussion to be had here. There was packing and leaving, and that was it.

Anger and resentment loosened my tongue, and before she could say anything, I snapped out, "You gonna call me a pussy too? Think I ought to go ahead and fuck Sienna, just to prove a point?"

Kiera cringed, and I instantly regretted saying it, but my veins were flooded with venom, and I couldn't calm down; my entire body was tight with tension. Stepping up to me, Kiera grabbed my curled fists. "Kellan...you can't give up now."

Bullshit, I couldn't. Yanking my hand free, I pointed at the door. "Were you in that meeting? Did you hear what they want me to do?"

Kiera swallowed as she nodded and grabbed my hand again. "Yes, and it's okay."

I felt like I'd just fallen into some alternate reality; that was the only rational explanation for what she'd just said. "It's...okay? How is me 'film fucking' someone okay?"

Kiera minutely flinched at my words, but instead of agreeing with me, she stepped into my body. She ran her hands up my arms, and it did something to me, extinguished some of the rage, cooled some of the fire. Her fingers laced around my neck, and her body pressed against me. The tension in my muscles was slow to release, but as her thumb stroked the back of my neck, I felt the pressure begin to soften. In its wake, pain and uncertainty leeched in. *How can I do this to you? Why would you want me to?*

At feeling me relax, Kiera gave me a little shrug and an encouraging smile. "Well, all right, maybe 'okay' isn't the best word. The thought of you being with her is actually a little horrifying."

Exactly. And that's why I can't do this.

Kiera noticed my body tightening and immediately added, "But it's a necessary evil."

Necessary? She was the only thing in my life that fit that

description. Shaking my head, I wrapped my arms around her. "No, it isn't necessary." The residual anger faded as I held her, shifting into frustration, reluctance...fear. Wanting to absorb her comfort, I rested my forehead against hers. "I don't want to hurt you. And I don't see how any of this won't hurt you."

She pulled back to look at me. "And I don't want you to give up on your dream because of me."

I instantly understood what would motivate her to say okay to this, and it hurt because it was so selfless of her. I didn't want to take advantage of that selflessness. I didn't want to allow *Nick* to take advantage of that selflessness. My dream wasn't worth losing her, and this...even if she was on board with it, this could break us.

Shaking my head, I looked away from her. My dream wasn't worth *us*.

She grabbed my cheek, refocusing my gaze on her. "You're so close, so very close. Just do this one thing to jumpstart your career, to jumpstart the guys' careers. Then, when you've completed your contract terms and you're the most sought-after band in the industry, find another label. *That* will prove your point much better than...you know."

Her comment brought a small smile to my lips. It was short-lived. Feeling a heaviness inside me, I exhaled a long breath and contemplated her argument. I hated that I was even thinking about it, but I supposed I had to at least consider it. Could I suck it up and do this one thing? For our future? For the guys' future? If she was truly okay with this, did that make a difference? I really wasn't sure. There were pitfalls along both paths, and I didn't know how to avoid them.

Finally, after a long moment of silence, I told Kiera, "I don't want to let the guys down, I really don't, and I see what you're saying. But when I said I was through with other girls, I meant it. You're it for me. I don't want to touch her."

Adoration in her eyes, she told me, "I know. And I love you so much for that. But this doesn't have to affect us if we don't let it. You're still my husband. I'm still your wife. Acting like you feel differently on camera doesn't change any of that. Okay?"

I supposed it didn't. In theory. But still...

Damn it. *Do I give up everyone's dreams? Or do this and pray that Kiera and I can survive it?* The guys would end up hating me if I walked away now. But Kiera could end up hating me if I stayed. *But she's saying she won't. She's saying she understands. She's saying she'll stay. Will she? Can I do this?* Fuck. I really didn't feel like I had a choice.

Feeling defeat wrap firmly around me, I gave Kiera a slow nod and a sad sigh. "I'm not even sure if I can film a love scene with someone other than you." Just the thought made me ill.

Kiera ran a hand through my slicked-back hair. "Sure you can. Just pretend she's me. It wouldn't be the first time."

She gave me a teasing smile, and I grinned at her for a second. My smile fell as my mood crashed. "You really want me to do this?"

Kiera bit her lip, and I saw the conflict in her eyes. She didn't want this to happen, but she *did* want success for the band. She was torn, same as me, but strangely...she was stronger. "Yes, I do," she finally said.

I closed my eyes and nodded, accepting her decision. And I hated to admit it, but there was a part of me that was glad she was the one deciding this and not me. It soothed a small portion of the guilt. But then she kissed me and told me she wanted to be there, she wanted to watch it.

"No," I instantly told her.

She gave me a decisive nod before kissing me again. "I have to, Kellan."

"Why? Why would you want to see that, Kiera?"

"Because it will be so much worse in my head if I don't," she said with a sigh.

My chest ached at the image of her watching me with another woman. If it bothered *me*, then there was no way I could let her see it. "Kiera, I don't want this, but if I have to do it, then I want you as far away from it as possible." I pushed her back and squatted down so I could look her in the eye. "I don't want to hurt you, and if our roles were reversed, I couldn't handle watching you with another man."

"You already did," she whispered, and the grief and sympathy in her expression nearly brought me to my knees. The pain her words invoked in me was sharp and deep, and for a second, the memories threatened to drown me. She pulled me back from the brink before I was swept under. "I love you."

She ended her statement with a soft kiss. And another. And another. And before I knew it, my heart was racing, and I was clutching the back of her head, holding her mouth to mine as I deepened the kiss. She moaned in my mouth, and my body surged with need.

Kiera's breath was as fast as mine as she pulled on my shirt, wanting it off. I quickly stripped it, then sought her mouth again. Her fingers explored my bare skin, each stroke filling me with fire. She tugged on my shorts, and I yanked them off too. Her heated eyes scanned my body for a moment, and I felt completely absorbed by her. I desperately hoped she understood that this was something Sienna would never have. This moment, this intimacy, this connection—it was *only* Kiera's.

Her arms aggressively wrapped around my neck, and she pulled me toward the bed. The minute we were on top of it, I started tearing off her damp clothes. I wasn't sure if it was because I wanted to convince her that no other woman would ever have me, or if it was because I wanted to convince myself that this video wouldn't change us, but I didn't think I'd ever wanted her more. I delighted in every section of skin that was revealed to me, but almost as soon as her clothes were gone, I pushed inside her, too eager to wait any longer.

She groaned the word, "Yes," in a loud, unselfconscious way that made me throb. I murmured her name before pulling back and pressing against her, and I felt the electric energy of our connection in every single part of me. My thoughts evaporated as the profound sensation of making love to her overwhelmed me. Kiera's hands clenched my skin, her legs rubbed against me, and each time we came together she let out the most erotic noise...I couldn't help but respond in kind.

Before long, we were both close, letting out fast, noisy breaths, trembling with the building pressure, desperate for a release yet not wanting the euphoria to end. Then Kiera gasped, stiffened, and let out a long, satisfied exhalation. Her nails dug into my back, scraping down my shoulder blades, and I immediately fell over the edge. My climax hit me hard, and I buried my head in her shoulder, groaning into her neck as I came.

We stayed that way a moment, relishing, recovering, then I rolled off her so that I wasn't crushing her. My eyes drifted closed as peace washed through me. Kiera softly kissed my cheek, and I gave her a small smile. I could feel the tug of relaxation pulling me under, and I didn't fight it. I wanted to let go for a while, wanted to feel nothing but bliss and contentment. Just for a few minutes.

Chapter 12

NO COMMENT

The day of the video shoot was here, and I was *not* ready. My heart pounded as I walked toward the bed surrounded in bright lights. Sienna was already lying on top of it, not a single piece of clothing on her. I didn't want to look at her, but shock froze my gaze. I hadn't realized we'd be naked for this. *I can't do this naked. That's just...no.*

From somewhere, a guy yelled, "Get his clothes off!"

I turned my head to tell him to go to hell, but hands grabbed me before the words came out, and before I even really knew what was happening, things were being pulled off me. I swung a punch at the person trying to remove my boxers, but somehow, they managed to get them off.

Sienna sat up on the bed once I was naked. She smiled at me in a way that turned my stomach, then she patted the spot next to her. *Don't do it. Turn around and walk away.* But my feet weren't listening to my head, and I trudged forward. Sitting on the mattress, I grabbed the rumpled sheet and covered myself. Sienna's grin grew.

"I didn't peg you as the shy type," she said, pulling on the sheet. I fought her, and she frowned. "It's going to have to come off sometime, Kellan."

"Why are we naked? It's supposed to be fake." I looked around the room, but I couldn't see anything past the glare of the lights.

Sienna sighed as she rested her wrist on my shoulder. "It's a love scene. Making love is typically done naked." She leaned forward and kissed my neck. "I truly thought you knew that."

Her eyes scanned my body, and I pushed her away. "We haven't started yet. Don't kiss me."

She suddenly threw herself on top of me, and caught off guard, I fell back against the mattress. "Of course we've started, Kellan. We started a long time ago."

Then she was all over me, kissing everywhere, grinding against everything. I tried to keep her away from me, but it was like she had a half-dozen arms and legs; I was as firmly trapped as a person could be. My stomach churned, and I felt bile rising in my throat as all my muscles locked up. *I don't want to do this.* And then Sienna was moving my hands, making me touch her ass, her chest. I wanted to run, but I couldn't get free.

Someone stepped up to the bed and stopped. As I twisted to look, hoping for help, Sienna ran her tongue up my neck, bottom to top. I opened my mouth to ask the person to push her off me, but the words died on my tongue when I saw who it was. Kiera. Tears were dripping down her pale cheeks, and her eyes were bloodshot. She could barely breathe through her sobs, but she managed to squeak out, "Why?"

That one word cut me to the core, and hot tears burned my eyes as I stared at her. I wanted to rush to her, explain that I didn't want any of this, but I couldn't get Sienna off me; everything I did seemed to draw her closer somehow. And then, over Kiera's shoulder, I saw my father step inside the ring of lights. He was laughing.

"How did I raise someone so stupid? Thank God you're not really mine," he sneered.

Seeing him...relaxed me. *I'm dreaming. Thank fuck, I'm dreaming.*

I woke with a start, my heart pounding, just like in the dream. I quickly scanned the room, just to be sure, but it was the bedroom Kiera and I were using at the label's house, it was early in the morning, and most importantly, we were alone.

Kiera's fingers moved to my stomach as I sat up on my elbows. "You okay?" she mumbled, her words thick with sleep.

Inhaling a deep breath, I forced myself to shove the dream from my mind. I was just panicking. It wouldn't be like that. *God, please don't let it be like that.* "Yeah, just...bad dream."

Kiera stirred, sitting up a little. "Do you want to talk about it?" she asked, concern in her eyes. Kiera knew my bad dreams could be exceptionally horrific. In comparison, this one wasn't, but still, it had shaken me, and I really didn't want to talk about it.

Leaning over, I kissed her head. "No. I just want to hold you until we need to get up. Which is..." I peeked at the clock. "Fuck...which is now. Sorry, babe. Time to get going."

She yawned, then pulled me into her. "Five more minutes," she murmured, nestling against my chest.

I laughed and let her snuggle. She needed it, I needed it. The label could wait. For a little bit. Today was the beginning of our hectic promo tour, and we had several places we needed to be. I didn't want to think about our tight schedule, didn't want to think about the *real* video shoot happening soon, didn't want to think about anything except my wife's arms and legs wrapped around me, warming me, comforting me. I never wanted to leave this bed.

But all too soon, we had to go. Kiera and I were both a little slow as we grabbed our bags and left our room. Evan stepped out of his room at the same time, lifting a hand in greeting as he yawned. Matt was banging on Griffin's door, yelling at him to hurry up. We'd all stayed up way too late last night, easing the anxiety by, well, by having a water fight and trashing the house. We really shouldn't have, but everyone had been a ball of restless energy, and it had helped. A lot.

When everyone was ready, we headed downstairs. Nick was waiting by the front door when we got there, along with a tall, blonde woman in a suit. I waited for Nick to be angry about the water everywhere, but he merely asked if we were ready to go. After I nodded, he indicated his companion.

"This is Tory. She'll be your handler for all of the media interviews."

Her face was a steel mask with harsh angles, tight lips, icy blue eyes...not a lot of warmth or compassion there. She thrust her hand in my direction. "Nice to officially meet you. Nick has told me many nice things." Her eyes briefly scanned my body before returning to my face.

I shook her hand, then asked Nick, "A handler?" I didn't know what that was, but I didn't like the sound of it. I wasn't a child.

Not waiting for Nick, Tory answered my question. "I'm the one who lined up all of your interviews. I'll be checking you in for each one and letting the interviewers know which questions you won't be allowing. I will also end the interview if I feel they are not respecting the label's wishes."

That instantly struck a nerve. "The label's wishes. Not mine, then?"

She gave me a cold, professional smile. "Nick has requested that you not talk about your personal life." Her eyes shifted to Kiera, and I suddenly knew exactly why she was really here. To gatekeep *me*. Fuck that.

Anger stirred in my stomach as I shot Nick a look. "You don't want me to talk about my wife? So when they ask what's going on with Sienna and me, I'm supposed to say...?" I raised my hands as disbelief washed through me. I had to still be dreaming.

Nick's smile was smooth and untroubled, like he did this all the time. "You tell them no comment and let them stew on that any way they want to."

My hands slapped to my sides. "'No comment'? I might as well tell them I'm screwing her brains out on a daily basis."

He shrugged, unmoved. "I'm not asking you to lie. I'm merely asking you not to respond and not to divulge any...unnecessary information. Think you can handle that?" he asked, an edge to his voice.

Kiera grabbed my hand, and I could feel all the guys staring at me, waiting for me to lose it. With the heat simmering in my body, I felt like I might. This was ridiculous. Absolutely ridiculous. *First, they want me to film-fuck Sienna, and now they want me to let everyone think I'm* actually *fucking her?* Why? What the fuck did it matter?

I was just about to tell Nick that I would say whatever the hell I wanted to say when he spoke again. "We're expecting this single to reach number one. When your album releases in a few weeks, I wouldn't be surprised if it debuts in the top twenty. All of that is due, in large part, to the fact that the public has a soft spot for you and Sienna together. You've become a couple in their eyes, and that sort of publicity cannot be bought. When your video hits the market, the buzz around you two will be out of this world. And if we don't take advantage of that, ride the tidal wave while it lasts, we'll lose the momentum, and your album will sink like a rock to the low hundreds. It's a very crowded market, jampacked with talented, gorgeous individuals, such as yourself. Do you want to start your career on top of them, or on the bottom of them...crushed into the oblivion of obscurity?" He paused to shrug. "The choice is yours."

The choice was mine? *Agree to this fucked-up plan or be the reason the band fails.* Some choice. Great. Just fucking great.

Not waiting for a response from me, Nick and Tory left the house. Kiera squeezed my hand tighter, just as speechless as I was. The guys were silent, but I felt what they wanted, felt it deep in my bones. It felt like a ton of weight being placed solely on my shoulders. It felt like compromising everything I cherished for success. It felt like I was stuck, hovering between two horrible options: staying the course or going home. And that was a nauseating feeling.

Since I had no idea what else to do, I headed outside. I'd figure it out in the car.

The first place we were scheduled to play was right here in L.A. The guys were excited on the ride to the radio station. Not because of the crazy promo tour we were about to embark on, but because of what Nick had said—that he believed our single would reach number one, that our album would debut in the top twenty. That the hype would keep it there. Because of Sienna and me. Because of the whirlwind of gossip surrounding us and the public's weird obsession with us being a couple. It was already a shitshow, and it hadn't even truly started yet. *How can I possibly say no comment to that?*

It annoyed the hell out of me that our success was now tied to something so fake and meaningless. And it really pissed me off that Nick didn't want me to refute it, didn't want me to tell the truth—that Sienna was just a collaborator on a song, that I was very happily married, that everything being tossed around out there was wrong. And he'd brought in a fucking handler, just to make sure I stuck to the script. Asshole. That right there made me want to quit again, but I couldn't do that to the guys. Because Kiera was right. We were so close to having what we wanted, what we'd been working toward for so long, what the guys deserved. I didn't want to be the reason we failed. I also didn't want to be the label's puppet.

I had no idea what I was going to say during the interview.

Matt and Evan looked at me as I sat in the third row with Kiera. Awe was clear on their faces. "Do you think he's right?" Matt asked me. "Do you really think we'll debut that high?"

I gave him a half-hearted shrug since I wasn't in the mood to celebrate. "I don't know, maybe." As I turned to look out the window, retreating from the conversation, I heard Griffin exclaim something about being number one, and Matt and Evan shifted back around to talk to him. Good. I couldn't fake excitement right now. My mind was spinning, doubt and guilt churning inside me like a turbulent sea, battering my positivity. With a sigh, I rested my head against the glass to stop my thoughts; it didn't help.

I felt Kiera resting her chin on my shoulder. She was oozing concern and sympathy. She knew I wasn't excited about this, knew I was still stressing about that damn music video. If she only knew the details of the dream I'd had last night, she might reconsider supporting this whole thing. But telling her would only make her worry, and I didn't want to do that. I just wanted all of this shit to go away.

"Hey, you all right?" Kiera asked.

No. Not really. Lifting my head, I watched my friends animatedly talking, watched their giddiness as they speculated about our success. It made me feel even worse. *I should be a part of their buzz.* "I just...I wish I could be as excited about this as they are." Guilt flooded my stomach as I looked over at her. "I feel like I'm letting them down because I'm not enjoying this."

She clasped my hand with both of hers. "It's different for you than it is for them. The label is asking you to do uncomfortable things. They understand. Well, Matt and Evan understand." She gave me an amused smile, trying to cheer me up.

It did, minutely. And she was right. Matt and Evan had both approached me about the video, both of them awkward and uncomfortable as they'd thanked me for going along with it, even though I hated it. Between then and now, they'd both apologized about five thousand times. Griffin had tried to high five me again. I'd shoved him into the pool since decking him had seemed a little over the top.

With a frown, I leaned down and told Kiera, "It's just so... fabricated. I don't see why there has to be all this hoopla-crap about some sordid imaginary romance. I just wish that the record and the music were enough to stand on their own. If we're going to make it, I want it to be because we're good, not because people are enamored with...my personal life." Because that fascination still made no sense to me. Why people even cared if Sienna was dating *me* was a mystery I'd never understand. *I'm not that special.*

Kiera studied me for a moment, then said, "And it *will* be about the music, Kellan. The high debut may be because of your celebrity status, but the album will stay there because you guys are amazing—one of the best bands I've ever heard."

That comment finally filled me with genuine amusement, and I cocked an eyebrow at her. "One of?" I teased. She rolled her eyes at me as I contemplated her words. I hoped she was right, hoped our talent would be the reason we succeeded long term, but I supposed Nick was also right, and the hype—no matter how ridiculous—*would* help us stand out in a crowded industry. My eyes drifted to the guys. I owed them the best start possible. "They've stood by me through so much. They were my family when I had...nobody. Literally nobody. And when I left everything in Los Angeles to move back to Seattle, they gave up everything we had down there to follow me, to stand by my side." I ran a hand down my face as my decision settled around me. "I owe them so much. We would have gotten signed ages ago if we'd stayed in L.A. I took this life from them once. I won't do it again."

With a sigh, I looked up at her. There was love in her warm, green-swirled eyes and no judgement. Feeling both lighter and heavier, I told her I owed them the chance to make it big, told her Nick was right about the competition, told her the guys didn't have as much to fall back on as me. "It's this or nothing for them, so..."

She gave me a small smile. "So...no comment?"

Feeling like my heart was cracking, I gave her a nod. "I don't want you to be offended or worried or hurt. And I'm not having an affair or even interested in having an affair. If all I have to do to make a...splash...is film a video and keep my mouth shut during interviews, then I owe them that much."

Kiera inhaled a deep breath. Her eyes flicked between mine

for a moment, and I wished I knew what she was thinking. Then finally, she said, "I understand, and it's okay."

A burst of shock went through me. I knew she was doing her best to be supportive, but I thought she might be a little upset. Maybe even hurt. "It is? If someone asks me if I'm married to Sienna, and I say nothing, that's okay?"

Resignation on her face, she shook her head and said, "Being a celebrity isn't as simple as it once was. It used to be that you had a talent, people liked it, and you excelled accordingly. Now it's almost more about being adept at traversing the social waters. You need talent *and* the ability to sway the public. Nick is good at the manipulation part, and you're really good at the talent part. You let him do his thing, you do your thing, and I'm sure everything will work out fine."

Her reasoned logic made me feel a lot better, and I gave her a bright grin as I teased her. "I can't tell if you're wise...or still naïve."

She lifted her chin with an adorable expression of cockiness on her face. "I'm gonna say wise." As I laughed at her comment, Kiera suddenly looked concerned. "Oh...will we still be able to get married? With a ceremony and everything? Because my mother will have an aneurism if I try to back out of it."

I kissed her cheek to soothe her worries. "We're still getting married, Kiera." Nick would have to lock me up somewhere to stop *that* from happening. "He only told me not to say anything to the public." I cupped her cheek, holding her close. "And I plan on saying 'I do' just to you." Grinning, I added, "And a few hundred friends and family."

Kiera groaned in a marvelous way. "Oh God," she murmured, looking a little pale.

Stifling a laugh, I poked her in the ribs. "You'll be fine. If I can do all this, then surely you can manage pledging your undying love, devotion, and fealty to me in front of a small crowd."

She snorted, amused by my word choice. "Fealty?"

"What? Isn't that one of the vows?" She certainly had my fealty. My heart. My soul. My everything.

When we got to the radio station, there was a surprising number of people waiting around outside. It was pretty early, and no one knew who we were...so why were they here? Evan asked if they were here for us, but no one knew. The crowd screamed when our car came to a stop. I looked over at Kiera, but she seemed just as confused as I was. I stepped out of the car, and the shrieking intensified. I wondered if they recognized me from the photo, or if they were just yelling because they thought I was a celebrity. Either way, it was weird.

I reached out my palm to Kiera, fully intent on holding her hand as we entered the building, but Tory grabbed my forearm and yanked me forward. I was about to pull away from her when the doors to the radio station opened and Sienna walked out. I hadn't realized she was going to be here, but the size of the crowd suddenly made sense.

Sienna ignored everyone but me as she floated our way. She was beaming at me with an odd expression on her face, like she'd been missing me and thinking about me the entire time we'd been apart. I was fairly certain that wasn't the case. Kiera had confessed that she'd called Sienna about the music video, but *I* hadn't heard from her since the day I'd asked her to say something about the photo.

She looped her arms around my neck once she got in front of me, then kissed each one of my cheeks. I wasn't sure what the hell was going on, but her greeting seemed like a lot more than a friendly custom this time. I was about to step away from her over-the-top affection when she gave me a sly smile and placed a soft kiss on my mouth.

My hands were instantly on her shoulders, pushing her away from me, but it was too late. The crowd watching was tittering, and I was sure every single one of them had just captured the kiss. Great. Fury was running through my veins as Sienna grabbed my arm and pulled me into the building. I was tired of getting jerked around, and I ripped my arm free once we were in the lobby.

"What was that?" I snapped.

She patted my cheek like I was a puppy she was rewarding. "That, love, was marketing."

My eyes narrowed as I scowled at her. I'd agreed not to say anything to dispute the rumors, but I'd never agreed to actively engage in a fake public relationship. Nick and Sienna could both go to hell if that was what they expected from me.

Sienna took in my expression with a small frown, like she was disappointed I was upset. "Relax. It's a harmless photograph to titillate the masses."

Reining in my anger, I told her, "Not on the lips. They belong to my wife."

Her lips twisted into a smirk that seemed to say she thought I was naïve. "Fine. How's your voice? Ready to do an acoustic set to kick off our single?"

I kept my expression neutral, but I was pretty surprised by her comment. From what we'd been told, the radio station was going to play the recorded version of our single with Sienna, then we were going to perform a song from our album. Clearly, Sienna wanted to be more involved with the release. Matt was going to flip.

Before I could say anything, Sienna and her bodyguards swept me away. I looked back at Kiera, and she gave me an encouraging smile and a small nod, telling me it was fine to go on without her. It didn't feel fine, but between Sienna and her muscle, I was kind of stuck.

We were shepherded into the room with the DJs, introduced to everyone, and given seats and headsets while our stuff was set up, and the entire time, my stomach was clenched with an anxiety that bordered on nervousness. Not for performing, not for talking to the DJs. No, all my nerves were centered around the *one* question I dreaded anyone asking me. The one question I was praying never came up. And so of course, because fate still liked fucking with me, it was one of the first questions they asked.

"So, Sienna, Kellan, rumor has it the two of you are an item?"

I felt my stomach sinking to the floor as the female DJ smiled at us. *Why do you care?* I wanted to ask. *No, never*, I wanted to tell her. Instead, I said nothing, did nothing, except clench my jaw and share a look with Sienna, silently begging her to deny it since I couldn't.

Sienna's expression was warm and worry-free as she shrugged and said, "Well, he is quite...edible." She looked back at the DJ with a knowing grin. "I would have to be an idiot to pass him up, right?"

I wanted to roll my eyes, wanted to deny it, wanted to snap at Sienna for not just saying *no comment* like we'd been told. Because what she just said and did—the look on her face, the innuendo in her voice, not to mention the kiss downstairs—it practically shouted that we were sleeping together.

The DJ still pressed her for a definitive answer, though, which of course, Sienna didn't give her. So naturally, the DJ turned to me for help. "So, come on, give me the scoop, Kellan. What's going on with you and Sienna?"

Nothing. Nothing at all.

I wanted to run, wanted to be anywhere but in that room, all eyes on me, all ears on me. This wasn't what I signed up for. This wasn't how it was supposed to go down. It was just supposed to be about the music. I scratched my head, desperately trying to think of a way out of this question that wouldn't make it sound even worse. I was coming up empty. Tory was watching me like a hawk, Matt and Evan were watching me with sympathy on their faces, the DJs were leaning in, waiting for breaking news to happen in their studio, and Kiera was sitting in the corner, watching me with sad encouragement on her face. Hating myself, I gave the rumor-boulder a good, hard shove.

"Ah...our single is out today...the album drops in September."

The DJs laughed, knowing looks on their faces. Tory relaxed, seeing that I was playing along. Evan discreetly touched my arm in silent apology. And Kiera...just looking her way made me sick to my stomach. She was still smiling at me, love on her face, but I felt horrid, like I'd betrayed her, betrayed *us*, and I vowed that I would set the record straight someday. When this was all over, when the hype wasn't needed because people knew us and loved us for our *talent*, then I would tell them exactly who had my heart. Who'd always had my heart.

The interview went on for a few more minutes, the DJs asking the other guys various questions, and I found it mildly interesting that none of them had restrictions on talking about their personal lives. Just me. I could tell Matt wanted to vanish and was probably reconsidering why he hadn't agreed with me about going home. Evan was calm and relaxed. Griffin looked like he wanted to stay here all day, telling everyone listening every little detail about his entire fucking life. Luckily, the DJs stopped him before too long. Once the questions were finished, we set up to play the single.

Matt was eying Sienna with a frown on his face as he grabbed his guitar. "You all right?" I quietly asked as I slipped behind him.

He frowned at me but nodded. "Yeah, just wish we'd had a heads-up about the song change," he muttered.

I clapped his shoulder. "Don't stress. We could pour a fifth of Jack down you, spin you around in a dozen circles, then randomly pull one of our songs out of a hat, and you'd nail it."

He smirked at me. "I highly doubt that, but thanks."

Griffin was suddenly there, leaning in between us. "What are we making Matt do? I heard fifth of Jack. We making him do this drunk?"

He looked way too excited about that prospect. Matt and I answered at the same time. "No."

Instead of looking dismayed, he grinned. "Yeah...okay."

Still grinning, he stepped away from us. Matt's eyes were wide when he looked at me. "*That* worries me way more than changing the song."

With a laugh, I left him to go stand behind my microphone. The song started, and I instantly fell into performance mode. It didn't matter that the audience was largely invisible to me, I felt their presence, even with the massive distance between us, and I fed off it. I fed off Sienna's energy too. She was as much of a performer as me, and by the end of the song, I was having fun, playing off her response to me, pretending like we hated each other. *Now this part isn't so bad.*

Kiera was grinning ear to ear when the song ended, and I knew she'd loved it. That meant even more to me than the stream of positive feedback the DJs were getting from listeners, and that was pretty damn awesome. I was both thrilled and relieved that people had enjoyed it, and despite everything, I was riding an exquisite high when we left the studio.

I kidnapped Kiera near the elevators, ducking her into a car and hitting the *close door* button before anyone could follow us. Tory scowled at me through the narrowing crack while Sienna frowned like she'd expected me to wait for her. I waved at them, then turned to the only person I wanted to be around right now.

Kiera was beaming at me, but even still, I couldn't help but ask what she thought. "How was it?"

Her face incredulous, she shook her head and tossed her arms around my neck. "Amazing! Perfect! Wonderful! I could go on and on."

Hearing her praise made me feel lighter than air. It amplified the adrenaline in my stomach, heightened every sensation, and instantly reminded me that privacy was going to be a scarce luxury for us on this tour; I wanted to take full advantage of our current isolation. "Maybe later," I murmured, pushing her back against the elevator wall. Her lips parted as she angled her head for me. I was almost to her mouth when I suddenly remembered something...distressing.

I frowned as I minutely pulled back. "Sienna kissed me...I feel like I should bleach my lips before I kiss you."

She smirked at me before grabbing my head and pulling me toward her. "I think I'll live," she whispered before we touched.

Her soft lips moved over mine so enticingly that I forgot all about Sienna kissing me. Kiera's hands tangled in my hair while mine slipped under her shirt to slowly stroke the ridge of her lower back. I could have stayed in here all day with her, our mouths moving together, our hands exploring each other, but sadly, the elevator reached the lobby, and the doors opened.

Seeing the lobby reminded me where we were and what I'd done. My lie of omission. An approved lie, but still...it ate at me. I felt ill, especially when I thought about what so many others were currently thinking about, the sordid rumor I'd let fester. Stepping back, I grabbed Kiera's hand and told her, "I'm sorry."

Kiera let out a deep laugh, her cheeks glowing with color. "You don't ever have to be sorry for that."

Her comment made me smile, but it quickly fell off me as I led her out of the elevator. "No, for earlier, in the interview... when I didn't say anything about you." Stopping us a few feet away, I sighed and faced her. "I really wanted to."

She instantly cupped my cheeks. Her face almost stern, she said, "Don't do that. Don't turn this moment into something you feel guilty about. I told you that I understand, and I meant it." Love in her eyes, Kiera told me I had to do what I had to do right now, then she reminded me that the listeners had loved the song, and once the album was released, she believed that I could say whatever I wanted because the fans would love *me*, not me and Sienna. Kiera's eyes glistened with tears as she held my gaze. "You just gave an acoustic performance at one of the biggest radio stations in the city. Your single is going to be all over the airwaves soon. I am so incredibly proud of you right now."

As I looked at her, all the lingering guilt vanished, replaced by the almost overwhelming warmth of her love for me. She was so damn amazing, and for the millionth time, I wondered how she'd wound up mine.

For a moment, I was stunned silent, then there was only one thing I wanted to say. "Will you marry me?" I whispered. Kiera laughed at my frequent question. Before she could answer me, Tory caught up to us and spoiled the moment.

She roughly stepped between us. "We have a plane to catch and more interviews to give, so there is no time for dawdling. You have eight minutes to spend with your fans outside."

I met eyes with Kiera over Tory's shoulder. Amusement on her face, Kiera mouthed, *Eight minutes?* I tried really hard not to laugh as Tory sternly pointed at the doors.

The crowd outside went nuts when they spotted the four of us again. They'd been listening to the radio station and had heard the single, and from their reaction, it was clear they'd loved it. "Kellan! Will you take a picture with us! Will you sign this!"

That sentiment was screamed at me from a dozen different places. With a laugh, I told the girls closest to me, "How about you guys first? Would you like me to sign something?"

They instantly shoved things in my face. I signed as much as I could, chatted with them for as long as I could, took as many pictures with them as I could. Even though they were new fans, I felt like I owed them more than eight minutes, but eight minutes was all I had. Tory let me know the time was up by snapping her fingers and barking at me to wrap it up. I had to say, I wasn't really a fan of that type of communication. I signed a few more things for fans, possibly out of spite.

A limo pulled up to the curb just as Sienna finally emerged from the building. She gave the fans a few moments of her time, then approached me. I was signing a piece of paper for a girl who looked kind of young to be here without parental supervision. She was staring at Sienna and me with wide, impressionable eyes. Cognizant of dozens of people staring at me, I stayed as neutral as possible. Sienna kissed my cheek, lingering a lot longer than I was comfortable with. As I moved to pull away, she retreated, telling me, and the listening crowd, "See you later." There was unmistakable heat in her voice, and the girls around me tittered.

Giving Sienna a stiff nod, I looked back at Kiera. She shrugged at me, and I knew what she meant by it. *Could have been worse.* I sighed, smiled at the fans in front of me, then told them I had to go. They all "awwed" like they were heartbroken. Grinning, I turned away, but then stopped when I noticed something. A girl nearby looked disheartened as she clutched a small bouquet of pink roses.

"Are you all right?" I asked her.

Her eyes went wide. "Yeah, I just...I brought these for Sienna, but she ran off so fast, I couldn't give them to her." Her expression brightened. "Could you give them to her?"

My smile turned tight. "I don't know when I'll see her again. But...could I have *one* petal?"

She looked confused by that but plucked one off for me. My grin grew as I took it. "Thank you." I twisted to leave, and all the girls screamed again.

Matt was nearby, hanging back, done with his part. Making sure Kiera wasn't watching, I sidled up to him. "Still have that Sharpie in your pocket?" I asked.

He rolled his eyes, then handed it to me, and I quickly wrote *Forever Yours* on the petal. Evan came up beside me before I was done. He snorted, and I glanced at him. Smirking, he shook his head and murmured, "Hallmark movie."

With a grin, I gave Matt back his Sharpie. "You say that like it's a bad thing. Trust me, it's not." I clapped him on the shoulder, then hurried to get into the waiting car so I could give the rose petal to my very understanding wife.

Chapter 13

PRETENDING

I had no idea what day it was, where we were, or where we were going, and I was a little fuzzy on where we'd been. I was just a dog on a leash being led from place to place, being told where to sit, where to stand, and what to say. It was exhausting on a level I'd never known before; it made the six-month tour with Justin seem like a leisurely vacation on a tropical island. God, that sounded nice. Maybe that was what Kiera and I would do for our honeymoon. When we got a chance to take one.

"Where are we going next, Matt?"

Matt had dark circles under his pale eyes; he looked just as wiped as me. He gave me a frown like he felt I should already know the answer to that. After a moment, he finally said, "Back to L.A."

That made me pause in the hallway of the hotel we were crashing in for the night. "Why are we going back to L.A? I thought we weren't going back until..." My voice trailed off as realization slammed into me. "Right...the video." I'd been so busy that I'd managed to completely block it from my mind.

Matt gave me a small, sympathetic nod. "Yeah, the video. Sorry." He cringed as he looked over at Kiera. She was a zombie walking beside me, but she managed to look up at hearing that. Her eyes were sad but accepting. I hated it.

"Maybe it's not too late," I said, trying to sound encouraging. "Maybe I can change their minds about the direction of the video. Maybe it can just be the four of us and her singing or something."

She gave me a tired smile. "You really think Nick will accept a video of you and Sienna just singing together?" Clenching my arm, she shook her head. "It's a nice delusion, but you know that's all it is. He wants...spice."

She let out a weary sigh, and my eyes drifted to the floor. "Yeah," I muttered. "I know."

Matt put his hand on my shoulder. "I know I've said this before, but I'm sorry, man. I'd do it for you if I could." I cocked an eyebrow at him, and he bit his lip. "Okay, yeah, I wouldn't. I don't think I physically could without throwing up...but I would definitely make Griffin do it if I could."

He gave me a slight smile, and I laughed. "I know you would. It will be fine." *It has to be.*

Matt nodded, then left Kiera and me alone in the hallway. Kiera sighed again, leaning her weight against me. "I could sleep for a month straight." Pausing, she looked up at me. "And at the same time, I don't think I'll be able to sleep at all."

I gave her a tight smile. "I know exactly what you mean." Now that I knew what was coming, dread was eating a hole in my stomach.

Kiera studied my face for a moment, then pulled on my arm. "Come on, let's try to get some sleep. We need it."

Nodding, I followed her to our hotel room. Kiera and I didn't have a lot of alone time on this chaotic tour. During the day, something always seemed to keep us apart, and whenever we did find a few minutes to ourselves, Tory was instantly there, either calling me away for something or being a really annoying third wheel. Kiera thought she'd been ordered by Nick to chaperone us, so no one would see something that might pop the rumor I'd helped inflate, and it seemed to be working. Every single interview started out with questions about my relationship with Sienna. It had pissed me off at first, but Kiera was helping me see the humor in it, and we usually ended the day with a good laugh.

Nighttime was when we really got to see each other since we always wound up in the same hotel room, although even that was something we had to force to happen. Tory always had Kiera assigned with her, but Kiera always ignored her and came with me to my room. Well, mine and Evan's; we were paired together most nights. It was a little crowded, sharing a small hotel room with three people, but Evan occasionally headed over to Matt and Griffin's room so we could have some privacy. That was not the case tonight, and he was already snoring when we opened the door. Kiera and I looked at each other, smiled, then walked inside to try to find oblivion like our roommate.

I didn't feel rested in the morning. Probably because I didn't ever fully fall asleep. Kiera either. She'd sighed and shifted about fifty thousand times. And she'd reached for me each time, running her thumb back and forth over my skin like she'd been trying to soothe me. Or more accurately, soothe herself.

When we got back to the label's house, the guys fell onto the living room couch with loud groans of exhaustion. "I. Feel. Dead," Griffin proclaimed, his eyes closed as he sprawled out. "Someone wake me when it's time to be awesome." Matt grunted something that sounded like an agreement, but his eyes were closed too. So were Evan's.

Kiera had a fond look on her face as she smiled at them. "At least we're getting a few days to rest," she said, shifting her gaze to me.

I nodded at her, then pulled her to our room. We dropped our bags to the ground when we got inside, and Kiera let out a joyful noise as she crawled onto the bed and snuggled into the pillows. I watched her for a moment before closing the door. The air felt thicker once we were sealed inside, alone, and I wasn't sure why. No, I knew why. Guilt. All I felt was an insane amount of guilt, and I hadn't even done anything yet.

With a sigh, I reached into my pocket and pulled out a rose petal. I'd found this one by happenstance at the airport, and I'd borrowed Matt's Sharpie on the plane ride over. My heart was heavy as I walked to the bed. Kiera softly smiled up at me. I tried to smile back as I handed her the petal, but I wasn't sure if I succeeded. Her expression brightened as she took it, though. She always got that look on her face whenever I handed her a note or a petal, like what I was doing was miraculous to her, more meaningful than simply saying the words. It made me want to leave notes for her everywhere again, but this note...this one wasn't sweet. Wasn't romantic. Wasn't anything but painful.

Kiera's smile fell as she read what I wrote. She frowned when she looked up at me. "You're sorry? Why are you sorry?"

I sat on the bed with a sigh, my head down. "You know why, Kiera." Everything about me felt weighted when I looked up at her, and for the millionth time, my nightmare version of her superseded the real-life version. Would she sob like that while she watched me? Would she hate me? How could she *not* hate me? *I'm going to ruin us.* My eyes burned as I stared at her. "I'm so sorry. For everything that might happen tomorrow, I'm just so—"

She instantly sat up and flung her arms around my neck. "Don't. Just stop. You don't need to feel guilty. You don't need to worry." She swallowed, then swallowed again. And again. "We'll be fine. Just fine." I shook my head, and she tenderly cupped my cheek. "Yes," she softly said.

My brows bunched in confusion. "Yes...what?"

Her eyes shimmered as she smiled. "Yes, I'll marry you. You slipped me a petal a while ago with the words *Marry Me* on it, and I never got a chance to answer you."

A small laugh escaped me, and it severely lightened the load on my chest. "Oh good, I've been stewing over that. Way to keep me in suspense...Mrs. Kyle."

She giggled, then pulled me down on the bed with her. "I think passing notes with you might be my favorite part of the tour." She sighed as she wrapped her legs around mine. "No, it was hearing your song on the radio for the first time. That was something I'll never forget."

I smiled as I wrapped my arms around her. That was a moment I would never forget either. We'd just finished an interview and had been half-dead in the car when we'd faintly heard our song playing. The driver had turned it up for us, and we'd all instantly freaked out. Everyone had called their loved ones, and me...I'd called Gavin. I hadn't even thought about it, I'd just done it. Gavin hadn't heard it yet, and his excitement had matched mine. And then he'd said...he'd said he was proud of me. A fact that still left me with this weird feeling of peace. I'd never realized just how much I'd wanted to hear those words from my family until that very moment.

"We're really doing it, aren't we?" I murmured, feeling sleep pulling me under.

Kiera snuggled into my side, and I felt her nodding. "You are. And we're going to be okay, Kellan. We'll get through this, and we'll...we'll be fine."

I held her tighter and prayed she was right, but I heard the slight desperation in her voice, the wistful hope, and I could feel a lingering sadness in the air. Neither one of us wanted tomorrow to come, but there was nothing we could do to stop it.

My dreams that night weren't pleasant, and I kept waking up in a panic, desperate to disengage from the nightmare. Sometime in the night, though, my body simply gave up on me, and I slipped into an exhausted, dreamless slumber. I was roused from it by the feeling of lips on my neck, and for a horrifying split-second, I wasn't sure who was kissing me. Then I sensed Kiera, smelled Kiera, heard her specific sighs, and I relaxed.

My hand touched her back, and she instantly crawled on top of me. Breath faster, she found my lips. "Kellan," she murmured, her hips grinding against me. My cock was more awake than I was, and it instantly hardened in response to her. Kiera groaned as she rubbed against me, her kiss desperate and needy.

It didn't take long for my breath to match hers, for my heart to pound, for my body to surge with frantic, restless energy. I was nearly panting as I pulled off her clothes, and she was gasping for breath as she tugged on mine. But even with the heat sizzling between us, there was an awareness, a disheartening reason behind the sudden fire. Every kiss, every touch...it felt like we were saying goodbye. It squeezed my chest just as much as it made me hunger. Painful euphoria.

We held each other for a long time afterward, until a timid knock on the door signaled it was time to get ready, time to go. That knock echoed in the stillness of the room, lingered long after the person who'd made it had left. Finally, with a heavy sigh, Kiera and I got out of bed, and it was really hard not to feel like I was leaving a piece of my marriage behind as I moved away from the rumpled sheets.

Evan gave me a look of concern when Kiera and I trudged into the living room. Not wanting to discuss my feelings, I minutely shook my head at him. His expression didn't change any, but he didn't ask me that dreaded question that I knew he wanted to ask: *How are you?*

Shitty. That's how I am.

My mood sank as we got into a waiting limousine, and it continued to decline the closer we got to the studio. Kiera helped me out of my funk when we arrived at the studios. She was looking around at all the massive buildings with uncontained wonder and joy on her face. Her response made me chuckle and laughing about something—*anything*—made me feel a little lighter. I tried to hold onto that feeling as we stopped at a building labeled B7.

Sienna was in the doorway of the building, waving at us. She looked like she was having the best day ever, and for a moment, I was envious of her happiness. But of course, today meant nothing to her. She wasn't risking anything by filming this video with me, while I was risking *everything* to film it with her.

When Sienna got close enough, she tossed her arms around my neck and gave me her standard greeting of a kiss on each cheek. "So good to see you all again," she said. Even though the words were directed at everyone, her gaze stayed on me. Already uncomfortable with this, I gave her a polite nod as I twisted out of her embrace and held out a hand for Kiera.

Kiera took my palm, her eyes briefly studying Sienna before shifting to me. As our eyes locked, Kiera's words from last night flashed through my brain: *We'll be fine, just fine.* I clung to that and prayed with everything inside of me that she was right.

Sienna attached herself to my elbow and started pulling us into the building. The inside of the studio was organized chaos, with people running around everywhere. I had no idea what everyone was doing, but they all seemed to understand their role here. I felt out of place around them, not because I didn't understand my part, but because I understood it all too well. And unlike them, I didn't want to be here.

Looking overjoyed that we were here, Sienna took all of us on a short tour of the place, showing us the two sets we'd be using—the stage set and the bedroom set. The stage set brought a smile to my face, but the bedroom set filled me with dread. The giant bed was garish under the lights, a blatant ode to sex. Its only adornment was a couple of pillows and a messy sheet that already looked like someone had been tangled up in it. Nerves assaulted me, and I squeezed Kiera's hand, both seeking comfort and trying to provide it. Kiera gave me a small smile, but she looked really pale and kind of queasy, like she might be sick at any moment. *Jesus. How can I do this to her?*

Sienna sat on the bed and giggled in a flirty way, like all of this was a joke, a joke she couldn't wait to partake in. I wanted to tell her that nothing about this was funny, but I wanted to reassure

Kiera more. I opened my mouth to tell Kiera for the millionth time how sorry I was, but before I could, Nick and another man stepped up to us.

Nick, dressed in his typical suit, grinned at Sienna and spread his arms wide. "Sienna, baby, you look fantastic."

Sienna jumped off the bed and gave him a kiss on the cheek. "As do you, Nicholas."

Nick wrapped an arm around Sienna, then turned to acknowledge me. "Good to see you, Kellan." His expression was smug, condescending, like he'd won something, like he thought I was foolish for ever believing this would turn out differently. That one look made me want to turn around and leave, but I couldn't give up now. So I supposed Nick's smugness was justified; he *had* won.

I gave him a slight nod in greeting since that was all I had in me. Nick ignored the resentment in my eyes and indicated the man beside him; he was tall, slim, with long, blond hair that was pulled back into a ponytail that damn near reached his ass. "Boys, this is Diedrich Kraus, visionary genius." He then went on to introduce all of us. Everyone except Kiera.

Before I could introduce her, Diedrich stuck out his hand to me. With a thick Scandinavian accent, he told me, "It is very excellent to meet you." Joy in his pale eyes, he clenched my hand with both of his. "The camera is going to love you! You and Miss Sexton are going to sizzle every piece of equipment in this place."

That one sentence killed any hope I had of getting Nick to change his mind about this video. It was clear from Diedrich's excitement and the dollar signs in Nick's eyes that nothing I had to say mattered. They wanted what they wanted.

A man with a clipboard approached our group, informing us that it was time to get ready. Sienna walked off with a wave. Griffin bounded away with a huge smile on his face. Matt and Evan were slower to leave, tossing me sympathetic smiles before heading out. I released a heavy sigh as I looked down at Kiera. She was staring up at me with a carefully crafted expression. One that was trying to radiate warmth and love and hope, and nothing else. I drank it in for a moment, wishing I wasn't speeding toward a brick wall. But that was exactly what it felt like. I was in an out-of-control vehicle, with no way to halt it or redirect its course, and I was rapidly approaching a dead end.

I leaned down to kiss Kiera's cheek. "I'll be back in a minute," I told her, pausing to breathe in the scent of her floral shampoo.

Then I left before I was too tempted to grab her hand and run away with her.

By the time I reached wardrobe, I was feeling extremely... pissy; everything and everyone was irritating me. It got especially bad when I received my "outfit."

Looking bored, the guy helping us casually said, "Put these on, then go to hair and makeup."

I couldn't stop stupidly staring at the package he'd just handed me. A pair of black boxer briefs. That was my wardrobe. Underwear. I supposed I should be grateful they were new. But I wasn't. "This is it? This is all I get to wear?" I knew it was a dumb question, but I was in the mood to argue.

The guy blankly looked at me for a moment, then pointed. "There are robes in the dressing room. You can take one of those too." From his tone of voice, it was clear he wanted to roll his eyes, but he was refraining, since he was a professional and all. Good thing. Because I was pretty sure I'd slug him if he did. My hand was even curling into a fist.

Evan grabbed my shoulder. "Come on, Kell. Let's go change."

I relaxed a little as I looked over at him. His eyes were begging me not to start something. Since I really didn't have a reason to be angry at the random guy assigned to hand us our clothes, I nodded and let Evan lead me to the changing rooms.

Griffin was bouncing around like a toddler when we got there. His energy wasn't doing anything to improve my mood. "Just change already," I snapped.

He frowned as he looked me over. "What crawled up your ass and died?"

I narrowed my eyes at him. Before I could say anything, Matt grabbed his shoulder and whispered something in his ear. Griffin sniffed at me but kept his mouth shut. Matt gave me a tight smile, then the three of them started changing into their normal, nice, rock star clothes. I was done long before they were since all I had to do was strip and change my underwear. As I stood there in my tight, foreign clothes, I started fuming.

"This is so fucking stupid. Why the fuck do I have to look like this, while you guys get to look like that? Who the fuck cares if the song is about a 'fiery romance?' Doesn't mean we have to act it out. I mean, fuck, one of our songs is about a guy overdosing. Are we gonna act that out too? Should we start doing drugs now to prepare?"

Matt and Evan looked down but didn't say anything. Griffin snorted. "Dude, if it's pot, count me in."

"Fuck off, Griffin."

Griffin scowled at me as he pulled on his shirt. "You fuck off. All you have to do is make out with her." He raised an eyebrow. "And I forgive you for that because *I* am a team player. And I get to watch." He grinned at me in a way that made me want to injure him. Just a little.

Matt shook his head as he pulled on a jacket. "No, you don't. They're filming our scenes at the same time."

Griffin's jaw dropped, and he finally looked as upset as I felt. "What? Why the fuck would they do that? The whole point of this video shoot is to watch Sienna Sexton roll around naked. If we don't get to do that, then Kell's right...this is stupid."

Matt snuck a cautious look at me before smirking at Griffin. "You'll just have to watch the finished product, like everyone else."

"Well, that fucking sucks," Griffin muttered.

Yes. Yes, it does. It all does.

Because I didn't want to get into it with him, I didn't say it.

Instead, I picked at the bottom of my too tight boxer briefs. "What sucks is this underwear."

Griffin shrugged. "Just take 'em off."

"Shouldn't you be getting to hair and makeup so they can do something with that?" I indicated his face with my fingers.

He smiled at me. "I don't see how they can possibly make me look any better, but I guess so." He looked over at Matt. "You ready, cuz?"

Matt nodded, and the two of them left the room. As they went, I heard Griffin say, "Are you sure they're filming us at the same time?"

I rolled my eyes, then turned back to the mirror and frowned at my reflection. Evan came up to me with a fluffy, white robe in his hand. As he offered it to me, he said, "You should probably leave your ring here."

With a sigh, I looked at my fingers as I took the robe. "Yeah, I suppose they won't let me keep it on, huh?"

He gave me a sympathetic smile in answer. Feeling heaviness settle over me, I popped off my wedding ring then stuffed it into the front pocket of my discarded jeans. Wrapping the robe around me, I looked out the door, to where the future I dreaded was waiting for me. "I don't want to do this," I told Evan.

He sighed, then put a hand on my shoulder. "I know. And I'm sorry. And if you need me to, I'll talk to Kiera. Every day if I have to. If she's not okay with this, I won't let up until she is."

Fire burned in my chest; it felt like a bomb was exploding. *If she's not okay with this? Jesus...what if she isn't? What if I'm setting a match to my marriage? What if we're never the same after today?* I looked over at Evan, pure panic on my face. His eyes widened as he studied my pained expression. "But she's going to be fine, Kellan. She knows what to expect, she knows how you feel about it, she knows how you feel about *her*. It will be fine. Okay?"

Swallowing the lump in my throat, I nodded. "Yeah..." *That's what I keep hearing.*

I went to hair and makeup with a heavy heart. They didn't do much with my hair, probably because Sienna was just going to fuck it up anyway. Makeup was more intensive. Voice courteous, my artist said, "Please disrobe so I can check your body for flaws."

Sighing, I shrugged the robe off my shoulders and set it on the nearby chair. The woman's eyes widened when she looked up from her assortment of supplies. "Okay, um, not much to do here." She took a walk around me, inspecting me. "I'll touch up that small scar along your ribs, but honestly, it's barely notice-able." Continuing around, she stopped at my chest and pointed at my tattoo. "Really, all you need is that covered, and you're good."

"Excuse me?" I said with a frown.

She indicated my chest. "The tattoo. It will have to be covered." She paused to point at a clipboard on her table. "You're supposed to be in a relationship with Sienna for the video. So either the 'Kiera' tattoo goes completely, or I have to change it to say Sienna. Your choice."

"Lucky me that I have a choice," I muttered. She frowned at me, and I sighed. "Cover it." The last thing in the world I would do was walk in there with Sienna's name on my chest.

Covering it took longer than I thought it would, and that made me happy. Kiera's name should be difficult to remove. Once the makeup artist was done with me, and my chest was pris-tine again, I felt oddly naked. I hated the tattoo's absence almost as much as what I was about to do.

Grabbing my robe, I slipped it on and sulked my way to the set.

Sienna was already on the bed when I got there. She was sitting up on her elbows, her dark hair spilling over her shoulders. Her outfit for today was a skimpy, overly erotic bra and under-wear set that didn't leave much to the imagination. I hated seeing her like that, hated the fact that I had to get in bed with her, and I wished with all my might that Kiera could somehow take her place. Or that we could all just go home. Yes, I would give anything to go home right now.

I knew I needed to get into that bed with her, but I couldn't move. Sienna frowned as she studied me, then she patted the bed in invitation. That just made me feel sick. Thankfully, Diedrich approached me, and I turned my attention to him. "All right, we're going to start out slowly, let you two get comfortable with each other. Then when you're ready, I want you to make it as fiery as you can. You want this woman, you can't wait to have her, you're going to explode if you don't get her...got it?"

No. Because I don't feel any of that for her.

I nodded, because what else could I do, then I removed my robe and handed it to a crew member. I could feel eyes on me, Sienna's included, but there was only one set of eyes that I cared about. Looking around the place, I searched for Kiera. She was halfway across the room, intently staring at me. She looked paler than normal, but maybe I was imagining that. I tried to smile for her, but it came out weak, pained.

Kiera inhaled a deep breath and gave me a reassuring nod as she stepped closer. I wanted to ask her to leave, wanted to get down on my knees and beg her to go, but I understood what she meant about making it worse in her head if she didn't see it. I didn't want her imagination to be the thing that tore us apart. *So how do I make reality tepid? How do I make out with Sienna, sell it for the audience, but downplay it for Kiera?* I had no idea.

I was stewing over that when I finally laid out on the bed beside Sienna. She was instantly all over me, her leg over mine, her arm over my stomach, her breasts pressed against me. The musky perfume she was wearing was strong, cloying, and I could practically feel it seeping into my skin, overpowering any lingering trace of Kiera on me. Something darkened inside my chest, and it took all my willpower not to shove her off me.

People around us started moving lights and panels; someone else adjusted the sheet so it just covered our hips. All the lights and people reminded me of my dream. And Kiera's face. And the pain I caused her. The pain I was going to cause her.

Stop. Just stop. Don't think. Relax.

But I couldn't. My mind was on a downward spiral, and there was nothing I could do to stop it. Sienna popped up on an elbow to look down at me, and I swallowed the nervous lump in my throat. My heart was racing, and I wondered if she could feel it. And if she could, I prayed she didn't misinterpret it as me wanting this.

Someone said, "Action," and icy panic flooded me. *I can't do this. I change my mind. I want to stop.* But Sienna was a professional, and she wasn't stopping. Her lips touched mine, and I wanted to turn away. Instead, I forced myself to kiss her back. *Don't think about the act, just think about the mechanics. You're not kissing her; you're just pursing your lips in time with hers. It's just another weird greeting, that's all.*

Sienna scowled at me, then climbed onto my stomach. My hands were rigidly locked to my sides; I couldn't move them if I wanted to. Sienna grinded against me like she was trying to turn me on. It was having the opposite effect, and I would have paid her good money to stop. She made an annoyed sound, then tried to shove her tongue into my mouth. I instinctually clenched my jaw and firmed my lips, sealing my mouth shut.

An irritated voice suddenly shouted, "Cut!" and I was flooded with relief. And guilt. And the undeniable sting of failure. *I actually* can't *do this.*

Sienna rolled off me, anger on her face. "He's not giving me anything to work with!" she snipped.

Her words struck me in a way that none of this had before. Whether Sienna was enjoying herself or not, she was here to do a job. Everyone here was just trying to do their job, and I was making it impossible. I was letting everyone down. Literally *everyone.* I'd always been good at my job before, sucking at it was a new feeling for me. One I didn't like. But the alternative...

Feeling stuck and lost and uncertain, I told her, "I'm sorry. I'm trying." *I'm failing, but I am trying. Aren't I?*

"Get with the program, Kellan!"

Nick shouted that at me, and there was true anger in his words. I hated every single feeling in my chest right now, and I searched for Kiera, for some help, for some guidance. I spotted her by the monitors. She still looked really pale, and her eyes were glossy, but she smiled at me, nodded, and mouthed, *It's okay.* I could tell it wasn't, but she was trying too.

With a sigh, I looked away from her. That was when I heard Diedrich say, "Remove the bra, sweetheart."

Wait. What? He's not serious...right? Isn't this supposed to be PG-13?

But from the corner of my eye, I could see Sienna shrug, could see her unclasp the tiny fabric. I immediately looked up and away so I wouldn't see any more. Kiera was barely handling what was happening, anything more might be the breaking point for her. And then what? Would she leave, storm out? Never speak to me again? I just wanted this hell to be over with. That was all I wanted. *Just let me be done already.*

Sienna climbed on top of me again, and I could feel her bare breasts pressing against my skin. *Jesus Christ, every second this just gets worse. Kiera is watching a nearly naked woman writhing around on my chest. There's no way she's okay with this. There's no way she's not hurting right now. Fuck, I'm hurting her right now. I can't do this. I just can't.*

Sienna squirmed against me, and I stared at the ceiling, exhaling a long, even breath as I resisted the urge to push her off me and run. *How do I stop this? How do I get through it so it's behind us already?*

Goddamn it. *What do I do? Kiera...what do I do?*

Crew members adjusted us into their desired positions. Someone made me put a hand on Sienna's ass. Then they took my other hand and put it on the low ridge of her back. Thoughts of Kiera flitted through my brain as I remembered the feel of my fingers on her spine. God, what I wouldn't give for it to be her body that I was touching. *Let my wife replace Sienna. Please.*

"Relax, love," Sienna whispered. "This is supposed to be fun."

For you, maybe. This is hell for me. Not feeling up for words, I just gave her a tight smile. Diedrich yelled action again, and Sienna immediately bent to kiss me. Still unwilling, I had to force myself to kiss her back. I knew if I didn't stop resisting, we would never get through this day, but I didn't know how to relax, didn't know how to seem like I enjoyed this. I wasn't enjoying this. I didn't want to fool around with Sienna. I didn't want to kiss her, didn't want to feel her body, didn't want to press against her, didn't want to act like she meant something to me. She didn't. The only person who meant something to me was currently getting her heart ripped out of her chest. Fuck. *I want to disappear.*

The lukewarm kissing lasted for a long time while I struggled with how to get through this, and then my finger unintentionally moved against the ridge of Sienna's back, and I was again flooded with thoughts of Kiera. And that was when I recalled something Kiera had told me when I'd first declined this shitshow. *Just pretend she's me.* I had zero interest in being with Sienna, but... could I turn her into Kiera? Just for today? Just to get through this? Fuck. I had to try, right? *This will never end if I don't try.*

I just want this to stop.

Kiera...I'm so sorry. Please forgive me.

Needing my imagination more than I'd ever needed it before, I inhaled a deep breath, squeezed my eyes shut, and made myself remember. *I love you. I love you...so much.* Kiera's voice saying those words wrapped around my mind, soothing me inside and out, and that vivid memory of our first time making love, my first time *ever* making love, swept through me. I allowed it to carry me away, used it to willfully escape the cold room I was in, and within seconds, I was mentally transported back to my warm bed.

My hands moved over Kiera's body, lingering on the indent

of her spine. My jaw relaxed, and my lips began working in tandem with hers. I pictured Kiera's hair, her smile, her eyes, her body...her soul. I felt her tongue in my mouth, and I welcomed it, stroking her with my own. She let out a soft, foreign noise, and I shifted it in my brain to match Kiera's erotic exhales.

Sensation started flaring to life inside me, but I stopped it cold. I was aware enough to know that my fake Kiera was just that —*fake*—and I refused to let her have a real reaction from me. I could act, I could pretend, I could control my body. I could ride that fine line between fantasy and reality, and not let myself fall. Because I had to...it was the only way I could look Kiera in the eye again.

Banishing that thought, I focused on my memory. Kiera sprawled on my bed, kissing her, touching her, loving her. Someone shouted directions on what to do, where to put my hands, where to kiss her. I integrated it into my fantasy so that the present wouldn't destroy me, imagined it was my internal voice I was hearing. *I love you, Kiera. You're my only.*

Eventually I had her on her back, and I was on top of her, thrusting into her. But not really. I slipped from my fantasy just long enough to make sure I was grinding a few inches below where she needed me to be. Sienna tried to scoot down so we would rub together, and in her ear, I growled, "No." She stopped after that, and I let the present fade away so I could retreat into my mind. With Kiera.

My breath quickened as I kissed my wife. Again my body wanted to respond, and again I let a sliver of reality enter my thoughts to beat it back. It was a difficult line to maintain, fantasizing about Kiera without desiring her, and it was sharp as a knife. I felt like I could slip at any moment, and that fall would kill me.

Diedrich finally yelled, "Cut," and I instantly rolled off Sienna. Reality battered me and guilt rose like a tidal wave. As much as I wanted to believe I was in bed with Kiera, I wasn't, and I was going to be sick. *How much does she hate me right now?* I could feel the tears stinging my eyes, could feel the bile rising in my throat. *Jesus. What did I just do?* I couldn't open my eyes to see if Kiera was still watching. I couldn't handle seeing the pain on her face. I just lay there with my eyes squeezed shut, trying not to break down.

And then Diedrich yelled, "Action," and my nightmare continued.

Chapter 14

NEVER AGAIN

What felt like years later, Diedrich finally had enough footage and released us. I wanted to feel relief that it was over, but all I felt was sick. I jumped off the bed, grabbed my robe, and practically ran from the room. I didn't even look to see if Kiera was still there. I knew she was. I could *feel* her. But I couldn't face her. Not yet.

Fuck, fuck, fuck. Flashes of what I'd just done leapt through my mind. My tongue running up Sienna's throat, smiling at her like I wanted her, all the grinding that must have looked like I was...

And Kiera watched it all.

Jesus, she watched it all.

I didn't make it to wardrobe. I came across a bathroom first, darted inside, and immediately threw up the small amount of food in my stomach.

When I finally made it to the dressing room, I felt like I'd run a marathon; I couldn't recall the last time I'd ever felt this exhausted. The room was empty, thankfully. I didn't think I could face the guys right now either. I stripped off those godforsaken boxer briefs and pulled on my own clothes. Reaching into the front pocket of my jeans, I grabbed my wedding ring. I had a hard time putting it back on my finger. Did it still belong there?

Feeling lightheaded, I slipped it on. Until Kiera demanded that I remove it...it wasn't leaving my finger again.

Still feeling like I was going to be sick, I headed outside. Once there, I dropped my head back and inhaled deep breaths. I could feel the grief welling in me, the desire to drop to the ground and sob. I held it inside. If by some miracle, Kiera was fine, I didn't want her to see me...broken.

The limo pulled up while I was deep breathing. The driver opened the door for me, and I instantly stepped inside. Time dripped forward, and every second made me feel worse and worse. Finally, the car door opened again, and my heart started thundering in my chest like I was running flat-out up a steep hill. I wasn't ready to face her, but at the same time, I needed to see her, needed to know she was okay.

Evan got in first. His face was...cautious as he studied me. "Hey, Kell," was all he said.

Matt was next. He just gave me a tight smile and then glanced outside. Fuck. Where Kiera was. I swallowed a thick lump in my throat.

Griffin got in next. He grinned at me like everything about today was awesome. "Hey, how was it?" he asked, wriggling his eyebrows. I ignored him and stared at the door, willing Kiera to come inside. *Don't run. At least give me a chance to beg at your feet before you run.*

It took a long time, but she finally climbed into the car. Her eyes were down, her hair was partially hiding her face, and she was curled inward like she was collapsing inside. *Oh my God...I did ruin us.* She took the empty space beside me, then instantly twisted her head to look out the window. My eyes burned as I stared at her cheek. *Look at me. Kiera, please...look at me.*

But she didn't. The entire car ride she studiously *didn't* look at me, and I felt the sting of that rejection all the way through my body. *She hates me. She fucking hates me. And I hate me too.*

The tension in the car rose with every mile. All conversations dried up until only thick silence remained. I could feel the guys staring at me as I relentlessly stared at Kiera, and Kiera ceaselessly stared out the window. I wanted to touch her, but I was terrified of her pulling away from me. I could see her reflection in the glass, could see the moisture in her eyes, could feel it building in my own. Griffin started to ask if we were fighting, but I heard one of the guys elbow him, and he shut up. *Yes. We are fighting. Because I destroyed her.*

We finally got back to the label's house, and Kiera fled the car the second the driver opened the door. I hopped out after her but stopped when I saw her running to the house. *Running* away from me. My jaw dropped as I saw our entire relationship dissolving. My breaths came in frantic pulls, and my vision wavered. Evan was suddenly in my face, his dark, concerned eyes studying me.

I felt hysteria coming over me as I stared at him. "You said she'd be fine. You *promised* me she'd be fine! She's not fine. She won't even look at me. What did I do? Jesus, what the fuck did I just do?"

Evan grabbed my shoulders and dug in, hard. "Stop. Stop it, Kellan. Stop spiraling and go talk to her."

I swallowed three times, nodding the whole while, and then I was rushing past him to chase after her.

My pace slowed as I trudged up the stairs to the second floor. I just couldn't handle this being the end of us, the end of everything. We'd gone through so much together, faced so much, grown so much. If she walked away from me now, I wasn't sure if there would be anything of me left.

When I got to the living room upstairs, all the bedroom doors were open except for Kiera's and mine. I stopped in front of it, my hand lifting to the knob, then falling in defeat. Everything could change after I opened this door.

I heard the guys walk into the room, heard Matt talking to Griffin about going down to the pool. I felt Evan behind me, but I was still just standing at the door, staring at the wood. He sighed, and I turned my head to look at him. "What if this is the end?" I whispered.

He shook his head. "I won't let it be, remember?" His frown deepened. "Not over this. Do you want me to talk to her first?" he asked, indicating the door.

Fuck. A part of me did. I wanted him to pave the way for me, take the blow, so to speak, but she was my wife...and I was the one who did this. I had to be the one to fix it.

Shaking my head, I made myself turn the knob and step inside.

The room was empty. I heard water coming from the bathroom as I carefully shut the door behind me. Heart pounding in my chest, I slowly walked that way. My eyes drifted to the bed as I passed by it; the tangled sheets, the remembered feel of Kiera's body wrapped around mine, it drove a hole right through me. Was that panicked, desperate act this morning the last time she'd love me?

Jesus. I can't do this.

I forced my hand to knock on the closed bathroom door, forced myself to begin the conversation that might end with goodbye. *I don't want to say goodbye.* "Kiera..." My voice was strained with barely contained grief. The water shut off in the bathroom, but the door didn't open. *She still won't talk to me. She must hate me so much.*

Knowing I was the cause of her pain was too much to bear. Knowing we wouldn't survive this was tearing me to pieces. "Kiera...please." My voice broke as I begged, then my body broke, and I couldn't stop the sob from escaping me. I sank my head into my hands and let the tears come. *Don't leave me. Please don't leave me. I'm so sorry.*

The despair wrapped around me tight, sinking its claws in deep. If she wouldn't even talk to me, then we were definitely over. The door finally opened, but I couldn't move, couldn't stop crying. Then, impossibly, I felt Kiera's arms wrap around me. Her comfort snapped the remainder of my sanity. Resting my head on her shoulder, I begged for us. "I'm sorry. I'm so sorry. Please don't hate me...please don't leave me."

The strangest words left her lips as she stroked my hair and shushed me. "It's okay...I'm not mad...it's okay."

The sympathy and empathy coming from her soothed the guilt-shattered remnants of my heart, but I knew she didn't mean it, I knew she was lying. I pulled back to look at her, my eyes burning from the emotional release. "How can you not be mad after what you saw? How can you not...hate me?" My voice cracked, and I could feel another sob rising.

Kiera grabbed my cheeks, holding me together with the intense look of love in her eyes. "Who were you kissing today?"

I didn't understand at first, and for a moment, I was horrified that she was going to make me say it—confess my sin even though she'd witnessed it—but then I understood what she was referencing, and I suddenly knew she was aware of what I'd done, of the fantasy I'd created for myself. A small, hopeful smile touched my lips. "You...I was kissing you. I was thinking about the first time we made love...after you told me that you loved me."

Kiera smiled and nodded, and the love in her eyes lightened the load on my chest. "I know. I could tell...and that's why I'm not mad. I know you were with me...and I love you so much."

Her words, her absolution, almost crumpled me to my knees. Kiera held my weight as I murmured, "God, thank you. I was so scared I'd just lost you. You wouldn't even look at me in the car..."

She cradled my head, rubbing her cheek against me. "I'm sorry. I just needed a minute. That was...intense."

No. It was wrong. A violation. One I would never allow to happen again.

Pulling back, I gave her my oath. "Never again. I don't care what's at stake. I don't care who I have to let down. I won't ever do that to you again. You...or me. I'm done playing their game."

Now Kiera sagged against me, relief clear in her body

language. I leaned down to seal the deal with a kiss, but she pushed me away from her. Panic instantly flared inside me. Oh, God...did she want to forgive me, but when push comes to shove, she couldn't? What would that mean for us?

Kiera got a strange look on her face, one of apology mixed with disgust. "You...smell like her."

Relief hit me again, but it was quickly replaced with anger. She was right. I did smell like Sienna. Her fucking perfume was over every inch of me, like even now she was trying to stake a claim on me. *I don't think so.*

"Not for long," I told Kiera, then I strode to the shower and turned it on.

I tore off my clothes and stepped inside the shower, feeling the bite of cold water before it shifted into warm. Kiera watched me for a second, then began removing her clothes, setting them on top of mine. It relieved me that she was willing to do this with me, willing to be vulnerable with me while I rid myself of Sienna.

Giving her a flick of a smile, I held out a bar of soap. "I want every trace of her off of me."

Kiera nodded, her face serious, like the task I'd given her was monumentally important. She started on my back, running the bar and her soapy hands over my neck, shoulders, ass, legs...even my feet. I felt better with every section she touched, felt the horror of today sliding down the drain with those tainted bubbles. I began washing my hair when she switched to my front. She scrubbed the makeup off my tattoo while sticking her tongue out of the corner of her mouth. It was adorable. Then she kissed the reappeared ink and gave me the sweetest smile. I smiled back at her, reveling in feeling our connection tightening again. Thank God.

She continued down my stomach, then darted down my legs. I thought she'd leave it at that, but after working her way back up my legs, she ran her soap-covered fingers over and around my cock. I instantly hardened at her touch, and I did nothing to try to stop it from happening. Fuck. *This is what today should have been*. Closing my eyes, I savored the feel of her caressing me.

Wanting to lighten the mood, ease the lingering stress of the day, I languidly told her, "That's the one part she didn't touch." I cracked an eye open to smile at her. "But I do appreciate your thoroughness."

She giggled, an adorable expression of delight and embarrassment on her face. She popped up to kiss me, but I held up my hand to stop her. "Wait. One more spot."

Kiera scanned my body like she was searching for what she'd missed. Knowing this was going to suck, but ultimately be worth it, I grabbed the shampoo bottle and squeezed a dollop into my mouth. Kiera's jaw dropped as she let go of the soap. "Kellan!" she screeched.

I held up a finger while I swished the vile, burning, flowery shit in my mouth. I regretted my melodramatic decision instantly, and I was pretty sure I was going to puke if I held it in any longer. I leaned over to spit it out, which did nothing to help me since my mouth was coated with the crap. As I coughed and gagged on the fumes and acerbic taste, Kiera started laughing.

Her eyes watery, she shook her head. "I cannot believe you just did that!"

I can't believe that was worse than I imagined. Needing the taste out of my mouth, I held my face up to the showerhead. Then I brushed my tongue with the loofah. Kiera held her sides as she giggled, and I loved seeing nothing but pure joy on her face again.

Once my mouth and body were as rinsed as I could get them, I turned off the water. "God, that was nasty," I told her.

Struggling to breathe, she wiped the tears off her cheeks. "That was *not* necessary, Kellan."

I grinned as I studied her, as I noted the absence of any pain, guilt, or jealousy on her face. All I saw was happiness, and seeing it evaporated all the pain, guilt, and regret inside of me. "Yes, it was."

Kiera looped her arms around my neck, then jumped up. I caught her and held her to me as she wrapped her legs around me. "I love you...even if you are insane."

Laughing, I opened the shower door. "Good, because I think I'm going to be burping soap bubbles for a week." And tasting it for much longer. But as I'd predicted, it was absolutely worth it. Kiera's eyes were locked on mine, her fingers threading through my wet hair. I paused a moment to absorb the love I felt coming from her, to feed it back to her. "I love you too, Kiera. Just you. You're my always."

She sighed, then laid her head on my shoulder. I laid my head against hers, hugging her the best I could as I held her, then walked us out of the shower. Kiera grabbed some towels as we passed by the hooks, but I didn't stop my progress so we could dry off. I led us right to the bed, then laid her down on top of it. Kiera laid the towels on the pillows, then held out her arms for me. I smiled at her invitation, admiring the beautiful woman stretched out before me, then I climbed in beside her.

Our bodies instantly tangled together, arms and legs cinching tight, and I inhaled a deep, relieved breath. As I released it, exhaustion swept in to take its place. "I'm so tired," I murmured, nuzzling into her neck. A good night's sleep had been difficult on the tour, impossible the last couple of nights.

Kiera made an agreeing sound, then started playing with my hair in a way that was quickly pulling me under. She kissed my damp cheek, then softly said, "I'm so sorry, Kellan."

I pulled back to look at her. "Sorry? What do you have to be sorry about? I'm the one who—"

She put her finger to my lips, stopping me from saying it. Then she shook her head. "I saw how hard that was for you. I saw your pain. I think I'm the only one who did, and I'm so sorry you had to go through that." Her brows furrowed with compassion, and my heart ached at seeing it.

Smiling, I gave her a tender kiss. "You're always the only one who truly sees me. Thank you."

She cupped my cheek, then pulled me back to her neck and resumed stroking my hair and periodically kissing my head. Surrounded in bliss, sleep was quick to claim me, and I spent the entire night wrapped in her arms and in her love.

My best friend, my partner, my soulmate...my wife. Thank God, I hadn't lost her.

Filming the rest of the music video promised to be a lot less stressful, and I woke up the next morning with a bounce in my step. Evan noticed my improved mood right away, which made me rethink my words to Kiera last night. She wasn't the only one who saw me; Evan saw a lot more than I gave him credit for.

"Things good?" he asked, raising his pierced eyebrow.

Grinning like an idiot, I nodded. "Yeah, no help needed. But thank you for the offer."

He smiled, nodding. "Of course. But don't think I was being entirely altruistic. I just don't want to lose the bet on the two of you."

The smile instantly fell off my face. "What bet?" He grinned at me in answer, then patted my shoulder and turned to head downstairs. "What bet?" I called out after him, but laughter was his only response. "Asshole," I muttered, right as Kiera joined my side.

"Who's an asshole?" she asked, wrapping both her arms around one of mine.

I grinned at hearing her swear, then frowned. Sweeping my hand to indicate the house, I told her, "All of them." I focused my gaze on Matt and Griffin across the room and raised my voice so they would hear me. "You're all assholes."

Matt looked confused by my pronouncement. Griffin started laughing. Then he nodded and flipped me off with both hands. Kiera giggled, and I smiled as I looked down at her. "Do I want to know?" she asked.

I shook my head as I shifted my arm to wrap it around her. "Nope." I was pretty sure *I* didn't even want to know.

When we got to the studio, I thought things might be a little awkward with Sienna, but she was a complete professional and acted like our love scene never happened. I was grateful for that. It made it a lot easier to brush it off and move forward. The rest of the video shoot was a breeze. I joined the guys on the stage set, and we ran through the song a few times. That didn't even feel like acting, we were simply performing for the crew. And Kiera. She had a huge grin on her face the entire time, and I loved seeing it.

After that, I finished up the bedroom scenes with Sienna. Fully clothed, thank fuck. We sang the more solemn lines staring down at the bed where the previous versions of us making out would be added later. They even brought in a man and woman dressed in head-to-toe green suits and had me stroke the green girl's arm. In the video it would look like I was touching Sienna *while* making out with her, and I had to admit, I was a little curious to see that.

Then we got to the angry part of the song, and Sienna and I ignored the bed and sang directly at each other. That was my favorite part. Sienna had a perfect sneer on her face as she practically spat the words at me, and I let all my frustrations out as I snarled the words at her. It was kind of cathartic, especially at the end, when we stalked off the set in opposite directions.

Finally, it was all over, and Diedrich thanked us for our time and effort. I kind of wanted to be a jackass to him for being a part of the machine that had made me do that, but I forced a smile to my face and gave him a polite nod of acknowledgment. While I hated my role in it, I could see the artistry in what he'd done, and I supposed I could be nice about it. Plus, in the end, I was the one who'd said yes.

Nick approached me once we were finished, looking happier than I'd ever seen him. He smacked my shoulder like we were friends. "See, now, that wasn't so bad, was it?" I opened my mouth to tell him exactly what it had been, but he steamrolled right over me. "This video is going to be smoking hot! Scorch everything else out of the water." He rubbed his hands together like he couldn't wait.

I wrapped my arm around Kiera's shoulders, pulling her tight to me. "I'm glad you're happy with it...because I'm never doing anything like that again."

Nick's expression instantly darkened. "Never say never. You're awfully new to this business."

True. But if this was what the business was really like, then I'd be just fine without it. I looked down at Kiera, then back up at Nick. "No, I'm never filming anything like that again. I'm done. I made a promise, and I'm keeping it. I'll help you promote the album in any way I can, because I owe that to my bandmates, but my wife comes first, and you need to accept that." I stared at him unflinchingly. If he told me he was done with us, then fine, I'd beg the guys to forgive me, and we'd start over. But I was *never* begging for forgiveness from my wife again.

Nick looked pissed as he stared back at me, but he also looked contemplative, like he was weighing pros and cons in his head, and the pros were winning. "*Any* way you can?" he finally said.

I nodded. "Within reason...of course. I won't let you play with my personal life anymore. I prefer to be private, but I'm not staying quiet. If someone asks me about my relationships, I'm going to give them an honest answer." Leaning in, I lowered my voice. "And I reread my contract. I know what my job entails, and I know what I have to do and *don't* have to do for you."

He smirked at that, and the smug look sent a wash of dread through me. But then he shrugged and smiled, like nothing I'd said bothered him. "Well, it's good to know where you stand." He strode over to Sienna after that, and the two of them left the room with bent heads and harsh whispers.

Kiera looped her arms around my waist, squeezing me tight. "I don't think he liked that," she told me with a grin.

I shrugged as I smiled down at her. "Oh fucking well. He got what he wanted, now I'm going to get what I want."

Kiera twisted to face me, then shifted to lace her fingers around my neck. "Oh, and what do you want?"

Wrapping my arms around her waist, I grinned and said, "You, by my side, in front of the world, consequences be damned." She smiled for a split-second, then all the blood drained from her face. I frowned at seeing the anxiety in her eyes. "What?"

"Don't take this the wrong way, but I don't want your fame. And I definitely don't want your spotlight. Just the thought makes me want to..." She didn't say it, just grimaced and put a hand to her stomach.

Frowning, I tilted my head. "What do you want me to do then? Because I'm done saying no comment, Kiera. I have comments. Lots of them."

She laughed a little, then shook her head. "And I want you to say them. Deny the rumor about Sienna, tell everyone you're in love and off the market, just don't mention me specifically."

I lifted an eyebrow at her as I pulled her close. "Are you sure? I don't think it would be as intrusive as you think. I'm still a nobody, remember?"

Now she lifted an eyebrow at me. "Your single is doing amazing, your album's release is going to be amazing, and Nick is right about the video—it's going to get attention. Your days of being a nobody are already gone, Kellan." I frowned at that, and Kiera smiled as she cupped my cheek. "And honestly...you were never a nobody." Her thumb stroked my cheek as she gazed at me with love in her eyes. "You've always been special, and you will always *be* special."

I smiled as I stared at her. "You really make me want to marry you. Do you know that?"

She laughed, then brought her lips to mine. "The feeling is mutual," she murmured.

We kissed for about five wonderful seconds, and then Tory

was there, snipping that we had to get back to the house, grab our things, and get back out on the road to finish the promo tour. *And so it continues.*

By that evening, we were halfway across the country. The following morning, we were at a radio station to do yet another interview and live performance. Tory yanked on my arm as we walked through the lobby.

I stopped with her, then stared down at where her fingers were digging into my skin. "Do you mind?" I said, ice in my voice.

Apparently, she didn't, because she didn't let go of me. Cold blue eyes narrowing, she stared me down. "Nick informed me that you might be a problem. You know what to do up there, right?"

I gave her a small smile as I pulled my arm free. "Don't worry. I know *exactly* what to do."

She analyzed my words for a moment, then nodded and indicated the elevators. "Well, go on then. You're going to be late."

Rolling my eyes, I stepped away from her. Kiera approached me, her gaze on Tory, her expression cautious. "What did she want?" she quietly asked.

"To scare me into submission," I told her. Then I grinned. "Too bad for her that I'm used to that tactic." And Tory wasn't nearly as frightening as my father.

Kiera's eyes softened in compassion; she knew what I meant by that comment. She tenderly held my hand as we stepped into the elevator. Tory came in next, followed by the guys. She narrowed her eyes at Kiera and me, and there was a clear warning being broadcasted in her stare. I ignored her, focusing on the doors instead. We got to the studio, and Kiera stepped away from me to sit on a stool in the corner. I wanted to grab her hand again, have her sit beside me during the interview, but I knew she didn't want that. She wanted invisibility, and the least I could do was give that to her.

The guys and I were introduced to the DJs, shown where to

sit, and given headsets to wear. After a minute of polite small talk, we went live, and the DJs introduced us to their audience. I couldn't quite keep the smirk off my face as I waited for the question that I knew was coming. As predicted, it was one of the first things they asked me.

Smiling at me with an interested gleam in his eye, one I was all too familiar with, one of the DJs smoothly said, "So, Kellan, tell me...what is it like dating the hottest pop star on the planet?"

Well, I personally wouldn't call Kiera a pop star, being on a stage might actually kill her, but she is the hottest woman *on the planet. And dating her is fantastic, thanks for asking.*

Knowing Kiera would kill me if I said that, I replied, "If you mean Sienna, I wouldn't know because we're not dating."

The man smirked like he thought I was feeding him bullshit. "Are you sure? Because it seems like you're dating."

Really? One random shot of us walking together, a few photos of Sienna kissing me against my will, and multiple "no comments" during interviews is somehow proof we're dating?

I didn't want to argue with the man, so I didn't say that either. I could see Tory in my peripheral. She was making a cut gesture across her throat and giving me stick-to-your-lines eyes. The frustration on her face made my lip curl up, and I told the DJ, "Sienna is a colleague that I collaborated with on a song, nothing more. I'm in a relationship, but not with her."

The DJ looked both intrigued and skeptical. "Oh, and who is this lucky person?"

"Ahhh..." I made a casual glance around the room, my gaze momentarily pausing on Kiera in the corner. She frowned at me, narrowing her eyes, and I could practically hear her yelling, *Don't you dare.* With a laugh, I glanced over at Evan before looking back at the DJ. "I'd rather not say, but did you know, Evan here is only dating someone because of me? He'd still be silently pining for her if I hadn't interfered."

Evan's dark eyes snapped to me. "That is categorically untrue."

I tilted my head at him. "Is it, though? Really?"

He started laughing. "Yes."

As I was hoping, the DJ latched on to our mild argument and forgot all about my love life. "This sounds interesting," he said. "What really happened then?"

Since Tory didn't care if the guys talked about their relationships—apparently, that restriction was just for me—Evan dove into the story of how he'd gotten together with Jenny, completely omitting how I'd nudged him along with threats of Griffin's sweaty spandex, of course.

As the conversation shifted to Matt and Griffin, I could feel Tory's stare burning a hole in me. I met eyes with her, and I could tell she was really pissed. I smiled at her, and her expression darkened even more. She practically attacked me when the interview was over, and we were back in the car. "That will *not* happen again, do you understand me?"

"What, messing with Evan? It's all in good fun, I doubt he's mad." I twisted to Evan. "You're not mad, are you?"

He flipped me off. "No, not at all," he said with a smile.

I turned back to Tory. "See? It's all good."

She was glaring at me so hard that I thought she might burst a blood vessel. Then she proceeded to rip me a new one for denying a relationship with Sienna. Since arguing with her was pointless —I would never change her mind, and she would never change mine—I simply smiled at her as I held Kiera's hand.

And then, when we got to the next interview, I did the exact same thing. I did it over and over and over. Tory yelled at me every time, but it didn't change my actions. I wasn't staying quiet anymore, and unless she was going to duct tape my mouth shut, there wasn't a damn thing Tory could do about it.

Chapter 15

BACK AT PETE'S

Finally, the album was done, the promo tour was done, and we all got to go home and recover before the actual tour began. I almost cried when Kiera and I stepped inside our house, and that was a weird feeling for me since I'd never had any true attachment to my parents' home before. Living here with Kiera had changed things for me, in more ways than one.

I did cry when we picked up the Chevelle. God, I'd missed my car.

Kiera and I crashed the minute we got back. Okay, we showered, made love, then crashed. We spent most of the next day in bed either sleeping or taking advantage of our privacy. We were in between those two things when my cell phone rang. I frowned as I grabbed it from the nightstand and glanced at the screen. Looking over at Kiera beside me, naked under the sheets, I debated letting it go to voicemail and giving her my full attention.

She smiled like she knew it. "Aren't you going to get that?"

I shrugged. "It's just Matt. I've spent enough time with Matt, but I'm still not satisfied with the amount of time I've spent with you."

She laughed lightly, then indicated my phone. "You should get it. If it wasn't important, he would just text you."

I rolled my eyes. "You don't know Matt." I sighed. "If this is about us getting together to rehearse, I might do him bodily harm." Kiera rolled into her pillow as she started giggling. I grinned at her, then answered my phone. "You realize we've spent the last several months practically in each other's laps, right? I know you love me, Matt, but I was—"

"So, Griffin and I were talking to Evan," he said, cutting me off, "and we're all gonna go to Pete's tonight, to celebrate the album's release. Wanna come?"

The album...damn. Remembering the moment when we'd found out just how well our album had debuted still floored me. We were nobodies. How in the hell did we debut in the top twenty? "Number nineteen...I still can't believe it. Are you sure that wasn't a weird, non-fever, fever dream?" Because that was exactly how it had felt at the time. We'd all screamed and jumped around and hugged everyone nearby, and it just didn't feel real. Still didn't.

Matt laughed. "Nope, we did it, man. And we're celebrating tonight. So get up, get dressed, and come out with us."

I grinned at my phone. "How do you know I'm not up? Or dressed?"

He snorted. "Because I'm not an idiot. So you comin'?"

I looked over at Kiera, sitting up on her elbow, watching me; the sheet just barely covered her breasts. "I don't know," I murmured.

Kiera bunched her brows at my answer. Matt whined. "Come on, man. It'll be fun!"

"What will be fun?" Kiera asked, overhearing him.

With a shrug, I told her, "The guys want to go to Pete's tonight to celebrate the album."

Her eyes lit up at the news. "That *will* be fun, we should go."

"Are you sure?" I asked, my gaze dragging down her body.

She sat all the way up, pulling the sheet higher around her. "Yes," she said with a smile. "We should definitely celebrate, and we should do it while everyone is together. And who knows when we'll have another chance like this." She shrugged.

That was true. We were leaving on the official tour soon. We wouldn't be here in Seattle for long, so missing this opportunity to celebrate with everyone was a real possibility. Nodding at her, I told Matt, "Yeah, okay, we'll be there."

"Awesome!" He then told me what time to meet them and warned me not to be late. It made me smile that at least some things hadn't changed.

Hours later, we were walking into Pete's with the guys, and as we strolled through the double doors, the strangeness of my life melted away. Things were like they always used to be, and a feeling of home wrapped tightly around me. The feeling didn't last long. We weren't in the bar ten seconds before the place exploded with shrieks and whistles. It was like we were about to do a show for a bunch of diehard fans who'd never seen us in person before, but a lot of the people here used to see us all the time, so it was really...weird.

Regulars that I'd known for ages came up to me with awe on their faces, telling me their names like I'd somehow forgotten who they were while we'd been gone. Some of them even asked for my autograph. It was as if we'd never shared beer, played pool, or made fun of Griffin together. It made the whole reunion feel odd, surreal. *Is this what they mean by you can never go home again?* I hadn't changed, but everyone around me had.

I met eyes with Matt and Evan as people crowded around us, and my friends had the same bewildered expression on their faces. Griffin looked pleased, like he'd wanted this from the first time he'd stepped in here. Kiera had removed herself from the chaos and was standing beside the bar with Jenny, Kate, and Rachel. She looked amused by the attention we were receiving, but maybe a little sad too. Being at Pete's was different now, for all of us.

Then I glanced across the bar and met eyes with Rita. She gave me a flirtatious wink that actually relieved me. Some things were the same.

"So, Kellan...Sienna Sexton, huh? Damn. I figured you'd trade up when you hit it big, but I had no idea you'd go right to the fucking top! Nicely done, man."

I turned to look at the guy on my left who'd said that. He was one of those regulars that I knew by sight, but I hadn't really spoken to him all that often, and so of course, he was one of the few who hadn't offered up his name. I was pretty sure it was Peter, though. I seemed to recall him constantly hitting on college girls, even though he looked closer to Rita's age. He'd pissed off Griffin one night by trying to pick up a girl while Griffin had been talking to her, and Griffin had lovingly given him the nickname Peter Pecker. No, Peter the Peckhead Pecker. That was it.

With a smirk, I shook my head. "Never pictured you as someone who followed the tabloids, Peter. Don't believe everything you read."

Peter grinned, pleased that I remembered him. I grinned internally, pleased that I'd gotten his name right. He shook his head. "I'm not talking about the tabloids. I'm talking about that smokin' hot music video. Magazines lie, but tongues down throats don't."

The smile instantly left my face. I hadn't realized the video was out. Great. I looked around, and that was when I noticed something I hadn't before. People were looking between Kiera and me with confusion and disbelief on their faces, like they didn't understand why we were here *together*. "It's not like that. Sienna and I are just...friends." That kind of felt like a stretch, but I didn't think Peter would believe me if I told him we were just co-workers. Not with what we'd done in that video. Although the friend label didn't justify it either. *I never should have agreed to that.*

Peter started laughing. "Yeah, I could tell. Great friends."

I scratched my head as I debated how to clear things up with this person I barely knew. And that was when I decided it wasn't worth the effort. If all those DJs who understood the business didn't believe me, then I couldn't expect him to. "I'd rather not talk about it, okay?"

He gave me a secretive smile as he flicked a glance at Kiera. "Yeah, sure, I get it." He leaned in close. "She won't hear nothing from me, man." The conspiratorial look on his face made me want to slug him, but I refrained.

Luckily, he went back to his table after that, and a few minutes later, I was finally able to escape to mine. Sam had cleared the band's traditional table for us, and he indicated my usual seat with a broad smile on his face. Since it had been a while since we'd forcibly removed customers from our table, I thought people would be mad, but everyone around us seemed almost gleeful, like the four of us were something special and deserved the royal treatment. The surrealness, combined with everyone staring, made me feel like I was in a fishbowl. It made me want to go on stage, just so I could give them something in return, something more interesting than me sitting on my ass, talking to Sam.

That was when I spotted Denny and Abby at a nearby table. Denny was watching the fawning with a smirk on his face. When our eyes met, he slowly shook his head at me, his smile widening. I immediately stood up and walked over to him. "Guess what?" I said, leaning on the back of his chair.

"Other than you're back? No idea," he answered.

Grinning, I yanked on the back of his chair. "You're sitting with us." He laughed as I loudly pulled his chair over to the end of our table. Kiera laughed as she watched me, then she nodded at Denny in greeting. I headed back to the table to grab Abby, but she lifted a hand at me and stood. I moved over her empty chair, then grabbed their food and drinks.

When we were all seated around the table, drinking the beers Kiera had grabbed for us, it felt more like old times. Until Pete came out, pride on his typically weary face. "My boys!" he said, opening his arms. "Welcome home! Drinks are on me." He paused a moment, then said, "*A* drink is on me. One."

Matt snorted at his comment. He twisted to say something to

Rachel beside him, making her giggle. "Thanks, Pete," I said for the group. "How's the new band working out?" I already knew Poetic Bliss was good, so I was pretty sure things were going just fine, but I wanted to hear him say it. I needed to know he was okay. If he wasn't happy with our choice, I'd do whatever I could to make it right. I owed him that much. Honestly, I owed him far more than that.

His grin didn't falter. "They're great. I think." He shrugged. "Music isn't really my thing, but we're packed most nights they play, so I can't complain." He looked at a chunky watch on his wrist. "They're playing tonight, so you'll get to see for yourself. If you're staying?" He raised an eyebrow, his expression hopeful.

As I studied his face, a slight disappointment washed through me. He was looking at me like the rest of the bar was, like I was something more than what I'd been when I'd left. But I could clearly remember all the times Pete had gotten on our asses for something: being late to play 'cause we were goofing off, Griffin dancing on the tables, me ripping the felt on the pool table, Evan breaking the jukebox, Matt dropping not one, but *three* full glasses of beer. Pete had always treated us like his rowdy children, but now it was like we were his betters or something. I kind of missed the disgruntled look.

Trying to accept the change in our relationship, I made myself smile. "There is nowhere else we want to be, other than right here." Wondering if I could make the look I missed return, I leaned forward and said something I knew he would hate. "Hey, how do you feel about karaoke night instead? Matt knows a guy. We could have it set up in an hour."

Pete instantly gave me a picture-perfect scowl. I couldn't even count the number of times I'd heard him gripe about karaoke, saying he'd rather die than allow it in his bar. He didn't even like people singing along to the jukebox. "Pete's has never—and will never—have karaoke. Ever." Rolling his gray eyes, he walked away.

Grinning, I yelled out, "Are you sure? Griffin is surprisingly good at rap!"

Griffin instantly got excited. "Fuck, yeah, I am! We doing karaoke? Sweet!"

Pete stopped and looked back at me with an expression on his face that was both annoyed and horrified. He darted out of the room, and I had a feeling we wouldn't see him for the rest of the night. Now *that* was the look I'd missed. Priceless.

Evan was laughing so hard that he had to wipe his eyes. "You're such an asshole," he muttered.

Jenny instantly pinched his arm. "Language." She turned to me with a frown on her face. "You're such a bad influence, Kellan. Whenever Evan spends a lot of time with you, he comes back swearing like a sailor."

My jaw dropped in mock indignation. "Me? I'm the saintly one, remember?"

Denny nearly spat out his beer, then he started laughing. Hard. I frowned as I looked over at him. "It's not *that* funny."

Everyone started laughing as Denny dropped his head to the table. "Saintly," he snickered.

As they all laughed at, well, me, Griffin scratched his head and asked in a confused voice, "Does this mean we're not doing karaoke?"

Our group grew when Anna joined us after she got off work, and the warmth and laughter around our table was almost palpable. Kiera was right, and I was glad we'd come out. Even if there were far too many people either gawking or gossiping, we'd needed this, and I savored every minute of celebrating with my friends.

I was on my way to rejoin them, coming back from a quick pit stop to the bathroom, when Denny approached me in the hallway. Eyes full of intent, he pointed at the far end of the hallway where there was a little more privacy.

"Can we talk for a minute?" he asked, his voice as serious as his face.

"Uh, sure." I walked with him to the back of the hallway. "What's up?" I asked. I tried to sound casual, but it came out laced with concern.

He glanced back down the hallway, making sure we were alone. "You and Sienna. Kiera says nothing is going on, but I don't think you would..." He paused to take a deep breath. "I don't think you would tell her if you were screwing around on her. I doubt you'd tell me either, but I can't sit on the sidelines this time, like I did a few months ago. At the very least, I have to ask...are you cheating on Kiera?"

A long sigh escaped me. I wanted to be angry at him for asking, but with our history, how could I be? "No, I'm not. I have no way to prove that to you, and I know there is a lot of pseudo-evidence that suggests otherwise, but...I'm not." Pausing, I looked him square in the eye. "Being with Kiera cost me your friendship. What it used to be, at any rate. I would never betray her when it cost me so much to have her. Does that make sense?"

He tilted his dark head, assessing me. "Yeah, I get it." Frowning, he shook his head. "But that video...?"

Closing my eyes, I bowed my head. "I didn't want to do it. When the label made it clear that it wasn't a request, I was ready to give it all up and walk away. Kiera is the one who convinced me to go through with it." I raised my head and opened my eyes. "I never would have done it if she hadn't approved. But even still, doing it made me feel so...sick. I can't...I won't ever..." My throat was closing up, and I had to swallow to release the pressure. I could feel my eyes begin to burn as I stared at him. "I won't *ever* do anything like that again. I can't."

That seemed to convince Denny more than anything else, and he cracked a small smile. Then he looked down. "Would you... would you have been honest with me?" He looked back up, an eyebrow arched in question. "In the beginning, if I'd asked you directly if you'd slept with her, would you have told me the truth?"

My breath caught in my chest as I realized that we weren't

talking about Sienna anymore. I swallowed again. "Yes. I think so. I hope so," I said with a shrug. "Now that the moment is past, I honestly can't say for sure what I would have done, but...I know there were times when I *wished* you would ask. Hiding it from you hurt, it hurt almost as much as..." I sighed, then shook my head. "It wasn't easy for me. None of it was easy for me."

A small smile touched his lips. "Good."

I lightly laughed, and I was a little surprised that I could. "I'm glad you were here tonight."

His smile grew. "Yeah, me too." Then he frowned. "Maybe a heads-up next time, huh? Mate?" There was a question in his tone, a request for reassurance, and maybe a sprinkling of apology too.

Grinning, I nodded. "Yes, absolutely. Mate." I sighed and rolled my eyes. "It's been a bitch of a few weeks. If you ever release an album and they want you to go on a promo tour for it, for fuck's sake, say no."

Denny chuckled, his dark eyes radiating humor. "No chance of that ever happening. I have no musical talent whatsoever, remember?" He grinned. "Jenny's right, you are a bad influence." Then he started laughing. "Saintly..."

I rolled my eyes at his amusement, then I clapped his shoulder, and we headed back to the table.

Eventually Poetic Bliss showed up for their set, and Rain freaked out when she spotted us. Grabbing my arm, the tiny, energetic, raven-haired girl pulled me up onto the stage with her. We got into a playful mock fight when she tried to push me in front of the microphone. The waiting crowd went nuts, and I let the fight go on for a little bit, to rile them up even more. Rain grinned at me as I finally took my old spot on the stage. It felt like putting on my favorite pair of worn jeans: comfortable, familiar, a perfect fit.

"Hey," I playfully told the multitude. The scream they let out was deafening. With a laugh, I briefly scanned the crowd before settling my gaze on Kiera. She was beaming at me with tears in her eyes, like she'd missed the sight of me up here just as much as I'd missed being up here. Her expression choked me up a little, so I quickly looked back to the crowd.

Holding up a hand to quiet them, I said, "It is so fucking good to be back here at Pete's!" Would anything ever feel as good as playing here? I honestly wasn't sure. All I knew was that I didn't want to leave without performing for them. That would be a form of torture, to be this close and not get to play. Hoping Rain had intended for me to take over for a bit when she'd pulled me up here, I asked the crowd, "You guys mind if the D-Bags take over for a song or two?"

By their reaction, they were as excited about the idea as I was. I glanced over at Rain and the girls, and every single one of them was giving me enthusiastic support—clapping, grinning, nodding, whistling. Having Poetic Bliss's okay, I looked over at the guys and tilted my head in invitation. They instantly left the table and joined me, Griffin almost upending Anna in his haste. I understood his eagerness but scowled at him when he bounded up the stairs. If Matt hadn't already smacked him, I would have.

Poetic Bliss handed the guys their very feminine instruments, making the crowd snigger. I shared a look with Evan, and he gave me a tiny nod. He knew what to do. As a group, we'd talked about something like this happening, needing just a few songs to perform when and if we were ever asked onstage as guests. It was more a daydream on our part, but Matt, ever the planner, had insisted on making it official, and we'd hammered out a five-song setlist. Hopefully, Griffin remembered which songs we'd picked.

Evan started the intro to the first song, and we were off. Grabbing the microphone from its stand, I let myself fall back into the countless memories I had of performing at Pete's. I stalked the stage, I flirted with the fans, I poured my soul into the words, and I fed off the massive amount of energy coming from the crowd. It gave me such a high. I could have stayed up there all night, but I was very conscious of the fact that this stage, in all its worn glory, wasn't mine anymore. I called it quits after two songs, worried that if I let myself do a third one, I wouldn't be able to stop.

After the second song, I briefly shook my head at Evan, then I bowed to the crowd, thanked them for being incredible, and hopped down to join them. I was stroked and fondled on my way to Kiera in the center, but I didn't let that deter me from getting to my girl. Once I was in front of her, I wrapped her in my arms and squeezed her tight. There was nothing quite like coming off my high with Kiera in my arms. A perfect end to a great night.

As Kiera and I softly kissed, Rain said into the microphone, "Thank you, boys, but it's the girls' turn to kick ass now!"

I laughed at her comment, tossing her a smile. Poetic Bliss started playing, and I shifted all my attention back to Kiera. Looping an arm around my neck, she pressed her body close to mine as she moved with the beat. Kiera and I hadn't had a chance to dance together in a long time. I'd almost forgotten how arousing it was to move with her. Making love to Kiera was my favorite thing in the world, but dancing with her was a close second.

As one song slid into the next, I slipped around behind Kiera. Dancing with her this way flooded me with memories—wanting her, needing her, aching for her. My hand was low on her stomach as we shifted together, and I had to resist the urge to unbutton her jeans. Desire shot through me as the movement, the music, and my memories collided. My breath picked up, my heart raced, and blood surged to all the right places. As Kiera's back pressed against my chest, I wondered if she also felt it, the building heat, the almost unbearable hunger. *Is she ready to leave too?*

My lips moved to her neck, and I ran my nose up the side of her throat. She shuddered, her head dropping back to my shoulder. I kissed her jaw, then said in her ear, "Wanna go somewhere with me?" My hands slid to her hips, and I gently pulled her into mine so she could feel how ready I was for her.

She turned her head to look at me. There was heat in her sea-green eyes and a mischievous smile on her lips as she nodded at me. I thought we'd go out to the car, I thought we'd go home, but she grabbed my hand and pulled me toward the back hallway. Looking like a woman on a mission, Kiera weaved us around curious people, stopping for no one and ignoring every question or comment tossed our way. Her determined focus almost made me laugh, but I was too turned on to find it funny. It was just hot.

Kiera pulled us into the back room, quickly closing the door behind us. I pressed her against the door as I locked it. "New lock still works," I murmured. Then I found her mouth. There was something about being in this room that ignited me. Maybe it was all the various times when being back here hadn't worked out for us, maybe it was the residual high from being on stage at Pete's again, or maybe it was just the fact that I was touching her in public and no one was scowling at me, but I was almost desperate to be inside her.

Kiera seemed just as fired up as me. Her kisses were frantic, her fingers clutching at my clothes. Her hands slid down my chest to my jeans; she had them unbuttoned and unzipped in seconds. I had hers undone in record time too. I was just starting to shove her pants down her hips when Kiera reached inside my jeans and wrapped her hand around me. The sensation hit me so hard that I had to stop what I was doing. Then she squeezed me, and I actually whimpered in response. I felt electrified and oversensitive, on the verge of either caving into the pleasure and letting it sweep me away, or taking a step back from her so I could force my body to calm down enough that I'd be able to give her something in return. *Fuck, I'm not gonna make it. This room is cursed. Has to be.*

That thought became especially true when Kiera released me and stopped my hands from ripping off her clothes. A desperate, frustrated noise came out of me as I clutched her jeans. *Okay, she doesn't want this here. That's fine. I'll calm down, then we'll go home. And then I'll take her on the floor of the entryway because I really don't think I can wait until we get upstairs.*

Just as I had resigned myself to that fate, Kiera gently pushed me away...then started sliding her back down the door. *What the hell is she doing?* "Kiera...?" *Shouldn't we be leaving?*

But then she stopped at my waist...so her head was at my waist. *No. No way. She's not...? She hates that. She wouldn't...? Would she? Holy fuck, would she?*

Not wanting to sway her decision either way, I didn't say anything. I just stared at her, staring at me. Then I reached down and traced her jaw with my finger; my hand was trembling, and I really hoped she didn't notice. She stared at me a moment longer, then she freed me from my clothes. My breath released from me in a rush, and it was only then that I realized I'd been holding it. I thought I might die if she didn't touch me, but I didn't want to push her into anything. If she stopped right now and wanted to go home, that was absolutely fine. I might need to relieve this building pressure myself, but it would be absolutely fine.

But fuck, I really hoped she didn't stop.

The anticipation of it was killing me, and I could feel myself shaking. It was hard not to touch her, not to beg her, but I wanted this to come from her, be *her* choice. And then, thank God, she lowered her mouth and took me in. As her warm lips wrapped around me, as her tongue brushed against me, I almost lost it. My head hit the door as I groaned in relief and ecstasy. I'd had my fair share of blowjobs in my day, but nothing like this, nothing even came close to this. Probably because I wanted it so much. Probably because I was still shocked she was doing it. Everything about this was undoing me.

I cupped her cheek as I slid against her, trying to somewhat make this romantic for her. But fuck, it felt so good. I was already so revved up from just the thought of this, that it didn't take long for my breaths to become pants, for the movement to become faster, for the tightening in my stomach to begin as I felt the wall approaching. Approaching fast, too fast. I needed to stop her. I didn't want her to have to go through *all* of this. If she released me right now, we could finish this together, but fuck, it had to be *right now*.

"Kiera..." I pushed on her shoulder, hoping she understood.

She seemed to, but she also seemed to disagree. She grabbed my hips and pulled me deeper. That was enough to make it impossible for me to stop, and the pleasure slammed into me, forcing me to release into her. I grabbed the door handle as I came, needing to steady myself against the waves of euphoria. It hit me so hard; I felt like I might crumple to the floor. It took a long time for the bliss to fade, and a little guilt trickled in once it had. I hadn't wanted that for her, but like all of this, it had been her choice, so I shouldn't feel bad about it. And honestly, I was pretty sure stopping would have killed me.

As I recovered, Kiera tucked me away, then slid up the door. I couldn't move. I couldn't do anything but slump against the door with my eyes closed, trying to breathe normally. Kiera wrapped her arms around my neck, cuddling into my body. I knew I should be doing something, should be returning the favor, giving her an orgasm that was equally mind-blowing, but I just...couldn't. I needed a minute.

I shifted to rest my head in the crook of her neck. I didn't think I'd ever been so satisfied in all my life. "Holy...oh my... fuck." I sagged against her body like all my muscles had stopped working. And they kind of had. I felt completely useless.

Kiera giggled as she stroked my back. "Don't swear," she murmured.

A tired laugh escaped me. "Sorry."

We stayed like that for a moment as I tried to find some motivation to help her with her situation. But then I felt Kiera zip up her pants. When her fingers moved over to mine, zipping and fastening them, I pulled back to look at her. "What are you doing?" I asked. Clearly, we weren't done here. A few more minutes and I'd be fine to go again. Maybe.

An amused smile on her face, Kiera gave me a soft kiss. "I'm making you presentable so we can finish celebrating with our friends."

I tilted my head in confusion. "But you didn't...don't you want me to satisfy you?" I knew exactly how turned on she'd been when we came in here, and I hadn't even touched her yet. Even if my body was being slow to recuperate, I could give her a release. She shouldn't have to...suffer.

But she gave me a joyful smile and shook her head. "You did satisfy me."

I was 100 percent certain that wasn't true. "I did? Are you sure? Because you're usually more vocal when you're satisfied," I said with a teasing grin. *Don't you want me to make you scream?*

She bit her lip as she studied me, rubbing her legs together like she was dying for me to take her. I wanted to kiss her, unfasten her jeans again, and give her everything that she'd just given me. Like she could see that on my face, she pushed me back a little. "I may not have...finished...but you definitely made me happy." Her finger came up to brush some hair away from my eyes. "I want to give you this."

The comment made me smile while the look in her eyes made my chest tighten. *God, I love her.* Kiera smirked as she unlocked the door. "You can return the favor later," she added. *God, I really love her.*

I softly laughed as she opened the door and led us back into the hallway. Yes. That was definitely a favor I would be returning later. Over and over again.

Chapter 16

BACK AT IT

We had a handful of days before the official tour for our album started. We were hitting the road with Justin and his band again, a fact I was excited about. We all got along really well, and after having toured with Paul, that fucking asshole, I understood just how important that was.

Kiera and I spent our free time catching up with friends or lounging in bed. Actually, we spent a lot of time lounging in bed. It was shameful of us really, but we were resting up for the exhaustion coming our way. And enjoying our privacy while we had it.

I was just about to head downstairs to make us a late-afternoon snack when my phone rang. Worried it was Matt again, I cringed as I looked at the screen. Seeing Hailey's name made me smile, and I instantly picked it up.

"Hey, Hails," I said, scratching my bare stomach. I briefly looked at my pants on the floor and wondered if I should be dressed while talking to my sister. But I had boxers on. Good enough. It wasn't like she could see me anyway.

The line was silent for so long that I thought the call had dropped. I opened my mouth to say Hailey's name again, but I was interrupted by a shrill screech and the words, "Oh my God, oh my God, oh my God!"

I had to pull the phone away from my ear, the scream was so loud. Kiera paused in typing on her laptop when she overheard Hailey's exclamation. She gave me a questioning look, and I shrugged since I had no idea what was going on. "Hailey?" I asked. "Everything okay?"

There was another loud shriek in my ear. "I'm talking to Kellan Kyle. I can't believe I'm talking to Kellan Kyle!"

A soft sigh escaped me as I realized that I was *not* talking to my sister. "Actually, you're more yelling in my ear than talking to me. Who is this?" Kiera's brows bunched, and I shrugged again.

The person on the phone giggled. "I am your biggest fan."

I glanced at the screen, but it was still Hailey's number on the display. "Did you kidnap my sister?" I asked, half serious.

"So you're really her brother? For real?"

"Yeah, pretty sure. And who are you?" I asked again.

She let out a dreamy sigh. "Your future wife."

A small laugh left me as I met eyes with Kiera. Not likely. *I'm already married, and I have no intention of ever letting go of my wife.*

There was an alarmed squeak on the phone followed by indistinct murmuring that sounded angry. Then a voice I recognized said, "I am *so* sorry, Kellan. She stole my phone."

I laughed in earnest at the annoyance in my sister's voice. I supposed I should have been prepared for that happening, especially since Hailey's friends already had a waiting line for me. "It's fine, Hailey," I told her.

"No, it's not." Louder, clearly talking to her friend, she yelled, "I'm pressing charges!"

I heard her friend shout back, "Worth it!" and I laughed even harder.

Kiera smiled at me, shook her head, then went back to typing. I gave her a kiss on the cheek before turning to head downstairs. "So what happened?" I asked my sister.

She sighed. "Your music video happened. I swear my friends were bad enough before, but after seeing that they're practically rabid." She let out a long sigh. "You could have warned me."

I cringed as I stepped off the stairs. "Sorry, I've been trying not to think about it. I guess I'll have to be suspicious of every call from you from now on."

"Oh no," she said, "I've got my phone on lockdown. They'll have to pry it out of my cold, dead hands. And I don't think they'd kill me to talk to you. I hope..." I laughed as I walked into the kitchen. Hailey's voice turned oddly serious. "Hey, I watched the video too. I don't want to ask but...are you and Kiera...? Are you guys...?"

Closing my eyes, I sighed. First Denny, now Hailey. Just how convincing was that damn video? "We're fine. She was there when I filmed it. She's the one who talked me into doing it."

"Oh," she said, sounding genuinely surprised. "Wow. She's a lot stronger than me. I'd probably claw Sienna's eyes out. I kind of want to, actually."

I smiled as I leaned against the counter. "Well, I don't think Kiera would stop you. It hasn't been easy for her. Even still, she's been so incredible with all of this. I couldn't do it without her."

"I'm so proud of you, Kellan," she said, joy in her voice. It shifted to a sigh. "But please, for the sake of my sanity, do *not* film another love scene. I just about died. That was *so* weird for me to watch."

"Why *did* you watch it?" I asked with a laugh.

"It was like a bad car accident. I wanted to look away, but I just couldn't. I told Riley he was grounded if he watched it."

I could practically see her shuddering. That didn't help my guilt, not at all. "Is it really that bad?" I asked, already cringing.

She was silent a moment before she spoke. "It's pretty...well, my friends are printing out screenshots and wallpapering their dorms with them, so you do the math."

"Great," I murmured, regretting it for the millionth time.

"Why did you do that, Kellan?" Her voice was cautious, like she didn't want to offend me, but she just had to understand.

I tilted my head back to look at the ceiling. *Good question.* "For my friends. For our career. I didn't...I didn't have a choice. Not really."

Once again, she was silent for a moment. Finally, she said, "I'm sorry."

My lips lifted into a small smile. "Thank you."

"Everyone thinks you guys are together now. Like *everyone*."

I shook my head as a burst of anger washed through me. I should have resisted Sienna and Nick from the beginning, and now it was just too late. "I know," I told her. "But we're not."

"I know," she said. "Well, *now* I know."

Her comment made me laugh, then sigh. *One down, only a few million more to go.* Oh well. It didn't really matter what people thought. Kiera knew the truth, and she was the only one who needed to know it.

Still, it would be really nice if people would stop asking me about Sienna. I barely knew the woman. Maybe now that we'd gone our separate ways, now that we wouldn't be seen together anymore, the rest of the world would figure that out. And Kiera wouldn't have to constantly hear about me and another woman. I longed for that day.

It wasn't too much later that Kiera and I decided to watch the video. I'd been content with never watching it—just the idea made me nauseated—but Kiera felt it was something we should do, especially since it was the band's first video. I understood that sentiment and reluctantly agreed, so Kiera pressed play on the video, and we watched it together. And it was horrible. Not visually...visually it had a sensual kind of beauty to it, but internally, it was awful. I had to stop watching it after a few seconds and fixated on Kiera instead.

Watching her watch it wasn't much better, and the harder she squeezed my hand, the higher the guilt rose inside me. Once it was over, I was almost scared to talk to her, scared that I'd reopened a wound. Kiera was still staring at the computer, lost in her thoughts. I cleared my throat to gently break the spell on her, and she twisted to look at me.

As I searched her face, hoping for a clue on how she was feeling, she told me, "The two of you look amazing together. I can see why the fans are so in love with the idea." I shook my head, wanting to object, but she cupped my cheek and stopped me. "Were you really thinking about me throughout that entire thing?"

I gave her a firm nod. "It was the only way I could get through it."

The smile she gave me was soft, warm, loving, and tears grew in her eyes as she studied me. Tears of joy, I hoped. And they had to be, considering the peace I saw on her face. "Kellan Kyle, will you marry me?" she asked.

My heart felt like it was going to burst into a thousand pieces. God, I loved those words. Grinning, I moved the computer off her lap and slid my body over hers. "I thought you'd never ask," I said, teasing her a little.

My lips moved to her neck, and she giggled. "Is that a yes?"

Pressing my hips against hers, I whispered in her ear, "With you, it's always yes."

I wandered down her neck, kissing and lightly licking the sweetness of her skin. Desire started burning inside me, and my breath and pulse both quickened in response. I'd just passed Kiera's collarbone when she stopped me with a gentle nudge. I lifted my head to look at her, and she swallowed twice, like she needed a minute to recover before speaking to me. I kind of loved that just the look on my face had momentarily thrown her. Then she said something a little odd. "How long is the break in the tour schedule for Christmas?"

My gaze wandered over her shoulder as I thought. "Ah, I'm not sure. Four or five days, maybe a week?" Soft smile on my face, I looked back at her. "Why?"

She wrapped her arms around my neck as she shrugged. "Want to go to a wedding with me in Ohio?"

Everything about that sentence made me happy. *Yes. Absolutely, yes.* Shifting to her side, I sat up on my elbow. "Anyone I know getting married?" I asked, amused at how she'd phrased it and playing along.

She shrugged again. "Just some annoying wishy-washy girl that half the world hates."

I had to raise an eyebrow at her. That statement was far from true; she must be worried about what the fans would think if they ever did know about her. I gently kissed her, easing a fear she didn't need to worry about yet. Or ever. I'd never let anyone hate her. If she'd let me, I'd spout her greatness until everyone loved her just as much as I did. She just had to give me the freedom to speak about her.

"They don't hate you," I said, then I softly laughed and reminded her about her own restriction. "They don't even know about you. And you're not annoying or wishy-washy. At least, not anymore." I laughed again, and she smacked my shoulder and frowned. Leaning forward, I kissed the corners of her mouth. "I would love to marry you in December...in Ohio...in front of your entire family. In front of my family." Just the thought made me deliriously happy, and I loved the fact that we were making definite plans to solidify our symbolic marriage with a genuine one.

Kiera asked if I could find out the exact dates. I looked for my phone, ready to get things started, but she stopped me. "Could you do it a little later, though? I'd like to have sex with you first."

A mixture of things coursed through me at hearing her bluntly say that. Pride was the first thing. Kiera had always struggled with telling me she wanted me, and she hadn't paused or fumbled those words. She'd even said them seductively, a small half-smile on her face as she flirtatiously peered up at me. The second thing that hit me was happiness, and it was closely followed by attraction. Because damn, that was hot.

Still, I had to tease her a little.

Opening my mouth like I was stunned, I told her, "Why, Mrs. Kyle, I am shocked at your brazenness." I shifted my expression to an eager grin. "I'm also incredibly turned on."

I moved to slide on top of her again, but she pushed me onto my back and climbed on top of me. Her aggressive move made me laugh. But only for a minute.

Sooner than I would have liked, our quiet time in Seattle was over, and we were again saying goodbye to our significant others. Well, everyone was except for me. My significant other was coming with me this time, and that made the entire leaving process so much easier. Still, I felt bad for Matt and Evan. They'd barely spent any time with Rachel and Jenny. There would be a longer break once this tour was over with, but I knew firsthand how difficult it was to be separated. I would have felt bad for Griffin and Anna too, but I still couldn't tell what the deal was between those two. For all I knew, they liked being separated since it made their reunions so...combustible.

We were in the Pete's parking lot again, saying goodbye at our favorite place. Kiera and I had dropped off the Chevelle at the auto body shop below Evan's loft, then gotten a ride over here with Evan and Jenny for a proper send-off with everyone. I might have teared up after dropping off my baby. Maybe. A little. Damn it, I missed my car already.

I hugged Jenny first, giving her an extra-tight squeeze. "This won't be forever," I told her, hoping she understood what I meant by that.

She wiped tears off her cheeks as we released each other. "I know. And I know this is important. You don't need to worry about us, Kellan. Evan and I...we're good."

Her smile was sad but untroubled, and it made me happy to see that while she missed him, she wasn't worried about him. "Good. Because you two are kind of my role models for a healthy relationship."

Jenny laughed, and her eyes drifted to Kiera saying goodbye to her sister. "I don't think you need role models anymore. I think you're doing just fine."

Considering all the things Kiera and I had kept from each other last tour, I wasn't sure if that statement was true, but I appreciated it, nonetheless.

Jenny started to move away from me, then stopped. Stepping closer to me, she lowered her voice. "Hey, Evan told me about how hard the music video was for you. He told me what it put you and Kiera through." Unwanted memories popped into my head, and I averted my eyes. Jenny placed a hand on my arm, and I looked back at her. "He also said the only reason you did it was for him. For him and the guys, so the band would have a real shot at making it, and I just..." She swallowed and looked like she might cry again. "I'm sorry you and Kiera had to go through that, but I'm...grateful that you did. The band means so much to Evan. You, the guys, you all mean so much to Evan. To both of us," she added with a smile.

My gaze drifted to our feet as a weird feeling of warmth and acceptance went through me. It meant a lot to me that she understood, especially since I'd been feeling the weight of judgement on me ever since that video had released. Not sure if I could speak through the sudden knot in my throat, I nodded and pulled her in for another hug.

Rachel approached me once Jenny moved over to Matt. I opened my arms in invitation. Her tan cheeks flushed a little, but she stepped in for a quick hug. After we separated, she smoothed her sheet of dark hair, then bit her lip and quietly murmured, "Keep Matt safe?" She eyed Griffin after she said that, like she was sure if any harm came to Matt, it would be his fault. And honestly, she wasn't wrong to think that.

I stopped myself from laughing and nodded at her. "Of course. Although he's usually the one keeping us safe." Louder, so he would hear, I said, "Matt *loves* being our babysitter."

Matt looked over from where he was talking with Jenny. He

instantly frowned and flipped me off. Rachel giggled, then gave me a shy smile. "Maybe let him have a little fun then."

This time, I did laugh. "I will," I said with a nod. If anyone deserved a break, it was Matt.

Anna stepped up to me next. "I'm going to miss you, Hot Bod," she said, yanking me into her for a hug.

I laughed at her old nickname for me as I held her tight. When we released each other, my eyes drifted to her stomach, and I frowned. "Are you going to be all right here on your own?"

She twisted her lips at me. "One, I'm not alone." She paused to indicate Jenny and Rachel. "Two, of course I'll be fine. I'm pregnant, not an invalid." She rolled her eyes, then leaned in to squeeze me again. "Take care of my sister, okay?"

"Always," I whispered, looking over her shoulder at Kiera saying goodbye to Denny. She was my primary responsibility. Higher than anything else. I'd die before I let any harm come to her.

Anna wandered off to be mauled by Griffin, and I walked over to Denny and Kiera. Denny gave me a small smile. "Thanks for letting me know when you were leaving."

With a grin, I told him, "Well, I didn't want to get ambushed again for not being communicative."

Kiera furrowed her brow as she looked between us. Denny rolled his eyes, then frowned like he was remembering the rest of that conversation. "You might want to clear up this mess with Sienna sooner rather than later, mate."

That made me frown too. "I'm trying, but nobody believes me." I had a feeling the denial would have to come from Sienna for people to believe it, and I also had a feeling she'd never deny it, not if keeping it going helped her career. With a sigh, I shook my head. "It's just a phase. It'll pass soon, it has to."

Denny's worried eyes shifted to Kiera. "Yeah," he murmured, but I could see he didn't entirely believe that. I gave him a quick one-armed hug, then the large SUV Matt had arranged for us pulled up, and it was time to leave. Again. And even though I wasn't leaving Kiera behind this time, I still found it difficult to leave Seattle. That feeling of loss was reflected on every face around me. The guys looked especially glum as we drove to the airport. Even Griffin seemed somber, and that was kind of shocking. Stuff like this usually had him bouncing off the walls.

"We'll be back soon," I told them. "And for longer next time. Much longer."

They all looked over at me, then they each smiled and nodded. It always helped to have something to look forward to. The last tour had taught me that too.

But honestly, as soon as we stepped onto our new tour bus, a bus we were sharing with Justin and his band this time, everyone's mood shifted to excitement. We were good at this, we were comfortable with this, we were born for this, and we were going to have a good time. A great time.

Our first concert was in L.A. and the energy backstage was exactly how I remembered it. Most of the bands joining us on the road were from the last tour, so I got to catch up with Kurt, Benji, and their bandmates. But thank fuck, not Paul. I had a feeling Justin would never invite him on a tour again.

This tour was much smaller than the previous one. It was a lot shorter too and had fewer perks. In other words, no hotel rooms this time. We'd be stuck on the buses between shows, but that was fine. We'd survive.

Some things were the exact same, though. Everyone freely mingled backstage with the fans, and there was still a surprising amount of alcohol to be found. Matt's lucky bucket had made the journey with him, and while it was always within his reach, he looked at ease as we waited for our turn. A far cry from the first show of our first tour. His growth made me proud.

There was one major difference between this time and the last time, though—the number of people wearing D-Bags merchandise. Even though Justin was once again the headliner of this tour, almost every single fan had something with our band name on it: shirts, bracelets, and some people even had stickers on their cheeks. They definitely knew who we were this time, and it was no happy accident that they were advertising our name. It was so surreal.

As was the fact that Sienna's name was almost as widespread as our own. I couldn't seem to escape the gossip as I wandered backstage. The gossip or the direct questions. Everyone wanted to know the truth, but no one believed me when I told it to them. "I'm not in a relationship with Sienna" and "Sienna and I are just colleagues" wafted from my mouth on autopilot, but it didn't make a lick of difference. The fans wanted us together, so in their minds, we were.

I tried to point out Kiera to them, to make it official to *someone*, but Kiera put a stop to that real quick with a painful pinch to my back. She didn't want to be subjected to their curiosity, didn't want her name somehow getting leaked to the media, didn't want the spectacle of being newsworthy. She just wanted to lie low until the gossip died down. I understood that, so I did what she asked and kept my responses as vague as possible.

When it was our turn to go onstage, I was already buzzing with eager energy. Kiera gave me a soft kiss before I followed the guys to the staging area. Her eyes were practically glowing with excitement for the show. I loved that she still enjoyed watching us perform, even after all this time. I loved that she was here this time, sharing the moment with me. I loved everything about this.

"Good luck," she told me.

My grin was uncontainable. I couldn't wait to go out there. "Thank you. Back in a bit."

I practically jogged my way to where the guys were already being prepped by crew members. As one of them handed equipment to me, I asked my friends, "You guys ready for this?"

Griffin smirked at me. "Born ready, dude." His expression shifted to a frown. "Although..." He turned to look at Matt. "I think it's time you gave me a shot at lead."

Matt immediately shook his head. "Give it a rest, Griff."

Griffin splayed his hands. "What? I'm just saying, you know the first show of a tour is hard for you. Let me take the load, in case you get sick."

Matt shook his head again. "I'm not gonna get sick. I'm fine." Right after he said that, though, he glanced at the stage and the massive crowd beyond it. His face paled, and he immediately looked away.

Griffin laughed, the sound almost lost in the noise coming from the audience. "You are so gonna hurl, dude. You should see your face right now."

Matt actually did look a little sick as he inhaled a deep breath and exhaled slowly out of his mouth. I smacked Griffin across the stomach to get him to shut up, then stepped in front of Matt. "You all right?"

He gave me a stiff nod. "Yep. It'll be fine. It's always fine."

Evan put a hand on his shoulder. "You got this. Nothing to worry about."

Matt nodded again. He was looking a little better now that he was deep breathing and avoiding looking at the crowd. Glancing at Griffin putting his earpiece in, I told Matt, "You know, if you start picturing Griffin's face on every person in the crowd, it might not freak you out anymore. It might even make you want to go out there, just so you can see thousands of Griffins worshipping you."

Matt snorted. "I'm not sure picturing thousands of Griffins would help anyone."

Griffin heard that and flipped him off. "Thousands of Griffins would help everyone. Except we wouldn't worship you. We'd storm the stage and rip that fucking guitar out of your hands."

A smirk crossed Matt's lips. "No, I think you'll worship me. Crying, screaming, down-on-your-knees worship me."

The satisfied look left Griffin's face. "Don't you dare make thousands of me worship you."

Matt just grinned, then he surprised us all by being the first one to hop onto the stage. Evan laughed as he looked at me. "You might have just cured his stage fright."

I grinned back at him. "Who knew tormenting Griffin was the answer."

Evan pursed his lips. "Huh, that's actually not very surprising. We really should have thought of that one years ago."

Griffin was not amused by us. "Hey, Evan, I got you something." He raised his clenched fingers, then slowly unfurled his middle one. He turned to me. "Don't be jealous, Kell, I got you one too." He repeated the gesture to me with his other hand, an annoyed smirk on his face. "Assholes."

Evan and I looked at each other, then started laughing. Griffin rolled his eyes, then followed Matt onto the stage. Evan, still laughing, followed close behind him. Someone handed me my guitar, and I grinned as I slung it over my back. Showtime. I stepped onto the stage right behind Evan, and I was rewarded with a shriek so loud that I was certain it could be heard from blocks away. I sauntered to the microphone as the guys got into position.

Leaning forward, I told the crowd, "Evenin'." They screamed like I'd just given them all their dream homes or something. I grinned as I scanned the crowd. Guys were hollering through their hands, girls were jumping up and down, everyone was ready for the show to start.

The noise died down somewhat, and in the comparative silence, I heard a cluster of girls shout, "We love you, Kellan!"

Being singled out like that was relatively new for me. Last tour, people hadn't known my name. At least, not until I'd told it to them. And even though I knew Sienna was the reason this crowd knew it—my name had been leaked not long after that first photo—seeing their affection warmed me. Real or not, it was sweet. "I love you guys too," I told them, meaning it in the general sense of the word. I had a profound appreciation for all our fans. I owed them everything, and that was a form of love. Some of the girls in front grabbed each other and screamed, taking my words literally, and just for them. It made me laugh.

Unslinging my guitar, I asked the crowd if they were having a good time. They screamed that they were, but I wasn't done playing with them. Flipping my guitar around to the front, I said, "Hmmm, I don't know. Doesn't really sound like you guys are having fun." While the crowd erupted with noise, I quickly glanced at the guys. They were all in place, all ready, all watching for my cue. Well, all except for Griffin, of course. He was busy making obscene gestures to the girls closest to him. And that was why we never began a show with one of the very few songs where Griffin played first. We'd learned the hard way that he was too easily distracted on stage.

Shaking my head at the crowd, I told them, "Let's try that again. I said, is everybody having a good fucking time!" I shouted that, and my energy transformed the crowd's energy into something truly chaotic. If it went on for too long, they might damage the building.

I looked back at Evan and nodded, and he started the song. The guys and I had spent a considerable amount of time while recording the album planning which songs to use on the tour. They were all on the album, and since the album had already released and was doing really well, a lot of the crowd knew the songs and sang along with me. I loved it. It made me feel like we were back at Pete's, performing for a crowd that truly knew us. It electrified me, and I was still flooded with energy when our last song finished, and we gave the crowd a bow. I didn't want to get off the stage—I could have stayed up there for hours—but this was Justin's show. We were just here to warm them up for him, and it was time for me to step back and let that happen.

After stepping off the stage and handing my stuff to the crew, I found Kiera. She was beaming at me as I tossed my arms around her. I held her tight, savoring the feel of her, the smell of her. Even though I knew I was sweaty and should probably give her some space, I rubbed my cheek against her neck and murmured, "Let's go back to the bus." If I couldn't be on a stage, being alone with her was the next best thing. Or *the* best thing, really.

Kiera pulled on the belt buckle loops of my jeans, her fingers digging into the denim like she desperately wanted me. Just that small reaction revved me up even more, and I decided right then and there that Kiera and I were claiming the bedroom on the bus. If I had to guard it to keep Griffin out of it, then so be it.

I was just about to grab her hand and pull her to the parking area when the crowd started chanting something. Lifting my head, I looked toward the stage to hear them better. Whatever they were saying was disjointed; they weren't saying it together, so it was just a cacophony of sound.

"What are they chanting?" Kiera asked. "I can't make it out."

I couldn't either until they finally synched up, and it became a clear word. I was surprised when I understood. And disappointed. Because what they wanted, I couldn't give them. Turning to Kiera, I told her, "They're saying 'Regretfully.' They want to hear the single." Damn it. The guys and I hadn't considered this happening. I hated the fact that I was going to have to let the fans down. And fuck, if this was the trend, I was going to have to let them down every single show. That darkened my mood, killing some of my buzz. Kiera nodded as I looked back at the stage. "We don't have her vocal track. We can't perform that song without Sienna...unless..."

I knew Kiera would never go for it—she would *never* willingly go out on that stage—but truly, it was our only option. I gave her a mischievous smile. She instantly knew what I was thinking, and immediately freaked out. Eyes wide, she tried to shove me away, then tried to extract herself from my arms. Tightening my hold, I laughed. "Sorry, babe. You know I don't like disappointing the fans, and you're the only one here that can fill in for Sienna."

She managed to twist herself around so that her back was to

my chest. That only made it easier for me to hold her, though; I had a firm grip around her waist. "No way in hell, Kyle! I am not going up there!"

There was an edge of hysteria to her voice. I would never actually pull her on stage, but I backed up like I fully intended to. "I'm sorry, but you're gonna have to sing with me tonight."

She started struggling and screaming in earnest. Her screeching was so loud that it wouldn't have surprised me if the still-chanting crowd could hear her. I spotted several crew members watching us while they prepped Justin and his band-mates. Justin was smirking at me, shaking his head of shaggy blond hair. *Asshole*, he mouthed.

Knowing he was right, and I was going to give Kiera an aneurism if I continued, I let her go. Then I held up my hands, just in case she smacked me. "Don't you want to live out your girl band fantasy? I'll help you through it, and if you get sick, there's usually a bucket in the corner." Matt's trusty bucket was almost always tucked right by the stairs.

Her eyes seemed to darken as she glared at me. "You're sleeping in your own cubby tonight," she stated.

There wasn't an ounce of teasing in her tone. Oh, shit. Did I actually piss her off? Would she seriously make me "sleep on the couch" so to speak? Damn it. Didn't she know I would never actually do that to her? Kiera turned away from me, and I backpedaled as quickly as I could. "I was joking, Kiera." Ignoring me, she stormed off with her fists tight to her sides. Shit. "Kiera? You know I was kidding, right?"

She tossed a sly, suggestive smile over her shoulder, and I instantly relaxed. Oh, thank fuck, she was messing with me. I gave her a devious grin in return. I kind of liked her messing with me; I was definitely claiming that bed now.

I took off after her. Quickly catching up, I wrapped her in my arms again. She giggled as I brought my lips to her ear. "That was not very nice," I said, nibbling on her earlobe.

She tilted her head, relaxing in my arms. "Neither is what you did." She gave me a stern look, and I laughed.

Grabbing her hand, I started leading her away. "Come on. Let's go find the bus." We had a good hour until tear down, and I planned on making the most of every single second.

Chapter 17

SURPRISE

On our way back to the bus, we passed by an open maintenance closet. Something caught my eye, and I stopped at the doorframe to peer inside. There was a bright yellow roll of *Do Not Enter* caution tape on one of the shelves. A great idea struck me, and I grinned and looked around to see if anyone was watching us.

Kiera frowned at me and asked, "What are you doing?"

Seeing that the coast was clear, I darted into the room and grabbed the roll. Tucking it under my arm, I told her, "You'll see." Then the two of us hurried away before someone yelled at me to put it back.

Once we were inside the bus, I found some tape, a thick marker, and a piece of paper. Then I blocked off the back bedroom with a sign that read: *Reserved for Mr. and Mrs. Kyle. Stay Out. That means you, Griffin*. I hoped Justin and his band-mates weren't annoyed by me presumptuously claiming the only real bed, but I remembered all too well how many people had "shared" Griffin's bed on the last tour, and I wasn't about to subject Kiera to used sheets, especially sheets used by Griffin. That thought made even *me* shudder.

Most of the guys laughed when they saw my sign later that evening, once we were all back on the buses, on our way to the next location. Griffin pouted. Pointing down the hallway, he said, "You're not serious about the bedroom, right?"

I raised an eyebrow at him. "I'm dead serious. You got the bed last time."

With an expression of *So?* he shook his head. "I shared my bed with anyone who wanted it. You know that."

Kiera gagged a little, then started coughing. I glanced at her sitting beside me before looking back up at Griffin. "Yeah, I do know that, and while it was nice of you, it was gross, and we're not sharing."

Griffin rolled his eyes while some of the other guys on the bus laughed. "Wuss," he said, then he muttered something about just what he would share with me before leaving to go claim a cubby.

Justin had a weird look of amusement and disgust on his face as he stepped up to us. I cringed as I met eyes with him. "I probably should have asked *you* first, though, since it's your tour, your bus."

With a smile, he shook his head. "Nah, go ahead and take it. I don't mind the cubbies. They're homey." His grin turned mischievous, and his pale eyes glowed with amusement. "Besides, I wouldn't dare stand between two newlyweds. And I definitely wouldn't make you have sex in those cubbies every night. Homey or not, it's more fun if you have space to roll around."

Kiera's eyes widened, and she instantly looked away from Justin. Peeking up at me, she said, "I'm gonna...go to bed." She gave me a kiss on the cheek, stood from our table, then muttered, "Goodnight," to Justin and fled as quickly as she politely could.

Justin laughed as he watched her retreat. "Oops. Forgot she was shy. Sorry."

I chuckled as I watched Kiera escaping. "It's fine. By the end of this tour, I doubt comments like that will even faze her."

He laughed again, but as I turned to look back at him, his expression changed. The humor left him, and he seemed contemplative. He chewed on his lip and furrowed his brow as he glanced back at where Kiera had gone and then at me. He wasn't saying anything, but I heard his thoughts in the silence.

With a sigh, I told him, "It's not true. Nothing is going on between Sienna and me."

His lips tightened, then he shook his head. "I wasn't going to ask. I've been in this business long enough to know not to ask." I nodded at that. I supposed he had. He nibbled on his lip again as he watched me. "But since you brought it up, what *is* going on? It's all anyone is talking about. That video..." He looked back down the hallway. "Does she...? I mean, are we supposed to make sure she doesn't...?" He looked lost, like he wasn't sure what he was supposed to do or how he could possibly manage doing it.

I gave him a soft smile. "She knows everything. She was there for the video; she's been there for all of it. I'm not hiding anything from my wife."

Justin collapsed a little, the relief evident. "Oh, thank God, because I honestly didn't think I could keep her in the dark about that. Someone's going to bring it up."

I ran a hand down my face with a sigh. "I know. Believe me, I know." Fans wanted to talk about it, DJs wanted to talk about it, even my friends wanted to talk about it. Shaking my head, I said, "Has the label ever asked you to do something like this? Something...you didn't agree with, but you felt like you had to do it anyway?"

Justin's expression became concerned. "Are you saying the label forced you into doing it?"

Another weary exhale left me. "My choices were...limited."

Justin studied me for a moment before slowly shaking his head. "Sorry, man. They've never asked me to do something I wasn't comfortable with, and I wasn't in a relationship when I signed up, so..." He shrugged with his palms out, guilt that he couldn't relate on his face.

I nodded again, appreciating his attempt, but understanding that he'd probably had a much different experience than me. The way he'd phrased his comment struck me as odd, though, and I suddenly remembered something Kiera had told me. About Justin texting Kate. A lot. Half-smile on my face, I said, "Are you in a relationship *now*?"

He grinned and looked away. "I don't know. Maybe. We'll see." He clapped my shoulder, then made his way to the cubbies, smiling the whole time.

We fell into an easy, familiar rhythm with the new tour, and it was almost like we'd never left the last one. Everyone hung out, everyone helped out, everyone encouraged each other. It was the same sense of family and camaraderie that I'd felt before, and now that Kiera was with me, I'd be happy doing this every day of my life.

The only part I wasn't especially enjoying was doing interviews at the radio stations. Now that we were more popular than before, we were being asked to go down to the station to perform live. That was fine with me—I loved performing—but there was always that awkward moment when people wanted a definitive answer on whether I was with Sienna or not, which led to that awkward moment when they didn't believe me when I said no. It was getting to the point where saying no was aggravating people, like they were annoyed I was lying to them or something. They were respectful enough not to say anything to my face, but after I left, they made sure to share their thoughts with all their listeners. And that included me sometimes.

It was really getting on my nerves. The DJs, the fans, nobody was listening to me, and I wasn't sure what to do about it. Some of the nonsense had died down since Sienna and I had parted ways, but every concert, the fans talked about her backstage and chanted a request for our song. And held up signs with our godawful combined name: Kell-Sex. That was how they'd chosen to portray us as a couple. Just seeing the word annoyed the fuck out of me, and I made a point of ignoring any sign that started with that moniker.

It would stop soon. Sienna and I were both incredibly busy, so the odds of our paths crossing again were low. And without any new fuel, the gossip-fire would die. It had to.

But...I'd forgotten how tenacious Sienna was.

We were in Texas, lounging on the bus before the show. Griffin had just hit me hard with a Hacky Sack, tossing out an insult to my manhood, all because I'd been playfully flirting with my wife. Apparently, Kiera had a cowboy fetish, and I'd been giving her my best southern drawl. Griffin had called me an "embarrassment to penises everywhere," so I grabbed the ball and nailed him in the junk with it. The way he doubled over was extremely satisfying. *Better to be an embarrassment than to be broken, huh, Griff?*

While the guys all cringed, joked, and laughed, grateful that it wasn't them, Justin's bassist, Mark, hopped onto the bus. His face was full of excitement and disbelief as he searched the bus for his friends. Seeing Justin by Griffin, he said, "You are not going to believe who's here."

As Justin said, "Ah, okay, who's here?" Kiera and I looked at each other. The expression on her face matched the feeling in my stomach, and before Mark even said her name, we both knew exactly who was here.

"Sienna Sexton, man."

Kiera and I both sighed at the same time. Yep, we were right. Twisting to look at Mark, I frowned and said, "She's here? Why?" Sienna was on her own tour right now. I didn't know her schedule, but the chances of us being in the same city at the same time seemed...slim.

He shrugged at me. "I don't know. She's got some uptight blonde bitch with her who told me to find you, stat. Who the hell actually uses the word 'stat'?"

I knew exactly who would use that word. I'd heard it barked at me several times during the promo tour. A weary exhale left me. "That would be Tory." Looking over at Kiera, I said, "I guess we should go see what Sienna wants." Kiera's face matched the reluctance in the pit of my stomach, but she nodded.

Evan and Matt came with us to find Sienna. Griffin, still cupping his junk and grunting in pain, stayed on the bus. We were early for the show tonight, and the venue was relatively quiet. A couple of staff members pointed us in the right direction, and it didn't take us long to find a private office being watched by Sienna's bodyguards. Even though they knew who I was, since they were the same guards she'd had with her at the label's house, and even though they had to know Sienna was looking for me, they wouldn't let me by them until I'd been officially cleared. It was annoying, but I tried to keep in mind that Sienna was extremely well known. If she always had tight security around her, there was probably a good reason for it.

Walking into the office, I spotted Tory leaning against the far wall, scowling as she flipped through a too-full planner that would give Matt stomach problems if it was his. Sienna was in front of her. She turned to face us, and her neutral expression instantly shifted into a flawless, megawatt smile as she met eyes with me. Once again, she looked like she'd been missing me every day since the last time we'd seen each other. And once again, I hadn't heard from her since that same time. Her face didn't mesh with my experience, and that made me wary. Or maybe it was just the fact that she was *here* that was making me paranoid.

"Oh my God, Kellan! It's been so long." She moved toward me with her arms open. Knowing how intimate her greetings could be, I held up a finger to stop her. She didn't hug me, but she still managed to peck my cheek. "It's absolutely lovely to see you."

Her habit of singling me out was making me uncomfortable. I hadn't entered the room alone, but she hadn't even looked at Kiera or my bandmates. I waved my hand, indicating them and the venue. "What are you doing here? Shouldn't you be on your tour?" I knew I was being kind of rude, but my suspicion was growing with every passing second.

She gave me a small, almost embarrassed smile as she shrugged one shoulder. "I'm playing nearby and had the night off. I just couldn't miss out on an opportunity to see you perform."

So she *was* in the area? If that was true, then I supposed it wouldn't be too odd for her to stop by. Right? I honestly didn't know her well enough to know for sure. It wasn't like we were friends who talked all the time. But she *had* mentioned she was a fan...and it *had* genuinely seemed like she'd meant it when she'd said it. "Well, it should be a good show," I told her with a nod.

She clasped her hands together, beaming just like my eager fans. "It's going to be fabulous. I can't wait!"

I wanted to believe her, wanted to take everything she was saying at face value, but I just couldn't shake the feeling that something deeper was going on here. "Did you want to see me, just to tell me you were watching the show tonight?"

Her face morphed into a dark expression of arrogant annoyance. And then it instantly evaporated into a delighted smile. It happened so fast that I almost wasn't sure it had happened at all. "Actually, I had a brilliant idea, and I wanted to run it by you."

There it is. She wants something from me. As wariness filled me, I crossed my arms over my chest. There were certain things I was *not* going to agree to, so if she thought I was still an easy sell, she was mistaken. "Yeah? What's your idea?"

She briefly frowned at my chest before smiling again. "Well, I don't know about you, but I'm being hounded nonstop to perform the new single at every show."

Her eyebrow lifted in question, and I nodded. "Yeah, I'm getting that a lot too."

She bit her lip and lightly pressed her fingernail against my chest. "I can't really perform it without you."

I deliberately looked down at her finger, wanting her to remove it. If she thought flirting with me would give her an automatic yes to whatever she wanted, she was again mistaken. "Nick can give you my vocals, or you can hire another guy to sing my part." I wasn't sure what else she expected from me.

Sienna looked irritated that I wasn't falling all over her, begging her to tell me what I could do for her. "It's not the same," she said, a slight whine in her accented voice. "I'd like to perform it again with you. Really wow the fans. Blow the lid off this place."

Understanding flooded me, followed closely by surprise. I looked around at where we were. If she was suggesting what I thought, I was floored. This venue was tiny compared to where she routinely performed. "You want to perform the song tonight? Here?"

Looking like she was planning the greatest surprise in the history of surprises, she nodded. "Wouldn't that be wild? Nobody would expect it. What do you think?"

I had to admit, I was torn. The fans asked for that song every show, and we were never able to give it to them. Guilt followed me after every performance. The chance to alleviate that guilt, even if it was just this one time, was a strong temptation. But there had to be more to it for Sienna. Unless maybe she felt the same guilt, and she wanted to do something about it? Something more meaningful than playing recorded tracks or hiring a stand-in.

Still, I looked back at Evan and Matt before answering her. Evan was frowning. He wanted Sienna to be more vocal about the nature of our "relationship." He was just as annoyed by all the questions as I was. Matt was smiling. He knew what a guest appearance like this could do for the band. Everyone would be talking about it tomorrow. And yes, that was great for the D-Bags. But for me? I wasn't sure.

Like Sienna could see me vacillating, she leaned in and said, "Just imagine the headlines tomorrow, and what that could do for your friends' careers. *'Sienna Sexton surprises the audience on Avoiding Redemption's sold-out tour...'*"

And that was when I realized that this could benefit Justin just as much as it could benefit the D-Bags. Maybe more so, especially if it was worded in that way. But would it be? I looked down at Kiera, trying to gauge her thoughts. She studied me for a moment, her eyes focused as her mind spun through the potential problems. After a moment of contemplation, she nodded. The possible good here was outweighing the bad. And it was only one night, then Sienna would be gone again. It might rekindle the gossip mongering, but I'd just continue answering the questions the way I always answered them. It would be fine. Annoying, but fine.

"All you want from me is one song?" I asked Sienna, wanting to be sure I understood her intentions.

She nodded as she giggled in excitement. "This is going to be great. For all of us."

I hoped that was true.

Everything was surprisingly normal after that. Sienna stayed hidden in the office to make sure the surprise wasn't accidentally spoiled. All the bands and everyone who worked on the show knew she was here, of course, but everyone stayed tightlipped about it. The only thing that marked tonight as special in any way, was when the tour manager informed me that the D-Bags would be closing the show.

"What?" I asked, stunned. "No, this is Justin's tour. We're here in a supporting role, and it should stay that way."

The haggard looking man shrugged. "This came from up top. It's not up to me, and it's definitely not up to you." He clapped my shoulder, his face both an apology and an order.

I sighed as he walked away. "This isn't right," I muttered.

Kiera squeezed my hand. "No, but it makes sense for the..." she looked around to make sure no one could hear her, "...for the encore to happen right after your set. And it *should* be the last song of the night. Justin going up after that might feel like a letdown. For the crowd and for him." Her face scrunched in a guilty cringe, then she shrugged. "Plus, it's just this one show. I'm sure Justin understands."

She made good points, but even still, I had to let him know this wasn't my call. Or my top choice. Giving Kiera a kiss on the head, I left to go find him. My gut twisted when I did come across him. He was sitting in a chair, an astonished expression on his face as he ran a hand through his layered hair. Guilt swirled inside me. Maybe I should have said no after all. But this could help him too.

"Hey," I said, cautiously approaching him. If he blamed me, this could turn violent. Or very vocal, at least.

He blinked a few times before looking up at me. "Hey. You heard?"

Swallowing to ease the tightness in my throat, I nodded. "Yeah. I'm so sorry. I asked them not to move us. I told them it was wrong. I told them your band should still—"

Justin raised his hand to cut me off. "Nah, I get it, man. It makes sense if you think about it."

"Yeah, but that doesn't mean it doesn't suck."

Justin smirked. "True. I don't know how to tell my guys. Although I suppose I don't have to. They probably already heard. James is gonna flip."

A long sigh left me. "Want me to go with you when you talk to them?"

He shook his head. "No. I honestly don't think that would help."

The guilt rose even higher as he slowly got to his feet. "I'm so sorry. Please tell them I didn't want this."

Justin eyed me for a moment, then nodded. "We know, Kell. This is bigger than you. Bigger than us too. Don't worry, this isn't the first time I've given the guys hard news, and it won't be the last. We'll be fine. We always are." He shrugged. "It's one of the reasons we work so well together."

I nodded, completely understanding. I'd had to do the same thing for my guys on multiple occasions. "At least it's only for one show."

Justin smiled and shook his head. "Your naïveté is cute." He sighed. "Trust me, changes this big aren't usually temporary."

He patted my arm like there were no hard feelings, then he

wandered off to find his bandmates. I had no idea if I should feel relieved or not. He understood, he wasn't upset, but he also wasn't happy. Even though it wasn't my decision, I felt like I'd just stabbed him in the back.

It was weird to go up last. Weird to listen to Avoiding Redemption's set, knowing we hadn't played yet. Usually, by that point, we were all buzzing with a post-performance high. Now we were all buzzing with pent-up energy. Griffin was being especially obnoxious. Not spilling the secret to the numerous fans backstage was a struggle for him. He was bursting at the seams to brag, and his patience was wearing thin.

Matt was clearly feeling the tension as well and was being snippier than usual. "Stop bouncing around. You're driving me up a fucking wall."

Griffin immediately started hopping in front of him, exuding energy like an overwound toy. "Oh yeah?" he said. "This bugging you?" He beamed at Matt like he was delighted his cousin was providing him with a distraction.

Matt groaned and turned around. Griffin instantly hopped in front of him again. "What, Matt? What's wrong?"

"Stop it," he ground out.

"Or what?"

Matt turned again, Griffin following again. Matt shoved him away. "Or I'll punch you in the balls."

Griffin grinned. "No, you won't. Not before a show. Come on, Matty, hop with me. It'll help your nerves."

Matt rolled his pale eyes. "I'm not hopping around like an idiot with you."

"Come on, do it."

Matt looked over at me, his expression clearly asking me to save him. I laughed, and he rolled his eyes again. "If I do it, will you leave me alone?"

Griffin shrugged. "Sure."

Matt reluctantly bounced on his toes. Once. Griffin snorted. "Wuss." Matt narrowed his eyes, then began bouncing in earnest.

That made Griffin laugh, which made Matt finally laugh, and then the two of them were jumping around like idiots, giggling like they were high.

Kiera slowly shook her head as she watched them, but there was fondness on her face, like she was happy to see Matt letting go a little bit. And maybe even happy to see that Griffin wasn't always a creep.

Finally, it was our time to go up, and we all bounded onstage, eager to get started. Once I was in front of the crowd, microphone in hand, I had just as much trouble not spilling the beans as Griffin. It was so tempting to tell the sea of elated faces what we were keeping from them. Holding back made me giddy and restless, and that energy translated into a searing performance that gave me goosebumps.

We'd barely begun walking off the stage when the chanting for "Regretfully" started. I shared a smile with the guys, then rushed over to Kiera to give her a quick squeeze. The chanting grew in intensity with every passing second. If Sienna hadn't been here, about to perform with me, the guilt would have been excruciating. But *finally* being able to do this for them had me flying high.

I gave Kiera a long, tender kiss before I had to return to the stage. As our mouths moved together, pleasure began mixing with the excitement of the moment, and a different kind of need filled me. Not wanting to get too carried away with *that* desire, I forced myself to stop the kiss. "I better go up there so I can get this over with and take you to bed." 100 percent not joking.

Kiera peered up at me with interest gleaming in her eyes. "I like that plan."

To be honest, I was starting to like that plan more than the surprise, but no...alone time with Kiera could wait. This was a once-in-a-lifetime treat for these fans. I smacked Kiera's ass, for good luck, of course, then hopped back onstage. The chanting turned to shrieking when the crowd spotted me.

I gave them all a bewildered expression as I approached the

microphone. "What are you guys still doing here?" I said over the noise. "It's over." I made a playful shooing motion with my hands, and while the crowd laughed at my antics, none of them appeared to be leaving. Good.

I was about to announce our surprise guest to the crowd when the energy of the audience shifted. Instead of laughter and the occasional scream, now they were yelling, cheering, and jumping as wildly as Matt and Griffin had been earlier. Their focus was behind me, and I knew, without a shadow of a doubt, that Sienna hadn't waited for her agreed-upon cue; she was making her own surprise entrance. A quick peek behind me confirmed that I was right. Wearing a playful smile, Sienna was stealthily walking up to me, like she was about to goose me. I straightened as I stared at her, surprised that she would go against an introduction plan that *she'd* set up. That was when I realized what this looked like to the crowd—an actual, genuine surprise. Like I hadn't known, until this very moment, that she was here. Like she was doing this to surprise *me*. I wasn't sure if it was clever of her or just plain annoying.

Sienna waved to the crowd as she closed the distance between us. Then she wrapped her arms around me, kissed my shoulder, and laid her head on me. The audience was a sea of cell phone lights, and I knew that moment had just been permanently captured. Damn it. That was definitely not going to help the rumors. I slipped out of her embrace as subtly as I could, but I already knew the damage was done.

Keeping a professional smile on my face, I introduced her to the crowd. "Ladies and gentlemen, Ms. Sienna Sexton."

A crew member handed her a microphone, and she bowed and thanked the energized audience. While she did, I looked back at Evan as he got into position behind his drums. He was frowning. He met eyes with me and shook his head, annoyance clear on his face. Since he was sort of hidden back there, he could be the most visually honest out of all of us. I gave him a tight smile in return.

After Sienna finished acknowledging the crowd, I signaled for the song to begin. Then I let the irritation fade and focused on giving the fans the encore they'd been begging to hear for so long. And even though I hated the gossip, hated the manipulation, hated the "marketing" as Sienna put it, I loved finally being able to perform the song again. The crowd ate it up, loudly singing along the entire time. It was hard not to smile through the lyrics, but the tone of the song was angry and aggressive, so I made my face match. Sienna did too, and I got goosebumps again while performing it.

When the song was over, I gave the crowd a wave while Sienna blew them kisses. I looked over to where Kiera was waiting for me. She seemed just as blown away as the crowd had been, her face a mixture of pride and joy. She locked eyes with me, and I slightly shook my head and shrugged. She nodded at me, and I knew she understood. Sienna was frustrating at times, but she certainly knew what people wanted, and she knew exactly how to give it to them.

Chapter 18

AN UNWANTED CHANGE

It didn't take long for me to regret doing the song with Sienna. The gossip the next morning was firmly centered around Sienna and me, with headlines like *Sienna Sexton Surprises Boyfriend on Tour,* and no mention of Avoiding Redemption anywhere. It shouldn't have upset me so much that Justin was snubbed, but it did. I'd really wanted to do some good with this absurd rumor mill and shine some light on him as well as the D-Bags. But the world only seemed to care about my relationship status. I didn't understand, but I was done playing along. If Sienna tried that again, disappointed fans or not, my answer was no.

But as the tour continued, I tried to let it go. Sienna was gone again, and eventually the hype would die down. I could endure the endless questions, innuendo, and requests to sign the photograph of Sienna kissing my shoulder until then. And being on tour certainly helped with forgetting about those things. The guys and I were having a blast. Kiera and I were having a blast. It was so much better having her with me, and as I saw homesickness on the faces of my friends—even Griffin—I wished they could somehow have this too. Maybe one day, when we were the true headliners of a tour, everyone could bring their loved ones with them. I hoped so.

We were in one of the Dakotas, getting ready to head out to a radio station for some sort of contest. Something about darts and pool. I did *not* anticipate winning, especially at the pool portion, unless my teammates could compensate for my complete lack of skill. Regardless of how many times I'd played the game, I never seemed to improve. Probably because I didn't care enough to improve.

Evan was standing in front of his bunk as I edged past him. He was playing with a flattened box of Jujubes. I didn't know what the box represented, but I'd heard him call Jenny Jujube before, so I assumed the box had something to do with her.

I clapped his shoulder as I walked by. "You all right?"

He blinked out of whatever thought he'd been having and tucked the box into his back pocket. "Yeah, just...thinking about home. Jenny's keeping busy with work and her art, but it's getting to her; I can tell." He sighed. "We weren't home very long."

Guilt squeezed my stomach as I saw the sorrow on his face. I'd been blessed with Kiera joining me, a gift I never wanted to take for granted. "The holidays will be here before you know it. Just keep that in mind. You'll see her soon."

He inhaled a deep breath, nodding. "Yeah, I know. Thanks."

I smirked as I shrugged. "Just doing my part to win the bet on you."

Evan rolled his dark brown eyes. "Please, there isn't a bet on Jenny and me."

True, there wasn't, but I wasn't about to let him know that because he still hadn't confirmed whether there was a bet on *me*. I stared at him with an amused smile on my face, and his expression darkened.

"Is there a bet on me?" he asked, an annoyed edge to his voice.

My grin widened. At least he wasn't missing Jenny anymore. "Ready for pool?" I asked, changing the subject. "I'm feeling lucky today. I think I might win this whole thing."

Matt and Griffin stepped into the sleeping area as I said that. Griffin loudly scoffed at my show of confidence. "Oh please, the day you become good at pool is the day my balls shrivel up and die."

Matt's eyes widened as he gaped at me. "Oh my God, Kellan. For the sake of all mankind, you *have* to win this thing."

Griffin flipped off Matt just as Kiera stepped into the room. She eyed the cousins warily, but it didn't seem like she'd heard any of that. I held out my hand for her just as Evan smacked my shoulder. "Is there?" he asked, still focused on his question.

Kiera took my hand, and I pulled her through the group of D-Bags. I shrugged at Evan, still grinning. He smirked at me, then flipped me off. Griffin seemed to think our conversation was about him, and he gave me the bird too. Matt glanced between Evan and Griffin, shrugged, and then he also gave me the finger. Kiera frowned at the group flip off while I laughed my head off. Once we were at the front portion of the bus, she quietly said, "Are they mad at you? Is everything okay?"

Still laughing, I nodded. "Everything's fine. They're just terrified I'm gonna win this thing. Griffin especially." Kiera snorted, and I twisted to frown at her. "What? I could win this."

She patted my stomach. "Of course you can." That should have been assuring, but her tone had way too much fake encouragement to it.

I smirked as I led her off the bus. "If you only knew what was at stake, you'd be more excited about me winning," I murmured.

She just laughed at that, and I smiled at seeing her joy. Definitely blessed.

Griffin surprised me by giving me pointers on the way to the pool hall. Of course, all his pointers were sexual in nature, so I figured he was just talking to talk. Either that, or he'd forgotten what he'd said about his balls and was actually trying to be a good friend. But no. He just wanted to make a crude remark about how girls bending over the table was code for "Grab me now and do naughty things to my no-no places." Fucking Griffin. I gave him a good smack for that one.

The contest was way more entertaining than I'd expected. The four of us were each crowned captains of a team, with the contest winners randomly divvied up among us. Kiera and I ended up on the same team, and I quickly forgot about trying to win this thing and focused all my attention on messing with her. It was so damn easy. She was so intent on doing well, like she truly wanted our team to win. Maybe she'd heard Griffin's pronouncement after all. But she was so cute, with her tongue sticking out as she aimed her dart...I had to try to distract her. It wasn't even optional for me. My hand instinctively found her thigh or her neck or her ass. I literally couldn't stop myself. Especially since it worked so well—I made her miss the dartboard three times in a row. One time, I scared her so badly that she twisted and tossed the dart into the teams playing pool. She nailed Griffin in the ass, and I almost died laughing.

She scowled at me every time, but there was heat in her eyes too. She loved the attention just as much as I loved being attentive. The only real downside to flirting with my wife, besides our team being dead last, which really didn't matter at all, was that the sight of me flirting with a woman made all the other women on my team think it was their turn next. When I wasn't playing or messing with Kiera, I was pushing aside friendly fingers.

"Sienna must be the most laidback girlfriend in the world if she doesn't mind you flirting with other women," one of the girls said, nodding her head at Kiera, who was studying the complicated winner's bracket.

I stifled a sigh as I looked at the contestant. She'd wrapped her fingers around my arm, and there was an excited energy in her eyes, like she was amazed she was here, touching me, and equally amazed that it wouldn't hurt my "girlfriend" to do so. Like Sienna had somehow given her permission to fondle me. "Sienna's not...we're not together," I said, unwrapping the girl's fingers from my arm.

She pursed her lips but nodded. "Right. I know, it's a secret. I won't tell a soul. Promise," she said with a wink. Then she stroked my shoulder. "But just how far does she let you go?"

The excitement was back in her eyes, and I did my best not to roll mine. Why didn't any of them believe me? I pulled the girl's hand off my body just as another girl put a hand on my chest. Then another girl put a hand on my back. They were all giggling, and I was suddenly reminded of the time Rita had cornered me behind the bar at Pete's. At the time, it had felt like Rita had six hands. Now there *were* six hands on me, and it felt like three dozen. I tried to move away, tried to sweep them off my skin, tried to ignore all the comments about how great Sienna was for allowing crap like this, all while trying to be polite and professional, trying to keep in mind that ultimately these were fans, and I didn't want to piss them off. It was a very fine line. It helped that Kiera was now looking my way, smirking at my predicament. *Smirking.*

I mouthed, *Help me,* to her and she openly grinned at me. It was a beautiful sight and a surprising one because there wasn't a trace of jealousy in her expression. Just amusement.

She sauntered my way with her hand extended. I grabbed it, and like magic, the girls around me backed off. "Come on, rock star," she said. "It's time for pool."

Holding her close, like she was a shield, I said, "Oh good. Pool is where I really shine."

Kiera snickered while the girls around us sighed. I loved the fact that only Kiera knew just how funny that comment was. Well, I supposed the rest would know soon enough, but for the moment, the joke was just for Kiera.

What made it even more amusing was the fact that Kiera wasn't any better at pool than me, so when she brazenly said, "Twenty bucks says I sink more shots than you," my reply was a given, because here was someone I might actually beat.

"Forty bucks says you just lost twenty bucks."

The instant I said it, I wanted to take it back. Not because I regretted the bet, but because I had a way more interesting counteroffer for her. Kiera laughed at my comment and stuck out her hand to accept the deal, but I wasn't interested in that deal anymore. Giving her a devilish smile, I leaned in and said, "No, let's make this interesting. If I win, we have sex backstage tonight. If you win, we have sex backstage tonight."

Her mouth popped open, and it was really hard to resist leaning down and sucking that lip into my mouth. I was suddenly ready for this contest to be over with. For tonight's show to be over with—whatever got me into a position where Kiera's arms and legs were wrapped around me.

"Um...I don't think you understand how betting works," she quietly told me.

I shifted my mouth to her ear, letting my lips brush against her skin as I said, "Don't I?" My hand was on her stomach, and I felt her muscles contract, shifting her hips like she was willing my fingers to drift lower. Damn. Could we forfeit the game and leave now?

She murmured, "Okay. Deal," and my cock instantly started hardening. Fuck. I shouldn't think about it here, with eyes and hands all over me, but now it was *all* I could think about. Win or lose, Kiera and I were sharing a moment backstage tonight. I couldn't fucking wait.

The anticipation was throwing off my game. Okay, not really. I was doing about as well as I usually did, missing shot after shot after shot. But then, fate threw me a bone, and an easy shot lined up, and I actually fucking made it. I instantly thrust my hand into the air, yelling, "Yes!" loud enough to get everyone's attention.

People were looking at me like I was insane, since the shot didn't affect my team's standing at all, but I didn't care. I got one in! I started playing the pool cue like a guitar, celebrating my personal victory. Kiera shook her head at me, rolling her eyes with an adoring smile on her lips. "I win," I told her while the girls on our team giggled at me, and the guys on our team intently watched them.

Kiera looked like she wanted to argue, since she still had a turn left, but she didn't because she knew, either way, sex was in our future. God, I loved a bet I couldn't actually lose.

At the end of the contest, we all gathered around the board, waiting for the results to be tabulated. It was very clear that my team wasn't in the running, though. Matt was beside me as we waited. He looked at me, then the board, then back at me. "Did you even try?" he asked.

I gave him a broad grin. "You have no idea how hard I tried." Maybe not at darts, but I was definitely invested in the pool portion of the game.

Matt just shook his head at me. "When you're good at something, you're *really good*. But when you're bad at something, you're *really*—"

I shoved his shoulder before he could finish that thought, and he started laughing. He was still chuckling when one of the DJs lifted the prize into the air. It was a trophy shaped like a giant D, and I had to admit, a part of me really wanted it. "All right, we have our winner!" His gaze shifted to the four of us. Griffin started preening, clearly expecting a victory. "And the Bag with the largest D is..." The DJ paused dramatically, then looked over at the winner. "Evan Wilder! Congratulations!"

Griffin instantly dropped to his knees, threw back his head, and yelled, "Noooooo!" as loud as he could.

Matt and I blankly stared at his theatrical display while Evan laughed so hard that he had to clutch his stomach. Then Griffin fell forward and hunched over his knees as he mock-cried on the floor. Matt slowly shook his head as he looked over at me. "We're gonna hear about this for the next sixty years." Then he grinned. "I'm giving him D-shaped trophy cookies for every birthday after this. With Evan's name frosted on the bottom of them." He rubbed his hands together, an almost maniacal gleam in his eyes.

"And for Christmas, St. Patrick's Day, Easter, Flag Day." He was still muttering holidays as he walked away.

Griffin was mopey and petulant the entire ride back to the venue. He even accused Evan of cheating. Instead of listening to him complain, I teased Kiera with an implied promise of the bet I was soon going to collect on, telling her I could *hard*ly wait. She surprised me by returning the innuendo with a delightful comment that included the word "rager." I couldn't let it go after that, and we tossed suggestive words around until Kiera said something so blatantly obvious that even Griffin knew what we were talking about. "I'm sure you'll reach your climax."

We'd been getting out of the car when she'd said that, and everybody stopped and stared at her. Stunned expressions were on Matt and Evan's faces; Kiera didn't usually make sexual comments. At least, not intentionally. Griffin was looking at Kiera like he was seeing her through new eyes, and he was impressed with what he was seeing. Kiera looked like she'd just stepped out of the car buck naked. Her cheeks went fire engine red as she quickly scanned my friends before locking eyes with me. I tried not to laugh at her failed attempt to be sneaky, but suppressing the giggles was like trying to shove bubbles underwater; they just kept oozing up.

Kiera cringed and said, "That wasn't subtle enough, was it?" and I completely lost the battle. I laughed so hard that I couldn't even answer her. All I could do was shake my head and fall even more in love with her. She adorably dropped her face into her hands, and I wanted to comfort her, especially when the guys started laughing too, but then she peeked at us through her fingers...and laughed along with us. At *herself*. And seeing her turn the could-be mortifying situation into a humorous one made me so proud of her.

Everyone was in a good mood when we entered the venue, even Griffin. He'd perked up after Kiera's goof, amusing himself even more by making his own suggestive remark...something about him coming. I wasn't sure. I really wasn't paying that much attention to him; all I could think about was making love to my wife. I figured we could squeeze in a couple of times before I needed to focus on my job.

Coming up behind Kiera, I wrapped my arms around her. "Where shall we go?" I murmured into her neck.

Kiera looked around the bustling room for a moment before peeking back at me. "Were you serious about that bet?"

Amusement on my lips, I spun her to face me. "Was I serious about the sex? Always." *With her, always.* Remembering something, I leaned down and whispered in her ear, "And I'm pretty sure I have a favor to return." Oh yeah, that was definitely happening. Just thinking about tasting her was making me inappropriately hard. We needed that privacy *right now.*

Grabbing her hand, I pulled her away. I wasn't entirely sure where I was going, but I'd know it when I saw it—somewhere with no people and a door that I could push her up against. Fans approached me while I searched for my haven. I always stopped and gave them my full attention for a few moments, but then I steadfastly resumed my quest.

My relentlessness made Kiera giggle. "Shouldn't you be helping set up the show, rock star?"

Yes, probably. I smiled at her over my shoulder. "When I can concentrate properly, I'll—"

Someone smashed into me, cutting off my sentence. Justin. I put my hand on his shoulder, steadying him as I steadied myself. His pale blue eyes were wide when he looked up from his phone. Giving me an embarrassed smile, he said, "Oh, hey, sorry, wasn't watching where I was going." He showed us his phone; he was clearly in the middle of texting someone. Probably Kate.

I would have told him to say hi for me, but I had other things on my mind. "No problem, we were just...running an errand."

Justin's confused expression almost made me laugh. There weren't a lot of errands to be done backstage. I could almost feel Kiera's embarrassment beside me, like she thought I'd just blatantly told him what we were doing with my admittedly horrible excuse. Oops.

Not wanting Justin to ask any questions, I clapped him on the shoulder, and we started walking around him. We'd only made it a few steps when Justin said, "Hey, I just wanted to let you know, I totally understand, and there's no hard feelings. We're cool, dude."

That stopped me cold, and icy dread immediately raced up my spine. "What are you talking about?"

"You leaving the tour," he said, closing the distance between us. "I just wanted you to know that I get it. You guys are bigger than this. Even I'll admit that."

I felt like he'd just walked up and sucker-punched me. Was he joking? Because I most definitely was not leaving the tour. I was so stunned that words failed me for a moment. "I'm...leaving... what? What the hell are you talking about?"

Justin's face morphed into an expression of *Oh shit*. "You don't know? I just assumed you knew. Fuck, sorry, man."

Anger simmered in my stomach as his words triggered an awful suspicion. *She wouldn't. She wouldn't do that to me. Or to Justin. Right?* "Know what? What the hell happened since this morning?"

Justin suddenly looked like he wanted to be anywhere but here, telling me this. "Ah, crap. Well, it went down while you guys were doing the thing with the radio station. Some, ah, bigwig from the label showed up and started barking orders at people. He said that he'd be sending people over after the show tonight to 'collect' your things, and if anybody else touched your stuff, there'd be hell to pay."

Kiera stroked my arm, and it was only then that I realized how tightly I was gripping her. "And where exactly are they sending our stuff? Where the fuck are we going?"

Justin cringed as he shifted. "Uh, back to L.A. You're playing Staples Center tomorrow night...with Sienna Sexton. The label's putting you on her tour."

Well, of course they were. God-fucking-damn it. She really *did* do this to us. Her and Nick. It had to be them. Kiera came to the same conclusion, and a loud, "That bitch!" escaped her before she could stop it.

Justin looked at her, then back at me. "I don't think it was her. It's just, you know, you guys are huge now. I mean, you could be selling out venues ten times as big as the places we're going. The label knows that. They're just doing what makes sense, and they're right. It really doesn't make sense for you to be on tour with us. I knew that the minute Sienna showed up for the duet." Soft smile on his face, he put his hand on my arm. "You're beyond this, man. We're holding you back."

No, they weren't. They were the entire reason we were anything of importance to begin with. We'd already been permanently moved to the closing position of the tour, just as Justin had predicted, and I was already struggling with the guilt of that decision. This, this was too much. It wasn't right, and it wasn't the way I wanted it to go down. What did it matter if we'd outgrown the tour—we'd make up for it on the next one. We owed it to the bands to stay. We owed it to the *fans* to stay. Moving us screwed over *everyone*.

I couldn't articulate that to Justin, though. He took my stunned silence as acceptance and gave me a pat on the back before leaving me with my thoughts. Mind spinning, I turned to Kiera. "What the fuck just happened?" I asked her, even though I already knew the answer.

Kiera let out a weary sigh. "Sienna and Nick. That's what happened."

"I don't think so," I stated, reaching into my pocket for my phone. Nick had called me once during the beginning of the promo tour. He'd said it was to make sure we were doing all right, but at the time it had felt like he was subtly reminding me to stick to my lines. I'd saved his number, just in case I needed it in the future. A future like today when I was being blatantly jerked around. As my phone rang, I told Kiera, "This is bullshit, and this is *not* how this is going down." She gave me a half-hearted smile, like she agreed, but she didn't think it was up to me. The fact that she might be right made my blood boil.

"Kellan, what a surprise." From the amused tone of Nick's voice, it wasn't a surprise at all. He'd been expecting me to call him.

Everything inside me tensed, ready for a fight. "What did you do?" I snapped.

"My job," he flatly intoned. "And if you wish to discuss it civilly, then come talk to me. I'm here at the venue, waiting for you."

Surprise washed through me that the "bigwig" Justin had mentioned was Nick. He'd come all the way out here to personally remove me from the tour? That seemed beneath the status of his job. He could have just called the tour manager and made it happen. "You're where?" I asked, certain I'd misheard him.

"I'm here, backstage, waiting for you." He vaguely described the direction he was in and told me to look for his security outside an office door. I told him I'd see him in a minute, then shoved the phone back into my pocket.

Still tightly holding Kiera's hand, I stormed down the hallway. There were a few doors along the way, but only one was being guarded by a large man with his arms crossed over his chest. The guy knocked on the door behind him as we approached, telling Nick, "He's here." He opened the door for me, and I barged through without even acknowledging him. Getting to Nick was the only thing on my mind.

Nick was leaning back in an office chair behind a huge desk piled with paperwork. His hands were casually resting on the arms of the chair, and he looked completely relaxed and comfortable. I was neither of those things. "Why the hell did you pull us from the tour?"

He smiled at me like I'd just asked him how he was doing. Indicating two chairs in front of the desk, he said, "Why don't you have a seat?"

Kiera started to move toward the chairs but stopped when I didn't follow her. "I'm not sitting, and I'm not leaving Justin's tour," I informed Nick.

With a weary sigh, he loosely folded his hands over his lap. "You seem to be under the impression that you have a choice on the matter. You don't. I decide where the acts play and who they play with." He showed me his palms like he had nothing to hide. "Now I'm usually a very flexible man, and I strive to give my artists as much free range as possible." Kiera squeaked out a laugh, and Nick shot her a look that had me tightening my fist. Luckily, he continued without saying anything to her. "But in some cases, when my talent is being wholly underrepresented, I feel the need—no, I feel it's my *duty*—to step in and make things right."

Standing, he tucked his hands into his pockets and walked around the desk. "The hard fact here is that you're too big of an act. You belong in stadiums. It's a waste of our money and a waste of your talent for you to be playing anything smaller. And I'm not a man to waste...anything." He sat on the edge of the desk and shrugged. "Sienna's tour is where you belong. That was made quite clear to me after that duet she performed on stage with you. It's magic whenever you two are together, and we're going to capitalize on that magic."

Inhaling a steadying breath, I told him where I stood on the matter. "No. I'm staying."

The asshole completely ignored me. "Sienna's been informed, and she's graciously made room for you. Your stuff is being moved over tonight, which I'm assuming you already know. A car will be picking you up and taking you to the airport the minute your set is over. When you arrive in L.A. a limo will be waiting, courtesy of Ms. Sexton."

Letting go of Kiera's hand, I crossed my arms over my chest and repeated my intentions. "I said we're staying."

Nick stood up and walked my way. Every step oozed confidence and superiority. "And I said you didn't have a choice. If you read your contract, like you said you did, then you should know that the label has final say over your schedule. If we want to pull you from one tour and put you on another, we will. If we want to send you on an over-fifty singles cruise in Alaska, we will. And you'll go because what you still don't seem to grasp is..." He paused dramatically as he got right in my face. "We own you."

My body started vibrating as I tried to rein in the rage rushing through me. Nick smirked like he knew it. He patted my arm as he stepped back. "And besides, you told me, and I do believe this is a direct quote, 'I will help you promote the album in any way I can...within reason.' I think asking you to perform in the hottest concert tour on Earth is very...reasonable." He lifted a questioning eyebrow. "Don't you?"

There was nothing I could say to that, and he fucking knew it. All I could do was glare at him, clench my jaw, and stop myself from exploding. Assaulting him would only get me fired and arrested. Nick gave me a condescending smile, then left the room.

I was seething as I stood there in the silent office. I could feel Kiera's gaze on me, but I couldn't look at her yet. My body was shaking with pent-up adrenaline, and I didn't want to go off on her. She didn't deserve it. Needing an outlet, I grabbed one of the chairs in front of the desk. With a grunt of frustration, I heaved it against the far wall. It left dents in the drywall, and I instantly felt bad. The venue didn't deserve my rage either.

Kiera timidly put a hand on my arm. "It will be okay, Kellan."

I knew she was right, but I was so tired of not having a voice. Turning to look at her, I said, "I thought I was done being manipulated, but every turn I take another string gets pulled."

She nodded, then cupped my cheek. Her tenderness cooled some of my fire. "I know this sucks," she told me. "Believe me, I know. But...Nick may actually have a point."

More of my anger fizzled as I studied her. "What do you mean?"

She laced her arms around my neck, hugging me. "As much as I love Justin and the guys, you are bigger than them. I mean, you've already replaced them as the closing act. You do belong in a stadium. And Staples Center, Kellan. That's...as large as it gets."

There was so much pride in her smile, like she truly did want this for me, even if the way it had happened was dirty and underhanded. I supposed I wanted it for my band too, but I'd really been enjoying what we had *right now*. I wasn't ready to give it up. "I like small," I told her. Letting a suggestive smile curve my lips, I added, "I like intimate."

Heat lit her eyes for a moment, and she leaned up to kiss me. "I know," she said against my lips. "But you might like this too. You won't know for sure if you don't try. Maybe this will be a good thing."

Again, a part of me knew she was right, but I still didn't see why we couldn't finish this the way we'd started it, and then take a step up on the next tour. This felt more like a publicity stunt than a genuine concern about the D-Bags being "wholly underrepresented," and I was tired of being Nick and Sienna's prop. I shook my head at Kiera, not wanting to voice the concerns that I knew she had too. "I think you're being naïve again," I told her instead.

She frowned at me, her eyes mirroring my thoughts. "I'm trying to look on the bright side."

Right. I let out a long sigh. "Guess we better go tell the guys the 'good' news."

I held out my palm for her, and she took it with a smile. I cringed as I looked at her fingers. "Sorry if I bruised you earlier." I'd been holding her hand pretty tight when we'd stepped into the room.

She warmly smiled at me. "If it stops you from hitting him, squeeze me anytime."

I crooked a grin at her. "Duly noted." She giggled as I opened the door, and I made myself absorb that sound instead of pointlessly worrying about whatever Nick and Sienna had planned for me.

Nick and his security were nowhere to be seen, and the

hallway was surprisingly empty. Annoyance flashed through me that Kiera and I had privacy now, but the desire to take advantage of that privacy was completely gone. Cockblocked by Nick. I almost believed that had been intentional.

Kiera and I trudged back to the main backstage area, and I spotted my friends talking to Justin. He was telling them something, shrugging and shaking his head, then he pointed toward the hallway we'd just come from. Matt was the first one to spot me. He bumped Griffin to get his attention, which got Evan's as well, and they all looked my way. Their faces were stunned, worried, and more than a little confused. They gave Justin a goodbye clap on the arm, then rushed my way. I inhaled a deep breath as they approached.

Justin met eyes with me while the D-Bags weaved through the room. I gave him a small nod in apology. He returned the gesture with a tiny smile, then he turned away from me and walked over to his friends. Just that brief interaction filled me with guilt. This wasn't right.

Matt reached me first, Griffin and Evan right behind him. "What's going on, Kell? Everyone is saying we got pulled from the tour. Justin mentioned something about Sienna?"

I sighed, then told them about my "meeting" with Nick. When I was finished, they all just stared at me with their mouths popped open. Griffin recovered from the shock first. He smacked Matt across the chest. "Dude! We're doing a stadium show! Holy shit, we're doing a stadium show! In our home-fucking-town!"

While Evan shook his head, murmuring, "Damn," Griffin jumped up and down in excitement.

All the color drained from Matt's face. "Oh my God..." he muttered. "Oh my God..." Then his hand went to his mouth.

Griffin instantly turned and shouted, "Bucket!" and like magic, Matt's lucky bucket was tossed into Griffin's hands. He shoved it under Matt's face right as he leaned over and started breathing heavy. Griffin patted his back, talking him through the panic attack. "It's okay, cuz. It's not that much bigger than this place."

But Matt knew that was a lie. We *all* knew that was a lie. Staples Center was much, much bigger; it was like comparing a boulder to a mountain. I honestly never thought we'd play there. Or if we did, I thought we'd have years to prepare for it—years to prepare *Matt* for it. But everything was happening so fast.

Too fast. Much too fast. And I had no idea how to slow it down.

Chapter 19

STAPLES MOTHERFUCKING CENTER

The guys were as torn as me once they processed the shock of doing a stadium show. It was a shitty thing to do to Justin and the fans, but it was a huge opportunity for our band. Both good and bad. God, I hated double-edged swords.

Sienna met us at the airport and instantly claimed she had nothing to do with moving us. She even went so far as saying that she'd wanted Nick to leave us on Justin's tour, but I didn't know if I believed her or not. And I really hated not knowing for sure. I'd heard someone once say in an interview that Sienna couldn't act, but I strongly disagreed since I could never tell how she genuinely felt about anything. Especially when she showed us our new, much nicer tour bus, with a surprisingly roomy bedroom in the back of it. With a warm smile on her face, Sienna said it was for Kiera and me. She said she wanted the arrangement to work for everyone, and I really wanted to believe that she meant it.

Maybe I was being the naïve one now.

I could tell right away that Sienna's tour was going to be a lot different than Justin's, and not just because of the size of the audience. For starters, Tory was here, and she had the backstage chaos streamlined into a well-oiled machine with no unnecessary components. I swear, no one even breathed without Tory's permission. Unlike before, we were all told to stay out of the way instead of encouraged to help out. It was strange not to have anything to do. And while there was press loitering around behind the scenes, there weren't any fans to talk to; any listeners who had been allowed backstage were restricted to certain areas and were highly watched over. When Tory explained the "meet-and-greet" portion of the evening to us, it sounded like it was going to be one of the most awkward things I'd ever experienced. On Justin's tour, once a fan was cleared to be backstage, they could go almost anywhere they wanted, could freely mingle with other fans and rock stars, like we were all hanging out at a bar. It was fun and natural, and it made it feel like home, even though it wasn't. This...this was just ridiculous.

"All right, listen up!" Tory bellowed, her pale eyes scanning our band and the other band on Sienna's tour, Holeshot. Their lead singer, Deacon, discreetly rolled his eyes at Tory and gave me a small, knowing grin. Having experienced Tory firsthand before, I grinned back at him. The three members of Holeshot—Deacon, David, and Ray—had been surprisingly easygoing about us crashing their tour. They weren't even upset that they had to share their bus with us, or that Sienna had given Kiera and I the plush bedroom. They'd just seemed happy to have more guys around. I was really glad they were so cool.

"Most of you know the drill," Tory told the room. "But for our new members, pay attention to how this works." Tory narrowed her eyes at me after she said that, like she thought *I* was going to be the problem here. I wanted to indicate Griffin to her, because out of any of us, he was the one who wasn't going to listen, but I really didn't feel like helping Tory do her job. She'd figure it out soon enough.

Shifting to scan the group, she said, "In ten minutes, security will lead you into the meet-and-greet room. Holeshot will go in first, followed by the D-Bags, followed by Sienna. You will stand in your appointed three-by-three area, on the X that has been taped to the floor. Do not move away from your specific X. That will be your home for the next sixty minutes."

I looked over at Kiera at hearing that. We had to stand on an X and stay there? I suddenly felt like I was at a weird rock star exhibit at the zoo or something. Kiera pressed her lips together as she studied the face I was making, like she was stopping herself from laughing.

"Kyle! Are you going to be a problem?" Tory snapped.

Feeling like I was back at school, being reprimanded by my math teacher, I shook my head. "Nope." Evan and Matt both softly snickered behind me.

Ignoring them, Tory continued. "The fans are already in place, waiting for you to arrive, and they've already been instructed on what they can and cannot do with you, basically, no hugging, no touching. I need all of you to enforce those boundaries if they forget. And they will forget." She paused to roll her eyes. "The fans will be formed into an orderly line and will make a pass by each artist on their way out of the room. You will have fifteen seconds with each person, and then you will encourage them to move down the line."

That got my attention. "Fifteen seconds? That's...that's nothing."

Tory narrowed her eyes at me. "That's all the time that has been allotted for them. If you keep them longer, the people behind them won't get any time at all." I clenched Kiera's hand tighter, already hating this. Tory looked at our laced fingers. "Those of you who are not going on stage tonight, will stay out of the way and will not interfere in the process, or you will be escorted from the room." Her eyes locked on Kiera's. "Understand?" she asked.

Kiera nodded, her eyes wide. Heat ran up my spine as Tory tried to intimidate my wife. I was just about to tell her that *no one* would be escorting Kiera anywhere when Tory snipped, "See you in ten minutes," and left the room.

Matt let out a low whistle behind me. "Damn. While I think

she's probably the biggest bitch I've ever met, I do respect how she gets things done." He smirked at me. "Wrangling rock stars isn't easy."

Evan laughed at his comment, then shook his head. "So they're just gonna say hi as they're paraded past us? How is that a meet-and-greet?"

I sighed in agreement as I looked over at Kiera. It wasn't a meet-and-greet. It was a pointless, rushed, walkthrough. If we were ever big enough to headline our own show, things would be different. Because this—this wasn't worth *anyone's* time.

Kiera gave me a sympathetic look, and I could tell she understood exactly how I felt. I was about to lean down and kiss her when a hand landed on my shoulder. I looked over to see Griffin frowning at me. "Hey dude, I spaced out for like thirty seconds, and I missed all of that. What was the high-strung chick saying?"

Yep. I knew Griffin was the one she should have been worrying about. "She was just explaining the meet-and-greet."

Griffin grinned. "Ah, yeah. I can't wait to French some fans."

Kiera glared at him, but he was too busy preening to notice. Matt sighed. "It's not that kind of meet-and-greet, cuz. There's gonna be an X on the floor. Stand there and wave while people pass by you."

Griffin pursed his lips at him. "Please, I'm not falling for that. You're usually more creative when you lie to me. The anxiety getting to you?"

Matt's eyes widened as he put a hand on his stomach. I almost smacked Griffin for reminding Matt what was waiting for him tonight. Matt was currently riding the denial train, and so far, it was working for him. Not wanting Matt to think about it, I told Griffin, "He's not making it up. That's pretty much what she just said."

Griffin's jaw dropped. "I don't do drive-bys. I need interaction." He frowned, then grinned. "You know what I think?" Before anyone could even answer, he said, "I think we need to get Tory laid so she'll chill out. Now, normally, I'd volunteer for that, but that chick scares me. I feel like she'd cut off my balls afterward for a trophy or something."

Matt smirked at that. "No one wants your balls as a trophy, Griffin."

Griffin gave him a smooth smile. "Dude, you have no idea how many girls have said they wanted my balls."

Matt snorted, and Evan started losing it. "I don't think they mean it as a compliment," Matt laughed.

Kiera covered her mouth as adorable giggles escaped her. Hearing her and the guys' amusement made me laugh too. Griffin glared at all of us, then sighed and said, "It's too bad Paul's not here. We could make him sleep with her."

I held up my fist for that one. "Abso-fucking-lutely," I told him.

As Griffin bumped my fist, Kiera softly asked, "Who's Paul?"

Shaking my head, I answered, "Someone who deserves to sleep with Tory."

Griffin nodded as he looked at Kiera. "And come out of it ball-less."

I fist-bumped him again, then all four of us were laughing. Kiera watched us with an amused smile, but she didn't ask anyone to clarify.

A few minutes later, security came to collect us, and we were escorted into a room ripe with eager tension. The too-fast procession was just as awkward and unsatisfying as I'd thought it would be. And the only thing I really got out of the experience was that I learned every single person wanted to say two specific things to me: *I love your music* and *I love you and Sienna together*. I didn't even have time to tell them that we weren't together, not that it would have mattered if I had. One, they wouldn't have believed me anyway, and two, Sienna was at the end of the line, and by the way she kept smiling in my direction as I stood between Evan and Griffin, I knew she wasn't about to deny anything.

When our allotted time with the fans was done, we were escorted to smaller rooms where we could quietly wait for our turn to go onstage. The insulated isolation was a really strange way to start a show for me. I was used to interaction and noise and drunk people and flirting and laughter, and without all that, it was kind of boring. I couldn't even use the downtime to make out with Kiera because Deacon was hanging out with us. He was easy to talk to, though, so we shot the shit and watched as Kiera practically crawled out of her skin; she was so anxious.

It was amusing to observe her escalating nervousness, especially since she wasn't even the one going onstage. Was she stressing out for me? She knew this stuff didn't bother me. I was instantly glad that Matt and the guys were in a different room. Kiera's energy would have fed Matt's anxiety, and he was probably a nervous wreck as it was. If him and Kiera were in a room together right now, Matt probably wouldn't play tonight. Hopefully, Griffin was doing a good job distracting him. Or pissing him off. Either one was fine as long as it got him on that stage.

Smile on his face, Deacon pointed at Kiera. "Is she always this nervous?" he asked.

I glanced at Deacon as I brought a bottle of beer to my lips. Deacon had long, black hair that almost reached his waist. He also had the palest eyes I'd ever seen; the intense darkness of his hair almost made his irises look white. There was amusement in those otherworldly eyes as he watched my fretting wife. Smiling around the bottle against my lips, I shifted my gaze to Kiera. She'd been pacing the room for a while now, yanking on her guitar necklace so hard that I worried she might break the chain.

Swallowing my beer, I told Deacon, "Pretty much." Kiera frowned at me, but she didn't argue with my absolutely true statement.

The door to our room opened as Deacon softly laughed at my comment. We all looked over to see a man in a headset lean into the room. He locked eyes with Deacon and said, "Show's starting, sir. You're up."

Deacon acknowledged him with a nod, then stood and

stretched. Looking just as laidback as me, he said, "Catch you guys on the flip side," and left the room.

Once Deacon was gone, a part of me wanted to go see how Matt was doing. But if there was truly a problem, someone would call me, and honestly, all of us coddling Matt right now would only remind him that he *should* be nervous. Best to just let him be.

Putting Matt from my mind, I focused my attention on the ball of anxiety in front of me. "Would you sit down, please?"

Kiera stopped her pacing and stared at me with frazzled eyes that were way more brown than green today. She pressed a hand to her stomach like she was about to be sick. "Aren't you nervous? Even a little bit?"

I casually took another drink of my beer before answering her. "Well, watching *you* is making me a little nervous." Getting a great idea, I set down my beer and patted my lap. "Come over here and help me relax." Making out with me usually got her mind off of *everything*, and we were finally alone, so I didn't see a single reason why we couldn't enjoy each other's company.

Kiera seemed to agree, even if she did smirk at me for my comment. She strolled right over to me, then she straddled my lap and tangled her fingers in my hair. Well, damn, game on. A light laugh escaped me as she gave me a soft kiss. "There, I feel better already," I told her, and that was 100 percent true. My body had started firing up the minute she'd suggestively sat on me.

Kiera ground her hips against mine, coaxing a groan out of me. Fuck, she felt good. How much time did we have, and how much would she let me do back here? And why wasn't she wearing a skirt?

Our soft kisses turned much more passionate, and our breaths quickened as our tongues brushed together. My hands ran up under her shirt, tracing her spine as blood surged through me, hardening me. Kiera rubbed against me, softly moaning in my mouth, and I began to rethink my plan of distracting her back here. Maybe we should go back to the bus? My hands had other plans, though, and before it even registered with me that I'd done it, her bra was unhooked.

She instantly pulled away from me, her lips pursing in cute displeasure. Ignoring the desire to suck on her bottom lip, I gave her a devilish grin. "Oops." On second thought, we didn't need a bus for privacy. We were alone in a room that locked. She just needed to hop off me for a moment, and then I could properly distract her.

Just as I was about to tell her my master plan, the door opened. Kiera jumped off my lap like I was on fire. I quickly made sure my shirt masked the rock-hard erection I had going on, then twisted to see who was here. It couldn't be our turn already, could it?

But it wasn't a crew member who walked in, it was Sienna. Kiera's cheeks were bright red as she fumbled with her bra strap. Now I genuinely did feel remorseful. Guess we should have locked the door first; we really should have learned that lesson by now.

Sienna hesitated as she glanced between the two of us. "Sorry, did I interrupt something?"

Wanting Kiera to see the humor in this moment, I locked eyes with her and gave her a soft smile. "Don't worry about it," I told Sienna. "We're getting used to it." A flicker of a smile played on Kiera's lips as she remembered all the times we'd been interrupted. At least we were basically fully clothed this time.

With an amused laugh, Sienna sat in a nearby chair. She made a comment about wanting to hear that story while Kiera finished with her bra and sat beside me. I smiled at Kiera as her nervous energy returned; she was bouncing her toes like the floor was hot. I wished Holeshot's set was done already, just so Kiera could relax.

Sienna asked if I was ready for the show, returning my attention to her. It was a little odd to me that she was here, killing time with us. But I supposed she probably got a little bored waiting for her turn, same as me. As we made polite small talk, a part of me wanted to grill her about me being here, ask her again if she'd had anything to do with it. Or ask her why she wasn't doing more to deny the rumors, why she was letting the media circus blow up around us. But she was being warm, open, and friendly, and it just didn't feel like the time or place to get into it with her. And besides, she'd already answered all those questions. I doubted I'd get a different response from her, so I tried to let it go and just be respectful and professional.

Then she started talking about her past and her family, about how controlling and relentless her parents had been, and I was reminded that beneath it all, Sienna was just a regular human being who'd been deeply hurt by the people she loved. It was something we had in common, and finding common ground with her made me sympathetic to her struggles. It softened me, made me feel like maybe we could be friends. It made me think that, pushing all the media bullshit aside, Sienna was a good person. A good person with a lot of armor around her. I could understand that, so when she told me a story about how her parents liked to send her onstage a little terrified, my response was sincere.

"I'm sorry you had to go through that." No child should be afraid of their parents.

Her smile was soft as she said, "Thank you." Then she reached over and put a hand on my thigh. I genuinely couldn't tell if she was being friendly, or if she was blatantly flirting with me, and that swung me right back around to the biggest problem I had with Sienna. I couldn't read her, couldn't gauge her true intentions, and because of that, I couldn't trust her. I couldn't ever let my guard down around her, and I definitely couldn't let her into my inner circle. We were friendly, but we were *not* friends. I needed to remember that.

Sienna offered to escort me to the stage when it was my turn to go on. I rejected the elbow she offered me but let her lead the way. Almost instantly, people from a local radio station spotted us; they practically salivated, seeing the two of us together. The part of me that sympathized with Sienna's stories about her parents didn't want to be bitter and jaded, but the rest of me couldn't help but wonder if this moment was the entire reason Sienna had been spending time with us.

The group wanted an interview with Sienna and photos with me. I told them I had to go—one, because I didn't want any more photos of Sienna and me being misconstrued by the public, and two, because the guy who'd been sent to fetch me was frantically waving toward the stage—but the woman with the camera wasn't having it.

"Just a quick photo of the happy couple?" she asked.

Rolling my eyes, I looked over my shoulder at Kiera. She was slightly behind me, but she was holding my hand. I wanted to lift our fingers and show the woman that, but I knew Kiera wouldn't want me to draw any attention to her. Instead, I pointed at Sienna and said, "We're not together."

The woman gave me a look that I was really sick of seeing. It was an expression of *Sure, you're not. It's so cute that you still deny it. What a sweet boyfriend.* That fucking look made me want to tear my hair out. Sienna's soft smile and silence didn't help either. I wanted to snap at Sienna to say something, I wanted to pull Kiera forward and show her off to them. Maybe if I turned around and gave Kiera the kind of private kiss that she hated getting in public, this group would finally understand who truly had my heart.

Like she could sense my thoughts, Kiera yanked on my arm. Knowing she didn't want to be a part of this circus, I ignored my instincts and walked away.

I had to leave Kiera at the staging area. She had a bright smile on her face as she darted away to find a good place to watch the show. I grinned the entire time crew members got me ready, happy she was happy, eager for the show. Until I saw Matt. Then my smile faded a little bit. He was greener than I'd ever seen him, and he was visibly shaking. Evan was giving him concerned glances, but what was even more alarming was Griffin's face. He genuinely looked worried for his cousin, and seeing his concern was like seeing a scared flight attendant—it just confirmed that everything was going to shit.

I approached Matt cautiously, not wanting to spook him. He looked up at me with wide, terrified eyes. "Kell?" he said, his voice shaking. "I don't think—" He grabbed his stomach, and Griffin instantly handed him his bucket.

"He's thrown up three times already," Griffin told me. "I've tried pissing him off, but nothing's working." Pursing his lips, he poked Matt in the side. "I flashed Rachel before we left. She liked it. Said I put you to shame."

Matt just blankly stared at him. He was clinging to the bucket like it was the only real thing left in the world. Griffin shrugged at me. "See?"

The stadium lights started going crazy, angling away from the stage and sweeping out over the crowd. I knew that was our cue. We were supposed to head out there while the stage was dark and surprise the crowd when the lights came back. We didn't have time for this.

"Matt, we have to go." He instantly shook his head. Grabbing his shoulders, I pulled his face close to mine. "Listen to me. We have to go. *Now*." I could feel the vibrations of Matt's trembles, could see the naked fear in his eyes. I sympathized, but there wasn't time to coax this out of him. Narrowing my eyes, I said, "What did you tell me? Way back in Seattle, when I said I couldn't go on tour, what did you tell me?"

Matt's brows bunched as he shook his head, like he couldn't remember. "You told me that you couldn't believe our chance had finally arrived, and I was saying no. Well, that's exactly what you're doing right now, Matt. You're scared, and I get that. More than you know, I get that. But you have to do it anyway. You *have* to because we're counting on you. The D-Bags will fail if you don't go out there. It's all over unless you go out there. Do you want this to be over?"

Matt swallowed, inhaled a deep breath, and shook his head. "No," he whispered.

"Do you want our dream to die? *Your* dream to die?"

His eyes narrowed, and a little color returned to his cheeks. "No," he said, his voice stronger.

I nodded at him, stepping back to give him room. "This is it. This is our chance. Are you gonna let fear take it from you? Are you gonna say no?"

Determination filled his face. He set down the bucket, lifted his chin, and firmly told me, "No."

Griffin snorted. "But you just said no?"

I wanted to slap my hand over Griffin's mouth, but Matt actually smiled at him. "Fuck you," he muttered, laughing.

Seeing his humor returning made me grin. He could do this. Wide smile on my face, I looked at each one of my friends and took a second to absorb the moment. "Let's go show them who we are."

The guys nodded at me, then we darted onto the dark stage. The lights swung our way just as I picked up my guitar and slipped the strap over my shoulder. The crowd lost it when they spotted us. The noise was so intense that I felt it echoing in my chest. The enormity of the crowd was mind-boggling—the lights, movement, and signs seemed to stretch on into eternity. I'd been to huge concerts before, been a part of that swarming mass of people, but the vantage point from the stage made it completely different. I felt tiny up here, a mere speck of dust in the cosmos compared to the vastness of them, but they were the ones losing their minds. For *us*.

Damn. This was cool.

Stepping up to the microphone, I addressed the crowd, then gave them a playful smile. I swear the noise tripled, and a couple of girls near the front collapsed into their friends. While I was glad they were excited, I hoped they were all right.

I glanced back at the guys getting into position. Evan was standing behind his drums, taking it all in with a bright smile on his face. Griffin seemed subdued for once as he strolled to his guitar, gaping at the crowd instead of making his usual obscene gestures to them. Matt was intent on his instrument, looping it over his shoulder and double-checking the equipment, blocking out everything else while he waited for his cue. Whatever got him through it.

Returning my focus to the fans, I flirted with them for a little bit, giving the guys a few more minutes to prepare. As I scanned the crowd, I saw D-Bags shirts and signs everywhere. That was so strange to me since our band being here was a last-minute change up; aside from the signs on the building announcing us, I didn't think the fans knew beforehand. It made me wonder if all Sienna's shows had been like this up to now, and that made me reconsider my anger at being switched. Maybe Nick was right after all, and being here was exactly where I was supposed to be.

I felt better about everything as our set began, and I could feel the guys' energy as they adjusted to our new reality. They nailed it. *We* nailed it. And the crowd ate it up so much that they didn't want to let us go. I had just rejoined Kiera offstage, her beaming face lifting my mood even higher, when the audience we'd left behind started calling out for more.

Griffin smacked my shoulder as we listened to them chanting our name. "We gotta give 'em an encore," he said.

I shook my head at him. "We don't have time to play another song. It's Sienna's show, and she's big on structure."

He frowned as he grabbed my arm. "What the fuck do I care about Sienna? It's our time to shine, baby," he said, shoving me toward the stage.

I resisted him since we really didn't have time for this, but then Matt and Evan started shoving me too. "Just pop your head out and wave," Matt said. And I was so impressed that Matt, of all people, wanted to go out and acknowledge the crowd that I relented with a shrug.

Matt was grinning, looking totally relaxed, and I loved seeing it. He looked over at Kiera with a laugh, telling her to plug her ears, then we dashed back onstage before any of the crew could stop us. The crowd went absolutely nuts as we stood at the front of the stage and waved.

This. This moment was going to live with me forever. And I was so happy that Kiera was here to share it with me. That my best friends were here to share it with me. When it looked like we were about to give the panicked crew an aneurism, I grabbed Griffin's arm and told the guys, "We should go now."

Evan and Matt nodded in agreement and helped me pull Griffin off the stage. "Fuck, that was awesome!" Griffin exclaimed as we handed the crew our equipment.

"We have some time, we should go celebrate," Matt said. Then he frowned and added, "Somewhere close. We're doing the song with Sienna at the end of the night."

Evan nodded. "I think I saw a bar across the street. But...are we allowed to leave?"

Griffin snorted. "I'd like to see them keep me here. Come on, let's go."

I nodded at them, then tilted my head toward where Kiera was waiting for us. The guys followed me, still laughing and bursting with energy as they recalled the show. When I got to Kiera's side, I wrapped my arms around her, told her the plan, and asked her if she wanted to come with us. Kiera grinned and nodded as she hugged a notebook to her chest. Seeing it made me curious.

"Were you writing?" I asked her. She nodded, and a strange mixture of warmth and fascination spread through me. "While I was singing?"

"You're very inspiring to watch," she said with a smile.

That was both amazing and mystifying. "I...inspire you?"

She looked at me like I'd hung the moon or something. "Daily," she sighed.

I was used to seeing love on her face, and I was getting used to seeing pride on her face, but being the source of her creative spark was something else entirely. I had *never* been anyone's inspiration.

I could barely wrap my mind around it. "And you say I'm absurd," I told her. She laughed at my comment, even though I wasn't really joking.

Wanting to keep her art as safe as possible, I pried it from her hands and gave it to a crew member. "This is priceless, literary genius, and you need to guard it with your life."

The guy looked at me like I'd just handed him the Mona Lisa. "Yes, sir," he said.

"Make sure it ends up inside my guitar case, please," I added.

"Yes, sir." He took off to complete his task before I could even thank him.

Twisting to Kiera, I said, "Did he just call me sir...twice?" That was just weird, overly formal, and completely unnecessary. Dude could have called me by my name. Or douchenoodle. I'd answer to that too.

I laughed at the thought, and Kiera lightly tapped my stomach. "Don't let it go to your head," she told me.

"Wouldn't dream of it," I said with a grin.

Since we really weren't sure if we were allowed to leave or not, the five of us stealthily snuck out of the venue. Once we were on the street, Griffin found the bar Evan had spotted and pointed it out with a "Bar, ho!" The guys took off down the street, laughing as they ran.

I looked over at Kiera beside me. "Last one to the bar has to sit by Griffin." She didn't even let me finish before she took off. I knew nothing would get her moving like using Griffin as a threat.

She just barely beat me to the bar, stepping on the mat a fraction of a second before I did. Hands on her knees, she panted as she recovered. "Beat 'cha," she beamed.

My breath was quicker too as I pulled open the door. "I let you win," I told her. "I liked the view." Mostly true and very true.

We walked inside, and even though this place wasn't Pete's, it had a similar vibe to it, and I felt a kind of homecoming wrap around me. Griffin found a table in the back, and we all followed him. Once we were there, he looked at each of us with a solemn expression on his face. "Same rules as last time," he stated.

Evan laughed while Matt rolled his eyes. A spike of unease shot up my spine as I glanced at Kiera. I knew exactly what Griffin was talking about, the stupid bar game he'd invented last tour. While it was amusing to watch Griffin lose his shit when he inevitably lost the game, it was not a game I wanted to play around my wife. Even though I'd never actively sought out phone numbers, I didn't think Kiera would be too happy about it. "We're not playing that game tonight, Griff."

His pale eyes were full of challenge as he scanned my body. "Uh, yeah, we are." He gave me a shit-talking smirk. "What? Afraid you'll lose?"

"When has Kellan ever lost?" Evan said to Matt, making him laugh.

"What game?" Kiera asked, reluctant curiosity on her face.

"It's stupid," I told her, not wanting to explain. "Griffin came up with it." And if she knew anything about Griffin, then she knew not to ask for an explanation.

Griffin let out a derisive snort. "You're a pansy. All intimidated 'cause your girlfriend's here?"

"Wife," I told him for the millionth time.

He rolled his eyes. "Whatever, we're playing. Turn out your pockets."

That was a new requirement. It almost made me laugh; Griffin was still so convinced we were cheating. I looked to Kiera for guidance since I wasn't sure what I should do. Looking more curious than anything, she nodded at me. I turned out my pockets along with Evan and Matt, all of us showing Mr. I-Refuse-to-Believe-I-Can-Lose that we were playing by his stupid rules. When Griffin was satisfied that we hadn't pre-stuffed our pockets, he quickly re-explained the rules—that numbers were one point, condoms were five, the loser picked up the tab, and the winner got a shot from everyone. I cringed the entire time he was talking, hoping Kiera didn't ask what any of it meant and just took it in stride as Griffin being Griffin. But I could see revulsion mixing with her curiosity as Griffin reminded us—again—not to cheat.

As Matt sighed at Griffin for singling him out as the cheater, Kiera asked, "Wait, what game?"

Griffin squatted in front of her, looking her directly in the eye. I kind of wanted to grab her hand and leave, but he was already talking. "The dude who fills his pockets with the most chick's phone numbers wins."

She looked over at me with wide eyes and a raised eyebrow. "And you haven't ever lost this game?"

Fucking Griffin. Knowing he was making it sound worse than it actually was, I lifted my hands in a gesture of innocence. "Completely unsolicited, I swear." She couldn't be angry because people flirted with me. Right? She pursed her lips at me, displeasure clear on her face, but there was also amusement pulling at the corners of her mouth. Wanting to change the subject, I slowly said, "You, uh, want a drink?"

Her lips pressed into a firm line, but the edges were still curled up a little, and her eyes were broadcasting love...mixed with mild annoyance. "Mmm-hmm," she said.

Both wanting away and wanting to make her happy, I made a beeline for the bar. I heard her soft laughter as I left, and relief flooded me. She was choosing to see the humor in the situation— to trust me—and I appreciated that so much.

I was grinning when I reached the bar, and the bartender did a double take when she noticed me. "What can I get you, handsome?"

"I need a drink that will make my wife forgive me."

She looked both disheartened and amused by that. "One 'Apology' coming your way."

I ordered beers for the guys and me, then waited while the bartender made Kiera's drink. It looked both sweet and strong. I hoped she liked it, and I hoped she truly wasn't bothered by Griffin's ridiculous game.

A couple of girls stepped up to me while I waited. They were giggling. "Excuse me," one of them said. I looked over to see a cute strawberry-blonde with bright red cheeks staring at me. "I don't usually do this, but I've had three drinks already, and you are the hottest human being I have ever seen." I pressed my lips together, so I didn't laugh, while she grabbed a napkin nearby. Her friend handed her a pen, and the girl instantly wrote down her phone number and slid it over to me. "Just in case you're interested," she said, then she pushed her friend, and they both sped off.

From the back of the bar, I heard Griffin yell out, "You're a whore!"

I looked over at our table. Griffin was glaring, Matt was laughing his ass off, Evan was shaking his head...and Kiera was grinning. Seeing that she wasn't angry with me, I figured it was okay to tease Griffin. Grabbing the napkin, I waved it at him, then shoved it into my pocket. *One down.* Griffin's glower intensified, and he stormed off to find his own phone numbers. I wished him luck; after that outburst, he was going to need it.

Evan helped me bring the drinks to the table, and I gave Kiera hers with a reproachful look on my face. "It's called an Apology," I told her. She smiled and shook her head at me, and I took a chance and kissed her cheek. She only giggled in response, thank God.

Matt called Griffin back to the table, and we took a moment to mark the occasion. Holding my beer out to the middle of the table, I told my friends, "Here's to playing Staples motherfucking Center."

We all clinked drinks and shared a look of surreal disbelief. All except Griffin. He just smirked and nodded, then he raised his beer and clapped Matt on the shoulder. "And here's to my cuz, grabbing life by the balls and riding it hard."

Kiera instantly grimaced while Evan and I just stared at Griffin. He looked at us and shrugged. "What?"

Matt slowly shook his head as he quietly laughed at his

cousin, then he lifted his beer and touched it to Griffin's. "Cheers," he said, and I couldn't help but notice the pride in his pale eyes. He'd faced his demon, and damn if he hadn't conquered the hell out of that beast. I doubted he'd ever be that nervous onstage again, and I couldn't have been happier for him. He deserved some peace up there.

Chapter 20

ENCORE

We settled in for some drinking, lounging, and laughing; there were numerous joking comments made about Griffin's dumb game, mainly to piss him off. I watched Kiera carefully as the night wore on, but she never seemed upset by what we were doing. She just seemed amused and curious as she watched women come on to me. I hoped she realized that it largely happened because alcohol gave people courage. If we tried this game at say, a supermarket, then Griffin and his incessant badgering would probably win. But there were several clumps of really drunk women here, and whenever I passed by a group of them—especially if they were older and didn't give a shit—someone handed me something or shoved something into my pocket. And since I wanted Griffin to go apeshit, I left them there.

Occasionally, Kiera asked how many I had, but I always told her I didn't know. It was more fun to wait and find out at the end, which snuck up on us way too fast. I was content to spend another hour chatting with strangers, and laughing with my wife and friends, when suddenly, Matt's watch started chiming. We all just stared at it for a moment, the memory of our job gone from our minds.

Matt remembered first. "Shit, Sienna's set is almost over. We have to go."

We all quickly finished our drinks, feeling the weight of urgency. When we stood to leave, Griffin exclaimed, "Wait! We need a winner. Pockets."

We really should have ignored him and left—if we were late, there would be hell to pay—but honestly, this was everyone's favorite part of the game...if Griffin's ridiculous game *had* to have a favorite part. Even Kiera looked excited for the outcome as she leaned into my side, an expectant smile on her face, like she knew I was going to win. Her support, even in something like this, was both mystifying and incredible. God, she was amazing.

Evan started us off by throwing down a piece of paper with a phone number haphazardly scribbled on it. "Just one," he said with a shrug.

Smug look on his face, Griffin tossed down his collection. "Ha! Three! Read 'em and weep."

He crossed his arms over his chest and gave me a defiant sneer. Kiera nudged me in the ribs when I didn't do anything right away. I shook my head at her eagerness, then emptied my pockets. I unfolded them as I counted, and when I passed Griffin's number, I grinned internally. "Uh...five," I said, tossing them on the pile.

Griffin instantly lost it. "Damn it, Kellan! I fucking hate you."

Evan smirked as he looked at me. "Just five? Slow night, Kell?"

Even if it was kind of true, I knew he'd said that just to piss off Griffin even more. As I laughed at his comment, Griffin rolled his eyes and said, "Fine, prick, what shot do you want?"

I was about to tell Griffin that we didn't have time when Kiera surprised me by saying, "What about Matt?" She turned to him with a smile. "How did you do?"

Matt had an odd look on his face, like he was about to expose a huge secret or something. He opened his mouth to tell us, but

Griffin steamrolled right over him. "Pfffft, no way Matt beat Kellan...it's over." He paused, then raised an eyebrow. "Unless... someone slip you a condom?"

Small smile on his face, Matt shook his head. "No..." He reached into his pocket and pulled out a key card. "I got a motel key."

We all just stared at the plastic card he tossed on the table, the name of a local motel chain plastered in bright colors on the front. In all the times we'd played this game, none of us had ever been slipped a room key. And the fact that it was quiet, shy Matt, who rarely talked to anyone outside of our group, was damn impressive. When the shock wore off and Matt's win registered, we all hooted and hollered so loud that more than a few heads turned our way.

Griffin was beside himself. "Holy shit! That's an instant win!" He grabbed Matt's shoulders as he bounced on his toes. "Oh my God, you beat Kellan!" He twisted Matt to face the bar; almost everyone was looking our way now. "Everybody! This is my cousin right here, and he just dethroned God's Gift to Women!"

He gave him a noogie, and Matt looked like he wanted to melt into the floor. I'd never seen him so embarrassed, and I had a feeling he regretted showing his winning hand. Matt ducked out of Griffin's grip and fled the bar. Griffin looked after him with raised hands. "Dude? Your shots?"

Evan and Kiera were both laughing hysterically, and I couldn't help but laugh with them. I paid our tab, bypassing Evan's attempt to pay; technically, he'd lost Griffin's game and was required to pay, but the game was stupid, and I wanted to treat my friends. Once we were square, we hurried out of the bar to make it to our final song of the show.

Our group had consumed more than I'd realized, and we were all a little unsteady as we rushed back to the stadium. Hopefully, the guys could still play, and I could still sing. I'd really hate for tonight to end on a sour note, especially since Kiera wasn't mad at me for what happened at the bar. I'd double-checked with her once we were outside, and after teasing me a little, she'd jokingly told me that she only would have been mad if I'd lost to Griffin. It meant a lot to me that she was finally trusting me, that we were finally trusting each other. It made me feel a little...invincible.

Getting back into the show took some finagling since dipshit forgot his credentials. Luckily, Deacon was nearby and grabbed them for Griffin; otherwise, we would have had to leave him behind, and Kiera would have had to learn to play bass real fast.

We made it back just in time for the encore. The crew looked frazzled and frantic as they waved us into position, and the part of my brain that wasn't airy and lightheaded thought maybe we shouldn't do that again. For their sanity, if nothing else. I gave Kiera a searing goodbye kiss, then followed the guys into the staging area. Crew members got us ready, and seeing the scowls on their faces made me feel even worse.

I told the guy helping me, "Sorry we're a little late," but he waved it off like it was no big deal, like he dealt with drunk, irresponsible rock stars all the time. I made a mental note to do something nice for him, right as Sienna announced us to the crowd.

The guys and I stepped onto the stage to a mind-numbing volume of screams. The guys swapped places with Sienna's band while I joined her up front. Sienna grabbed my hand and leaned toward me like she was going to kiss my cheek. Even though my mind was slower than usual, I easily sensed the photo-op she was going for and turned away to acknowledge the crowd.

Wanting to limit our time on stage together, I discreetly motioned for Evan to start the song. Even though he was buzzing as much as I was, he saw and understood, and a heartbeat later, he began to play. Matt and Griffin hit their marks, then it was my turn. My vision was a little hazy—having a few rounds of celebratory shots was probably the worst idea we'd had tonight—but I nailed my part. Thankfully, singing was as automatic as breathing to me, and 99 percent of the time, the words were there when I needed them, stuck to the ridges of my brain like barnacles to a boat.

Instead of engaging the crowd, like I usually did, Sienna and I kept the song insular, facing each other as we sneered through the words. It was Sienna's idea to do it that way, to mimic the video, and I had to say, it was both effective and fun. While I hated the stunts Sienna sometimes pulled, performing with her was an altogether different story. If our relationship was only about this, I wouldn't mind it at all.

The end of the song came up, and with fury on my face, I stormed past her so we could walk off the stage in opposite directions, just like in the video. Sienna grabbed my arm as we crossed, though, and yanked me toward her. Confusion ran through me as my dazed body stumbled into hers. I was just trying to catch my balance when I felt a hand thread through my hair, clench the strands, and pull me forward. In my drunken haze, I went with no resistance. Then I was suddenly colliding with warm lips. Everything went pitch black, and screams pounded against me, drowning out all rational thought. A tip of a tongue brushed my lip, and my mouth instinctively moved to welcome the sensation. That was when my brain caught up to my body, and I realized just what had happened.

I simultaneously shoved Sienna away from me and stepped back.

She made me kiss her. On stage. In front of everybody. Fuck, in front of Kiera.

It was still dark on stage, dark around the crowd except for the cell phone lights, but I could see Sienna in the flashes, standing there with a small, victorious smile on her face. She'd wanted another photo-op, so she'd taken it. I had no doubt that several fans had caught that moment, and even now, they were sharing it online. Goddamn it.

Rage boiled inside me. Lifting a finger, I told her, "Don't ever fucking touch me again." Then I hurried toward the exit. I needed to get off this stage before I blew up.

I yanked my earpiece and receiver pack off me, tossing them to a crew member that I knew I should be nicer to, but the fury wasn't settling down. Neither was the feeling of being violated. She had no right to do that, especially since I'd already made it perfectly clear where my boundaries were.

Evan and Matt were making a beeline for me as I forced people out of my way so I could get down the stairs and to the bus. I didn't want to be back here anymore, and I didn't want to talk to my friends. I just wanted to grab Kiera and run. Maybe run all the way back home. Was this the breaking point for me?

I heard Evan call my name, but I ignored him. Then I heard a breezy, unruffled voice say, "You're overreacting, love." Everything about Sienna's tone implied that I was being a child, throwing a tantrum. Not a hint of remorse over the fact that she'd broken my trust. Again.

It made the anger inside me twist into something dark and ugly: wrath. Pausing on the steps, I closed my eyes and took a second to attempt to calm down. What she'd done was awful, yes, but she was vastly more influential than me. Like it or not, she held my career in her hands, and I had to be careful. I needed to be firm but civil. Unless, of course, I really was throwing in the towel right now. And I couldn't do that without discussing it with the guys first. This wasn't just about me, even if it felt like it was sometimes.

Opening my eyes, I turned around and faced her. The smug smile was gone, but now she was looking at me like she was resisting rolling her eyes. Like I was being completely unreasonable. "I told you," I said, pointing at her. "Not on the lips!" You wouldn't think that would be a difficult request to honor, but here we were.

She gave me one of her trademark smiles. Then she started walking my way. My body tightened with every step she took toward me, and I had to believe fire was dancing in my eyes right now. The tense way Evan was studying me suggested as much. Sienna didn't even seem to notice. Stopping at my side, she had the balls to put a hand on my arm. "I got carried away by the heat of the moment. Won't happen again."

Damn straight it wouldn't; otherwise, we'd be singing that song from opposite ends of the arena. If we sang it at all.

I was about to tell her that when Kiera suddenly stepped in front of us. Her cheeks were flaming red; it matched the fury in her eyes. I'd been struggling to hold the lid on my anger, but it was clear Kiera hadn't been as successful as me. Her hands were even clenched into fists, like she was two seconds away from clocking the superstar. If it wouldn't ultimately make Kiera's life more difficult, I might have let her. I held up my hands to stop an assault, but I couldn't stop her mouth as her anger bubbled over into an unfiltered outburst. "Hell right, it won't happen again! He doesn't belong to you!"

Kiera lurched forward, but hands on her shoulders instantly hauled her back. My gaze shot up to see that it was one of Sienna's silent bodyguards restraining her. *You have five seconds to let go of my wife, douchewad.* Before I could pry Kiera free, Sienna stepped up to her. "He's a person, love, so he doesn't *belong* to anyone." Her haughty gaze swept over everyone before returning to Kiera. "And in case you didn't notice, he didn't exactly pull away from me."

Sienna's eyes met mine then, and I saw a clear warning in the dark depths. *Drop this, or I'll make it so much worse.* As if she already hadn't made it worse. Goddamn it. When I didn't say anything in response, Sienna gave me a small smile that clearly said, *Good boy,* and that fire in my stomach burned even hotter. Until she left with her bodyguard and Kiera twisted to stare at me with a questioning devastation in her eyes. Then the fire turned to ice. Fuck.

People around us dispersed like they could sense the emotional bomb about to go off. Evan gave me a sympathetic smile, gave Kiera a pat on the shoulder, then helped Matt drag

Griffin away. Now that no one was around, the tension in the air felt suffocating. I didn't know what to say, didn't know what she wanted to hear, didn't know what she absolutely *wouldn't* want to hear. The guilt was excruciating. As was watching the moisture build up in Kiera's eyes. *How do I fix this?*

I didn't even know where to start, and Kiera was done waiting for me to begin. She spun on her heel and stormed away from me. I instantly rushed after her. "I'm drunk, Kiera. It happened so fast; I didn't have time to—"

She jerked around so quickly that I almost collided with her. "I know!" she screeched, pointing her finger in my face.

She again turned around and stomped away from me. Confused, I followed her. "Then why are you mad?" I asked.

Pausing, she sighed and faced me again. "Because I'm drunk too!"

Her body started turning away again, and I grabbed her arm. "Would you stop walking away from me, please?" She did as I asked, but her face told me she wasn't happy about it. "Are you mad at me?" I pressed.

Her brows bunched with confusion. "I don't know. Did you kiss her back?"

Fuck, fuck, fuck, fuck. That was a question I did *not* want to answer. At least, not 100 percent truthfully. This was one of those moments where a little white lie would go a really long way, but we were trying to live a lie-free life. That was our agreement, complete and total honesty, and even though that honesty was going to hurt us both, it was the only way I could strengthen the trust between us. And that trust meant everything to me.

Feeling my eyes begin to burn, I told her a misleading truth that I wished I could deny. "Just for a micro-second." The instant moisture in her eyes filled me with dread and panic, and I rushed my explanation. "I'm drunk, she caught me off guard. It was instinct. I moved my lips once, just a tiny fraction of an inch, but I didn't do it again. I pushed her away when I realized what was happening, but the lights had already blacked out by that point."

Desperation shifted into frustration, and I tossed my hands in the air. "Griffin's gotten more action out of me, but I have to say yes to be honest with you." *It was nothing. Please believe me, it was nothing.*

Kiera studied me for an achingly long moment, then she wrapped her arms around my neck and pulled me close. "It's okay," she whispered. "I'm not mad at you. I'm mad at her."

Relief washed over me in calming waves. Thank God, she believed me. I held her tight to my body, never wanting to let her go. "So am I," I told her. Sienna had gone too far. And if she tried it again, then the guys and I were going to have a talk about our future...because it wouldn't be with her anymore.

Kiera and I headed to the bus after that. Along the way, we passed a cart filled with flowers that fans had brought for Sienna. Reaching out, I discreetly popped the heads off a couple of roses and shoved them in my pocket. If there was ever a time to show Kiera a little Hallmark-worthy romance, it was now.

She was quiet as we stepped onto the bus, acknowledging my friends with a brief smile and a small wave. Evan frowned at me after she wordlessly passed by him. He lifted his pierced eyebrow, and I heard the question in his expression: *Do you want me to talk to her?* It made me happy that he was so willing to fight for us, but I shook my head at him. *We're fine. I think.*

But she was still unnaturally quiet as we got ready for bed, and my heart was beating a little harder as I slipped under the covers with her. "Kiera?" I whispered in the near darkness.

"I'm fine," she responded. "Just...tired."

Her words weren't filling me with confidence, but I didn't want to badger her either. Instead, I wrapped my arms around her, holding her back firmly to my chest. "You know I love you, right?"

"Yes, I know."

I could hear the smile in her answer. I smiled too, kissing her head. "More than anything?"

She pulled my arms tight against her body. "Yes, I know."

"Good," I said, kissing the curve of her ear. "Because you're everything I've always wanted, everything I never knew I could have, and everything I hope to have from here on out. You are my past, my present, and my future."

She twisted to look at me, and I could see the reflection of the soft nightlights glistening in the wetness of her eyes. But her expression was happy this time, and seeing these tears filled me with warmth. "I love you so much," she said, cupping my cheek.

I smiled as I leaned against her hand. Closing my eyes, I took a moment to just absorb the love I felt radiating from her. It was better than anything I'd felt in my entire life. But then I felt her soft lips against mine, and I reconsidered. *This* was better than anything. Better than everything.

We spent a long time just kissing and holding each other until eventually, Kiera fell asleep in my arms. I resisted following her into slumber—I just wanted to keep staring at her—but finally, the pull became too insistent, and I gave into it.

Multiple weird dreams woke me up during the night—one about Sienna trying to put a collar on me, one about Kiera getting sick of it all and going back to Denny, and one about my father being his usual, assholish self. Surprisingly, that one was the least troubling of the bunch.

When my body gave up on sleep and I was fully awake, I instinctively knew it was early and no one else would be up. I quietly eased out of bed. Wanting to get to work on my romantic project, I skipped my typical morning workout. Instead, I tossed on some clothes, grabbed my stolen petals, and made my way to the sleeping area.

As predicted, everyone in here was asleep. I made my way to Matt's bunk, then crouched down and pulled back his curtain. He was on his side, away from me, and his light breathing told me he was deeply asleep. Hopefully, he wasn't too mad at me for this, but he had something I needed. "Matt," I whispered.

He didn't respond, so I said his name again and lightly shoved his shoulder. That earned me a grumbled, "What?"

"I need your Sharpie."

He let out a string of whiny, muffled noises that sounded like, "Get your own."

"I will get my own, but I can't right now, and there's something I need to do." I tried to keep my voice down as I said that, but I heard a groggy, "Shut the fuck up," from Griffin's bunk. I figured I had about two seconds to get what I wanted before I was violently forced to leave.

Thankfully, Matt grunted and flung his hand toward the slots in the far wall of his cubby. I reached over him and felt along the pockets until I found the familiar cylinder. "Thanks," I told him, stepping back.

As I replaced the curtain, he said over his shoulder, "I want that back." The fact that it was the first coherent thing he'd said, made me want to laugh. I refrained since Griffin might kick me in the face if I made any more noise.

Grinning, I left my sleepy friends and made my way to the lounging area so I could turn on a light without pissing people off. I waved at the bus driver, then tucked into a seat and pulled out my petals. I plucked them off one by one and started mapping out what I wanted to write. A part of me wanted to apologize on every piece, but Kiera and I had ended the evening really well, and I didn't want to remind her about what had happened onstage. I wanted to remind her about how good we were together, about how much I loved her. I wanted to watch her eyes light up, to make her smile, to bring her joy. And most of all, I wanted her to have some fun. After the mess of last night and the shitstorm heading our way thanks to that photo, a little fun was exactly what she needed right now. Honestly, I needed it too.

When I was done, I gathered up the petals, then returned Matt's Sharpie to his cubby. He made a grunting noise that sounded an awful lot like, "Thanks," which again, almost made me laugh.

I quietly returned to my bedroom. Kiera was still sound

asleep, curled up facing where I would be. It was tempting to crawl back into bed with her, but I wasn't tired, and she clearly was. Sleep was a luxury on tour, and I wanted her to get as much as she needed, so I set down my petals instead, tossing them haphazardly around the bed before heading back to the lounging area.

The minutes felt like years as I waited for Kiera to wake up. I was excited to see the spark in her eyes, eager for her to see what I'd done. Sitting there staring at what I wanted felt like standing at the edge of a stage, waiting for my turn to perform; I was practically vibrating with expectant energy.

Just when the waiting was becoming more than I could bear, I finally heard the sleeping-area curtain rustle and saw it begin to move. Kiera stepped through a second later, and the vision of her momentarily stole my breath. She was still wearing her pajamas—loose pants and a tank top—her dark hair was crazy from just waking up, and she was radiating happiness like there was a spotlight shining inside of her. With the world's most beautiful smile on her face and pure joy in her eyes, she walked over to my table.

Sitting on my lap, she tossed her arms around my neck and said, "I love you too."

A soft smile curved my lips as I stared at her. "Did you get them all?" I asked.

She laughed, then pulled her hands back to show me the pile of petals clutched in her palms. "I think so, but...what does it mean?" Her brows furrowed as she looked at her hands.

A soft laugh escaped me as I removed the petals and placed them on the table. I hadn't written a message on each one, like I normally did. In fact, I hadn't written a message at all. I'd written random words on each petal, front and back. There were common words, loving words, and words specific to us. "It says whatever you want it to say," I told her, then I pulled out three petals that spelled out *I love you*.

Kiera smiled at me with such warmth on her face; it melted every part of me. "You're amazing, you know that?"

I smiled back at her, then reached down and pulled out the petal that said *yes*. Then I quickly added petals that spelled out *I'm hot too*.

Kiera snort-laughed so loud that she slapped a hand over her mouth and looked up at the curtain. She softly elbowed me in the side, then got to work sorting through the surprising number of petals. She laughed when she came upon words that were important to us: Pete's, Chevelle...coffee. Then she found a petal that made her cheeks flush with color. She twisted to look at me as she held it up. "And what sentence am I going to make with this?" she asked, a small, embarrassed smirk on her face.

Grinning, I started piecing together a sentence she could make with it. *Can. I. Suck. On. Your.* She immediately scattered my petals and glared at me. Keeping my expression even, I raised an eyebrow at her. "Can I finish?"

She sighed, but she was smiling. Biting my lip, I found the word that I had specifically written to go with the *suck* petal. I held it up to her, and she giggled. "Lemon? Really?"

"Of course," I said with a shrug. "What were you thinking?" She immediately turned bright red, and I chuckled at her. "You have such a dirty mind," I teased.

She poked me in the ribs again, harder this time, and I had no choice but to tickle her.

We flirted, laughed, and made sentences for hours. Sometimes they were gushy and romantic, sometimes they were weird and funny, and sometimes they were ripe with innuendo, but they were always entertaining, and they completely obliterated the situation we were in. For a moment, Kiera and I were just two people in love. Nothing more, nothing less.

The guys eventually woke up and joined us. Evan smiled and shook his head when he saw what we were doing. Matt frowned. He was probably still annoyed that I'd woken him up to borrow a pen. Griffin sat down and immediately started spelling out the filthiest sentences my options would let him make. Kiera quickly shooed him away from the table. Griffin grudgingly sat down with Matt, but he was in no way defeated. He had Deacon give him some paper, made Matt give him his marker, then he made his own words. And they were anything but romantic. He eventually had every guy on the bus joining him in making sentences that should never be uttered out loud.

They were all laughing, genuinely entertained, and Kiera was frowning, genuinely *not* entertained, so I scooped up the petals, grabbed Kiera's hand, and led her back to our bedroom where we could make the most of our busmates being distracted. I scattered the petals over the bed, stripped off Kiera's pajamas, then my own clothes. She smiled as she lay on the petal-strewn bed, and I had to pause to swallow the sudden lump in my throat. She was so beautiful.

Before joining my wife on the mattress, I picked out some choice words from among the petals and strategically placed them on her body. And damn, I'd never been so grateful to myself for writing the word "lick." By the time I'd finished removing each petal, diligently following every prompt I'd been given, Kiera was writhing on the bed, pulling at my skin, wanting me with an almost frenzied desperation. I felt the same animalistic need pulsing through my body, and I groaned in relief when I finally sank inside her.

She cupped my cheek as we moved together, prompting my gaze to meet hers. The connection between us intensified along with the building pressure, the insatiable need for more. Our eyes stayed locked, our mouths close enough that we shared the same air. I was so in the moment with her that I could almost tangibly feel her love wrapping around me, holding me so securely that I knew it would never untangle. I both wanted the euphoria that I knew was coming and didn't want anything about this moment to change. Then Kiera closed her eyes and bit her lip, containing the sounds I knew she wanted to make. I felt her clench around me, and it shoved me over the edge. I groaned as I came, and Kiera held my head, pulling me into her neck, into her warmth. I rode out the bliss with her, cherishing every second of it. Cherishing every second of her. Then I locked her in my arms and held her tight as we recovered, as we fell even deeper in love with each other.

We didn't leave our love nest until it was time to get ready for the next show. And it was absolute heaven.

Chapter 21

I'M SO STUPID

Sienna didn't try to kiss me again onstage. She seemed to realize where the line was with me, seemed to understand that she was already straddling it. But it didn't matter that she was keeping her distance now; the photo of us was everywhere, and me ditching Justin's tour to "run to her side" was all anyone was talking about. It was infuriating, especially since Sienna was staying quiet about the whole damn thing, and my refusal of our relationship was falling on deaf ears. Nobody fucking believed me. Even my friends were starting to lose faith in me. Not the guys, they saw too much not to believe me, but my friends back home, my family back east...they were all beginning to doubt me.

'Are you sure you and Kiera are all right?'

A long sigh escaped me as I looked at the text from Hailey. Another text came in while I debated what to say to her. *'You can tell me the truth. No judgement.'*

I laid my head back on the seat and tossed my phone on the table. I was probably making her suspicions worse by not responding right away, but goddamn...I was sick of everyone thinking something was going on with Sienna and me. I'd heard Evan talking to Jenny about it, heard Matt talking to Rachel. Gavin had asked *how I was doing with everything*, then told me he was around if I *wanted to talk*. Denny's message had been somewhat hopeful, somewhat reproachful: *This looks bad, Kellan. I'm choosing to believe what you told me at the bar, but if you want the rumors to end, mate, you should probably stop kissing her.* All of it was driving me batshit crazy.

Evan looked over at me when I let out a loud groan of annoyance. "That good, huh?" he said.

I rolled my head his way. "I'm over this. I'm so fucking over it. Everyone thinks I'm banging her." I tossed up my hands. "Everyone."

Evan frowned, then shook his head. "I don't. Matt doesn't. And most importantly, Kiera doesn't. And that's all that really matters."

I closed my eyes and nodded. "Thank God she came with me. If she was home, listening to this..." My throat clenched so hard that I couldn't keep speaking. Opening my eyes, I looked back at our bedroom, where Kiera was happily getting some work done. Jesus. Would she believe me if she wasn't here to see it?

Evan touched my shoulder, bringing my attention back to him. Like he could read my mind, he told me, "She'd believe you, Kellan. I'm not saying it would be easy, or that it wouldn't cause its own problems, but in the end, she would believe you." His lips twisted into a smirk. "And if not, then she'd believe me. I'm a pillar of trust. And I'd one hundred percent throw you under the bus if you *were* cheating on her."

Humor rose in me as I shook my head at him. I didn't think he would since he hadn't mentioned anything to Denny when I'd betrayed him, but still, I appreciated the sentiment. "Good to know," I told him. I frowned as something he'd said struck me. Or rather, something he hadn't said. "You mentioned you and Matt...what about Griffin?" I'd already had to convince him that nothing was going on. He hadn't given me shit in a while, but who knew what he really thought.

Evan rolled his eyes. "Griffin thinks everyone is doing everybody." I nodded at his assessment of our friend, and he smiled at me. "But...rumor has it, he told Kiera you'd never actually do anything with Sienna. Rumor is, he was *comforting*."

I was briefly concerned to hear that Kiera *had* been worried about me, but the feeling was quickly overridden by shock. My jaw dropped. "Comforting? Griffin?" Evan nodded, and I shook my head. "No way. I'll believe I'm banging Sienna before I believe that."

Evan started laughing, then he held out his fist for me. I laughed as I bumped knuckles with him, and the release made me feel a lot better. Picking up my phone, I told my sister, yet again, that Kiera and I were just fine. And we were. None of this shit really mattered.

I left Evan to go see Kiera after that. When I opened the door to our room, I found her typing on her laptop with tears in her eyes. "Are you okay?" I asked.

She sniffed, wiped her eyes, then smiled at me. "Yes," she said, closing her laptop. "Just a hard part." She shrugged in apology, but I was the one who suddenly felt guilty.

"I'm sorry," I told her, sitting on the edge of the bed.

She laughed a little as she wrapped her arms around me. "You don't even know what part it was."

That was true, but still, I was sorry for all of it. Not wanting to get into it right now, I changed the subject. "I heard a rumor today."

She instantly groaned. "Now what? Is she pregnant with your baby yet?"

That should have been funny, should have made me laugh, but I actually *had* heard that rumor, and it wasn't funny at all. "Not about Sienna. About you." Her eyes snapped to mine, and they were wide with fear. I knew exactly why she was panicking and mentally slapped myself for not phrasing it better. Shaking my head, I told her, "About Griffin being nice to you. Comforting you about Sienna and me."

She visibly relaxed, then she smirked. "Oh, yeah. That one is true."

An odd combination of shock and pride went through me. Damn if Griffin couldn't still surprise me. Maybe I might win the bet on him after all. My delighted smile fell off my face as I realized what all that being true meant. "You were worried about me? About Sienna and me?"

Kiera sighed as she studied my face. "The music video had me freaking out a little. I thought...I worried that once you got a taste of her, you'd...you'd want her over me."

My eyes drifted to the sheets as guilt pummeled me. I never should have agreed to that damn video. It was going to haunt me forever. "Kiera, I'd never..."

Her fingers touched my chin, lifting my gaze. "I know. I don't feel that way anymore. It was just a random fear, a voiced insecurity, and Griffin happened to be there to talk me through it."

"Damn it," I said, smiling. "Now I feel like I owe him an apology for almost kicking him out of the band."

Kiera laughed and looped her arms around me again. "Don't worry about it. His inconsiderate moments far outweigh his sweet ones. Just keep refraining from kicking him out, and that will be repayment enough."

I laughed at her comment, then pulled her tight. "Very, very true. You're so wise, Mrs. Kyle."

"I'm trying to be," she said with a shrug.

"Well, you're succeeding." In this, and in everything else.

She inspired me every day, and I tried really hard after that not to let the rumors get to me so much, to use her strength as my example. And for the most part, it worked. Until the day it all... spiraled out of control.

Kiera and I were in the lounging area of the bus, relaxing after a rather rousing lovemaking session. It had involved an intense level of teasing that I'd never experienced before. I'd confessed how I sometimes drew the alphabet while I was going down on her, and she'd playfully tried it out on me. And holy fuck...just thinking about it made me want to take her back to the bedroom so we could do it again.

I was contemplating that very thing when I heard Griffin's voice from the sleeping area. "Oh my God! Oh my fucking God!" He kept saying it over and over, and dread instantly washed through me, dousing every spark of desire.

Setting down my guitar, I stood up and looked over at Kiera. We'd both been working a little, her on her book, and me on a new song, but we were both going to be distracted until we knew what Griffin was freaking out about. "Why don't you stay here?" I told her. There were very few things that shocked Griffin, and every single one of those things was something Kiera would *not* want to hear about. She knew that too, and she nodded that she'd stay put.

Griffin was still swearing exclamations as I stepped through the curtain. Others were grumbling at him, shushing him, and snapping at him to shut up, but he was beyond caring. I started feeling queasy as I replaced the privacy curtain. I wasn't sure how yet, but I was pretty sure this involved me. Or maybe that was just my paranoia talking.

"Griffin? What the hell are you freaking out about?" I quietly asked.

The curtain on his cubby instantly pulled back, and he leaned over the edge on his elbow. "Dude! What the fuck, man?"

More curtains opened as curious people looked between Griffin and me. "What?" I asked, hopelessly confused.

Griffin hopped out of his bunk and showed me his phone. "I can't believe you. You totally lied to me, and I bought it. You suck, man. You totally suck. You knew I wanted her first."

I grabbed his phone since I still didn't have a clue what he was talking about. There was a paused video on the screen. A video that looked alarmingly familiar. "Oh...fuck," I murmured.

Griffin instantly pulled his phone back. "Yeah, fuck. What the hell, dude? I thought you were doing the whole monogamy thing, and you've been screwing Sienna this whole time? I stood up for you, man. I don't mind lying for you, but I like to *know* when I'm lying."

Now Matt and Evan were scrambling out of their beds to check out Griffin's phone. They looked between the video and me, confusion clear on their faces. I could understand why. Even in the freezeframe, it was obviously me. "It's not what you think," I said, trying to keep my voice down.

Griffin pressed play on the video, and instantly, the sound of fucking, combined with my name being moaned, filled the small space. "Really?" Griffin said, a mixture of glee and annoyance on his face. "That seems pretty self-explanatory, even for me."

I quickly grabbed his phone and frantically tried to stop the stupid thing. Matt eventually reached over and helped me. His eyes were hard, though. So were Evan's. Great. Now even they believed the rumors. God-fucking-damn it. "Yes, it's me. Yes, it's a sex tape. But it's not Sienna."

Matt and Evan shared a look, but I couldn't tell if they believed me. Griffin scoffed and showed me his phone. "Dude, it says it's Sienna right there." His finger went to the top of the tiny screen where the header of the video stated *Sienna Sexton and Kellan Kyle Sex Tape Leaked*.

All the blood drained from my face. Oh...my God. It wasn't being leaked as my sex tape with a random woman, it was being leaked as Sienna's sex tape with *me*. No wonder Griffin jumped to that conclusion. I put a hand to my mouth, then said something I never thought I'd say. "Press play again."

Griffin looked at the guys, then shrugged and pressed play. I studied the video as it played, trying to make out Joey, but it was so damn dark and grainy, all I could tell was that it was me with a dark-haired woman. And fuck if Joey didn't look a lot like Sienna in the video. Feeling sick, I told him, "Shut it off."

He did, then he gave me a look of disbelief mixed with excitement. "You fucked her! You actually fucked her! I'm super-pissed that you got her first, but, dude, I have to know, how was she? On a scale of one to ten...like a twenty, right? I totally fucking hate you for this, but damn, man, thanks for recording it for the rest of us."

"Jesus, Kellan," Evan said. He opened his mouth to say more, but nothing came out. Matt just frowned at me. As I looked around the cubbies, Deacon and his bandmates were studying me with frowns on their faces too. They'd been around Kiera long enough to have grown to like her, and they all believed this shit. Because fuck, this wasn't a rumor anymore. This was proof. Except...it wasn't.

I held up my hands as I looked around the room filled with judgement. "It's Joey, okay. I wanted you to play it so I could show you, but you can't fucking tell from the video because her camera was a piece of shit. But I swear to you, that's Joey." I paused to look around again. Deacon and his friends looked skeptical since they didn't know who Joey was, but the guys were changing their expressions. Matt and Evan looked contemplative. Griffin looked...confused.

He scratched his head of dirty-blond hair. "You cheated on Kiera with *Joey*? When? And why? I mean, don't get me wrong, Joey's hot, but if you're gonna torch your relationship, do it with the hottest girl you can find, you know?"

I inhaled a deep breath. Then I counted to ten. When I finally didn't feel like hitting him, I said, "I didn't cheat on Kiera. That video is years old. *Before* Kiera."

Matt and Evan nodded; they seemed to believe me. Griffin still wasn't convinced. "Are you sure? Because that really seems like Sienna."

I narrowed my eyes at him. "Am I sure who I made a sex tape with? Yeah. Yeah, I'm sure."

He crossed his arms over his chest. "So you're telling me there's been a sex tape of Joey out there for years, and you didn't tell me about it? Dude, I thought we were friends?"

Ignoring him, I turned to Matt. "Please tell me this is just on one random website, and no one but him knows about it?"

Matt started searching his phone, but Griffin was already laughing. "Nah, man, it's everywhere. I wasn't even searching for porn, and this popped up. Best. Day. Ever."

I ran a hand down my face and sighed. "Goddamn it. Does everyone think it's Sienna?"

Griffin said, "Yep," but I ignored him and waited for Matt's analysis.

He scanned his phone for a minute, then cringed and met eyes with me. "Uh...yeah. It's pretty clear it's you..." He paused to show a shot of my face looking directly at the camera since, yeah, I'd turned it on. Pulling his phone back, he scanned for more and shrugged. "No one else has claimed it's them, so the general assumption is that it's Sienna. Sorry," he added with another cringe.

I scrubbed my face with both hands now. I knew this would come out eventually, but I never imagined, not in a million years, that it would come out in *this* way. "I basically gave them proof," I muttered. "They'll never believe me now." Not that they were believing me anyway.

"Yeah," Griffin said, putting a hand on my shoulder. Then he lightly smacked me. "Good job, by the way. I haven't watched it all the way through yet, but what I did see was super-hot." I lifted my eyes to glare at him, and he raised an eyebrow at me. "Are you sure it's not—"

I lunged for him, and Evan instantly interceded. "Maybe you should go warn Kiera?" he said, keeping me away from Griffin.

I groaned a little, then nodded. Pointing at Griffin, I told the room, "Find a way to make his phone block that."

Matt grinned. "On it," he said, snatching Griffin's phone from him.

"Hey, that's my porn. Give it back, Matty." They started scuffling, and Deacon and his friends started laughing. "I have to know how it ends," Griffin complained.

"How do you think it ends?" Matt said with a laugh as he dodged Griffin's hands.

"I don't know," he said, trying to get the phone from behind Matt's back. "Maybe he didn't stick the landing. Maybe that's the *real* reason Joey moved out. How will I know if I don't watch it?"

The guys in the cubbies laughed even harder at that, and Evan grabbed Griffin to try to keep him away from Matt. I sighed, rolled my eyes, then fortified myself to face my wife. At least she already knew about the video. If *this* was how she'd first found out about it, well damn, I didn't think she'd be as forgiving as she was back at the house.

When I stepped into the sitting area of the bus, Kiera had her hands on the table like she was about to stand up. She froze when she saw me, and there was so much trepidation on her face that I was again bombarded with guilt. This one was entirely my fault. I never should have filmed myself like that. I should have known it wouldn't stay private. Nothing stayed private anymore.

Words tumbled through my brain as I sat beside Kiera, but none of them were sticking. I didn't know what to say to her except that I was sorry, and that just didn't feel like enough. Griffin peeked his head into the room, his face eager, like he wanted to see Kiera lose her shit on me. Matt pulled him back, and I rolled my eyes again. Through the sudden silence, I heard a cell phone ringing. I had a feeling that would be a common sound today.

"What?" Kiera whispered, her face pale, her eyes wide.

I wanted to tell her, but I still couldn't decide where to start. *You were right, I was wrong. I completely fucked up, and if you thought the rumors were bad before, well, just you wait.*

Just the thought of saying that made me frown. I really wasn't ready to confess the mess I'd made. Why couldn't we rewind time and go back to before all this craziness began? And then freeze the moment and live there forever, trapped in an eternity of bliss? Was that really too much to ask?

Kiera's phone was still incessantly ringing. Since I still hadn't answered her, she looked toward the back and said, "Maybe I should get that. It could be my sister."

"I wouldn't be surprised," I murmured, annoyance filling me.

If just the photo of Sienna kissing me had caused everyone back home to freak out...God, I didn't even want to think about what people were going to say to me today.

"Kellan?" Kiera said, clearly wanting an explanation.

With a sigh, I put a hand on her knee. "Joey leaked the tape. It's all anyone is talking about this morning."

A mixture of relief and sadness crossed Kiera's face. "Oh, you had me worried for a minute."

I really wanted to leave it at that. I wanted to say, *Yep, it sucks but oh well*, and drop it for the rest of our lives, but I hadn't told her the full story, and I didn't want Kiera to be unprepared. By my expression, Kiera could tell there was more. "What?" she asked.

There was a throbbing ache behind my eye that I knew was going to be a full-on headache in about five minutes. As I rubbed my temple, I told her, "Joey's camera was...fucking fabulous. It's so grainy that she's hard to make out, so because of Nick shoving me onto this tour, and all of the stories, photos, and speculation, everyone is just assuming that I'm doing—"

Kiera's jaw dropped as she got it. "They think you made a sex tape with Sienna."

Wishing I could deny it, I nodded. "They look enough alike that it's a really easy mistake to make. Plus, the angle wasn't that great, and there's no date on the tape. The only clear thing about it is that it's definitely me. There is this one clear shot of my face since I...started the recording...and Joey says my name a lot." I cringed internally right after I said that. *She doesn't need details, dumbass.*

Kiera looked ill as she stared at me. Then she blinked and said, "Oh, should you say something?"

"Yes, absolutely, but..." I shrugged as a wave of hopelessness rushed through me. "I'm not so sure that it will matter. People will believe what they want to believe." I closed my eyes as the weight of it all pressed in on me. "Even Griffin believes it's Sienna on the tape." And somewhere inside, he probably always would.

Right along with everyone else. Opening my eyes, I gently cupped Kiera's cheek. "I'm sorry, but I think I just unintentionally gave them the irrefutable proof they were looking for. I don't think it's possible to stop this now."

Goddamn it. I never should have skirted around the issue, inflaming everyone's curiosity. From that very first interview, I should have pulled Kiera onto my lap and said, "This is my wife, and I'm head over heels in love with her." But I hadn't. I'd played along, and now everyone had this image of me that was so wrong; I couldn't stand it.

Kiera sighed and pushed her computer away. "I should get my phone. Try to explain..."

I nodded at her. "Yeah, I probably should too." I just didn't feel like it. I didn't feel like doing anything but wallow in anger. Mostly at myself.

Kiera kissed my cheek, then made her way to the back of the bus to start fielding phone calls. I stayed where I was, staring out the window. It was beginning to rain outside, and that felt really appropriate.

Eventually Evan joined me at the table. He had my cell phone in his hand. "Kiera gave me this to give to you. She says it keeps going off." I took it from him, saw about ten missed phone calls on the display, then turned it over and set it on the table.

"I'm so stupid," I told him.

He gave me a laugh that didn't have any humor in it. "For a minute there, I really thought you were." I looked over at him, and he shrugged. "It does seem like Sienna. I thought you cheated on Kiera. I don't think I've ever been that shocked in all my life."

I laid my head back on the seat with a sigh. "I don't know what to say about it. To the public, I mean. Everyone is going to ask, and I don't know what to say. I never thought...I never thought it would be like this."

Evan sighed and rubbed his dark head. "Yeah, I don't get it. They want you to be with her so bad; it makes me wonder..."

Lifting my head, I looked over at him. "Wonder what?"

He cringed like he didn't want to say it. "What would happen if they did know about Kiera?"

I frowned at him. "What do you mean?"

He chewed on his lip, silently studying me for a moment. "Despite everything you've said, they think you and Sienna are in love. And now this, this is documented proof of everything they've hoped for. So if they catch wind of Kiera *now*, she won't be the wife you've had all along, she'll be the—"

"Holy fuck," I said, finally catching on. "She'll be the other woman. She'll be my mistress. They'll...eviscerate her."

Evan shrugged. "Maybe. I honestly don't know, but I think... I think you two should be careful. At least until this blows over."

I dropped my head into my hands, then dug my thumbs into my skull so hard that I thought I might dent something. "Jesus Christ," I murmured. "How do I fix this?"

An idea popped into my head, and I grabbed my phone. Ignoring all the missed calls and texts, I found Sienna's number and called her. She picked up instantly, like she'd been on her phone all morning too. "Kellan, love. What a pleasant surprise."

There was something in her voice that crawled right under my skin. Joy. Glee. Delight at an unexpected turn of events that was working out perfectly for her. "I'm sure you've heard by now," I said.

"Heard what, darling?"

My hand clenched. Both her term of endearment and her fake ignorance was pissing me off. "Don't play games with me, Sienna. I'm not having a good day. And out of everyone, *you* should understand how I feel right now."

She let out a long sigh that was heavy with weariness. "I do. And I'm sorry. Being betrayed is no easy thing. I feel awful that someone has done this to you."

I analyzed every single syllable, looking for a lie, but I couldn't hear one. She seemed genuinely sympathetic to what I was going through, and it relaxed me to hear it. "Thank you. I hate to ask, but I need your help with this. I need you to say something. Deny it's you, tell them we're just colleagues...*something*."

She let out an amused noise. "Funny how they instantly jumped to it being me, isn't it? They do love us together."

That wasn't the response I was looking for. "Sienna, *please*."

She was silent a moment, then she said, "I'll talk with my people, and we'll work out the best way to deal with this. Don't you fret."

I had no idea what that actually meant, but it sounded positive, so I told her, "Okay, thank you."

"Of course, love." She paused, then added, "Can I offer you some advice?"

Unease instantly pooled in my stomach. "Sure."

"Never record *anything* that you don't want *everyone* to see."

I closed my eyes as shame and annoyance heated my face. "Yeah, I think I've got that one now. But thank you."

She giggled a little, then said, "See you tonight," and disconnected the call.

Evan raised an eyebrow as I set down my phone. "She gonna help?"

I sighed as my phone chirped with a text message. "Who knows." Because I sure as shit couldn't tell what any of that conversation truly meant. And that really pissed me off.

Three more texts came in while Evan and I sat there. Evan looked at me every time I got a message but didn't say anything when I ignored them. I just wasn't ready to deal with it yet, and I was seriously regretting exchanging numbers with everyone I saw the last time we were home. Damn nostalgia. I could hear Kiera's phone ringing every once in a while, but it never rang for long. She was answering hers, because again, she was stronger than me.

Just as I was thinking that I should respond to somebody, my phone rang, and Jenny's name appeared on the screen. Evan sat up straighter and fidgeted in his seat, like he was restraining himself from answering it. He stared at me while it continued to ring, and I could tell it was annoying him that I was ignoring her.

I glanced at him, then turned to look out the window. I still wasn't ready.

Evan sighed but didn't chide me for it. My phone finally silenced, and almost immediately, Evan's started ringing. He didn't hesitate to answer it, not even when I snapped my head around and glared at him. "Hey, Jujube," he said, locking eyes with me.

He was silent for a long time, and I sighed as I imagined all the horrible things Jenny was saying about me. Then Evan frowned and said, "I'm not gonna do that." I heard a response from Jenny that sounded really angry, but I couldn't make out the words. Evan sighed, then reached over and lightly smacked my chest. "That's from Jenny," he said. "She's really mad at you."

A weary exhale left me. "Tell her I didn't cheat on Kiera."

He relayed my message, then said, "I don't think he wants to...Yeah, I know, but...Jenny..." He stopped, sighed, then said, "Okay, but be nice." Right after saying that, he handed his phone to me. "She wants to talk to you."

I just stared at him. She couldn't talk to me if I didn't pick up the phone. Evan sighed again, then waved his cell phone at me. "Come on, man," he said, his dark eyes begging me not to get him in trouble.

I let out an irritated huff, then grabbed his phone. Bringing it to my ear, I pretended today was just a normal day. "Hey, Jenny. What's up?" Evan rolled his eyes at the pep in my voice.

"Oh my God, Kellan. What did you do? And why would you do it? And why would you film it? And why aren't you answering your phone?"

Wishing I'd never woken up this morning, I exhaled a five-second breath. "Which question do you want an answer to first?" I asked her.

"Kellan!" she snapped. "This is serious."

"I know it's serious, Jenny," I snapped back. "That's why I'm not answering my phone. I need a minute to figure out just what the fuck I'm supposed to do."

Jenny sighed, and for once, she didn't reprimand me for my language. "Kiera told me it's the tape you made with Joey a long time ago. She swears up and down that you didn't cheat on her. Is that true?" She sighed again. "Would you even tell me the truth?" she muttered.

I closed my eyes as an aching hurt wrapped around my heart. "You know what I really can't stand? Everyone's complete lack of faith in me." I knew I shouldn't be upset that my friends questioned my honesty since I'd had such a breezy relationship with the truth in the past, but still, it killed me that they doubted me. Jenny started to say something, but I cut her off. "Of course I didn't cheat on her. I wouldn't *ever* cheat on her. It's not who I am, and I really thought you understood that."

I hung up before she could respond, then tossed the phone back to Evan. I instantly felt bad for snapping at her. My shady past wasn't her fault, and after everything I'd done with Kiera while she'd been with Denny, I really couldn't blame Jenny for wondering about me.

Evan stared at his phone for a second, maybe to see if she'd call back. Thankfully, she didn't. He frowned when he looked up at me. "Maybe I should have warned *you* to be nice."

"Sorry," I sighed. "*That's* why I'm not talking yet." Shaking my head, I shoved my phone away from me. It shot across the table and landed on the floor. I seriously hoped I'd just broken it, but then I heard three new message alerts, back to back to back. Fucking phone.

"You could just turn it off," Evan murmured.

I flipped him off. He softly chuckled at me, then started texting someone. Probably Jenny, to apologize for me being an asshole. I was about to tell him to let Jenny know I was sorry when Matt and Griffin joined us. Matt gave me a small smile. "Rachel, um...I let her know it's not as bad as it seems."

Shaking my head, I looked out the window. "Does she believe my story?" I asked.

"Uh...yeah. Of course."

I sighed again. That wasn't a ringing endorsement of my innocence, and I could easily read between the lines. She wanted to believe me, but she wouldn't be shocked if the opposite proved to be true. Great.

"Hey, Kell."

I looked over to see Griffin smiling at me. He lifted his hand in a high five, and I just blankly stared at him. Looking annoyed, he grabbed my hand and made me slap his palm. Kind of. "That's from Anna," he said. "She watched the video, and she said you totally stuck the landing, so nice job, man."

Rolling my eyes, I asked, "And does *she* believe me?"

He shrugged. "Yeah. She believes everything I say." I had a hard time believing that was true, but I didn't feel like arguing with him. Especially when he grinned and said, "I can't believe my best friend is a porn star. It's like today's my birthday or something."

Right at that moment, I regretted shoving my phone to the floor. I would have loved to nail him in the face with it. Matt snorted at his comment. "If it was your birthday, wouldn't *you* be the porn star?"

Griffin rubbed his chin as he thought about that. "Hmmm, you make a good point. Damn, I *should* be a porn star. New life goal, when the band breaks up, that's what I'm gonna be. The world's greatest porn star."

Matt shared a look with Evan and me, and seeing the mischief on his face actually made me feel a little better. "That's a good plan, Griff. There's just one little problem with it."

Griffin shook his head. "And what's that?"

Matt shrugged. "Shouldn't you be good at sex if you're gonna be a porn star?"

Evan started cracking up, and that made me crack up, and damn, it felt good. Griffin scowled as he looked between all of us. "Dude, I'm great at the sex. I'm incredible at the sex. I'm glorious at the sex. No worries there, cuz."

Matt grimaced. "Please stop calling it *the* sex. And please don't ever film yourself. I have enough nightmares about you as it is."

Griffin looked over at him and smiled. "Are you saying you would watch me?"

"Not willingly," Matt stated, suddenly looking a little green.

Griffin's grin widened. "I can work with that."

Evan and I were both laughing at the disgusted look on Matt's face when my phone chimed again with another message. Griffin reached down and picked it up. "Hey, Kell, you know your phone's on the floor?" He started scrolling through it like it was his. "Damn...people are mad at you." He looked up at me with a raised eyebrow. "You want me to respond to some of these?"

I instantly felt weary again, and with a shrug, I told him, "Sure." Matt and Evan immediately shot me startled looks, and I quickly amended my statement. "No! I meant no!" I hastily grabbed my phone.

"Too late," he said with a grin.

Cringing, I looked down to see what he'd done. "Jesus Christ, Griffin. You sent Kate a winky face?"

He laughed a little as he shook his head. "No, it's a winky face with its tongue out. You're welcome."

"Goddamn it," I muttered, then I got to work fixing his callous response...and responding to all the others.

It felt like years later when the calls and texts finally stopped coming in. I'd apologized to Jenny, reassured my sister, told Gavin it was all a misunderstanding, begged forgiveness from Kiera's parents, who'd insisted on getting my number from Kiera, and even called the bar to apologize to Pete, who I'd heard was getting bombarded by gossip magazines that wanted an inside scoop on me. It all sucked, and I was just about to flush my phone away when I got one last call.

I was at a bar with the guys and the members of Holeshot, relaxing before tonight's show. Evan's idea, to get my mind off things. Kiera had stayed on the bus. I'd offered to turn the guys down and stay with her, but she'd wanted to be alone. I'd left an apology petal for her, but it hadn't felt like enough. Nothing was feeling like enough.

When I saw who was calling me, I genuinely contemplated letting it ring. But avoidance hadn't gotten me anywhere today. Feeling like I could sleep for a thousand years, I reluctantly answered the phone. "Hey, Denny."

"I'm kind of surprised you picked up," he said with a laugh.

A small, tired chuckle escaped me. "Don't think I didn't weigh my options first." I sighed, then told him, "It's not true, please don't yell at me."

He laughed again. "Is that what your day's been like?"

"Pretty much," I grumbled, watching my friends talk to each other with happy, carefree expressions on their faces. Lucky bastards. "Everyone thinks it's Sienna on the tape. Everyone thinks I cheated on Kiera." I braced myself, then asked a question I really didn't want to ask. "Do you think that?"

He didn't answer right away, and I felt that ball of disappointment getting heavier in my stomach. Then finally, he said, "No, I don't think that."

"You don't?" I couldn't keep the amazement out of my voice, and Denny laughed again.

"Kiera told me about the video a while ago. It's with Joey, right?"

I simultaneously felt both relief and shame. "Yeah, it was way back before you guys...before she and I..." I stopped explaining since he already knew our fucked-up history.

"Yeah," he said. "The minute I heard about it, I figured that was what it was. Well, ninety-nine percent of me figured that."

"And the other one percent?" I asked, cringing.

He sighed at me. "You know I'm trying to let things go, mate, but in the back of my mind, you'll always be capable of hurting the people you care about. A small part of me will always think the worst about you, but I try really hard not to listen to that part."

Well, damn. At least he was being honest with me, and I couldn't fault him for that. And truly, only one percent of him doubting me wasn't too shabby. "I know I deserve a lot worse from you, so...I can live with that."

He laughed softly, then he sighed. "Hey, I told Kiera this would die down soon, but I don't know...I think you should lay low for a while. And avoid Sienna as much as you possibly can."

Evan's comment about Kiera being perceived as my mistress flashed through my mind, and I wholeheartedly agreed with what Denny said. Problem was, avoiding Sienna wasn't as easy as it sounded. Not until this damn tour was over with. "I'll do whatever I have to do to keep her safe," I told him, meaning every word.

I could hear the smile in his voice when he responded with, "I know you will, Kellan. *That* I believe one hundred percent."

And for the first time that day, I actually felt better after getting off the phone with someone.

Chapter 22

AN UNEXPECTED VISITOR

The next couple of weeks sucked. I felt like I was in hiding; I was avoiding people so much. Only, I really wasn't because I still had to be present for the show, for the meet-and-greets, and for the bane of my existence...interviews. I was quickly growing to hate anyone who wanted to ask me questions, especially when those questions had to do with my personal life. And they always asked about my personal life. No one cared about boundaries anymore. They just wanted me to say *Yes, I'm frequently having sex with Sienna. It's great, thanks for asking me about it.* And when I didn't say that, when I denied it, they mocked me. *Sure, right, you're just friends. I've heard that before.*

I felt like I had explained the sex tape fifty million times already, telling everyone that the woman in the video was someone that I used to date, but it wasn't Sienna, and it would *never* be Sienna. Because we *just worked together*. And that was it. But I might as well just record myself saying it and play that at every interview since they all still asked me about it.

It didn't help anything that I was the only one talking. Sienna's "plan" to help me was to act offended whenever anyone brought it up, going so far as to walk away in a huff sometimes. And all that did was make it seem true. I tried talking to her about it again, but she always gave me the same response: *Of course, I'll see what I can do*. And then she never actually did anything. Eventually I stopped asking and just did my best not to be seen with her. If only the DJs could see how little we actually saw of each other, then maybe they'd believe me, although they'd probably just call our distance a *lovers spat*, then ask when we were getting married. Fuck my life.

It also didn't help anything that Joey had disappeared from the face of the Earth. I had to believe she'd released the tape for attention, but she hadn't said a word to anyone about being the woman on the tape. She was happily letting Sienna steal her thunder, and that seemed so unlike her to me. Joey wanted to be worshipped, wanted to be lusted after. She *lived* for it, so her silence now—when this golden opportunity had fallen in her lap —was mind-boggling.

I was beginning to wonder if Joey had been paid to be silent. That made the most sense, but at the same time, I just couldn't believe it. The only people to benefit from her silence were Nick and Sienna. And considering everything that Sienna had been through with her ex, I just couldn't believe that she would orchestrate something like this. And Nick doing it just seemed so... unprofessional. I mean, he was the VP of a major label. Surely, he had better things to do than manipulate public perception to create a frenzied, cultish type of obsession for a fake relationship that would probably result in boosted sales for both of us, and fuck...yeah, he probably was behind it. Sienna too, sadly. But like everything else, I didn't know what to do about that. Again, fuck my life.

The rumors were so crazy right now, and the public was so certain of my relationship with Sienna, that Kiera had finally asked me to take off my wedding ring. She'd brought it up a couple of days after the tape released, when it was clear that the frenzy wasn't going to die down anytime soon, and even though I understood why—and agreed with her—the conversation had still been a difficult one.

"It's not forever, it's just for right now. While they're so stuck on you and Sienna being a couple."

The sadness in her eyes was almost too much for me to bear, but I popped the ring off anyway. "Yeah, Evan mentioned something about them seeing you as my mistress, and I just can't—" I looked up at her with a sigh. "I don't know what I would do if someone said that about you. And if it was a fan..." I let that trail off as I shook my head. I'd probably get arrested for assault, and there'd be a massive public backlash, and my career would be over. Definitely, permanently over.

Kiera sighed and grabbed my hand. "We'll be more careful in public. They won't know, and you won't have to hit anyone."

I smiled as I peeked up at her, but it quickly fell off my face. "How do we get married like this?"

She opened her mouth, but nothing came out, and when she closed it, there were tears in her eyes. She didn't know, and I didn't know, and I hated it. I fucking hated *all of it*.

Pushing that memory aside, I played with my ring, sitting forlornly on my right hand, and contemplated what I could do to put things back on the correct course. By myself? Not much. I needed Sienna's help and cooperation, and I just wasn't getting it.

We were leaving a particularly annoying interview, and my mood wasn't improving, even though it was over. I just wanted my life back. Kiera was giving me sad but reassuring glances as we drove away from the radio station. I could probably switch my ring back now, but we were staying at a hotel tonight, so I still had to be mindful of public perception. Kiera and I usually skipped out on the hotel rooms, letting the guys have the two rooms reserved for the D-Bags, giving them some much-needed space, but this particular hotel room had a jacuzzi in it, and the minute we'd heard that, we'd opted to leave our love nest behind for the evening. And since I didn't want to risk someone photographing me wearing a wedding ring while I walked from the car to the hotel, I left it on the wrong hand. Because that was my life now.

Kiera's phone rang while I was stewing. She dug through her bag, found it, then smiled as she answered it. "Hey, sis. What's up?"

Griffin was in the front seat of the enormous SUV we were in, and I saw his eyes in the rearview mirror instantly lock on Kiera as she talked to her sister. Anything about Anna usually caught his attention right away, a fact that I found really interesting.

As far as I knew, Griffin hadn't slept with anyone other than Anna since he'd found out about the pregnancy. Granted, I didn't keep track of Griffin twenty-four-seven, so there was no way I could know that for sure, but Griffin was usually pretty vocal about his sex life, and I hadn't heard anything recently to make me think I was wrong. He was either striking out a lot—a genuine possibility—or he was subconsciously being faithful to her. I was hoping for the latter, but considering how often he'd tried with Sienna, it was probably the former.

Curious, I watched Griffin while he watched Kiera. She was telling Anna where we were, somewhere in Atlanta, heading to the hotel. Then Kiera said, "You're in Georgia?"

Griffin latched on to those words and instantly twisted around in his seat. "Anna's in Georgia? Awesome. Where is she?" His eyes were damn near glowing as he said it, the eagerness and anticipation clear as day on his face.

Kiera murmured, "Airport," to Griffin, then continued her conversation with Anna, asking her why she was in Georgia. While Anna presumably answered her, Griffin turned to the driver. "Dude, we need to turn around and go to the airport to pick somebody up." He looked over at the speedometer and added, "I'll give you a thousand dollars if you go double the speed limit."

His comment made me laugh, and I heard equally amused chuckles coming from Matt and Evan. The driver didn't respond to Griffin's offer, or change his speed any, but he did start the process of turning the car around, and eventually we wound up at the airport.

The first thing I noticed when I spotted Anna was that her stomach had dramatically swelled in size, and for the life of me, I couldn't remember when she was due. And that was a bit concerning when I took in the number of bags she'd brought with her. How long was she staying? Was she having this baby on the bus? Fuck, was she having this baby *in my bed*? Although I supposed it really wasn't my bed anymore. There wasn't a single part of me that could make Anna sleep in a cubby, and I had no desire to take the bed back after Anna and Griffin were done with it. Those two horndogs could have it, keep it, and take it with them when they left.

Oh well. At least Kiera would enjoy having her sister here, for however long that might be. And Griffin would be thrilled if she stayed, which meant the rest of us would be happier too since Griffin was slightly less annoying when he was getting regular sex. Slightly.

Kiera wrapped her arms around Anna, holding her as close as she could with the baby between them. Kiera's smile was huge, lighting up her entire face. Anna's expression was similar, and it did something to me to see that bond. In the past, whenever I'd watched people with their families, there had been a...hole inside of me. An empty part that acknowledged what I was seeing, but couldn't quite understand it. I'd never had a bonding moment with my family, not until Hailey, Riley...Gavin. Now seeing the affection filled me with warmth, made me miss my siblings. And my father. And fuck if it wasn't weird to feel that way. *I should call them.*

"Hi, Max," Kiera said, welcoming her unborn nephew.

"It's Maximus," Griffin interjected, then he brushed Kiera out of the way and started getting busy with Anna. Okay, all he did was kiss her, but it wasn't a public friendly smack. No, it was a closed-door, I'm-about-to-plunge-it-into-you, we're-not-stopping-'til-we're-screaming kind of kiss.

They were both nearly panting when they broke apart, staring at each other like they were absorbing each other's sexual energy. I shared a glance with Evan. He was grimacing, and I knew he was thinking the same thing I was: *The hotel is too damn far. Maybe we should give them the car and grab a taxi?*

I laughed at the look on his face, then grabbed Griffin's shoulders. Pulling him back, I said, "Simmer down," then I leaned in to give Anna a brief hug. "It's good to see you," I told her.

She smiled at me, her face changing from lust to fondness. Then she frowned. "I'm sorry for the shit you're going through right now." She glanced at her sister. "Both of you."

I sighed as I looked over at Kiera. She was studying the ground, avoiding even looking in Anna and Griffin's direction. "Thanks," I murmured.

Anna squeezed my arm, then leaned forward and quietly said, "That video is hot, though. Turned me on." She pulled back, and there was playfulness in her green eyes as she winked at me.

Shaking my head, I gave her an amused smile as I opened the door to help her into the car.

We were on our way soon after that, and so were Anna and Griffin. They were all over each other in the car, Griffin fisting Anna's dark hair as he tried to suck her soul out of her mouth. At least, that was how it seemed to all of us watching them. Or, bare minimum, listening to them.

Matt had lost the car seat roulette and was turning a little green as he sat beside them. Leaning as far away from them as he could, he scowled and said, "We *are* going straight back to the hotel, right?"

Evan and I laughed while Kiera scrunched her face just as much as Matt. She was avoiding looking, but it was hard to block out the heavy-breathing and moaning. Maybe we should have gotten a taxi after all.

Eventually our quiet, unfazed-by-anything driver got us to the hotel. The second he stopped the car, we all fled the vehicle like it was on fire. All except for Anna and Griffin, who were apparently content to get reacquainted right there in the backseat.

Matt grabbed his stomach, making a face like he was about to vomit. Evan and I shared a laugh as we started grabbing Anna's bags from the back. Our driver shooed us away from the luggage when a guy from the hotel stepped up with a cart. The two of them began loading it, ignoring what they could see and hear from Anna and Griffin. When they were finished, our driver returned to the front seat, and Matt and Evan followed the bellhop into the hotel with the cart. But Anna and Griffin *still* didn't get out of the car. Kiera was getting red with embarrassment as she waited for Anna beside me. I could almost hear her incredulity: *Are they seriously going to have sex in the car, in the drop-off area of the hotel, while the driver sits there listening to them?*

Honestly, it wouldn't surprise me if they did.

Finally, when it was clear Anna and Griffin wouldn't be getting out on their own, Kiera turned to me and said, "Can you...?"

She indicated the car with her hand, but I already knew exactly what she meant, and I was more than happy to do it. Especially when I remembered the look on Griffin's face when he'd ogled my naked wife while she'd been underneath me. Fucker was lucky he was still alive.

"I would love to," I told Kiera, then I walked over to the door and swung it wide. That didn't even faze Anna and Griffin. He had her laid down on the seat, his hand up her dress, her hand inside his pants, their tongues deep down each other's throats.

Reaching in, I grabbed the back of Griffin's shirt and tugged. "Come on," I said, glancing at the driver. He had his hands on the wheel and was just sitting there patiently, staring straight ahead. The label had provided us with the car and the driver, and by this guy's placid exterior, he'd been doing this a while, and he'd seen much, much worse.

Griffin grunted in annoyance when he released from Anna

with an audible pop. "Fuck off, Kell," he growled, trying to swat my hands off his clothes.

"You can't have sex here," I told him, switching my grasp to his arms and yanking.

We stumbled out of the car. Griffin knocked me off him and gave me a look that clearly said, *Oh yeah, watch me, fucker.* He was about to say it too, but Anna stepped out and kissed his cheek, and all he could do was stare at her with lust in his pale eyes.

Anna adjusted her clothes and walked over to Kiera like nothing remotely sexual had just happened. Squeezing her sister, Anna squealed, "This is going to be so much fun, Kiera!" Then the two of them started walking toward the hotel entrance. Kiera looked back at us, saw the expression on Griffin's face, and immediately twisted back around.

I didn't blame her. Griffin was staring after Anna with his mouth open, his pants open, and his eyes simmering. He was still breathing heavier than normal, and he looked like he was about to do something that would definitely get him arrested. I smacked his back to snap him out of it, because we really didn't need the scandal of Griffin jacking off in public.

Griffin shook his head and looked over at me with confusion on his face, like he'd forgotten I was there. "Hey, Kell...I might miss the show tonight. Tell Matt for me, 'kay?" He smiled and thumped me on the chest like he was thanking me for letting people know he wasn't coming to a party or something.

With a frown, I sternly told him, "You're not missing the show tonight."

His jaw dropped, and he made a scoffing noise. Then he tossed his hands toward the lobby, indicating the only person he cared about at the moment. "Duuuuude," he said in a whine, and I interpreted that to mean *But Anna is here, and I haven't had sex in forever. How can you ask me to be somewhere when all I want is to be balls deep in her for the next six hours?*

I gave him a hard stare. "You're *not* missing the show. You can have sex before and after, but you're gonna be there." My eyes flashed down to his crotch. "Now zip up your pants so we can go inside."

Surprisingly, he did what I asked, but he grumbled the entire time.

The girls beat us to the elevator once we were in the hotel, and we had to wait for the next car. Griffin was a ball of restless energy as he watched the numbers on the wall. He kept adjusting his junk like every position was uncomfortable. I sympathized, but the asshole was going to have to wait a little bit longer.

"Fuck, man. I need to have sex, like, right now." He looked at me after he said that, and I raised an eyebrow at him. He instantly scoffed at me. "You wish," he muttered.

An elevator finally opened with a ding and Griffin rushed into it. He hit the *close door* button before I was even all the way inside. "Jesus, Griffin," I said. "Have you heard the phrase *playing hard to get*?"

He scowled as he squeezed his junk. "Have you heard the phrase *fuck you*?" He twisted to look at me. "Because fuck you."

I laughed the entire ride to our floor.

When we got to the two rooms reserved for the D-Bags, Griffin didn't hesitate. He went straight to the room I'd planned on sharing with Kiera, then straight to the bed Anna was lying on, where he immediately shoved his hand up her dress again. His determination made me laugh, but I was also seriously impressed that he hadn't shucked his pants before lying down.

I tipped the guy who'd helped with the luggage while Kiera hastily averted her eyes from the bed. She was grabbing my hand a second later, pulling me from the room while telling her sister, "Catch you guys later." I was still chuckling as we headed over to the other D-Bag room.

Damn, guess we weren't staying there tonight. Oh well, there would be other jacuzzi nights, I was sure. And it was pretty clear that Griffin really needed this. Anna too, probably.

I was *so* going to win that bet.

. . .

Having Anna on the bus changed the mood, and not just with Griffin, although that was certainly the biggest change. With Kiera's sister around to distract him, the rest of us were getting a much-needed break from his toddler-level energy. And there was something about him...it almost seemed like he was finally satisfied, like for the moment, he wasn't looking for anything else. He was just enjoying being with Anna, and it was weird seeing him so content. And really nice, to be honest. Even if we did have to listen to them having sex nonstop. Or at least, that was how it felt.

Kiera was really enjoying having Anna on the bus too, and if Kiera wasn't writing or spending time with me, then she was usually with her sister. I'd overheard them talking about friends back home, their mother's crazy plans for our wedding, and of course, the fans' chaotic obsession with Sienna and me. Kiera seemed a little less annoyed about the gossip now that she had her sister to complain to, especially since Anna was so breezy about everything. I constantly heard her telling Kiera not to worry about it, that everything was going to be fine. And even though the craziness over the sex tape wasn't dying down, I was starting to feel like Anna was right. As long as no one ever found out about Kiera, the hype wasn't so bad. *I guess.* I just didn't see how I'd be able to hide Kiera forever. And that worried me.

"Hey there, hot stuff."

I turned my gaze from the window to see Anna sitting down in the seat beside me. "Hey. How are you feeling?" My gaze drifted to her stomach. I swear it was larger every time I saw her.

She rested a hand on her belly with a sigh. A happy sigh. "Griffin found, like, six different positions for us that are all extremely comfortable for me, so I'm great. Better than great. I'm orgasmically fantastic."

I laughed as Anna grinned. A part of me wanted to ask her what her plan was—how long she was staying, where she was going to have the baby, what she was going to do once the baby was born—but after listening to Kiera talk about it, I already knew the answer. Anna wasn't looking that far ahead. Her only concern was right now, and right now everything was *orgasmically fantastic*.

Anna got a conspiratorial look on her face, then glanced around the bus. I had the distinct feeling she was looking for Kiera, but Kiera was in our cramped cubby, getting some work done. Or taking a nap. Sleeping in that small space together every night was challenging. Having sex in that small space was even more challenging. In fact, we hadn't yet, and I was really starting to miss making love to my wife. And my bed. And making love to my wife on my bed. Damn it. *Greater good, Kellan. Greater good.*

When Anna saw the coast was clear, she leaned in and said, "Did you know that men are using your sex tape as an instructional video for how to put on a condom really fast?"

I was *not* expecting her to say that, and a loud laugh burst out of me that got everyone's attention. Griffin was in the middle of a poker game, but he paused to eye me. The look on his face was a mixture of *Be nice to my baby mama* and *Stay away from my baby mama*. Since I really didn't want him joining us, I stifled the laughter. Shaking my head, I told Anna, "Um...no. Hadn't heard that." And I wasn't sure if I wanted to have heard it.

Anna giggled. "Yeah. That was pretty impressive." Her eyes moved to my lap, and she grinned like she was picturing it *right now*. I cupped myself like I suddenly had modesty, and she snorted. "I meant your speed was impressive, not your funstick. Although that was damn fine." She sighed. "But I suppose I can't say that for sure since I haven't seen it in real life. For all I know, you could have photoshopped yourself."

I started laughing uncontrollably. I wouldn't even know where to begin trying to alter a video, and if I did, I would have blurred out my face, not enhanced my cock. But still, that was funny.

Anna laughed with me, and Griffin half-stood from his seat. "Kyle!" he snapped. "Don't make me kick your ass."

Still laughing, I pointed at Anna. "She's the one making me laugh. Kick her ass."

He screwed up his face like I'd just suggested he circumcise himself or something. "I'm not gonna kick a chick's ass." His expression shifted into a sly grin. "But I'll certainly tap that ass." Focusing on Anna, he tilted his head toward the back bedroom. "You wanna?"

Anna looked at him, then shrugged and nodded. Griffin instantly abandoned his game, throwing his cards on the table as he stood up. Anna laughed at his eagerness, then turned to me. "Just wanted you to know that you're a rock star...rock star," she said with a wink. She turned her entire body to get out of the chair, then tossed over her shoulder, "Now go have sex with my sister. She misses you."

That made me sigh. I missed her too.

Getting up from my seat, I made my way to the cubbies. The curtain was closed on my cubby with Kiera, and I could hear her in there, typing. I cleared my throat and the clicking paused, then the curtain opened. Her dark head peeked out, and she smiled when she saw it was me. "Hey," she said.

"Hey," I answered, squatting down. "So, I hate to be the bearer of bad news..." Her expression instantly fell, but I didn't let her plummet for long. "But Anna just ordered me to have sex with you, so..." I shrugged in an expression of *It sucks, but what can we do?*

Kiera both flushed and giggled, then she scooted over so I could join her. Closing her laptop, she shoved it to the back corner of the cubby. "It has been a while, hasn't it?"

I gave her a soft smile as I settled by her side. "That depends on your definition of 'a while.' I remember going months without you. *That* was a while, this...this is nothing."

Smile on her face, she leaned over to kiss me. It was a soft, drawn-out kiss that ended with her gently sucking my bottom lip into her mouth. Blood instantly surged through my body, hardening me, and I wanted more. So much more. My eyes felt heavy when I looked up at her, and she inhaled a shaky breath when she saw the heat on my face.

"Is everyone...busy?" she asked, darting a look behind me, at the open curtain.

I blindly reached over my shoulder and closed it. "Yeah," I told her, my voice low, my gaze returning to her mouth.

There was laughter in the main cabin as the poker game resumed, and there was the unmistakable sound of Anna and Griffin enjoying themselves coming from the back bedroom. Kiera sighed as she flicked a glance that way. A light laugh escaped me as I touched her chin. "We could take advantage of this... everyone will think it's them."

She bit her lip and cringed. "Unless they come back here."

I shook my head as I leaned forward to kiss her. "No one wants to get closer to Anna and Griffin going at it. Trust me."

She laughed, but only until my lips met hers. Then she moaned and murmured, "Okay."

Our kiss turned heated after that, and every other sound on the bus vanished as Kiera became my entire world. Every breath she released, every sigh, every gasp...it surrounded me in a cocoon of her presence. My hands slipped under her shirt, feeling the ridge of her low spine, the softness of her stomach, and I couldn't get enough of her. I could *never* get enough of her. My breath was fast as the ache for her grew almost painful. She murmured my name as she fumbled with my jeans. Cursing myself for wearing them, I helped her unfasten them.

I was trying to shove them and my underwear down my hips when her warm hand wrapped around my cock and squeezed. I sucked in a breath, releasing it in a groan. God, she felt so good. I was hitting everything around me as I tried to get my pants down far enough. Kiera started working on her clothes too, then we were hitting each other as much as everything else.

I laughed, and Kiera giggled with me. "These fucking cubbies," I murmured, looking for her lips again.

Kiera chuckled against my mouth. I blindly helped her with her jeans, but I quickly gave up because I needed to feel how much she wanted me. I ran a finger between her legs, feeling the wet warmth that was just for me. Kiera cried out louder than she normally would in this situation, and it made me throb to hear it, to feel it. Fuck, I wanted her so bad. I might have to tear her jeans off her.

Finally, with a lot of banging and cursing, her bottom half was free of clothing, and then mine was as well. I didn't waste any more time. I settled myself on top of her and slid into her in almost one movement, and it felt so fucking good that it stopped my breath for a second. I was completely conscious of the fact that Kiera and I were at an angle, that both of our legs were sticking out of the curtain, but I was choosing to trust that no one would be coming back here for a few minutes. *Jesus, please just give me a few minutes of peace with my wife.*

Kiera and I started frantically moving together, both of us all too aware that we didn't have much time. Or we were just too fucking turned on to go slowly. She clutched my shoulders as she whimpered, and I clenched her hip as I panted. Fuck, I felt like I was about to come already, and we'd barely begun. *Make it last a little. Not too long, but damn it, a little.* My head dropped to her shoulder as I felt my body tightening in preparation. *Shit. Not yet.*

"Kiera," I groaned, my voice strained as I tried to hold on.

But thankfully, she was just as worked up as me, and she arched and murmured, "God, yes," before letting out an erotic noise that completely ruined my control.

She clenched around me, and I hit the wall hard, groaning as the ecstasy exploded throughout my body, sending shivers of delight *everywhere*. We kept moving together as we both came down, slower, gentler, until finally, I couldn't do it anymore, and I slumped against her, spent. She threaded her fingers through my hair and kissed my cheek, her breath fast, her heartbeat fast. I slid my arms underneath her, holding her to me for just a moment before we had to move.

"I love you," I mumbled, barely coherent.

Kiera chuckled, then I felt her look down. "Oh my God, pull your feet back in."

"I can't." I literally didn't think I could move yet.

She smacked my shoulder, squirming under me until I laughed and rolled off her so I could bend my knees and hide my legs. Kiera lifted her head and looked around; her eyes were wide as she listened for evidence that someone had heard us. But the front half of the bus was still playing poker, and the back half of the bus was still...preoccupied.

Kiera relaxed back down, settling into my arms with a quiet laugh. "See," I said. "We could probably do that three more times before someone needs the bathroom."

I felt her laugh against my chest, then she lifted her head and kissed me. "Maybe just one more time," she murmured.

I instantly cupped her cheek and deepened the kiss. "Yes, ma'am," I said, shifting her to her back. Whether she wanted ten more times or just a hug, her wish was my command. Always.

Chapter 23
GOING OUT

As the tour continued, not much changed. I kept on denying everything in regard to Sienna, and she kept remaining as coy and aloof as always, neither confirming nor denying anything, letting the world decide whatever they wanted about us. And the fans still saw us as a rabidly-in-love couple, a couple they wholeheartedly supported. Promoted even, with banners, T-shirts, buttons, montages online...it was kind of insane. They didn't even know us. Why the fuck did they care so much?

While I was doing my best not to create any new content for the *Are they or aren't they?* discussion groups, going so far as singing our duet on the opposite side of the stage as Sienna, she wasn't being as careful. If we were together and there was a camera nearby, she'd find a way to get a shot with me. I outright refused to pose with her for the media, but Sienna seemed to realize that I had a weakness for making fans happy, and she frequently used that to her advantage.

"Can I please, please, please get a photo with you *and* Sienna?"

The begging fan in front of me had tears in their eyes. *Tears*. How was I supposed to say no to that? Even still, I looked over at

Sienna standing beside me. She gave me a shy smile in return, and I resisted rolling my eyes. She wasn't even supposed to be standing next to me. Matt had been beside me, and Sienna's X was on the far side of him, by the door. But she'd completely ignored her assigned spot and had squeezed in between Matt and me, and of course, Tory didn't say a word about it. Unlike us, Sienna could do whatever she damn well pleased.

"I would absolutely love that," Sienna said, her eyes fixed on my face.

Knowing she truly meant that, just not for the reason the fan thought, I fought off a scowl. My gut was telling me to say no, but I couldn't deny a fan, especially after Sienna had already said yes; I'd come across as a dick. So with a forced smile on my face, I told the trembling girl in front of me, "Sure, a quick one." The sooner we got this over with, the better.

Sienna grinned and stepped closer to me. While the fan situated herself between us, Sienna smiled at me with a warm look on her face, like she was cherishing every freckle on mine. Like she loved me. But she didn't. We barely spoke and rarely saw each other outside of moments like this, and everything on her face right now was just part of the show. Clenching my jaw, I faced front and ignored her fake fawning. Making a fan's day was the important thing here, and as long as there was a respectful gap between us, the photo shouldn't be all that remarkable. Hopefully.

But then, right before the fan's friend snapped the picture, Sienna scooted closer and put her head on my shoulder. Goddamn it. I pulled away, but it was too late, the moment was captured and would be all over the Internet soon, part of a collage glorifying our "inspiring" love affair. It made me want to scream.

With a sigh, I tried to remind myself that eventually the tour would be over, and the interest would most likely die out. I just wished it would happen before my wedding next month.

Like I'd wished my wife into existence, Kiera was suddenly

the next fan in line. I blinked in surprise at seeing her in front of me. "Hey." My face relaxed into a grin, and I felt a million times better. Wanting to flirt with the woman who *actually* had my heart, I leaned forward and gave her my sexiest voice. "Is there anything you'd like me to sign?" I briefly dropped my gaze to her chest and pumped my eyebrows.

Kiera seemed distracted, though, and she shook her head as her hazel eyes shifted to Sienna. She'd seen that then. She had to be wondering why I'd agreed to a joint photo since she knew I was trying to publicly keep my distance from Sienna. Easier said than done.

I frowned when she looked back at me. "A fan begged. I didn't want to be rude."

Kiera nodded at me, and I saw genuine understanding on her face. She knew what the fans meant to me, and she knew how much I hated this assembly-line version of a meet-and-greet. I couldn't properly thank the fans here, couldn't give them anything but a few fleeting seconds of my life. And apparently, a photo-op with the woman who was manipulating *all of them*. I wished I could tell them the truth, that the goddess in front of me right now meant everything in the world to me...but that was the one thing I couldn't tell them. Not here, not like this. Possibly, not ever. It killed me to stay silent, but for Kiera's sake, I'd do it.

Kiera flashed a glance at Tory, then motioned for me to come closer. The curiosity was almost eating me alive as I lowered my head next to hers. Pointing at a fan down the line, she said, "She gave me something special. Can you thank her for me?"

Special? I was instantly intrigued. "What did she give you?"

A delightful, mischievous smile curved Kiera's mouth, and it took a lot of willpower to stop myself from sucking on one of those lips. "You'll see later," was all she would tell me.

Kiera took a step away from me as a fan nudged her. I was dying to know what the surprise was because by the look on

Kiera's face, I was going to like it. A lot. And that reminded me that I'd gotten us our own hotel room for the evening since we were staying in the city tonight. I could *not* wait.

Wishing the show was already over, I told her, "I'll see what I can do."

I ended up giving the fan and her friend a backstage tour. I didn't even bother asking for permission; I just did it. And while it was difficult, I refrained from asking the two girls what they'd given my wife. One, because Kiera went on the tour with us, and I didn't want her to see me trying to ruin the surprise. And two, because if it was anything even remotely sexy, I didn't think I'd be able to keep the desire off my face, and that might clue the girls in on the fact that Kiera was more than just my personal assistant, which is how she'd sold our relationship to them.

I concluded the tour by showing the girls the stage. The two of them were amusing to be around. Every time I looked in their direction, they squealed and giggled. And they damn near fainted when I gave them my hand to help them onto the stage. It was humorous to watch, but at the same time, it was also a little unsettling. Underneath it all, we were basically the same. I could understand being nervous, but they should be able to look me in the eye and have a conversation with me, just like they would anyone else.

Kiera made a comment about it when I offered her my hand next. She hopped up by herself, then told me I should keep my hands free in case one of the girls passed out and fell off the stage. "I wouldn't want you to get sued," she teased.

She pointed at the girls. I looked back at them and sure enough, they screeched. Turning back to Kiera, I gave her a crooked grin. "I'm glad you don't squeal when I look at you." Stepping forward, I softly added, "I like having to earn it." Straight up fact.

Twisting back around, I left her with that thought, but not before I saw a delightful, soft pink flush rise from her chest to her cheeks. Damn. It. There were still hours to go before I could get her to that hotel room. This was going to be a long night.

I was just finishing showing the fans the stage when Sienna suddenly appeared. She sauntered over to us, motioning to security to come collect the girls, and I knew, with absolute certainty, she was only here so the fans could snap a photo of us together, one they would share with all their friends. And that was exactly what they did.

"It's time, love," she told me, her voice so suggestive that it left no doubt as to what she really meant by that. Only she didn't. Because she was pretending.

I was so sick of her orchestrating misleading moments. If she wasn't going to say anything, then she could at least stop fanning the flames. I was about to tell her that when the fans suddenly bubbled over with excitement. "We adore you so much, Sienna. You're amazing. And we think it's so awesome that you and Kellan fell in love while recording a song together. They should make a movie about you two."

Now would be a perfect opportunity for Sienna to set them straight, but no, she smiled and said, "I would love that! I could even play myself!" She gave me a playful smile while she shared a giggle with the girls, but I could tell she actually meant that. If someone approached her to forever memorialize our "love" on film, she'd absolutely say yes, and she'd fight for the lead. Jesus, where was the line with her?

"Sienna and I are not in a relationship," I told the fans. If she wasn't going to deny it, then it was my duty to let them know the truth. Not that they believed me. They just smiled at my statement like they thought I was being chivalrous by repeatedly denying that we were together.

Security was on them then, politely but firmly leading them away. Sienna gave me an amused smile before turning to leave the stage. I followed her, not feeling half as amused as she was. She had basically confirmed everything those two believed with that one little comment. And it wasn't the first time I'd heard her say stuff like that. Her response to getting asked *anything* about me, was to start complimenting me. And talking about how great I was, wasn't helping to clear things up. I was so sick of all this fake bullshit.

"We need to talk," I said, stepping in front of her.

Giving me an untroubled smile, she said, "Sure thing, love," then she motioned for us to follow her. She disappeared into her dressing room, not even looking back to see if we were trailing behind her.

I was about to burst into her room and tell her exactly what I thought about all this nonsense, but Kiera put a hand on my chest, stopping me. "If you don't mind, I'd like to speak with her alone, woman to woman."

Seeing that she was calmer than me, I nodded. Kiera might actually get through to Sienna if she went in there to talk to her like an equal. I'd probably just yell at her, and then she'd yell at me, and then things on this tour might get really uncomfortable. For everyone.

Indicating behind me, I told Kiera, "I'm gonna go blow off some steam. Find me when you're done. And don't feel like you need to go easy on her either." And just me saying that was proof that Kiera really should go in there instead of me. As much as Sienna's actions annoyed me, she had the power to send Kiera home. I couldn't ever forget that because having Kiera here with me was the reason I was getting through this chaos with my sanity intact.

Kiera cupped my cheek, her eyes silently telling me that she loved me, but she fully intended on playing nice with the superstar who held our fate in her hands. I swiftly kissed her wrist and walked away before I gave her any more bad advice.

Hoping to unwind the coil of irritation in my chest, I went searching for the guys. I came across Griffin first. Oddly, he was all alone, standing in the recess of some stairs, nearly invisible.

Griffin was *never* invisible. I was pretty sure he was allergic to being invisible, so seeing him almost hiding was downright startling.

"Griffin?" I said, approaching him cautiously.

He gave me a blank look. "Kellan."

I frowned at the flatness in his voice. "What are you doing?"

He looked around himself. "Standing."

"Everything...okay?" It felt weird to ask him that. Griffin was always okay. I mean, unless he was pissed off at something, but him being mad was as natural as him being crude—neither thing even fazed me. But right now, he seemed almost pensive, and that was concerning.

Rolling his eyes, he stepped out from the shadow of the stairs. "Leave me alone, Kell. I'm not looking for a hug."

"Okay," I said as he brushed past me.

Wondering what the hell was wrong with him, and if it was going to be a problem later, I watched him the entire time he walked away from me. Evan stepped up to me as I was staring after Griffin. "What did he do now?" he asked.

I looked over at him with a frown. "I have no idea. And that terrifies me a little."

Evan chewed on his lip for a second, then nodded. "Maybe we should go find Matt. He'll know."

I let out a sigh. "I'd rather not worry about Griffin right now. I've got my own problems."

He tilted his head as his brows furrowed. "What's going on?"

"Sienna, fans, gossip, my wife being my dirty little secret. Take your pick."

Evan nodded, then put a hand on my shoulder. "I know exactly what you need." He smiled as he said, "It calms *me* down whenever I'm worked up about something."

That made me raise my eyebrows. Laidback was practically Evan's middle name. "*You* get worked up about things? What? When?" I couldn't stop the smile growing on my face. It got larger the deeper Evan's frown became.

"I *do* hang out with a bunch of assholes, so yeah, on occasion, I get worked up." He slapped my back, a little harder than necessary, then said, "This way, smartass."

I was laughing as I followed Evan to a staging area where our instruments were being stored. At first, I thought he wanted me to play my guitar, maybe do a little jam session with me, but then he reached into an open case and handed me a pair of drumsticks. Pointing to a set of drums nearby, he grinned and said, "Bang it out."

"I'm going to ignore the fact that sounded really dirty and remind you that I've never touched a drum in my life."

Evan chuckled. "I know. That's why I'm so excited to see you try." He tapped the tip of the drumstick. "Hit the flat part with this."

I frowned at him as I clutched the sticks. "You're not the only one surrounded by assholes, you know."

Wide smile on his face, he nodded, then showcased the drums. I sighed, then smirked. I'd seen him do this a million times...how hard could it be? And besides, it did seem really cathartic. While Evan watched me with amusement in his eyes, I settled onto the stool behind the drums and tried to picture Evan going through one of our songs. The first thing that struck me was how many different fucking options there were back here. I swear, there were fifteen thousand different things to hit. And I swear, Evan hit them all during every single song, sometimes all at the same time. Or so it seemed.

Pursing my lips, I tried to think of a song with a simple beat. There weren't many, but one popped into my head. I started a mental countdown, then dove into it. Almost immediately, Evan snickered at me. I ignored him and tried to remember the beat... and duplicate it with my fifty thousand options since the drum set had somehow expanded since I first sat down.

A crowd gathered around the drums as I butchered the song I was trying to play. My only saving grace was the fact that we didn't play this song on the tour, and it wasn't on the album, so nobody but Evan knew how badly I was performing it. I blocked out Evan's merciless laughter and tried to remember our countless rehearsals. Why hadn't I paid more attention to him? Because I couldn't remember half of the rhythm, and I hadn't even touched the cymbals yet. I was just fucking around with the bass, toms, and snare while Evan lost his ever-lovin' mind.

While it wasn't exactly as cathartic as I'd hoped, the level of concentration it required did evaporate my irritation at Sienna. Now I was just mad at these fucking drums. It didn't take long for me to completely lose the rhythm. I was so far off that I wasn't even sure how to get back on track, so I tossed the sticks away from me and admitted defeat. "Fuck! I give up!"

Then I laid my head on a drum and listened to everyone around me laugh at my expense. I didn't blame them. That was fucking awful. I saw Kiera's legs appear in my sideways line of vision, and I peeked up at her with a pathetic pout on my face. "I suck."

Smiling warmly at me, she held out her hand. "You can't be a pro at everything, Kellan."

She helped me to my feet, fingering the wedding ring on my right hand and looking at me with so much love in her eyes. I wished I could kiss her, wished I could hold her, but there were too many people around, so I settled on teasing her. Heat in my voice, I murmured, "You're right. I'll just stick to what I'm really, really good at." Then I caressed her with my vision since that was all I could do at the moment.

It worked, though. Her eyes sparkled with interest, even as she frowned at me in silent warning. Before she could verbally tell me to behave myself, I switched subjects. "What did Sienna say?"

Kiera's brows bunched as we walked through the busy backstage area. "She said we were overreacting."

Of course she would say that. To her this was just one big game, and her only goal was to push the pieces around in a way that made her look good. But this was my *life*, mine and Kiera's, and the thought of people attacking it, without understanding anything about it, really bothered me.

Kiera continued as I stewed. "She also said she'd ease up on the cuddling."

I gave her a wry smirk. "She's said that before. But then a camera gets pointed in her direction, and she...forgets." Intentionally forgets. Because it benefitted her not to remember that little promise. Because it was what the fans expected, what they wanted, and she would never deny them what they wanted. I rolled my eyes as I remembered her commenting about how much they loved us together. If the fans ever decided they hated us together, then she'd probably freeze me out. Because ultimately, all of this was up to them. "Gotta give the fans what they want. She's a performer to the core."

"It's how she was raised," Kiera said. "It's how she survived the transition from child star to superstar."

She seemed surprised after saying that. I was too. Kiera didn't often defend Sienna, mainly because Sienna had the power to make all of this go away, and she refused to use it. But Kiera was right in her assessment. I hadn't been in the business long, but I already understood that it involved a lot more than just being able to sing. It couldn't have been easy for Sienna, growing up in a spotlight. I was struggling with the scrutiny, and I was an adult who didn't have stage parents breathing down my neck.

"I get that," I said, holding open the door to my dressing room. "I think the only thing I really *do* get about her is that her childhood sucked just as much as mine did."

The door closed behind us, and Kiera immediately wrapped her arms around my neck, holding me close. "No, her childhood was nothing like yours, Kellan. Not even close."

I tried to fight back the images that instantly flooded my brain, but it was impossible to keep them all at bay. I saw myself crying as I tried to sleep on my stomach because I literally couldn't roll over. I saw my father calling me a worthless waste of space as he struck me for some stupid infraction. I saw my mother's impassive expression as she told me to stop whining about a little "smack." I saw their anger, their hate, their misery. From what I'd pieced together, Sienna's parents were really overbearing, but yeah, I would have paid good money to have had *that* be my only problem with my parents.

I nodded at Kiera in agreement, then held her tight, savoring the fact that we were alone for a little bit. This was all that really mattered. Kiera and me. Together.

After the show, I felt a lot better. Of course, that might have been the hotel room calling my name. Kiera and I could stretch out in an actual bed again. And make love in a bed again. We'd done it in the cubbies a couple of times now, including once this morning, and while it was still satisfying and amazing, it was also cramped and a little awkward. Kiera accidentally kneeing me in the junk earlier had solidified my decision to always spring for a private room whenever we had a hotel night, and that was tonight.

I practically had a spring in my step when I rejoined Kiera backstage. She briefly smiled at me, but most of her attention was on Griffin, for some reason.

She frowned when Griffin said, "Let's go drink," to Matt.

Matt was on board with Griffin's idea and looked over at Kiera and me. "You guys want to go out?"

I told him, "No," right as Kiera told him, "Sure."

Surprise and disappointment flooded through me. I'd really been looking forward to some quiet cuddle time. And honestly, ever since the tape was leaked and the fans had turned rabid, Kiera and I hadn't gone out much with the guys. Evan had dragged me out that first night, to help calm my nerves, but I'd kept a low profile since then, typically staying behind with Kiera whenever the guys left. Kiera wanting to brave the exposure was really odd, and so was the look on her face as she studied Griffin.

Sienna had followed us off the stage, and she included herself in Matt's invitation. Looking overjoyed, she said, "Drinks sound bloody fabulous! I know just the place." She lifted her hands like she was going to wrap her arms around mine, but then, to my absolute surprise, she stopped herself. Was she serious about easing up this time? Maybe she realized my patience was wearing thin. Maybe she'd finally say something soon.

That thought gave me hope, but I still looked at Kiera with a question in my eyes. *Are you sure you want to go out? When a bed and four walls are waiting for us?*

Kiera smiled at me, but it looked forced, like she was trying to convince herself that she wanted to go, but she really, really didn't. Had she said that accidentally? Her mouth moving too quickly again? I didn't think that was it, though, because she kept looking at Griffin, and I had a feeling she wanted to go out because of *him*. I just had no idea why.

I thought over Griffin's behavior as we freshened up. He *had* been oddly reserved all night, introspective almost, and it was a little jarring once I realized that. Damn, maybe there *was* something wrong with him. I stepped up to him as he was putting on a clean T-shirt.

"Are you okay?" I asked, again feeling weird for saying it.

"Why do you keep asking me that?" he said, looking annoyed.

I shook my head. "I honestly don't know."

"Well then, stop it. I'm fine. Ready to get my drink on." By the way he wriggled his eyebrows, it was clear that he wasn't actually talking about alcohol, and that was when it all snapped into place.

Ah, fuck. Griffin was looking for sex, but clearly, not sex with Anna since she wasn't coming with us. Damn it. Kiera must know that, or suspect it anyway, and she'd said yes to try to prevent him from scoring. But I knew from experience just how difficult that was. Detracting Griffin from his goal was near impossible. She'd have to chase the girl away from him, and depending on the girl, that wasn't always as easy as it sounded. Griffin was going to break Kiera's heart tonight, shattering this illusion she was building that he was Anna's faithful, committed partner. He wasn't. Even with my hopeful bet, I knew that. Anna too. No one here had any delusions about Griffin...except my wife.

I wondered how to talk to her about it the entire time we waited for Sienna to get ready. Then I decided it wasn't worth bringing up. Griffin wasn't always successful when he was pursuing a woman. In fact, he struck out more often than he succeeded, so honestly, Kiera didn't have as much to worry about as she thought.

But then again, we weren't flying under the radar, going to a local bar where we'd be relatively hidden and unknown. No, we were going out with Sienna, who'd lined up a limo and was taking us to one of the hottest clubs in town. We were practically broadcasting celebrity status, and that...might improve Griffin's chances.

It also helped Sienna create a buzzworthy event for the two of us, a fact that was made very clear to me when we pulled up to a club that was surrounded by waiting photographers. Damn it. I should have known she hadn't had a change of heart. She was still very much playing the game. But I was not about to play along. Not anymore.

Flashes were already going off when the driver got out, like every single person holding a camera knew who was inside. Irritation shot up my spine as I tossed a glare at Sienna. She had a small smile on her face as she preened. Had she arranged for this? Or was paparazzi typical for...where the fuck were we...somewhere in North Carolina? Charlotte, I recalled from the concert. I could feel Kiera shaking beside me. She had to be stressing over how she would be portrayed in this circus. As a friend? As Matt or Evan's girl? Or as my side piece? And I supposed the answer to all of that would depend on me. If I walked in with Kiera, they'd definitely wonder. If I walked in by myself, they still might wonder. But if I walked in on Sienna's arm...they wouldn't give Kiera a second thought.

And that was exactly what Sienna wanted me to do. *I don't think so.*

The driver opened our door and held out a hand for Sienna. She took it and exited the car as gracefully as a swan. The flashes were nearly blinding. Sienna briefly smiled for them, then turned and waited. For me.

Evan and Griffin moved like they were going to leave, but I held out a hand to stop them. I was not playing this fucking game. Leaning forward to meet the driver's eye, while also making sure I couldn't be seen, I firmly told him, "We're not walking through that, take us somewhere else."

The driver nodded at me, respecting my wishes. Then he turned to Sienna. "Would you like to stay or go, Ms. Sexton?"

Sienna looked genuinely torn as she glanced back at the frenzy waiting for her. But finally, she got into the car, and the driver closed the door. "Really? That was the best club in town," she pouted.

Smile on my face, I told her, "You were welcome to stay, if you wanted to." Wouldn't hurt my feelings at all.

She rolled her eyes at me but didn't comment any further. The next club we arrived at was completely empty, all but confirming my suspicions. I could feel Kiera's relief when the driver opened the door. This was much, much better.

Sienna was recognized the second she stepped inside the club, and we were all swept away to a private VIP room. That was an additional relief, especially since I didn't think anyone had recognized *me* yet. The less gossip after this, the better.

The room we were in was very secluded. Sienna ordered expensive champagne from one of the two waitresses before settling herself onto a plush looking lounge chair. It made me happy that we were so alone. Sienna couldn't turn this into a promotional moment, and Griffin couldn't scratch whatever itch he was feeling. He seemed really annoyed by that as he studied the limpid wall separating us from the rest of the club. No one on the other side of it looked our way, so it was clear they couldn't see us. We could see them, though, grinding away with roaming hands and eager mouths.

After studying the wall for a moment, Griffin muttered, "We need chicks."

The man who'd brought us in here heard him and immediately snapped his fingers to get the attention of the remaining waitress. "Do you prefer blondes, brunettes, or redheads?" he asked Griffin.

Griffin's smile was creepy. Pervy. I wanted to smack him, but he was too far away. "All of the above," he said to the guy, and I rolled my eyes. Jackass.

The guy flashed a glance at me, like he thought I wanted in on the women ordering or something. I did not. "I'm assuming nothing less than a perfect ten?" he said, his eyes returning to Griffin.

Griffin nodded, his smile getting even wider, creepier. The waitress left to go "get his women," but before she got too far, Griffin called out, "I need at least a dozen!"

I could feel Kiera's simmering anger as she glared at him. Matt and Evan were both rolling their eyes at Griffin as they sat down, but they didn't look annoyed or upset, not like Kiera. While Kiera and I took a seat, I met eyes with Griffin, giving him a questioning *What was that?* face.

He ignored me. And that concerned me. Typically, when Griffin was being an ass, he owned it. He'd nod, make devil horns, and say something like, *"Dude, what? I'm increasing my odds to get laid tonight. Chill."*

But there was something in his expression as he sat there waiting, something...uncomfortable. Like he didn't want to be here either, but he felt like he had to be. Like anything less than this was completely unacceptable. It was such an odd look, and he was in such an odd mood, that I suddenly wanted to yank him aside and make him talk to me. But experience told me he wouldn't. He'd get belligerent before he opened up...and even more stubborn. If Griffin was going through something right now, he needed to get there on his own, or he would never get there at all.

Shifting my priorities, I focused on Kiera instead. Watching this might be more than she could handle, and I wanted her to know that she didn't have to see it. Wrapping my arm around her as we sat on a couch, I leaned in and said, "We can leave any time." I felt her nod, but her gaze never left Griffin.

Chapter 24

ENOUGH

The champagne arrived and was followed not too much later by a large group of beautiful women. Griffin was over the moon as the small space was flooded with girls who could definitely be models. Kiera eyed them all with a crease between her brows, and I wondered what bothered her more—that the club owner had found so many women so fast, or that they were all incredibly attractive and dressed like they were ready to party. Or maybe she was worried about what the other D-Bags were going to do. I had a pretty good idea what they'd do, and that was confirmed as I watched my friends.

Evan looked indifferent when a girl sat down next to him. Matt was red in the face when a girl squeezed beside him. He looked like he wanted to be anywhere but in this room, and he kept eyeing Griffin with an annoyed scowl, like he was mentally killing his cousin for putting him in this situation. It made me want to laugh. Griffin had his arms wide, welcoming all the women to sit on his lap. That made me roll my eyes again.

A few of the girls headed Sienna's way, the rest headed mine. And now *I* was eyeing Griffin with a scowl on my face. *I could be in a hotel room right now, making love to my wife instead of batting off unwanted attention while you work out whatever issue you're working out. You owe me one after this.*

I tried to catch Griffin's gaze, but he was still ignoring me. Honestly, he was ignoring *everyone* but the women. And while it wasn't unusual for him to singularly focus on what he wanted, he still had that odd expression on his face. Like he was faking it. Or forcing it.

I was about to shift my attention to Matt, to see if he could try talking to Griffin, when Kiera suddenly leapt onto my lap. All thoughts of Griffin vanished from my brain as Kiera wrapped her arms around my neck and glared at every woman who was making their way over to me. Kiera hadn't been this friendly with me in public since the tape came out, and I had to admit, I really, really liked it. Of course, this wasn't all that public—no one could see us from the main dancefloor, and none of the people they'd let inside appeared to have phones. They'd probably all been warned about taking photos of the celebrities. Still, this almost felt like our lives were normal again, and that made me happy.

Wanting to make a joke out of this weird situation, to calm Kiera's hackles a little, I leaned in and said, "I like you possessively sitting on me. Maybe we should hire the girls to follow us around everywhere?"

Kiera instantly gave me the most amazing put-out expression. I felt a laugh bubbling up, but before it escaped, she gave me a devilish smirk and wriggled her butt, rubbing against me in the *best* way. My cock immediately started hardening as a shot of desire went right through me. *Fuck, yes.* Regardless of who was watching, I wanted her in my arms, wanted to move with her to the heavy beat coming from the other side of the wall. I just wanted to enjoy my wife for a minute.

Grabbing Kiera's drink, I set both of ours on a nearby waitress's tray. "We need to dance," I told Kiera. *Right now.* I stood up with her in my arms, not really giving her a choice in the matter.

Setting Kiera down, I led her to a clear area of the room. She wrapped her arms around my neck while I pulled her hips into mine. We moved together in a provocative way that had my heart racing and my breath quickening. Damn, I'd really missed dancing with her. I felt eyes on me, but my gaze never left Kiera's face. She was the only thing that mattered right now. Kiera was studying me too, but every once in a while, her eyes, a dark brown in this light, would dart around the room. Keeping an eye on the women? Or keeping an eye on the D-Bags?

Several girls had followed us onto the dancefloor, and the more intimate Kiera and I danced, the friendlier their fingers became. I felt hands on my back, my arms, drifting over my pecs. Kiera removed palms from my body while I batted a few away from my ass. Seriously? I wasn't sure why these girls had no issues invading my personal space, but by the way they kept tossing curious glances at Sienna, I had a feeling it was because Sienna wasn't getting mad at me. Like that made me fair game for everyone. *God, what a laidback girlfriend. If she really doesn't care, then we might as well get what we can!*

Ignoring it all, I focused on Kiera. Her fingers were in my hair and almost every inch of our bodies was molded together. Our mouths were so compellingly close. It made me ache to resist kissing her, but I felt like the girls would become even more brazen if I did. Even still, I couldn't stop my hands from exploring her body. Up her sides, down her back, over her ass. Every circuit was turning me on more and more. I was pretty sure it was turning Kiera on too, and I thought she might take me up on that offer to leave early. Until her body went completely rigid.

I was confused until I noticed her gaze. She was staring at something off to her left. I knew what it was even before I looked. And yep, Griffin had found a couple of girls willing to say yes to him. He was deeply kissing a blonde while a redhead had her hand down his pants. There were a couple of other interested girls in his proximity, and I knew, without a doubt, Griffin was going to fuck at least one of them tonight.

Kiera started pulling away from me—toward him—but I

held her back. She was so angry that she was vibrating, and I put my lips to her ear so she could hear me over the music. "Making a scene with him isn't going to help anything. I'll talk to him later." Because something was definitely going on with him.

Kiera turned her anger toward me. She shoved me away from her, heat in her eyes. "Later? What, after he's screwed them?"

Yes. Because he's going to do it regardless.

I shook my head as I thought of some way to tell her that without sounding like I was condoning it. Sienna stepped up to us as my mind spun. "Problem?" she asked. She had a man on each arm—her gift from the club owner.

My smile was tight when I answered her. "Everything's fine."

Kiera opened her mouth, most likely to yell at me, but Griffin walked by us just then. He had a girl on each arm and a determined look on his face as he strode toward the VIP bathrooms. He was going to go for it right here, but oddly, he didn't seem as thrilled about that as he usually did. He wasn't even smiling.

Kiera didn't seem to notice that, though. She just saw him escaping to have sex, and she was enraged about it. "That son of a bitch!" She started storming his way, but I held on tight to her hand. Her angry eyes snapped back to mine when she couldn't move any further. "Let me go, Kellan."

I pulled her back to me as I shook my head. "You can't make him change, Kiera. He has to want to. And he's not going to stop...whatever he's doing in there just because you barge in yelling and screaming. Trust me. You'll just end up seeing way more than you want to."

I hoped she believed me, because that would be exactly what happened if she walked in on him. I'd walked in on Griffin enough times to know that. He only stopped when he finished.

Kiera yanked her hand out of mine. She shoved my chest, taking her frustration out on me—which was fine. I'd rather have her smack me a few times than have Griffin screwing another woman permanently lodged in her brain. "Then you go stop him," she snapped. "Drag him out of there like you dragged him away from those two girl-looking guys in New Jersey!" Tears stung her eyes as she said that, and a part of me wanted to do it, just so I could hurt him for hurting her. But the fact was, I hadn't dragged him away from anyone, I'd convinced the girls to leave, and I knew I wouldn't be able to do that this time. It was already a done deal. And besides, it would only be a temporary fix.

Stepping into Kiera, I cupped her cheeks. "*He* has to make the choice, Kiera. It means nothing if I force him." I couldn't watch over him every second of every day. And I wouldn't. As much as she hated this, she needed to accept it. And move on. Because if she didn't, she would never be happy.

Her chin wobbled, and I again wanted to punch Griffin in the nuts. "He won't get away with it, Kellan. I'm not going to lie for him."

I stroked her cheek, wishing I could somehow make this easier for her. "Anna knows what he's like, Kiera. You don't have to lie." That was the only bright spot in all of this. Technically, Griffin wasn't cheating on Anna because they weren't actually a couple. Although even *I* thought he'd wait until after she left the tour to sleep with other women. And that was the conversation I intended to have with him. It was a matter of respect.

Kiera looked like she was about to be sick as she stared at me. "I want to leave now."

I absolutely didn't blame her. Wrapping my arms around her, I held her to my chest and got the attention of a waitress nearby. "Can you call me a cab?" I asked her. She nodded while I rocked Kiera in my arms and tried to make all of her pain go away.

Sienna was watching the two of us with a strange expression on her face. Almost wistful. "We're gonna go," I told her.

She nodded, flicked a glance down at Kiera, then lifted her eyes to the bathrooms. I almost told her she was welcome to bust apart Griffin's little sex party, but getting Kiera away from here was my primary concern.

Arm around Kiera's shoulders, I shifted us over to Matt and Evan so we could tell them we were leaving. The two of them were having an animated conversation about music. They probably hadn't even noticed Griffin taking off with his conquests. They looked up when I stopped directly in front of them. "We're gonna take off," I said.

They both shifted to look at Kiera, then they both frowned. She was still obviously upset. They looked around the room, like they just now remembered where we were and how awkward Griffin had made it with his "order."

"All right," Evan said. "Everything okay?"

Kiera sighed, then looked up at me. "I'm going to go wait by the door." Her gaze shifted to the bathrooms. "I can't be in here anymore."

I nodded at her, letting her escape. Then I looked back at Evan and answered his question. "Griffin's an asshole, and I'm pretty sure I just lost that bet."

Matt's lips twisted as he looked over at the bathrooms. "You want me to do something about that?" he asked, looking back at me.

I again contemplated it, but in the end, what I'd said to Kiera was right. We couldn't force monogamy on him. He had to choose it. Feeling exhausted, I tossed up my hands. "What's the point?"

Face serious, Matt told me, "Blue balls. Blue balls is the point." Then he smirked.

A weary laugh escaped me, then I sighed. "Do what you want. I'm gonna try to calm Kiera down."

I told them both goodbye, then I found Kiera waiting at the rear exit. She still seemed upset, like she wanted to scream and sob at the same time. There was a taxi waiting for us when we stepped out onto the street. We were all alone out here, no one around to notice me holding Kiera's hand as we slipped into the taxi together, but for once, I didn't care how it might have looked. My wife was hurting and helping her was the only thing that mattered to me.

Once we were in the cab, I told the driver where to go, then twisted to face Kiera. She was crying, and it broke me to see it. "I hate him," she said, her voice thick with pain. I didn't know what to do, didn't know how to fix this. And I didn't know what this might mean for the band from here on out. If she really, truly couldn't be around Griffin anymore, would she leave? Would she be miserable if she stayed? Fucking Griffin.

Not knowing what else to do, I placed my hands on her cheeks and gave her the tenderest kiss I possessed. *He might hurt you, but I never will.* That was the only promise I could make her; that while I might make questionable jokes like Griffin, he and I were nothing alike where it truly mattered.

Kiera was still in a sour mood when we got to the hotel room. I wanted to hold her all night, gently stroking her skin, calming her down, but I was more tired than I thought, and it wasn't long before sleep pulled me under.

I groggily woke to the sound of people yelling in the hallway. "Shut the fuck up," I murmured, hovering the line between awake and asleep. There was a perfectly good sidewalk outside where the angry couple could shout at each other all they wanted. But then the voices registered with me. My eyes shot open, and I was instantly wide awake. My hand instinctively reached over to the spot next to me, but it was empty—because it was Kiera in the hallway having a yelling match. With Griffin. Damn it. I should have seen that one coming.

Jumping out of bed, I flung open the door. Evan was holding Kiera back, keeping her from physically assaulting our bassist. She struck him with words instead. "My sister is going to have your baby any second, and you're out screwing whores in bathrooms! I hope Anna finally wises up and kicks your ass to the curb!"

The stunned look on Griffin's face immediately hardened. "Yeah, like Denny kicked yours?"

Anger shot up my spine at hearing him go there. He didn't get to comment on that when he didn't have all the facts. "Griffin!" I snapped, reminding him that I was right here, and he needed to watch his fucking mouth.

He looked up at me with annoyance on his face but wariness in his eyes. I could take him in a fight, and he knew that. He also knew I really could kick him out of this band if I wanted to. Or if he forced me to.

Kiera's anger filled the brief silence. "Minutes after Anna admits that she loves you, you find some cheap floozies to go down on you? What the hell's wrong with you?"

That comment absolutely stunned me, and everything suddenly made sense. Griffin's odd behavior, Kiera's almost over-the-top anger. Anna had finally broached the subject of having a deeper relationship with Griffin, and he'd...freaked out. I almost wanted to walk over to him, smack him across the head, then repeat Kiera's question. Because she was right. That was fucked up, even for him.

Deciding it was more important to keep Kiera from punching him, I indicated for Evan to let me take over. He stepped back, and I wrapped my hands around Kiera's arms. I could feel her trembling; she was so angry. Evan stayed close, watching Griffin just as much as Matt was. Both of them had stunned, uncertain expressions, like they weren't sure what to do. I honestly wasn't sure either, but I knew this was something Kiera needed to get off her chest, and as long as it didn't turn violent, I was going to let her say her piece.

And that was when Griffin took a step forward. A menacing step. Matt and Evan were right there, each one putting a hand on his arm, warning him not to do anything stupid. My body tensed, ready to shove him back, but he kept his hands at his sides, his posture agitated but unthreatening. Leaning into Kiera, he snarled, "I didn't do anything with either of those girls, okay? So back the fuck off!"

I wasn't sure if I believed him. Kiera wasn't either. "Right. And I'm supposed to believe that. I *saw* you."

As Griffin stepped back and sighed, I noticed a hotel room door opening. Anna stepped into the doorway. Leaning against the frame, she studied the fight in front of her with furrowed brows. I wondered how much she'd already heard...if she knew what they were fighting about. If she felt just a fraction of the anger Kiera felt, this would be it. They'd be over.

"Yeah," Griffin said, his voice quieter. "We started going at it. I had both girls primed, panties on the floor, dying to jump me, but all I could think about was Anna."

Griffin lifted his hands like he was exasperated, and I flicked a glance at Anna. She looked shocked, and I didn't think it was because of what he'd said about the women.

Voice stronger, Griffin snapped, "I didn't want to fuck either of those girls because I'm in love with your fucking sister! Are you happy now, bitch! I'm fucking whipped...just like these other pussies." He indicated the three of us, and we all frowned at him. Seriously. And did he just call my wife a bitch? *I don't think so.*

Kiera didn't have a response to that. In fact, all of the rigid-ness seemed to leave her body, and I had to imagine she was gaping at him. If he hadn't just pissed me off, I'd be gaping at him too. He just said he loved Anna. And he *meant* it. Damn. Never thought I'd see the day.

Anna took that moment to let Griffin know she was listening. "You're in love with me?" She still looked stunned.

Every other head in the hallway turned her way, noticing her for the first time. The mood in the air shifted again, but for the better this time. Matt and Evan released Griffin as he sagged like he was utterly defeated. "Yes," he muttered. "I'm in love with you, and I don't want anybody else." That should have been a really romantic line, but by the sound of his voice, you'd think he was telling her they'd just canceled his favorite TV show.

Anna didn't seem fazed by the dejected look on his face. She stepped into the hallway with a smile. Moving to stand in front of him, she said, "I love you too, and I don't want anybody else either." She paused to cup his cheek. "You're enough for me."

Griffin's entire expression changed, brightened, like she'd just said the magic words that made him okay with his feelings. His grin was damn near contagious. "You're enough for me too."

Anna grabbed his hand and backed them toward their room. "Good, then come be enough for me right now. I'm horny as hell."

Griffin surged forward, grabbing her ass. "God, me too." Then they were kissing.

Kiera turned around, ready to go back to our room, but I was still blocking the propped-open door. While I was happy that he'd worked things out with Anna, I couldn't just let what he'd said to Kiera slide. "Hey, Griffin!"

He slowly pulled away from Anna to look at me. There was heat in his eyes, impatience on his face. Wrapping my arm around Kiera's waist, I told him, "Don't call my wife a bitch again."

Fucker smirked at me—*smirked*—then twisted back to Anna. Asshole.

I almost wanted to break up their joyfest, but Kiera pushed on my shoulder. I looked down to see her smiling at me. "It's fine," she said. "Let them...enjoy this." She cringed after she said it, like she didn't want to think about what they were going to do to celebrate this milestone.

I glanced back at them. Anna hadn't propped her door, and Griffin had her pressed against it while she fumbled in his pants for his wallet. If she didn't find his key soon, they were absolutely going to have sex in the hallway. Matt and Evan had apparently reached that same conclusion; they were both speed-reaching for their wallets. Evan found his key first, and Matt smacked him on the back, telling him to hurry. I laughed as I pushed open my door and led Kiera inside. I'd smack Griffin for that smirk later.

Kiera was giggling when I closed the door behind us; she looked joyfully happy now. "Did you hear him, Kellan? He loves her. And he only wants to be with her. I think he might be a good boyfriend now." Her smile shifted into a frown. "Maybe."

Reaching down, I scooped Kiera into my arms, making her laugh again. "I did hear that. I woke up hearing that." I lifted an eyebrow at her as I walked her to our bed. "All alone."

She wrinkled her nose in an adorable way. "Sorry, I couldn't sleep knowing what he was doing, and I just...I heard him out there, and I couldn't, I couldn't let him get away with it. He needed to know he sucked." She rolled her eyes. "Just in case he wasn't aware of it."

I laughed as I set her on the bed. She scooted over, leaving room so I could join her. The sheets had already cooled, and her body was an irresistible source of warmth. I wrapped her in my arms, reveling in her soft heat, and we both sighed in contentment. Then she peeked up at me. "I'm sorry I yelled at your bandmate. I know I overstepped."

"It's fine," I said, shaking my head. "I think he would have kept on denying it if you hadn't confronted him like that. You gave him the shove he needed to get his foot out of his ass."

A tired giggle escaped her. She leaned up to kiss me, then stopped so she could yawn in the crook of her arm. Chuckling, I put a hand on her head, coaxing her to my chest. She settled in, her cheek on my skin, and another content sigh left her. "I'm so glad I'm here with you," she said, squeezing me tight.

I wrapped a leg around hers, rubbed a circle on her back. "I'm so glad you're here too. I love you," I added, kissing her hair.

She mumbled some sort of response, then she went still. Within moments, her breathing changed, and she was out cold, her work for the day done. And what a task it had been, making Griffin finally admit the obvious feelings that he'd worked so hard to ignore. A damn miracle.

I could have slept in that super-comfy bed for three days straight, but it seemed like I only got a few minutes of rest before Tory was banging on my door, telling me I had a radio interview in ten minutes. I sat up, annoyed but also grateful. All my interviews were over the phone today, so I didn't have to go anywhere until the show. Fuck, I didn't even have to get *dressed* until the show. And that thought led me to a wonderful idea. Ten minutes was plenty of time to make love to my wife...

Kiera was in a much better mood now that she wasn't pissed at Griffin, and it didn't take long for us to be breathing heavy, clawing at each other's clothes like we hadn't had sex in years. Kiera let out an uninhibited moan of pleasure as I sank inside her. She wrapped her legs around me, drawing me in tight, and I let out my own satisfied noise as I dropped my head to her shoulder. God, she felt amazing.

It wasn't long before Kiera was gasping and groaning, shuddering with her release. The feeling of her clenching around me was intense, but I wanted to give her more, so I focused on my breath and distracted myself with her pleasure. She came a second time as Tory was pounding on my door with a five-minute warning. I grinned as I kissed Kiera's jaw. She wasn't pushing me away or begging me to finish, so I felt like I had an opportunity here...if I could just hold out.

Kiera moaned, "Yes," clutching my back as we rocked together. It took every ounce of willpower I had not to lose control and let myself come, but I could tell she was escalating again, and I was not about to leave her hanging. But damn, the restraint was making me shake, and I knew I wouldn't make it much longer.

My breath was fast as I kept up a steady rhythm. Kiera's was too as she matched my pace. She was letting out the most fantastic erotic noises and everything inside me started tightening, tensing, preparing. *Please come for me again, Kiera.* Because I desperately needed relief. Like she heard me, Kiera stiffened, arching her back as a satisfied moan left her. Her body clenched around mine again, and I almost sighed in relief as I dropped my control and let myself finish with her. The euphoria hit me hard, and I groaned as I came, vaguely hearing Tory yelling something about sixty seconds.

I slumped against Kiera, wishing I had time to revel in the bliss with her, but if I didn't get on the phone soon, Tory would have my ass. Kiera was languid beneath me, like all her bones had turned to Jell-O. Smiling at the peace on her face, I kissed her cheek, then grabbed my phone so I could do my job.

The morning went peacefully enough, even with having to

inform people for the millionth time that Sienna and I were not a couple. Kiera and I dressed in robes while she had our laundry cleaned. Well, she dressed in a robe; I laid mine over my lap since I was busy on the phone. She ordered us room service, and I had to smirk at the Denver omelet she got for me. *Cheeky. I like it.* Once my interviews were done, we lounged, being as lazy as possible until it was time to get ready for the show. And that was when I saw something...amazing.

"What's that?" I asked Kiera, pausing mid-zip on my jeans.

Kiera noticed where my gaze was—firmly on her underwear, her underwear that had the initials KK on the front—and she gave me a flirty smile as she turned around so I could see her ass. And damn, that was a fine ass. Even without the words *Rock God* embroidered on the back, I was enjoying the view.

"This is what the lucky fan gave me. Do you like them?" she asked.

Did I like them? Fuck, that was an understatement. Crossing my arms, I gave her a firm look. "My initials are on your underwear. Of course I like them."

She frowned at my posture, then asked the question I'd hoped she'd ask. "Then why are you scowling at me?"

I flipped my expression into a sultry grin. "Because you could have been wearing those earlier today, and I could have ripped them off of you with my teeth." Damn, now I really wanted to do that. But we had to go. My sigh was genuine as I zipped up my pants. "But it's too late now...you missed out." *I* missed out.

Kiera rolled her eyes at me, but her cheeks were flushed. "I'll still be wearing them later," she murmured.

My grin widened at that, and I couldn't stop myself from picturing it. Kiera's flush deepened as she absorbed my expression, and it took her a solid minute before she could pull herself away from my gaze to finish getting dressed. Oh yeah, that was definitely happening later.

We left our plush, private room after that, joining the guys in the waiting SUV. Well, all the guys except Griffin. And Anna.

The two of them were nowhere to be seen, and nobody could get them on the phone. Matt was freaking out about it when we got to the venue, but I had faith Griffin would be there. He wouldn't miss a show. At least, I didn't think he would. Fuck...he better not.

After security escorted us to the dressing rooms, where we could relax for a bit before the meet-and-greet, Kiera kissed my shoulder and told me she was going to go search for Anna, make sure she was okay. I assured her Anna was most likely fine; wherever she was, I was positive she was with Griffin, and he wouldn't let anything happen to her. I was pretty sure they were just caught up in a sexual marathon. Tory would find them, and she'd get them to the venue in time.

Before Kiera left, I tossed out a tease. "See you later, KK."

She froze in her tracks and color rushed up her cheeks. She knew what I meant by that, and she looked stunned that I'd said it. She shouldn't be. That sentence was so vague; no one in the room could possibly know that I was referencing her underwear.

A slow smile crossed her face as she realized that. Then she said, "I look forward to it, KK." And damn if my cock didn't instantly respond.

I pressed hard on the ache, willing it to simmer down for a while. Deacon noticed my move and cocked an eyebrow at me. I smiled at him and shrugged. *Hazard of traveling with your sexy-as-hell wife*. Deacon laughed at my gesture and nodded.

Kiera didn't return to the room, and the longer she was gone, the more I worried. If she wasn't here, it was because Griffin and Anna weren't here. Fuck. What if he didn't show up? I thought about texting Matt but decided to message Evan instead. He'd be calmer.

'*Any sign of Jackass yet?*'

'*Nope. Matt's about to lose his mind.*'

'*Fuck. What do we do if he doesn't make it?*' We couldn't cancel. We just...couldn't.

'*I'll talk to David. See if he can cover,*' he responded.

Fuck. David was Holeshot's bassist. He was good, but he didn't know our songs. Still, it was better than nothing. '*Matt might actually kill Griffin for this.*'

'*Yep. Do we stop him or let him?*'

I smiled as I texted him back. '*Damn it. Don't ask me questions I don't know the answer to.*'

He responded with a laughing face, and I put my phone away and prayed Griffin showed up soon.

But he missed the meet-and-greet, and I'd honestly never seen Matt so mad. And worried. As the minutes narrowed and our time to go up grew closer, Matt started losing it. We were all waiting in the same dressing room, needing to be together while we stressed over Griffin's absence. Kiera kept asking me if she should call her parents. Every time, I told her to wait ten more minutes because I just couldn't believe that they'd bail on this. Kiera had already called all the local hospitals. Anna wasn't in labor, so they were just fucking around. They'd realize what time it was and show up. No need to worry her family. No need to cause them the kind of stress that Matt was currently experiencing.

He was yelling into his phone for the umpteenth time. "We're on in twenty minutes, Griffin! Wherever the fuck you are, get back here now!"

Stepping in front of where he was pacing, I tried calming him down. "Relax, he'll be here."

His cheeks were bright red when he locked eyes with me. "And what if he's not, Kellan? Do we bail on the show or go up there without a bassist?"

Evan sheepishly told Matt our plan. "David said he would play with us if Griffin didn't show." He cringed after saying it because we both knew Matt wouldn't like it.

"Does he know any of our songs?" he asked, his jaw dropped.

Evan's cringe deepened. "He said he'd fake it."

Matt tossed his hands in the air. "Fake it? Wonderful!" He started calling Griffin again, and that was when Griffin finally fucking showed up. The second Matt spotted him walking into the room, he threw his phone at him and yelled, "Where the fuck have you been!"

Griffin hastily caught his cousin's phone. "Jesus, Matt! You almost nailed me in the face!"

Anna walked in after Griffin, and Kiera instantly rushed to her side, asking her where she'd been. Anna looked oddly guilty as she pulled back and said, "Well, don't be mad, but I sort of…"

She shared a look with Griffin, and that was when Kiera noticed something. She grabbed Anna's hand and pulled her ring finger up to her face. "Oh my God! You got married?"

My jaw dropped as Anna confirmed that they had, in fact, gotten married. As she showed us her wedding ring, as Griffin twisted his hand to show his own, I looked over at Evan and Matt; they both had the same startled expressions on their faces. This was the last thing any of us would have ever expected from Griffin. I honestly thought they'd just been breaking into hotel rooms all day, having sex on as many beds as possible. That was way more believable than this.

The room was stunned silent for a moment. Kiera was the first one to break the stillness. "You got married?" she asked again.

"Yes," Anna said with a pout.

"To *him*?" Kiera asked, pointing at Griffin.

Griffin frowned at her while Anna put her hands on her hips. "Yes," she stated, annoyed.

Hoping to deter a potential fight, I stepped up to Kiera's sister and gave her a hug. "Congratulations, Anna."

Her mood shifted into exuberant giggles as she thanked me. I turned to Griffin, a little dumbfounded. How did he go from reluctantly accepting commitment to rushing to the altar, in the span of one day? Go big or go home, I supposed. "You too, I guess." I smirked as I patted his shoulder.

He beamed at me with his chin raised. Boastful, even in this.

"Thanks." His grin turned devious. "The bachelor party is at the next stop."

Evan congratulated the couple next, then Matt murmured something positive before grabbing Griffin's elbow and saying, "We have to go."

Matt hurried us out the door, rushing us to the staging area. He visibly calmed when we arrived on time. A little early in fact. As we waited for the crew to be ready, Matt turned to Griffin with a frown. A typical, annoyed frown, not an I'm-going-to-kill-someone frown. "You got married? Without me?" He gave him a *What the hell?* expression.

Griffin shrugged, looking sheepish. "It just sort of happened. Wasn't a snub, dude. We'll party it out later." Matt pursed his lips, still looking annoyed, but he let it go. Griffin patted his back, then shifted to me. "Oh, hey, Kell, before I forget...it turns out it's really hard to get married in a day. There's some bullshit about needing an appointment." He paused to roll his eyes. "I tried to pull the 'famous person' card, but it didn't work as well as I thought it would." He shook his head like he was genuinely baffled by that. "Anyway, after I proved I was in the band, the chick at the counter said she'd pull some strings for me, but only if I gave you her number and promised that I'd make you call her." He reached into his pocket and handed me a business card with hearts drawn around the girl's number. "Here you go." He clapped my shoulder. "She's expecting phone sex, so make it good, dude."

"Griffin," I bit out. I was not having phone sex with another woman as a favor.

Griffin snorted. "Just kidding. Say hi or whatever. Just work your Kellan Kyle magic on her."

I sighed as I shoved the card in my pocket. "Why did you involve me?"

He grinned while Matt and Evan both snickered. I was glad Matt was in a better mood, but goddamn it. Griffin smacked my shoulder again. "'Cause she likes you. And you're the 'monogamy is the key to life' guy, so I thought you'd appreciate and support my efforts to join your cult."

I frowned at his use of the word "cult," but I couldn't really argue with anything he'd just said. Guess I was making an awkward phone call later. Super.

Chapter 25

THE BEST SURPRISE

Something was different about Griffin after he married Anna. I couldn't quite put my finger on it, but there was an aura of tranquility around him that hadn't been there before. He still had way too much energy and an incessant need to be constantly entertained, but he wasn't as manic about it. And it was pretty clear that whatever turmoil he'd felt about being monogamous was gone. He seemed to be completely at peace with his decision. In fact, the only girl he ever talked about wanting to bang now was Anna, and there was a softness in his eyes when he said it. It was weird. Matt constantly teased him about it.

"So you'd really turn down every woman who wanted to have sex with you?" Matt asked.

Griffin looked up from his phone with a frown on his face. "Yeah, duh. Have you seen my wife? She's a fucking goddess and as horny as me. Why the hell would I say yes?"

Matt started laughing, because if he'd asked that same question just a couple of days ago, he would have gotten a very different answer. "What about if Sienna finally said yes to you? Begged you to do her?"

Griffin scoffed, his eyes going back to his phone. "She would beg. I'm a fucking genius in bed. But no...she's got nothing on Anna. I'd tell her no thanks and go fuck my wife."

God, it was so weird to hear him say *my wife*. Those were two words I wouldn't have imagined his mouth could even form. As Matt laughed again, I happened to glance at Griffin's phone. My brows instantly furrowed, because I swear to God, he was watching a kids' show.

"What the hell are you watching?" I asked him.

"It's called *Handy's Helpers*," he said, not looking up.

Matt laughed even harder; he could barely breathe now. Confused, I asked Griffin, "Are you watching it in preparation for your kid or something? Because I don't think you have to prescreen programming for kids. They're kind of...aimed at kids."

He gave me a quick side-eye before returning to his show. "One, I'll be prescreening everything my kid watches, thank you very much. And two, this is the only shit that will play on my phone now." He jerked his thumb at Matt. "He put some goddamn parental blocker on it. I can't get rid of it, so I'm embracing it. And actually, this shit's pretty good."

Matt snorted, then sank his head to the table as he died laughing. I laughed with him for a moment while Griffin ignored us and watched his new favorite show. That was when I noticed Anna coming out of the sleeping area, a content smile on her face as she spotted Griffin. His back was to her, and he hadn't noticed her yet. Perfect. I needed to talk to her alone. I'd had an idea after Griffin's bachelor party comment, and I was going to need her help to pull it off.

I looked up the bus to where Kiera was sitting with her computer, working. Wanting this to be a secret meeting, I stood up and swiftly walked toward Anna. "Hey, Kellan," she brightly said.

Tilting my head back to the sleeping area, I asked, "Can I talk to you for a second?"

Her eyes lit up as she flashed a glance at Kiera. "Ooooh,

secrets." She dashed back behind the curtain without another word.

Shaking my head, I looked around to make sure no one was watching, then joined her. She instantly rubbed her hands together. "Okay. You want to whisk Kiera away for a romantic elopement in Paris, right? Because you've seen the crap my mom picked out for the wedding, and you would never force Kiera—or me—to wear that shit, right? Please say I'm right."

I laughed at her comment, then shook my head. "No, we're still getting married in Ohio, with all the crap your mom picked out."

She sighed. "Goddamn it, Kellan. Is it really too much to ask you to save us from the puffy sleeves?" I frowned at that, and she nodded. "Yes, exactly! Puffy fucking sleeves! Picture that being immortalized in your wedding photos and tell me you don't want to whisk her away to Europe. And me too, of course. We're a packaged deal when it comes to your wedding."

She smirked, and I shook my head again. "Whatever Kiera is fine with, I'm fine with. Even if it is puffy sleeves." Anna let out a dramatic sigh, and I laughed again. "I do need your help with something, though." Her deep green eyes lit up with intrigue. Leaning forward, I said, "Griffin wants to go out and celebrate your marriage, and that got me thinking about Kiera and our upcoming wedding, and I thought maybe we could kill two birds with one stone and—"

She clapped her hands. "If you're saying joint bachelor/bachelorette parties, then yes! I'm so in!"

I shushed her, looking back toward the main room. "I want it to be a surprise, though. And I want it to be with everyone. Do you think you could help me get the girls here?"

Her smile was a mile wide as she nodded. "Oh, yeah. We'll be in D.C. soon; we'll do it there." She did a little excited dance, trying to stay as quiet as possible. "This is going to be so much fun!"

I laughed at her eagerness. "Let the girls know I'll pay for everyone's tickets and handle the hotel rooms. I don't care what it costs, I just want them here. Kiera needs this."

Anna bit her lip and nodded. She knew exactly how much Kiera needed a little normalcy. We all did, honestly. I held up my fist to Anna, my partner-in-crime, and she grinned and bumped it. I was just about to leave when Anna's eyes suddenly lit up again. She grabbed my elbow to stop me.

"Are you cool with me taking her anywhere I want to?" she asked.

I instantly frowned. "What did you have in mind?" She was way too much like Griffin for me to just blindly say yes to that.

Anna giggled, looking absolutely delighted. "Kiera would lose her shit if I took her to see male strippers. Would you have a problem with me doing that?" Before I could answer, she added, "Please let me embarrass her with half-naked men. I've been waiting my entire life for this moment."

I laughed at that, then shrugged. "It's fine with me, but good luck getting her to stay." I had a feeling she'd bolt after the first hip thrust...and I kind of wanted to see that.

Anna snorted. "Don't worry, we'll tie her down if we have to."

I shook my head at her, marveling at her wicked side; she was worse than me when it came to teasing Kiera. I was just about to tell her that I'd help her find a place, and ask her to let Kiera leave if she really wanted to go, when she suddenly got a look on her face that exactly mirrored an expression of Griffin's, an expression that usually led to bad things. It was a mixture of *I just had the best idea* and *You're going to hate this, but we're doing it anyway.* I was immediately wary.

"Do you know the most amazing thing you could do for her?" she asked.

I shrugged. "Get all her friends here for a surprise bachelorette party?"

She swished her hand. "After that." When I didn't say

anything, she raised her eyebrows at me. "*You* be the entertainment. She would die."

I scrunched my brows in confusion. "Entertainment? What kind of entertainment?" Because it sounded like she wanted me to...

Anna's smile grew just as devilish as her husband's. She didn't clarify, but her eyes slowly scanned my body, and I had my answer. Yes, it was exactly what it sounded like. She wanted me to get on stage for Kiera, but a vastly different kind of stage.

Leaning closer, I said, "You want me to strip for her? At the club?"

Her face tightened like she was suppressing a squeal. "Yes! I'll get her there, and I'll get her to stay, and you crash the stage! It would be the ultimate surprise!" She started laughing. "For everyone."

The eagerness on her face made me laugh too, but then I shook my head. "While I'm not entirely opposed to the idea, they're not going to let me just walk on stage and start stripping."

Her eyes roved my body again. "Yeah, Hot Bod...they will."

I debated it for a moment, pictured the look on Kiera's face if I did that for her—the desire, the mortification. It was a tempting vision but also an impossible one. I shook my head with a sigh. "I can't, Anna." I waved a hand at my face. "Someone would recognize me." And if I couldn't be seen in public with Kiera, then I definitely couldn't be seen stripping for her.

Anna smirked at me. "You know the best thing about male strippers? The costumes. I'm absolutely certain you could find something that would hide your face."

Even as she said it, ideas flooded my brain. *Oh yeah...that would totally work.* Shit. Was I actually considering this? A part of me wanted to laugh it off and tell her no—it was an absurd idea —but the thought of surprising Kiera in *that* way...fuck. It was already turning me on. Plus, Anna was right, Kiera would absolutely die, and how could I possibly say no to such a great opportunity to tease her? I gave Anna a sly grin. "All right, let's make it happen."

She made a high-pitched shriek of excitement, then slapped a hand over her mouth to stifle it.

"Not a word to anyone. Got it," I said, pointing at her. "It's a secret." She zipped her lips, still giggling. Smile on my face, I rolled my eyes. "How did I let you talk me into this?"

She grinned. "Because you love my sister, and you'd do anything to make her happy. And I know Kiera; if there's any man on this planet that she actually *wants* to see stripping, it's you. Seeing you like that would make her *very* happy."

I looked at the floor, a soft smile on my face. With as much as Kiera loved looking at my body, I had to believe that was true. Anna lightly socked my arm. "And you owe me for the puffy sleeves." She smirked, then added, "I can't wait to see what Mom picked out for you. Payback is a bitch, Kellan Kyle. Just you remember that."

She turned and strode out of the room, and I lightly laughed to myself as I watched her leave.

That was when I heard someone clearing their throat. I twisted around to see Deacon partially hidden in his bunk. He was staring at me with a cocked eyebrow and an amused expression. He'd heard all of that then. Oops. Guess I should have checked the cubbies first. I pointed at him with a stern finger. "Not a peep to anyone. It's a surprise."

He started laughing. "I definitely think she'll be surprised." He shook his head. "You're going to strip in a club full of rabid women? You're a far braver man than I am."

I laughed at that. "Brave or stupid?"

He shrugged. "Sometimes they're the same thing, right?"

True. Very, very true. Oh well, it would be worth it to see the horrified yet enraptured look on Kiera's face. I couldn't wait.

I was anxious about it as we got into D.C., more excited for that performance than the concert. Anna did her part well, and between the two of us, we got everyone flights and hotel rooms.

And of course, as soon as the girls knew about the surprise, the guys knew too. At least, they knew part of it. No one but Anna—and Deacon—knew about my stripping plan. That really wasn't something I should sit on, though. I'd learned my lesson after the photograph incident, and I had to tell at least two of the guys what was going to happen, had to make sure they were okay with it. Griffin, I wasn't worried about. I already knew he wouldn't care, but if I brought it up to him, he'd insist on going onstage with me, and that was *not* the type of surprise Kiera would want.

"I can't believe you sprang for everyone to fly over here, Kellan. That was really cool of you."

I shrugged at Matt, looking around to make sure Kiera wasn't nearby. She was stepping off the bus with Anna, though, so I turned back to him. "I want it to be the best night of Kiera's life, and it wouldn't be if her friends weren't there. Just make sure you don't say anything around her. I want it to be a surprise."

Evan and Matt both grinned and nodded. They looked happier than I'd seen in a while; this was as much a gift for them as it was for Kiera. Three birds with one stone. Hopefully, they were still happy after I told them about the second half of my surprise.

"So the night they all go out, I want to...Anna had this idea... I'm going to..." Fuck. This was weird to explain.

Evan furrowed his brows at me. "You're going to what?"

Damn. He didn't hit me the last time I was half-naked around Jenny, but would he hit me this time? "Okay, don't be mad..." They both instantly looked annoyed. I hastily spat it out, just to get it over with. "Anna wants to take them to a male strip club, and I'm going to surprise them there." I cringed after I said it; even I knew that didn't explain a whole lot.

"Surprise them with what?" Matt asked.

Biting my lip, I indicated my body with my hand. Matt's jaw dropped. "You're going to strip for them?"

I held up my hands, just in case he was thinking about punching me. "I'm stripping for Kiera...they'll just happen to be there while I do it. Are you guys cool with that?" I looked between the two of them, but I couldn't get a read on how they felt.

Evan frowned at me. Matt slowly shook his head as he said, "First you ask my girlfriend to help take a nude photo of you—"

"I wasn't naked," I interrupted. "And technically, I asked Jenny, not Rachel."

Evan's frown deepened, and Matt continued like I hadn't spoken. "And now you want to strip in front of her? Why do you keep taking off your clothes in front of other people's girlfriends?"

He lifted a pale eyebrow at me, and Evan crossed his arms over his chest. Shit. Were they mad? I lifted my hands, my smile small and innocent. "For love?"

They both stared at me a second, then they started laughing. No, howling.

When their chortling died down some, Evan sighed and said, "Whatever, Kellan, it's your body."

Matt nodded in agreement. Wiping his eyes, he said, "I'll have Rachel take pictures so we can update the website."

I scowled at him, but that only made him laugh harder. "Don't mention anything to the girls, okay? Or Griffin. I don't need that headache."

They looked at each other, still chuckling, and I was glad they were choosing to make fun of me instead of being angry at me. I was sure they understood that Kiera was my entire world, and even if I was completely naked, their girlfriends were safe in my hands. And besides, I wasn't going to be completely naked. It was nothing both girls hadn't seen already. Nothing most of the world hadn't seen already; I'd practically be fully dressed compared to what was out there.

I mentioned that to the guys, and Evan shook his head. "It might be time you rethink your life choices, Kell."

"Already done," I said with a smirk. Then I handed Matt my

phone. "Will you help me find a club where guys are performing so I can tell Anna where to go?"

Matt's expression turned sullen as he took my phone. "What would you do without me? Like literally, what would you do?"

Evan laughed while I solemnly shook my head. "I don't even want to think about that."

Finally, the day of the party arrived, and as far as I knew, Kiera had no idea all her friends would be visiting her soon. It was hard not to give it away, to act nonchalant, like today was just another day. I was calm on the surface but bouncing around like a little kid on the inside. But then Kiera did something that sent a spike of trepidation straight through me. We were relaxing on the bus, Kiera working on her book while I worked on lyrics, when the sound of typing stopped, and Kiera reached across the table and wrapped her fingers around mine. The look on her face was one of intense relief and utter satisfaction, and I knew exactly what it meant; I often had the same look on my face when I finished a song. She was done with her book, and if she was finally done, then she might let me see it. I really wanted to read her thoughts on how we got together; I was also full of an almost catatonic terror.

"You're finished? Do I finally get to read it?"

Kiera looked torn as she locked eyes with me. I saw a matching terror in the depths of her hazel eyes, but even still, she turned the laptop toward me. It made it a little easier to know that we were both facing our fears when it came to this book. And she loved me. I couldn't ever forget that.

Setting down my notebook, I held Kiera's gaze a little longer, then turned my attention to the computer. I scrolled to the top of the document, and Kiera shot out of her seat like she'd been stung. I instantly stopped what I was doing and looked up at her. She was visibly trembling as she shook out her fingers. Maybe this was great in theory, but in reality, it was just...too much. Because she looked ill, and I kind of felt the same way.

"I can't just peacefully sit here while you read it," she said, then she scanned the bus like she was looking for an escape.

Feeling bad that I was obviously hurting her, I started closing the laptop. "If it bothers you, I won't read it."

She shook her head at me. "No, I want you to. I just...can't watch you do it."

I reopened the computer. She was being strong; I could be too. Kiera started heading toward the cubbies, but a sound outside stopped her. There were fans hovering around the parking area, hoping to catch a glimpse of one of us. They were typically quiet, but now they were yelling and screaming like a mini concert was going on outside. Maybe one of the guys was back? Although they usually didn't scream quite so loudly for them. But then someone knocked on the bus door, and I knew it wasn't one of the guys. They wouldn't knock. Unless it was Griffin. He was still knocking around Kiera and me, and even if he was doing it to be a jackass, I fucking loved him for it.

I went over to open the door for Griffin, but it wasn't him. "Sienna? What are you doing here?" There was literally nothing she needed on this bus. She could just call me if she needed to tell me something.

"Can I come in?" The look she was giving me was sweet, shy...weird. By her face, you'd think she was standing in the doorway of my bedroom, demurely asking me to make love to her.

I stepped back, indicating that she could come inside with a sweep of my hand. She paused beside me, looking like she was a breath away from kissing me. "Thank you," she murmured, and that was when I realized...the way the bus was parked, all the fans could see us. And from the show she'd just put on, they all had the same incorrect assumption about what we were going to do in here. Damn it. She'd just photo-op'd me on my own bus. Had she come over here just for that?

Because there was nothing I could do about it now, I kept my expression neutral as I closed the bus door. I even made myself ignore all the shouted questions and remarks coming from the fans: *How long have you and Sienna been together? When are you getting married? We love you two together! Please don't ever break up!*

Sienna's demeanor was entirely different once she was on the bus. She was bright, bubbly, friendly, and no longer looking like she utterly adored me. She greeted Kiera like they were best friends. "Kiera! Lovely to see you."

Kiera's response was a lot less enthusiastic. "You too."

"What is it?" I asked Sienna, positive she'd had yet another "brilliant" idea that she wanted to run by me.

She turned to face me, her smile a mixture of playfulness and innocence. "Can't a girl drop in on her friends? I'm used to having people around me, but this tour it's just been my security and me on the bus. Gets a little lonely."

I was sure that was true, and while I sympathized, I didn't let myself forget that she was a major part of the manipulative force in my life right now, as that moment outside had just shown. Along with her next words.

"Would you two like to ride the next leg of the tour with me?"

My mouth opened to tell her no, but Kiera beat me to it. "No, it's all right, we're fine here." I pressed my lips together, glad that Kiera had taken that one for me. I probably wouldn't have phrased it as nicely.

Sienna pouted like she was truly disappointed, then she said something about the offer always being open to us. And of course it was. The fans would go crazy if I hopped on her bus.

Wanting out of this mess, I edged past Sienna and grabbed Kiera's laptop. Turning to our "guest," I said, "I was actually going to rest a little bit before the show. Hope you don't mind." *But if you do, I don't really care.* Sienna shook her head and shrugged, because regardless of her expression when we were in public, she didn't have a thing for me. I was simply a tool for her to use when it was convenient to use it. Annoyed, I twisted back to Kiera. "You okay?" I asked her, indicating Sienna with my eyes.

Kiera gave me a firm nod, then lightly touched her laptop. "I'm more worried about you reading this."

Completely understanding that feeling, I leaned over and kissed her cheek. "It won't change how I feel about you." It might change how I felt about *myself,* but definitely not her. I'd felt her internal struggle during that time. I already knew how conflicted she'd been and how much worse I'd made it by not communicating. If I'd only told her how I felt about her—that first night, before anything had happened between us—everything would have been different. Still painful, but very different.

Already hating myself, I ducked behind the curtain. I heard Kiera mention something to Sienna about the random photographers that had been stalking that club in North Carolina, and I paused to listen to Sienna's response. She brushed it off like it was a completely normal occurrence for her, and maybe it was. I honestly had no idea what her day-to-day life was like. All I knew was that she hadn't looked surprised or upset to see them, and that was a giant red flag for me.

Suppressing a sigh, I sat on our bunk and opened Kiera's laptop.

My pulse raced as I began Kiera's story, and I wasn't sure what was making me more nervous: reading about me or reading about Denny. Probably both. It was clear to me right away that Kiera had been overly interested in me, even from the beginning, from that first moment when she'd seen me on stage. And I was struck by the fact, that even back then, she had seen deeper inside me than any woman I'd ever known. She saw me on that stage, the real me.

Her thoughts on our first official meeting made me laugh. She'd been just as embarrassed as I'd thought she'd been. And more attracted to me than I'd realized. The way she described me...I knew I was good-looking, I wasn't blind, but she made me sound like a god, like some mythical creature that couldn't actually exist. It was surreal the way she saw me, the way she watched me from that day forward. She'd noticed...everything. She just hadn't interpreted it correctly.

Like me leaving her after our first time together. Jesus. She'd thought I'd screwed her and then fled to avoid dealing with her. Pump and dump. She hadn't realized there'd been feelings involved for me. She hadn't realized she'd broken my heart when she—

I almost shut the computer when I got to her "reunion" with Denny. I couldn't read it. I couldn't stand the fact that if I hadn't left her, if I'd come back earlier, then maybe that wouldn't have happened. Or maybe it would have. She'd loved him, heart and soul, and it had taken her a long time to trust me enough to let go of him. A really long fucking time. Because I'd made her doubt me, time and time again.

Skipping past their love scene, I came across my stumbling-drunk scene. I was floored as I read it since I didn't entirely remember that night. I'd come home wasted, then I'd been an asshole, and she'd still helped me, still longed for me, in a way. She'd wanted me to care about her, to care about our night together, and I had—so fucking much—but I'd successfully hidden that fact from her, and it had hurt us both. Because after that drunken night, I was just a straight up dick to her.

Reading about all the jerk comments that I'd said to her made me want to slap myself. God, this was harder to read than her sex scene with Denny would be. I kind of wanted to skip it too, but I knew I had to read it. I'd done it, I had to take ownership of that fact. Instead of talking to her like a fucking adult, I'd verbally attacked her over and over again. Why did she ever fall for me? I certainly hadn't made it easy for her.

A voice in the real world just about made me jump out of my skin. "Sienna left."

Adrenaline rushed through my veins as I looked up to see Kiera standing by our bunk; my heart was thudding in my chest. "I didn't hear you come in. You scared the piss out of me."

She gave me a brief smile, then her expression turned solemn as she sat on the edge of the bed. "Do you hate me?" she asked, looking extremely nervous about my answer.

I stared at her for a long time, not sure what to say. Did I hate her? No, absolutely not. Did I hate myself? Fuck yes. Closing her computer, I crawled out of the cubby to sit beside her on the edge. I could feel her nervousness as she waited for my response, and I hated myself even more for putting her on edge. I just... needed a minute.

"I'm so sorry...for all the pain I put you through."

Her eyes glistened as she stared at me in disbelief. "For all the pain you put *me* through? I'm the one who cut out your heart, then handed it back to you in pieces."

Very, very true. And still not her fault. Not entirely. "I haven't gotten that far in the story yet. I'm still at the part where I'm an asshole."

Small grin on her face, she bumped my shoulder with hers. "I kind of like it when you're an asshole."

I knew from reading the book that her comment was *not* true, but it made me smile regardless. "I'll keep that in mind," I told her. The humor faded as the guilt resurfaced. Wishing I could rewind time, I studied her face. "But I mean it. I really am sorry. I should have just been honest with you. I wanted to tell you how I felt...I just...couldn't. It was too hard."

Looking remorseful, she nodded. "I know. But you don't have to apologize. What I did to you was so much worse. Sorry isn't a big enough word to cover it."

There was nothing I could say to that, so I lifted my lips into a semblance of a smile and wiped the tear off her cheek. Kiera cringed, her eyes heavy with regret. "I'm so sorry about the scenes with Denny. I shouldn't have let you read those."

I put a finger on her lips to stop her. "Don't. I understand. I knew going into this that a story about us was also going to be a story about the two of you. And it should be. He was a big part of your life, and I'm okay with your history. It made you who you are. And I happen to be in love with who you are." And that was a truth I couldn't deny. Being with Denny had shaped a part of her personality, helped form the person sitting beside me, and while I sometimes wished I could be her first real love, like she was mine, I also understood that we might not have ended up the same—if we'd even met at all. Events had to play out the way they did so we could be who we were now. And I loved who we were now.

Still, I had to confess what I'd done. Letting out a tension-relieving laugh, I told her, "I couldn't read about it, though. I, uh, skimmed a few parts. I hope you don't mind."

Shaking her head, she tossed her arms around me and held me tight. She nuzzled against me for a moment, then she kissed my neck and said, "I love you, you know?"

I let the pain of the past slip away as I rubbed her back. Seeing a golden opportunity to tease her, I smirked and said, "I know you love my hair." She pulled back to look at me, and I could barely keep my expression even as she pursed her lips in irritation. "I mean you *really* love my hair...almost obsessively so. I had no idea." I was stretching our honesty pact by saying that. I knew she loved playing with my hair, and she was constantly looking at it, but it *had* surprised me to read just how much she liked it. Honestly, my hair was almost another character in the book. I was really glad I'd never taken George up on his offer to cut it.

Kiera's cheeks reddened. Because I couldn't resist, I gave her a playful grin. "And my abs." Referencing an internal comment she'd made during our infamous hallway meeting, I said, "Would you like to try etching them with a marker? I'll let you. Although edible paint is a lot more fun."

She pushed away from me, annoyance on her face as she stood up. Laughing, I pulled her onto my lap. She giggled when she collided with my body, and I delighted in the fact that the past was far enough behind us that it was getting easier and easier to let it go.

Kiera brought her hands up to the hair she loved so much,

tangling her fingers around the long strands. Voice deep and sensual, she told me, "I'll etch you if you etch me."

Abso-fucking-lutely. That sounded even better than the night I'd already mapped out for her. Shifting her around so she was straddling me, I murmured, "Deal." Then I sealed it with a kiss. The girls would understand if I told them plans had changed...right?

My hands darted under Kiera's shirt, alternating between caressing her and tickling her. She giggled between kisses, and I wondered if we had time to sneak away before the girls arrived. So of course, that was when the girls arrived.

"Well, this is familiar."

Kiera only mildly startled at being walked in on. Sadly, we were getting pretty used to it. But when she noticed who was here, her jaw dropped almost to her chest. "Jenny?"

I smiled at Jenny as she laughed and said, "Surprise!"

Kiera let out a shriek of joy and shoved off me to get to her friend. I grunted at the force she'd used, then grinned as I watched my wife's exuberance. Tears were in her eyes when she squeezed Jenny tight. And then she noticed that Jenny wasn't alone. She listed off her girlfriends as she spotted them: Kate, Rachel, and her friend from school, Cheyenne. I was so glad that we'd managed to get them all here for her. It made my chest ache to see the happiness on Kiera's face.

Kiera looked between her girlfriends and me, like she knew I was behind this. "What's going on?" she asked.

Griffin and Anna were back from shopping. Griffin looked exhausted as he crashed into a chair, bags falling from his arms. Anna looked like she'd just taken a six-hour nap and was ready to go all night long. She wrapped an arm around Rachel and handed Kiera a solid black bag. I noticed Griffin smirk as Kiera took it, and I could only imagine what was inside it.

Kiera opened the bag and almost immediately closed it. Her face bright red, she turned to me and said, "Okay, seriously, what the hell is going on?"

Standing, I walked over and put an arm around her. "We're officially getting married next month, and Anna and Griffin just tied the knot, so we"— I motioned toward Anna—"decided a little celebration was in order."

Anna cradled her stomach so she could bounce on her toes. "Dual bachelorette party, Kiera!"

Kiera looked absolutely stunned, floored that all of her closest girlfriends would drop everything to fly out here and help her celebrate. She hugged each of them, then turned to me with awe on her face. "You arranged all of this?"

I gave her a smile and a shrug. "Our lives are crazy. When moments to remember happen, you have to pause a second to appreciate them. Otherwise, none of this is worth it," I said, indicating the bus and our surreal situation. "And getting married to you is definitely a moment to remember." One I was going to cherish forever.

Kiera's eyes turned watery as she gazed at me. I wanted to hug her, kiss her, hold her forever, but Griffin spoiled the moment by saying, "And while you guys are drooling over dudes, we'll be swimming in a sea of half-naked babes."

He'd gotten up from the chair to stand behind Anna, and she elbowed him for his comment. Kiera looked back at me, unease in her eyes, and I shook my head. "We're just going to a bar after the show tonight." The last thing I wanted was for her to spend the entire night thinking about me being surrounded by nearly naked women. I wanted her to have nothing on her mind but her friends. And *me* half-naked. Or fully naked, in her mind at least.

Griffin instantly tossed me a put-out look. "I said I wanted a strip club."

He had. Loudly. At every opportunity. He might be practicing monogamy now, but he still loved leering at half-naked women. "And I said I wanted a bar. If you want to do separate bachelor parties, then by all means, go to a strip club tonight. But I don't feel like celebrating my marriage with overpriced alcohol and glitter."

Griffin eyed me with annoyance. We'd discussed this enough that he knew I meant it. I'd rather we celebrate together, but I wasn't going with him if that was his choice. He also knew none of the other guys would go either, not even Deacon or his friends —he'd already asked—so unless he wanted to go alone, which he didn't, then he'd be joining us at a regular bar. Where he'd probably pout until we got him wasted. After that, he'd be fine. Needless to say, getting him fucked up was our top priority.

Griffin rolled his eyes in reluctant acceptance, then made a *You're so whipped* noise. I grinned at him. I didn't mind being whipped, not one tiny little bit.

Kiera turned to her sister, her brows still bunched in concern. "And what exactly are *we* doing tonight?" she asked. There was wariness in her voice, because she also knew Anna and Griffin were a lot alike, and she had to suspect what Anna had in store for her, especially after Griffin's "drooling over dudes" comment.

And yet, I was certain she wouldn't expect *me*.

Anna flashed me a quick glance, then told Kiera, "Oh, don't you worry about the details. I've got everything under control."

Chapter 26
FULFILLING A FANTASY

The girls took over the back half of the bus, and none of us guys were allowed to cross the curtain line until they were done getting ready. Jenny and Rachel were the last ones to disappear behind the curtain, lingering to visit with Evan and Matt for as long as possible. Before Jenny joined my wife in her makeshift dressing room, she pulled me aside.

"Hey, Kellan, I just..." Her pale eyes drifted to the floor as her words trailed off.

"I know what you want to talk about, and I'm sorry." I'd already apologized a dozen times for snapping at her—for hanging up on her—but I'd say it a dozen more times if she needed to hear it. I didn't want any issues between us.

She lifted her eyes to mine and shook her head. "No, that's not..." She sighed, took a moment to collect herself, then started over. "I wanted to apologize. What I said was rude, and I shouldn't have doubted you. I've seen you change over the past couple of years, and I know you're not...who you used to be."

She cringed after she said that, and a soft laugh escaped me. "You mean a douchebag who would sleep with anyone who wanted me? Whether they were in a relationship or not?" My smile faded. "And then lie about it, to all my closest friends." I paused to sigh. "I don't blame you for doubting my honesty, Jenny. I will never blame anyone for that. I haven't lived a very honest life. But I'm trying to, I swear to God, I'm trying to."

A tender smile graced her lips as she studied my eyes. "I know you are. That's why I'm sorry. I need to respect you for the man you are today, not treat you like the man you were back then. So please...forgive me?"

Shaking my head, I wrapped my arms around her. "There's nothing to forgive. You're allowed to call me out when I've done something really fucking stupid. But if you need to hear it, then yes, I forgive you."

We pulled apart, and she gave me a bright, friendly smile. "Language, Kellan," she told me, a teasing light in her eyes, and that was when it struck me—I had three sisters: Hailey, Anna, *and* Jenny. The realization was enough to choke me up, even as I laughed at her remark.

Jenny patted my arm, then joined the girls behind the curtain. I twisted around to see Evan staring at me. He raised an eyebrow when he caught my attention. "You two work things out?" he asked.

I nodded as I sat down across from him. "Yeah, we're cool." *We're family. All of us.*

Evan grinned as his gaze darted to the curtain. "Good, because I was starting to get sick of how often our conversations became about you." His dark eyes returned to mine, and he gave me a smirk. "I love you, man, but sometimes I want to talk to my girlfriend about *me*."

I laughed at the look on his face, then felt bad. Again. I hadn't realized just how guilty Jenny had felt for what she'd said to me. It hadn't even been that bad really. Jenny was just a genuinely good person. "Won't happen again," I told him. Hopefully.

He sighed, and there was heavy annoyance in the sound. "It'll happen at least *one* more time. Are you still planning...what you're planning?"

I grinned at him in answer, and he sighed again, but this

time the sigh was a fake one; there was a hefty dose of humor beneath it. I had a feeling Evan was going to get a kick out of Jenny's reaction to my performance for Kiera, and they'd spend a good chunk of time laughing about it later. Jenny wasn't shy like Rachel, so I didn't think me dancing provocatively would bother her. Honestly, I had a feeling she'd find it...kind of sweet. But if it became too much for her, then she could close her eyes. I fully expected that from Rachel, unless of course, Matt had actually convinced her to take pictures for the website. Damn it.

Just as I was considering telling Anna to steal Rachel's phone, Griffin sat down next to me. "What are you planning?" he asked, having heard Evan's question.

"Nothing much," I said with a smile.

He frowned at me, but his next words had nothing to do with my surprise. "Are you serious about going to a bar? Or are you just saying that to throw off Kiera?"

I sighed at him. "I don't lie to my wife, and yes, I was serious about a bar. And separate parties." I raised an eyebrow at him, and his pout grew deeper.

Looking up the bus, he spotted his cousin and shouted, "Matt!"

Matt tore his gaze from the curtain, locked eyes with Griffin, and immediately said, "No."

Evan and I started laughing while Griffin tossed his hands in the air. "I didn't ask you anything yet."

Matt gave him an annoyed look. "You've only asked me one question for the last six hours, and my answer hasn't changed. I'm not going to a strip club with you, I'm going to the bar with Kellan."

Griffin crossed his arms over his chest. "You all suck," he muttered.

With a laugh, I patted his shoulder. "First round is on me," I told him.

He smirked at me. "Every round's on you, fucker."

I sighed, then nodded. It was the least I could do for his...sacrifice.

What felt like several hours later, the girls were finally ready for their adventure. When they stepped out from behind the curtain, a part of me wanted to pull Anna aside and thank her for making an unknown fantasy come true. The rest of me wanted to toss Kiera over my shoulder and take her straight to our hotel room without letting anyone else lay eyes on her, because damn, she looked good.

She was wearing a skintight black dress that showed off all her curves and left most of her legs exposed. Her makeup was pure seduction—bright red lips, dark eyeshadow, mile-long eyelashes. But the kicker, the part I couldn't stop staring at, was the neon pink wig she was wearing. The shorter bob style framed her face in such an appealing way, and the color was doing something to me. Fuck. I had a thing for pink, and that was something I hadn't known before. But the longer I looked, the harder I got, so I couldn't ignore it. I liked pink. Or I liked *her* in pink. Either way, fuck our plans. We could celebrate together in our hotel room, and I'd be perfectly happy with that.

The other girls were dressed similarly to Kiera, but I barely noticed them as I stood and stepped up to her. "I am not going to be able to concentrate on stage tonight with this image of you in my mind." And wasn't that the truth? Even now, I couldn't think of a single fucking lyric. "You are unbelievably hot."

She glanced down, and I fully expected her to deny or brush off my compliment. Instead, she told me, "Thank you."

I grinned at her, happy she'd owned her attractiveness, then I leaned in close and whispered, "You're keeping the wig, right?"

My fingers glided down a strand, and I sucked on my lip as I pictured all sorts of amazing things. Kiera studied my face for a moment, then put her lips against my ear. "It's the only thing I'll keep on when I get back."

Fuck. Me.

I didn't think I could let her leave now; there was way too

much that I wanted and needed from her. Wrapping my arms around her waist, I pulled her into me and told the bus, "Change of plans, we're canceling the show tonight and staying in."

All the guys agreed with my idea, even Matt, which was kind of shocking. Kiera gave me a soft smile. "Nice try, but you know you can't do that."

A wistful sigh left me as reality crashed around me. "I know, but it was a nice thought."

Eventually it was time for the band to go inside the venue. We each said goodbye to the girls, and I told Kiera that the newly arrived limo was for them. I told her to have fun on her night, and she returned the sentiment. Then she grabbed my arm and said, "Hey, if you really want to go to a strip club, I would be okay with it. I trust you."

I saw the discomfort on her face as she said it, but I also saw the conviction. She truly did trust me, even around a bunch of half-naked women. I smiled at her, warmed by her faith in me. But seeing other women wasn't what I wanted tonight. Or ever. I just wanted her.

"I'm glad to hear that," I told her. "I don't need a club, though." Not wanting her to feel like she was entirely influencing my decision, I confessed that clubs had never done much for me anyway. And that was true. I'd tried it a few times when I was younger, mainly out of curiosity, but it was more fun for me to flirt with girls at a bar. And honestly, that had a better payoff, although I didn't think it was necessary to mention that to Kiera. And by the smirk she gave me, I knew she was well aware that finding women to take their clothes off for me—for free—hadn't been terribly difficult.

Kiera was on my mind every second after that, and I was antsy for the show to be over...for my second show to begin.

When we were finally done with our set, I rushed down the stage stairs so I could get to my other performance. Matt rushed down with me. Putting a hand on my arm, he said, "You know when to be back, right?"

I nodded as I tossed stuff at the crew. "Yeah, don't worry."

He ran a hand through his spikey hair. "Don't worry? There are a million things that could hold you up. Are you sure you want to do this?"

I nodded for a second time, then patted his shoulder. "It'll be fine. I won't be late."

He sighed, already looking stressed, and I knew he'd be a mess of nerves until I returned. I'd repay him later, at the bar.

Matt opened his mouth, looking like he wanted to object, but I clapped his shoulder and took off before he could. If I wanted to make it back in time, then I didn't have time to spare. The car Matt had helped me arrange was waiting out back, and I dashed inside it. I told the driver the name of the club, then pondered how I was going to convince someone who worked there to let me go onstage.

When we got to the club, the driver pulled right up to the front of it. I smiled when I saw Kiera's limo waiting in the lot. Looking up at the front entrance, at the feminine neon legs that were alternately blinking so they looked like they were kicking, I wondered how to get inside without being noticed. If it was a typical night, the front door probably wouldn't be a problem, but it was ladies' night, and the place was packed with women who just might recognize me.

Leaning forward, I asked the driver, "Can you see if there's a back entrance?"

He nodded, not looking at all fazed by my question. He drove around the building, and sure enough, there was a door in the back by the Dumpsters. It didn't look like a discreet entrance, though, it just looked like a quick way to get to the alley. Sighing, I decided to give it a shot. Maybe someone nearby would hear me knocking.

I told the driver to wait there for me, then I sped over to the door. There was a camera above it, but I couldn't tell if it worked or not. I banged on the door, but nothing happened. I tried again, then again, then again. Sighing, I debated wrapping my jacket around my face and risking a walk through the front door. That was when the back door popped open. A guy stuck his head out, his face a mask of confusion and curiosity.

"Hey," I said when he spotted me. "This is gonna sound weird, but I was—"

The guy opened the door wider. He wasn't wearing a shirt, and his abs were as chiseled as mine, so I figured he was a performer. "Oh my God, you're Kellan Kyle!" he blurted, interrupting me.

The grin on my face was sheepish. I'd never considered the dancers recognizing me. This could really backfire. "Yeah...hi. I was wondering—"

The guy stepped aside and urged me indoors. "Tell me inside, wouldn't want people to see you back here and start swarming."

I breathed a sigh of relief that the guy cared about discretion. I was again about to tell him what I wanted, but he again spoke before I could. "Uh, if you're here to use the club, it's ladies' night." He showcased his body with his hand. "There aren't any girls working tonight, just guys." Tilting his head, he added, "But if that's why you're here, I could find a discreet place for you to watch backstage?"

It was genuinely touching that he was so considerate, but that wasn't why I was here. Smiling, I shook my head. "No, actually, I have a request. My girl is in the crowd, celebrating with some friends, and I wanted to surprise her. *On the stage.*" I lifted my eyebrows as I waited to see if my plan was possible.

The guy's eyes widened. "Sienna is here?"

It was really hard not to close my eyes and groan. "No, I'm not...I'm not with Sienna."

His face twisted in confusion, but then he shrugged like it didn't really matter to him. "That's cool that you want to do that for her, and I wish I could make it happen, but we...well, we've got a standard when it comes to body types and—"

Knowing exactly what he meant, and being impressed by the fact that he hadn't seen me naked yet, I lifted my shirt and showed him my abs.

He stopped talking. Pursing his lips, he said, "Yeah, that'll work. You can take my spot."

Grinning, I smacked his shoulder. "Thanks! And maybe we could keep this just between us?"

He grinned. "Give me the tips you make, and yeah, I won't say a damn word."

"Done," I told him. And I already knew I'd throw in whatever cash was in my wallet. This guy deserved the largest tip I could get him.

He led me to a nearby dressing room where a bunch of guys were either changing into outfits, rubbing some sort of oil on themselves, or...making themselves look bigger. Everyone was busy doing their own thing, and nobody paid me any attention. My amiable helper led me to a private corner of the room, then said, "You know what you wanna wear?"

Smiling at him, I nodded. "I need to hide my face, and my wife has a thing for cowboys."

An inquisitive look crossed his face when I said "wife," but he didn't question me. He just smiled and said, "Stay here. I've got the perfect thing."

He came back a couple of minutes later with a black cowboy hat, a bandanna for my face, a leather vest, spandex briefs, black boots, and...fuck...chaps. I laughed as I held up the pants, and my friendly savior grinned at me.

"They're tearaway," he said with a wink.

"Thanks, man, this is perfect." He showed me where I could put my stuff, and then he handed me a bottle of oil.

"Goop up with this once you've got the shorts on."

I cringed as I took it. "Do I have to?"

With a smirk, he nodded. "You're supposed to be me up there, and I never go on without it." He shrugged. "It makes your muscles pop under the lights, and it makes it harder for women to latch on. Their hands slide right off," he said with a laugh.

"Does it wipe off easy?" I asked.

His grin grew. "Nope." He patted my shoulder, then moved away to give me privacy. I stopped him before he got too far. "Hey, what's your name?"

"Derrick," he said.

"Thanks for the help, Derrick. If you ever want to come to a D-Bags show, message me through our website. I'll get you in." I was pretty sure Matt monitored that stuff, and I made a mental note to ask him to keep an eye out for anything from Derrick.

Derrick's grin widened. "Thanks! I'll definitely do that. You guys are amazing." With a laugh, he indicated the club. "Now let's see if you're any good on *this* stage."

"Right," I said, frowning, and for a split second, I wondered what the hell I was doing. But then I remembered that Kiera was out there, and excitement flooded me again. Even if I sucked at this, she'd still lose her mind. This was a win-win for me. And for her. And for Derrick.

When it was time, Derrick stealthily led me to the stage; he didn't want to be spotted by anyone in management. He made a shushing motion to some of the overly curious performers, but thanks to my outfit, none of the dancers knew who was replacing him for a song. Derrick gave me some last-minute instructions while I scanned the crowd. Finding Kiera and the others wasn't hard—their outfits stood out like a spotlight was on them. They were right in front, hollering and laughing, having a great time. I grinned as I watched them, then Derrick said, "All right, that's your cue. Good luck."

I gave him a nod, then stepped out onto the stage. I made sure to keep my head down as I got into position; I didn't want Kiera recognizing me too quickly. I couldn't see her as I stood with a hand resting on the tip of my hat, my gaze on the floor, but I could feel her watching me. I could feel everyone's eyes on me;

the energy of their stares was crawling up my spine, making my heart race in anticipation.

The music started, and I lifted my head, looking out over the crowd. I really wasn't sure if Kiera would recognize me just by my eyes, but before I even looked her way, I clearly heard her screech, "Oh my fucking God!" *Yep, she definitely knows it's me.*

I instantly laughed, but thanks to the bandanna, nobody could tell. Still chuckling, I began seductively moving in time to the music. The crowd was already going nuts, and I was grinning when I finally met Kiera's eyes. She was bright red, and she looked like she wanted to strangle me. Sitting beside Kiera, Anna was holding her stomach; she was laughing so hard. The other girls were staring at Kiera, wondering why she'd just sworn so loudly. I knew Jenny and Rachel would figure it out the second I removed my vest; they'd both seen my tattoo before. Kate and Cheyenne would probably figure it out then too since Kiera's name was kind of a dead giveaway.

Wanting to get Derrick as many tips as possible, I seduced the entire crowd. To my surprise, it felt exactly like singing—I absorbed the crowd's energy, then fed it right back to them through my movements. When it seemed like it was time to ramp things up a little, I made my way over to Kiera's table. I slid the vest off my shoulders, running a hand down my chest. Grabbing the fabric, I tossed it at Kiera. I didn't think she'd give it back, so I made a mental note to pay Derrick for it afterward.

Kiera's eyes widened as the vest dropped on her. She was so absorbed in what I was doing that she almost didn't catch it. The club went crazy when my chest was exposed, and I scanned Kiera's table. Anna gave me a wink and a thumbs up. Cheyenne spotted my tattoo, giggled, and looked over at Kiera. Kate was staring fixedly at the ink over my pec, her brow furrowed in confusion. Then she suddenly widened her eyes and locked gazes with me. The recognition made me laugh, and I wanted to wave at her, but I had a job to do. Jenny and Rachel were gaping at me, slack-jawed, and I saw Jenny lean over to confirm my identity with Kiera, who pursed her lips as she nodded at Jenny's question. Rachel instantly covered her eyes. Jenny started laughing. Shaking her head, she met eyes with me, and I could clearly see her thinking *You're unbelievable.*

I laughed again, then got to work. I split my attention between Kiera and the rest of the crowd, lingering near the edges so the women could touch me, then backing off when they got a little too friendly; it didn't take long for me to completely understand what Derrick meant about the oil. When I felt like the crowd was at the peak of their frenzy, I ripped off the chaps. And damn, tearaway clothes were fun. I needed to get some for when Kiera and I were back at home.

The crowd went ballistic when I was just in my briefs. Kiera buried her face in her hands. Jenny and Anna were dying laughing. Rachel still had her eyes covered, although I did notice her peeking every now and then. Keeping it sexy, I ran my hands over my skin as I rolled and flexed my body. I felt money being shoved in my spandex, and I was a little shocked at how many women went for the front of my briefs. Turning at just the right time truly was an artform.

Eventually the song approached its end. I sauntered back to Kiera, wanting the finale to be hers and hers alone. I jumped off the stage to land right beside her table. Several women nearby rushed my way, but before they could get to me, I grabbed Kiera's hand and pulled her to her feet. Moving to the beat, I grabbed her leg and hooked it around my hip. Her arms laced around my neck as she molded herself to my body. I dipped her when the song finished, then slowly pulled her back up. Our faces were inches apart as she clung to me, as I clung to her. Staring at her made my breath quicken, made my pulse race. Kiera's eyes were alive with heat as she searched mine, and then she leaned forward and kissed me, right over the bandanna. The crowd watching us screamed in excitement, but their energy was nothing compared to what I felt coming from Kiera. My hands drifted to her ass as I cursed the stupid fabric separating our mouths. I wanted to tear it off and feel her lips on mine, but I knew this would quickly turn into a nightmare for Kiera if people recognized me.

Kiera finally pulled away from me, and I saw the same wishful desire in her eyes. *Later. We'll get to finish this later.* Wanting to cool myself down, I jokingly told her, "You probably shouldn't turn me on in this outfit. I may get arrested." I was already harder than I should be, considering who was watching me. Luckily, thinking that quickly evened my blood flow.

Kiera pushed me back with a laugh. "I cannot believe you just did that."

I gave her a playful bow and a chaste kiss on her hand. "I couldn't resist." Straightening, I pointed at Anna. "It was her idea."

Kiera instantly glared at her sister. Anna grinned, then motioned up and down my body with her hand. "Sex on a Stick," she stated, like that explained everything.

The announcer rattled off another dancer's name, and even though I wanted to stay, I knew I needed to wrap this up. I gave Kiera one last hug, then told her, "I have to go finish my *other* performance or Matt will have my head." I glanced down at my shining body. "And I need to go wipe this oil shit off." Or try to anyway.

Kiera laughed, then kissed my cheek. "You're something else, you know?"

I smiled at her under the bandanna. "So are you. It's good to see you having fun. I'll see you back at the hotel."

She gave me a look that instantly ignited me. "Yes, you certainly will," she murmured. Damn. I was supposed to be teasing her, but she was the one undoing me. Fuck, I couldn't wait until later.

We pulled apart, and I made my way back to the stage. Women stroked me the entire time, shoving more bills in my briefs and brazenly trying to cop a feel. I stopped them from groping me but let them leave a tip for Derrick. I owed him that much. When I got to the stairs at the edge of the stage, I glanced back at Kiera. She was grinning at me, joy on her face, peace in her eyes. I paused a moment to appreciate everything about her, to let the love I felt for her permeate every cell of my body, then I tipped my hat and forced myself to go backstage so I could change.

Derrick was waiting for me just offstage. He grinned when he made eye contact with me. "That was good, man. You could do this for a living if you wanted. I know half a dozen places that would hire you on the spot."

With a laugh, I shook my head. "That was fun, but I think I'll stick to my other stage."

Derrick laughed and nodded, then led me back to the dressing room. I thanked him again for letting me crash his stage, then gave him all the bills that had been shoved down my shorts. After changing and wiping the shit off me as best I could, I offered him the handful of hundreds that I happened to have in my wallet.

"Oh, hey, you don't have to do that. Tickets to a show are more than payment enough."

I shook my head at him. "I owe you big time. Please, take it."

He shrugged, then took the bills. Then he grinned. "I saw how much your girl loved the outfit. Keep it." He lifted the bills. "In exchange for this."

With a grin, I grabbed the boots, hat, briefs, and the bandanna. I was definitely on board for that exchange. Derrick helped me covertly walk to the back door, and I smiled when I saw that my driver was still waiting. As I walked outside, Derrick said, "If you ever get tired of being a rock star, that job offer is always open."

I laughed, nodded, then hopped into the car.

I told the driver to hurry back to the venue, then hoped and prayed I wasn't late. Grabbing my phone from my jacket pocket, I checked to see if there were any panicked messages from Matt. There wasn't anything from him, but there was a text from Kiera. I laughed when I saw what it was. She'd sent me a photo of a receipt with a guy's number written on it, and her text beneath it said, *'I won!'* like the girls had been playing Griffin's game or something. I was pretty sure they hadn't been, but it amused me that Kiera was making a joke about being hit on. And it made me so happy that we were comfortable enough to kid around about that kind of thing; we both knew neither one of us was going to stray.

Grinning, I texted her, *'No, I get you tonight and every night, so I'm pretty sure I won.'* No, I knew I'd won. I'd won big. A fact that still surprised me sometimes.

When I got back to the venue, Matt was on me the instant I stepped into the dressing room. "Oh good, you made—" He stopped talking when he noticed what was in my hands. Then his mouth quirked like he was trying not to laugh. "Did you...dress up...like a cowboy?" His eyes watered as he struggled not to snicker.

I looked down at the boots, hat, and clothes in my hands. "What's wrong with being a cowboy?" I asked. He let out a stran-gled semi-snort, then stifled it. I smirked at his restraint, then said something that I knew would break him. "You should have seen my chaps."

A laugh burst out of him, and he giggled so hard that he had to clutch his stomach. "Oh my God, please tell me someone got pictures." Tears were streaming down his cheeks now as he bent over.

Griffin appeared beside me, his expression puzzled as he watched his cousin lose it. Then he glanced at the objects I was setting down and scratched his head. "Uh, we doin' this in costume tonight?"

While Matt laughed even harder, I told Griffin, "No," and took off my jacket.

Griffin tilted his head as he examined my bare arms. "Dude, why are you...greasy?" Matt snorted, then crashed onto a nearby couch and buried his head in the pillows as he laughed. Griffin watched him, then leaned over to me and whispered, "Is he high?"

I couldn't contain my laughter anymore and around chuckles, I told Griffin, "Yes, yes he is." High on my ridiculousness.

Griffin frowned. "Damn it, Matt. You're supposed to share that shit, cuz. We talked about this."

Matt laughed the entire time we waited to go onstage. And possibly while we were *on* the stage. Definitely after we got off the stage. He laughed for so long that by the time we got to the bar, he had the hiccups. Which made the rest of us laugh.

"Fuck. All. Of you," he said between spasms.

With a grin, I tipped my hat. I'd worn it to the bar to prolong Matt's giggling problem. He teared up every time he looked at me, then he flipped me off since he knew I was purposely egging him on. I appeased him with a round of drinks, but because I enjoyed being a dick, I ordered us something called a Flaming Lasso.

Matt clutched his stomach as he glared at me. "I hate you so much." Between laughing and hiccupping, he could barely say the words.

Griffin scowled at him. "I want to know what you took. And I want to know why you didn't give me any. You're supposed to be the responsible one. *I'm* the fuck up." Matt just snorted and shook his head. Griffin's frown turned into a pout. "Plus, it's *my* bachelor party," he murmured.

"*Our* bachelor party," I reminded him.

He rolled his eyes at me. Evan smiled as he looked between us. "I still can't believe that out of all of us, you two are the ones who got married first." He pointed at Griffin. "Especially you. You getting married defies the laws of nature. It's like the sun has started rising in the west."

Griffin tilted his head, and he got an expression on his face that I knew was him trying to remember where the sun was supposed to rise. He quickly gave up and flipped off Evan. "Don't hate on us because you two are chickenshits." Smile on his face, he leaned forward on his elbows. "You're just jealous that we had the balls to do it."

Evan rolled his eyes, but Matt suddenly looked introspective, like he was genuinely wondering if he was a coward. I tossed a napkin at him. He looked up at me, and I nodded my head at Griffin and rolled my eyes. The last person Matt should listen to when it came to relationships was Griffin. It was fine if Matt wanted to wait to get married, or if he never wanted to get married at all. The choice was entirely up to him. It was his life, not Griffin's, and he shouldn't feel guilted or rushed into anything. With a small laugh, Matt gave me a discreet nod of understanding.

And that was when our Flaming Lassos arrived. The waitress set down Matt's in front of him, and he instantly scowled at me. Then hiccupped. Then laughed.

We were all pretty tipsy when last call came around. Everyone at the bar—from management to the staff—told us we could stay as long as we wanted. Even wearing a cowboy hat, I'd been noticed right away. For the most part, my friends had kept the crowd at a respectful distance, but I'd signed a lot of napkins and posed for a lot of selfies. Hopefully, I didn't look too trashed in those photos.

Turning down the bar's offer, we left when it officially closed. The guys and I had places to be and very special people waiting for us. I was giddy when I got to my hotel room, wondering if Kiera had kept her promise about just wearing the wig. Fuck, just thinking about it was making me hard. I hoped I hadn't overdone it with the alcohol, or else this might be a very disappointing night for Kiera. I knew my body, though, and I was nowhere near that stumbling-drunk, inoperable level of intoxication. I just felt...good. And I couldn't wait to make her feel good too.

It was incredibly dark when I shut the door behind me. I shuffled my way to the bed, dropping my jacket to the floor as I went. A light on the nightstand popped on, blinding me for a second. When my eyesight stabilized, the vision in front of me took my breath away.

Kiera was lying on the bed with the covers off, letting me see all of her body. And fuck...she'd done it. She had her arm resting over her breasts and her legs demurely twisted, but yeah, she was only wearing that damn sexy, neon pink wig. My cock turned concrete-hard so fast that it actually hurt a little.

"Hey, cowboy," she murmured. She bit her lip, and her eyes drifted down my body, and I couldn't take it anymore; I needed to touch her.

I kicked off my boots while simultaneously unfastening my jeans, giving myself some fucking room, then I dove onto the bed with her. She giggled when our bodies collided, then removed my hat so I could kiss her without hitting her with it. My lips instantly sought her mouth while my hands slipped over her smooth skin. "Fuck, you're so hot," I murmured, feeling like I was gonna lose it already.

An amused laugh left her, then my hand cupped her breast, and she moaned when my thumb circled her nipple. Her kiss turned eager and hungry, and her fingers pulled at my shirt, wanting it off. I helped her remove it, tossing it to the floor. Her hands on my skin sent bolts of delight sizzling through me. My lips shifted to her neck as her fingers started pushing down my jeans. Fucking clothes.

With a grunt of annoyance, I paused to remove the confining fabric. When I was finally completely bare, I rejoined her warm body. She closed her eyes when every piece of us met skin to skin. I explored her body with my fingers, but I couldn't stop staring at her face. That perfect, beautiful, loving face. I knew every freckle, every line, every emotion that flickered across it, and every day I grew to cherish it more and more. The love I felt building inside of me as I absorbed her was almost too much to bear.

Acting on their own, my fingers slid between her legs. She gasped, arching her back and releasing her breath in a moan. My body pulsed with need as I drank in her reaction. "Kiera," I whispered.

She opened her eyes, and my breath caught in my throat at the level of love that I saw reflecting back at me. Her hand touched my cheek, and she gently drew me in for a searing kiss. As our mouths moved together more intensely, our breaths grew frantic, and my heart raced in my chest. Kiera suddenly grabbed my hips, urging me onto her, into her. Adjusting my position, I sank inside her. Our mouths separated as a groan escaped me. My head dropped to her shoulder as her hands tenderly cradled me. She was perfection, fucking perfection.

I felt delirious as we began to move together, more intoxicated from her than the alcohol. My name left Kiera's lips in a whisper, and the passion in the quiet pleading almost undid me. I wanted to give this woman everything that I could, every second of every day. Our slow, teasing pace quickly morphed into something more frenetic as pure need drove us. Kiera clutched my back as the erotic noises she was making escalated. I felt it too, that maddening need for more.

One of her hands searched for mine. I grabbed it, cinching her tight as I felt the crest approaching. I prayed she was almost there too because I didn't think I had enough control to delay it. Her breathless pants mimicked mine, and her aching cries matched my own. I felt the rush of my release at the exact moment that she stiffened beneath me. Her grip tightened around my hand as she reached her climax, and mine tightened around hers as I joined her. Our bodies completely in sync, we finished together, and that familiar sense of completion and unity filled the void as my high ebbed.

I sank into her body, into her embrace, as the bliss wrapped around me, around her, around *us*.

God, I love this woman.

Chapter 27

GOODBYE

I woke up with a start, my heart thundering in my chest. Fear was rushing through me, but I wasn't sure why. I looked around the darkened space I was in and tried to get my bearings, tried to understand why I was freaking out. From the cramped position I was in, from the warm body lying beside me, I knew I was in my cubby on the bus. My body relaxed as I put an arm around Kiera and gently pulled her toward me. I must have been dreaming, and from the adrenaline I'd felt when I'd woken up, I was sure I didn't want to remember it.

Kiera murmured something that sounded like, "It's okay," and an unamused laugh left me. She was so used to me startling awake from a nightmare that she was responding to me in her sleep. I wished I could stop the dreams, wished I could make peace with the past, I just didn't know how.

I supposed that was where talking to someone would help, but I wasn't ready for that. I just wanted to move on and forget it. My parents were dead. Why couldn't my subconscious leave them in their graves? What was the point of me reliving the torture?

Not feeling tired anymore, I kissed Kiera's shoulder, then carefully got out of the bunk. I knew my dreams intensified when I was worried or anxious. So...was I? I certainly wasn't happy about the situation I was in. It pissed me off that I couldn't hold Kiera's hand in public, that I couldn't talk about her at every interview, that I had to stomach all the fake news about Sienna and me. It was draining me, and I didn't see a way out of that either.

Annoyed, I headed into the main part of the bus to start my workout routine. Maybe sweat would drive the demons away. For a while at least.

I was still going at it when Kiera woke up and joined me. She eyed my bare chest as I stood up to greet her, then she frowned when she noticed just how sweaty I was. Glancing down, I saw that I was dripping with it, beads running down my arms, along the lines of my abs, and that was when I realized just how hard I'd pushed myself; my entire body was trembling, and I felt a little nauseated.

"Everything okay?" she asked, putting a hand on my slick chest.

Nodding, I cupped her hand with my own. "Yeah, I just...bad dream," I confessed.

Concern marked her features as she gazed at me. "Do you want to talk about it?"

I shook my head. "I honestly don't remember it. I just woke up feeling...anxious. Needed to burn off the energy," I said, pointing to the floor.

She nodded, then leaned forward and tenderly kissed me. "You're loved," she whispered against my lips, and fuck if my eyes didn't instantly water.

Swallowing the knot in my throat, I smiled at her and nodded. "I know." While my dreams often tried to prove otherwise, deep down I knew the truth. Kiera loved me, the guys loved me, even Denny loved me. Grudgingly at times, but still, he cared about me.

Instantly feeling better, I told Kiera, "I should go shower."

Kiera wrinkled her nose and nodded. "Yes, you should."

I lifted an eyebrow at her. "You could join me?"

She laughed and shook her head. "Not in that shower."

I laughed with her, understanding what she meant. The shower on the bus was microscopic; it was hard for *one* person to fit inside, two would be physically impossible. Even still, it was a million times better than the shower on Justin's bus. I left her with a kiss, then hurried to get clean so I could rejoin her.

My arms shook as I washed my hair. I was going to be so sore today. Weird that I hadn't even noticed that I was overdoing it. I'd just been enjoying the mindlessness of not thinking. Because the last thing I'd been thinking about before bed was...

Pausing with my hands in my hair, I remembered Matt telling me that our next concert was in Philadelphia. That was where the bus was headed; we might even be there already. Matt had shown me where the city was on the map, and I'd instantly been struck with how close it was to...somewhere else. Somewhere I hadn't wanted to go. Somewhere I thought I'd *never* go. But now that I was here, now that it was *right there*...well, fuck. No wonder I'd had bad dreams last night.

I finished rinsing, turned off the water, and just stood there as indecision filled me. I began to tremble with the cold, but I didn't care because the thought that wouldn't leave me alone had me shaking on the inside. *I shouldn't. They don't deserve it. I should ignore where I am, ignore that they're here, and pretend that none of this affects me. Pretend they don't matter to me. They shouldn't matter to me. Why the fuck do they still matter to me?*

The tears in my eyes grew heavy as I contemplated that, and suddenly, like a dam bursting, the memory of my dream flooded me. It had been a real memory I'd relived last night. I'd been much younger...eight, maybe nine, and my father had told me, he'd *actually* told me, that if I wanted to end my life, he wouldn't stop it, he wouldn't mourn me, he wouldn't care. He'd even *help* me. He didn't usually take his hatred that far, but even now I could remember smelling the alcohol on him. And in this case, the alcohol had loosened his tongue with his true feelings.

His words had made me cry; I'd been too young to keep it in.

The second the tears had started falling, he'd backhanded me across the cheek. It was one of the rare times that he'd actually struck my face; he'd preferred less obvious places. His own face had been twisted in a look of disgust as he'd told me that *real men don't cry*.

Jesus. *That* was the person I was contemplating visiting? Because that was my dilemma. My parents were buried nearby, in New Jersey. I had the afternoon off, and their graves were within driving distance, and I couldn't stop thinking about it.

No. There was no point. Even if they could somehow realize that I was there, it wouldn't matter to them. I'd ignore it, ignore them. Treat them the way they treated me.

But damn, that didn't feel right either.

I was emotionally numb when I finally got out of the shower and got dressed. Time sped up on me, swallowed by my internal conflict. Jenny and Rachel were still with us, having stayed a couple of extra days to visit Evan and Matt; they were all going out to do some sightseeing in Philly. Deacon and his bandmates were visiting friends and family in the area. Anna and Griffin were going out to find some gross combination of foods for Anna and her cravings. Every group invited Kiera and me to go with them, but we declined every offer. Kiera probably thought that was because of the media frenzy, or so we could have some alone time together, but that wasn't my entire reason for saying no to my friends. Because I was still fucking thinking about it, and the longer I stewed on it, the harder it was to ignore.

Damn it. If I didn't do this, it would haunt me for the rest of my life. As much as I wanted to let this opportunity pass me by, as much as I knew they didn't deserve my respect, I had to go. For me. For closure. I needed to make peace with them so I could move forward.

Once everyone left for their outings, Kiera turned to me with a flirty smile on her lips. "So now that it is just you and me, Mr. Kyle, what would you like to do?" Her voice dropped into a seductive range that normally would have had my blood boiling. "Maybe return that favor you still owe me?"

God. I knew what she meant by that. Hearing her say it should have had me climbing the walls, but my mind and my heart were somewhere else.

My eyes dropped to the floor as nerves crawled up my stomach. Was I strong enough to do this? "Actually...I have a favor to ask of you."

The earlier concern instantly reappeared on Kiera's face. "What is it?"

I leaned forward over my knees as I struggled with wanting to do this and *not* wanting to do this. How was it possible to feel both of those things so strongly? I ran a hand through my hair, peeking up at her as I partially confessed my desire. "I've been debating doing something. I wasn't going to do it, so I didn't even bother mentioning it, but the longer we sit here, the more it eats away at me, and I just feel like...I have to do it. I need to do it." Saying it out loud made my path even clearer, and I exhaled a slow breath as my body struggled to accept my decision. "But I can't do it alone. I need you." Because I fully expected this to tear me apart.

Kiera instantly grabbed my hand. "My answer is yes. Whatever the favor is, my answer is always yes. Whenever you need me, I'm there, Kellan...I'm always here for you."

Her words squeezed my heart, made my eyes burn with pain. In *one* statement she had shown me more love than they ever had. If I got through today, it would only be because of her.

An empathetic ache in her eyes, Kiera brushed some stray strands off my forehead and whispered, "What do you need to do?"

My throat instantly tightened. *Say goodbye to my parents.* I wanted to say the words, release them so they would stop having so much power over me, but I couldn't. I literally couldn't. I swallowed, waited, then told her in the only way that I could. Vaguely. "I need to visit someone." Just saying that much tore me open, and I could feel a breakdown trying to rise to the surface. I had to look away from her, focus on something else. My eyes locked on my guitar across the bus, and I started counting the strings.

Kiera kissed my shoulder. "Okay," she told me, and I could hear the encouragement in her voice. It gave me the strength to look back at her, and I gave her a sad smile as a thank you.

I tried not to think about what I was about to do as I called for a cab to pick us up, and I kept my mind as blank as possible as I waited for the taxi to arrive. Kiera didn't ask me any questions as we waited. She just stroked my hand, kissed my forehead... soothed me as a mother would soothe a troubled child. Well, as a good mother would. Mine never did. My mother hated it when I was upset, and she would order me to my room until I "got a hold of myself." Occasionally, I'd faked being in a bad mood, just so I'd be left alone. Of course, that often backfired since my dad loved making my bad moods worse.

But fuck, I wasn't supposed to be thinking about any of that.

It was almost a relief when the cab finally came. After Sienna had forced that last photo-op, I'd talked our bus driver into parking our bus so that the door was hidden from any loitering fans' view by the other bus. The taxi parked by the crack between the buses, so the odds of Kiera and me being spotted leaving were slim. I didn't want any part of today being exploited by the public. If ever I'd needed privacy, it was today.

I thanked Kiera for doing this for me as I helped her with her coat. Any time we went out together was a risk for her, and I was fully aware that my request wasn't as simple as it sounded.

She locked eyes with me; hers were a deep, sympathetic green today. "It's not a problem, Kellan. You're not ever a problem."

I nodded at her, then we headed out to the taxi. We snuck inside with zero fanfare, and I felt confident that no one knew we were leaving. My stomach churned when the driver asked me where we wanted to go. I was afraid my voice would falter as I said it, but I pulled from a lifetime of pretending and gave him the address like there was nothing special about our destination. "Saint Joseph's Cemetery in Gloucester Township, New Jersey."

The driver nodded and started pulling away. I could feel Kiera's curiosity beside me. Still feeling that well of courage that came from acting, I turned to her and quickly explained, while I still could. "It's where my parents are buried."

Her eyes widened with understanding, and she put a hand on my thigh in support. I immediately grabbed it and laced our fingers together. As I looked out over the passing landscape, Kiera asked me why my parents were buried here, and not in Seattle. Good question. Both of my parents were originally from the East Coast. They'd moved to the West Coast for work. Dad had come back alone when his last remaining family member, his mom, had died of a stroke. He'd stayed longer than necessary to handle things with her estate. That was the "family emergency" that had resulted in my conception. My mom's last remaining family member, my aunt, was the one who'd called me in Los Angeles to tell me they were dead. Mom and Aunt Margaret had been fairly close, but even still, Mom and Dad had left everything to me. Everything. That fact still shocked me. My aunt had blamed me for it, like I'd somehow manipulated them into doing that. She'd even tried, unsuccessfully, to contest their will. She'd brought them both back here out of spite, to prove that she loved them, and I didn't. Maybe she thought taking them away would hurt me, but it had actually been a relief.

With a shrug, I told Kiera the basic facts. "My aunt brought them here after the funeral. She said there was nothing left in Washington for them, so why bury them there. She buried them *here*, near where she and my mom grew up." And as far away from me as she could get them.

Kiera looked shocked and saddened by that, like she was just now realizing how alone I'd truly been. She asked if my aunt lived here, and my gaze snapped back to the window. "Don't know, don't care. We don't talk...never have." That was one bridge I was content to leave burned.

I knew Kiera had more questions, but she didn't ask them, and I was grateful for the silence.

As we drove, I spotted a flower shop. Before I even knew what I was doing, I told the driver, "Hey, man, can you stop here at the corner for a second?"

He nodded and pulled over. Before I could overthink it, I kissed Kiera on the cheek and told her I'd be right back. Head down, I hurried through the soft rain to get inside. The bell chimed when I opened the door, and an older woman turned and smiled widely at me. She didn't seem to recognize me, and I was thankful for the anonymity; I just couldn't deal with that kind of attention right now. I felt like my chest was about to rip open, and the only thing that was keeping me stitched together was not having to answer any questions.

Now that I was in the shop, with the fragrant scent of the flowers so thick in the air it was a little nauseating, I wasn't sure why I'd come. Wasn't my presence, just the act of being there, enough? But even as I thought it, I grabbed two bouquets of bright red roses and trudged to the counter. If I was going to say goodbye, then I was going to do it properly.

The woman at the counter rang me up with a bright smile on her face, like today was a joyous occasion. Like every day was. I drank in her happiness, letting it calm me, reassure me. Then I spotted a Sharpie on her counter. "Do you mind if I borrow that?" I asked her.

"Of course not, dear," she said, pushing it my way.

I gave her a small smile. "Can I also buy one white rose petal?"

Her brows bunched together in confusion. "One white rose?"

I shook my head. "Just a petal."

She shrugged, walked over to a display, and grabbed one for me. I rubbed the velvety softness for a second, then wrote, *I'm glad you're here* on it. "Thank you," I told the woman. Then I grabbed my purchased flowers and headed back to my wife.

Kiera's eyes were heavy with moisture when I got back inside the cab. Her gaze locked on the roses, and her face twisted with pain, like seeing them physically hurt her. I understood the feeling; they felt like a brand in my hand, burning all the way up my arm to deep inside my chest. Not feeling capable of words, I handed Kiera the white petal. She read it, quickly swiped her eyes, then gave me a tight nod and a heartbreakingly sad smile. The emotion on her face was getting to me, so I shifted my gaze to look out the window while Kiera clenched my hand, silently giving me her support.

The rain intensified as we drove into the cemetery; it was like the entire world was mourning with me. As the cab stopped beside a giant angel statue, I was suddenly struck by the size of this place. A sense of hopelessness filled me as I looked out the rain-streaked window. I only knew they were buried here. I had no idea where, and time was not on my side.

"Please wait for us," I told the driver. He nodded that he'd stay, pulling out a book to read while he waited.

Kiera and I got out of the cab, and despair filled me as I looked around the wet, dreary landscape. They could be anywhere. The rain was a brutal downpour now, and Kiera and I were both soaked within seconds. Part of me wanted to give up. Another part of me knew I'd never make it this far again. It was now or never, and I needed this weight off my chest.

Slicking back my hair, I confessed to Kiera, "I don't know where they are."

Her hand slid into mine, and she gave me a squeeze of reassurance. "We'll find them."

I looked at her, grateful for her support, grateful for her understanding, grateful for her *soul*. Inhaling a deep breath, I nodded in agreement. We'd try, it was all we could do. We separated so we could search for them more effectively, but it still felt like a long shot. We got through half of the cemetery with no luck, and shaking from the cold, we made our way to the other half. The much larger half.

Kiera didn't make one word of complaint as we searched, but I knew she had to be miserable and tired. I was. I was completely soaked through, rain running under my jacket. My jeans were saturated, and my hands were shaking as numbness set in. How much longer could we search before we physically couldn't do it anymore?

The melancholic air of this place wasn't helping my mood either. Everywhere I looked, I saw a life that had been cut away from someone else. I saw husbands and wives who'd died years apart from each other. I saw children who'd barely lived. I saw whole families ripped away by time. My spirit was already at the breaking point, and we still had a lot of the cemetery to cover. *This is impossible. We should just leave.*

And that was when I heard Kiera say my name.

I looked over to see her a few rows behind me. Her eyes were wide with surprise, and I knew she'd found them. My gaze drifted to the gravestone at her feet, and I suddenly felt like the entire world was contracting, focusing in on that one spot. A shiver ran through me, and I wasn't sure if it was from the cold, or from fear, regret...remorse. I inhaled a deep breath and forced myself to walk over to her. This was it. This was why I'd come.

My feet felt heavier with every step. Could they see me now? Did they know I was here? Were they laughing at me?

No. They were gone, and I was alone. Only that wasn't true. I wasn't alone, not anymore.

I could feel Kiera's eyes on me when I reached her side, but I couldn't tear my gaze away from my parents' graves, from their headstone. *John and Susan Kyle: Beloved Friends, Family, and Parents.* A vague memory reached out for me as I stared at the etched words. Of me, feeling numb as I'd talked to the funeral director, as I'd ordered weird shit that I'd never thought about having to order before—caskets, tombstones, flowers. I hadn't wanted to do any of it, had been content to shove my parents into a box in an unmarked grave, but even still, *I'd* chosen these words. I'd picked the sentiment that I wished was true, instead of carving the reality. Or was it true? They'd been loved by friends; Gavin was proof of that. And they'd been loved by their families —both of them had spoken fondly of their parents, and regardless of her hatred for me, Aunt Margaret had loved my mother. And they had been loved...by me. Stupidly, hopelessly, unrequitedly loved by me. After all, wasn't love the real reason I was here?

Feeling like my chest was cracking open, I squatted in front of their graves. My throat tightened as I ran my fingers over my mother's name, over my father's. *I loved you. Did you ever love me*? I searched my memories as I placed my hand on the grass, looking for something good, *anything* good. And there, buried deep in my mind, I found pockets of contentment. My mother's laugh when I said something funny. My father giving me an extra cookie after dinner, just because. My mother listening to me play guitar, a slight smile on her face. My father reluctantly but effectively teaching me how to drive. My mother rubbing my back in appreciation when I went to the store for her when she was sick. There were slivers of kindness in the cruelty of my past. I typically overlooked them because they were too rare to be truly meaningful, but still, they *were* there.

And remembering those times made the pain...so much worse. Sometimes hate was easier than love. I felt the tears rolling down my cheeks as I struggled to keep a hold of my emotions. Like Kiera sensed I was losing it, she tenderly touched my shoulder, focusing me, calming me. Feeling strengthened, I opened my eyes and placed a bouquet under my mother's name, then my father's. *I can't say I miss you, but I do miss what we could have been, if you'd only let us.*

Sitting back on my heels, I stared at their names and contemplated what to say to them. I knew that somewhere in their past they were not the same people who'd raised me. I'd changed them, hardened them. I knew it wasn't my fault, but I also knew they would have been very different without me. They might have even been happy. While I couldn't forgive them, I could acknowledge that I'd been the catalyst, an undeniable truth that had placed a wedge of hatred between them. A wedge that had cut into me at every opportunity.

"I'm sorry I wasn't what you wanted, what you needed," I said to them both. I shifted my gaze to Mom. "I'm sorry I ruined everything for you." My eyes recentered on Dad. "For both of you." A heavy breath escaped me as genuine remorse filled me. What would they have been without me? What could we have been together if John had been my biological father? I ached for that knowledge, for that dream, for that hope, and I couldn't help but wonder if they'd ached for it too. "I wish things had been different for us, but...wishing doesn't change anything. So, I just wanted to say goodbye...and—"

The words locked in my tight throat. Everything inside of me felt tight, on the verge of exploding, breaking into a thousand pieces that would never properly fit together again. A part of me wanted to hold onto the words, keep them locked inside me until the day I died, but I knew that was spite talking. Anger. Hatred. Those weren't things I wanted to keep holding on to, so I made myself tell them how I felt. How I really felt. "I love you both."

I felt both lighter and heavier when I stood. The rain was easing up, but I was still shaking, and I didn't think it was the cold that was making me vibrate. My eyes watered as I stared at my parents. Kiera wrapped her arms around me, silently comforting me. I held her tight and savored our connection; she was my life raft in this turbulent ocean of mixed feelings.

As I stared at the sodden flowers on their graves, I thought about how far I'd come since the last time I'd seen them. I was just a kid when I left home, barely of legal age. I'd been through so much since then—discovered who I was without them, learned who I *wanted* to be. There had been high-highs and really low-lows. I'd failed, I'd succeeded. I'd lived, I'd loved. Should I tell them that? Would they care about anything I'd done? Anything I'd accomplished? I honestly didn't know.

I knew Kiera wouldn't know either, but I needed to hear her

voice. Needed to hear an answer to an impossible question. "Do you think they would be proud of me? Even just a little?"

My voice failed on me as I said it, and I felt the child inside of me begging for someone to say yes. I thought Kiera might, just to appease that inner craving that she knew I had to be feeling. But instead, she told me something better, something *true*.

"I don't know...but *I* am so proud of you. For everything you've done, for what you just did."

She started crying after she said it, like she couldn't bear my pain anymore. Seeing the tears flowing down her cheeks was too much for me. I fought it, but I felt the torment rising to a point where my body just couldn't handle it anymore. My fingers went to my eyes right as the sob escaped me. The pain, the neglect, the rejection, the loneliness, it all crashed through me at once, overwhelming me. Kiera's hand went to the back of my head, urging me to her shoulder, to her shelter. I clung to her as the sobs relentlessly tore from me. I couldn't control it, I couldn't contain it, and I didn't want to. This was a pain I'd been fighting against my entire life, and fully giving into it, completely lowering all my walls, was surprisingly healing.

I let it all pour out of me, as harsh and vicious as the earlier rainstorm had been, and by the time there were no tears left inside me, the clouds had eased up as well, parting and clearing, so a little sunlight could finally peek through.

Feeling more at peace than I'd felt in a really long time, I rested my head against Kiera's and breathed in deep. When I could speak, I said, "I love you, Kiera...so much." I never would have made it through that without her.

She raised her chin, her cool lips finding mine. We softly kissed, and I felt the well that I'd just emptied being filled by her. Being overfilled. Because her love was a hundred times more potent than my lifetime of pain. And as our mouths moved together in the silence of this solemn place, I felt joy rekindling inside me.

Until I heard something odd. A familiar, repetitious click

that was wholly out of place here. Kiera and I broke apart at the same time, twisting toward the sound. There was a man with a camera standing at the edge of some trees, snapping photo after photo...of us. He didn't seem fazed at all that we'd caught him peeping; if anything, his movements became even more frantic, like he was giddy.

"You have got to be kidding me," I bit out. This place wasn't a trendy location where I expected photographers to be waiting. There was just no way he'd randomly come across me here. Had he followed us from the venue, and I just hadn't noticed? It really didn't matter how he'd gotten here; he'd been taking pictures of Kiera. Of me *kissing* Kiera. Fuck.

As angry as the intrusion made me, it seemed to push Kiera over the edge. She stormed his way with her fists clenched. "Have you no common decency!" she yelled. I took off after her while she kept screaming at the guy. "We are at a freaking cemetery! The man is clearly grieving! Show some goddamn respect!"

The man was only a few feet away now, grinning as he captured Kiera's anger. She made a move like she was going to rush him, and I grabbed her arm to stop her. Her shouting at him was one thing, her getting physical with him was another; the guy easily had a hundred pounds on her. And I'd beat the living shit out of him if he so much as laid a finger on her.

"No, don't—" I warned her.

The guy shifted his attention to me. Snapping pictures the entire time, he said, "You stepping out on Sienna? This your dirty little mistress, Kellan?"

I instantly saw red. Shifting Kiera behind me, I shoved a finger into his chest. "She is *not* my mistress! You watch your fucking mouth!"

The guy backed up, his camera still documenting the moment. "Sure looks like you're banging this bitch behind Sienna's back. Can't hide your little secret anymore. I got you, man! Gotcha red-handed! Your little slut is about to make headlines!"

I gave the guy a smirk. *If you think you're getting out of this unscathed after that comment, you're so fucking wrong. No one calls my wife a slut. No one.* I knew I was about to make things worse, but I didn't care. My fist clenched and swung in almost one movement. The asshole wasn't expecting it, and I knocked him right to the ground.

He landed hard on his hip, but it didn't even faze him. He grinned at me, scooped up his camera, and resumed taking pictures. "You just fucked up, man! I'm suing your ass for assault now!" There was blood dripping down his chin, but he looked like he'd just won the lottery. And maybe he had. Fuck.

Oh well. In for a penny, in for a pound, right? I lunged for him, fully intent on wiping that fucking smile off his face, but Kiera pulled me back. "Come on. He's not worth it, Kellan."

My eyes locked on hers. "He's got your picture." And unless we did something about that right now, Kiera would be exposed by morning. And in the worst possible way.

She sighed at me, and I saw defeat in her eyes. And determination. Shaking her head, she told me, "Then he's got my picture. It's not worth getting arrested over."

That was debatable, but I could tell Kiera really didn't want me to go down that path. And I had a feeling it would be an intense battle if I did try to force the issue. This guy wasn't giving up his camera for anything short of a concussion.

Hating that our cathartic moment was now tainted, I grudgingly let Kiera pull me away. The man had the audacity to laugh as we left. Furious and frustrated, I snapped, "You're scum, you know that, right?"

Shaking his head, the guy gave me a look of contempt, like he was the virtuous one here. "I'm not the one dicking around on the hottest girl in the world! What the hell are you thinking?"

Turning my back to him, I said under my breath, "I'm married to the hottest girl in the world, and I would never dick around on her, asshole."

Kiera smiled up at me, love mixed with unease in her eyes. Firmly wrapping an arm around me, since distance didn't matter anymore, she said, "Maybe it wasn't the smartest move...but I'm so glad you decked that guy."

In a show of unity and protection, I wrapped my arm around her too. Fuck him, fuck everyone. Looking back, I saw the creep was still taking our picture. Asshole. Clenching my jaw, I told Kiera, "Me too." I just wished it had changed the outcome because Kiera's anonymity would be gone after this. And that killed me.

With nothing left to hide, Kiera and I walked out of there locked together with our heads held high. There would be a firestorm of misplaced anger and incorrect assumptions after this, but there was no one else I'd rather have beside me in the chaos than Kiera. I just hoped that I could handle all the hurtful things people were going to say about her. Because hitting *everyone* probably wasn't a viable option.

Chapter 28

PERMANENT

I was fuming as we drove back to the venue, upset that Kiera's one wish in all this craziness—to maintain her privacy—had just been burned to ash. And I really wanted to know what the hell had just happened because there was no way that guy had found us by happenstance. Deep down in my gut, I had the horrible feeling that Sienna had something to do with it.

After the taxi dropped us off, I led Kiera to Sienna's bus instead of ours. I had to know for sure. Kiera gave me a questioning look, but she didn't pull away as I pounded on Sienna's door. One of her security guys opened it, examined us, then let us inside. I noticed Kiera taking in the luxuriousness of Sienna's place, and I had to admit, her bus *was* way nicer than ours, but I really didn't fucking care. If she'd messed with my wife, that was an uncrossable line with me.

Sienna brightened when she spotted us, like she was delighted to see us on board with her. Lounging on a leather couch, she said, "Kellan, Kiera, what a nice surprise." She glanced out the window like she was looking to see if anyone had witnessed my visit. That did not help my suspicions any. Or my anger. Was everything a game to her? "What can I help you with this fine afternoon?" she asked.

Kiera's hand still in mine, I stormed right up to her. "Did you set us up?" I immediately asked.

Sienna's bodyguards tensed, clearly not liking my aggressiveness, but Sienna just looked confused. It was either genuine or she was an outstanding actress. "What on Earth are you talking about? And did the two of you take a fully clothed shower? You're absolutely soaked."

She had her security get us towels while I told her what happened. She smirked after hearing my story. "Those little insects can be quite intrusive, can't they? Well, don't worry too much about hitting him. I'll have my people take care of it. Toss them enough money, and nine times out of ten the paparazzi won't seek legal damages."

That was definitely a weight off my shoulders, and I felt myself minutely relaxing, subconsciously starting to trust her thanks to her generous offer. But then I remembered that she might be the reason he was there in the first place...and she'd just skillfully avoided answering my question. Heat filling me again, I said, "You tip him off?"

She gave me an offended frown. "I had no idea where you went. How could I possibly give someone your location if I didn't know it?"

She made a really good point, one that made doubt start to eat at my anger, but even still, I just couldn't make myself 100 percent believe that she was completely innocent in all of this. Once again, I couldn't get an accurate read on her. "I never know if you're telling me the truth, or if you're feeding me bullshit," I snipped.

Sienna didn't like being called out, and her face got stormy as I tossed aside our towels and turned to leave. "I had nothing to do with this," she reiterated. "I'm not some mastermind out to sabotage your relationship. I just roll with whatever life gives me, and I suggest that the both of you learn to do the same."

Her advice had real merit to it, but still, my distrust of her wouldn't let me drop it. Turning back to her, I firmly and plainly stated my position on the matter. "If I find out you had anything to do with this, we're done. I will pack up my shit and walk away from this tour, and I don't give a fuck what Nick does to me. Let him sue me for breach of contract. I won't be played anymore."

Kiera and I went back to our bus to change before the show. The guys had returned from their excursions into the city, and everyone paused their conversations to look at us when we stepped inside. Griffin immediately returned his attention to Anna, but Matt and Evan eyed me with curiosity and concern. I was still struggling to rein in my anger, and I had to imagine that battle was reflected on my face.

Anna studied Kiera while Griffin jabbered in her ear. Brows furrowed, she said, "What's wrong?"

Kiera swallowed as she looked between Jenny, Rachel, and her sister. "We went out, and there was a guy...and he...he..."

Looping my arm around her, I spat out what she was having trouble saying. "The asshole took a picture of us." My gaze settled on Evan. "He took a picture of us *kissing*," I said with a raised eyebrow.

Evan paled, and his dark eyes widened. He knew what that meant, understood what the public was going to do to Kiera once that photo came out. Everyone started asking questions at once, most along the lines of *Did you get rid of the photo*? The girls swarmed Kiera, giving her physical comfort, while I ran a hand through my slicked-back hair. Panic was already welling inside me and hearing their questions was making it worse. "No, we couldn't get it back," I told them. "Not without knocking the guy out. I hit him...I wanted to kill him...but we had to let him go with it." And I already regretted that decision.

Kiera reached through her friends to put a hand on my arm. "It's not worth going to jail over."

I gave her a weary sigh. She might feel differently about that in the morning. Griffin scratched his head as he took in the concern swirling around him. "Okay, I'm definitely missing something. Who cares if he's got your picture?" he said to Kiera.

Kiera opened her mouth, but Anna answered him first. "The fans want Kellan with Sienna. They're going to be all over Kiera for this, and she wanted to stay out of the public eye." Her expression softened as she smirked at him. "I know this is hard for you to imagine, but some people don't want attention."

Griffin grinned and shook his head. "Yeah, that makes no sense to me." Turning to Kiera, he said, "Hey, if you want, I'll get a picture of Kell and me kissing? Then everyone will be talking about us, not you."

Matt started snickering, and Evan looked at him and grinned. Rolling my eyes at my friends' amusement, I frowned at Griffin. "No thanks. I've kissed you enough for one lifetime."

Griffin smirked at me. "No one could ever kiss me enough for any lifetime. My mouth is like a drug. One taste and you're addicted."

Just as I was about to tell him that was most definitely *not* true, Anna told the room, "He's not lying. My man has got some serious mouth skills. And his tongue, Jesus Christ—"

Kiera instantly slapped her hand over her sister's mouth. "Stop," she said. "Please, stop."

Anna giggled beneath Kiera's hand. Griffin smiled and nodded like Anna's praise had just confirmed everything he believed about himself. Everyone else grimaced; Matt and Rachel had such matching looks of disgust on their faces that a light laugh escaped me.

"We'll consider that an emergency-only backup plan," I told Griffin. He nodded, winked, and gave me finger guns. Yeah, there was no way in hell I was kissing Griffin. Again.

Things felt lighter after that, almost back to normal as Kiera and I relaxed with our friends before the show. But then Kiera decided to stay in the dressing room during our set, stay hidden as long as possible, and I remembered that nothing was normal anymore. And it bothered me. All I'd wanted was to protect her and make her happy, and I felt like I'd failed on both counts. I didn't know what to do anymore, except sit down and tell the world that they had it wrong. The only option left to me was to tell my truth and hope that people believed it.

So that was what I was going to do. First chance I got. And since they were going to know about Kiera soon anyway, I could be specific this time, and maybe that would make a difference. Maybe for once, people would *listen*.

When our set was over, Kiera was gone. I was concerned until I saw her text telling me that she'd gone back to the hotel with Anna. Then I was a little defeated. She wasn't obligated to watch me every time or anything, but I knew her bailing on the show had nothing to do with her being tired or her wanting to get some work done. She'd just wanted to get away from the drama for a moment. I really wished that I could join her, press pause on the chaos a little bit longer, but I still had a job to do, so I hung out with the guys until our encore with Sienna.

It was weird being up on stage with her, knowing what the crowd thought about us right now, knowing what they were going to think about us in the morning. Or think about me. That thought actually brightened me a little. Maybe they would shift all their anger toward me, and Kiera would be blameless, a victim of my charm. I could handle it, absorb their hate and judgement; I vastly preferred it to them hating Kiera. But by the way they were staring at me, screaming at me, crying over me...I didn't think that would happen. They'd put me on a pedestal, and they'd knock everyone else over before they touched me.

I was exhausted when the show was over, dead on my feet from the emotional day. In fact, I started to fall asleep in the car on the way to the hotel. Evan had to nudge me awake when we got there. I thanked him, then trudged up to my private room with Kiera. No matter what, at least I'd still get to fall asleep with her every night; one small positive in all this crap.

I'd grabbed Kiera's laptop from the bus, along with our bags, just in case she wanted to work in the morning. I set them near the closet, then softly closed the door. Our room was dark and quiet, peaceful, so I figured Kiera was sound asleep.

Careful not to wake her, I stepped into the bathroom to get ready for bed. When I turned on the bathroom light, I saw just how much of a mess I was. Circles under my eyes, lines of exhaustion on my face, my hair unusually limp and lifeless. It was like today had sucked the life right out of me. Even still, I was glad I'd gone to the cemetery. Glad I'd said goodbye. It felt like a weight had been lifted from my chest, like I could finally breathe.

Wanting to wash away the trauma, I took a quick shower, then dried off and slipped on a fresh pair of underwear. Just doing that much made me feel better. The heat from the shower cooled on me as I finished getting ready, though, and by the time I slipped under the covers with Kiera, I was fairly chilled.

Kiera stirred when she sensed me, and the warmth emanating from her body was an irresistible draw. I wrapped my arms and legs around her, pressing my chest against her back. "I'm cold," I whispered. "Warm me up."

I thought she might instinctually shy away from me trying to steal her heat, but she flipped around and pulled me into her body. She led my head into the crook of her neck, kissing my cheek as she shared everything she had with me. I groaned in contentment as my hungry skin quickly absorbed her generosity. "You're so warm…" I murmured. She was heaven. Absolute heaven.

Her hot hands ran up and down my back, and the fatigue in my body began to dissipate as she caressed me. I pressed my lips to her neck, sucking her heat into my mouth. Her body responded instantly, her hands clenching my back, her hips squirming against me. My heart pumped harder, and I began generating my own warmth as an urgent need rose inside me.

Kiera felt it too, and she started pressing against my body to intentionally rile me up. It worked. As my lips ran over her neck and my hands slid over her ass, I was wide awake and rock hard. I eased her to her back, positioned myself on top of her, then ran my lips across her throat to her ear. "I love it when you make me hot," I told her. I pressed my cock right where she needed it, and the most fantastic moan left her lips.

I needed her so much; I was throbbing. Kiera seemed just as desperate. Her lips were frantic against mine, her fingers clawing at my boxers like she would rip them apart if she could. The passion coming from her drove me absolutely crazy. I yanked off her shirt, then shoved her underwear down her legs, tossing them to the ground along with mine. My lips cherished her skin while my hands explored her body. Her moans made me wild, and after feeling how ready she was for me, I was certain I would explode if I didn't press inside her soon.

Breathing so hard that I was almost dizzy, I adjusted our position so I could take her. I'd just barely entered her when she grabbed the pillow under her head with both hands, and I noticed something that completely distracted me. My eyes had adjusted to the darkness, and I could just make out a bandage over her wrist. Was she hurt?

She didn't seem hurt. Eyes closed, voice breathy, she said some of my favorite words. "Yes, God, please...yes."

Damn. I desperately wanted to plunge inside her, but I had to know if she was okay first. And the type of bandage...it almost looked like...

I shifted to her side so I could think, so I could ask her. She groaned, the noise heavy with annoyance, then she kissed my chest and tossed her leg over my hip, ready to climb onto me if I didn't finish what I'd started. I grabbed her hands, my body both burning with need and aching with concern. "Kiera?" It was all I could get out.

Kiera ignored the question in my voice and shifted her hips around until I was pressing inside her again. God, she felt so good. I wanted to shove her onto me, take her, but I needed to know what had happened to her. I moved one of my hands to her hips, stopping her from pushing herself onto me. With my other hand, I stroked her bandage with my thumb. "What is this?" I could barely get the words out as an animalistic urge to satisfy the ache ate at my restraint.

Kiera pushed herself onto me, my one hand not enough to keep her desire at bay. "It's for you," she murmured, then she sank me all the way inside her.

And fuck, I wanted to stop caring. I wanted to ignore it and focus on the feeling of her clamped around me, but I couldn't quite let it go. I also couldn't ignore the fact that she felt so fucking good. I gave up on trying to hold her back and pulled her onto me, deeper, harder. "Oh God," I murmured, curiosity and heady desire alternating inside me. "What is it?"

Our fingers laced together as our bodies started moving with true purpose. The heat was rising inside me as Kiera cried out with every thrust. "Your name," she finally murmured.

I was struck with the realization of what she'd done just as I felt the buildup reaching that intense, glorious spot of pure bliss mixed with white-hot need. "What...why...?" I tried to focus, but my thoughts were scrambling. "Oh God...God, Kiera...you feel so good..." More. I needed more.

I abandoned words and thoughts and gave in to the pure pleasure. Finding Kiera's lips, I kissed her as our bodies strove for completion. Our pace quickened, and we both started shaking with need. I felt the edge approaching, and I was desperate to get there, to feel the euphoria as Kiera clenched around me. Kiera let out a long cry as she hit the wall, and I gave in to the tension, climaxing a second behind her. The bliss flowed through me, satisfying me, satisfying her.

Kiera collapsed in my arms, spent and happy. I rolled onto my back, pulling her onto my chest. I could feel her heart rapidly beating against my skin, could feel my own keeping pace with her. It was a long moment before I could recenter my thoughts, and even then, my sentence came out unfinished. "What...?"

She giggled as she pushed herself up to look at me. "What, what?" she asked, peace in her eyes.

I swallowed, trying to collect myself, then grabbed her hand with the bandaged wrist. "What did you do?"

She sat up, then turned on the bedside lamp. I flinched in the sudden brightness, then blinked so I could see if she had done what I suspected she'd done. And yes, as soon as I saw the bandage clearly, I knew...and I was floored. Because that was a tattoo bandage, and she'd said it was my name...

She pulled it back to reveal angry skin with bright black ink that did, in fact, spell out my name. Holy shit. *She etched my name on her*. She was claiming me as loudly as someone could claim me, and I really didn't know how to process that. My eyes instantly burned with the significance of it, and when I looked up at her, I was momentarily stunned speechless. My own father had refused to claim me. He'd grudgingly given me his last name, but he'd refused to put himself on my birth certificate, and she'd just...

My mind felt stuck, and all I could think to say was, "You know that's permanent, right?"

With a soft smile, she rebandaged her wrist. "You know *you're* permanent, right?" she countered.

I looked away from her as the old demons instantly reared their heads. It was surprisingly easy to beat them back, though, because Kiera showed me every day just how much she loved me. I looked back at her with an easy smile. "Yeah, I know."

She dropped her mouth in a show of sarcastic surprise. "You're not going to argue with me, call me absurd?"

Smartass. I cupped her cheek, amused and warmed. "Well, I still think you're absurd, but I'm not going to argue with you about spending the rest of your life with me."

She lifted her eyebrow, a pointed look on her face. "Because you know I'm head over heels in love with you."

"Yes," I told her. I truly did know that.

"And you know you're a good man," she added, testing my self-acceptance.

That one was harder, but...yes. I'd made mistakes, sure, but I wasn't horrible. I wasn't my father. "Yes," I told her.

Kiera paused, and I saw her weighing something in her mind. Then she said, "And you know you're worthy of being loved."

My lips instantly curled down, and again those demons rose up to try to choke me. Was I worth loving? I wasn't sure, and contemplating if I was worthy or not made me very uncomfortable. Maybe if I looked at it in reverse. Was I worthy of being hated? Loathed? No, I didn't think so. Denny was the person I'd hurt the most in my life, and he still cared about me. If he still cared, if even *he* couldn't hate me, then maybe I wasn't worthy of being reviled. And if I wasn't worthy of being hated, then the opposite must be true.

Looking up at Kiera, I told her, "Yes." She beamed at me like she was proud of me, and a surge of something that felt like healing went through me. And damn, it felt amazing.

Kiera leaned in to kiss me, but I pulled away from her; I wasn't the only one with demons. "And you know you're sexy, intriguing, adorable, and the only person I'll ever be in love with. You know you're the most beautiful girl I've ever seen."

She didn't even hesitate. Just grinned wider and said, "Yes, I do." And now I was beaming at her, pride flushing through every cell of my body. It almost felt better than the sex.

"Good," I proudly stated, then I gave her a soft kiss. "I love hearing you say I do." She let out an adorable giggle, warming me in all the right places. Damn...I could *not* wait to marry her. Smiling, I told her, "And I really love your tattoo." More than she could possibly imagine; it meant everything to me that she'd done that.

She cupped my cheeks, then fell back to the mattress, pulling me with her. "Good," she said. "Because I really love *you*."

She did. And there wasn't a single part of me that had any doubts about that. Not anymore.

. . .

When we woke up the next morning, things were perfect. For a few minutes. Both of our cell phones ringing at almost the same time was the first indication that things had irrevocably changed. *They know about Kiera, and they're all hating on her.* I didn't know how to handle that. She was my entire world, and I couldn't stomach the thought of all the cruel things that were probably being said about her *right now.* It made me want to scream. It made me want to punch something. It made me want to punch everything.

I definitely needed to avoid the Internet today. Luckily for me, that was exceedingly easy.

Kiera and I both ignored our phones, reluctant to leave the quiet solitude of our bed. We would be on the defensive the moment we got up, and just the thought exhausted me. After another long moment, I whispered to Kiera, "Why did we get cell phones again?" Honestly, the minute Kiera joined me on tour, I should have flushed mine. I supposed it wasn't too late. Would anyone really miss me if I permanently unplugged? Fuck. Matt would kill me. And I did enjoy talking to Hailey, Riley, and Gavin. *Fine. I'll keep the stupid thing.*

Kiera laughed at my question, then kissed my nose and told me we should be responsible and start talking to all our worried friends. A long sigh escaped me as I nodded. I moved to get up, but Kiera cupped my cheek, drawing my attention. Holding my gaze, she said, "Whatever happens from here on out, I want you to know that I don't regret anything. Being with you, loving you, experiencing this with you...it's all been worth it, and we'll get through this together. We're a team. It's us against the world."

Her words lightened the load on my heart, eased the tension in my body, and slightly lessened the urge to harm anyone who said a cross word about her. It meant so much to me that even though the thing she'd feared this entire time had finally happened, she had no remorse; she'd do it all over again to be with me.

Feeling better, I murmured, "Us against the world? That sounds like wonderful odds."

She giggled and gave me a soft kiss. "It's better than no odds at all."

Very true.

Kiera and I had become one with the bedsheets during the night and untangling ourselves was trickier than it seemed. It was like the bed didn't want us to go, and I kind of agreed with it. *I'd stay if I could, comfy mattress. Trust me.* We both laughed as we ripped ourselves free, and it was nice to have a second of fun before all the stress began.

Once I was out of bed, I pulled on my boxers and picked up my phone. Seeing who it was, I instantly answered it. "Gavin...hey."

"Are you okay?" he said, concern heavy in his voice. "Is Kiera okay? Have you seen what people are saying?"

I sighed and felt the weight of this nonsense returning to my shoulders. "I'm fine, Kiera's fine, and I really don't want to know what people are saying. It might make me lose my mind."

"There are photos of the two of you everywhere. Intimate photos. People are...angry." He paused to sigh. "Is there anything I can do?"

His offer and his concern touched me, and I found myself smiling, despite it all. "Just ignore it for now. I'm gonna fix this, I just have to figure out how."

There was a long pause on his end, and in the silence, I heard Kiera snort and say, "Yeah, fleeing back home and hiding out with my ex and his girlfriend—that wouldn't be awkward at all."

I caught her eye and smirked at her. She had to be talking to Denny. Nice of him to offer her a refuge from this chaos. A part of me wanted her to take him up on his offer, so she'd be safe, sheltered, but the rest of me couldn't imagine getting through this without her.

Gavin spoke and I returned my attention to him. "You

looked...very emotional in the photos. Are you sure everything is all right?"

Remembering where I'd been, and what I'd been doing, made my throat close up. I swallowed a couple of times to relieve the pressure, then told him, "I was...I visited my parents' graves. I was...saying goodbye."

He was silent again for a moment, and I vaguely heard Kiera greeting her father. God, Martin was probably so pissed at me for letting Kiera get exposed like that. Just as I was debating calling him later, Gavin quietly said, "That must have been extremely difficult for you. I'm sorry I wasn't there."

My gaze drifted to the floor as his words filled me with warmth. "It was. But it was good too. I think I needed to do that." And now I kind of wished Gavin had been there too. His presence would have been calming. A reminder that I did have a loving parent in my life now. And damn if that still didn't feel a little weird.

"My offer to come stay here with me still stands. If you ever need a moment away from that life, if it ever gets to be too much for Kiera and she wants to come here to rest up...my door is open to both of you. Anytime."

Jesus. My throat filled with emotion again, and I nodded, even though I knew he couldn't see me. "Thank you. That means...so much to me." *It means everything to me.*

We talked a little longer before disconnecting, and I could tell Gavin was genuinely afraid for me, for Kiera, and that really made me wonder just how vicious the fans were being. Kiera was still talking to Martin, but she'd grabbed her laptop and was studying something at the same time. I saw photos of us splashed on her screen, and I instantly averted my eyes. Just seeing it pissed me off. That guy had no right to do that. I wished there was some way to get the photos taken down, but I already knew there wasn't. Nothing ever completely disappeared from the Internet. Even I knew that.

Someone softly knocked on our hotel room door, and I

walked over and opened it. Jenny and Rachel were standing there, concern etched deep on their faces. "Hey," Jenny said. She glanced at Kiera on her computer. "I take it you guys have seen what's happening?"

Exhaling wearily, I stepped aside so they could enter. "Kiera has. I refuse to look. I don't want to know what people are saying. She's my *wife*," I bit out.

Jenny put a hand on my arm, sympathy in her sky-blue eyes. It was only then that I remembered I was still just in my boxers. Oh well. It wasn't like they both hadn't seen them before.

Kiera finally got off the phone with Martin, and Jenny walked over to give her a hug. Jenny told her that she and Rachel were just about to leave for the airport, then she told Kiera that she hated what the media was saying about her. Just hearing her say that boiled my blood. There was a trace amount of curiosity in me, a desire to know how deep the vitriol went, but I knew it was better if I didn't know a thing.

My phone rang again as the girls were saying their goodbyes. The screen showed my sister's name, and I weakly smiled. "Hey," I said in answer.

"Oh my God, do you know what's happening today? I have been ranting at people all morning! I'm about to lose my shit. People suck!"

Her comment made me laugh. "I haven't seen it for myself, but I know about the photos. You don't have to engage them, Hailey."

"Uh, yeah, I do. You're my brother, and I will defend you until the day I die. And the shit they're saying about Kiera—"

"Don't tell me," I quickly interrupted, running a hand through my hair. "I'll start ranting with you if you tell me, and I don't think that's the best way to handle this."

She softly sighed. "I'm so sorry, Kellan. I know Kiera didn't want the spotlight. I know you wanted to protect her. I know everything they're saying is a lie. And I'm just..." She paused, and her voice was rough with emotion when she continued. "I'm scared for Kiera. They hate her so much. I'm scared they're going to...lynch her or something."

The emotion in her voice made a wash of fear go through me. I beat it back, but it was surprisingly difficult. "Don't worry. I would never let *anyone* touch a hair on her head. She's safe here with me."

"All right, but...don't let her out of your sight, Kellan. Not until this blows over. I'm serious...it's bad."

"I won't," I assured her. "But honestly, nobody is going to take it that far. It's just people blustering online. It won't be like that in person. People are more respectful in person."

She sighed. "I want to believe that, I really do, but I don't know...people are crazy. Especially when it comes to you." She groaned. "My friends are driving me nuts."

I frowned. "Don't they already know about Kiera?"

She made a disgruntled sound. "Oh yeah, they're not mad for the same reason that everyone else is mad. They're mad that you're in a committed relationship because, and this is a direct quote, 'How will we ever have a chance if he's off the market?' Can you believe that they actually want me to break you two up?"

I had to laugh at that. "At least they don't hate Kiera. Today, I'm calling that a win."

She laughed, then sighed. "I love you both. Stay safe, okay?"

I assured her I would try, then hung up the phone. Looking around, I saw that Jenny and Rachel were gone. "The girls leave?" I asked Kiera.

Looking forlorn, she said, "Yeah."

Lifting my phone, I told her about the calls from Gavin and Hailey, their mutual concern. Kiera wrapped her arms around my neck and told me we'd get everything sorted out. Then she reminded me that I had shit to do today, a private performance that had completely slipped my mind.

"God, I'd forgotten all about that," I told her. "I was hoping to sit down with someone this afternoon, make a formal statement about that picture, but I'm not going to have time." And that really pissed me off. There just wasn't enough time. A fact that was further proved by both of our cell phones going off and Tory pounding on the door, telling me I had ten minutes. Fuck my life.

Chapter 29

A LITTLE MIRACLE

When the private performance was over, the car took us back to the hotel so we could pick up Kiera, Anna, and our things, and then it took us to the venue. The group for the private performance had been all right: nobody had asked me anything, made any comments, or yelled anything derogatory. They'd given me hope that maybe things wouldn't be so bad for Kiera. But then we stepped out of the car at the venue, and the vibe was the complete opposite. The crowd clustered around the fence was full of guys with cameras, and it was almost like they knew Kiera was with me; they immediately started taking pictures the second the car door opened.

Kiera didn't want to hide anymore, so she held my hand, and we walked inside together. Seeing the two of us as a unit drove the photographers into a frenzy. It also angered the handful of fans in the group, and they yelled things that made a vengeful sort of adrenaline surge through my body. Hearing them made me want to turn around and give them a piece of my mind. I knew I couldn't, I knew it would only make things worse, but man, it was difficult to ignore words like *whore, slut, bitch*. I clenched Kiera's hand tighter and tighter to stop myself from assaulting somebody.

Kiera stayed in the dressing room when it was time for the meet-and-greet. I didn't blame her at all, in fact, I was glad she wanted to stay somewhere safe and quiet. I needed to be professional and respectful with my fans. After all, they were the reason I was able to do what I loved for a living. But Kiera was my entire world, and if it came down to respecting them or protecting her, well, it wasn't even close. I'd burn it all to the ground for her. But I really hoped it didn't come to that, and I was sure, once I had a chance to explain things to the fans, they'd let her in and leave her alone. Fuck, I hoped so.

When I stepped into the room for the meet-and-greet, I braced myself for a cold or lukewarm reception. I thought I might hear someone call *me* a whore or something, but no one did. All I got from the fans was screaming, giggling, jumping up and down...the normal reaction. It floored me that no one was mad at me for what they thought was infidelity. But maybe it was just the rush of being in the same room as me. Maybe I was being ripped apart online just as much as Kiera. I honestly didn't know.

Sienna and I ended up standing next to each other. We usually did, but for once, it didn't bother me. If Sienna and I seemed cordial, unruffled, then maybe the fans would connect the dots. But Sienna ignored me the entire time. She wouldn't even look in my direction, and that reaction sent a wave of tension into the crowd. When she discreetly wiped her eyes—like she was fucking crying over me—I just about lost my shit.

I was three seconds away from forcing her to look at me so I could tell her to knock it off...when I noticed Kiera run into the room. My heart dropped to the floor as I met eyes with her. What the hell was she doing? Or more accurately, what the hell was wrong? Because she wouldn't come in here unless she absolutely had to.

I tried to move forward, to go over to her, but I was stuck behind a wall of people. Kiera wasn't angling for me, though. She was cutting through the lines toward Griffin. Griffin. Shit...this had to be about Anna then. Fuck, something was wrong with

Anna. That would explain why Kiera was as pale as a ghost, why she was being aggressive with the fans who wouldn't let her through. By the looks on the fans' faces, it was clear she'd been recognized, and my heart surged with worry.

Powerless to help, I watched in frustration as the crowd around Kiera reacted poorly to her attempt to squeeze through them; they started pushing back. I again tried to step forward, but the bodies blocking me weren't giving way. Things around Kiera turned rough, and pure panic sliced through me. Then a girl with a bright pink fauxhawk slapped Kiera, and suddenly, I wasn't in a room with fans anymore. Everyone in here was a potential threat to my wife, and I needed to get her out.

"Hey!" I shouted at the pink-haired girl, then I shoved in earnest. Some of the fans squeaked and stepped back. One almost fell down, so I stopped pushing. "I need through," I told them.

Sienna put a hand on my arm. "What's going on?" she asked. She scanned the crowd, and I couldn't help but note that any sign of sadness was gone from her expression. She only looked mildly alarmed now.

"I don't know," I told her, then I sought out Kiera again. She'd made it to Griffin and was explaining something to him. Whatever she was saying, he was stunned by it. He looked toward the exit. The fans who had been waiting in organized lines were now a disorganized mob. Tory was attempting to regain control, but there was a frenzied feeling in the air. I called out Kiera's name, but she didn't respond—her entire focus was on Griffin. She pulled on his arm, then the two of them started moving.

Griffin barreled his way through the crowd, shouting, "Get the fuck out of my way!" Freaked-out fans let him pass, and he pulled Kiera with him.

When they got close enough, Kiera looked at me and yelled, "Anna! Hospital!"

My jaw dropped as I suddenly understood. Anna was in labor. Holy shit. I instantly turned to Sienna; they were going to need help getting Anna to the hospital quickly and quietly.

Sienna could easily get one of the label's cars for them; we were only allowed to use them for official tour business.

"Anna's in labor," I told her. "Can you call a car for her?" Sienna's dark eyes briefly widened, then she nodded and pulled out her phone. As she made the call, the crowd suddenly surged forward, pressing us against the wall. The girls directly pressing against me were a mixture of pleased and petrified; they were being squished too. Shit, this was how people in crowds suffocated. In fact, I couldn't inhale deeply enough, and I was starting to feel lightheaded. I also couldn't lift my arms to push people back. I couldn't do a damn thing.

Right as panic was really starting to kick in, people were suddenly yanked off me. I looked up to see one of Sienna's bodyguards creating a bubble of protection around me; the other bodyguard was already hurrying Sienna out of the room. "Thank you," I told the wall of solid muscle.

He gave me a stiff nod, then indicated for me to get into the hallway. I hustled out of the room, glancing back to check on Matt and Evan. They were in the corner of the room now, behind the mass of fans, but not being bothered by them. Sienna's bodyguard was already working on reaching them, and I wondered if Sienna had asked him to do that since technically, none of us were under his protection. It made me both grateful and irritated because she was a major reason for the escalation in the first place. If she'd just fucking say something, all of this chaos would go away.

But talking to her about it had proven to be a waste of time. Conversations with Sienna were always so circular. It was maddening to never get the response I wanted from her—the response I *needed*. She was both the helpful ally supporting me in my skyrocketing career and the roadblock I could never get around in my personal life. A blessing and a curse.

Matt and Evan joined me a few moments later in a quieter spot up the hallway; security from the venue had tightened around the meet-and-greet room, and for the moment, none of the fans were being allowed to leave. The members of Holeshot were the last people to exit the fray.

Matt's eyes were wide as he looked back at the chaotic room. "Holy shit, that was nuts." His eyes went even wider. "Holy shit, Kiera said Anna's in labor." His face went pale white. "Holy shit, Griffin left with her, didn't he? We don't have a bassist!"

None of us knew the answer to that, so Matt ran to the dressing room; Evan and I hurried after him. Once he saw it was empty, Matt started combing his fingers through his short, spikey hair. "Shit, shit, shit! What do we do? What the fuck do we do?"

Evan put his hands on Matt's shoulders. "Calm down. We planned for this, remember? David has been learning our songs, he's going to fill in."

Matt slowly nodded, like he was just now remembering that. "We were supposed to have more time. She's not due for another week. David's not ready."

I almost smirked at Matt for thinking he could schedule when Anna would give birth, but none of this was funny, and Matt did have a legitimate concern. David *had* been learning the songs during his free time, but we hadn't all played together yet, and learning a song and performing it with a group were two very different things.

Evan lightly shook Matt. "He *is* ready, and he can do this. We'll have an emergency practice right now. Will that make you feel better?"

Matt visibly relaxed. "Yes, yeah, let's do that. Kell?" he said, turning to me, a lingering panic in his voice.

I nodded, then held up a hand. "Just let me call Kiera first." Matt gave me a *Seriously?* face, and I made myself not scowl at him; he was just stressed. "I want to make sure *everyone is okay*," I told him, stressing the words. He blinked, like he'd just remembered what had caused our D-Bag deficiency, then he nodded and let me do what I needed to do.

Grabbing my phone, I called Kiera. She answered right away. "Hey, you're okay," she said, gratefulness in her voice.

A sigh of both weariness and relief left me. "I was going to say the same thing. I can't believe that bitch hit you." I kind of wanted to wade back into that chaos just to find the woman who'd smacked Kiera. But that was definitely a bad idea.

"I'm fine," she firmly told me, like she knew I needed to be reassured and redirected.

Letting it go, I asked her, "How's Anna?"

Kiera hesitated before saying, "She's...okay."

I had to imagine Anna was in a lot of pain. And I also wondered how Griffin was holding up. He wasn't exactly the most comforting person, but then again, he had his moments. "I wish I could be there with you, but Matt's freaking out about the show." I told her about our plan to have David fill in, how we were cramming in an emergency practice session, then told her I'd skip the encore and see her after our set. Surely, Sienna would understand if we missed it *one* time. And if she didn't, well, I wasn't too concerned with that at the moment. My family needed me.

Kiera told me she'd see me then and wished me good luck. With a dose of dry humor in my voice, I returned the sentiment. I just had to deal with Matt, Sienna, and disappointing the fans. Kiera had to deal with Griffin.

When I disconnected the call, Matt and Evan were both staring at me. "How is she?" Matt asked, concern on his face.

Knowing he meant Anna, I smiled and said, "She's fine. She'll be fine."

Matt nodded, then grabbed my arm and pulled. "We need to find David."

I sighed, nodded, then let myself be dragged away.

Practice went smoothly. Our set went smoothly. David was a professional, and talented to boot, so stepping in for Griffin wasn't as much of a problem as Matt had feared. I decided to wait and tell Sienna that we weren't sticking around for the encore until after our set, mainly because I didn't want to argue with her. I just wanted to tell her, then leave. She was in the staging area when we came down from the stage, and I walked over to her to deliver the bad news.

She smiled brightly when she saw me. "How is Anna doing, love? I haven't heard any newborns crying, so I'm assuming the car arrived on time?"

I mentally cringed. I probably should have thanked her for that already. "Yeah, Kiera texted me; they made it to the hospital. Anna and the baby are fine. Thank you for your help." Without that car, they probably wouldn't have made it, and Anna would have given birth waiting for the cab. Everyone was relieved that she'd made it on time, and that was all thanks to Sienna.

Her grin grew even brighter. "Of course. Anything I can do to help."

I instantly wanted to tell her exactly what she could do to truly help us...but now wasn't the time for that conversation. "I'm glad you said that," I told her. "Because the guys and I are leaving for the hospital. We won't be back for the encore. I just wanted to let you know."

Her smile instantly vanished. "What?"

I shrugged and smiled. "Thank you for helping us with this. We realize it isn't the most ideal situation, but I'm sure if you explain it to the fans, they'll understand." Leaning in, I couldn't help but add, "They go along with everything you say, after all."

She blinked and pulled back, and for a second, I saw uncertainty on her face. It was quickly replaced by annoyance, then completely erased by cool composure. "Of course. Do what you need to do, love." I started to leave, and she tossed out, "Give Anna and the baby my best. I'll have some things sent to the hospital for them. They rushed out of here so quickly that I doubt they remembered to grab everything."

Stopping in my tracks, I looked back at her in stunned confusion. "Thank you. That's very generous."

She shrugged. "It's what I do for my friends." She winked, then turned away to get ready for her set.

I watched her for a moment as my mood toward her spun. It

would be so much easier to dislike her if she'd stop doing really nice things for us. I opened my mouth, wanting to take her moment of kindness as an opportunity to come up with a real solution to my problem with Kiera and the media, but Matt clapped me on the shoulder before I could start the conversation.

"Ready, Kell?"

There was a relaxed eagerness in Matt's eyes; he was relieved our set had gone well, and he couldn't wait to meet his newest relative. I let my thought of begging Sienna for help go and gave him a smile. "Yeah." I looked down at my shirt, damp with sweat. "Maybe we should change first, though."

Matt agreed with a laugh, and we all took a moment to clean up before heading to the hospital. It was pretty late when we got there, and I worried that they wouldn't let us visit. But then I noticed the nurses looking at me, saw their eyes widen in recognition. I hated to take advantage of my pseudo-celebrity status, but I had people that I really needed to find.

"Hi," I said, leaning against the counter, soft smile on my face. "I was wondering if you could help me?"

One of the nurses giggled, then coughed to stop herself. "Of course. What can we do for you?"

I heard one of the girls in the back quietly say, "Need a bed?" The nurse beside her softly snorted, but I ignored them. "I'm looking for Anna Hancock. She just had a baby."

"Ah, yes. Down this hallway, room 515," the first nurse said. Then her eyes brightened. "Would you like me to show you the way?"

I heard Evan snigger behind me. Ignoring him, I told the nurse, "That's all right. We can find it. Thank you."

As I walked away with Evan and Matt, I swear to God, I heard a collective sigh coming from the nurses' station. Matt said something to Evan, but they were both far enough in front of me that I couldn't hear him. I just saw Evan nod and laugh, and I was positive they were making fun of me. Jackasses.

That was when someone rushed up behind me and pinched

my ass. I spun around, fully expecting to see one of the nurses assaulting me, but to my delight, it was Kiera. My heart was still hammering in my chest from the surprise, and Kiera's eyes danced with mischievous glee. "Hey, stranger," she said. "Come here often?"

Willing my body to calm down, I smiled at her. "Not if I can help it." Hospitals were my least favorite place on Earth.

Kiera looked like she was containing a secret as she showed us Anna's room. I couldn't even begin to imagine what she wasn't telling us. Maybe Anna had twins? Matt was the first one to rush through the door, and by the time I walked in, Griffin was show-casing his son to Matt. Only...he wasn't calling the baby a boy.

"She's totally got my nose, right?"

Matt's jaw dropped as he examined his newest family member. "You had a girl?" he asked. I looked over at Kiera for confirmation, and she nodded and smiled at me. Damn. Anna had been right all along. We never should have doubted her.

We all congratulated the new parents, and I had to laugh at the look on Griffin's face. By the pride in his eyes, you'd think he'd chiseled his daughter out of clay, then magically made her come to life, all by himself. Anna watched his reaction with amusement in her eyes. And tears. And I had to admit, as I watched Griffin pass his child to Matt, I was nearly moved to tears myself. It overjoyed me to see that there was one thing in this world that Griffin actually took seriously, for there was no mistaking the love and adoration on his face as he stared at his daughter. And the reluctance as he handed her over.

"So...Myrtle?" Matt said, gently rocking her. He tried to hide his grimace, but he wasn't all that successful.

Anna snorted. "No. That was never happening. We named her Gibson."

Matt let out a long noise of relief. "Oh, thank God." He glared at Griffin. "What were you thinking? Even Grandma Myrtle hated the name Myrtle."

Griffin shrugged, then indicated for Matt to pass her along.

Evan took her next, and a really weird feeling started building inside me. She was so tiny and looked more fragile than anything I'd ever seen in my entire life. I didn't typically have butterfingers, but I could easily imagine my fingers slipping, or not holding her in the right spot to protect her, or some other catastrophe that would result in her being permanently damaged. Fuck. I didn't want to permanently damage a baby.

Evan held her for a long moment, then looked over at me with a raised eyebrow. Fuck, I was already sweating. That wasn't going to help anything. Wiping my clammy palms on my jeans, I quietly said to Kiera, "I'm so nervous right now. What if I drop her?"

Rubbing my shoulder, Kiera whispered in my ear, "Don't worry, you're good with women."

Smirking, I rolled my eyes at her. Then I sucked it up, said a quick prayer, and took the baby from Evan. And damn...I forgot all about the possibility of dropping her once she was in my arms. She fit so perfectly cradled against me, and I'd never felt anything so...natural. I couldn't stop smiling at this beautiful, tiny little child in my arms. Everything about her was perfect. The pudgy cheeks, the tiny fingers clutching the blanket she was wrapped in, the cute little quirk her mouth did, like she was trying to smile, the way her blue-gray eyes ceaselessly stared at me, like she was absorbing every little thing about me. It filled me with an ache I'd never had before, and it was easy to picture my own child looking back at me like this one day. God, I wanted that so much.

I gently stroked her cheek, and her skin was so soft that it almost didn't feel real. And she had this smell to her that was so oddly appealing. Mystified, I said to Kiera, "She smells good. Why does she smell so good?"

Kiera shrugged in answer, but there were tears in her eyes and a soft smile on her face, and I wondered if she was also picturing our future, when the baby in my arms would be equal parts her and me. I hoped so because I couldn't stop thinking about it. We'd talked about children before, but we'd never discussed *when* we'd have them. I supposed we should handle getting legally married first, then broach that topic, although if she wanted to say *screw it* and have a baby now, I'd happily give her one. I was ready whenever she was.

I held Gibson far longer than the others, swaying her, making weird faces at her, rubbing her nose and watching her try to suck on it. Now that I had her, I was really reluctant to let her go. People were taking pictures while I held her, but I was mostly oblivious to it. I vaguely heard Matt ask Griffin if he'd called his parents yet. Griffin mentioned something about visiting them in L.A. when the tour was over. Then Matt said something that snagged my attention.

"The tour is moving on tonight. What are the two of you going to do?"

I looked up to see Griffin look at Anna with anguish in his eyes. I'd never seen him make that face before, and it punched me right in the gut. "We have to be on the bus when it leaves. I have to go with them."

Anna had tears in her eyes as she nodded. "I know."

Just as I was wishing there was something I could do for them, I heard Kiera say, "I'll stay here with you, Anna." My eyes snapped to hers. She gave me a pained smile, then turned her attention to her sister. "I'm sure you'll be discharged tomorrow if everything looks good. Then I'll take you home...to Mom and Dad. You can stay there and rest up until the wedding."

My heart sank as I absorbed Kiera's plan. I wanted to argue, but it made too much sense. It was the best thing for Anna, one airplane ride with an infant instead of multiple, and it might be the best thing for Kiera too, a chance to take a break from all this craziness. Maybe when she took Anna home, she should stay there with her. At least with her parents, she'd be safe. Because I really couldn't handle someone slapping her again.

Kiera was avoiding looking at me, like she didn't want to see if there was hurt on my face. Anna bowed her head, not happy, but realizing it was probably for the best. Matt and Evan looked equally glum, and it struck me then, that nobody wanted Anna to leave. We all knew that was going to be the outcome, though. What other choice was there?

Surprisingly, Griffin was the one who came up with an alternate plan. "No, I don't think so." He walked over and took Gibson from me, and I had to fight the urge to resist him. Holding her was really comforting, but she wasn't mine. She was his. And he didn't want to leave her. Eyes glued on Anna, he said, "I don't want you to go. I want you to stay on the bus with me." His eyes were hard when he focused them on Kiera. "After they let her go, you bring her to me."

Kiera's eyes widened in shock, and I felt a similar sensation run through me. "You want a newborn on a tour bus with you?"

Griffin shrugged like he didn't see anything wrong with that. "Sure. Why not?"

Anna bit her lip, staring at Gibson with apprehension, like one wrong choice might completely destroy her daughter's life. "I don't know, Griff. It seems unsanitary."

With a snort, Griffin said, "I'm probably the dirtiest thing on the bus, and you sleep with me every night."

Kiera started giggling, and amused, I nudged her with my elbow and shook my head at her.

Anna still seemed unsure, and it was an odd expression to see on her. She usually leapt first and thought about the consequences later, if at all. But everything had changed now that her daughter was the one who might suffer. "What do you think, Kiera?" she asked.

Griffin instantly glared at Kiera, and I had a bad feeling about this. If Kiera didn't agree with him, I wasn't sure what he would do. But I could tell from the way Kiera was studying Gibson that whatever she said would be for *her* benefit, and I would back her up, 100 percent.

"I think in most cases, having a baby on a bus, living the life we live, is absolutely insane." Griffin instantly started objecting, but Kiera held up her hand to stop him. "But in this particular case, I think it works." She smiled at Anna. "Your baby was never going to have a typical childhood, and I can't think of anywhere else that she could possibly be loved more than on that bus." She shrugged. "Besides, didn't the nurse say they mainly sleep, eat, and poop for the first few months anyway?"

Griffin nodded like it was settled, then he looked over at Matt, Evan, and me, like he just then remembered that we existed and might have an opinion on the matter. "You guys...cool with that?"

Smiling, I wrapped my arms around Kiera and swiftly kissed her neck. "I think it sounds great," I told him.

Evan nodded, not in the least worried about it. Matt smirked at his cousin. "Loud crying coming from your room at all hours of the day and night?" He paused to look at Evan and me. "I think we're already used to that."

We all laughed at that, but then I remembered that we shared our bus. Frowning at Matt, I said, "We'll have to have a talk with Holeshot."

He nodded at me. "Deacon is pretty easygoing. I'm sure he'll be fine with it."

Kiera twisted to look up at me. "They can always hop on Sienna's bus. Didn't she say she was tired of riding alone?"

That made me burst out laughing. "That is an excellent idea."

Griffin glared at me with an intensity I'd never seen before. "Dude, keep it down. You freaked out my daughter."

I smiled at the man who'd finally learned what the word "responsible" meant. "Sorry." Then I made a whipping sound because the hypocritical fucker deserved to hear it. He rolled his eyes at me, then smiled down at his daughter, and I already knew she had him completely wrapped around her finger. Good.

We stayed as long as we could, but inevitably, we had to rejoin the show. After saying our goodbyes to Anna and Gibson, we moved into the hallway so Griffin could say his goodbyes in private. I already knew I was going to suffer while Kiera was gone, so I couldn't even begin to imagine how Griffin was feeling right now.

Squeezing Kiera, I said, "I'm going to miss you."

She put her chin on my chest and peeked up at me. "I'm going to miss you too, but you're only going to East Rutherford. That's not far."

"Feels far," I told her, especially since I had no idea where that was. Looking back at Anna's door, I asked Kiera if she thought Griffin would be a good father. Her answer matched my gut feeling: that he was going to be surprisingly great at it. I turned back to her and asked the question I was really curious about. "Do you think *I* would be a good father...one day?"

Kiera tightened her arms around my neck and beamed at me. "I know you will be," she said, not a trace of doubt in her voice.

It warmed me that she felt that way, that she still wanted that future for us. That it *was* going to be our future. I couldn't wait.

Griffin emerged from Anna's room a few minutes later. His pale eyes were red and watery, and he was trying to wipe them dry as subtly as he could. I stared at him, shocked, because I'd never seen him grieve before, and that was exactly how he looked—like he was mourning. He scowled at us gaping at him, then said, "What?" and moodily started walking down the hallway.

Matt and Evan hurried to catch up to him. Evan tossed an arm over him while Matt playfully punched him in the shoulder. I knew I had to join them, but all of a sudden, I felt like I was grieving too. There wasn't a single part of me that wanted to leave Kiera behind. But like Griffin, I had to. Turning back to her with a sigh, I said, "Guess I'm off to work. I'll see you soon. Please be careful."

She gave me a soft, unworried kiss. "I'm always careful. I love you."

"I love you too." Then I made myself turn around and leave.

I caught up to the guys by the elevators. Griffin still looked distraught. "This doesn't feel right," he said. "I shouldn't be leaving right now. I should stay." He nodded like he'd decided something, then he stepped forward.

Matt grabbed his elbow. "You can't. We've got that thing at that high school tomorrow, and David's got his own stuff to worry about. He can't cover for you. You *have* to come with us." Face sympathetic, he added, "I'm sorry."

Griffin studied him for a long time, and I truly thought he was going to say *fuck it* and stay anyway, but when the doors chimed open, he followed us inside the elevator. He closed his eyes when the doors closed, and his entire face contracted with pain. "This sucks," he said. "This sucks so fucking much."

I put a hand on his shoulder. "Kiera will get her back to you. Both of them. It's going to be okay."

He opened his eyes and looked at me, and I was taken aback by the depth of pain in his expression. I never would have guessed he had the emotional maturity to feel agony, but I was dead wrong. "You promise?" he whispered.

I gave him a firm, solid nod. "I promise." He inhaled a deep breath, relaxing some.

He was quiet as we made our way to the front doors. Looking up, I spotted something outside and stopped. The guys stopped with me, looking confused. "We can't go that way," I told them. "Look, there's a crowd of fans forming out there."

Matt scanned the loitering people. "How do you know they're fans?"

I sighed. "The T-shirts." I could just make out the band's name on some, and others were sporting the godawful Kell-Sex moniker.

Matt instantly saw what I'd seen. "Ah. Yeah. The cab I called is waiting right behind them. I'll call again, have the driver move around to the emergency room doors. They won't see us over there."

I nodded at his plan, then started to worry. Leaving Kiera behind when I thought nobody knew she was here had been hard enough. Leaving her behind when I knew for a fact that fans were hovering outside was...more than I could bear.

Evan must have seen the fear on my face. Leaning close, so Griffin wouldn't hear, he said, "They're not going to do anything to her when she's got a newborn baby with her. She'll be okay."

Swallowing a hard knot in my throat, I prayed he was right. Even still, the second we were inside the cab, I called the hospital to let them know to step up their security, and then I called Kiera to let her know to be careful when she left tomorrow. She didn't seem as worried about it as I was, and I had a hard time sleeping when I got back to the bus. No, an impossible time. I just kept hearing Hailey telling me to never leave her alone, and my promise to her that I never would. But I had. And it disturbed me all night long.

I needed to fix this shit. Now.

Chapter 30

WINNING AND LOSING

Finding time to fix anything the next day was virtually impossible. Matt was right about the high school thing. We were doing a mini concert with a lengthy, drawn-out meet-and-greet for a school that won a contest to see us. I wasn't about to complain about it, though, since how they'd won was by donating the most food to their local food bank. They deserved every minute of time we could give them.

Tory went with us, to make sure everything stayed civil and organized, and during the day I must have asked her fifteen thousand times if she could help me make a statement to the public. Whenever I did, her answer was, "We don't have time to deal with that right now. Focus on your current assignment, Kyle."

That pissed me off for several reasons. One, her calling aspects of my job "assignments" made it sound like I worked for her. I didn't. Two, the way she used my last name sounded demeaning instead of respectful, and it annoyed me every time it came out of her mouth. And three, it was a bullshit answer because if anyone could effectively handle juggling a hundred tasks at a time, it was Tory. She was just "handling" me again, and I fucking hated it.

I was in a bad mood by the time it was over, and then I felt guilty for feeling pissy because I'd wanted to give those kids a much happier version of me. Especially since they'd all been really nice, and none of them had said a word to me about Kiera. Although I'd seen a lot of whispering from the groups watching me from afar, and by the looks on their faces, there was little doubt as to what they'd been discussing. It made me wonder if they would have acted differently if Kiera had been there. Probably.

Kiera and I talked throughout the day, and she gave me multiple updates on how things were going with Anna. When the guys and I finally got back to the venue, they were still at the hospital but getting ready to leave. I had a couple of hours before tonight's meet-and-greet, and my mood lifted as I thought that I might actually have time to talk to...somebody. But then Tory stopped me in the parking lot and smashed all my hope.

"Kyle, I have a stack of promotional photos that I need you to sign. The label has immediate plans for them, so you need to do it now."

God, I just loved being politely asked to do stuff. Shoving my sarcastic thoughts aside, I indicated the rest of the D-Bags; Griffin had already hopped onto the bus, but Evan and Matt were nearby. "You just need me? Don't we all need to sign them?"

She pursed her lips, annoyed, then she tilted her head at Matt and Evan. "I've already gotten signatures from the others." I glanced at Evan, and he nodded at me. Rolling her eyes, Tory turned around and started walking toward the building. "Follow me," she tossed over her shoulder.

Still standing there, I circled my hands in the air like I was wringing her neck. Matt softly laughed at me. "Like I said, biggest bitch in the world, but she gets shit done."

Dropping my hands, I sighed. Then smiled. "How long do you think she'll wait for me before she storms back out here and drags me inside."

Matt smirked. "Three minutes. On the nose."

I laughed at that, then clapped his shoulder. Evan walked up to us as I stood there debating if I wanted to be a shit and eat up all three of those minutes, or if I wanted to be mature and just go do my job. Matt shared a look with Evan, then reached into his pocket and grabbed something. A second later, he handed me a folded hundred-dollar bill. "Here," he said.

My brows furrowed as I took it. "What's this for?"

Evan grinned, then he also reached into his pocket and handed me a hundred-dollar bill. He looked over at Matt as he said, "We've decided that you won."

"Won?" I asked, holding up the money.

Matt nodded, then he tilted his head to indicate our bus nearby. We were standing in a spot where the fans' view of us was blocked, but I could hear screaming on the other side of the fence. "The bet on Griffin and Anna. You won."

Shaking my head, I gave him a smirk. "Isn't it kind of early to call it?"

Grinning, Matt shook his head. "He's in there right now taking measurements for the back bedroom. Then he's making me go shopping with him, to get Gibson everything she might possibly need."

I opened my mouth to tell him that didn't really count—Anna could get Griffin to do all sorts of unexpected things—but Matt negated my argument before I could even voice it. "Anna didn't ask him to do it. He's doing it because he *wants to*. He wants to surprise her." He paused to laugh. "So, yeah, you won. I think you won the moment he married her." His laugh trailed off to a sigh. "And I'm really glad you did."

With a grin, I handed them both back their money. "I'm glad too, but I can't take this."

Matt laughed again. "Keep it. I'm going to make way more than that off of you."

They both snickered, and my smile shifted into a scowl. "Did you guys seriously bet on Kiera and me?" They just looked at each other and laughed even harder.

I opened my mouth, determined to get to the bottom of this,

but the door to the venue opened, and a red-faced Tory stepped out. "Kyle! Now!" At hearing her, Matt checked his watch and smirked.

Shoving their money into my pocket, I told them, "To be continued," then I turned toward Tory. Matt and Evan chuckled the entire time I walked away from them. Assholes.

Kiera still wasn't back by the time the show started. After our set, I checked my phone and saw a text from her saying they'd finally arrived. I headed to the bus to see her, but she was sound asleep in our cubby. I left her alone to catch up on her rest, slipping out of the sleeping area as quietly as I could. The relief of having her back with me was palpable, and I saw the same relief on Griffin's face when he joined me in the lounging area just a few seconds later.

"They're both passed out," he said, a peaceful smile on his lips.

I smiled at him, then held up my fist. "Congratulations, Griff," I quietly told him. "Your kid is truly beautiful."

He scoffed at me as he bumped my fist. "Did you think she wouldn't be?" He indicated himself with his hand. "Look at the genetic material that made her, dude." He swirled his hand around his junk. "My swimmers don't do ugly. It's a scientific impossibility. Every single one of these little dudes is a god or goddess waiting to happen."

"Yeah, okay," I said, slapping him on the back just to get him to shut up. "How about we let them sleep and go finish our show?"

Grinning at me, he nodded. We made our way back into the venue, and the entire time we walked, Griffin told me all about the cute shit he bought for his daughter. Damn, Matt was right... the bet was over. Griffin was officially a family man. I never thought I'd see that happen.

I was exhausted when I finally slipped into bed with Kiera.

She was still out but stirred when my arms and legs wrapped around her. "What time is it?" she murmured, nestling against me.

"Late. They're still tearing down the show. We'll leave some-time tomorrow." Squeezing her tight, I softly told her, "I missed you last night. I couldn't sleep without you next to me." Not having her safe in my arms had been a constant burr in my side. I'd read her book about us to pass the time but reading about her falling in love with me had just made me miss her even more.

Kiera twisted around to face me. Not wanting to be kneed in the nuts again, I swiftly backed away from her body. Once she was facing me, I rejoined her. "Hey," I whispered, cupping her cheek before giving her a kiss.

"Hey," she said against my lips.

Our mouths moved together for a moment, my tongue lightly seeking hers. The second we brushed together, she clutched at my shirt, then started yanking it up. Partially sitting, I pulled it off one-handed. Kiera shoved it somewhere, then ran her hands up my bare back as I moved over her. I could hear the smile in her voice when she again said, "Hey."

Smiling myself, I whispered, "Always so eager to undress me." I felt the happiness emanating from her as my mouth tasted her neck, as my hands slipped under her shirt. Tracing her ribs, I said in her ear, "Any troubles leaving the hospital?"

Sounding distracted as my hands drifted farther up her chest, she said, "Aside from some fans telling me that they wished I'd never been born? No. No problems at all."

That stopped me dead cold. "What?"

I pulled back to look at her, and she shook her head and wrig-gled her body like she was trying to get my hands moving again. "It was fine. I'm fine."

No, she wasn't. Someone saying that to her wasn't fine. None of this was fine. Shifting my body to her side, I withdrew my hand from her shirt. With a soft sigh, Kiera propped herself up on her elbow. "They threatened you?" I asked, my voice hard.

She shook her head. "No...they just expressed their dislike. Nobody touched—" She paused, and that pause spoke volumes. "Nobody hurt me," she amended.

My mind spun as I sat up on my elbow, matching her posture. Head down, I thought over every horrible thing that could have happened to her. Hailey was right, I never should have left her alone. I should have found a way to stay behind or snuck them out of the hospital with us. Neither of those ideas were actually plausible, though, and I hated the thought of Anna staying at the hospital alone, but fuck...they'd *threatened* her.

"Kellan, nobody hurt me."

My eyes flashed up to hers as a rush of anger flooded through me. "This time. Nobody hurt you this time." I looked out over the secluded darkness of our cubby, hating how far this had gone. "This is such bullshit. You're my wife." Returning my eyes to hers, I told her about how busy I'd been today, how I hadn't had a chance to say anything yet. "I hate that this has festered for so long. My silence isn't helping anything." It was probably just confirming everyone's assumptions, making the entire fabrication seem true. Would saying anything at this point even matter?

Kiera kissed me, then pulled the two of us back down to the mattress. "It's only been two days, and it's not your fault."

I knew that, I really did, but it didn't help me to hear it. I needed to do something, say something, scream at someone. But I was being leashed and caged by obligations and responsibilities, and in the meantime, Kiera was the one suffering. The one being yelled at, the one being *struck*. It wasn't right. None of this was right.

Kiera suddenly threaded her fingers into my hair and pulled me into a heated kiss. I'd been softly kissing her, but my mind had been a million miles away. By Kiera's aggressiveness, it was clear she wanted my full attention. I tried to release my anxiety and give it to her—intently kissing her back, grinding our bodies together in a way that quickly fired me up—but damn if I couldn't completely shut off the worry. Even still, desire had sprung to life, and I was hard, aching, ready. I shoved my hand down the back of her pants, inside her underwear, wishing I could rip them off, wishing I could push everything aside and just enjoy this moment, wishing I could keep her safe...wishing I could keep her with me.

A different kind of ache rushed through me as I said in her ear, "I want you." She let out a groan, and her hands shifted to my jeans. She started unfastening them, and as much as I wanted her to continue, my sentence wasn't finished. "But I want you...safe."

She stopped her hands and stared at me. I knew she could see the desire on my face, hear how fast my breath was, maybe even feel my rapid heartbeat, but I also knew she could see the concern too. She frowned at me. "Kellan, don't worry—"

"I heard you talking to Denny about fleeing back home. You were joking, but...maybe that's a good idea. Maybe you should head home until I have a chance to set this straight."

She gaped at me, clearly shocked. "No, I want to be with you. Home is wherever you are."

I was touched by that, truly, but right now, her safety was my primary concern. Shifting to her side again, I told her, "I want to be with you too, but I can't stand the way people talk about you. It makes me want to kick every single one of their asses. And I don't want you around me if it's dangerous for you."

"It's not—"

My eyes narrowed. "I saw that girl slap you, Kiera, so don't tell me it's not dangerous."

She paused a moment, and when she spoke again, her words were calm and confident. "You said we needed to carve out time for each other; otherwise, none of this mattered. You remember telling me that?"

A weary sigh left me. "I know, but that was before things got so messed up." I ran a finger down her beautiful cheek as sadness filled me. "And who is to say that anything will change when I do make another statement. They're so curious about my life, they might still hound you. They might still hate you, call you names. I can't handle that. I can't do my job if I'm constantly worrying about you. I just want you safe, even if that means we have to be apart."

God, I hated to say that. And even more, I hated that it was true. As much as I might fantasize about leaving all this crap behind, I had an obligation to the guys, and I had an obligation to the fans, even the ones who were currently causing me grief. And besides, it wasn't *all* the fans who were making me miserable. Just the very vocal, very passionate Kell-Sex-forever fans. I couldn't give up on all of them because of a handful of them.

Kiera absorbed my words for a moment, then said, "And I just want to be with you. I can handle being mobbed. I can handle being photographed. I can handle being ridiculed. And I can even handle being slapped...on occasion." She cupped both of my cheeks. "What I can't handle is people forcing us to behave in a certain way. People forcing us to be apart. We're not playing their game anymore, remember? We've fought too hard to be together. It's us against the world, Kellan, and they don't dictate our relationship. We do."

Damn. She was right. She was strong, and she could handle more than I gave her credit for. She made me want to be strong too. Whatever it took for us to stay together. "This attitude you've got right now is very attractive," I told her.

Smile on her face, she looped her arms around my neck and pulled me back to her. "Then stop trying to send me away and make love to me."

Well, damn. How could I possibly argue with that?

After making love to Kiera, I passed out hard, and even though these cramped cubbies sucked, it was the best sleep I'd had in a while. I felt like I could have slept all day, but I was nudged awake by an insistent finger in my side.

"What?" I mumbled.

"Kellan? Are our clothes on the floor?"

I peeked an eye open to see Kiera clutching the blanket to her chest as she looked around our cubby. "What clothes?" I said with a yawn.

She giggled and tossed me an amused look. "The clothes neither one of us are wearing."

With a grin, I rolled over and put my head on her chest. "Those are my favorite kinds of clothes." My hands wandered up her bare body, and *my* body was suddenly wide awake. *Definitely my favorite kinds of clothes.* I pulled down the blanket with my teeth, exposing her chest, then I sucked a perky nipple into my mouth. Waking up like this was even better than coffee.

Kiera didn't seem to agree. She pushed me back, an adorable scowl on her face. "Could you take a peek and see if they're on the floor?"

My gaze drifted to the breast I hadn't had a chance to greet yet. "You sure you want me to do that?" I asked. Seemed wrong to leave things uneven.

Laughing again, she pushed my shoulder back. "Yes, please find them."

Smiling to myself, I peeked out the curtain, but there wasn't a damn thing on the floor. "There's nothing out there," I said with a frown.

Kiera began searching our cubby in earnest, all the corners, under the blanket, under us, but there was nothing in here either. "Where's our stuff then?" she asked.

"I don't—" Sudden insight hit me, and I stopped talking. If our shit wasn't in here or out there, that could only mean someone had taken it. And there was only one jackass on the bus who would leave us stranded in our cubby, naked. With a sigh, I said, "I'm gonna kill that fucker, new dad or not." If he snuck a peek at Kiera, he was definitely a dead man.

Kiera yanked the blanket up, covering her chest. "Griffin stole our clothes?"

I simply cocked an eyebrow in answer. *He's the only one who would.* I expected Kiera to be so mortified that she'd start crying or something, but instead, she started cracking up. I was so surprised by her reaction that I just stared at her. That made her laugh even harder. Then she pushed me with her knees. "Go get some new clothes for us."

I let out a morose sigh as I stuck my legs out of the curtain; it was cold outside the blanket. "You want me to go out there naked?" I asked Kiera.

She smirked as she clutched the blanket to her. "Do you care if you're naked, Kellan?" she asked.

I returned her smirk. "Not really." Just not excited about freezing my ass off. Oh well, I'd rather be cold than steal her blanket and leave her sitting there buck naked. I gave her a quick kiss, then hopped out of the cubby and told her I'd be back soon.

Kiera softly laughed, probably embarrassed for me, as I made my way to the curtain separating the sleeping section from the bathroom area. I'd just stepped inside the space when Anna came out of her bedroom. We stared at each other for a second, then her eyes snapped to my crotch; I was so stunned to see her that I didn't even think to cover myself. Anna's gaze immediately returned to my face, but her smile was a mile wide. With a sigh, I walked over to the closet by the bathroom. "Your husband's an asshole," I said as an explanation.

She giggled. "An asshole? Or the best human being ever? Because I've been waiting for the money shot for *years*. And damn, Kellan, it's nice to know you didn't photoshop yourself." She smacked my ass as she passed by me on her way to the bathroom.

Shaking my head, smiling to myself, I opened the closet and quickly got dressed. I was nearly finished when Anna reemerged. She eyed me a moment, then gave me a crooked smile. "Now that I've seen it all, I have to say, clothes do you a disservice. Your body was meant to be naked."

I laughed as I grabbed clothes for Kiera. "I think your sister would take issue with that. And the guys. And, well, everyone else."

She laughed as she shook her head. "Not *everyone* else. Trust me."

Still lightly laughing, I headed back to the sleeping area. Kiera had been waiting for me to reappear, her head sticking out of our privacy curtain, and she furrowed her brows when she saw me; she had to be wondering why I was laughing. Anna stepped out behind me, and Kiera's jaw dropped. That only made me laugh more. Anna smirked as she snuck by me. She leaned down and said something to Kiera, then she turned back to me and winked. By the look of mortification on Kiera's face, I was pretty sure Anna had just told her that she'd seen me naked. Oh well. At least her remarks to me had been nice, and considering how chilly it was on the bus, I appreciated her kindness.

I gave Kiera her clothes, then stayed with her while she got dressed. When she was ready, we walked into the lounging section. The second I saw Griffin, I thanked him for his practical joke by rapping him on the back of the head. He was, of course, completely clueless as to why I'd smacked him. After I told him, he laughed and said it was his and Gibson's idea. And yeah, him including his daughter in his devious little plan was pretty adorable. I gave him a pass for it.

The morning was surprisingly peaceful, and a part of me just wanted to stay like this forever, all of us together on the bus, happy, healthy...isolated. But it couldn't last, and before I was ready, we were entering our next stop: New York City. Kiera was staring out the window, worrying her lip, and I had to wonder if she was thinking about the amount of people here, the increased potential for her to be attacked again, both verbally and physically. I knew I was thinking about it. Over and over again.

My phone started ringing, and thinking it was Gavin or Hailey, I pulled it out of my pocket. When I saw who it was, I genuinely considered just letting it ring. Sienna. She didn't often call me; private phone calls weren't good publicity stunts. Stifling a sigh, I answered the phone. If nothing else, I could ask her to say something. Again.

"Sienna," I flatly said.

"Kellan, love. I have the best news. Is everyone there with you?" Her voice was bright and cheerful, completely unaffected by the frenzy she'd helped create.

Annoyed and curious, I told her everyone was around but Griffin. He was in the back, changing Gibson's diaper. A fact that still shocked me because I'd gotten a whiff of that, and it was *not* pleasant.

I asked Sienna why she wanted to know if we were all here, and she said, "I want to tell all of you at once! Put me on speaker."

Rolling my eyes at her melodramatics, I told her, "Fine," then I pulled the phone back and studied the screen. I'd never had to put anyone on speaker before, and I had zero idea how to do it. I also wasn't in the mood to figure it out. I asked Kiera for help, and with a small smirk, she adjusted the phone for me. I motioned Evan and Matt to our table, then told Sienna, "You're on, go ahead."

Voice full of sunshine, she said, "Well, first off, I just want to say how much I miss all of you! Things have been so hectic; I feel like I rarely see you."

I shared a look with Kiera at hearing that because while it wasn't a lie, it also wasn't entirely the truth. Sienna was playing up the role of a woman betrayed and hurt. The meet-and-greets were awkwardly full of tension, and last night when we'd performed our duet together, she'd cried at the end. *Cried.* It made me look like the biggest d-bag to ever walk the planet.

"I just couldn't wait until the tour stopped to tell you all the fabulous news!" she continued.

"What news?" I tentatively asked. I could feel caution building inside me already.

She giggled, then said, "I just got off the phone with Nick... and your album shot to number two on the charts, right below mine."

She squealed like she couldn't believe it. I also couldn't

believe it, but for an entirely different reason. It worked. All the marketing, scheming, and fake publicity worked, and Sienna and Nick got exactly what they wanted.

I met eyes with Kiera, and she had the same stunned expression on her face. "You reached number one?" she asked, her voice full of disbelief.

"And the D-Bags are at number two! Isn't that fabulous?"

Leaning back in my seat, I tried to take it all in, tried to be excited, but I just kept getting stuck on the fact that they'd *won*. They'd lied to the fans, created a completely fake frenzy about Sienna and me, just to capture the public's interest. They'd disregarded my feelings about it, disregarded my wife's feelings, and they'd fucking won. I knew I should feel some happiness over the fact that it had benefitted the D-Bags too, that we were sitting in the second spot right now—something I'd never truly imagined happening—but I was just...exhausted.

I scrubbed my hands over my face, through my hair, then I wearily said to Kiera, "I really miss Pete's."

Sienna heard me say that, and her voice instantly changed. Now she sounded irritated. "This is incredible news. You should all be jumping up and down, screaming your bloody heads off, not pouting like I just told you your best friend moved away."

Anger shot up my spine. "The public thinks my wife is a whore. I'm really not okay with that. And now that you got what you wanted, and Nick got what he wanted, it's my turn. And I want you to admit the truth. All of it. From the very beginning."

She inhaled a deep, noisy breath. "Here's the thing, love. If we confess that we fabricated our entire relationship to bump sales, there will be a public backlash that will negatively affect us both. The scandal will stay with you for the rest of your career. Do you really want that monkey on your back?"

I didn't want to do that to the guys, but damn it, I was tired of this shit. Closing my eyes as frustration filled me, I bit out, "This *scandal* was your doing from the very beginning. And now you're asking me if I'm okay with it? I was never okay with it!"

Her voice changed again to crisp coolness. "You went along with it, Kellan. No one forced you."

I couldn't believe she'd just fucking said that to me. "No one forced..." I'd been pushed around and threatened from the very start. Surely, she understood that.

Sienna sighed, clearly frustrated as well. "Look, I only said that the truth couldn't come out. I didn't say that Kell-Sex couldn't end. If you're so bent out of shape about it that you can't even enjoy being on top of the world, then we'll 'break up' after the tour. I'll be heartbroken, but I'll quickly move on, and when everyone sees how happy I am with my new beau, you and your wife will be free to date in peace. Problem solved."

Oh my fucking God, did she actually think that was a viable solution? Kiera seemed just as flabbergasted as me. She sputtered on her words, then spat out, "How does that solve anything? I'll still be the other woman who broke you up."

Sienna let out a weary exhale. "We'll be at the venue soon. I just wanted to call and...congratulate you on your success." She sighed again, then hung up the phone since her end of the conversation was finished.

Everyone stared at the phone for long, silent seconds. Then Anna said, "She's really not going to help you guys at all, is she?"

I shook my head. "No, she was never gonna help us. We have to fix this on our own." And I was pretty sure I'd just thought of a way to do it. If Sienna wouldn't come clean, then I would. About everything. Because the truth was the only option left for me. I would tell everyone what I'd done, what the label had coerced me into doing, and what I'd knowingly and unknowingly helped perpetuate. They'd crucify me, but at least they'd stop hating Kiera.

Griffin and Gibson returned while I mulled over my idea. Griffin looked at our solemn table and asked us, in his own special way, what was wrong. "Why the fuck does everyone look constipated? Bad coffee or something?"

Evan filled him in on the phone call with Sienna, and Griffin instantly flipped out. Kiera quickly rescued Gibson from his exuberance, and Griffin tossed his hands in the air as he jumped up and down. "Whoooooooooo! Number two, baby!" He started running up and down the aisle, screaming his head off, and seeing his joy finally melted my melancholy.

Evan and Matt joined his happiness, Matt telling me, "Number two, Kell! We're number two!"

Feeling worry-free for a moment, I snatched Gibson from Kiera and said, "I know, man. It's crazy." And it really was. We'd come so far, so fast; my head was still spinning. I bounced Gibson in my arms as the guys ruminated over our success.

"Number two," Evan said, looking dazed. "Right behind Sienna Sexton. Six months ago, I never would have pictured that happening."

Griffin instantly started humping the air. "Not me. I always knew I'd be banging on Sienna's backdoor one day." He kept going with his simulated sexual act. Kiera grimaced and looked away. Deacon stumbled out of the sleeping area, smirked at Griffin, then sat down with his bandmates. Griffin dramatically, and loudly, finished his performance, then took a bow. I smiled as Kiera unplugged her ears, then we both cracked up. The rest of the guys did too, and Anna giggled as she clapped for her husband. Fucking Griffin.

Matt smacked him on the back as his laughter died down. "It's nice to see that becoming a husband and father hasn't changed you in the slightest, cuz."

Griffin gave him a haughty sniff. "Did you think it would?"

Nope. Not really.

Once everyone stopped laughing, I locked eyes with my band members. I had something to tell them that they weren't going to like, something that was going to affect all of us, something I needed their support in. The mood in the air changed as they each noted the seriousness on my face. Well, Matt and Evan noticed it; Griffin had to be smacked by Matt.

When I had their complete attention, I said, "Tomorrow

morning, we're going to a radio station to perform. We're scheduled to play two songs, pimp the album and the concert, and leave. I don't want to do that. I don't want to sing." I shifted my eyes to Kiera. "I want to talk, and I want to tell them everything."

Kiera's eyes widened and she thickly swallowed. "You want to go on air, behind Sienna and Nick's back, and tell the world what they did? How they manipulated you?"

I nodded at her. "And I want to tell them exactly who you are to me."

Her face went pale white, but she gave me a soft smile. "Then I'll talk with you. We'll do this interview together."

Surprise went through me, followed by pride. That was huge of her to even suggest doing it with me. "Are you sure? It's one of the largest radio stations on the East Coast."

She frowned, and looked a little green, but nodded. "Yes, I'm sure. If you're going to do something as reckless as throw your record label and the biggest pop star on the planet under the bus, then I'm going to be right beside you." Lifting her wrist, she showed me her tattoo. "I'm done hiding." She paused as she grimaced. "And now I have to go throw up."

I laughed, then gave her a kiss. When we pulled apart, I shifted my attention to the guys. "This affects you too. If I tell everyone what we did to boost sales, it could hurt us. Sienna was right about that—the stigma could follow us for years. Are you guys okay with that?"

My heart thudded in my chest as I waited for their reply. If they weren't okay with it, then...we'd find another way. I just didn't know what that other way might be. Except maybe Sienna's idea, but I really hated letting my wife continue to be the enemy in the public's eye. It would chip away at me, make me bitter. It already was.

Evan was the first one to respond. He walked over and picked up Kiera in a bone-crushing hug. "I hated hearing all that Kell-Sex crap, so I'm thrilled it's about to be over."

A tiny bit of relief filled me at hearing him say that. I glanced at Griffin, and he was nodding, so I figured he was fine with it. Then I looked over at Matt. If anyone was going to object, it would be him. The band was his baby, and he'd worked his ass off to get us here. Matt stared at me for a long moment. Guilt filled me as I stared back at him until finally, I couldn't take the silence anymore. "I'm sorry, Matt. I really didn't expect any of this...and I won't come clean if everyone's not on board." *But please be on board. I need this to end, and I need your support.*

Like he heard my silent plea, he finally grinned. Then he playfully socked me in the shoulder. "You're doing the right thing, man. Don't worry about it." Eyes serious, he pointed at each of us. "We just have to make sure the next album rocks so freaking hard that all of this doesn't mean a damn thing."

I clapped his arm as pure relief filled me. "Deal," I told him.

Chapter 31

THE INTERVIEW

Kiera and I decided to sleep on the bus instead of going to the hotel. Even though a hotel room would have been more spacious, the bus just felt safe, cozy, and considering what we were doing in the morning, we both needed to feel that way for as long as possible. The guys surprised me by staying with us, and we all stayed up later than we should have, reminiscing about the good times we'd had and coming up with a plan in case all of this backfired badly. Saying *screw it* and going back to Pete's to live out the rest of our days playing there was the top contender.

Once we all called it a night and crawled into our cramped beds, I had a hard time sleeping. I couldn't stop worrying that I was doing the wrong thing, and yet, I was also filled with an eager kind of hope that it would work, that people would be understanding about the situation, sympathetic even. We'd been so clueless in the beginning, so overwhelmed by everything...so voiceless. I supposed we still were. It made me wish Lana had been able to stay by our side the whole time. She'd always felt like an advocate, a friend, but handholding us wasn't her job, and I already knew she didn't have the authority to contradict Nick.

I'd reached out to her a few times during all this, asking for help, asking for advice, and she'd always told me the same thing: *I really want to help you, but my hands are tied*. She'd always followed it up with, "Stay strong." I understood. In a way, she was just as trapped as we were. Too far down the ladder to make a difference. Hopefully, that fact would save her from any potential backlash from this upcoming interview.

Since sleep wasn't happening, I crawled out of bed and decided to finish reading Kiera's book. Comparatively, that pain was easier to bear; at least I knew how that story ended. Time sped by as I got caught up in our history, and I wanted to smack myself a dozen times for all the stupid shit I did. Like the fight in the rain. That was particularly difficult to read. And taking those two girls up to my room after that fucking party. Just reading about Kiera struggling through that made me feel sick. Of course, Kiera made her mistakes too...like having goodbye sex with Denny. Like panicking in the parking lot, changing her mind about us, forcing a goodbye between us that neither of us wanted. Things that still sometimes hurt and baffled me were so much clearer after reading them through Kiera's perspective. I got it. I got her. And I loved her even more for it, something I didn't even realize was possible. But love truly had no limit; there was *always* room for more.

Anna joined me in the early morning. Yawning repeatedly, she waved a greeting, then sat across the aisle from me and started feeding Gibson. I closed Kiera's laptop, feeling nothing but a sense of accomplishment and pride for my wife. What she'd just written down was raw, real, gut-wrenching, and messy. Exactly how it had been. I'd understand if she didn't want to release it to the public, but I really thought she should. Because I was pretty certain Kiera wasn't the only one to ever feel that way, and I knew how good it felt not to be alone in your pain.

When Anna was done feeding Gibson, burping her on her shoulder, a thought struck me. Smiling, I leaned over the aisle and asked, "Hey, did you bring any flowers back from the hospital? Any roses?"

She thought for a moment, then nodded. With a smirk, she

said, "One of the nurses brought me a small 'congratulations' bouquet. You should have seen his face." She swirled a finger around hers. "Bright red. Adorable."

A light laugh escaped me. Leave it to Anna to get hit on by a guy just moments after having someone else's baby. We really were a lot alike. "This is going to sound weird, but do you think I could have a petal?"

She lifted an eyebrow at me. "More romance?" she asked. Then she smiled. "I think you've got her, Kellan. I don't think you need to keep trying so hard."

I softly smiled at her. "It isn't about trying to get her or trying to keep her. I just can't contain how much I love her."

Anna stared at me a moment, and I swear her deep green eyes grew glossy. Finally, she blinked rapidly and murmured, "Damn, pregnancy hormones." She swished a hand at me. "Yes, go get your damn petal."

I stood up with a bright smile on my face. "Thanks." Then I leaned over and gave Gibson a quick kiss on the forehead before quietly making my way to the back bedroom.

Griffin was out cold when I stepped inside, snoring away like he hadn't slept in ten years. Careful not to wake the fucker, I spotted the flowers and plucked a petal off a rose. I turned to leave, then paused and considered messing with Griffin. I did owe him some payback after all. I scanned the room, looking for an appropriate retaliation, and that was when I spotted the perfect prank. It was childish, stupid, and absurdly messy...and that made it just right for Griffin.

Suppressing a maniacal giggle, I grabbed Gibson's baby powder, unscrewed the top, and carefully poured a thick layer over Griffin's chest. Then over his hair. Then I carefully lifted the covers and squeezed a bunch down there. God, I hoped he was naked. Already the white shit was getting everywhere, and I glee-fully imagined Griffin looking like a powder puff. I'd help him clean up his room later, because I wasn't a total dick, but I was going to get a really good laugh out of it first.

Petal in hand, I went back to the lounging area to wait for Matt to get up so I could borrow his Sharpie. He woke up not long after Kiera, yawning as he waved a tired greeting to us. Since Kiera was cooing at Gibson, I took the opportunity to approach him.

"Hey, can I borrow your—"

Before I even finished my question, he grunted in annoyance and thrust his hand into his pocket. "Oh my God, just keep it," he said, shoving the marker at me.

"Are you sure?" I asked. "I know how much it means to you."

His pale eyes narrowed into a glare. "I'll get another one."

The look on his face made me chuckle. He shook his head at me, and that was when I heard a loud exclamation from the back bedroom. "What the fuck? Who the...? Goddamn it, Matt!"

Matt's eyes widened, and I started losing it. He tilted his head at me. "What did you do?" he asked.

I couldn't answer him, and I didn't need to—Griffin burst into the room a second later. He was only wearing boxer briefs, and he had splotches of white powder all over him. Matt saw him and instantly started laughing. Griffin pointed at him. "You're dead!"

Matt held up his hands. "It wasn't me."

Griffin scanned the room. Anna was wiping tears from her eyes; she was laughing so hard. Kiera was gaping, shocked by the sight of him. Evan peeked into the room from the sleeping area, then he laughed too. Matt was dying, but he was looking at me. That seemed to clue Griffin in on the real culprit. "Kyle," he stated. "Did you do this?"

"I'll help you clean it up," I got out between giggles.

"You bet your ass you will." He ran a hand through his hair, noticed all the powder in his fingers, then smirked and blew the shit in our faces. Matt and I started coughing. And laughing. Griffin got a vicious gleam in his eye, and I—too late—realized my mistake. I'd wanted to piss him off a little, but I'd inadvertently given him a weapon.

Matt and I raised our hands. "Don't!" we said together, then Matt pointed at Gibson. "Baby in the room! Baby in the room!"

Griffin hesitated as he glanced at his daughter. Then he sighed. "I'm gonna go wash this crap off," he told Anna. Then to us, he said, "Consider today your lucky day, shitheads."

With that, he turned around and stalked off, leaving a light trail of powder along the floor. Oops. I might have gotten carried away with that prank.

Matt raised his arms, letting them fall back to his sides with a heavy thud. "What did *I* do?" he called to Griffin. He was ignored. Matt turned back to me with a frown. "Thanks for that." He held out his hand. "I want my Sharpie back."

Grinning, I slid it into my pocket. "What Sharpie?" Matt pursed his lips at me, and I pointed to his cheek. "You got a little something right there."

He wiped the white dust off with his sleeve, looked at it, then started laughing. "You're an asshole," he muttered, then he smacked my shoulder. "Make me coffee."

He sat down next to Kiera so he could play with Gibson. Evan strode over to stand behind him, peering down at the newborn with a soft smile on his face. The shower in the back kicked on, and I heard Griffin singing to himself...something about tying me to a park bench, covered in maple syrup and birdseed. I smiled as I looked around this bus full of mischief and love. At least we were all in this together, and no matter what this day brought, I was sure that wouldn't change.

A car from the label arrived a little while later to take us to the radio station. Kiera was a bundle of nerves as we drove. I smiled as I watched her anxiety, both proud and amazed that she was going to do this with me. Then, to ease her fears and tell her how much I loved her book, I gave her the message I'd written while she'd gotten dressed.

Kiera looked at the petal in her palm with confusion on her face. I'd written *You are a,* then drawn a little star. When she peeked up at me, I explained. "I finished your book. It's amazing, Kiera. You really should get it published."

She smiled in a way that was both shy and grateful. "Thank you. I wasn't sure how you'd feel about it after you read it all."

Putting my arm across her shoulders, I drew her to me. "I didn't think it was possible, but I'm pretty sure I love you even more. How you see me...I never thought anyone would ever..." I couldn't even finish saying it. Being unloved and unwanted for so long had hollowed me out, and having her warmth fill that hole... it was still too much sometimes. A joy so bright it burned. On really dark days, I still felt undeserving of it. But those days were few and far between now.

Kiera looked up at me with understanding and compassion in her eyes. "That's because you don't see yourself as clearly as I see you," she said.

Knowing I'd said similar sentiments to her made me laugh. "God, we really are peas in a pod, aren't we?"

She snuggled into my side with a smile. I fingered her wedding ring, feeling nothing but contentment. Today was the first time in a long time that I was going out in public with my ring on my left hand, where it belonged, and I already felt great about that decision. I honestly hoped someone asked me about it because I knew exactly what I'd tell them. *Yes, I am married, and this is my wife right here, Mrs. Kiera Kyle.*

I was lost in that daydream when Kiera suddenly asked, "Where the hell do you keep getting these petals?"

With a devilish grin, I told her, "I'm a man of many mysteries, Mrs. Kyle." Damn, I loved saying that. Kiera gave me such a cute pout after my noninformative statement that I had to laugh. And the amusement felt good. It made me think that maybe Griffin was right. Maybe today was our lucky day and everything was going to turn out just fine. Honestly, we should have done this ages ago.

When we got to the radio station, the crowd was a lot bigger than I'd expected. People were waving signs, sporting our shirts, screaming, crying...it was so surreal. Still. I honestly didn't think it would ever feel normal, and it shouldn't because this was in no way a normal life.

Tory tried to get us to bypass the fans and go into the building, but I had a feeling these people had been here for a really long time, and none of us were going to just walk by them like they didn't exist. That wasn't our style. Evan was first out of the car, and he immediately stepped up to the crowd, welcoming and thanking them. Matt followed suit, not being as overtly friendly as hug-happy Evan but shaking hands and signing things. Griffin ran up and down the sidewalk, getting the crowd to lift their hands in a wave. He instantly had them laughing instead of crying, and I loved him for it.

I waited for Kiera before I walked up to the masses. I wanted us to approach them together, show them, right now, that we were a united front. Kiera took my hand after exiting the car, and I could feel her shaking. I gently tugged her toward the crowd; she resisted for a second before walking beside me. I knew she was terrified to approach them with me. Like Matt, she didn't enjoy this level of attention. Especially now that the attention was usually negative. I hoped people would be kind to her with me standing right beside her. Because fan or not, *no one* was going to get away with telling my wife she never should have been born.

There were a lot of gaping mouths as Kiera and I stepped up to the fans. They clearly didn't know what to do with this situation. I helped them out by not making it a big deal. "How are you guys doing this mornin'?" I asked.

They screamed in answer, and I assumed that meant they were doing great. With a laugh, I released Kiera's hand and started autographing things for them. I made small talk while I signed, joking around with the outgoing ones, engaging the shy ones with playful words and flirty smiles—whatever I could do to make them happy, to make this moment something worth their time and effort. My repayment for their devotion. After a few minutes of interaction, they all seemed way more relaxed around me, and I was pleasantly surprised that none of them were giving Kiera any grief. Well, no one did until we got to the end of the line.

Scowl on her face, a girl in a Kell-Sex shirt finally asked the question I'd seen in far too many eyes. "Why is *she* here with you?"

I studied the girl for a moment, careful to keep my expression neutral as a rush of irritation flooded me. It wasn't this girl's fault that she'd bought the lies, and I could tell from the hurt on her face that her question came from a place of concern. She clearly adored Sienna, and she thought I was cheating on her. And her question, taken from that perspective, wasn't completely unwarranted.

Forcing the frustration aside, I gave her my response in the calmest voice I could muster. "She's my wife. She goes where I go." With that, I grabbed Kiera's hand and we walked into the building together. Once inside, I grinned at Kiera. "It felt really good to say that."

She grinned, then went pale white. "Just think how good it will feel to say it to millions of people in a few minutes."

She looked like she was going to throw up, and I cursed myself for not bringing Matt's bucket. Wrapping my arm around her, I said, "It's not millions. I'm pretty sure it's not millions." It might be millions. Shit. I hoped she didn't get sick on air.

Tory got us through security, then we all squished into an elevator car. Tory started giving instructions the second the doors closed. It was all the basic stuff she said every time we had an appearance: *Keep the interview about the tour, don't talk about your personal life.* In other words, no comment, no comment, no comment. She was going to lose her mind when I did the exact opposite of that. Not wanting to give her any indication of my plan, I simply smiled at her and let her talk to her heart's content.

The DJs were live when we walked into the studio. The lead DJ, a tall, lean, middle-aged man, smiled when he spotted us. With a deep, pleasing voice, he immediately introduced us to the audience listening. And watching. This particular radio station had several web cameras around the room so people could see the interview as well as hear it. I wondered if Kiera had remembered that little detail when she'd agreed to this. I shook the man's hand in greeting; he'd been really decent to me the last time we'd been here. Actually, all of them had been kind, and I was happy we were doing this here, with them. Some of the other DJs I'd met, well, I'd be happy if I never saw them again.

The DJ told us to have a seat and indicated four chairs set up for us. Nodding my head at Kiera, I asked if we could get another chair. They all stopped and stared at me for a moment, and I could tell they all recognized Kiera from the photo, and they were all dying to ask why she was here.

The younger male DJ said, "Sure, no problem," and hopped up to get Kiera a chair. Tory was glaring at this point; she hadn't wanted Kiera in the room, but for now she was staying in her corner, silently fuming from a distance.

As the guys and I were set up with headphones, the female DJ said, "It's so nice to have you back. How have you been?" Her gaze went from me, to Kiera, to the guys, then back to Kiera, and I could see the curiosity eating at her.

A microphone was set in front of me, and I figured now was as good a time as any to get right into it. "Not so great, actually."

Interest sparked in all the DJs' eyes. The woman was glancing between Kiera and me, and I could see her debating what she should say. Tory had already mentioned that she'd specifically instructed them not to ask anything about our personal life. I could see the DJ both wanting to pry and wanting to be respectful. Finally, she pointed at Kiera and said, "I can imagine things have been...rough...lately?"

She looked over at Tory after saying that. Tory was giving her a cut gesture and a nasty scowl, but this wasn't up to Tory anymore. This was up to me, and this time, I *wanted* to talk. I held up a finger to Tory. She looked stunned for a moment, and I took her distraction to answer the DJ. "I need to clear the air about a few things. I know we were supposed to perform for you today, but I would like to do an interview instead. Do you mind?"

None of them did. I asked them for headphones for Kiera. People leapt up to get her some, but Evan handed her his first. Kiera was shaking as she thanked him and put them on. She wasn't the only one shaking. Tory was so pissed; her energy was almost vibrating the entire room.

Stepping over to me, she ripped the headphone off my ear and hissed, "Do *not* say another word! End this. Now!"

Anger flashed through me as I pulled away from her. "No! I won't be quiet. I'm done with this."

Adjusting my headphone back over my ear, I turned away from her. I could feel her fury behind me, but honestly, there wasn't anything she could do to stop me from talking, and I didn't care if she was pissed. I was too. I heard her leave the room, and I knew she was going to call Nick. There would be repercussions from this, but I'd deal with that later, after I confessed.

The room filled with anticipation as Kiera was given a microphone. She clasped my hand, and her palm was clammy with nerves. I locked eyes with her, letting her know she wasn't alone. Our stance against the world started right now. Kiera seemed to relax the longer I stared at her, so eyes still on her, I pulled the microphone forward and said, "I'd like to formally introduce you to this beautiful girl at my side, Miss Kiera Michelle Allen." I paused to look back at the DJs. "My wife."

Everyone's eyes widened and their mouths dropped. It was almost comical how floored they all were, especially when they all looked at our hands at almost the same time. In the stunned silence, Kiera murmured, "Hi," into the microphone. It was adorable.

The woman snapped out of it first. "Oh, well...congratulations. Is this...recent?"

Feeling better than I had in a really long time, I shook my

head. "No. We actually got married last June before any of this craziness started."

Kiera frowned as she looked at me. "Well, we aren't technically married yet. We had a small ceremony...sort of, but we haven't legally gone through the proceedings."

Peaceful smile on my face, I shrugged. "I married you in that bar. That's all that matters to me."

The younger, bearded DJ smiled at hearing that. "You got married in a bar? Nice. That's my dream wedding location. Not that I'm ever getting married."

Kiera giggled, and I felt the tension loosen in her grip. Looking more relaxed, she kissed the back of my hand. "We married in June, but we've been together...well, it will be two years now in March." Even longer if you considered us together when she was still with Denny. Not that I wanted to get into that mess on the air.

Looking confused, the woman asked me, "If you've been engaged this whole time, why has nobody heard about Kiera before now?" She smiled at Kiera. "Where have you been hiding?"

Kiera laughed, then shrugged and said, "I was hiding right by his side. We've been almost inseparable this entire time." She went on to describe how she'd been in the room while I'd mentioned being in a relationship, and the DJ instantly asked me why I hadn't just pointed her out. Sheepish look on her face, Kiera raised her free hand. "That would be because of me. I'm not...comfortable being the center of attention. Kellan was trying to keep me out of the spotlight." Twirling her finger around the room, she added, "All of this makes me want to either vomit, pee my pants, or some horrible combination of the two."

Kiera's cheeks flushed with color, and I knew she was berating herself for saying that out loud. Everyone in the room chuckled, but I could tell it was because they thought she was cute. And she was. She was freaking adorable.

While I rubbed Kiera's palm with my thumb, the female DJ

gave her a conspiratorial smile. "It's okay. This makes me want to pee too," she said.

I laughed at the DJ's comment and Kiera smiled, looking relaxed again. Shaking my head, I told the DJs about how I'd tried to steer the public away from Sienna and me as a couple, how I'd told them I was in a relationship, but they'd twisted that to mean I didn't want to talk about Sienna, how I couldn't specifically mention my wife because she didn't want me to. Kissing Kiera's hand, I gave her a sad smile. "I was as vague as I could be about you. Maybe I was too vague. I should have at least said I was engaged."

Kiera shook her head. "You did what you knew I was comfortable with; you don't have to feel bad about that." She laughed. "And you know Sienna just would have started wearing an engagement ring anyway."

I smirked. "Yeah, I can see her doing that." Honestly, I was a little surprised she hadn't.

The air in the room changed as the DJs instantly comprehended what we were implying. "Are you saying that Sienna Sexton orchestrated the Kell-Sex phenomenon?"

Fuck. This was it. The point of no return. A part of me didn't want to throw Sienna under the bus; she wasn't completely evil, just...driven. But I needed people to understand my side. I needed the truth to come out. I was sick and tired of all the misunderstandings.

With a sigh, I ripped off the Band-aid. "It's not entirely Sienna's fault, but yes, she definitely did her part to make sure the fans saw us together."

The confused DJs asked why, and I paused to look back at the guys. What I said next wasn't going to paint us in a good light. We'd played along because it benefitted us. Yes, it was more complicated than that, but regardless of the reasons, in the beginning, we'd done it. Griffin was just staring at me, looking confused, like all of this was news to him. Matt gave me a small, encouraging nod, and Evan put a hand on my shoulder. With a squeeze and a nod, he let me know that they had my back. *Time to throw us all under the bus.*

I slowly looked back at the DJs, then confessed something that I probably shouldn't. "To boost sales. The record label decided early on that Sienna and I as a couple would create a buzz that would help us both. It was their idea to make the music video so...explosive. And I'll never really forgive myself for doing it," I said, looking at Kiera.

"I talked you into it," Kiera said, her eyes reminding me that I had nothing to feel guilty about. I still did, but I appreciated the support.

I nodded at her, then continued to explain everything that the label had set in motion. How I'd been told to let the rumors go, told to hold my tongue. How I'd gone along with it to help out my band, my family. How I'd eventually changed my mind, but it had been too late, nobody had believed me. Kiera took over from there, telling them how the label had pulled us off Justin's tour, forced us onto Sienna's tour. How Sienna had made sure we were photographed together, how I'd been evasive in interviews to protect Kiera's identity, her privacy. "It's no wonder that the fans didn't believe what you were telling them. No one's at fault there," she told me.

The female DJ made a scoffing sound, then surprising the hell out of me, she said, "No one but your label and Sienna. You were green to the business, probably overwhelmed, and they completely walked all over you. It's disgusting, and I for one am outraged for you."

Relief hit me strong and hard; I honestly hadn't been sure anyone would understand the pressure we'd been under. It was easy to say you'd never compromise your beliefs for anything, harder to do when reality was bearing down on you.

The conversation opened up after that as we started explaining the myriad ways we'd been manipulated. And then, the younger DJ finally asked about the sex tape. "I'm behind everything you're saying, man, but I gotta ask...what about the sex tape? You've already confirmed it was you, and I'm sorry, but it really looks like Sienna. Did you...make a sex tape with her?" He glanced at Kiera after saying that and lifted his hands as he cringed in apology. Kiera smiled and nodded at him. She'd probably been expecting that question.

A weary sigh left me as I answered him. "No, that wasn't Sienna. That was an old roommate of mine. We made it several years ago. She leaked it for money, and since she's never once spoken up about being the girl in the video, I'm assuming that she got paid a great deal of money." Because it would take at least seven figures for Joey to walk away from fame. Of that, I was certain.

Once the DJs ran out of questions, they opened it up to callers. Those were harder to deal with. I hated disappointing fans, and some of them were crying as I popped their Kell-Sex bubble. It broke me, and I felt even worse about everything. When we got to the angrier callers, I quietly let them say everything they needed to say. And when they were done venting, I simply told them, "I'm sorry. I never meant to hurt anyone."

But a lot of the callers did understand, and there was a surprising amount of sympathy and compassion. It gave me hope that I hadn't just set a match to the D-Bags.

When we finally left the studio, I felt lighter. I felt guiltier, but also lighter. At least everything was out in the open now.

Tory was bright red and stone silent when we joined her in the hallway. She pointed at the elevators, too furious to even speak. I was certain her tongue would loosen up in the car. Not worried about being chastised by her, I walked over to the elevator with Kiera. My phone went off, and knowing it was either Nick or Sienna, I grudgingly pulled it from my pocket. *Time to face the music.* Seeing Sienna's name on the screen made me cringe, but I'd rather be yelled at by her than Nick.

A second after I answered the phone, Sienna yelled, "What the bloody hell did you just do?"

"Something I should have done a long time ago," I told her. "I said my piece."

"You just admitted that we manipulated the public for money! Are you trying to ruin both of our careers?" She screamed that so loud that my ear started ringing.

Holding the phone away, I told her, "Our albums will speak for themselves. And that's the way it should be. If our music isn't good enough to stand on its own, then we shouldn't be at the top. And if we fall...I'm fine with it."

"You are the biggest bloody fool I have ever met! Get your ass back here. Now!"

She hung up after that, so I tucked my phone back into my pocket. As the elevator doors opened, I leaned over to Kiera and whispered, "You think she's mad?"

Wrapping her arms around me, she pulled me into the elevator and kissed me. "I don't really care if she is," she said during a brief break.

My phone rang the entire time the elevator descended, but I ignored it, choosing to savor the moment with Kiera instead.

When we stepped outside, there was a chill in the air that wasn't entirely caused by the weather. The crowd had grown since we'd entered the building, and from the looks on the fans' faces, they'd all heard the interview, and they were shocked, angered, saddened...confused. It hurt my heart to see their pain, to know I was the cause of it. I never should have agreed to any of this. I should have said no to the song with Sienna, let the D-Bags find fame slowly and naturally. All of this was my fault.

I wanted to explain things to the crowd, beg their forgiveness, let them vent at me, but it wasn't just fans in the multitude anymore. Press was here too. And gossip-hungry paparazzi. There were microphones and video cameras amid the numerous people taking photographs, and questions were being tossed at me left and right. Reporters asking me to comment, asking me what I was going to do now, asking me if I was going to sue, asking me if

I'd violated my contract. My head swam as I felt the pressure of their very-good questions driving into me.

The reporters were stepping into us, wanting answers. The fans were too. Their questions were more emotional, full of disappointment and disbelief. "You're really not a couple?" "That was fake?" "Are you sure you're not in love with Sienna?"

I opened my mouth to say something, but there were too many people with too many questions, and they were all crowding in on us, filling the air with tension. It almost felt like that moment before a fight started, that buildup of expectant energy right before the first fist swung, and my body instantly tensed in preparation. I needed to get Kiera out of here, now.

Security and interns from the radio station were trying to hold back the crowd, and they managed a small enough gap that Matt, Evan, and Griffin were able to slip into the car. The gap wasn't wide enough for Kiera and me to walk side by side, so I grabbed her hand and led her through the narrow space. It was difficult since the crowds surged against security with every step I took. I was bumped and jostled, and questions were tossed at me the entire time.

Then a pair of aggressive photographers broke through security to stand right in front of us, completely blocking our path to the car. I tried to move around them, but there wasn't room. I tried politely asking them to move, but they didn't give a shit what I wanted.

I looked up at the car to see Evan standing there, half in, half out. Matt was behind him, sticking his head out with a frown on his face. They both looked like they were about to come get me and start swinging if they had to. I shook my head at them. The photographers would press charges if anyone hit them, and I didn't want my friends to have to deal with that headache. Kiera and I would get through. Somehow.

That was when a gap opened in the sea of fans. The channel through the people led to a spot several feet behind the car, but if Kiera and I could make it to the street, maybe I could hail a taxi.

That seemed like a better course of action than waiting for more security to arrive.

Clenching Kiera's hand, I faked out the photographers, darting right before swinging left, then I ran for the gap, wanting to get through it before it closed. The body of fans shifted back into position after Kiera, effectively blocking off the aggressive photographers. I was patted and stroked as I hurried to the curb, but I could deal with that. I hadn't anticipated the energy of the crowd following me, though. With no security on this side to keep them at bay, they pressed in around me, excitement in their eyes, questions on their lips. They blocked us off from moving up the street toward the car or down the street toward potential freedom. We were trapped in a half-moon of affection.

I held up my hand, desperate to flag down a taxi, but of course, since I urgently needed one, none were around. Reporters behind the fans held microphones my way, still trying to get an answer to their numerous questions. The paparazzi behind them started shoving to get a better shot. The girls around me looked elated that I was so close, and yet, I clearly wasn't close enough.

There was a fevered energy to the air that was making my heart race, and beside me Kiera whimpered, "Kellan, I don't like this, let's get out of here."

"We'll get a cab in a second." Almost exactly after I said it, the fans surged forward, the brief space between us and them vanishing. Hands ran up my chest, arms circled my waist, pens were shoved in my face, and cell phones were raised, recording it all. Kiera was pushed away from me as people squeezed between us, and even though I tried to hold her tight, our fingers eventually slid apart.

And then, the entire crowd moved forward as the fans were pushed by the reporters who were pushed by the paparazzi. I was shoved in a clearly unintentional way, and a couple of fans screamed as they realized how precarious their position was. I resisted their shove, absorbing the bodies pressing into me, but Kiera was swept away by them. I tried to lunge for her, but there were too many people in the way, and I couldn't stretch far enough to grab her. I watched in helpless horror as she was accidently pushed off the edge of the sidewalk, as a fan tried to grab her but missed, as she harshly landed on the busy street.

Icy adrenaline hit me hard as I watched a nightmare playing out before my very eyes. *This can't actually be happening.* I instantly surged toward Kiera, violently breaking away from the people around me, driving through the few who'd snuck behind me, who were almost standing in the street themselves. Kiera was struggling to get to her feet, clearly disoriented. My heart thundered in my chest; there was a truck speeding toward her, and there was no way on Earth she could possibly move fast enough to avoid it.

No.

Running to her side, I yanked on her arm with all my strength to get her to her feet, then I shoved her away from me and took her place. It was all I had time to do. In the span of a single heartbeat, as I instinctively lifted my hand, as I waited for the truck to inevitably hit me, every single moment with Kiera flooded my brain: meeting her, loving her, losing her, loving her again, every look, every sigh, every smile—everything. My last thought was a prayer, a hope that I'd pushed Kiera far enough away to keep her safe.

Let me take it all. Let her live. That's all I ask. Let her live.

Chapter 32

FEELING LOVED

I was aware of sound first. A soft, incessant beeping, the occasional whir of a machine, the rustling of sheets. Someone sniffling. I inhaled a deep breath, minutely stretching, and instantly regretted it; there was a stabbing pulse of pain deep inside me. Careful not to move too much, I worked my eyes open. It was surprisingly hard. They were so heavy, like I'd been in the middle of a really deep sleep. I heard someone say, "Kellan, baby?" but I couldn't focus; my mind felt splintered, fractured, and thoughts were hard to hold on to. I was so tired, and everything was so blurry. I blinked until my vision stabilized, but when the room came into focus, nothing made sense; I didn't recognize the bed, the walls, the lights, the floor. *Where the hell am I? Why can I barely keep my eyes open? Why does it hurt to move?*

"Kellan?"

A finger stroked down my cheek, and I slowly turned my head to see Kiera sitting beside me. She was beaming at me, her smile bright and happy, but her eyes were bloodshot, like she'd been sobbing. Why? It was frustrating, not being able to remember.

I opened my mouth to speak, and that ache of pain hit me again. My mouth was dry, like it had turned to dust from disuse. I swallowed three times, trying to work up some moisture, but it didn't help much. "Kiera?" I whispered. "What happened?" I tried to push through the fog, tried to sift through my memories, but the only thing I could clearly recall was leaving the radio station, trying to get through the crowd to the curb.

Kiera filled me in on the parts that were just...gone. "I got pushed into the street," she said. "You raced out to help me, and a truck hit you. You're in the hospital."

Her voice wavered as she said it, as she relived it in her mind. I struggled to remember, but it was still just a blurry wall of shapes and shadows. Her words terrified me, though, and I finally noticed the bandage at her hairline. She was hurt. "Are you okay?" I asked, worry stinging me.

Love in her red eyes, she shook her head. "You're alive. I'm perfect." She leaned over to give me a soft kiss.

The more my body woke up, the more I was aware that something was wrong with me. There was a constant dull ache inside me that shifted into a sharp, shooting pain if I moved wrong, if I breathed too deeply. I was still more tired than I should be, and my brain felt like it was lagging behind my thoughts. Eyes closed, I told Kiera, "I don't feel good."

Kiera ran a soothing hand over my hair. "I know. They had to operate on you because your spleen ruptured. They were able to save it, but you're going to be sore for a while."

I forced an eye open to look at her. It was so weird to think that just a little while ago, complete strangers were rooting around my insides. Guess this wasn't my lucky day after all. Or maybe it was. Small smile on my face, I told her, "Oh, good, I'd hate to be spleenless." My eyes drifted closed. "What the hell does a spleen do anyway?"

Kiera laughed at my comment, and the sound did more for me than whatever they'd given me to take the edge off my pain. "From what I remember in school, it's like the oil filter of your immune system...and it was once thought to be the source of anger. I'm not sure about that one, though."

I started to chuckle, but the second my abs contracted, a white-hot burst of pain shot through me, and I immediately stopped. "Oh, don't make me laugh," I told her.

She kissed my cheek. "I won't. We'll never laugh again, I promise."

That instantly made me start to laugh again, and I opened my eyes to half glare, half cringe at her. "I said don't make me laugh."

She smiled, then carefully bent over to rest her forehead against mine. "I love you so much. I'm so glad you're okay."

I tried to lift my arms, tried to pull her down next to me, but everything hurt. Sensing my intention, Kiera put her hand on mine to stop me. Then she adjusted herself so that she was lying beside me, in the crook of my arm. She tenderly rested her arm as high on my chest as she comfortably could, then she squeezed my shoulder in a hug. I exhaled a small sigh of contentment as she wrapped me in her warmth. "I love you too," I told her, feeling the tug of exhaustion.

Kiera kissed my head and squeezed me a little tighter. "You saved my life," she whispered, her voice trembling with emotion.

"I was returning the favor," I murmured. She had saved me in multiple ways.

I started fading in and out of consciousness, both resisting the pull of sleep and wanting to cave into it. I felt Kiera start to move away from me, and it partially snapped me back to alertness. My hand on her back tensed and tightened, holding her to me the best I could. "It's okay," she whispered. "I was just going to let the others come see you. They're all so worried."

Right, the others. I wanted to see them too, wanted to let them know I was mostly fine, but I wasn't ready for her to leave me yet. Not even for just a few minutes. I just needed a little more time with her. Reassurance that she really was okay. "Stay...just... for a minute." I was so tired that I had to force the words from my lips.

Kiera kissed my shoulder, whispering, "As long as you want, Kellan. As long as you want."

Forever. I want forever.

But my body had other plans, and I drifted off again what felt like just a few seconds later. I was almost instantly woken up by the sound of people trying to be silent. Trying...and failing.

"Shhhh, be quiet. He's trying to sleep."

"I *am* being quiet. It's not my fault someone put a cart full of shit right here by the door. What is this stuff anyway? Think there's any good drugs in here?"

"Shut up, Griffin. And leave that shit alone. It's just bandages and bedpans anyway."

"Bedpans! Why the fuck didn't you tell me those were bedpans before I picked one up!"

"He's joking. I'm pretty sure those are barf trays."

"Dude, how is that any better?"

Smiling, I cracked an eye open to see everyone crowding around my bed. And I mean everyone. Matt and Evan, Griffin holding Gibson, Anna and Kiera, Deacon, David, and Ray, and surprisingly, Justin. They were all looking at Griffin, trying to get him to stop talking.

Trying hard not to laugh, I murmured, "The first person to shut him up gets a hug." They all swung their attention to me, and I gave them a sleepy smile. "Hey," I said.

Anna instantly started crying, and even Matt and Evan swiped their eyes, but they were all smiling. Shaking his head, Evan leaned over me to give me a quick, careful hug. "Jesus Christ, Kellan," he murmured as he straightened back up. A tear rolled down his cheek, and he hastily brushed it off. "That was too fucking close."

I nodded at him, then looked at the friends that were struggling to keep it together. "I'm fine," I whispered. My eyes landed back on Evan's. "I'm just fine."

He scanned my covered body, swallowed, but nodded. Anna came up to me next. "I know you need to sleep," she said. "But I need a fucking hug."

I motioned her forward with my fingers since that was all I

could do at the moment, and she gingerly ducked in, wrapping her hand over my shoulder like Kiera had. She kissed my cheek, then said, "I hope you know...I would have killed you if you hadn't survived that." I smiled at her, and her expression turned somber. "Thank you for getting Kiera out of the way. You saved her life."

My eyes drifted to my wife as I carefully shook my head. "I saved *my* life," I told her.

Kiera smiled at me, and Anna giggled and kissed my cheek again. "Yep, there's my sickeningly romantic brother-in-law." Straightening, she said to Kiera, "He really is fine."

Kiera laughed and nodded, and the others moved closer for their pseudo-hugs. Matt was next. His eyes were as red as Kiera's as he shook his head at me. "Don't ever do that again, please."

Blinking slowly, I told him, "I make no guarantees." I'd do it a thousand more times if necessary, anything to protect Kiera.

The members of Holeshot hugged me next, telling me how happy they were that I was okay. I fought the sleep trying to reclaim me as I told each of them thank you. Then Justin stepped up to me. "You're here?" I said, grinning.

He shook his head. "I came the second I heard." His eyes started filling up. "Fuck, man." Then he gave me a hug that was a little too exuberant. I sucked in a quick pain-filled breath, and he cringed and let me go. "Sorry."

"It's fine," I said, trying not to laugh at the look on his face.

He backed off, and the last person in the room finally walked up to me. Griffin looked uncertain as he stood there with Gibson nestled in the crook of his arm. He glanced down at his daughter, then looked back up at me and shook his head. "I've never almost lost someone like that before. I don't...I don't like it." His light blue eyes watered as he stared at me, and I knew he was gonna lose it if I didn't lighten the mood.

With a smirk, I slowly told him, "Don't worry. You can't kill a god, remember?"

He instantly grinned. "Dude, you're not a god. Nice try,

though." As I struggled not to snicker, Griffin looked around the packed room, then leaned in and said, "Hey, so...I know this is shit timing, but...you still have to help me clean up my bedroom." Pulling back, he lifted an eyebrow at me. His expression clearly said *It sucks to be you, but a deal's a deal.*

The urge to laugh was so strong that I had to blow out a soft steady stream of air. "Sorry," I told him, smiling. "I don't think I'll be able to help after all."

Griffin sighed. "Yeah, I figured. Hell of a way to get out of it. I'd kick your ass, but a truck beat me to it."

A laugh stubbornly escaped me, and a wave of pain shifted it to a groan. "Ugh. Goddamn it, Griffin," I said through the discomfort. "Hug me, then go away."

He grinned, handed Gibson to Kiera, then darted in to give me a firm squeeze. "Glad you're okay, man."

"Me too," I murmured, looking at all of them. I opened my hand for Kiera, and she readjusted Gibson so she could take it. "Me too." Then I closed my eyes and stopped fighting the exhaustion. And as I drifted off again, the last thing I heard was someone snapping at Griffin to be quiet.

My room was flooded with people all day long. Just about everyone who worked on the tour came by to check on me. I quietly thanked them, addressing all the ones I knew by name. They seemed touched by that, surprised and pleased that I remembered them. Tory checked on me too, and I was a little surprised to see that all the anger was gone from her face, like she'd forgotten what I'd done in that radio station. But then she started animatedly mapping out the statement she was going to give to the press. Some overly dramatic piece about how I was on Death's doorstep, but I'd valiantly held on to life, and I was going to be just fine. She seemed ecstatic about it, like today was Christmas for her. The second Tory left, I looked at Kiera and rolled my eyes. She giggled in the most adorable way.

The small space was boisterous and noisy, but I still managed to nod off every once in a while. When I was in the tranquil space between awake and asleep, I heard bits and pieces of various conversations: Kiera on the phone, telling people I was all right, Matt and Evan asking Justin about his tour, Griffin complaining that I didn't have a cast for him to sign this time. I vaguely heard him mutter something about signing my face instead, then I heard a scuffle. Not long after that, the room was cleared out by the hospital staff.

By that evening, I felt more or less like myself again. Still in pain, still a little groggy, but more alert and awake than I was earlier. One of the nurses brought me a tray of food, but I wasn't hungry, and the food looked so unappealing; I wasn't even sure if I could make myself eat it. Kiera and I were currently alone in the room. The guys were downstairs with Anna and Justin, giving us some space. They said they'd pop back in to say goodbye before heading to the hotel for the night. That made me wonder what was going to happen with the tour now. The show would be starting soon, and we definitely weren't going to be there. I honestly didn't think I'd be able to finish the tour at all, and I really hated that. So many fans were going to be so disappointed. Hopefully, they understood.

Thinking of the tour made me realize that there was one person who hadn't checked on me today. And I was kind of thrown that she hadn't. As Kiera stepped toward the window, I asked her about it. "Have you heard from Sienna? She didn't come by. I'm kind of surprised by that." It would have been a great opportunity for a big splashy photo, and a way for her to begin repairing the damage I'd done during the interview.

"I'm kind of surprised by that too," Kiera said. "She sent flowers."

I peeked up from stabbing my Jell-O to see Kiera pointing to a small vase of flowers resting among the more opulent ones; the one from Nick was especially garish. "A subtle get-well bouquet isn't exactly her style. I was expecting her to hand deliver them to me in a sequined, floor-length gown." Even her card had been lowkey, merely saying, "I'm so sorry," and discreetly signed with an S.

Kiera smirked at my comment, then turned back to the window since she didn't understand Sienna's motives any more than I did. I was trying to convince myself that eating the Jell-O was a good idea when Kiera suddenly said, "Kellan, you have to see this."

There was an odd amount of reverence and awe in her voice. She raised the blinds, and I angled my head as much as I could to see what had her attention. When I spotted what she'd spotted, I dropped my plastic spoon. It was just getting dark outside, but the night was being kept at bay by dozens of people holding softly glowing candles. "What is that?" I asked, unsure I was seeing what I was really seeing.

"Those are your fans. They're here for you." She waved at the sea of lights, and the candles waved back.

Mystified, my gaze drifted to her face. "That's for me?" Because that looked like a vigil, and who the hell was I to have earned a vigil?

Kiera walked over to the bed, sat down, and tenderly ran a hand through my hair. "You're very loved," she said. "And not just because of what you are. Your fans see you. Through your music, they see you. And they love you." She put a hand on my jaw and stroked my cheek with her thumb. "It's not just *this* that they love, you know? It's you."

She leaned down and kissed my forehead while I tried to process that. Tried to accept it.

There was a soft knock on the door then, and when I peeked up to see who was here, my heart stuttered in my chest. "Gavin, Caroline...Martin? What are you doing in New York?" I couldn't keep the amazement off my face at seeing my father and Kiera's parents here. And behind them, I could see Hailey and Riley grinning at me. It blew me away.

Gavin stepped up to me, and there was moisture in his dark

blue eyes and fear on his face. "I'm sorry we're so late. We got on the first flight we could." He put a hand on my shoulder, and I could feel my eyes burning as I stared at him. "We were all so incredibly worried about you," he said.

Stunned stupid, all I could respond with was, "You were worried about...me?" I'd never had family who worried about me before. Ever. I couldn't even wrap my mind around it.

Gavin smiled at me. "Of course I was, son. When I heard you were in an accident, I was terrified." Pain flashed over his face, and I saw the truth in his words.

Hailey and Riley had moved to the end of my bed. Hailey rubbed my foot while Riley nodded and said, "We love you, bro."

It slipped so simply from his mouth, so easily, like it was something he was used to saying, used to hearing. It wasn't for me, and my entire body was choking with emotion. The tension made physical pain wash through me, but I ignored it as I bathed myself in their love.

Caroline and Martin approached the bed. Martin was smiling warmly at me, like he really did care about me. Caroline was holding Gibson, and she shifted her in her arms so she could touch my leg. "We came as soon as we could too." She glanced at Kiera, then looked back at me and pointedly said, "You're family, Kellan."

It was too much, too overwhelming. It was everything I'd been wanting, hoping, and searching for my entire life. And it was all being tossed at me at the exact same time, and I just couldn't take it. I looked up at Kiera because I knew she knew what this meant to me. I thought maybe she could put it into words for me, but the minute she locked eyes with me, she burst into tears. Seeing her lose it for me, because she was *happy* for me, calmed me down. I relaxed against my pillows, accepting the warmth in the room, as Caroline wrapped her arm around her daughter.

When Kiera grunted in annoyance and pulled herself

together, I gave her a soft smile. "So adorable," I told her. *So perfect. So wonderful. So incredible. And all mine.*

Our families stayed long into the night, and I had a chance to talk to each and every one of them. Riley told me he now officially had a girlfriend, which made Gavin sigh. Guess my little brother had gotten over the g-word. Good. Caroline told me she'd picked out my tux, then she told me it "had a little color to it." I wasn't sure what that meant, but I thanked her all the same. Martin told me he'd heard a recording of the interview, and he was proud of me for doing the right thing by his daughter. And fuck if that didn't choke me up. Hailey was the last one to have a heart to heart with me. With a sigh, she lay down on the bed beside me.

"You know, there are less drastic ways to get me to visit you," she said with a smile.

I bit my lip after a laugh escaped me. "Why do I know so many smartasses, and why are they always trying to make me laugh?" I said with a cringe.

She grinned, then sighed. "Hey, I was thinking...when I'm done with school, I want to—" She paused and looked over at Gavin, but he was busy talking with Martin and Caroline. Hailey returned her eyes to me and dropped her voice. "I want to come out west with you. I want to live in Seattle." She cringed. "Would that be okay?"

My jaw dropped. "You do?"

She nodded. "I'll visit Dad and Ry as much as I can, but...I want to spend some time with you."

Smile on my face, I dropped my eyes to the sheet covering me. "I'd like that," I told her. "I've never had family around me." Cringing, I looked back at her. "Even when I lived with my parents, I never had...family."

She bit her lip, her deep blue eyes watering, then she nodded. "I know." I lifted an eyebrow at her, surprised. I'd never told her about my life with John and Susan. Hailey softly sighed as she studied me. "That night you and Dad met, when we got back to the hotel, he was really upset. I hadn't seen him cry since Mom died, and he was...sobbing. He told me what you said to him, about your parents. I know...what they did to you." I averted my eyes as a mixture of shock and sympathy went through me. It did something to me, picturing Gavin in tears...over *me*. Hailey placed her hand on mine. "Don't be mad at him. I made him tell me, and he...he needed to talk about it. He feels so guilty..."

Lifting my eyes, I smiled at her. "I'm not mad. And I'm glad you know." I sighed. "I should have just told you when you asked why I didn't want to talk to him." Hiding it from her hadn't helped either of us.

She gave me a sad smile. "It certainly helped explain why you didn't want to meet him, why you were so mad at him." She shook her head. "I've been wanting to tell you that I knew for a while now, but I didn't know how to bring it up. I'm so sorry, Kellan."

Soft smile on my face, I shook my head. "Don't be sorry for me." My smile grew as I looked around the room. "I have everything I want." My eyes settled on Kiera. *Almost* everything. Marrying her, having children with her, that was next on my to-do list. Once I got out of here, of course.

Eventually Justin, Anna, and the D-Bags came back in to say goodnight, and Kiera and I made them take our families with them when they left. Because honestly, I got the impression they were going to steal some blankets and sleep in my room, and while sweet, it wasn't necessary. I'd see them in the morning.

Kiera stayed behind with me, and I was grateful for her peaceful presence. We were enjoying the quiet, enjoying each other's company, when I finally reached the point where I couldn't ignore my body's needs anymore. Damn it. "Crap," I told her. "I have to pee." I looked forlornly at the bathroom. It wasn't all that far from me but just laughing had sucked; I couldn't even imagine how painful getting up was going to be.

With a soft chuckle, Kiera kissed my cheek. "I could help you?" she offered.

It was sweet, but I had to at least try this on my own. Pride and all. "Uh, no, I got it. I can do this." I let out a slow, calming breath. "The nurse said I should get up and move around anyway." I leaned forward, and when everything inside me shifted, a deep pulsing ache told me to lie back down. I couldn't, though; I absolutely refused to use a bedpan.

Kiera put a supportive hand on my back. "She said tomorrow you should."

I fought back the pain, but it leaked out of me in a groan. "It's just a couple of hours shy of tomorrow," I told her. Ignoring the fact that my body was telling me this was a bad idea, I pulled back the covers, inched my legs around, and made myself stand up. Kiera had moved the IV stand over for me, and I clenched it tight as a burst of pain shot through me. It was so intense; my vision wavered, and I felt dizzy. I knew falling would hurt even worse, though, so I fought through the agony and lightheaded-ness until my body adjusted to my new position.

Once I was stable, it wasn't as bad as I feared. My eyes drifted to the window and shock replaced the pain. "Oh my God, Kiera. They're still here." Outside, in the chill of the night, was a swarm of candlelight, and I swear it was bigger than before.

Kiera patted my hand on the pole, indicating the bathroom with her other. "Of course they are," she told me, her voice soft. She might have accepted it, but I was so touched by the display that I couldn't even feel my pain anymore. Until I moved. Then I felt it in each stabbing step.

I shuffled my way to the bathroom, Kiera opening the door for me. I thanked her, then slid inside. Kiera took the opportunity to check out my ass, and the small smile on her face made me chuckle. Which made everything hurt. "Stop making me laugh and close the door," I told her.

She laughed in a way that I couldn't, then did what I requested.

Going to the bathroom, well, it sucked. But I was really proud of myself for accomplishing it without falling or passing out. I was softly smiling, reveling in my personal victory, when I opened the bathroom door and spotted a newcomer in my room...and it was someone I never would have expected to see here. Denny. Denny was here, squeezing Kiera in a friendly hug. What the hell was he doing here?

Denny and Kiera both turned to look at me, and I tilted my head in confusion. "Are you a figment of my pain meds? Or are you really standing right in front of me?"

The corners of his warm brown eyes crinkled as he gave me a beaming smile. "I'm really here. It's good to see you in one piece, mate." He walked over and tossed an arm around me, and I wobbled, both shocked and really fucking tired.

Denny steered me toward my bed, and I looked back to see a familiar blonde behind him, standing by Kiera. Abby, Denny's girlfriend. No, his fiancée. He'd proposed recently. She'd come too? "You're here? You both came all the way over here? For me?" I still couldn't quite believe what was in front of me. I must have fallen asleep. I must be dreaming. That made more sense to me.

Once Denny got me repositioned in bed, the flaring pain in my stomach subsided. I wouldn't be in pain if I was dreaming, right? With a sigh, Denny ran a hand through his dark hair. "Yeah, we came here for you," he said. He looked at Abby before returning his eyes to me. "It scared the piss outta me when I found out you were hurt. All I could think was that..." He averted his eyes and swallowed, and I recognized that movement as pain. No, grief. "We used to be close. We used to be like brothers. And if you died...it would be like a part of my family had died. And I don't think you realize that." He looked back at me, his eyes glossy. "I hate the idea of you dying without knowing how much I..." He paused to collect himself. "I don't know, I feel like, maybe I haven't been the greatest friend to you."

There was nothing he could have said that would have surprised me more. "Denny," I started to object.

He held up a hand to stop me. "I knew what was going on,

Kellan, with you and your dad, and I didn't say anything to anybody. I didn't help you like I should have."

His accented words were thick with guilt, and it made a different sort of ache rip through my stomach. "You were a kid," I told him. What was he supposed to do?

Denny locked eyes with me. "So were you," he said. "And when I moved away, I didn't keep in touch like I promised." Anger flashed over his face as he shook his head. "You needed me, and I wasn't there for you. And I'm really sorry. That was pretty shitty of me."

Okay, *now* I couldn't have been more shocked by his words. "Are you kidding? I slept with your girlfriend...repeatedly." If one of us was an asshole, hands down it was me.

Denny's lips curved into a frown. "Well, that was pretty shitty of you." His expression darkened. "But I left you alone in hell... and I almost think that was worse." He stared at me for a long moment, then he stuck out his hand. "I know we've already put the past behind us, and I know we're friends, but I want you to know, without a doubt in your head, that we're still brothers. You understand me?"

My eyes watered as I stared at him. I'd never met anyone with his level of compassion and understanding, and I hated what I'd done to him with Kiera, hated that he blamed himself for anything my father had done to me after he'd left. But more than that, I loved what he was saying, I loved that he still wanted us to be family. Thick or thin, real, even if chosen, we were blood.

Stunned but accepting, I took his hand. "Yeah, yeah, okay."

Chapter 33

I DO

Denny surprised me by spending the night at the hospital. Honestly, him being here at all surprised me, but him sleeping in an uncomfortable chair by my side all night long was shocking. We stayed up late, catching up, and I had to admit, it was really nice having him around again. Feeling like family again.

By mid-morning the next day, everyone else had reappeared, and my room was once again filled with warmth. I was ready to leave the hospital, but I also could have stayed here forever, surrounded by the people who meant the world to me. Once everyone was gathered, Kiera asked people how long they were staying. There was an odd mixture of excitement and hopefulness in her eyes when she talked to her mom, then Gavin, then Justin, and finally Denny and Abby. I wasn't sure what was going on, but I knew she was trying to plan something.

After everyone confirmed that they were sticking around for a few days, a fact that truly surprised and moved me, Kiera stood up and announced to the room that she had a proposition. She didn't explain her idea any further. Instead, she walked over to my bag of belongings on the nightstand and dug through it. Everyone watched her with curiosity on their faces as she rummaged through the bag, looking for something. I was baffled until she grabbed my wedding ring from the bag and showed it to me. Sitting on the edge of the bed, she reached for my left hand. Something about the movement, about the look in her eyes, the way her hand slightly trembled, made my heart race.

Voice low, she told me, "Kellan Kyle, you are the love of my life. You have my heart from now until the end of forever. Will you please make me the happiest woman on Earth and marry me...Thursday."

She slid the ring on my finger, and I had to swallow the sudden lump in my throat. I could feel the tears building in my eyes as I clenched her hand. *Yes. A thousand times yes.* I'd marry her this very second, but I kind of thought she wanted something a little more elaborate than a hospital room. "You want to get married on Thanksgiving...*here*?"

Soft smile on her face, she nodded. "The where doesn't matter...just the who. I can't wait another month to officially marry you, and what better way could we celebrate a day of giving thanks than by becoming husband and wife?" She swished her hand around the room. "The most important people in our lives are already here." She paused to frown. "Except Jenny and the girls. We'll just have to fly them back out to us. They should really be here for this."

"Not a problem," Evan said. I looked over to see him leaning against a wall, smile on his face and tears in his eyes. "I'll have Jujube gather the girls and head on over. She wouldn't want to miss this. And I would never hear the end of it if she did."

I chuckled at that, then immediately stopped myself. I really couldn't wait for laughing not to hurt anymore.

Kiera looked back at me, her smile radiant. "See? This is how we were supposed to get married."

My eyes scanned her face, my gaze catching on the ever-changing color of her eyes; they were almost bright green today, practically glowing. "You'll really be my wife," I murmured, hardly believing it.

She leaned forward and kissed me. "And you'll really be my husband."

I was reveling in how good that sounded when I heard Caroline let out a sad sigh. "Here, Kiera? Really?" Kiera and I looked over to see her frowning. "But we already sent out the invitations. We have family coming in from out of state, cousins you haven't seen in a decade or more. And everything is ready at our church. There's going to be a potluck after the ceremony. Polly is bringing her world-famous baked beans, and Gertrude is so excited to play the organ for you. She's ninety-eight, Kiera. She's only got a year or two left in her..."

Just beyond Caroline, Anna was quietly laughing her ass off. I tried not to watch her since seeing her giggling was starting to infect me. Biting my lip, I stared at the ceiling and tried to think of things that weren't funny. *War, death...baked beans.* Fucking baked beans. Damn it.

I felt Kiera get off the bed and looked down to see her put her hands on Caroline's shoulders. "Mom, I almost lost my husband yesterday. I don't want to wait another minute to become his wife. Will you please help me get married on Thursday?"

A tear dripped down Caroline's cheek; I figured it would be the first of many. "Of course I will," she said.

Kiera grinned. "Good, then find someone who can marry us on really, really short notice."

Caroline instantly rattled off things that needed to be done. She only looked sad when she mentioned not being able to use the dress she'd bought for Kiera. The puffy-sleeved dress that had Anna wanting me to run off with Kiera to elope; Anna looked thrilled that it had been left behind. Caroline got super-focused on making this happen, going so far as to give Gibson back to Griffin, while Kiera and Anna made plans to go dress shopping.

Kiera looked euphoric when she gave me a parting kiss. "We'll be back in a little bit. Will you be all right here?"

I nodded at her in answer, and she pulled away, giggling.

Tilting my chin up, I grabbed her hand and said, "One more before you go? Please?"

Knowing what I meant, she returned her lips to mine. I savored the moment, kissing her about six more times. As I did, I heard Griffin say, "Your wedding day is Thanksgiving. That's convenient." I broke away from Kiera to see Griffin pointing at me. "You probably won't forget your anniversary." He looked back at Anna. "We shoulda done that. I already forgot ours."

My stomach instantly tightened as humor coursed through me. I struggled to relax, struggled not to laugh. Fucking Griffin. "Uh, it won't always be on Thanksgiving, Griff."

He looked genuinely confused by that. "Huh? Yeah, it will."

My abs twitched, and I bit my lip, refusing to laugh. "Thanksgiving isn't on the same day every year. It moves around."

He narrowed his pale eyes and glared at me. "Don't even try fucking with me, Kell. I'm on to you," he said, tapping his head.

Everyone in the room snickered. Everyone except Martin. He stared at the ceiling and shook his head. I had to breathe out slowly and calmly to control my reaction—*I will not laugh...I will not laugh*. I started to explain to Griffin that I wasn't messing with him, but Kiera suggested I let it go, and I figured she was right. Some battles just weren't worth fighting, especially when I was trying not to laugh. And failing. One escaped from me, and I gently put a hand on my stomach as the pain ripped through me.

"Damn idiot," I muttered under my breath. Kiera laughed, squeezed my leg, then headed out the door with Anna.

Matt stepped up to me once they were gone. "Need anything, Kell?" he asked, looking me over.

I started to shake my head, then stopped and told him, "Can you help Evan get the girls here? I'll cover everything. My wallet's...in there somewhere." I pointed to the bag holding all my stuff, and Matt grinned at me.

"Are you sure you don't want to do it? I've only shown you how about sixty times," he said with a smirk.

I smiled at him. "I never said I didn't know how. I just like it when you do it."

Matt rolled his eyes. "Uh-huh."

Opening my bag, he rooted around for my wallet. Voice casual, I told him, "Don't touch the Sharpie."

Matt sighed but nodded. "It probably broke in the fall anyway," he muttered. Then he found it and held it up to me. Surprisingly, it was intact. "See why I love this shit?" he said.

I minutely pressed on my stomach as a small laugh got by me. "Put it back," I said with a grimace.

He frowned, but he did it, and I made a mental note to order him a brick of them for Christmas. Or maybe I'd enroll him in a Sharpie-of-the-month club. There had to be one somewhere. The thought had me dying inside, and my eyes watered as I tried not to laugh again.

Matt found my wallet and lifted it to Evan. "Let's call the girls," he said, tilting his head toward the hallway; they'd get better reception downstairs or outside.

They started to leave, but I motioned them back. They glanced at each other, then stepped up to the bed. "Need something?" Evan asked, concern in his eyes.

I stared at them both for a long moment, then gave them a solemn nod. "Yes." My face shifted into a playful scowl. "Do you two really have a bet on Kiera and me? I almost died...you have to tell me."

Matt started laughing. He looked up at Evan, who was grinning at me. "Oh yeah, that," Matt said. When he didn't elaborate, I narrowed my eyes at him. He laughed again, then nodded his head at Evan. "Yeah, we have an ongoing bet on you." He grinned. "We both bet a million bucks that you and Kiera will be together until the day you die." He frowned. "We never imagined you'd try to end the bet early by stepping in front of a flower truck." He raised an eyebrow at me. "We're both okay with the bet taking decades, dude."

My mouth tilted into an expression that was half amazement,

half amusement. "You both bet the same thing? That Kiera and I would make it?"

Evan shrugged, then nodded. "Of course we did, Kellan. We're not idiots. We know how this is gonna play out."

I grinned at them and slowly shook my head, moved by their confidence. And that was when Griffin entered our circle. "What are we discussing?" he asked in a whisper. Clutching Gibson to his chest, he pointed at me. "How to get him to a bar for a pre-wedding shot? Yeah, I've been wondering that too. What did you guys come up with?"

Shifting my smile to Griffin, I ignored his question and told him, "We were just talking about how excited I am to get married." I paused to sigh. "After Thursday, when I call Kiera my wife, she'll actually *be* my wife."

Griffin grunted. "Thank God." He raised his eyebrows at me. "No offense, but that shit was annoying."

While I frowned at Griffin's comment, Matt dramatically dropped his jaw. "Did you just say no offense?" he asked. "I've never heard you say those words before. I didn't even think you *could* say them." He gave Griffin a proud smile and faked wiping a tear off his cheek as he looked at Evan and me. "Guys, he's maturing."

Griffin immediately gave him the bird, and Matt pursed his lips. "Never mind," he amended. "Spoke too soon."

Evan and Matt left the room shortly after that, both of them chuckling. Griffin began pacing the room, gently swaying Gibson, smiling down at her like the entire world revolved around her. On the far side of the room, Denny was absorbed in a conversation with Gavin and Martin. Probably something about sports, by the look on Martin's face. It gave me a weird sense of peace to see my "brother" bonding with my father.

Justin was close to them, talking to Hailey and Riley about his show tonight. Somehow, he'd convinced Gavin to let Hailey and Riley go see Avoiding Redemption perform; they were both ecstatic about it. Knowing how protective Gavin was, I had to wonder if he was only okay with it because Justin was my friend, because he was here among my inner circle and therefore, trustworthy. That gave me a weird sort of peace too.

Caroline was working on the wedding, using the hospital's landline to make phone calls, and Abby was alternating between helping her and cooing at Gibson whenever Griffin got close enough. It was all so...perfect. Everything was right in my world. Except for the fact that I had to pee again and getting up still sucked. Oh well. I'd been through worse in my life. Even with the discomfort, this was heaven.

Jenny, Rachel, Kate, and Cheyenne joined us the following day. All the girls hugged in a circle of squealing that almost shattered the windows. Final preparations were discussed. Caroline had found a minister. Martin and Gavin had found food. Anna and Kiera had convinced a clerk from the city to come to the hospital so I could sign the marriage license. Matt was going to pick up my guitar so someone could play it during the ceremony. Everything was set except for outfits and decorations.

With bright smiles on their faces, the girls took off to go dress shopping. Looking a little less enthused, the guys headed out to go find suits. And I stayed behind, sitting on my ass and feeling useless. That feeling got even worse when everyone came back and started decorating the room, trying to make it as wedding-like as possible, and I couldn't do a damn thing to help them. I really hated just lying in bed while everyone was working so hard to make *my* wedding look nice.

I told Kiera as much and she joked, "Well, that's what happens when you go and tear an internal organ. Maybe next time you should be more careful."

With a smirk, I told her, "The next time we're hit by a floral truck, I'll be sure to do that." Her mom didn't find that funny.

At the end of the day, when the license was signed, the preparations were all in place, and my hospital room was as romantic as our friends could make it, Anna stole Kiera from me. Something about how Kiera shouldn't spend the night before her wedding with her fiancé. Kiera tried objecting, but Anna wouldn't have it, and the girls pulled her away from me. I missed her instantly, but knowing she'd legally be my wife soon made it easier. It also made sleep impossible. Luckily, Evan and Denny stayed behind to keep me company.

It was a little awkward at first, it being just the three of us. Evan still had mixed feelings about Denny. He was one of the few people who knew the truth about the night of the "mugging," and he'd never entirely forgiven Denny for beating the shit out of me. Even still, Evan wasn't one to hold grudges, and he tried to be as nice as possible to Denny.

"So, you and Abby...got engaged, huh?" Evan cringed as he scratched his head, like he didn't know what else to say to Denny.

Denny tightly smiled at him and nodded. "Yeah...she's great. We're really excited..." He averted his eyes, and I could feel the tension coming off him. The guilt.

Silence built in the room as I glanced between my two best friends. "Okay, you two need to knock it off." They both looked up at me, confusion on their faces. Eyes narrowed, I looked at Evan. "It wasn't his fault. He snapped, lost control, it could happen to anyone. I don't blame him, you shouldn't either." My gaze shifted to Denny. "We've already discussed this at length, and you don't need to feel guilty. Not when it comes to me. I took something that didn't belong to me, and I deserved to get my ass kicked for it." Denny opened his mouth, clearly about to object again, and I held up a hand. "This isn't about us, it's about the two of you. I need you two to get along. I need both of you to let it go."

Denny sighed, then looked over at Evan. Evan sighed as he met eyes with him. Denny swallowed, then shook his head. "I'm sorry," he whispered.

Evan looked down, then at me, then back at Denny. He

inhaled a deep breath, then said, "I know." Extending his hand out to him, he lifted his pierced eyebrow. "Don't do it again?"

Denny grinned as he took his hand. "Deal."

They shook hands, and I softly snickered. When they both looked back at me with puzzled expressions, I smiled. "Sorry, it's just...you two just made peace over a deal for Denny to never kick my ass again. I find that morbidly funny."

Evan rolled his eyes at me, then rolled his eyes at Denny. Denny started laughing, then we were all laughing. And it hurt. But it also felt great. Laughing meant forgiveness, and that was all I wanted right now. For everyone to forgive each other. We weren't the people we used to be, and we didn't need to hold on to the past anymore. Not when the future was so very, very bright.

We talked about weddings after that. Denny told us Abby had decided on Valentine's Day for their wedding. Apparently, she had a thing for holidays. In fact, Denny was taking her to see the Macy's Thanksgiving Day Parade in the morning. We badgered Evan about when he was going to ask Jenny to marry him, especially since he'd purchased her engagement ring months ago. With a shrug, he told us, "When the mood's right." That meant it could be in six minutes or six years, but I had a feeling Jenny wouldn't care when it happened. She'd take all the days with Evan that she could get, married to him or not.

That brought the conversation around to Matt, and we debated if he would ever ask Rachel to be his wife. "I bet he will," Evan said.

I raised an eyebrow at him. "I'll take that bet. I bet he will too."

Evan smirked at me while Denny frowned. "You can't both bet the same thing. Not if no one's betting anything different. How would you win?"

Evan laughed while I contained a chuckle. Looking over at Denny, I said, "You could bet against us?"

With a grin, he shook his head. "I'm not betting on someone *not* getting married."

Evan smiled. "Okay, I bet he asks her in some overly romantic way. Like an over-the-top, unnecessarily complicated way."

I furrowed my brows at him. "Quiet little Matt? You think he'll be elaborate? I think he'll do it when they're alone." I paused to smirk. "Right after they've had sex. He'll just blurt it out, not even realizing he's said it until it's out of his mouth."

Evan snorted, then extended his hand to me. "Okay, game on." I shook hands with him while Denny laughed at both of us.

Evan asked him if he wanted in on it, but Denny shook his head. "I'm not betting on my friends' relationships."

It warmed me to hear him call my friends his friends, and by the way Evan smiled at him, I figured he was touched as well. I smiled at his comment. "Your loss. I've already made two hundred bucks off these guys." I jerked my thumb at Evan, and Denny raised his eyebrows.

Smirk on his face, Evan shook his head. "I still can't believe Griffin beat us *all* to the altar. That asshole just has to win at everything, doesn't he?"

I laughed so hard that I had to gently press against my stomach to ease the shot of pain that ripped through me. Evan apologized, then he and Denny kept right on laughing. I joined them, ignoring the pain.

Needless to say, when I woke up in the morning, my stomach hurt, but I didn't regret it for a second. Sometimes a good memory was worth a little agony. Denny left to take Abby to the parade for a few hours. While he was gone, the rest of the guys showed up. Gavin and Martin chatted with me for a bit, then got to work moving all the furniture out of the room so there would be more space for visitors. Everything except my bed, the nightstand, and my IV stand were pushed out the door. Then they had the hospital put down some carpet, making an aisle to the window where a cluster of rope lights and twisted linens formed the arch where the minister would stand.

Watching the finishing touches made me giddy; it made this finally feel real.

When Denny returned, he took one look at the room and smiled at my two fathers. "I didn't think it could be done, but it looks really nice in here. Good job." Gavin and Martin grinned at him, appreciating his praise, and I shook my head, amused at how well Denny fit in with *everyone.*

After surveying the room for a moment, Denny decided it needed a pop of color and a bit of romance, so he tore apart Nick's gargantuan floral bouquet. I thought that was an odd choice if he was going for romance until he began artfully spreading the petals over the floor. As he did, I said, "Hey, Denny, can I have one of those?"

Question on his face, he held up a rose petal. I nodded and held out my hand, and he put a bright red one on my palm. I told him, "Thanks," then turned my head to ask Matt for a favor, but he already had a Sharpie in his hand and was holding it out to me with a smirk on his face. I blinked at seeing it, then smiled at him.

He rolled his eyes, then said, "This is my replacement Sharpie, and no, you don't get to keep it."

"But it's my wedding day," I said as I grabbed it.

Matt held onto it. "Regardless, I want it back."

Grinning, I told him, "I would never keep a man from his Sharpie." Matt's eyes instantly went to the nightstand where Kiera had stuffed my bag of belongings; his original Sharpie was tucked in with my stuff. "That doesn't count. That was a gift."

He rolled his eyes, released the marker, then watched as I wrote *Forever Your Husband* on the petal. Smirk on his face, he turned to Evan. "You're right," he said. "He *is* a walking Hallmark movie."

Evan grinned and nodded. I flipped both of them off, then gave Matt back his marker. "Hey, did you guys get me something to wear?" I asked, looking down at myself. I really didn't want to get married in a hospital gown, and my clothes from the accident were torn and covered in blood.

Evan and Matt both got the same stunned look on their faces as they locked eyes with each other. Frowning, I said, "You didn't get me anything to wear?" I settled my annoyance on Evan. "Aren't you my best man?"

Denny shook his head at them. "They did. Evan's got your stuff in his bag."

Evan frowned at Denny. "You were supposed to let him freak out a little longer. Then we were going to send Griffin to get some emergency clothes, and he'd come back with something godawful, 'cause he's Griffin, and then Kell would lose his shit, and *then* we'd tell him. Don't you know how this works?"

While I scowled at Evan, Denny looked at me with a grin on his face. "I'm the nice one, aren't I?"

I gave him a slow nod. "Yes. See why I need you around?"

Denny laughed, and that got Griffin's attention. "What are we doing? I thought I heard something about me getting Kellan something to wear." Looking over at me, he said, "You look fine. Just wear that." Then he smirked. "Actually, turn it around so it opens in the front. That'll be better."

My eyes returned to Denny, silently telling him, *See what I have to put up with?* He laughed again.

When it was time, the guys changed into their outfits. All of Holeshot had shown up by this point, along with all of Avoiding Redemption. Justin, Deacon, Matt, Griffin, and two others—all the people who knew both a mix of D-Bags songs and wedding songs—drew straws to see who would have the honor of playing guitar for the service. Deacon won, which was a relief because I was pretty sure Griffin was lying about knowing wedding songs.

Once everything was ready except for me, Evan helped me get up and get dressed. "Don't make me laugh," I warned him as I slowly stood. "I might fall over."

He didn't say anything, just calmly handed me a bag of adult Underoos. "Oh my God," I said, clutching my IV pole as I struggled not to laugh. "I hate you. I hate you so fucking much." The giggles slipped out as I removed the pair of Superman briefs. Oh well...I could be Superman for my wedding day.

Everyone who'd gone shopping with Evan started laughing; even my dad and Martin were chuckling. Shaking my head at them, I gingerly stepped into the underwear and tried my damnedest to pull them up without bending over. Evan snickered at me, then he did his best man duty and helped me put on my superhero underwear. The rest was slightly easier—black slacks and a white button-up shirt that I left untucked over the pants. I climbed back into bed after that, not even bothering with socks. I was dressed enough. And already tired. But excited too. And so, so ready.

Waiting for Kiera to arrive stretched every bit of my patience. Martin had arranged for a limo to pick up the girls from the hotel. When he glanced at his watch and told me they should be on route, my stomach shifted into this almost nauseating feeling of excitement and anticipation. I felt like I'd been waiting for this moment my entire life, and in a way, I had. Every day, for as long as I could remember, I'd wished for someone who could love me unconditionally. Someone who would care for me through the ups and the downs, who would always be by my side and on my side, and that was what today felt like—our official declaration of our unending, unlimited love. Kiera and I had already devoted our hearts and souls to each other, but today...today we became family. A true family.

Martin's phone chimed with a message. He read it, then smiled at me. "They're here. Are you ready?" he asked, genuine warmth on his face.

"Absolutely," I told him with a grin.

He nodded, squeezed my shoulder, then left the room to bring my wife to me. After he left, everyone else moved into place. The minister Caroline had found, a nurse who had helped stitch me up, was standing in front of the arch framing the window, her hands clasped together and a wide smile on her face. My bed was just to the right of her. Wearing dramatic black-on-black outfits, all the guys took up their positions: Evan and Denny to the right of me; Matt, Griffin, Gavin, Riley, and Justin on one side of the red-carpet aisle. The remaining band members and visitors were crowding the back of the room, hovering around the door.

For the moment, I was lying in bed, but getting married lying down just felt wrong. I knew I could stand long enough for the ceremony, and that was what I fully intended to do; I was just waiting until the last minute to do it. Everyone was holding candlesticks in a cup like the ones the fans outside were using. The main lights were off, but there were strung lights hanging over the tops and sides of the numerous long, white tablecloths hung around the room, and between those lights and the flickering candles, there was an appealing warm glow around the entire space. I had to say, even though we were doing this in a hospital room, the atmosphere was very romantic.

Deacon moved to the doorway, my guitar strapped over his shoulder, his long dark hair pulled back in a low ponytail. When he started a song, Kiera's favorite D-Bags song, I knew she was here. My eyes instantly watered, and I had to blink about twenty times to get myself under control. God, I was never going to make it through this whole thing.

The bridesmaids began entering the room, all of them dressed in deep red gowns of varying styles. Anna and Jenny were first, holding small bouquets instead of candles. Rachel and Cheyenne were next, followed by Kate, Hailey, and Abby. I glanced at each of my friends as the women they cared about appeared, and I smiled when I saw their reactions. Evan, Denny, and even Matt got a little glossy-eyed when they saw Jenny, Abby, and Rachel. Griffin grinned broadly when he saw Anna in her skintight dress, then he stuck his tongue out and curled it up in a provocative gesture that would have made Kiera blush if she'd seen it. Matt noticed and smacked him, carefully, since he was holding Gibson instead of a candle. Justin smiled warmly at Kate, and Kate gave him a shy smile in return. Hailey gave me a little wave when she spotted me, and Cheyenne gave me a playful wink.

Anna and Jenny took their positions on the left side of the minister while the other girls stood opposite the guys along the aisle. Once everyone was in place, all eyes fixated on the door, waiting for Kiera. My heart began thudding in my chest when Deacon started playing the wedding march. And moments later, when Kiera stepped through the door with Martin holding her arm, my breath completely stopped. She was gorgeous. No, she was radiant.

The dress she was wearing was stunning in its simplicity—a shining, shimmering white gown with thin straps and no extra adornments. It looked like it had been made just for her. Or just for me. Her dark hair was curled but left down around her shoulders, and she was wearing the guitar necklace that I'd given her as a goodbye. A goodbye that had ended in a new beginning, in a together-forever reuniting. Kiera's eyes were a heavenly green tonight, highlighted in light makeup and a sheen of unshed tears. She was holding a bouquet of calla lilies and trembling as her father led her down the aisle...led her to me.

Seeing her like this, watching her slowly approach me, it was overwhelming, and my eyes filled up on me. When she stopped at the foot of my bed, all I could think to say was, "You're breathtaking."

The tears in Kiera's eyes grew heavier as she smiled at me. Then she looked at the bed and moved like she was going to climb in with me. "Wait," I told her, then I started sitting up.

Kiera instantly took a step toward me. "No, Kellan, don't. You're still weak, you can lie down. You don't have to stand for this."

Grasping my IV pole, cringing as the pain washed through me, I told her, "I've been waiting my entire life to marry you, Kiera. I think I'll stand."

As I began the process of getting to my feet, Gavin was suddenly at my side, helping me. The tears in Kiera's eyes rolled down her cheeks as she watched my father escorting me to the altar. Gavin helped me shuffle my way over to the minister, then he moved back into place beside Riley. Martin kissed Kiera's cheek, then let her go. She rushed to my side, clutching me like she was afraid I was going to topple over. The intense flash of pain was gone, though, and while I was a little lightheaded, I was okay, and I told her as much.

Kiera smiled at me, then kicked off her shoes so we were both barefoot. I chuckled at the playful move, only mildly cringing as my body complained. The minister thanked everyone for being here, and I reached into my pocket and discreetly handed Kiera the petal I'd made for her. She read it, then she looked up at me with wonder and amazement on her face. And tears. So many tears. Seeing the love and joy in her expression made it really hard to hold in my own tears, to not sweep her into my arms and kiss her. But we weren't there yet, so I resisted the almost painful need to physically express my love for her.

Kiera took my free hand with both of hers when the minister directed her comments at us. "Kellan Kyle, Kiera Allen, your friends and family are gathered here today to watch your two separate lives merge into one. From this point forward, you will face the trials, tribulations, and triumphs of life as one being. You will be bound together, body and soul, and the desires of the one will be forsaken for the needs of the two. But there is strength to be gained from this bond, for each of you. Where one might break, two can stand tall. Where one might fold, two can hold firm. From here until the end of your days on Earth, you will have someone to support you during times of weakness, comfort you during times of grief, encourage you during times of fear, and celebrate with you during times of joy. That is a gift, one that should never be abused or taken for granted. Cherish each other as God cherishes you, and you will both know peace."

Kiera squeezed my hand, and I knew she was just as moved by those words as I was. The tears in her eyes grew heavy again, and back in the crowd I heard a couple of people sobbing already. I struggled to keep it together while the minister said to Anna and Evan, "Do you have the rings?"

They both nodded and handed us the rings we'd given them yesterday, mine to Kiera, Kiera's to me. Then the minister asked if we wanted standard vows, or if we wanted to say our own. "I'd like to say something," I told her, my eyes never leaving Kiera's.

Surprising me, Kiera nodded and said, "I'd like to say something too."

The minister smiled and gave me a small encouraging nod. I released the IV stand, pausing a moment to steady myself before grabbing Kiera's left hand. Holding her ring at the end of her ring finger, I opened my heart and let it all pour out. "Kiera Michelle Allen, my life was empty before you stepped into it. I thought I had everything I needed, but only because I didn't let myself want anything. And then I saw you, and you burned a hole straight through me. I have never wanted anything more in my life. And I have never been more terrified in all my life. In *all* my life," I repeated, meaningfully.

Kiera swallowed and minutely nodded, and I knew she understood how significant that comment was. There had been many things for me to be afraid of in my life, but loving her, at least in the beginning, had surpassed every fear I'd ever had. Kiera looked like she wanted to comfort me, but I wasn't finished yet.

The seriousness left my expression as awe filled me. "And then, beyond some miracle that I'll never understand, I got to keep you, and now...I'm only just beginning to understand what it means to *truly* want something. Because I want so much now. I want to make you happy. I want to give you the world. I want you to be proud of me. I want to comfort you. I want you to comfort me. I want to hold you when you're scared. I want you to hold me when I'm scared. I want to make you laugh. I want to make you blush." Smirking, I leaned in and quietly said, "I want to make you scream." She instantly flushed with color, making me chuckle.

Sliding the ring all the way up her finger, I continued with my desires. "I want to give you a home. I want to fill it with children. I want to take care of you. I want to grow old with you. I want you by my side, every day." I folded my hand over hers. "I just want you. Do you want me too?"

I could see the emotion choking her, could see her struggling to answer me. She swallowed, nodded, then said in a whisper, "I do."

I beamed at hearing her answer, then patiently waited while she composed herself. When she was ready, she grabbed my left hand and slowly slid my ring onto my finger. As she did, she said, "I never thought of myself as anything but plain and ordinary until you came along. The way you look at me, the way you see me...you pull something out of me. When I want to hide, you urge me forward. When I think I'm not good enough, you make me believe I am. When I feel anything but pretty, you convince me I'm beautiful. Just being around you makes me feel special. You don't think you're good at loving people, but you are. Your friends, your family...the level of love that you have for people astounds me. You don't think people love you back, but they do. They fiercely love you. *I* fiercely love you. I've never met anyone as passionate as you, as kindhearted as you...as amazing as you. You love with every fiber of your soul. You inspire me every day. And if you'll agree to be my husband, I'll do my best to make you proud of me, to inspire you."

Her words drove deep into my soul, filling a void that had been expanding my entire life. A tear rolled down my cheek as I marveled at this beautiful soul in front of me. *My wife. My beautiful, incredible wife.*

Then Kiera's face scrunched into an endearing expression of awkwardness. "So...will you...do you? Take me?" Her eyes widened and she quickly added, "As your wife."

The entire room softly laughed, and I couldn't hold it in. God, she was cute. Kiera chuckled along with everyone else, and I was happy to see her laughing at herself. She was getting better and better about letting the embarrassment go, and I was so proud of her.

I grabbed the IV pole as a wave of pain made me unsteady. "I do," I said. After blowing out a long, even breath, to try to stop the giggles from returning, I told her, "So damn adorable. I never stood a chance."

Kiera grinned at me, looking mildly self-conscious but ultimately unworried. Our vows completed, the minister said, "By the power vested in me, I now pronounce you husband and wife. You may kiss your bride now."

Feeling another tear slide down my cheek, I told her, "Thank God, 'cause I couldn't hold out another damn second." Then I dropped the stand, reached for Kiera's face, and kissed my wife. Kiera looped her arms around my neck, and the crowd of friends and family clapped. I barely heard them as my lips moved softly with Kiera's. There was a depth to the kiss that had never been there before—a promise, an encouragement, a belief in the hope of our future. It made the tears flow even harder down my cheeks.

And then, over the clapping in the room and the pounding of my heart, I heard the minister say, "Ladies and gentlemen, Mr. and Mrs. Kellan Kyle."

Then there was shrieking, whistling, clapping, and foot stomping. Kiera and I laughed between soft kisses, briefly gazing at each other between connections, our faces a mirror image of joy. A part of me couldn't believe this was actually happening, that this was real, but I'd done it; I'd finally married the woman of my dreams. I'd never felt such radiant bliss in all my life, and I was positive nothing would ever top this day. Nothing.

Chapter 34

AN OFFER

When my strength began to give out on me, I asked Kiera if we could lie down. As she led me back to my bed, I noticed the lights outside my window. The fans. They were still there, holding their candles, silently sending out prayers for my recovery. It blew my mind that so many people—so many strangers—would spend days out in the cold, give up time with their families on a holiday, just to show me that they cared. And like their prayers were working, I felt my strength returning, and I shifted course so I could be closer to them.

I stepped up to the window, and the people began moving their candles back and forth, waving with them. There were men, women, and even some kids in the crowd. Raising my free hand, I waved back, and even with the distance between us, I could hear them scream and cheer. Kiera was right, these people cared in a way that went beyond skin deep. There was something they saw in me, something they heard in my music, experienced in my voice, something that drew them in on a deeper level. It was probably something different for every person down there, but I knew, without a doubt, that I'd touched them in some way. I'd changed them, and they were here to thank me for it. I wished I could personally thank each one of them in return, but all I had to give them at the moment was a greeting and a smile.

"See how loved you are?" Kiera whispered from beside me.

Turning to face my wife, I paused a moment to absorb the love and adoration that was streaming from her; she was practically glowing with it. "Yes, I do," I told her. Then I did what I'd wanted to do for so long: I cupped her cheek, leaned forward, and kissed her in front of the entire crowd of well-wishers.

When we pulled apart, Kiera helped me back onto the bed, and I nearly groaned in relief when I was lying down again. Kiera climbed on top of the covers with me, and friends and family crowded around to congratulate us. Tears rolling down her cheeks, Caroline gave me a warm, gentle hug. Martin shook my hand and damn if there wasn't pride in his eyes and respect on his face. I didn't want to jinx it or anything, but I was beginning to believe that he might actually like me. Anna hugged me next, then Griffin leaned over Kiera and fucking kissed me. Again. And once again, I couldn't get away from him fast enough.

"Fuck, man," I said, trying to wipe the feel of his mouth off mine.

Griffin laughed as he smacked my thigh. "Congrats, dude." Then he added, "Hey, you took my advice. You're getting better at the tongue thing."

Jackass. Kiera's parents looked between us with confused and concerned expressions. Anna was laughing. And so was Kiera. She was laughing so hard that tears were rolling down her cheeks, and she was clutching her stomach. I smiled at her obvious glee, then flipped off Griffin. When Kiera was calmer, she motioned for Griffin to hug her, and that surprised me more than anything else that had happened so far.

She murmured something to him that I couldn't hear, and when Griffin pulled back, he had a mischievous smile on his face. "You love me," he stated.

Kiera's expression evened. "I didn't say that."

Griffin nodded as he released her. "But that's what you

meant," he said in singsong. "You totally love me!" Thrusting both hands in the air, he shouted, "Kiera totally wants me!"

Matt shoved him out of the way as I tried not to laugh at the horrified look on Kiera's face. Some of the nurses approached my side while Matt softly conversed with Kiera. The nurses congratulated me on my marriage while also openly flirting with me. That made me want to laugh too. Evan replaced Matt on Kiera's side; he scooped her off the bed, twirling her in a boisterous hug. Matt approached my side while Jenny and Evan hugged my wife.

"Congratulations, Kell," Matt said, leaning down to hug me. When he straightened, his face was oddly serious. "I know this isn't the right time, but...what about the tour? Where do we go from here?"

I sighed as I considered that. "I don't know, but I know I won't be able to go back for a while. And honestly, by the time I can go back, if I even feel up to it, there won't be much of the tour left." I sighed again, then shook my head. "We can figure that out later, but for right now, I was kind of thinking...you guys should just go home. No point hanging around."

Evan and Jenny approached as I was saying that. Evan furrowed his brow. "Go home? Now? But what about you?"

He scanned me, concern clear on his face. I smiled at seeing it, then shook my head as I looked over at Kiera giving Denny a friendly hug. "I'm already home." Looking back at Evan, I shrugged. "Kiera and I will be fine here until they release me. And then, I don't know, maybe I'll stay on the East Coast for a while, visit Gavin's side of the family. Hailey tells me I just *have* to meet our grandmother. Apparently, she's feisty."

I laughed a little, and Evan nodded as he leaned down to hug me. When he pulled away, he frowned. "Is it weird that I'm gonna miss you?"

Smiling at him, I shook my head. "You shouldn't miss me. You should worry about what I'm going to do as payback for the underwear."

His dark eyes widened. Matt snickered while Jenny looked

between Evan and me with confusion on her face. "Underwear?" she said. "Do I even want to know?"

Evan just laughed in response. Jenny rolled her eyes, then gave me a quick squeeze, telling me she was so happy for me. Abby took her place when she stepped back. She gave me a warm hug, then straightened and said, "I'm so glad we could be here for this. I know Denny would have hated to miss it."

I nodded at her. "And I'd hate to miss yours." I raised an eyebrow at her in question.

With a soft giggle, she said, "Of course you're invited. You and Kiera both. Did Denny tell you it's on Valentine's Day?"

Her expression was so animated, so joyful; I chuckled at seeing it. "Yeah, he mentioned that. I can't wait."

I asked her about the parade, and her gray eyes lit up as she told me about all her favorite parts. There were a lot of them. Denny was softly laughing as he stepped up to her side. Looking at me, he said, "I should have warned you not to bring up the parade." He glanced back at the line of people waiting. "Not unless you had a lot of time to discuss it."

Abby laughed at his comment, then kissed his cheek and stepped away, giving us privacy. Denny was smiling as he looked down at me. "Not exactly how I imagined things ending when Kiera and I moved in with you, but...I think this was the right ending." He held out his hand to me. "Congratulations, mate."

I stared at his hand, shook my head, and opened my arms. "Family doesn't shake hands, family hugs," I told him.

He laughed, nodded, then leaned in to hug me. After pulling away, he softly said, "I already told Kiera this, but Abby and I want to talk to you guys later, when things are quieter."

Eyebrows furrowed, I looked back at where Abby was smiling at Gibson. "Everything okay?"

Denny nodded. "Everything's great." He lightly patted my shoulder, then stepped away so others could congratulate me.

Other friends stepped up to me then: Justin, Kate, Rachel, Cheyenne. Hailey and Riley stepped up to me together. Riley partially climbed onto the bed to give me a hug. "This was cool," he said. "I mean...for a wedding." He shrugged after that, and Hailey laughed and rumpled his hair.

She hugged me next, lingering far longer than our brother. "I'm so happy for you two," she whispered in my ear.

Feeling my eyes sting, I told her, "Thank you. There were times when I thought we'd never get here."

Pulling back, she gave me a warm smile. "I know. I remember." Wiping her eyes, she shook her head. "But you made it, so there's only one thing left for you to do."

"What's that?" I asked.

She lifted her eyebrows at me. "Come visit us in Pennsylvania. After you get out of here." She pressed her hands together. "Please?"

Since I'd already been contemplating it, I nodded. "Okay."

Hailey squealed, then said, "Promise?"

Again, I nodded. "I promise." I still needed to talk to Kiera about it, but by the way she was smiling at me, I didn't think she'd have an issue with us spending some time with my family.

Deacon and the rest of Holeshot and Avoiding Redemption said their congratulations next, and Kiera thanked Deacon for playing for us. Once that group moved away, there was only one person left to see us, and he already had tears in his eyes.

Gavin's lip quivered as he said, "I'm so happy for the both of you." He paused to collect himself, then continued. "Savor this moment. Remember this feeling because it won't always be like this. You'll have ups, you'll have downs." He paused again to laugh. "You'll drive each other crazy. But it's worth it if you stick through it. I had so many good years with my wife before she died." His expression turned peaceful and reflective.

Moved, I grasped his hand with both of mine. "Thank you, Dad." I wasn't sure how it would feel to call him that. I never had before, not directly to him. But I was surprised to find that it felt completely natural, normal even.

Gavin was shocked, though, and his eyes both widened and

moistened. He looked uncertain how to respond and over-whelmed with emotion. Seeing it was tightening my throat, but I just kept smiling at him, letting him know that I felt it too. He gave me a nod and placed his other hand on top of ours, sealing us together, the way it should have been from the beginning.

Everyone hung around for the reception/Thanksgiving dinner, and Kiera giggled uncontrollably when the nurses brought in trays of turkey and stuffing. My wife was so cute. After a leisurely meal and lengthy conversations, people started leaving. My father and siblings hugged me as they said goodbye, and after Gavin invited me again to visit him, I assured him, and my sister, that I would soon; once I knew for sure when I was getting out of here, once I had a chance to talk everything over with Kiera, I'd make more definitive plans with him.

Kiera's bridesmaids nearly tackled her as they said goodbye in a boisterous, tearful group hug. Jenny made a comment about never wanting to see either of us in a hospital again, so naturally, I jokingly tossed out, "Guess you're having the baby on the bus, babe."

Kiera spent the next twenty minutes convincing everyone that she wasn't pregnant. My stomach flared with pain as I tried not to laugh and failed miserably. Kiera glared at me, but I saw a spark of desire in her eyes. She might not want to be pregnant right now, but she wanted to be someday. And once I was healed enough that it wouldn't be exceedingly painful, I was more than happy to practice making a baby with her. Over and over.

As Evan and Matt were herding Jenny, Rachel, Kate, and Cheyenne out the door, Justin told them to wait, then came up to me to say his goodbyes. He held out his hand and I shook it. "I'm glad you're doing all right, man. What the label did to you with Sienna was crap. Pure crap. I wouldn't blame you if you dropped 'em." Since I didn't know what I was going to do yet, I didn't have anything to say to that. Justin smiled, then leaned in and said, "Next tour, when the D-Bags are headlining arenas, we'll open for you." He twisted to point at the members of

Holeshot, who were leaving the room with the other members of Avoiding Redemption. "We'll both open for you."

Amused at his optimism, I smirked and told him, "I'm all for going on tour with you, but we're not going to be headlining stadiums anytime soon."

Justin laughed as he ran his hand through his layered hair. "You sure about that? The D-Bags are on top of the world right now. I'd say your days of playing anything *but* the large venues are long behind you."

I wasn't so sure about that, especially after the scandal I'd just confessed to being a part of, but who knew…I'd seen much stranger things. "Yeah, let's make it happen," I told him. Justin grinned, then headed over to Evan, Matt, and the girls. He left the room holding Kate's hand, and I had a feeling the next time I asked him if he was in a relationship, he'd have a much more decisive answer.

Kiera's parents said their goodbyes next. Anna and Griffin were leaving with them, mainly because Caroline was reluctant to part with Gibson. Anna was trying to get her mom to put Gibson in her car seat before they headed downstairs, but Caroline just wasn't interested in giving her up. "Mom, if you hold her nonstop, she's going to get used to it, and I'm never going to be able to put her down!" Anna complained.

Rocking Gibson, Caroline pursed her lips and told her, "She'll be fine, Anna, and I have to hold her. I just have to. I don't get to see her as much as you."

Griffin nodded. Then surprising the hell out of me, he said, "Babies should be held. It helps them form bonds and shit."

Kiera was staring at Griffin wide-eyed, clearly shocked by that too. It wasn't all that often that Griffin made a really good point, and the fact that he'd made it about parenting was kind of mind-boggling. Maybe the guys and I wouldn't have to intervene as much as we thought.

Once that group left the room, Denny and Abby were the only ones left. Remembering that they'd wanted to talk to Kiera and me alone heightened my curiosity. Kiera asked if they were going to head back to the hotel soon, and Denny nodded. Relaxing back in his chair, he grabbed Abby's hand and said, "Yeah, in a minute. Now that everyone is gone, there is something that Abby and I wanted to talk to you guys about."

Kiera sat up on the bed. "What is it?"

Before Denny could answer, my phone rang. I knew who it was without having to look. Kiera had changed the ringtone for Sienna, so now it played "You're So Vain" whenever she called me. It cracked me up, and even if I knew how to change it, I wouldn't.

Everyone looked over to the nightstand holding my stuff. "Sienna," I said. "I wonder what she wants."

Kiera got up to retrieve my phone. She quickly answered it so it wouldn't go to voicemail. "Sienna?" Kiera paused, then said, "Yeah, Kellan's a little out of commission right now, so I answered his phone for him." There was ice in her voice as she said that, and I couldn't blame her for feeling angry. If Sienna had just spoken up, told the fans the truth, I wouldn't be lying in a hospital bed right now.

Kiera listened to Sienna for a moment, then her eyes narrowed, and she told her, "You played with people's heads, drummed up a juicy story that wasn't even real. What did you think would happen?"

She again listened to something Sienna was saying. Her expression softened, then she sighed and said, "Hold on, Sienna. I'm going to put you on speaker." Kiera did something to my phone, put it on my lap, then told Sienna to go ahead.

Sienna's accented voice instantly filled the silent room. "Kellan, love, I'm so sorry about what happened to you. I feel awful, just awful. I don't even know how to fully express how horrid I feel."

I wanted to believe that, but I'd been fooled by her before. Many times. And if she truly felt guilty, wouldn't she apologize in person? "Yeah, I got your flowers," I dryly said.

She sighed. "Look, I know you don't understand, but everything I'm doing, I'm doing for you, for the both of you."

Narrowing my eyes at the phone, I told her, "You're right, I don't understand."

"You will never have to worry about being manipulated by me again. I give you my word. And you won't have to worry about Nick either. My contract was up after that last album. I've threatened to walk if he bothers you again."

Shock stunned me into silence. Glancing around the room, I finally managed to say, "You...what?"

"I also spoke with the president of the label, Nick's father. He's none too happy about how his son has been handling things lately. He doesn't want the label associated with scandals. You calling the label out on the radio got his attention. My admitting to him what Nick helped orchestrate...well, let's just say that Nick will probably have to get permission to take a piss from now on."

Denny softly laughed at that, but I was still so shocked; all I could do was gape. "Why would you do that?" Kiera asked.

Sienna paused for a long time before answering. "Because I wronged you—both of you. And I'm trying to make it up to you. I've been stewing about this for days, but I'm going to give a public apology. I'm going to confess my part in what was done to Kellan."

Kiera sat on the edge of the bed, surprise on her face. "You'll lose fans. They'll turn on you. Your career...?"

"I'll bounce back," Sienna brightly said. "I always do."

Kiera looked just as stunned as me. "Well, thank you for helping us," she said.

In a near whisper, Sienna replied, "If you knew everything I did to hurt the two of you, love, you might take that back."

"It's probably better that you never tell me then," Kiera said, shaking her head.

Sienna laughed. "Agreed. But I give you my word that I will completely leave your relationship alone from now on."

I looked over at Denny with a frown, because now I couldn't help but wonder just how much of that shitshow had purely been because of Sienna. Denny stared back at me with a thoughtful expression, and I saw a decision solidifying in his dark eyes as he minutely nodded to himself. I wanted to ask him what he was thinking, what he'd wanted to talk to us about, but before I could get off the phone with Sienna, she asked Kiera if her book was finished, if she could give it to her agent.

That instantly worried me. I didn't trust that Sienna would stick to her word; I'd heard too many empty promises from her. Kiera seemed to feel the same. In a quiet voice, she told her, "It's finished, but I, uh...I want to do it on my own."

Denny and I grinned at the same time. Sienna made a surprised sound. "Really? You think you'll get anywhere that way?"

With a laugh, Kiera told her, "I don't know...guess we'll see."

"All right then. Well, if you change your mind..."

Kiera smiled. "I know where to find you."

Still sounding stunned, Sienna wished Kiera good luck, then said goodbye to me. I grinned at Kiera after disconnecting the call. "Look at you, turning down an offer from one of the biggest stars on the planet."

Kiera instantly looked ill. "Crap, did I just make a huge mistake?" she asked, looking between Denny and me.

We glanced at each other, then answered her simultaneously. "No."

That made me laugh, then cringe in pain. Denny gave me a small, empathetic smile, then he looked over at my wife. "You'll get there your own way, Kiera, and you'll feel great about how you did it. I may not have read your story yet, but I've read your papers, and you're brilliant. I *know* you'll get there."

She smiled softly at him. "Thank you. That means a lot to me."

Silence fell on the room, but there was a charge to it, a feeling of unspoken importance, a palpable anticipation of whatever it was Denny and Abby wanted to talk to us about. Kiera and I looked at each other, then we both looked over at Denny. His expression was serious now, all business. Leaning forward over his knees, he clasped his hands together and studied Kiera and me before finally speaking. "Abby and I have been discussing something recently. We've been discussing it a lot actually."

"Discussing what?" I asked.

Denny smiled, then looked over at Abby. She instantly pointed at me and said, "You, mate."

The two of them sitting around talking about me was so odd that I couldn't even imagine it. Denny noticed the confusion on my face and laughed. "You and your band," he said. The humor on his face morphed into something close to anger. "Abby and I both feel that you are being poorly represented. The band isn't being looked out for. The people who are supposed to be protecting you aren't." His deep brown eyes shifted to my bed. "That much is clear."

Looking back at me, he indicated himself and Abby. "We both have a lot of experience in marketing things, people, brands, creating positive PR. If you're interested, we would like to manage you. We would speak for you, be your voice to the world. We would protect you." He pointed over to the window with his thumb. "And crap like what happened with Sienna wouldn't ever happen again. Not to that extent, at any rate."

I never in a million years would have anticipated those words coming out of Denny's mouth. It never even occurred to me that he would protect me like that, that he would *want* to protect me like that. "You want to be the band's...agents? You would do that for us?"

He gave me a warm smile. "Yes, of course we would."

Kiera seemed just as stunned as me. "But your jobs...?" she asked.

Denny shook his head. "The D-Bags would be my only clients, and I don't anticipate you needing my help full time. As long as we're able to, we would continue with our jobs on some level." He paused to put his hand on my arm. "But you would be my top priority, and if you needed me, I would be there for you. I would be honored to be the one standing up for you."

I was stunned and shaken, floored by his capacity for both forgiveness and loyalty. "Yeah, okay. I mean, I'll need to run it by the guys, but...yeah, let's do it. I'd be honored to have you guys represent me." I couldn't think of anyone better to have my back, to have all our backs. I stuck out my palm and shook hands with Denny, then Abby. I couldn't stop smiling and feeling like—finally—it wasn't all on me anymore. Glancing between Denny and Abby, I said, "And we'll pay you, of course." Because there was no way I'd let them do this for free.

Denny laughed. "We'll talk about that part later," he said. Then he waved his hand at my IV stand. "Maybe when you're not on drugs."

Everyone laughed at that, and I almost let out a sigh of relief. Just like that, Denny had lifted a huge burden off my shoulders, and I felt more confident, more relaxed, and more hopeful of the career I'd been stumbling my way through for years. With his help, Kiera's support, and my friends' talent...maybe we really could do this. Maybe Justin was right, maybe we would be doing stadium shows sooner than I thought. I really wasn't sure, but I was positive that together, with the help of my best friends and my soulmate, we'd figure it out.

Like Denny, I never would have imagined, back when he and Kiera had first moved in with me, that things would turn out this way. Also like my friend, I couldn't help but feel that this path we were on was the right one for us, for all of us. And considering all the shit we'd gone through together to get here, that was pretty fucking amazing.

Damn. I'd said it before, and I was sure I'd say it again, but I was one lucky son of a bitch. A fact I would never let myself forget. A fact I was reminded of when I was finally released from the hospital.

They made me leave in a wheelchair, something all the guys

delighted in teasing me about. Even though I'd told my friends that they shouldn't worry about me, that they should just go home, they'd all stayed until I was released. That meant a lot to me, so I tolerated their teasing and Kiera's amused grins. Although she pushed the limits of my tolerance when she patted me on the head like a dog. Smartass.

We were all heading to the airport—the guys were going back to Seattle, and Kiera and I were heading to Gavin's for a while. And once I was better...we wouldn't be rejoining Sienna on her tour. She'd made sure of that. The morning after her apologetic phone call, she'd shocked the hell out of me by living up to her word and confessing everything in a televised interview. She'd apologized profusely for her part of the scandal, told everyone that I hadn't wanted to go along with the deception, and then she'd given me an out by informing everyone that the D-Bags wouldn't be finishing the tour with her, that I would be taking time to rest and recover with my wife. I'd been really torn about going back to the tour or not, and right before the interview, the guys and I had been discussing the possibility of just staying home and starting on the second album. Having Sienna officially excuse us was another weight off my shoulders, and I found myself feeling grateful to her. And surprised that she'd done it since all of the backlash for it was falling on her. I felt bad for her, but then I remembered that she was the one who'd dug that hole to begin with.

There was a limo waiting for us when we got outside the hospital. A sort of apology from Nick, who was clearly trying to get back in his father's good graces. Everyone had a plane to catch, but the limo wasn't the only thing waiting for me outside, and I couldn't leave just yet. Every walkway was crammed with people, with fans. They cheered and screamed as they gleefully waved their signs, candles, and small bouquets of flowers. Seeing the affection brought tears to my eyes. I couldn't believe they were still coming out here every day, and I swear to God, some of them hadn't left since I'd been admitted.

People from the hospital were trying to keep them away from me, keep the path to the limo clear, but I couldn't just roll by them with a brief wave. These people had sacrificed for me, and I needed to acknowledge that, acknowledge them.

I held up my hand to stop the guy who'd bumped Kiera aside to take control of my chair. "Wait, I want to talk to them."

The staff seemed uncertain about my request, but Kiera grabbed my chair and turned me toward the crowd. The guys stayed by the car, giving me this time alone with the fans since they'd already had numerous opportunities to thank them. Well, Evan and Matt gave me time alone with them; Griffin was shoved into the limo by Matt. He didn't pop back out, so I figured he'd found something in there to occupy him. Probably Anna and Gibson. Or alcohol.

Once we were in front of the largest section of the crowd, I held up a hand to quiet them while also reaching back to cover Kiera's hand with my other one, slightly squeezing her in appreciation. "I can't thank you enough for your devotion and your prayers," I told the group. "I saw you. Every night I saw you standing out here in the cold...for me. You don't know how much that means to me, how much each and every one of you means to me." Emotion tightened my throat as I scanned the strangers in front of me. "I will never forget this." I squeezed Kiera's hand again, letting her know my words were intended for her too. We were married here. This place would always be special to me.

"Thank you," I told the fans.

Seeing that I was finished and knowing we needed to leave, Kiera began turning my chair. As she did, a girl in the crowd said, "Congratulations on your marriage!"

Happy to hear that from a fan, happy to finally be officially married, I looked back at the girl with a playful half-smile. "Thank you," I told her, genuinely meaning it. The girl's eyes widened as I made eye contact with her, and she suddenly looked so pale that I thought she might need my wheelchair. Oops. Hadn't meant to overwhelm her.

Kiera quickly wheeled me away, then leaned down and said, "You just can't help it, can you?"

Even though I was pretty sure I knew what she was referring to, I looked up at her with innocent eyes. "Help what?"

She grinned, then kissed my cheek. "Being ridiculously attractive."

Amused, and happy that the way the fans reacted to me no longer bothered her, I shook my head and said, "I'm pretty sure you're the only ridiculous one here." I grunted as I shifted into the car, and Kiera rolled her eyes as she got in beside me.

Grinning, I tossed my arm over her shoulders, then looked around at Anna and the guys. They were all holding glasses of orange juice. No, mimosas. Griffin was just finishing making one for Kiera. He handed it to her, then made me a glass of straight juice. I frowned when he gave it to me, and he shrugged. "Sorry, none for you. Doctor's orders."

I rolled my eyes but accepted my juice without complaint. Matt held his glass out to the middle of the car. "To the end of our first stadium tour. Not exactly how we planned on this turning out, but for the most part, the tour was a success." He frowned and looked at us. "Right?"

Evan shrugged. "We all lived. That's something."

We laughed at that, then we all clinked glasses and took a sip. Smiling at my friends, I said, "Let's make the next one better. Deal?"

They all heartily agreed, and we clinked again and drank again. Yes, hopefully the next tour would be much, much better. And honestly, as long as I didn't get hit by a truck again, it would be.

Chapter 35

RECOVERING

I was nervous on the plane ride, and I kept fidgeting in my seat, making my stomach flare with pain each time I repositioned. It baffled me that I was anxious. I'd met up with Gavin a few times now, and we talked or texted frequently enough that this shouldn't bother me. But this was the first time that I'd be in his city, in his *home*, and even though I'd been invited multiple times, I still felt like I was intruding.

"Are you okay?" Kiera asked, studying me with concern as I shifted for the millionth time. "Do you need a pain pill?"

Trying to relax back in my seat, I shook my head. "I'm fine, I'm just..." Furrowing my brows, I contemplated how to put what I was feeling into words. Frustrated at my confusion, I told her, "Do you think he wants me there? I mean, I know he offered his house a bunch of times, but maybe he was just being nice. Maybe we should get a hotel. Maybe we should go home."

Kiera put a hand on mine. "He wants you there, Kellan. He wants to take care of you. He wants to get to know you. He wants to be a part of your life."

"How do you know that?" I asked, searching her eyes. She looked so calm, so certain, but she was just guessing, same as me.

There was no guarantee that Gavin's words and wants truly matched.

Kiera gave me a soft smile and a small shrug. "I have faith," she said.

I rolled my eyes at that. "You've been friends with Jenny for too long. She's rubbing off on you."

She gave me a bright grin. "That's a compliment, and you know it."

I smiled at her. "True." Jenny was the absolute best.

Kiera's expression suddenly shifted into a frown. "Speaking of Jenny…"

She had a strange look on her face, one I couldn't quite decipher. It was amusement mixed with irritation mixed with adoration. "Yes?" I prompted.

She raised an eyebrow. "Jenny let something slip while she was visiting. She said it wasn't a secret, and she wasn't keeping it from me; she just assumed that you'd already told me. Imagine her surprise when I mentioned that you hadn't said a word."

"What are you talking about?" I asked, once again baffled.

Kiera pursed her lips. "The photo."

My confusion lasted for another three seconds…and then I understood what she was referring to. "I wasn't naked," I immediately told her.

She stared at me for a moment, then laughed. "I know," she said. "Jenny told me all about how she tortured you with freezing cold water." I grimaced as I remembered it, and Kiera giggled more. Then she said, "Why didn't you tell me she took it for you?"

Now it was my turn to raise an eyebrow at her. "A magician never reveals his secrets." She rolled her eyes at me, still more amused than anything. I laughed a little, then said, "I was just so happy you liked it that it completely slipped my mind. I'd planned on telling you later that Jenny had helped me with it, but it never came up, and honestly, when we were together, it was the last thing I was thinking about. Sorry." I shrugged in apology.

She shook her head at me. "Slipped your mind...only you would forget about asking your best friend's girlfriend to take a nude photo of you."

"I wasn't naked," I repeated. "Why does everyone keep getting that part wrong?"

Kiera snorted, then laughed so hard that the people around us turned to look at her. Although to be fair, they'd been turning to look at us every few minutes anyway. We were sitting in first class, another apology present from Nick, and the privacy curtain was drawn, so there were only a handful of looky-loos, but every person on the plane knew I was up here; they'd all gone bug-eyed when they'd spotted us while boarding. It made me think I should probably start wearing disguises when we went out: hats, sunglasses, maybe a fake beard. God. No. I would rather be stared at than resort to gluing fur on my face.

"Are you mad at me?" I asked Kiera when she finally settled down.

She gave me a look of incredulity, like she couldn't believe I'd asked her that right after she'd laughed her ass off. "No," she said. "I trust you, and I trust Jenny and Rachel." She paused to bite her lip. "And that photo's really hot."

She dramatically fanned herself, and a soft laugh escaped me. "Good," I told her, smiling. Then a thought struck me, and my smile turned devilish. "I wouldn't mind a reciprocal present, you know?"

Her eyes widened for a moment, color flushing her cheeks, but then she gave me a teasing smile. "I'll keep that in mind," she murmured.

Well, holy fuck. Just the thought of her taking a sexy, half-naked photo of herself was making me hard. I couldn't even imagine having sex right now, not in any way that wouldn't be painful, but I already knew the doctor's recommendation of waiting six weeks was *not* happening. Maybe two. Three tops. Less if she kept talking about that photo...

"My birthday's in April," I murmured.

She bent over as she laughed again, and I smiled as I watched her amusement. And then smiled wider when I realized I wasn't nervous anymore. At all.

The flight attendants let us off the plane first, large grins on their faces as they wished us well. Shuffling to the door was uncomfortable, but moving around didn't hurt nearly as much as it did before, and I was sure I could make it through the airport just fine. When I stepped off the plane, however, I was greeted by a man holding another freaking wheelchair. "Mr. Kyle," he said, indicating the seat.

I immediately glared at Kiera. "I can walk."

She practically beamed at me as she said, "I know. Please get in the chair." When I frowned at her, she leaned up and whispered in my ear, "The sooner you heal, the sooner we can consummate our marriage."

I gave her a crooked grin, then sat my ass down and let the man push me wherever he wanted.

Fans finally got the courage to approach me in baggage claim. They were polite, respectful, and very conscious of the fact that I was injured. I signed things for them and posed for photos while we waited for our things. They all left my side looking a little brighter, a little happier, and it gave me a profound sense of peace to know, that in just a few minutes, I could completely change the course of someone's day.

Moments later, Gavin arrived. He took one look at me in a wheelchair, and I could clearly see the sudden anxiety in his eyes, the worry, the fear of what could have happened. I waved off his concern with an annoyed frown. "I'm fine. I can walk. Kiera's just being overly careful with me."

Gavin looked at Kiera and nodded. "Good," he said.

I rolled my eyes at them, and I knew I was going to be mother-henned to death on this visit. And that actually sounded kind of...amazing. I'd never been cared for like that before. Not by family.

Kiera and Gavin helped me into the car, then we were off.

Gavin lived a little under an hour away from Pittsburgh, in a nice, upper-middleclass community. It was snowing outside, and there was a thick layer on the ground already. It made Gavin's two-story brick home seem even more idyllic.

We crunched to a stop, then Gavin hopped out of the car and rushed around to my door to help me get out. Even though it made me feel useless, I let him support me all the way to the front door; slipping and falling on the ice sounded excruciating.

Once we were inside, Gavin showed us to the room we'd be using. "On the first floor," he said, looking nervous, "so you don't have to deal with the stairs."

"Thank you," I told him.

He nodded, then explained that Hailey and Riley would be home after they were done with their respective schools. I thanked him again, then trudged to the bed to lie down for a bit. Gavin excused himself, letting Kiera and I have a moment alone while I rested. Kiera cuddled into my side, and I smiled as I looked around the guest bedroom. "Do you think this would have been my room? If I'd lived here, instead of Seattle?"

Kiera peeked up at me. "Maybe." She frowned. "I feel horrible saying this, considering what you went through, but I'm really glad you didn't grow up here. And now that I've said it, I feel even worse. I'm sorry."

I softly laughed as I squeezed her to me. "I understand what you mean," I said, moving my head so I was looking straight at her. "We never would have met if I'd lived here."

She smiled at me, then gave me a soft kiss. "Still, I wish you could have had this...but over there."

"Me too," I murmured, closing my eyes, feeling exhausted.

I must have fallen asleep because the next time I opened my eyes, I was alone, and there were voices echoing down the hallway, just loud enough for me to hear.

"Shush, he needs to rest. You shouldn't even be here. Why did I open my big mouth?"

"Because you love us!"

"That is seriously debatable. Can you guys please go?"

"Just a peek. Please. One tiny little peek at your rock star brother. Where's the harm?"

A smile formed on my face as I suddenly realized just what I was hearing. Hailey's aggressively fanatic friends. As I heard Hailey attempt to get rid of them again, I shifted my feet and gingerly stood up. It was getting easier and easier every day. *See, Kiera, I can walk just fine.*

I plodded to the now-closed bedroom door. Quietly opening it, I stepped into the hallway, then made my way to where the argument was coming from—the living room. Kiera was sitting on the couch, trying not to laugh as she watched Hailey arguing with two of her friends. Hailey had her hands on the back of one and was trying to shove her toward the front door. Her friend spotted me, and her jaw dropped wide open. "Oh my God," she muttered. "He's hotter in person..."

Hailey's other friend snapped her head around to look at me, and much to my amusement, her jaw dropped in the exact same way. "Holy shit," she said. "How is that even possible?"

Hailey sighed as she looked over at me, then cringed. "Sorry. I was trying to get them to leave. They followed me home after class got out."

I gave Kiera a smile, then shook my head at Hailey. "It's fine. I needed to get up anyway, or else I'll never sleep tonight." Small, amused smile on my face, I shifted my attention to Hailey's friends. "Hello. I'm Hailey's brother, Kellan...as you already know." Walking closer, I extended a hand to them. But the closer I got, the farther they backed away. I tilted my head. "I don't bite," I assured them.

The smaller dark-haired one giggled. Hailey rolled her eyes, then shook her head and introduced them. "This is Sara and Courtney. They're usually more articulate. I swear."

I grinned at them, raising an eyebrow, arm still outstretched, daring them to shake hands with me. Sara, the taller redhead, finally gathered her courage and took my palm. "I can't believe

I'm touching you," she murmured, then she flushed bright red like she hadn't meant to say that. She reminded me of Kiera, and I shifted my eyes to grin at my wife.

She knew exactly why I was grinning and rolled her eyes at me. Then she frowned. "Do you want to sit?" she asked, patting the spot beside her.

Hailey's friends instantly leapt into action. "Yes, sit, please! God, I forgot you were injured," Courtney said, cringing. "We suck. Seriously."

I laughed at them, then shook my head. "I've been sitting all day. I need to get used to this." They nodded, but now they looked concerned, like they thought I was going to drop at any moment. Not wanting any more caretakers, I looked between the two of them. "So...which one of you is at the top of the list?"

Hailey snorted while Kiera asked, "What list?"

Sara and Courtney both widened their eyes—one pair a deep green, the other almost black. Almost simultaneously, they both sputtered, "We didn't...there isn't really...it was a joke."

With a laugh, Hailey said, "Courtney is first. Sara gets you if anything happens to her."

Kiera frowned. "Gets you?" she asked.

Sara and Courtney went ghostly white as they swung their heads to look at her. "We're joking. It's just a joke," Courtney said.

Hailey smiled at Kiera. "They made a waiting list for him with a handful of other friends. Competition was fierce, but Courtney clawed her way into the top spot. Literally."

Both of Kiera's eyebrows raised, and Courtney looked a little ill. "That was an accident," she said to Hailey, then she locked eyes with Kiera. "It was before you were married." She forced a smile to her face. "Congratulations by the way. How was the wedding?"

I chuckled at their discomfort, then annoyed by my own discomfort, I finally conceded to taking a seat by my wife. "It was perfect," I said, kissing Kiera's cheek.

She smiled at me, then asked Sara and Courtney to sit and join us for a bit. They looked incredibly uncomfortable at first, but eventually, the longer they were around me, the more normal they acted. Especially when Riley showed up...with his girlfriend.

Sara gave him a hug the second the poor kid walked in the door with Gavin. "Riley! If it isn't my favorite ten-year-old."

She rumpled his hair, and he frowned at her. "I'm almost eleven," he said, like that somehow made a huge difference.

Sara just grinned wider. Then she noticed the young girl with Riley; she was adorable, with almost white-blonde hair and bright blue eyes. "Is this your girlfriend, Riley? Hi!" The girl's eyes widened, and she looked so uncomfortable; I felt bad for her.

"Give them some space, Sara," Hailey said. Then to me she added, "See, that's why she's second on the list."

Kiera quietly laughed while Sara scowled. Gavin watched the exchange with furrowed brows, then sighed and said to me, "Sorry. Katie's parents asked if she could visit for a bit so they could run some errands."

Grinning, I told him, "I'm glad they did. It's nice to meet you, Katie."

The poor girl flushed with color, then grabbed Riley's hand like he was the only thing keeping her in the house. Turning to him, she said, "Can we hang out in your room?"

Riley nodded, said, "Hey, bro," to me, then dashed up the stairs with his girl before I could even respond to him. Damn, he kind of reminded me of my younger self—eager to be alone with a beautiful woman.

While I chuckled at his hasty retreat, Gavin called out, "Leave the door open!" Sara and Courtney laughed at that while Gavin let out a long sigh. Looking over at Kiera and me, he said, "Think long and hard before you have kids. They age you."

Hailey rolled her eyes and smiled. "You gotta cut the cord, Dad." She looked back at me. "He won't even let Riley have a cell phone yet."

"Like he just told Sara, he's not even eleven. What does he need a cell phone for?" Gavin asked with a frown.

Hailey pointed upstairs. "To talk to his girlfriend."

I raised my hand. "And his brother. Passing messages through you and Hailey is kind of annoying."

Gavin sighed but nodded. "We'll see."

Gavin's house was fun and boisterous, with people coming and going all the time, constant laughter, endless affection. I loved it. It was how a home *should* be. And the way Gavin was with his kids, the warmth, concern, and care he showed them, he seamlessly extended that to me. At first, it was odd when he kept asking me if I needed anything, or when he brought me a sandwich just because he thought I might be hungry, but after a few days, it felt completely natural to be under his wing. Like I'd always been there, and I supposed I had, I just hadn't known it until recently.

"Kellan, son, we've got this; you don't need to help." Gavin placed his palm on my forearm to stop me from setting down a plate.

With a smile, I shook my head at him. "I'm feeling much better. It doesn't even hurt to get up anymore. I'd like to help. Please." He studied my expression for any sign of pain, but I wasn't lying. As long as I didn't bend over, twist my torso too far, lift anything even remotely heavy, or God forbid, fall down, I was fine. I could even tolerate laughing now.

His face softening into a smile, Gavin let go of my arm. "Just don't overexert yourself, okay? No need to go back to the hospital so soon."

I gave him a small laugh. "Trust me, the last thing I want to do is set foot in another hospital." My eyes drifted across the large dining room table, to where Kiera was setting down a bowl of mashed potatoes. "Not yet anyway," I murmured, a vision of helping a very pregnant Kiera through the hospital doors filling my mind.

Gavin tracked my eyeline, and his smile widened. Patting my shoulder, he told me, "All in due time, son. Like I keep telling your brother and sister, don't be in such a hurry to grow up."

I grinned at him, then nodded. Then marveled at the fact that I was getting sound fatherly advice. Until recently, I never would have imagined that happening.

The front door opened just as we finished setting the table, and a few moments later, an elderly couple stepped into the dining room. Everyone looked over, and almost at the same time, Hailey and Riley said, "Grandma! Grandpa!"

I swallowed a lump in my throat as I locked eyes with the people who'd created my father. Gavin's mother, Lucy, was tall, slender, and she was slightly hunched over as she supported herself with a cane. She had short, shockingly white hair...and the same dark blue eyes as me. Gavin's father, Jim, had pale blue eyes like Riley, dark gray hair, and a surprisingly fit frame, considering his age.

Nerves flashed through me as they both silently scanned my face. Meeting family was still an unsettling experience for me, and I was happy it was just the two of them joining us tonight; Gavin had an older brother, Tristan, who also had some children...my cousins. I had cousins. That still made my mind spin. They all lived nearby, but not wanting to overwhelm me, they were going to meet me another time.

Finally, when I felt the almost unbearable need to say something, Lucy lifted her free hand in a gesture of openness and warmly said, "There he is...Home at last. Come give your grandmother a hug."

Her greeting, her implied instant acceptance, relaxed me, and I tenderly wrapped my arms around the frail woman. From behind me, I heard Gavin say, "Mom, Dad, I would have picked you up. I was just about to leave, actually."

Jim shook his head. "No need for you to leave your family,

son. The retirement home has a ride service. They even walked us to the door." Releasing me, Lucy pursed her lips at her husband. He smiled as he looked down at her. "It's not because they thought you couldn't do it by yourself. They were just being nice, dear."

Lucy rolled her eyes, then looked over at Gavin. "And besides, you drive too slow. It would have taken an hour to get here, and I was in a hurry to see this beautiful boy." She tossed me a beaming smile. "My, my," she said, looking over at Jim. "We do have good-looking genes, don't we?"

Jim grinned at his wife, then turned his smile to me. "We sure do," he said. "It's nice to finally meet you, Kellan." Then he stepped forward and gave me his own welcoming, unreserved hug.

I patted his back, amazed and slightly overwhelmed anyway. "It's nice to meet you too," I said, my throat already tightening up on me.

Lucy sighed, and her expression darkened with sadness. "We're sorry it took so long. I wanted to visit you ages ago, when you were younger, but Gavin kept telling me not to interfere. Told me you didn't know who your real father was, so you wouldn't know who I was either." A fire flared in her eyes as she looked over at her son. "An absurd notion. He would have taken one look at me and instantly known the truth, Gavin." She rolled her eyes at him, then looked back at me. "I swear, the boy is just plain ridiculous sometimes. I don't know where he gets that from." She looked over at her husband and frowned. Jim smiled; Gavin sighed.

Grin on my face, I warmly told her, "I wish you had." I would have loved to meet a family member who cared about me. More than loved.

She instantly glared at my father. "See, Gavin. He wishes I had."

Turning my head, I saw Gavin inhale a deep, calming breath. "Yes, Mother," he said, clearly not wanting to get into it with her.

Hailey snorted and came up behind Lucy to give her a hug. "Oh, Grandma. The best part of your visits is watching you put Dad in his place." She tossed a grin at Gavin before adding, "You and Grandpa should live with us full time."

Gavin's eyes widened while Lucy made a scoffing sound. "As much as we love all of you, dear, we're never leaving Golden Pines. We have all our meals specially made for us, like we're royalty, and there's swim aerobics, bingo night twice a month, salsa on the weekends." She paused, and a mischievous gleam filled her eyes. "And they have an endless supply of little blue pills."

"Mother!" Gavin snapped, lifting his hands and shaking his head in disbelief.

While Jim chuckled, Lucy stared at her son a moment, then told Hailey, "Plus, your father can be exhausting."

Hailey started cracking up, and my grin grew a mile wide. Now I knew what Hailey meant when she'd called Grandma Lucy feisty. "I think I already love you," I told her, and I was mildly surprised to find that I meant it. And that saying it was as easy as breathing.

Lucy gave me a playful wink. "Of course you do." She put her hand on my chest, and her expression suddenly became more serious. "And I already love you. I have since the day you were born." She cringed a little, then raised an eyebrow and said, "I don't suppose you got any of my cards?"

"You weren't supposed to send him cards," Gavin said, annoyance in his voice.

She looked over at him with heat in her eyes again. "I'm not supposed to sneak fudge from the kitchens either, but I do."

Cards? She'd sent me cards? For a moment, I was so stunned by that confession that I could hardly process what she'd asked me. Finally, shaking my head, I told her, "Um, no...I never received anything...from anybody." Ever.

The intensity in her eyes suddenly reminded me of myself when I was angry enough to clock someone. "I won't speak ill of your mother," she said, "but that bit—" Inhaling a deep breath, she forced a small smile to her face and omitted the swear. "*She* must have intercepted them." Lucy looked back at Gavin again. "I still can't believe you had a child with her. Honestly, son, sometimes your life choices worry me."

Turning, I saw Gavin raise an eyebrow. "I'm not the only exhausting one, Mom."

Lucy's voice turned playful. "Good thing we love each other then, isn't it?"

Gavin finally smiled. "Yes, it is." He walked over and hugged her then, and despite all the bickering, I saw true affection pass between them.

Gavin let her go and hugged his father, and Riley swooped in to claim his own hug from his grandmother. Looking up at Lucy, he said, "What did you mean by little blue pills?" I heard Gavin sigh again, but Lucy merely smiled at Riley and smoothed back his hair. "Nothing, dear." She kissed his head, then said, "Be a gem and take my jacket?"

Riley nodded and waited while she removed it. As she did, Kiera stepped up to me. She was struggling not to laugh and subtly wiping tears from her eyes. Grinning at her, I grabbed her hand and gently pulled her closer. "Kiera, this is my grandmother, Lucy, and my grandfather, Jim. Jim, Lucy, this is my wife, Kiera."

Also handing his jacket to Riley, Jim smiled widely at us. "Already married? Any children?"

Kiera bit her lip and shook her head. "No, not yet," she said.

Lucy patted her hand, eagerness on her face. "Well, don't wait too long. You should enjoy children while you're young."

"Don't rush them, Mother," Gavin said. Lucy looked about to argue, but Gavin grinned and smacked his hands together. "Shall we eat?" he asked, clearly changing the subject.

Kiera finally let out the laugh she'd been holding. Watching her fall apart made me fall apart, and before long, all of us were giggling. And I already knew I was going to miss every single person here once I left. I also already knew that I would be returning to visit them as often as I could.

We stayed at Gavin's for a couple more weeks, then we hopped on another plane to spend some time with Kiera's parents. It was shockingly hard to leave my newfound family, and I found myself struggling with melancholy on the plane, especially when I pictured saying goodbye to Gavin.

He'd driven us to the airport, escorted us as far as he could, then wrapped his arms around me and said, "I'm so glad you came. I'm going to miss you." When he pulled back, there were tears in his eyes. It instantly made tears form in mine. It was still such an odd—but wonderful—feeling to be missed.

"I'm going to miss you too," I told him, meaning it more profoundly than I'd ever anticipated. "But we'll keep in touch."

He smiled, then told me, "Of course we will. I love you, Kellan. And I'm very proud of you. I want you to know that. I want you to *always* know that."

The lump in my throat almost made speech impossible, but I managed to tell him, "Thank you. I...I love you too."

He grinned even as the tears started sliding down his cheeks. I'd never told him that before, and after seeing how it affected him, I wished I'd told him earlier. Because it was true. I did love him. And I already missed him.

"It gets easier," Kiera said from beside me. I looked over at her, and she smiled at me. "Leaving home. It gets easier." She shook her head as she sighed. "The first time I left home, I cried off and on for at least three days, and I was really excited to leave. Because my parents are, well, you know." She shrugged.

I laughed as I nodded. Her parents, especially her father, gave the word "overprotective" a whole new meaning; Gavin seemed lenient in comparison. And remembering that brought up a whole new worry. Martin and I living under the same roof for an extended period...would he kill me by the end of this visit? And would I still have to sleep on the couch? Fuck, I really hoped not. That couch sucked.

Nerves once again ate at me while Kiera and I waited for our things in baggage claim. Eager fans approached, and I welcomed the distraction. Now that I was mostly healed, fans swooped right in for hugs and photos, and I was smashed in between two giggling girls when Martin and Caroline showed up. Martin immediately scowled when he saw what I was doing, and my spirit sank. *Fuck. I've already pissed him off.* But then the girls waved Kiera into the picture, smushing her into my side, and Martin's expression shifted into one of puzzlement and reluctant acceptance. I'd made Kiera famous, but at least it was a positive type of fame now.

Once the fans thanked us and moved away, Kiera's parents stepped up to us. Caroline squeezed her daughter, then me, while Martin grabbed our bags. I opened my mouth to offer my help, but Martin shot me a look that said, *Let me do this.* Forcing a smile to my face, I simply told him, "Thank you." Then I cringed at Kiera because this already wasn't going well.

Peaceful smile on her face, Kiera squeezed my hand in support, and then we were on our way. I tried to think of things to talk about the entire car ride there, but I wasn't coming up with anything. Luckily, Kiera and her mom had plenty to talk about, and their chatter filled the empty space between Martin and me.

When we got to the house, Martin again grabbed our bags. I clenched my hand as I bit my cheek, stopping myself from telling him that I could handle it. Clearly, this was something he wanted to do for us. With a sigh, I followed him into the house, Caroline trailing behind with Kiera, the two of them still chatting. We got to the living room, and Martin scowled as he looked between the couch and the stairs. Realizing his problem, I blurted out, "I don't mind the couch. It's really...comfortable."

Martin widened his eyes at me, and for a moment, I thought I saw respect on his face. Before he could say anything, though,

Caroline interjected. "Nonsense. The two of you are married. You'll share a room." She shifted to frown at her husband. "Martin." Her deep green eyes pointedly looked at the stairs.

Martin sighed, then began trudging up the stairs with our bags. And every step he took, I felt him getting further and further away from me. Turning to Caroline, I said, "I really don't mind. I don't want to cause problems." That was mostly true. I didn't want to sleep on a couch, didn't want to be apart from Kiera, but I didn't want Martin to resent me either.

Kiera was frowning at me, but Caroline just smiled. "He'll get over it," she said. "You two have every right to share a bed now." Eagerness flaring in her eyes, she added, "How else will we get grandkids from you?"

"Mom," Kiera groaned, color flooding her cheeks.

I stifled a laugh as Caroline said, "What? Just imagine how beautiful your babies will be, Kiera. I can't wait. I'd like at least four. Two girls, two boys. And twins would be amazing. Do twins run in your family, Kellan?"

I was about to tell her I had no idea, but Martin was back, and he looked about as pleased with the conversation as Kiera did. Seeing someone on her side, Kiera looked over at him and said, "Dad, please make her stop."

He sighed as he ran a hand down his face. "I would love to, Kiera. I would love to." Then he looked at me. "Kellan, can you drink yet? I think we should drink. And...talk."

By the way he flashed a glance at Caroline, I figured his suggestion was a request that she'd made. He must have promised to try to bond with me. Not wanting to make it any more difficult than it already was, I smiled and told him, "That sounds good. I'd love a beer."

Caroline grinned at him, then touched Kiera's elbow. "How about we get some drinks for them, then make an apple pie for dessert?" Kiera looked over at me, but I nodded at her. I could do this. Kiera nodded at her mom, and they started walking into the kitchen. As they left, I heard Caroline ask her, "Do *you* know if twins run in Kellan's family?"

Kiera groaned while Martin sighed. Then he pointed at the plastic-wrapped couch. "Have a seat." Once I sat down, he slowly lowered himself to sit beside me. Looking mildly uncomfortable, he asked, "So...how are you feeling?"

"Great. Well, better. Things are still sore...sometimes."

He frowned after I said that, and I had the weirdest feeling that he'd somehow taken my response as sexual in nature. I really hadn't meant it that way but clarifying just felt awkward. We sat in silence until our beers arrived. Caroline handed one to her husband with an expression that said, *Talk to him and be nice.* Kiera handed one to me with an expression that said, *I am so sorry. I'll make it up to you later, promise.*

Once the girls left, Martin took a long drink from his bottle. As I took a sip from mine, he said, "Your wedding was very nice. Caroline talked about it for a week straight."

I grinned at him, then said, "Thank you." My smile shifted into a frown. "I really didn't help much, but everyone else did a great job."

He nodded at that, then more silence. Fuck. I needed to find something we could bond over, but I was completely blank. Martin was too. Then he scratched his head and said, "So, how do you think the Reds are going to do next year?"

Fuck. Baseball. I honestly knew nothing about the sport or his favorite team, and I'd used up all the previous knowledge that I'd borrowed to impress him—I couldn't even remember half the stuff I'd told him last time. I either had to lie and fake my way through this conversation or come clean, and I had a feeling honesty would do more for me right now.

I let out a long sigh. "I'm sorry, I have to confess...I don't know anything about baseball. I don't even know all the rules, and I definitely don't know any of the players or how good any of the teams are or aren't." He seemed floored by that, and I cringed.

"I had help before. I knew you were a sports fan. I wanted to have something to talk about. I wanted you to like me."

"Oh." He looked down, and I saw the disappointment on his face. Then he peeked up at me and said, "I suppose that was very thoughtful of you. It was nice that you tried." He briefly grinned, then he looked disappointed again.

A thought occurred to me, and I decided to broach the subject with him. "Maybe...maybe you could teach me?"

He instantly perked up, his back straightening, his smile widening. "Yes. Yes, I could do that. It would be fun to teach you." He gave me a decisive nod. "Yes, you're a clean slate, and I'll teach you right. Won't have to convince you to give up on an inferior team; you'll start out loving the greatest team there ever was." Over his shoulder, he tossed out, "Caroline! Grab my old game tapes! Kellan's learning baseball!" He turned back to me with an excitement in his eyes that I'd never seen before. "No time like the present to get started."

I forced myself to smile, forced myself to look excited for this, but I knew, even if I never gave a shit about baseball, I would become the biggest Reds fan in the world to bond with Martin. Well, the second biggest Reds fan; I could never out-fan Martin. But I was already imagining going to games with him, having hot dogs and beer, and screaming until we were both hoarse, and all of a sudden, I didn't have to fake my smile or my excitement. This *was* going to be fun, and I couldn't wait.

Chapter 36

GOING HOME

We spent a few weeks with Kiera's parents, and by the time we left, I actually did have a working knowledge of baseball. Martin was a good teacher, and he was already making plans for us to watch games together. Over the phone for the most part, but also in person if we had a chance to get together during the season. And oddly, I found myself excited about it. His enthusiasm was infectious.

Kiera watched us bonding with tears in her eyes. Although those tears could have been because she was excited about her own future. She'd shared her book with Denny over our long break, wanting his opinion and approval before she did anything with it. He'd told her it was amazing, told her he wouldn't have a problem if she published it, and had encouraged her to go for it. The day she'd heard back from Denny, the day he'd signed off on the book, she'd squealed and attacked me with kisses. Her enthusiasm was infectious too, and I couldn't wait to hold her book in my hands, to see it on shelves, to watch readers lose themselves in her world. It was going to be a dream come true for her, and therefore, a dream come true for me.

But first, it was time to go home. And while I was sad to leave our families behind, there was something waiting for me in

Seattle that I'd truly missed, and I was a little giddy on the plane ride. Maybe *a lot* giddy. I practically leapt from my seat once the plane stopped, helping Kiera to her feet with an urgency that she clearly didn't understand. I thanked the crew, then hurried us to baggage claim where I scooped up our travel-worn bags with a huge smile on my face. And all the while Kiera watched me with amused confusion on hers.

After signing a few things for fans, pausing to take some pictures with them, I led Kiera to the taxis. Once we were settled, I gave the driver Evan's address. That was when Kiera's smile shifted into a frown. "Why are we going to Evan's?" she asked.

From the disappointment on her face, it was clear she had been hoping we'd go straight home. Maybe straight to bed. That made me reconsider my plans for a moment. We'd consummated our marriage several weeks ago. Very carefully since I'd still been pretty tender at the time. And we'd had a rousing round early this morning, but I had to admit, I was really intrigued by the idea of laying her out on our bed and doing things to her that I hadn't been able to do at either of our family's houses...because she absolutely wouldn't have been quiet enough. I fully wanted to make her lose control, but damn it, I really wanted to get my car too. *But wait, I don't actually have to choose. I can do both.*

Grinning at her, I said, "We're not going to Evan's, we're going to the shop."

My answer didn't immediately make sense to her, but once it did, she rolled her eyes and laughed. I just smiled because I knew, in only a handful of minutes, I was going to be back behind the wheel of my second favorite baby, driving her home so I could make love to my first favorite baby. Really, could today get any better?

The minute I stepped out of the cab, Roxie walked outside the open bay doors. Smile on her face, she reached into her coveralls and pulled out my car keys. The sight of them almost made me weep, and I scooped up Roxie in an exuberant hug of gratitude. Leaving the Chevelle with someone who loved her as much as I did was such a relief, and I knew my car would be in better condition than when I'd left her; Rox loved to tinker.

Roxie laughed as I set her down, then she indicated inside the garage, to where my car was resting under a sheet. A swell of emotion hit me as I took the keys from her. I knew it was a little ridiculous to be so attached to a vehicle, but I'd been through a lot with my car, and there were times, a lot of times actually, when the vehicle had been the only thing that felt like home to me.

"Thank you," I told her, wishing I had better words to show my appreciation. Rox nodded and smiled, and I moved over to my car. When I pulled off the cover, I saw that she'd been polished recently, and she practically glowed under the garage lights. I ran my hand over the sleek black, admiring the sexy chrome accents as I went. "Hey, girl," I murmured. "I'm home." And then, even though I knew Kiera would mock me for it, I laid my head on the roof of my car and gave her a warm hug. Damn, I'd missed my baby.

Kiera stepped up to me as I was lying on my car. Her smile was amused, but she didn't comment on the affection I was giving an inanimate vehicle. Instead, she extended her palm out to me like she wanted something.

"What?" I asked, lifting my head to frown at her.

"Seeing as how you're still recovering from a serious operation, I don't think you should drive."

Fuck that. I clenched my fingers around my keys. She would have to pry them from my dead body to drive right now. "I'm fine, and you know I'm fine. Sex takes way more energy than driving, and we've been doing that for weeks." Seeing a prime opportunity to embarrass her, I smirked and added, "And it didn't hurt at all when you rode me this morning. It felt pretty amazing actually."

Eyes widening, Kiera slapped her hand over my mouth while Roxie chuckled in amusement. I laughed too, and I knew Kiera could feel it under her fingers. Adorable scowl on her face, she let go and pointed at the car. "Just...get inside," she said.

I waved at Rox, then unlocked the doors so we could crawl inside, Kiera on the passenger's side, me in the driver's seat...as it should be. I briefly considered pulling the car out of the garage, then parking and running upstairs to say hi to Evan real quick, but the expression on Kiera's face made me want to take her home. I could see Evan and the guys tomorrow. Since Kiera still seemed a little peeved as I started the car, I said, "What? Am I wrong?"

She knew I wasn't. This morning *had* been amazing, and I'd seen the frustrated struggle on her face as she'd tried to stay as silent as possible. Now she didn't have to, and by the sultry smile that she gave me, I knew her thoughts were in line with mine. Damn, I couldn't wait to get home.

I sped as I drove us there. I couldn't help it. The look on Kiera's face, the growl of the engine, everything was pushing me onward. Then I got to our street, and I came to a dead stop at the top of the hill. The street was always packed with parked cars; they typically lined both sides, narrowing the road so that there was barely enough room for the Chevelle down the middle. But now, the cars were blocking the entire road, and there were people everywhere, spreading out from a point that I knew was my house. I could see phones being held up, flashes from cameras, and the look of stunned excitement on multiple faces. I'd seen that look before, from fans. *Fuck...they know where I live.* Guess my day had peaked with picking up the car. Damn it.

"Please tell me your neighbors are having a block party," Kiera whispered.

I looked over at her, disheartened, and as I noticed the horror in her eyes, I suddenly felt the full weight of constant travel settling on me. I'd just wanted to take her home to *our* place, *our* things, take a shower in *our* shower, lie down on *our* bed...and now I wasn't sure if that would ever happen. "I don't think this has anything to do with my neighbors," I told her, and even as I said it, my words were confirmed when a couple of my neighbors walked into their yards to scream at the crowd. Great. I'd never been particularly close to my neighbors, but I felt bad for inconveniencing them like this. Because if all these people were here for me, they might not go away any time soon. How the fuck had they found me? Where do we go now?

I could only think of one place, so I put the car in drive and said goodbye to my home from a distance. And fuck, the farther I got away from it, the more it bothered me. Yes, I had mixed feelings about my home, but...it was the only thing I had left of my parents. Literally, the *only* thing of theirs. And I hadn't realized when I'd left it months ago that I'd never be returning. Not being able to say goodbye properly was reopening that void, that need for closure. Visiting their graves was supposed to seal that hole for good, but mile by mile I felt it ripping back open.

When I finally pulled up to Matt's house, I wasn't sure how I felt. Other than disappointed. Luckily, Matt's place was quiet; nobody knew he was here. Yet. Maybe it was time we all moved.

I shut off the car, but I couldn't get out yet. This wasn't how I wanted today to go. Kiera put her hand over mine. "It will be okay, Kellan. Home is wherever we are. Home is the two of us. And if we can't go back to that one, then we'll find a new one. One without ghosts. One that works with who we are now, and who we'll be in the future. One we pick out together."

Her words were like the sun breaking through the clouds on a cold day, and my mood turned completely around as I smiled at her. She was right. A place was just a place, an object just an object. *She* was what mattered, and no one was taking her from me. My true home was always with me. "Thank you," I told her. "I think I needed to hear that."

She smiled, then gave me a kiss on the cheek. "Shall we go bug Matt? Oh, and Rachel. I just remembered that they moved in together. Did he tell you that? Rachel was so excited. Even more so by the fact that Griffin lives with Anna now. She never would have said yes if he still lived here, and I really don't blame her. I could *not* live with Griffin. The bus was hard enough." She closed her eyes and shuddered like she was having disturbing flashbacks.

Her expression made me laugh, and I felt a million times better as I opened my door. "Very true," I told her. She got out, and we met at the front of the car. Grabbing her hand, I said, "Let's go tell Matt we're homeless."

Matt grinned when he opened his front door and saw us. "Kell, you're back!" He stepped up and gave me a quick, one-armed hug, then he waved at Kiera. "I thought you guys were coming in today, but...why are you *here*?"

A long sigh left me. "We tried to go home, but my house is a shitshow. There were people everywhere, waiting around, taking pictures...it's probably just a matter of time before they break in and start stealing shit." And that made me frown. I didn't have a lot of things of value, but my old guitar was there, and my numerous journals full of lyrics, plus the Ramones poster Kiera had picked up for me. There were things I wanted to keep, and I hated the thought of someone swiping them.

Matt's pale eyes widened as he swung the door wide and gestured for us to come in. "Fuck, how do they know?" He popped his head outside to look around his front yard, like he thought his place might be next. And I supposed it might be.

"I don't know," I told him.

He closed his door once we were inside, then yelled toward the hallway, "Babe! Kell and Kiera are here. They couldn't go home. Their place is crawling with people." Then he grabbed his phone and started searching for something.

Rachel came out of the hallway a couple of seconds later. Her face did this weird smile-frown combination. She hugged Kiera, then shook her head, her dark hair rippling around her shoulders. "People were at your place? Like fans? Why? How?"

Matt sighed. "Fuck. I just found it. Didn't even take long." He sighed again as he looked up at me. "I'm sorry, man. I should have noticed this earlier."

"Noticed what?" I asked, leaning over to try to read his phone.

He showed me while explaining to the girls. "Joey finally opened her mouth. She did an interview, told them everything... including your address." His cheeks turned pink as he shook his head. "I can't believe those fuckers actually posted it. You should sue their asses, Kellan."

My jaw dropped as I read the article, as I saw my address just out there for the entire world to see. "Fuck. I guess that explains it." I sighed, then looked between Matt and Rachel. "I'm sorry to barge in on you without any notice, but can we—"

"Of course you can," Rachel said, not even letting me finish. Her gaze shifted to Kiera. "You're family."

Matt nodded. "You know my home is yours, Kell. And we'll do something about your place. At least get your stuff for you. Somehow."

I nodded, then smiled. "Thanks. I owe you."

He grinned at me. "No, you don't. Like Rachel said, you're family. You don't owe me anything." He frowned. "Except a Sharpie. You do owe me a Sharpie."

I grinned back. "No, I don't. That was a gift."

He sighed while Kiera looked between us with furrowed brows. Seeing her confusion, I explained. "He's emotionally attached to markers. Be very respectful if you see any lying around the house."

Rachel giggled and nodded. Matt pursed his lips. "I want to say *fuck you*, but actually...that's completely true. Please don't touch my Sharpies."

I could see Kiera holding in her laughter. I tried, but I just didn't have her fortitude. I started cracking up, and that broke her resolve too. Matt rolled his eyes as we all laughed, then he laughed too. And damn, even if we weren't technically home, it felt so good to be back. And now I really needed to find that Sharpie-of-the-month club. Or make my own. Yes, I'd have Kiera help me because that was definitely happening now.

The following morning, everyone got together and packed up my house for me. Not being able to help was a thorn in my side. No, a spear in my side. I grumbled a lot while Kiera coordinated things over the phone. All the guys were helping, plus Denny, Abby, Jenny, Rachel, Anna, and Sam, who apparently was keeping the crowd at bay with nothing more than menacing looks. I wished I could see it. Instead, I was sitting on my ass, watching Gibson for Griffin and Anna...and that wasn't a bad gig.

Since Kiera and I didn't have a whole lot, the house was emptied in a day, and all our things were squeezed into a medium-sized storage unit, waiting for us while we figured out just what the fuck we were going to do. Because living in that house again wasn't an option. Fucking Joey.

After a couple of days of indecision, Kiera and I started the process of looking for a place of our own. I didn't have a real estate person, so I asked my new agent for help...the band's new agent. The day after Denny had broached the topic with me, I'd asked the guys how they felt about him managing us. They'd all been on board with the idea, even Matt, who had technically been managing us for years. When I'd asked him specifically if he was okay giving up control, he'd given me a sigh that was heavy with relief, then said, "Dude, yes, I think it's great. The three of you are exhausting."

Denny had already been a huge help. Nick had called me while I was recovering at Gavin's house, wanting to set up a new tour for us. I'd told him all arrangements would need to be made through our agent, given him Denny's information, then happily excused myself from the call. Letting someone else deal with Nick and his crap was such an amazing feeling, and I was so grateful for Denny's offer. I was even more grateful when Denny called me back a couple of weeks later to let me know the details of the tour. Since Denny knew me, knew *us*, he'd fought for mid-level shows—smaller than arenas, bigger than Justin's typical venues— a place in between where we could reach a lot of people but still have that feeling of intimacy that I liked. We were leaving in April, and Holeshot and Avoiding Redemption were coming with us. I couldn't wait.

Denny, of course, had a real estate agent that he trusted, and he set up a meeting for us. The guy was amazing. He helped me get my parents' place ready to sell, arranging for small updates and fixes, then he listened to what Kiera and I wanted in a dream home and made a list of places for us to visit. For the most part, Kiera and I agreed on what we wanted: something outside of the city, something secluded, something with room for a growing family. Okay, that last one was my request, but it made sense in the long run. Kiera and I definitely wanted kids one day, so why not plan for it now? Thankfully, with the money and investments that my parents had left me, the house I would be selling soon, and the money from the album—which reached number one after the accident and was *still there*—Kiera and I had a pretty large budget to work with, and the houses we were looking at were kind of ridiculous.

"Kellan, don't you think this is a little...excessive?" Kiera asked, frowning as she looked up at what could only be described as a mansion.

"Maybe," I conceded. "But it's on eleven acres, it's in the middle of nowhere, and our closest neighbor is an elderly couple who have owned their home for, like, a hundred years." I turned to look at Will, the real estate agent. "Right?"

He smiled and nodded. "Pretty much. As far as seclusion, this is the top listing I could find while still keeping you somewhat close to the city. Plus, it has a fence around the entire property, cameras everywhere, a top-of-the-line security system, and an electronic gate at the entrance. It's also the most *secure* listing I could find, and in your case, that might be its most important feature."

Kiera bit her lip but nodded. "It's just so...big. And why is the driveway at the bottom of the hill? Look at all those steps." Her eyes traveled up the absurdly long stairway leading from where the cars parked to the front door. She was right on that count, but...that *could* be a positive.

"Just look at it as a workout," I said. "You won't have to worry about going to a gym when you have to go up those all the time."

She smirked at me, then said, "Okay, Rocky. You're definitely helping me with the groceries then."

I laughed at her comment, then nodded. "Of course. Let's go look inside."

Will led us up the stairs, and Kiera and I were both breathing heavier once we reached the top. She pursed her lips at me, but I just smiled and shrugged. "That was the hardest it will ever be." She smirked and rolled her eyes.

After unlocking the brick-red door, Will stepped inside and held it open for us. Kiera walked through first, her eyes scanning the entryway. It was huge compared to what I was used to; we could probably park my car in here. "Oh wow," Kiera murmured. Her voice echoed around the empty space, and I could already picture screaming kids, bickering relatives, and jackass friends standing here as we greeted them. I was already sold.

Will led us to a spacious, open living room where a huge sliding door along the back wall showed us an impressive outdoor entertaining space, complete with a pool. Behind the pool was another building. It was fairly large, much bigger than a simple shed. "What's that?" I asked the realtor, pointing to it.

He glanced back at the space, then said, "I believe it was originally designed as a storage shed for pool supplies, yard tools, Christmas decorations, that sort of thing. The previous owner modified it some, adding power and insulation. They used it as an art studio, but there are a variety of ways that it could be utilized."

I grinned at Kiera. "Like a recording studio. Or at the very least, a quiet place away from the house to practice."

She beamed at me, and I knew she loved both of those ideas. I did too, and I was already wondering if I could convince the guys to come out this far to rehearse. Matt and Evan, probably. Griffin might take some persuading. I'd think of something.

Kiera's jaw dropped when she saw the kitchen. It was one of those ridiculously huge, overdone, top-of-the-line everything kitchens that only professional chefs filming a cooking show truly needed. Kiera looked around at all the shiny stainless-steel appliances, then turned back to me and said, "If this is really going to be our kitchen, then one of us should probably learn how to cook."

I laughed at that, nodding. We went upstairs next, and Will showed us a seemingly endless number of bedrooms. They all looked more or less the same, and all of them were larger than our old bedroom at my house. Then he showed us the master suite. I swear to God, at first, I thought he was showing us a second living room...it was comically large. We could fit three queen-sized beds along the wall and still have space for nightstands. Kiera actually groaned when she saw the massive walk-in closet, and damn if that didn't make me want to sign the papers right there. Then Will showed us the master bathroom. Or personal spa; that seemed like a more fitting description. Kiera oohed and aahed over every luxurious detail, but my eyes were glued on the jetted tub that could easily fit three people all lying down next to each other. We could absolutely have sex in that tub. Why were we still taking a tour?

When we got back downstairs, I asked Kiera, "So? What do you think?"

She bit her lip like she was undecided, but her eyes were glowing with excitement. "It's gorgeous, Kellan, but...isn't it kind of much for just two people?"

Smiling, I wrapped my arms around her. "But that's the thing. It won't just be for two people." She furrowed her brows, and I could almost see her contemplating who else was moving in with us. My smile widened. "We'll have friends staying periodically. Family. Then kids...grandkids." She smirked at that, and I shrugged and added, "It might not be big *enough*."

She laughed as she looped her arms around my neck. "You're ridiculous. And I love you. And it's perfect."

"Even with the stairs?" I asked, cocking an eyebrow at her.

She nodded. "Even with the stairs."

An idea struck me, and I told her, "Maybe we'll get some dune buggies and bypass the stairs altogether?" She laughed at that, but I was being 100 percent serious. Seemed like a workable solution to me, and actually, that might be just the incentive I needed to get Griffin to come all the way out here. No...I'd never get him off the damn things. I would definitely need to keep them a secret.

As Kiera's laughter died down, as we quietly gazed at each other for a moment, I began imagining us being here together, entertaining our friends, our families, raising our kids. It choked me up to think that far ahead, but in a good way. Our life was truly beginning, right here, right now. Today. Over my shoulder, I told Will, "We'll take it."

"Excellent! I'll get started on the paperwork."

He began going into specifics on what we would need to do next, something about escrow and an inspection, but I was already tuning him out as I lost myself in Kiera's ever-changing eyes. Then Kiera squealed, kissed my cheek, and started taking pictures of the house to show our friends and family. I chuckled as I watched her run from room to room, outside, then back inside, covering every inch until finally we were at the driveway at the bottom of the hill, looking up at the generous amount of cement steps. With a content sigh, Kiera adorably said goodbye to our new home, then we made the drive back to Seattle.

We had rehearsal at Evan's that night. We had a new album to plan after all, and while I'd been recovering, I'd written a couple of new songs for it. Hopefully. We were still testing them out. Kiera decided to come to rehearsal with me so she could show off the photos. When we stepped inside Evan's loft, I was a little surprised to see that everyone was there—all the guys, all their girls, and even Denny and Abby.

Looking around at everyone, I cocked an eyebrow and asked, "Something going on?"

Abby grinned at me. "Hey! We were just going over wedding plans! It's getting close."

Denny smiled at her, then looked at me and the guys. "Thank you again for agreeing to play for us."

All the guys nodded. Except Griffin. He looked mildly confused until Anna leaned down and whispered something in his ear. Then I heard him say, "That's what we agreed to?" Anna snorted and handed Gibson to him. He grinned and instantly stopped paying attention to anything but his daughter.

Denny, having heard his comment, rolled his eyes, then looked back at me. "We were also going over your schedule for the Grammys."

My stomach sank as I remembered that. We'd been officially nominated back in November. I honestly thought we'd be dropped, but no, not only were we performing at the show, but we were also up for the *Best New Artist* award, which was ridiculous. Absolutely ridiculous. And nothing I wanted to think about right now.

Seeing the look on my face made Denny grin. "It's going to be all right, mate. No need to be nervous."

I smirked at that. "I'm not nervous."

"God, I am," Matt muttered from the kitchen area. He looked ill, and Rachel, beside him, rubbed his back in sympathy. Hope in his eyes, he asked Denny, "Are you sure we have to do it live? Couldn't we record our performance? And an acceptance speech type thing? Don't people do that all the time?"

Denny gave him a warm smile. "When they absolutely can't make it, sure." He raised his eyebrows at Matt. "But you *can* make it, and I already confirmed that you'd be there, and it really will be okay."

Matt deflated. Sagging against the counter, he murmured "Sure...yeah...fuck."

Damn. A part of me really didn't want to go either, but I

knew I had to be strong for Matt. If I fell apart, God...he probably wouldn't even get on the plane. I tossed him a carefree grin. "Don't worry, Matt. We'll pack your bucket."

He gave me a weak smile, then flipped me off.

As I laughed at him, Denny walked over to me. "There's just one more thing we need to talk about...and you're going to hate it." He gave me the same look he'd just given Matt. That *You're going to do it anyway* look. Fuck.

"What?" I asked, already annoyed.

He smiled, then said, "You need an online presence."

My response was immediate. "No."

Matt instantly snorted, and I shot him an unamused look. Denny sighed. "It's not optional anymore, Kellan. You need a way to interact with your fans instantly and directly, so you can squash rumors before they spiral out of control. So what happened with Sienna won't happen again. It's not a perfect solution, of course, some people will always believe what they want to believe, but it's better than doing random radio interviews here and there."

Matt started snickering, and now Evan was joining him. Kiera put a hand on my arm as I let out a long sigh. "He's got a point, Kellan. And I can help you with it."

I gave her a forlorn look, then said to Denny, "So what exactly are we talking about here?"

He went over a couple of sites that he wanted me to use. The more he explained how they worked, the deeper my frown got. And the more hysterically Matt and Evan laughed. Even Anna, Jenny, and Rachel were giggling now; Griffin was still cooing at Gibson. I shot all of them a look, then stared at Denny in utter disbelief. There was no way the words that had just come out of his mouth were real. "You want me to whatbook? And Tweet? Like a bird? Are you serious?"

Matt laughed so hard that he had to sit down. Evan shoved his face into a pillow as he lost it. Even Abby was struggling to remain professional, hiding her smile behind her hand. Denny just grinned at me. "Yes. I'm completely serious." I scowled at him, and he raised his hands. "It won't be as hard as you think. You can do it right from your phone."

At that, Matt lay down on the floor and clutched his stomach. "Stop," he told Denny. "You're killing me."

Kiera patted my shoulder, but she was giggling now too. "I'll help you. I promise."

I sighed at her, sighed at my friends, then bit out, "Fine. I'll do your stupid social media." Kiera discreetly took my picture after I said that. I rolled my eyes at her, but humor was quickly replacing my annoyance. Because I couldn't resist tormenting someone, I smirked and said, "Hey, Matt, can you—?"

Still lying on the floor, tears streaming down his cheeks now, he immediately flipped me off with both hands. "No! You're married. Holding your hand is Kiera's job now."

The entire room cracked up again, and Griffin finally seemed to realize something was going on. Lifting his head, he said, "Kiera's giving Kell a blowjob? Right now?" He held his hand above Gibson's eyes, blocking her view. "All right. Go for it."

Anna snort-laughed, but every other woman in the room got the same disgusted look on their face and instantly snapped at Griffin for being gross. I was positive the only thing keeping Griffin from being smacked by about a dozen different objects was the adorable infant in his arms, and when Griffin smirked as he looked down at her, I knew he knew it. Fucker had a shield now. We were all screwed.

Chapter 37

A DREAM COME TRUE

Sooner than I would have liked, we were back in L.A., getting ready for the Grammys. So many things had been going on recently that time had gotten away from me. We'd purchased the massive home on the hill and moved in all our stuff. That really hadn't taken very long since we didn't have much stuff to begin with. Kiera wanted to rectify that soon and had enlisted the help of Jenny and Denny, who both had an eye for decorating, or so she told me. I really didn't care what the place looked like. All I needed was her.

Once we were all moved in, I'd invited the guys over and broached the idea of using the back building as our new rehearsal/recording room. Matt's eyes had practically burned with enthusiasm, and right then and there, he'd started researching everything we'd need to transform it. Evan had been just as sold as Matt. The only holdout had been the one I was expecting.

"You want to meet here? In the middle of fucking nowhere?"

I nodded at Griffin's question. Again. He'd asked it at least ten times before I'd even shown them the building. "It's not that far. And it's private. It's perfect."

Scowling at me, he pointed at my front door. "I'm not

climbing up twenty thousand steps every time I visit you. You're gonna fix that shit, right?"

Wanting him to agree, I nodded and said, "Absolutely. I'll also keep a fridge full of beer, just for you. And when we're done for the day, you can use the pool."

He thought for a moment, considering. "Naked?" he finally asked.

With a bright smile on my face, I immediately told him, "Hell no."

He'd looked extremely disappointed about that, but he'd eventually agreed to come out to my place for rehearsals. Renovations were already in the works, and Matt was pretty sure everything would be ready for us in a month or two. So far, I'd resisted pointing out the fact that Matt had completely taken over the project for me, even though I was "married," and Kiera was the one "holding my hand" now. It was difficult not to tease him, but I really had no idea how to make a recording studio, so I was keeping my mouth shut. Almost. I did joke about it with Kiera on a near daily basis.

Kiera had also been busy on her own endeavors. She'd finally published her book, and I was the proud owner of the very first signed copy of her masterpiece. I'd intercepted her package of paperbacks when we'd still been living with Matt, then I'd led her on an entertaining scavenger hunt to collect her prize. She'd finally found me holding a dozen roses in one hand and her book in the other, and I still wasn't sure which one of us she'd wanted to hug more. Probably the book.

Her excitement was adorable, and I was so proud of her for chasing her dream. I wanted to pimp her book every day on my stupid social media sites, but she wouldn't let me. She wanted to make it on her own merits, not ride my fame—or her own—and I respected her decision. And honestly, she didn't need my help. The book, released under a pen name for anonymity, was doing really well. She was already planning her next bestseller, and I was going to be the first in line for a signed copy of that one too.

Kiera and I had also been busy helping Denny with his wedding. That was happening in a couple of days, and we still hadn't nailed down which song the D-Bags would be performing for Denny and Abby's first dance. Abby wanted either "Islands in the Stream" or "Endless Love," and I just...couldn't. Even if it was *their* wedding, *their* choice, I just...no. But if they really wanted those songs, I knew a half-dozen cover bands they could use, and I would be more than happy to line up one for them. But I should do it soon. And I couldn't do anything while I was stuck here in this ridiculously overpriced hotel, putting on ridiculously overpriced clothes, waiting for a ridiculously over-dramatic awards show to start. I *really* wasn't looking forward to this.

For the millionth time, I tried getting out of it. "Are you sure you want to go?" I asked Kiera. "You've been a little rundown lately. We could tell everyone you're sick, then stay here and spend the night lounging in bed, watching movies and eating ice cream sundaes. Doesn't that sound nice?"

She smirked at me. "I'm fine, and you know we have to go. We can lounge in bed when we get back," she added with a grin.

I frowned at her statement, mystified that she was so calm about all of this. Kiera hated the spotlight, and while she wasn't going onstage tonight, she was definitely going to have thou-sands, if not millions, of eyes on her. At the very least, she should be forlorn and resigned, but no, she was actually looking forward to this, and that made no sense to me. If it were a year ago, she would have been freaking out, backing out, begging me to back out, or a combination of all three. It was kind of annoying that she wasn't. The one time I really needed her anxiety as an excuse to bail, and she didn't have any. *Figures*.

Seeing my expression, Kiera walked over and put a hand on my cheek. "Why are you so nervous?" she asked.

My frown deepened. "I'm not nervous. I just don't see the point. We're not going to win. We shouldn't even be nominated. *Best* New Artist? As in the best of everyone who debuted this year? We're all right, but...the *best*? It just doesn't make any sense."

Smiling, Kiera rubbed my cheek with her thumb. "It does to those of us who aren't you."

I rolled my eyes at her comment, but then I was struck by how alluring her outfit was, and I instantly stopped complaining. Damn, she was gorgeous. The dress she'd been gifted for the evening was solid black and made out of a silky material that loosely flowed over her body but also clung to all my favorite curves. It only had a strap on one shoulder, and with her long, dark hair swept up, exposing all of her neck, showing off the guitar necklace that she still wore every day, the expanse of bare skin was calling to me. The arch of her neck, the ridge of her collarbone, the swell of the top of her breast—I wanted to taste it all.

"Are you *sure* you want to go?" I asked, dropping my voice to that seductive level that usually got her naked pretty fast.

She stepped away from me with her hands raised like she thought I was about to pounce on her. Which I might. "Yes, I'm sure. And whatever you're about to do, don't. I already got a text from Anna, and the limo is five minutes away."

I gave her a crooked grin. "Five minutes is plenty of time."

She narrowed her eyes at me. "It took Jenny and Anna thirty minutes to do my hair and makeup."

My grin widened. "And it will only take me twenty seconds to ruin it."

"Don't. You. Dare." The green flecks in her eyes were like jade shards of fire. It was hot. But I wouldn't actually do that to her right before we needed to leave. And yes, I was fully aware that I couldn't really get out of this. Still, teasing her was taking my mind off things.

I took one step toward her, and she shrieked and ran...for the bed. Really? Amused, I continued stalking her. And that was when someone started excessively pounding on our door. "Kell, we need to go!"

Hearing Matt's slightly panicked voice made me sigh, straighten, and step away from Kiera so she could put on her shoes. She grinned at me like she'd just won a major battle. "Later," I told her, then I opened the door before Matt knocked it down.

Ten minutes later, we were all slipping inside one of the longest limos I'd ever seen. The girls were all in fancy evening gowns, dresses that had been loaned to us by big designers that I'd never heard of. Anna assured me they were important, though, and I had a feeling their gowns probably cost more than our new recording equipment. The guys were dressed more simply, but in much nicer clothes than what they usually wore. Even I was dressed better than my average attire, wearing black slacks, a partially undone button-up, and a one-button jacket. I looked nicer than I had for my wedding, although I kind of missed the Underoos. I should have brought 'em. Evan would have gotten a kick out of that, and by the look on his face, he could use the distraction.

Because while everyone looked amazing, they also looked nervous. Things were being fidgeted with left and right—clasps on clutches, buttons on jackets, rings on fingers, and multiple bouncing knees. Wanting to ease the tension I felt building, I said, "Hey, when this is over, you guys want to go to The Rusted Pipe? It would blow Cody's mind if we showed up."

Matt and Evan grinned. Griffin frowned. "Do you know how many afterparties there's gonna be tonight? With celebrities and shit. And you want to go to The Pipe?"

I thought about it for a half-second, then nodded. "Yeah. Wanna come?"

He pondered it for a moment more, then shrugged. "Sure, why not."

Matt snickered at that, then relaxed back into his seat, and I knew he was finally looking forward to something.

The car quieted after that, everyone lost in their own thoughts, and once again, I felt nerves eating away at my stomach.

I wasn't sure what was going on with me, but I knew I didn't like it. Kiera pulled out her phone and started typing. At first, I thought she was checking in with Denny and Abby—they were back in Seattle, watching over Gibson—but then I saw the now-familiar design of the social media site Denny had made me join. The bird one. She sent something into cyberspace, and I knew it was on my behalf. Denny had said I could do it from my phone, but 99 percent of the time, the messages came from Kiera on her phone. No one seemed to notice or care, which made me think if she ever got tired of it, I could just hire someone to be me. But damn it, that felt like lying. At least if the messages came from Kiera, it was basically me talking. She knew everything I might want to say.

"What are you doing?" I asked her, just wanting to talk about something. Anything.

"Tweeting your fans," she casually said, like that sentence somehow made sense. Then she held up the phone and showed me what she'd sent. "About to head into the Grammys. Wish me luck."

The whole thing made me roll my eyes. I couldn't imagine that anyone really cared that I was sitting in a car on my way to not-win an award that we shouldn't be up for in the first place, but apparently, people did care. As I watched, comment after comment came rolling in. Reading all of them ate up a decent chunk of time, and before I knew it, the limo was pulling up to the venue. I glanced outside and felt my mouth fall open as I absorbed the absolute chaos: people, cameras, celebrities, more people, more cameras, more celebrities, all highlighted by a garish, bright-red carpet.

"Fuck me," I muttered, then I flashed a glance at Matt. He might not get out of the car if he noticed what was waiting for us. But apparently, he'd already considered that. While everyone else was looking around and letting out nervous-but-excited screeches, his eyes were glued on his shoes. Smart. I wished I'd thought of that. And I liked crowds.

The car stopped in the drop-off zone, and the driver got out to walk around and let us out. Knowing we didn't have much longer, I leaned forward and said, "Hey, no matter what happens tonight, I just want you to know, it's been an honor performing with you guys, and I already feel like we've won." I paused to grin at them. "We did it. We did everything we wanted to do. All of us." I shifted my focus to take in the girls. Without their support and encouragement, the guys would have fallen apart on the road. I'd seen it happen. They were just as much a part of our success, and winning or not winning some award didn't change that.

"Love you guys," Evan said, smiling.

"Love you too, man," Matt replied.

Griffin sniffed and dramatically wiped a non-existent tear off his cheek. Then he started singing "Can You Feel the Love Tonight," and as one, we all leaned over and shoved him against the wall. He was laughing when the driver opened the door.

Kiera and I were sitting closest to the exit, so we'd be doing this first. Kiera's eyes were wider than normal, and she looked a little pale, but she smiled at me and nodded; she was ready. I exhaled a quick breath, then slapped on a smile like this was something I did every other day. I stepped out of the limo to the roaring sound of screaming, and a million flashing lights. I was both blinded and deafened, and that actually made it a little easier. I extended my hand out for Kiera, and when she joined me, I swear the sound doubled. She laughed a little as she stood beside me, and I could clearly see the disbelief in her eyes. *How is this real life?* I laughed in agreement, because this was too surreal to be real, then I led her down the path to our future, clenching her hand the entire time.

Inside wasn't much better. Instead of being swarmed by strangers, we were surrounded by celebrities who looked vaguely familiar; I was much better with music than faces. The more I was approached by people, the more I wanted to just sit somewhere quiet and wait for our category to be over with. Or leave. Maybe we could go and come back when it was time to perform.

We'd already been filmed entering; who would notice if we weren't there for the bulk of the show? I thought to mention the idea to Kiera, but then a guy approached us with instructions to follow him to our seats. Feeling like it was too late to bail, I reluctantly let him escort us.

Kiera could sense my mood, or I'd complained enough that she knew I didn't want to be here. She spent a lot of time trying to engage me in idle chitchat, talking about things that were simple and easy—Abby probably wanting kids after babysitting Gibson, what songs we should play at their wedding, whether we should soundproof our bedroom. Well, that one was my suggestion, but I firmly believed we should seriously consider it, especially if our house was going to be constantly filled with friends, family, and one day, kids. Seemed like a no-brainer to me.

But as time wore on—as our category drew nearer—something happened to me. I felt sick, nauseated to the point where I was sure I was about to throw up. And I couldn't stop moving. It was like my fight-or-flight response was at a ten, but I couldn't do anything about it except sit there and stew. Conversation dried up as I stopped answering Kiera's prompts. Then I started kissing her wrist, over and over and over. Even I knew it was getting obsessive but feeling her skin underneath me helped calm me. If I could have sat in her lap with her arms around me, I would have. I wasn't even sure why I felt this way. It didn't matter if we won or not, but every time I thought that, a tiny part of me screamed in protest. A part that...wanted to win. It was stupid, meaningless, but fuck, it was definitely there. A desire to be wanted, appreciated, liked for something other than my face, my body, liked for something that truly mattered to me. I wanted to know my words mattered, my thoughts mattered, my talent mattered. And fuck, I was terrified I wouldn't measure up. But still...hadn't I already, just by being nominated? Why wasn't that enough? It made no sense.

My knee started bouncing when the two actors announcing our category walked onto the stage. *Fuck. I can't do this. I need to leave.* Kiera's hand went to my knee, stopping my ceaseless energy. Not able to stand it anymore, I leaned over and whispered, "I'm nervous. I'm really fucking nervous. I never get nervous. What the hell is wrong with me?"

She gave me a smile that was so calm; it was bizarre to me. "You're human," she said. "And I think it's pretty safe to say that everybody in here is nervous on some level."

Laughter filtered around the room as the announcers made some joke that I didn't even hear. The blood was rushing through my body so fast; all I could hear was my raging heartbeat. And still, Kiera looked peaceful, like we were sitting in our favorite movie theater back home watching a rom-com. It boggled me. "You're not nervous," I said, a little irritated.

Kiera gave me a smile that was full of warmth and mystery, like she knew something I didn't, like she had a crystal ball, and she knew exactly how this was going to play out. If she did, I'd appreciate a heads-up. Because they were playing clips of all the bands now, and I was genuinely going to hurl.

Then she leaned forward and whispered two words that evaporated every single nerve in my body. "I'm pregnant."

I was positive I hadn't heard her right, but I was too stunned to ask her to repeat it. I just stared at her with wide eyes and a dropped jaw. But like she heard me, she smiled and nodded, confirming my unasked question. *Oh my God. Oh my God. Oh my fucking God...we're having a baby.*

Reaching for her face, I pulled her to my lips, barely coherent of the audience screaming and cheering. My mind was whirling, dazed. *She's pregnant. Holy shit, she's pregnant.* I tenderly kissed her as I felt the tears burning behind my closed lids. I kissed her over and over, light, gentle kisses that felt like laughter. *I* wanted to laugh, I wanted to cry, I wanted to ask her how it was possible. I thought she'd been on the pill. I thought we were going to wait. I had a dozen questions, I had a thousand comments, I had a million kisses...but someone was trying to get my attention.

I could feel someone grabbing the back of my jacket, vaguely heard my name being said over the sound of hundreds of people clapping, but it was Kiera pushing me back and motioning for me to stand up that finally brought the reality of the moment crashing down around me. Everyone was looking at us, and the guys were wearing gigantic grins as they waved me up. I didn't think all this fuss was because they'd heard Kiera, which meant... holy shit...did we win?

Evan shoved me forward, toward the aisle, and the girls were all standing, clapping, and crying, so yeah, I was pretty sure that meant we won. Shit. We *won*. And Kiera was pregnant. And I couldn't deal with all of that happening at the same time. I felt drunk as I stumbled down the path toward the stage, and if my mind had been spinning before, it was a hurricane now. I kept looking back at Kiera, wondering if all that had really happened, or if I was dreaming right now. But by the smile she gave me, I knew I hadn't hallucinated that. She was pregnant. She was going to be a mom. I was going to be a dad. Fuck, I was going to be a dad. Fuck, I just won a Grammy.

Someone handed me a gold statue of a gramophone. Someone else congratulated me, gave me a quick hug. My eyes were watering so badly that I could barely see anything, but I did notice Matt and Evan step back, the pair of them holding Griffin by his shoulders so I could take centerstage. Fuck. I really wasn't sure if I could talk right now. But I had to try. I had to acknowledge this moment somehow. Damn it, why didn't I write a speech? I should have; my mind was too turbulent for coherency.

"Oh...wow...I don't know what to say." I genuinely didn't. And the moisture in my eyes was thickening, along with the lump in my throat. *Just get through this, then you can fall apart.* "I want to thank..." My voice broke on me as a tiny sob escaped. Retreating a step, I pressed the back of my hand to my mouth to stop myself from having a full-on breakdown. Swallowing repeatedly, I struggled for control. It wasn't happening. Shaking my head, I told the room, "I'm sorry. My wife just told me she's pregnant."

I stepped back as the tears dropped to my cheeks. The crowd erupted in another chorus of cheers, like they were all friends of mine, excited over the news. The guys cheered too, jumping on my back, socking me in the shoulder, and hugging me until I laughed. It relieved the tension, washing away the emotional dam.

Discreetly wiping my cheeks, I pulled myself together so I could do my job. Feeling like I was literally on top of the world, I stepped up to the microphone and tried to convey my gratitude in a few short sentences. "Well, I can honestly say that this is the best day of my life." I took a moment to find Kiera in the crowd, to absorb the loving smile she was giving me. With a grin, I swept my eyes over the whole room. "I want to thank every single person who has ever supported us. Your dedication has meant the world, and we wouldn't be here without you. I may be overly emotional right now, since I'm about to be a father, but I really do love each and every one of you. From the bottom of my heart, thank you."

I stepped back again with a small wave, then I glanced at Evan and Matt to see if they wanted to add anything. Matt, I was positive, wouldn't step up to that microphone if I paid him, and Evan shook his head, content with what I'd said. Even Griffin looked happy to leave it alone. Of course, he probably just wanted to get started on the celebratory drinking. Too bad he had to wait until after our performance. A performance I couldn't wait to give.

Damn. I never would have imagined tonight turning out like this, and as I tossed my arm over Evan's shoulders and left the stage with him, I was so glad I'd braved the nerves and done it, that we all had. We'd come so far, so fast. We'd made mistakes, but we'd done our best to correct them. We'd poured our heart and soul into that album, and we'd given our all at every single performance. We'd done our best, and we'd officially been recognized for it, and I was so fucking proud. Of my friends, of my family, of our fans...of all of us.

My phone blew up for the rest of the night, everyone sending me their congratulations. Hailey called me when we were back in the limo, heading over to The Pipe after a brief appearance at an afterparty sponsored by the label. We'd mainly gone to appease Griffin, but it had turned out all right. Justin and the rest of Avoiding Redemption had been there. Sienna too. She'd walked up to us, given us a brief congratulations for the win, then she'd left us alone, as she'd promised. I had to admit, I was impressed she was finally keeping her word, and I hoped she'd learned a lesson from all of this. Being on top didn't mean anything if you stomped on everyone around you to get there. There was something to be said for good, old-fashioned kindness and respect. Or maybe I was still being naïve. If I was, I was okay with it; I'd rather be naïve than jaded.

"Oh my God," Hailey said in a long, drawn-out sigh. "You killed me tonight. Killed. Me. That was the most amazing thing I've ever seen, and I'm so happy for you. For both of you." Then she squealed so loud that I had to hold the phone away from my ear. Kiera grinned, clearly having heard her.

"Thank you," I told her. "We're excited, and I can't wait for you to meet your niece or nephew."

She gushed some more, then we disconnected, and I just sat there, stunned. It still hadn't completely sunk in. Kiera smiled at me, her thumb running over the back of my hand. "You're really pregnant?" I asked. It wasn't the first time I'd asked her that either. More like the thousandth.

With a giggle, she nodded. "Yes. Doctor confirmed, I am most definitely pregnant."

I could only shake my head in wonder. "How?"

Unfortunately, Griffin heard me ask that. Leaning forward he said, "Seriously? You still don't know how to make a baby?" With a dramatic sigh, he shifted to look at Kiera. "I'm so sorry you've had such an inadequate partner for so long. I'd offer my services, so you'd know exactly what you're missing, but Anna and I don't share anymore. Sorry."

He shrugged while Anna grinned, and Kiera smirked. I

flipped him off. "I know *how*, obviously," I paused to indicate her doctor-confirmed pregnant body, then I frowned. "I just don't understand...how. I thought you were on birth control?"

Kiera flushed as she glanced at all the people listening to the details of our sex life, then she shrugged and said, "I guess there was a bad batch of pills. Packaged wrong or something. The odds were still pretty low, but...here we are. The baby is due in September," she beamed.

Still dazed, I just stared at her for a moment. Tonight certainly was a night of slim chances. As I leaned forward to kiss Kiera, I heard Matt quietly say to Rachel, "You don't take the same ones, do you?" I pulled back to laugh. Matt noticed my amusement and flipped me off. He loved Rachel more than I'd ever seen him love anything outside of music, but he definitely wasn't ready to be a dad yet. He might not ever be ready for that; Evan and I should start another bet.

The long, sleek limo looked massively out of place pulling up to the crumbling exterior of The Rusted Pipe. Like he agreed with that thought, the driver lowered the partition and asked, "Are you sure you want me to let you out here?"

Nodding, I told him, "Yep, thanks. And I'll get the door." It probably wasn't a good idea to leave a car running in this neighborhood, not even for the few minutes it would take to let us out.

Matt told him to come back at closing, then we all hurried out of the vehicle. We were ridiculously overdressed for this place, but I knew once we got inside, everything would be fine. A lot of the old regulars were still here, and I was expecting a warm reception. I wasn't disappointed.

Cody noticed us the second we walked through the door. Everyone did actually, and the room erupted into cheers, whistles, and claps. It was enough to make me shake my head in disbelief, but I tossed up a hand in a friendly wave of appreciation. We headed to the bar while everyone watched and whispered.

Cody shook his head. "Damn, Grammy winners in my bar. Never thought I'd see that. Congratulations, guys. We watched the whole thing on TV." He stuck out his hand, shaking with each of us in turn. Then he twisted around and grabbed a top-shelf bottle of whiskey, one that was clearly never touched; it was covered in a thick layer of dust. "Tonight, we bust out the good stuff," he said. As everyone sat down on rickety stools, Cody winked at Kiera. "Except you. We'll get you something without alcohol." He turned his eyes back to me. "A special congratulations to you, Papa Kyle."

Anna snorted and murmured, "Daddy Kyle."

Kiera shot her a look, but Griffin instantly brightened. "Fill our glasses, Cody. We gotta toast him."

I frowned at Griffin while Cody filled a shot glass for each of us, then filled a small glass with juice for Kiera. Griffin's toasts usually weren't very...good. After dramatically clearing his throat, Griffin raised his glass. He waited for us to do the same, then he held his glass out to me. "To my best friend, Kellan, who finally impregnated a woman."

Everyone but Anna and Cody frowned at Griffin; they both laughed. Griffin looked around and said, "What?" He raised an eyebrow at me. "Let's be honest, you should have gotten *someone* pregnant by now, so obviously, you've been shooting blanks for years. That's a miracle baby right there."

I knew I shouldn't have been surprised by anything he said, but I felt dumbstruck anyway. "That's not..." Matt and Evan were snickering now too, but instead of trying to explain things to Griffin, I rolled my eyes and said, "And what about you? Took you forever too."

He sniffed, then shrugged. "Beat you." Leaning forward, he quietly added, "And I bet I beat you again."

I had no idea if he was seriously making a bet with me about that, but I wouldn't be surprised if he was. Shaking my head, I made my own toast. "To our future. Because damn, it's looking good."

No one had a problem drinking to that, and everyone tipped back their glasses. Once we were done, Cody smiled and circled his finger at our group. "We need a new picture for the wall, one with everyone this time." He indicated behind the bar with his thumb, to where the photo of Evan, Matt, and me was resting between two bottles of vodka.

Griffin looked at it and frowned. "Where am I?" He looked over at me. "Did you guys come here without me? What the fuck, dude? I take back that best friend comment."

I laughed, then grabbed the bottle still sitting on the counter and poured him another shot. He instantly smiled. "Never mind. You are the best, sir."

Cody waved us together, and Matt and Evan came up to stand behind us. Cody grabbed his phone, then shook his head and said, "Wives too."

Anna and Kiera were already in the frame, sitting on either side of Griffin and me, but upon hearing Cody, Evan grabbed Jenny and yanked her into his arms. Matt's cheeks flushed with color, but he smiled and put his arm around Rachel when she stepped up to him. Cody arranged us so that everyone was visible, and my smile was uncontainable as he captured the moment with all of us. It just felt right, and my only regret was that Denny, Abby, and all our loved ones couldn't be here too. Because the D-Bags were more than just four people. We were a family that was growing larger all the time. And I loved it. I absolutely loved it.

This is everything I've ever wanted.

Or at least...it was about to be.

Chapter 38

A NEW BEGINNING

Denny's wedding was incredible and watching one of my best friends be *that* happy moved me. Seeing Denny's face when he said, "I do," damn near brought me to tears. Seeing Kiera's face right after he said it, did.

I'd never wanted to hurt Denny, and while I'd always feel a touch guilty around him, I was overjoyed that he'd bounced back from what we'd done to him in such a positive way. Everything about him was stronger than before—his confidence, his career, his relationship—but he was still the good-natured guy who'd befriended me as a kid. The only friend I'd ever had until Evan, Matt, and Griffin. I was so grateful I hadn't lost him. And oddly, I was grateful Kiera hadn't lost him either. He was a good friend to us both. A good manager too, and for the first time since all this craziness started, I felt safe, protected, and supported. It was such a relief.

I squeezed him so hard once the ceremony was over that I was sure I was hurting him; he just laughed, though. "Congratulations, man. Welcome to the club."

He grinned at me, his smile bright and carefree. "Thanks, mate." He shook his head. "I still can't believe you beat me."

"I get that a lot," I told him with a smirk.

He laughed again, then Kiera stepped up to him. She already had tears in her eyes as she hugged him and brokenly told him how happy she was for him, and I knew she was a breath away from completely losing it. I was proven right a moment later when she stepped back and there were tears on her cheeks.

Warm smile on his face, Denny brushed them aside and told her, "I'm so glad you're here. I love you, mate."

There was so much respect and friendship in his tone that even *I* got choked up. Kiera sobbed. Happy sobs, if such a thing existed. With a laugh, I pulled her away from him. She'd been crying at the drop of a hat lately. Just this morning, she'd deteriorated into tears because I'd kissed her stomach and told our child, "Mornin'." When I'd asked her if she was okay, she'd just nodded and kept right on crying. It was cute.

"Keep it together, you," I told her. I was feeling a little emotional too, and if she kept this up, I was going to fall apart with her, and I still had a job to do tonight. I doubted Denny and Abby wanted me sniffling through the song I'd written for them. A song that had flowed out of me after Kiera told me she was pregnant. I wrote the entire thing on the plane ride, then handed it to Matt and Evan, who'd instantly started coming up with a rhythm. I don't think we'd ever put a song together so quickly; even my rushed goodbye song to Kiera had taken longer. But it worked, and it was beautiful, romantic...perfect. I couldn't wait to perform it for them.

That happened about an hour later after a top-notch dinner, rounds of toasts, and Denny and Abby cutting their massive wedding cake. Griffin was annoyed with me when we set up for the song. I'd only let him have one glass of champagne, and I hadn't let him give a toast to the happy couple.

"I wasn't going to say anything bad," he murmured to me.

"What were you going to say?" I asked.

He grinned, and I knew just by his smile that whatever he was going to say would *not* be appropriate for a very formal wedding.

He opened his mouth, and I raised my hand. "Yeah, that's what I thought. You can tell him in private."

Disbelief on his face, he lifted his hands. "I didn't tell you yet."

I shifted my finger to point at each one of his mischievous, blue irises. "You *did* tell me. You told me everything I needed to know."

He rolled his eyes. "God, you sound just like Matt. I told him earlier, and he said if I said it, he wouldn't let me have any cake." He frowned. "He knows cake is my weakness."

Matt heard him say that and snorted. Griffin moved his hand, and I knew he was seconds away from flipping him off. I grabbed his wrist to stop him. God. I almost—*almost*—wished Tory was here. Because Matt was right, wrangling rock stars wasn't easy.

"Just get ready," I told him.

He grumbled, but he did what I asked. Once we were all set, I stepped up to the microphone. There was excitement in the air. A lot of the guests were either Denny and Abby's coworkers or friends that I didn't know. They knew me, though, and they were all eager for an intimate D-Bags show. I held up my hand, and the buzz of people talking quieted to hushed whispers.

"Tonight is a very special night for a very special couple." I locked eyes with my friend as he waited on the dancefloor with his incredibly beautiful bride. "Denny, Abby, I wish you endless love, bottomless happiness, and not too many nights of Denny sleeping on the couch." The crowd laughed at that, and smiling, Denny shook his head at me. "I'm so incredibly happy for the both of you." Abby started crying, and even Denny teared up. Not wanting to drown the room in emotion, I shifted my gaze to the audience and said, "Ladies and gentlemen, the first dance of Mr. and Mrs. Harris."

I indicated for Evan to start with a flick of my wrist. He began the song, and a beat later, Matt and Griffin joined in. I waited for my cue, and when I started singing, Denny and Abby started dancing. I smiled as I sang about finding your soulmate and falling more in love with them every day. My gaze eventually drifted to Kiera, and I sang most of the song directly to her since it was about her anyway. About how I felt about her, about how much I loved her, about how amazing it was that she felt the same way about me. Emotion tightened my chest as I sang to the love of my life, as I periodically glanced at my best friend dancing with the love of his. I was a little proud of myself for getting through the whole damn thing without my throat closing up.

Once it was done, I subtly wiped my wet eyes. Then I told the crowd, "All right, enough with this emotional crap. Let's dance!"

The crowd laughed again, and I was relieved to see Denny and Abby laugh too. Then Evan started a fast-paced song, and between the bride, the groom, and me, we got everyone to their feet.

I could have played until dawn, but eventually Denny and Abby stole my microphone and called it a night. They had an early plane to catch, and I imagined there was some private celebrating they wanted to do. I hugged them, telling them congratulations again, before they made their last rounds of the evening. Abby thanked me for the song with tears in her eyes. "It was beautiful," she gushed.

Once she moved aside, Denny leaned over and said, "You just didn't want to sing 'We've Only Just Begun,' did you?"

Raising my eyebrows, I nodded. "It would have killed me."

He laughed, then clapped my shoulder and retreated with his wife.

Kiera and I left not long after Denny and Abby. After saying goodbye to our friends, who seemed ready to shut down the party, we headed up to the hotel room where we'd gotten ready before the ceremony. I was grinning as I unlocked the door, and Kiera noticed.

"Why are you smiling like that?" she asked, her lips pursed in amusement.

Knowing she wasn't going to expect what was waiting for her, I simply said, "You'll see." Then I prayed that the hotel staff had done what I'd asked them to do. If they hadn't, I'd have to come up with something else to justify my cryptic statement. That could be really fun, though.

Happy with either scenario, I pushed the door in and turned on the lights. I was greeted with a sea of roses, and I smiled at seeing it. There were vases on every hard surface, along with loose petals strewn about; they were all over the bed, all over the floor. Mixed with the petals were wrapped chocolate hearts, and by the way they were all face up and perfectly arranged, I knew they'd been strategically placed by hand. On the bed was a tray holding two wine glasses and a bottle resting in a silver bucket of ice. There was also a bowl of strawberries and a container of fruit dip. Damn. I'd have to make sure to leave these guys a huge tip because this was pretty impressive.

Kiera's mouth popped open as she took it all in. She looked up at me with surprise and confusion in her eyes. "It didn't look like this when we left."

I laughed and nodded. "I know." Grabbing her hand, I led her to the bed. "Do you know the best thing about super-fancy hotels like this one?" I indicated the numerous floral arrangements; the flowers here almost equaled the number at Denny and Abby's wedding. Almost. "They really aim to please. I probably could have gotten some doves released in here."

She laughed at that, then shook her head. "What's all this for?"

With a shrug, I pulled the bottle out of the ice to check the label. Sparkling cider, just as I'd requested. "You and I, we never really had a wedding night."

Kiera bit her lip and raised an eyebrow. "I seem to recall that we did," she said.

I grinned at that, remembering the night after our bar-wedding. "I mean an official wedding night...after being legally married. And I know tonight wasn't our wedding, but it was *a* wedding, and I'm in a tux and you..." my gaze drifted to the incredible gown that clung to her in all the right places, "...you look like that. And I just thought, maybe this could be the night we didn't get to have. You know?"

Her eyes turned glossy as she stared at me. "I never know what to say when you do stuff like this."

Cupping her cheek, I shook my head. "You already said the most important thing."

Smiling, she leaned into my hand. "I do?" she said, her voice teasing.

Running my thumb over her satin skin, I shook my head again. "No...I want you." She pursed her lips at me, and I grinned. "And I love you. And I do. The trifecta of perfect words."

She smiled again, then reached up to kiss me. And damn, it was heaven. *She* was heaven. My eternal peace.

In the spring we left on the new tour, a tour we were headlining. Kiera was coming with me again, a fact that both overjoyed and worried me. I didn't want anything to happen to her or the fragile baby inside of her. But honestly, if she wasn't with me, I'd worry just as much. At least with her by my side, I could wake up every morning and verify that she was fine. And I did. Every single morning.

Denny had scored us a private bus for the tour. It seemed ridiculously indulgent, but it was a luxury Kiera and I quickly got used to. Although we weren't entirely alone on the bus. If we were moving, there was a driver present, and I'd hired a body-guard this time around. That also seemed ridiculously indulgent, but with my wife and my child's lives on the line, nothing was too exorbitant. I'd even enlisted Sienna's help to hire the bulky guy since I knew nothing about personal security. Surprising the hell out of me, she'd offered up one of the two men who typically watched over her. That was a relief for me. One, because I'd met the guy before, and two, because I knew from personal experience that he was good at his job. He was exceedingly serious, though, and insisted on always calling me "sir." And he never, ever smiled, not even when the guys were being genuinely funny. It was my newfound mission in life to crack his façade. Mainly because I needed the reassurance that an actual human being was protecting my family.

Kiera's body grew day by day, month by month, and I loved seeing the expansion. I frequently tried to picture how big the baby was, which meant I was frequently staring at Kiera's belly. She didn't seem to mind, and when I told her what I was doing, she found it more endearing than anything else. When I wasn't staring at Kiera's stomach, I was resting my head against it, listening for the baby, or running my hands over it, trying to feel the baby move, or singing to it, hoping the baby would know my voice before he or she was even born. Kiera thought my fascination was adorable, but I couldn't help myself. I wanted to know our child; the waiting period was killing me.

"Do you need anything? Chair? Pillow? Foot massage?"

Kiera smiled as she rubbed her stomach. We were walking around backstage at our last show in the U.S. After this, we were heading overseas. Australia first, then a few spots in Europe. I wasn't sure how I felt about it. I was excited to see a little more of the world, excited to see Denny's homeland, but nervous about us being so far from home with Kiera being so very pregnant. Every day I resisted the urge to cancel the last leg of the tour.

"I'm fine," Kiera said. Then she pursed her lips. "I'll take you up on that foot massage later, though."

Stopping us, I put my hand on her stomach. Like the baby knew what I wanted, I felt a small kick under my palm. I instantly grinned. Then I looked up and glanced at our ever-present shadow, our bodyguard, Kevin. "Hey, Kev, want to feel this? It's really trippy."

Kiera looked over her shoulder at him. He wasn't watching us. He usually didn't. He was watching the halls, looking for sudden or suspicious movement. There was a clump of excited fans at the other end of the hallway, and his eyes were glued on them like they were holding knives, not pens. I'd already signed autographs for them, but they were still watching Kiera and me as we went for a walk before the show. I figured they'd stand there watching until we were out of sight. Unlike Sienna's strict, regimented tour, we were keeping things more casual, and fans were allowed to freely roam around certain backstage areas. Under the watchful eye of security, of course.

Face still as stone, Kevin told me, "No thank you, sir."

"All right, but you're missing out." Kiera smirked at me. She found my attempts to engage Kevin entertaining.

There was a rush of movement up ahead, someone running my way, and like he had supernatural powers, Kevin was suddenly in front of us, one hand on his gun under his jacket, the other hand signaling us to stay back. But it was Griffin running our way. He slid to a stop when he noticed Kev's posture, then he raised his hands like there actually was a gun pointed at him.

"Whoa, dude, tell your pit bull I'm a friendly."

Kevin was already relaxing, but I cocked an eyebrow at Griffin. "Are you, though?" I asked him.

He scowled at me, giving Kevin cautious glances as the tank of a man moved behind us again. "Not cool, Kell. Not cool."

I grinned again. Having a bodyguard was kind of fun. "Were you running through the hallways to amuse yourself, or were you looking for us?"

He smirked. "Both. Matt told me to come find you. He needs to talk to you about something." He shrugged like he didn't know any more than that, and he probably didn't. He tended to tune out everything that didn't directly involve him.

Reaching for Kiera's hand, I indicated for him to lead the way. With Kevin a pace behind us, we made our way to a large room. I could hear whispering and movement inside, but for some reason, the lights were off. Kevin was instantly on high alert, but I held up my hand and told him, "I'm pretty sure I know what this is, and it's fine."

He frowned at me but nodded. I honestly doubted it was my

words that appeased him, though; it was more the fact that the door was heavily guarded by a security team from the venue. Kiera smiled at me as she clenched my hand tighter, then the two of us followed Griffin into the dark room. The lights flashed on the moment we stepped inside, blinding us both, and at least a hundred people shouted, "Surprise!" in unison.

I blinked until I could see, and once I could, I was floored. Everyone from the crew was in here, along with the guys and everyone from Avoiding Redemption and Holeshot. Even our drivers were here, and every single person was clapping and whistling. On the wall behind them was a huge banner that said *Congratulations!* There was a table overflowing with food, drinks, and cake—a blue and pink cake—and the ceiling of the room was practically hidden by a plethora of pastel balloons.

Matt and Evan stepped forward as I leaned over and said to Kiera, "It's not my birthday; is it your birthday?"

She laughed at my joke—she was well aware I knew when her birthday was—then she put her hand on her stomach. "I don't think this is for us," she said.

Grinning at the room, I shook my head, genuinely touched by the gesture. Matt explained when he was close enough. "Most of the crew won't be joining us for the last leg, but they wanted to do something special for Little Kyle before they left us." He indicated the room, and that was when I noticed that a lot of them were holding presents. Presents for my kid. It was so surreal, and it reminded me once again that my job, especially at this level, required a small army to make it happen. An army with lives, loves, and stories of their own, and the fact that they'd gone out of their way for my child, to show they cared like this...it choked me up.

"Thank you," I told the room. "This...this means a lot to me, to us. I just..." I couldn't even finish that, just shook my head in disbelief as someone handed me a beer and someone else passed presents to Kiera. Damn, I knew the best fucking people.

The show that night was one of the best we'd ever done.

Everyone was in a good mood, everyone was excited, happy... pumped up on a massive amount of joy and sugar. And even though we were saying goodbye, to the crew, to the fans, it didn't feel like goodbye. It felt like...*until next time*.

Not too much later, we were on a massive plane heading Down Under. It still concerned me that Kiera was traveling in her last trimester. I thought I'd feel better about it on the plane, but I really didn't. "Are you sure about this?" I asked her, shifting around to lean over the aisle between our two first class seats. "We could still go home."

She raised her eyebrows at me. "We're two hours into a bazillion-hour flight. There's no simple way to just 'go home' anymore."

I frowned as I studied her stomach. "I know. We'd have to immediately get on another plane, spend another day in the air, then I'd have to come right back after getting you settled..." I looked up at her. "I didn't say it would be easy. Or fun. But it's possible. You *could* go home."

Her smile was remarkably at ease. "I *am* home," she told me. Even though it was a sweet sentiment, I rolled my eyes. She frowned at me. "It's going to be fine, Kellan. My due date is a ways after the tour ends. By the time the baby comes, we'll be home and rested."

"What if the baby comes early?"

Her lip quirked. "Then they'll be born in another country. Would that technically make them a citizen of that country? Maybe they could get dual citizenship." She seemed excited by that, but my frown deepened. She sighed. "They have hospitals everywhere, you know? It's going to be fine."

Pursing my lips, I shook my head and scooted closer to her. "All right, Anna. How did you take over my wife's body...and how long have you been inhabiting her. Because if Kiera finds out what we did last night..."

She leaned over to smack my knee, and I chuckled. "You

should be grateful I've been taking some life tips from my sister," she said. "Otherwise...you'd never get your wings."

My eyebrows lifted in surprise. "Were you serious about that?"

She bit her lip and nodded. "Yeah. You wanna try?" she quietly asked.

All I could do was dumbly stare at her. When I'd first seemed uncertain about her coming with me, she'd hinted that we could have sex in the airplane. I thought she'd been joking. Semi-public sex wasn't her thing, and those bathrooms were a joke; it was a tight fit with just *one* person. But I could tell by the look in her eye that she was serious; she wanted to try. Well damn. It wasn't like I was going to deny giving my pregnant wife what she wanted.

Smile on my face, I stood and held out my hand to help her up.

We nonchalantly walked up to the pair of bathrooms, acting like we were each going to take one. People were drinking, talking, watching screens, or sleeping. No one was paying any attention to us, so we ducked into the same bathroom and quickly closed the door. I almost instantly laughed. While this bathroom was bigger than the main cabin bathrooms, there was barely enough room for two people in here. Kiera smiled when she saw the amusement on my face, then she started undoing my jeans. Was she really serious about this?

Apparently, she was, because her lips were on mine a moment later. I stopped thinking as she kissed me, stopped worrying about the logistics of it, stopped being annoyed that keeping my balance felt like surfing, stopped being frustrated that moving any part of my body made me hit a wall. I stopped thinking about all of it and just let myself *feel*. Her lips moving over mine, my hand cupping her cheek, her hand slipping inside my jeans...

She wrapped her fingers around me, and that was all it took for me to be 1,000 percent on board. A soft groan left me as my body instantly responded to her. She moaned in my mouth as she felt me come alive, and I knew, right at that moment, they'd have to handcuff us and drag us out of there to get us to stop. She was wearing a loose dress, which was incredibly helpful. Sliding my lips to her neck, I turned her around, hiked up her dress, and pulled off her underwear. She was fully ready for me too, and when I slid my finger between her legs, she grabbed my other hand and pressed it over her mouth. I smiled as I kissed the back of her neck, loving the fact that she knew she'd need help suppressing herself.

Having sex in a tiny, rocking room with a very pregnant woman was even more complicated than I thought it would be. Finding the right position, one that was comfortable for both of us, without fucking falling or cramping was the true challenge. But once we found that sweet spot, fuck, it felt so good. With Kiera bracing against the counter and me behind her, I could clearly see her face in the mirror. Mine too. With my hand still clamped over her mouth, I watched her face fill with ecstasy, watched her fall apart even as I felt her tightening around me. I drove into her a few more times as I felt my own wall approaching, then I dropped my head to the crook of her neck and tried to stifle my own groan as I came. God...damn.

I had to rest like that for a moment, catching my breath, and then I felt Kiera's hand on my cheek. She moved my hand on her mouth, resting it over her heart, and I felt her rapid pulse under my fingers. Smiling, I shifted my head to look at her in the mirror. Her cheeks were flushed, and she damn near glowed as she smiled back at me. I took a full thirty seconds to just stand there and cherish her before finally helping her clean up and get dressed.

There was a flight attendant waiting right outside the bathroom when I eventually opened the door. I stopped and stared when I spotted her, wondering just how much trouble a person could get into for having sex in a bathroom on a plane. She smirked at Kiera and me, raising an eyebrow, and I gave her a *Sorry, won't happen again* shrug mixed with a *Don't be mad at me, I swear I'm not a perv* smile. She giggled at the look on my face, then wordlessly reached into her uniform and handed each of us a pair of plastic wings.

Oh my God. When Kiera had mentioned earning my wings, I'd never imagined that I'd actually be given a pair of wings. With a bright grin on my face, I attached them to my shirt and wore the pin with pride for the remainder of the flight. Actually, for the remainder of the tour. Kiera looked mildly embarrassed at first, but then she gave me fond smiles, like she thought it was cute. Griffin sulked about it, wanting his own pair, and I was suddenly really grateful Anna had stayed home. They definitely would have gotten arrested.

When the tour found its way to Brisbane, I invited Denny's parents to the concert. I honestly didn't think they'd show; they really didn't have a reason to. Kiera was nervous as she sat backstage, waiting. "Is it wrong that I hope they don't make it? Is it weird that I hope they do? Am I crazy for wanting both things to happen?"

With a short laugh, I shook my head. "If you're crazy, then I'm crazy too. I feel like I did right before I met my dad for the first time." I blew out a long breath as I shook my head. "It will be fine. Worst case scenario, they'll try to kill me, and Kev here will stop them."

Kevin raised his eyebrows. "Are you expecting them to be violent?" he asked.

Just getting him to raise his eyebrows felt like a win. Wanting more, I told him, "I knocked up their son's girlfriend, so...yeah."

His mouth opened, just a fraction, and victory swam in my veins. But he immediately shut his mouth and nodded. "I'll keep them ten feet away at all times."

Kiera grunted and softly swatted my arm. "You make it sound worse than it was, and I didn't even think that was possible." She looked up at Kevin. "Kellan and I were married when he..." Stopping herself, she shook her head. "Denny is fine; he's happily married too, and I'm positive his parents aren't worried about whatever might have gone down between us. That was eons ago anyway."

"So why are you nervous?" I asked her.

She sighed, then looked back at Kevin. "Maybe three feet away."

He nodded, but I swore his mouth twitched.

Finally, not long before the start of the show, I got word that they'd arrived. Security was bringing them to us, and I had to scrub my hands on my jeans about ten times while I waited. Kiera played with her guitar necklace, yanking it back and forth, and I again marveled at the strength of the chain it had come with. Worth every penny.

A member of the crew popped in and said, "A Mr. and Mrs. Harris to see you, sir. They were on the friends and family list."

I nodded at him. "Let them in, thank you."

He stepped back, and my heart started thudding. Kiera stood up and clenched my hand, and I wasn't sure which one of us was clammier. Damn it. Why the fuck was I so nervous? Because I cared. Because I knew I deserved condemnation from them, but what I really wanted was approval. Acceptance. Love. But I knew I wouldn't get it. I'd torched that bridge long ago. *So why did they come?*

Seconds later, an older couple walked into the room, and damn if the resemblance to Denny wasn't clear as day. Their hair was mostly gray, but there was a darkness to it that implied it had once been a deep brown. Their eyes were both just as dark as their son's, but what really sold the familiarity...was the kindness in their expressions. The crinkles around their eyes, the way their lips curved up even before they smiled, like their mouths were incapable of forming frowns, the complete lack of judgement on their faces. It screamed *these are good people*, and that made sense since Denny was the best person I knew.

I held out my hand, conscious of the fact that my fingers were shaking. "Mr. and Mrs. Harris, it's an honor to finally meet you. Denny speaks highly of both of you."

Mrs. Harris grabbed me first, clasping my hand in both of hers. "It's nice to meet you, Kellan." She lifted an eyebrow. "He speaks highly of you too."

Of course he did. Now. I had to imagine there was a time when he didn't. "I remember calling you when he first came home, so I know that's not completely true," I told her.

She sighed and nodded. "Yes. He was...unhappy with you back then." Her eyes drifted to Kiera. "With both of you."

Kiera loudly swallowed, and I saw tears shining in her eyes. "I'm sorry," she whispered. "I never wanted to hurt him. I—"

Denny's mom shushed her, then hugged her. "Life happens," she said. "We learn, we grow, and if we're strong enough, we take the moments that hurt us and become better people." She pulled away from Kiera with a smile. "And what I learned when my son came home was that he was an incredibly strong person. And good. And kind. And forgiving. And I firmly believe he ended up exactly where he was *supposed* to. I'm incredibly proud of him, and while I'm not thrilled you broke his heart...I know my son... he wouldn't have loved you as much as he did, as much as he *does*, if you were a bad person." She looked back at me. "Either of you."

Denny's dad nodded in agreement, then said, "But try not to break his heart again, okay? Unlike my son, I only have so much forgiveness in me."

Kiera laughed at that, and I did too. Then we all hugged and moved on. Kiera and I took turns talking, letting them get to know the people we were *now* instead of wasting time reminiscing about the naïve kids we'd been years ago. And by the end of the night, I felt like I had another set of parents, and I was pretty sure Kiera felt the same way.

As the tour wrapped up, I could tell Kiera was ready to go home. She was ready to rest and be pampered, and I was ready to pamper her. I did everything I could to make her comfortable, but the closer she got to her due date, the more helpless I felt. I couldn't make her feet stop swelling, I couldn't take away her discomfort so she could sleep at night, I couldn't make the baby stop kicking her in the exact same spot over and over. There was literally nothing I could do for her, and I hated feeling useless.

"Do you want me to get you that special ice cream again?" I asked her.

With a long sigh, she rubbed her side and said, "No, it doesn't sound good anymore."

"Do you want me to try painting your toes again? I think I can do better this time." Last time, I got more of it on her feet and my hands than her nails.

She let out a soft giggle. "No, but thank you."

"Do you want me to check on your mom?" Caroline had come over early and was staying down the hallway in a guest bedroom. She hadn't wanted to take a chance on missing the birth like she'd missed Gibson's.

Kiera sighed and looked at our closed bedroom door. "No, she's fine."

Running a hand through my hair, I studied her as she lay on the bed looking miserable. "What can I do?" I asked. Because I needed to do something. This was killing me.

Kiera shook her head. "There isn't anything more you can do, Kellan. The nursery is ready, my mom is here, we've made all the arrangements...the only thing left to do is wait."

I sighed and rested my chin on her arm. "I hate waiting. And I hate that the entire burden is falling on you. I wish we could share the baby."

She cringed as she laughed. "That would be so weird." Her hand came up to stroke my cheek. "Don't worry, you'll have plenty to do once the baby is born."

That made me smile. "Do you think it's a boy or a girl?" I asked. I tried to picture it, tried to picture what our life was going to be like soon, but I still couldn't. It still seemed like some distant fantasy that wasn't ever going to happen.

Kiera grinned as she ran both hands around her stomach. "I

don't know. I'm glad we didn't find out, though. I'm looking forward to the surprise. And being able to bend over again."

The misery on her face made me sigh again. God, I wished there was *something* I could do. Sitting up, I shrugged and said, "Do you want sex?"

Honestly, it felt like the only thing I had left to give her, but she laughed as she shook her head. "I'm fine, Kellan. I promise."

I frowned at her. "I don't want you to be fine, I want you to be amazing." I paused as I thought, then I shrugged and pulled off my shirt.

Kiera eyed my chest, my abs, but she was frowning. "I love you, but I really just can't right now."

Standing up, I removed my jeans. "I know," I told her. Heading over to our dresser, I grabbed the cowboy hat and plopped it on my head.

Kiera's frown deepened as she watched me. "Then what are you doing?"

Strutting my way over to her, I stopped at the edge of the bed and just stood there. Her eyes roved over my body. Slapping on my sexiest smile, I told her, "All I can offer you now is eye candy, so...here you go. Drink it up."

She started laughing, then she giggled so hard that her eyes watered. "You're absolutely ridiculous," she told me between fits.

I turned around so she could stare at my ass for a while. "I know," I told her. Then I said, "Just let me know if you want the boxers to come off."

She snorted, and I just smiled as I posed. At least I could make her laugh. Maybe I wasn't so useless after all.

It was three days later when Kiera started having contractions. The minute she told me, I leapt into action. Or...I started having a nervous breakdown. That felt more accurate. I tried to remember our plan, tried to remember everything we might need, tried to remember how to walk and talk at the same time, but my brain instantly turned to jelly, and cognizant thought became utterly impossible. I wasn't entirely sure how, but I managed to drive her to the hospital. And her mom. *I think.*

As Kiera's pain intensified, my heart felt like it was shattering. *How could I do this to her? Was it even worth it? How the fuck do I stop myself from crying and begging for her forgiveness?* Caroline must have seen the desolation on my face. She pulled me to the side of the room, looked me in the eye, and said, "As scared as you are, she's feeling it more. Take a deep breath, collect yourself, then go be her rock. Because what she needs from you right now is *support.*"

I nodded, inhaled a deep breath, shoved down all my panic, and walked over to my wife. Grabbing her hand, I leaned down and told her, "You can do this, baby. You're the strongest person I know." Her eyes were wide with fear, pain, and worry. Swallowing the lump in my throat, I nodded at her. "I'm right here. I've got you."

Kiera minutely relaxed as she gave me a small nod. "I love you," she murmured, her voice tight.

Moving to the other side of her, Caroline told me, "Cherish that. It might be the last time she says it for a while."

The nurses softly laughed, and even Kiera smiled, but...Caroline was pretty much right. As things picked up, Kiera looked like she was cursing the entire world, and I was at the very top of her shit list. But my God, she was amazing. Strong. Focused. Determined. I didn't think I could do it, didn't think I could lie there and deal with that much pain for that long. And that was *with* drugs. She absolutely blew me away, and tears of pride were streaming down my cheeks long before the doctor told her to push one final time.

Kiera was more exhausted than I'd ever seen her, but she did it, and there was a flurry of activity and a sound that would forever be bound inside my head—a baby crying. *My* baby crying. I wanted to look, but I couldn't take my eyes off Kiera. "You're amazing," I told her, kissing her head.

She gave me the sleepiest smile I'd ever seen, and her eyes

closed in exhaustion. They sprang open when somebody said, "Congratulations! It's a boy!"

My gaze snapped to the nurse holding...my son. *Son*. I couldn't quite believe it. I heard myself say, "I have a son?" felt tears falling from my eyes, but it all seemed so surreal. A boy. A miniature me. A chance to correct the mistake life had made when I was born. An opportunity to set things right. Hope. That was what it felt like. Hope.

The nurse nodded at my question, beaming as she held the tiny bundle in her arms. She started to hand him to Kiera, then stopped and gave him to me. My hands were shaking as I let go of Kiera to take him. *Him. My son*. He was warm as I cradled him in my arms. His head was covered with a pastel cap, but his eyes were wide open as he watched me watch him; they were a deep, dark gray with a hint of midnight blue around the edges, and I wondered if they'd look like mine one day. I saw myself in the shape of his mouth, saw Kiera in his tiny nose. He was perfect. Stunningly, beautifully perfect, and I already knew I'd do everything in my power to keep him this pristine forever. To keep him happy, safe, protected, and most of all, loved.

A sound escaped me that was a strangled laugh mixed with a sob. The rush of love sweeping over me made it hard to talk, hard to see, but I needed him to know me. To instantly identify me as the person who'd been cooing at him for months inside his mom's belly. And I needed him to know how I felt about him. Even if he didn't understand yet, I needed him to know. I never wanted him to question my feelings for him. Ever.

"Hey, little man," I choked out. "I'm your dad, and I love you...so much. I'm so glad you're here."

Chapter 39

HAPPILY EVER AFTER

I loved being a father. No, loved didn't cover it. Whatever word surpassed love—that was how I felt. I was...whole. All the gaps erased, all the voids filled, all the shadows burned away. I wasn't *at* peace, I *was* peace.

Kiera and I settled on the name Ryder for our son. Ryder Carter Kyle. I thought it had a nice ring to it, and I liked that the first name was similar to my brother's and the middle name was my father's surname. Kiera thought it sounded appropriate for a rock star's kid, and I supposed it did, although that didn't matter at all to me.

Leaving the hospital with a newborn was one of the most stressful experiences of my life. I'd never really noticed before how insanely people drove, and I wanted to yell at everyone on the freeway. Especially the lane hoppers. *Leapfrogging through traffic to gain a meager thirty seconds doesn't help anyone and is really fucking dangerous, you fucking tool bags!* Needless to say, the first thing Kiera did when we got home was hand me a beer.

I felt so much better when Ryder was safe and sound in our house. Until it was bedtime. Then I felt like I was back on the freeway.

"Are you sure we should put him down in the nursery? Maybe we should bring the crib into our bedroom. Or maybe he should sleep in the bed with us. Is that safe? Is the crib safe? Maybe we should all sleep on the floor? Maybe we should take shifts watching over him? He's gonna be all right, right?"

I said all of that really fast in one breath, and both Kiera and Caroline were staring at me with wide eyes. Knowing I sounded a little crazy, I shrugged and cringed. "I just don't want anything bad to happen to him. And I don't want him to feel abandoned."

Kiera's face softened at that, her eyes glistening. Caroline smiled at me but shook her head. "He won't feel abandoned, and he'll be just fine. You have a monitor, and you can listen to him all night long if you want, but it really is better in the long run if he learns to do this on his own." She grinned. "And he'll be up every three hours anyway."

"He'll...what?" Kiera said, her mouth popping open.

Caroline laughed and patted Kiera's shoulder. "You should let Kellan put him down and go get as much sleep as you can."

Kiera sighed, stared at Ryder a moment, then nodded. She gave me a kiss, then shuffled to our bedroom, and I knew she'd be out before I got there. Caroline wasn't lying about the three-hour thing, and Kiera had been up with Ryder several times during the night. I was sure she'd been hoping that was a fluke, or a just-the-first-night type of thing. She must have blocked out everything Anna had told her about dealing with Gibson as a newborn. Denial. It was a powerful thing.

I was still standing beside Ryder's crib, gently swaying him, even though he was already sleeping. Caroline watched me, a soft smile on her face. "I know I need to put him down," I told her. "I just...can't yet."

She nodded. "It's all right. I'm a firm believer in cuddles. You hold him as long as you want, Kellan. It's important for both of you."

She stroked my arm, kissed Ryder's chubby cheek, then left

the room. I stared down at him, awed and amazed by how much I loved him. I'd never experienced anything like it before because it was different than what I felt for Kiera. Kiera was a piece of my heart, and I kept her inside of me everywhere I went, but Ryder... he was like a piece of my heart that was outside of my body. And that was terrifying because I couldn't protect something outside of me, not all the time. I'd only just met him, and I already was having such a hard time letting go. I suddenly understood Martin and Gavin so much better. And I was completely mystified by John, the man who'd raised me. Whether I was his or not, how could he have looked at me and instantly hated me? Staring at the tiny, trusting infant in my arms, I couldn't even fathom it.

Not wanting to dwell on the past, I started softly singing Kiera's favorite D-Bags song, the one I'd sung that first night at Pete's when she'd walked in with Denny. The one that had made her really notice me. Ryder stirred as I sang, then his mouth twitched like he was smiling, or trying to. It brought tears to my eyes, and I choked on a lyric. I wondered if he remembered my voice, remembered this song from when I'd sung it to him while Kiera was pregnant. I really hoped he did.

I held my finger under his little hand, and even in sleep, he curled his tiny digits around mine like he was claiming me. It killed me, and I had to stop singing, had to swallow the lump in my throat about a billion times. When I could finally speak, I told him, "I love you so much. You're probably going to get sick of me saying it. You're probably going to think I'm overbearing and overprotective. You'll probably even hate me sometimes. And that's fine, as long as you know that I love you. Every day, every hour, no matter what you do, no matter who you become, I love you, and I want nothing but the best for you." I sighed. "Which is probably sleep. I really should put you down. I just...don't want to miss a second."

Shaking my head, I rolled my eyes. "Damn it, I need to get a grip. Oops. I probably shouldn't say damn it. Damn it, I just said it again. Fuck. I'm gonna have to make a swear jar, I can already tell." I softly laughed. "Don't talk like your old man, kid. Or like Uncle Griffin. In fact, you should probably stay away from him altogether. And I should quit talking to myself because you're asleep and can't even hear me." Shaking my head again, I sighed and said, "Okay, I'm putting you down. I swear." Then I made myself turn around and put him in his crib, after a thousand kisses, of course.

He looked so tiny lying there, and my arms actually ached with him gone. But I made myself leave the room, made myself close the door, and made myself walk the short distance to my bedroom. And I instantly smiled when I stepped inside because I could hear him breathing through the monitor, and it filled me with relief.

Kiera stirred when I sat down, and when she twisted to look at me, the moonlight streaming through the window highlighted the tears in her eyes. "What's wrong?" I asked her.

She shook her head, sat up, and wrapped her arms around me. "Just when I thought I couldn't possibly love you any more than I already did, you became a father," she murmured. And that was when I realized she'd heard me talking to Ryder through the baby monitor.

Smiling into her shoulder, I eased her down to the mattress and kissed her head. "I know exactly what you mean," I told her. Because every moment I loved her more and watching *her* with Ryder only amplified the feeling. "What I said to him goes for you too, you know? I love you every day, every hour, every minute, and I want nothing but the best for you. And hopefully, that's me."

She softly laughed as she snuggled into my chest. "It is. And it will always be you. You're the best thing that's ever happened to me."

I had to swallow another lump at hearing that. "Same," I whispered, my voice shaky. Needing to change the mood, I added, "Now stop trying to make me cry and go to sleep. Our son will need you soon."

She laughed, then sighed, then faded into sleep. And I smiled as I held her tight, as I listened to my son's tiny breaths, and I thanked every fate there was that life had worked out this way for me. It was better than I ever imagined it would be.

And it just kept getting better.

As Ryder grew, he seemed less fragile, and so I worried less about him. Slightly. Maybe. Well, I worried about different things. I stopped overanalyzing every breath I heard on the monitor and started freaking out about tiny objects around the house. Buttons became the bane of my existence. I just kept picturing them coming off everything, and him swallowing them, and...ugh. It was a mental nightmare. I tried to channel my inner Evan and not worry so much. Still, I had the entire house babyproofed before Ryder could even hold his head up by himself.

The guys and I had recorded our second album over the summer, after returning home from the tour. It was releasing late-January, and we were hoping it did all right. Personally, I liked it even better than our first album, and there were a couple of collaborations on it that I was really excited for fans to hear. There was one with Avoiding Redemption that had turned out fucking awesome. I hoped that song became a huge radio hit because Justin deserved more recognition for his talent. I was really excited to tour with him again...but anxious too.

Honestly, I couldn't even think about the summer tour yet. Just the thought of the upcoming promotional tour was stressing me out. Because there was no way Ryder could come with me—it was too fast-paced and hectic—and the thought of leaving him behind, even for just a couple of weeks, was like a permanent rock wedged in my stomach.

"Maybe we don't need to do a promotional thing this time. Everyone knows who we are now, right?"

Kiera had Ryder propped on her hip, and he was just staring at her and grinning. His eyes had shifted into a deep blue like mine, and he had this crazy mess of light brown hair that Kiera was always trying to flatten, but like he was already imitating me, it stuck up everywhere. I loved it.

Kiera shook her head at me. "True, but you should still do it. It's a great way to advertise, remind people you're still around, hype up the album right before it releases..."

I nodded because I *knew* that, but still. "Yeah. I just can't imagine not seeing you guys every day. And he changes so fast." Like he knew I was talking about him, Ryder shifted his gaze to me; he was still grinning, and fuck, he was cute. I squatted down to look him in the eye. "You're not allowed to say your first words while I'm gone. Or walk. Or start dating. We have to have the birds and the bees speech before you start dating. And no, I don't know why it's called that."

Ryder just kept smiling at me. Kiera laughed. "He's not going to start dating while you're gone. Or walking. And his babbles aren't really words. You're not going to miss anything."

Straightening, I frowned at her. "That is absolutely not true. I'm going to miss a lot."

She gave me a soft smile. "We're going to miss you too. And that got me thinking...what if we came with you on the main tour this summer? It's not quite as chaotic, and we could get our own bus...and hire a second bodyguard. I don't want to take any chances."

I was already broadly smiling, in love with this idea. "Yeah? You'd want to do that?"

She grinned. "Yeah. It won't be feasible to join you on every tour, but this one seems doable. With some help."

"Yes, yes!" I gave her a long kiss, and I felt Ryder's little fingers grab my shirt. Pulling apart from her, I smiled down at him. "Speaking of bodyguards...what do you think about hiring Sam?"

As I pulled my shirt out of Ryder's grip, Kiera's jaw dropped. "Sam from Pete's?"

I nodded. "If we're going to hire someone to protect us, someone who's going to be around Ryder a lot, I'd rather hire someone we know and trust. And I think he'd be really good at it."

Her shock shifted into a smile. "I like that idea. A lot."

"Me too," I said, holding Ryder's hand. And suddenly, I didn't mind thinking about the upcoming summer tour anymore. This was going to be fun, and I'd get to share it with my family. It would be the best of both worlds.

Leaving for the promo tour still sucked, though, and even *I* would admit I was a miserable son of a bitch, cranky as fuck. All the guys snapped at me at some point, even Evan. They started putting me in time-outs. To be cute, cheeky. It just made me miss Kiera and Ryder even more, and when I wasn't in trouble, I spent an oddly exorbitant amount of time getting parenting tips from Griffin. Granted, I only half-listened to everything he said, because Griffin was still Griffin, but talking about our kids helped dull the ache. And maybe Griffin wasn't as clueless as he seemed. Not about this. None of us could deny that Griffin was a good dad. It shocked all of us. Daily.

Not long after we got back from the whirlwind tour, a slew of good things happened to everybody. Our second album released at number one. Kiera released her second book, and a huge publishing agency was interested in purchasing her first book. Evan finally gave Jenny the ring he'd picked up sixty million years ago, and they were now officially engaged. Jenny was pursuing her dream and opening an art gallery. Matt was working on plans to propose to Rachel before the summer tour, and damn if Evan wasn't right—quiet little Matt was planning something over-the-top elaborate. I was still shocked; I really thought I'd had that bet in the bag. Anna was pregnant again, and Griffin was over the moon that he'd won our bet, even though I'd never agreed to a bet about that. Hailey had moved to Seattle last summer, and she was loving her new city and having fun spending a ton of time with her nephew; she was our go-to babysitter whenever we needed one. Gavin had mixed feelings about Hailey living here, but he was choosing to see it as an excuse to visit me even more. And his grandson. He had come up with Riley over the holidays, and then again in February when we had a party for the album, and then again in April for spring break. I had a feeling once his parents passed away, he and Riley would move over here too. I both wanted that and didn't want that. I really liked Grandma and Grandpa.

But more important than all that good news...Ryder said his first word: Da-da. It was a mumbled, garbled mess, but he was looking right at me, and he said it three times in a row, so I was calling it. First word, right there.

"Did you hear that?" I said, twisting to look at Kiera.

She frowned at me. "He's babbling."

"No, he's not," I said with a bright grin. "He said 'dad.' He was talking to me."

She rolled her eyes, but she was smiling now. I was pretty sure she'd wanted Momma to be his first word, but I was also sure she wasn't upset about him saying mine. Now, if he'd said Griffin, well, Kiera would probably already be in the car on her way to kick Griffin's ass.

Wanting Ryder to say my name again, I looked at him and said, "Say it for Mommy. Say Da-da. Da-da." I repeated it about six more times while bouncing him on my hip.

Ryder was grinning, drooling, loving this game, but eventually he said it again. "Dahh...dahhh."

I grinned at Kiera again, victory on my face. She had tears in her eyes, but she was shaking her head. "Does it really count if he's just repeating you?"

Mock disdain on my face, I held him closer to me. "Yes. Yes, it does. And he knows." I looked back at him. "I know he knows."

And like he really did know, he put his wet little hand on my lip and said it again, clearer this time. "Da-da."

I hadn't prompted him, hadn't asked for him to say it, and by the way he was looking at me, I knew he understood that the word meant me. And he wanted me. My eyes instantly burned, and when I looked back at Kiera, she was wiping tears off her cheeks. "Kiera," I murmured, blown away. I'd never imagined that hearing my son acknowledge me would hit me so hard. I felt like I was flying *and* plummeting.

Kiera nodded at me. "I know. I heard it."

There was no arguing it this time. He knew me. He wanted me. *He loved me.* I let out a laugh, but it sort of came out like a sob. Kiera's arms were instantly around me, around us, and she repeatedly kissed my cheek, murmuring, "I love you."

Ryder started working on his words more and more after that, and Kiera was thrilled when he mumbled out a Momma. It was more like Mmmmommmmommma. There were a lot of mmms in it, but like with my name, he'd been looking at her at the time, and he'd said it unprompted. She cried when he did it, then attacked me with passionate kisses, like I'd somehow made him do it.

And that was when I started leaving Kiera notes written by Ryder. I wrote stuff like *You're the best Mommy ever*, and *I love you, Mommy*, and *Daddy says I need siblings*. I even wrote them with my left hand so it would look like a child had done it. She always cooed at him whenever she found one, then she'd come up to me, shake her head, and kiss me so fervently that I instantly felt intoxicated, drunk on her. I knew we weren't actually ready for a second kid yet, but damn, we were getting a lot of practice at making one.

I was a little nervous when the summer tour kicked off. It would be a lot of firsts for Ryder, a lot of firsts for us, and a lot of stimulation and exposure. I wasn't sure how he'd handle it. Or how *I'd* handle it, for that matter. It didn't help that there was tension between the guys. Griffin was being...I wasn't sure what was going on with him, but he'd been acting up more and more lately. Demanding lead guitar, wanting more attention, acting like all of us were keeping him down, but at the same time, not putting in a lick of extra effort. He was exhausting all of us, but things were getting especially bad between him and Matt.

I couldn't even repeat what he did during Matt's romantic

proposal. It was...anything but romantic. Matt fumed about it for *weeks*. But eventually, like always, Matt got over it, and by mid-tour he and Griffin were fine. I hoped.

Ryder, on the other hand, handled touring like a pro...like it was in his blood. He didn't have a speck of shyness in him, and he would happily interact with anyone who took an interest in him. That made me happy, but it also made me grateful that Sam had agreed to come along. Between him and Kevin, I felt like my family was in good hands.

We had a little time to kill before the concert, and I was showing Ryder the stage while Kiera spent some quality time with her very-pregnant sister. Sam was with me while Kevin went with Kiera. I'd wanted her to take both of them, but the girls had just gone out to dinner; some upscale place with valet service and beefy guys at the doors keeping out anyone who didn't have reservations. Kiera assured me they'd be fine with just Kevin, and she wanted someone to stay with Ryder. And me, I supposed.

Setting Ryder down on the empty stage, I squatted beside him and said, "What do you think? Want to be up here one day? Seeing thousands of people cheering for you? I'll be honest...it's pretty cool."

He grinned at me and slapped the stage, and I was taking that to mean *Hell, yeah, Dad! I can't wait to follow in your footsteps.* Ruffling his hair, I stood up and looked around. This was one of the larger venues on the tour. It still wasn't as large as anything we'd done on Sienna's tour, but it was impressive. The seats were all empty now, but I knew they'd start filling soon, and I knew they'd all be full. The entire tour had sold out. That still blew my mind.

I took a step forward, then glanced back at Ryder. He was looking out over the seats like he was envisioning it too. I instantly pictured him a little older, holding a guitar, singing along with me on the stage. Would Kiera be okay with that? If he wanted to do it? Still watching him, I took another step back. Now I was picturing him at my age, by himself on the stage, everyone cheering for him and just him. I didn't know if that was his future—he might not have any interest in music, he might not be able to sing to save his life, he might hate being the center of attention—and all of that was okay, but for just a minute, I visualized it, and fuck, the image was so clear to me. Picture perfect.

As my vision grew hazy, Ryder decided I was too far away. He slammed onto his hands, and I was positive he was going to start crawling my way. But then he juggled his weight back and forth, getting to his feet. I just stared at him in awe. He'd done this before, worked his way onto his feet, but he was usually holding onto something—a table, a chair, my pant leg, something. But he was doing it without any help, and I was freaking out.

"Oh my God, oh my God! You did it!" He grinned at me as he wobbled on his feet. He'd done this too. Wobbled on his feet, but that was usually where it ended. Knowing he was seconds from falling, I took a step forward. And so did he.

My jaw dropped as I watched him take a step toward me. "Oh my God," I murmured. Tears instantly stung my eyes as I smiled at him, as I watched him reach up for me, as I watched him take another step toward me. His face...it was pure, unadulterated joy. And I felt like sobbing. And then my eyes widened. "Oh shit, your mom's gonna kill me!"

Oblivious to what I was saying, Ryder took another gleeful step in my direction. I started patting myself. "Where's my phone. Where's my fucking phone!" I patted my chest, my ass, my thighs. My brain was frying because I knew he was going to crash any second, and I didn't want Kiera to miss it. She had to see this. Where the fuck was my phone?

Remembering I wasn't alone, I looked up and said, "Sam!"

Smile on his face, he already had his phone out; he was already recording it. He gave me a thumbs up, and I felt relief weaken my stance. "Thank you," I told him.

He nodded. "You hired me to protect you. That includes from your wife."

I laughed at that, then let the tears fall as I watched my son finally plop down to his padded backside. I immediately scooped him up, hugging him tight. "You did it, little man! You walked! Your mom's gonna die when she sees this!" I kissed him five thousand times as I walked over to Sam. "You got it all, right?"

He nodded, slipping his phone back into his pocket. "Yep, every second."

"Thank fuck," I told him. I grinned. "I knew hiring you was the best decision I'd ever make."

He nodded again, then raised an eyebrow at me. "That's thirty, by the way. Just in the last five minutes. You're up to sixty, just for today."

My smile slipped. "Well, fuck."

Sam grinned. "Make that seventy."

I'd made Sam my personal swear jar, and instead of it being a dollar per swear, I'd made it ten dollars per swear, paid out to him at the end of each day. I'd thought it would motivate me to watch my mouth, but honestly...I was just making Sam a very rich man. He loved it.

"This is why you always stay behind with me, isn't it?" I asked him.

He smirked. "I go where Ryder goes. But it *is* entertaining for me when you're there." His grin widened. "I can't wait until you have more kids. Because it's ten per swear per kid."

My eyes widened. "I never agreed to that."

He shrugged. "Kiera did."

I let out a long sigh. "Fuck."

With a laugh, he murmured, "Eighty."

I flipped him off because I didn't have to pay him for that. Although...I probably shouldn't teach Ryder that either. Fuck. Being a parent was hard.

It wasn't long after the tour ended that Anna had her baby—another girl, thank God—and Ryder turned one. Even though we both knew he wouldn't remember it, we had a massive party for him. All my family, all Kiera's family, all the guys, all the girls, all our friends from Pete's, anyone and everyone who might enjoy witnessing a milestone was invited. A surprising number of people showed up. Probably for the cake and booze.

Gavin and Riley were up visiting again, making good use of our numerous guest rooms. Hailey was here too. Honestly, Hailey practically lived here; she visited so much. In fact, she'd already claimed one of the guest rooms as being permanently hers. I loved it, and I let her do whatever she wanted with it. Martin and Caroline were visiting too. They'd both arrived a little while ago, around the birth of Anna's second baby. They were staying with us since Griffin's house was currently full of his side of the family. That and Martin didn't think he could share a home with Griffin. It gave me a weird sense of bliss to know that I was the favored son-in-law. I shouldn't be thrilled about that... but I was really thrilled about that.

Griffin shuffled into the house, looking half-dead, with his mom, dad, brother, sister, and her twin daughters in tow. Even though he'd been prickly lately, I felt bad for the guy. He had a lot on his plate, juggling two kids and his family, so I encouraged him and Anna to take advantage of the numerous babysitters and take a nap in my bedroom since it would be the quietest room. He'd groggily nodded at me and walked upstairs. Because I couldn't resist laying down some ground rules, I tossed out, "Just a nap, Griffin."

He turned and looked back at me with a smirk on his face, and I knew I would be changing the sheets before I climbed into bed later.

Sam showed up with some of the regulars from Pete's. Sam tried to work the party, but I forced him to relax and have fun. I felt pretty safe among these people that we'd known for years. Rita arrived with her husband, which shocked the hell out of me; a part of me had seriously doubted the man existed. Troy brought his new boyfriend and spent most of the afternoon firmly attached to his side. And I had to admit, it was both weird and nice not to be ogled by either Pete's bartender.

Matt and Rachel stepped in the door right behind Evan and

Jenny. Both girls were subtly flashing their engagement rings all over the place, and it made me so happy to see their effervescent joy. They deserved it, all of them. Kate arrived sans Justin, who couldn't make it up, but she told me he said hello. And then she flushed and giggled. It was cute.

Cheyenne arrived with her girlfriend, Meadow, who brought her bandmate, Rain. Rain gushed about how much she loved playing at Pete's. She must have asked me a hundred times if I was sure we weren't going to want our slot back one day. I always told her I was sure, and it was hers until she was ready to move on from it. Because honestly, we were too big for Pete's now, and Poetic Bliss was getting too big for them too. I'd already been approached by Lana, who had shown an interest in putting them on the same extended tour where she'd discovered us. I was pretty sure it was just a matter of time before Pete's would need a new band. Damn. Pete was gonna hate that. I'd have to talk to Evan and Matt soon about finding a new act for Pete. I just couldn't leave that man in a lurch. I owed him too much.

Ryder was still napping by the time everyone had arrived. I worried he might sleep through his entire party, but when I went to check on him, I heard him babbling to himself. Opening his door, I was instantly greeted with the word, "Up."

I smiled as I walked inside. Kiera and Jenny had painted Ryder's room so that it sort of resembled the stage at Pete's, and I thought of the bar every time I went in here. Ryder's crib was centered against a solid black wall, a wall we were going to hang guitars on when Ryder was older. The rest of the walls were white, but Jenny had drawn a perfect 5-line staff across each of them, complete with music notes that depicted an actual D-Bags song. The melancholy song I'd written for Kiera. The one I'd been singing when she'd walked back into my life. I thought of that every time I went in here too.

Ryder was standing in his crib, reaching up for me. "Da-da. Up," he said.

"Ready for your party?" I asked him. "People have been

waiting for you." He just smiled at me in answer because he had no idea what a birthday party was.

I changed him, dressing him in a fresh toddler-sized D-Bags shirt, then brought him downstairs with me. Like he was a magnet, people immediately surrounded us. His grandparents, his numerous uncles, his numerous aunts...everyone wanted to love on him. I tried to get him to the kitchen so we could get started on cake and presents, but I kept getting distracted along the way.

Jenny and Rachel were taking turns tickling his cheeks, making him cringe and giggle. Shaking her head, Jenny told me, "I can't get over how much he looks like you."

With a laugh, I looked over at Gavin and Riley, sitting on the couch. The three of us, now four of us, were so strikingly similar that we almost could have been clones. Even Uncle Tristan and his kids bore the family resemblance. And Grandpa Jim, of course. "Yeah, I guess the genes are strong on my side of the family."

Jenny grinned and shook her head. "He's going to be such a heartbreaker. I pity all the girls in his generation."

I frowned at that. "*All* the girls?"

She nodded. "Yep. There won't be a single one who doesn't fall for him. You need to make sure he knows to wield his power carefully."

I smirked at that. "His looks are a superpower?"

She glanced at Rachel, and they both nodded. "That and your fame," Jenny said.

That gave me pause, and as I looked down at him, I supposed they had a point. Money, fame, and good looks...that could lead him down a dark path. But as I looked around my home full of good people, I knew that wouldn't happen. He had too many amazing role models in his life, and Kiera and I would teach him how to be kind, how to be humble, how to be grateful. He was going to be just fine. But I nodded at Jenny and Rachel, telling them, "Yeah, I'll make sure he knows...that with great power..."

Jenny narrowed her eyes at me. "Don't."

"Comes great..."

Rachel started giggling. Jenny narrowed her eyes even more, and I didn't even know that was possible. "Kellan."

"Responsibility," I finished with a smirk.

She rolled her eyes at me, then laughed. "You're such a dork. I don't know how I missed that for so long."

I laughed as she shoved my shoulder, pushing me away from her. Still chuckling, I continued weaving my way to the kitchen. People tried to steal Ryder from me as I went. I had to keep telling them they could have him in a minute, but I needed to get him to Kiera first. Roxie came up to me just after I'd successfully gotten away from Abby. She grinned at me, and her smile was a mile wide. "Hey, mind if I take a look at the Chevelle? Make sure she's running right." Her grin shifted to Ryder, and she cooed, "Hey, cutie. Happy Birthday."

Smiling, I shook my head at her. "It's your day off. You should rest, relax."

All the D-Bags had moved since Kiera and I had purchased this place. Well, all of them except Evan. Much to my chagrin, he'd decided to purchase the entire building he lived in, but instead of keeping the auto body shop beneath his loft, he'd converted it into extra living space and an art studio for Jenny. At the time, I'd thought that meant I'd lost the only person I trusted with the Chevelle. Until I'd realized I could hire Rox as my personal mechanic.

Now technically, she didn't work exclusively for me, but she did make house calls for me. And she made them frequently because she loved that car almost as much as I did. She was actively trying to convince me to buy more classic cars, to fill up my entire garage with them. "Someone needs to save them, Kellan," was her typical argument. And damn if it wasn't starting to work on me. Was it too soon to buy Ryder his very first muscle car? Was that spoiling him? Or was it just a natural and normal rite of passage?

Patting Roxie's shoulder, I told her, "Have a birthday cake margarita. Abby made them."

She scrunched her face. "That sounds...disgusting."

My grin widened. "I know."

Abby had decorated my house for the party and provided all the food and drinks. She'd gone a little overboard, and it basically looked like the words "Happy Birthday" had thrown up everywhere, but ever mindful of my choking paranoia, nothing Abby had used for decorations was smaller than a Chihuahua. I appreciated that. Griffin too since Gibson still taste-tested everything. And I mean *everything*. Griff kept his "fun stuff" under lock and key now...and there were times when I wished I didn't know that.

Roxie shrugged and followed me into the kitchen to try a flavor of margarita that should not exist. When we stepped into the room, I instantly spotted Kiera chatting with her mom. Ryder spotted her too. "Ma-ma," he said, leaning over like he could reach her from six feet away.

Kiera brightened when she saw us, then held out her hands for Ryder. I brought him to her, and she scooped him into her arms. She kissed his neck, making him laugh in the best way, making my chest contract in the best way. "There's my birthday boy," she said. "Ready for cake?"

She strapped him into his highchair, then asked Sam to gather everyone for us. No one could wrangle people like Sam, and the room was overcrowded with friends and family just seconds later. We all sang the birthday song to Ryder, gave him the first piece of cake, and then watched in amusement as he smeared it all over himself while devouring it as quickly as he could; cake just might be his weakness too.

Several hours later, when I was crawling into my freshly made bed, I realized something: birthday parties were exhausting. And amazing.

"Do you think he had fun?" Kiera sleepily asked.

Pulling her curled body closer to mine, I told her, "He had

cake, a ton of attention, and a boatload of new toys to play with. I think it was his best day ever."

She laughed at that, then sighed. "Good." Turning her head to look at me, she asked, "Did you have a good day?"

I smiled at her beautiful face being softly caressed by the moonlight. "I had cake, a ton of attention, and a boatload of new toys to play with. It was my best day ever."

She laughed again, then leaned forward and kissed me. When our lips broke apart, I frowned at her. "What?" she asked.

"I just realized something." She lifted an eyebrow, waiting for an explanation, and I shrugged. "We never took that honeymoon I promised you. There was the accident, the pregnancy, the tour, Ryder, another tour...we sort of missed it."

She smiled at me, then bit her lip. "We've got a few hours right now. What if, instead of one long, elaborate trip, we just take little mini honeymoons each night?"

I grinned at her. "For how long?"

Her eyes, a deep brown in the darkness, slowly scanned my face. "How about...forever?"

"I can do forever," I told her, leaning down to find her lips again.

"I love you," she murmured.

I started to tell her I loved her too, but before I knew it, one thing led to another, and words just weren't necessary anymore. She knew how I felt about her, about our life together, and I knew she felt the exact same way. I fell asleep with a smile on my face, content and satisfied in every single way. Definitely my best day ever.

But even still, a hazy dream built up around me as I slipped into slumber. A dream I hadn't had in a while. I was back at the birthday party, standing alone in my living room, facing my mother and father. They looked different than they usually did in my dreams, almost black and white, almost transparent. We just stared at each other, silent for a change. Then my father shook his head. "You think you've won? That your life will just be perfect from here on out?"

A strange sort of grief washed over me as I alternated my gaze between the two of them. No, not grief. Pity. "No," I said. "Of course not. Life's not perfect, and I'm sure there are hard times ahead of me. For everyone I care about."

Dad tilted his head at me, and for once, he didn't look terrifying to me. Just...broken. "Then why are you smiling?"

I looked over at Mom, and she had the same washed-out weariness to her. "Because I know something now," I said. "Something I didn't know before. Something that took me a long time to learn, mainly because of the two of you."

Dad narrowed his eyes, but even as he did, his body flickered, like he was made of static. "And what's that?" he asked, his voice sounding far away.

My gaze shifted to take in the emptiness of the room. "This isn't right. This doesn't reflect my life." As I looked around, the space slowly started filling with people, with everyone who meant something to me. No, with everyone who had shown me that *I* meant something to them—the people who had a piece of me in *their* hearts. Kiera. Ryder. Evan. Matt. Griffin. Anna. Jenny. Rachel. Gavin. Hailey. Riley. Denny. Abby. They just kept appearing one after another, and with every person who materialized, my parents softened until I could barely see them.

I stared at their hazy shapes until the only thing I could see was the whites of their eyes. In a soft voice, I told them, "I learned I'm not alone. I learned I'm loved. And I don't need to keep holding on to you anymore. I can let you go."

Their eyes popped out of existence, and I inhaled a deep breath as I woke up. The remembered feeling of that dream-room filled with warmth echoed through my mind, bringing a smile to my face and a sense of peace throughout my entire body. I just felt so...safe.

Kiera shifted beside me. "You okay?" she murmured, putting a hand on my arm.

Smiling her way, I covered her hand with mine, our wedding rings rubbing together with a soft clink. "Yeah, I'm fine. I'm great." The future was bright, and the past had finally released me. Or more accurately, I'd released it. I was beyond great.

I was wonderful.

Acknowledgments

Ending a series is always bittersweet. Ending an alternate point of view of a series is even more so. I love these characters so much, and I'm so happy that I was able to finish telling Kellan's side of the story. And no matter how many times I read it, those last couple of chapters make me cry. Every. Time. I'm just so happy for him, and I hope you are too.

As always, a huge thank you to Lori and Becky for reading the story for me and letting me know your thoughts. Thank you, Madison Seidler, for helping me with the editing. Thank you, Hang Le, for yet another gorgeous cover (and that tattoo...ugh, perfection). Thank you, Mike at HMG Formatting, for your formatting magic (and I apologize for my obsessive need for things to match). Thank you, Kim and Mo at Audibly Addicted, for helping me with the audiobooks. I would be lost without you! Thank you, J.F. Harding, for giving Kellan such a great voice. And thank you, Lysa at Pegasus Designs, for making my website... wonderful (sorry, I had to).

To my readers, I am floored by how much you still love these books. Your undying support and enthusiasm—it means the world to me. I'm grateful, I'm humbled. You are the best! Thank you for letting me share these characters with you. Thank you for sticking with them until the end (even those of you who desperately wish Kiera harm). Thank you for posting about my books, for encouraging others to read them. Thank you for hanging out at Pete's Bar with me. Thank you for sharing your stories, artwork, tattoos! Thank you for the encouragement. Thank you for your patience! I know this one was a long time coming. I hope it was worth the wait.

And a huge thank you to my friends and family. Thank you for putting up with my endless hours in the writing cave. Thank you for understanding when I don't have time to do much of anything. Thank you for the hugs and the pep talks. Thank you for everything. I love you so much!

About the Author

S.C. Stephens is a bestselling author who enjoys spending every free moment creating stories that are packed with emotion and heavy on romance. Her debut novel, *Thoughtless*, an angst-filled love story featuring insurmountable passion and the unforgettable Kellan Kyle, took the world of romance by storm in 2009. Stephens has been writing nonstop ever since.

In addition to writing, Stephens enjoys spending lazy afternoons in the sun reading fabulous novels, loading up her iPod with writer's block–reducing music, heading out to the movies, and spending quality time with her friends and family. She currently resides in the beautiful Pacific Northwest with her two equally beautiful children.

You can learn more at:
AuthorSCStephens.com
Twitter @SC_Stephens_
Facebook.com/SCStephensAuthor
Instagram sc_stephens_